The
MX Book
of
New
Sherlock
Holmes
Stories

Part XIV – 2019 Annual
(1891-1897)

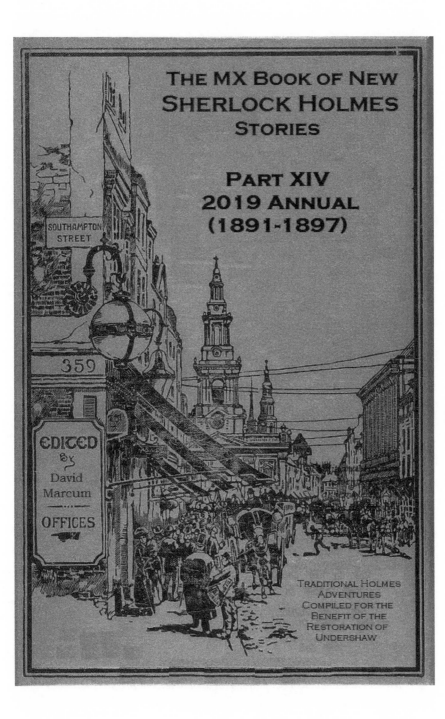

THE MX BOOK OF NEW SHERLOCK HOLMES STORIES

PART XIV
2019 ANNUAL
(1891-1897)

SOUTHAMPTON STREET

359

EDITED BY
David Marcum

OFFICES

TRADITIONAL HOLMES
ADVENTURES
COMPILED FOR THE
BENEFIT OF THE
RESTORATION OF
UNDERSHAW

First edition published in 2019
© Copyright 2019

ISBN Hardcover   978-1-78705-446-2
ISBN Paperback   978-1-78705-447-9
ISBN AUK ePub   978-1-78705-448-6
ISBN AUK PDF   978-1-78705-449-3

Published in the UK by
MX Publishing
335 Princess Park Manor, Royal Drive,
London, N11 3GX
www.mxpublishing.co.uk

David Marcum can be reached at:
thepapersofsherlockholmes@gmail.com

Cover design by Brian Belanger
www.belangerbooks.com and *www.redbubble.com/people/zhahadun*

CONTENTS

Forewords

Adventures

(Continued on the next page . . . .)

(Continued on the next page . . . .)

The following can be found in the companion volumes
The MX Book of New Sherlock Holmes Stories
Part XIII – 2019 Annual (1881-1890)
and
Part XV – 2019 Annual (1898-1917)

(Continued on the next page . . . .)

**These additional Sherlock Holmes adventures
can be found in the previous volumes of**
The MX Book of New Sherlock Holmes Stories

(Continued on the next page . . . .)

PART III: 1896-1929

PART IV – 2016 Annual

(Continued on the next page . . . .)

PART V – Christmas Adventures

(Continued on the next page . . . .)

PART VI – 2017 Annual

(Continued on the next page . . . .)

PART VII – Eliminate the Impossible: 1880-1891

PART VIII – Eliminate the Impossible: 1892-1905

(Continued on the next page . . . .)

Part IX – 2018 Annual (1879-1895)

(Continued on the next page . . . .)

The Confession of Anna Jarrow – S. F. Bennett
The Adventure of the Disappearing Dictionary – Sonia Fetherston
The Fairy Hills Horror – Geri Schear
A Loathsome and Remarkable Adventure – Marcia Wilson
The Adventure of the Multiple Moriartys – David Friend
The Influence Machine – Mark Mower

Part X – 2018 Annual (1896-1916)

Part XI: Some Untold Cases (1880-1891)

(Continued on the next page . . . .)

Part XII: Some Untold Cases (1894-1902)

The following contributions appear in this volume:
The MX Book of New Sherlock Holmes Stories
Part XIV– 2019 Annual (1891-1897)

The following contributions appear in
Part XIII – 2019 Annual (1881-1890)

The following contributions appear in
Part XV – 2019 Annual (1898-1917)

The 2019 Annual, Parts XIII, XIV, and XV of
The MX Book of New Sherlock Holmes Stories,
are dedicated to

Joel Senter

Joel passed away in July 2018.
He was a wonderful and very supportive
Sherlockian, and
he will be missed.

Editor's Introduction:
The Great Holmes Tapestry
by David Marcum

Way back in early 2015, when the world was a much simpler place, I woke up early one morning from a very vivid dream where I had edited a Sherlock Holmes anthology. Instead of going back to sleep, I arose and started thinking about it. What a wild hansom cab ride it's been since then!

Who would have then suspected the future of *The MX Book of New Sherlock Holmes Stories*? Since that time, we've had over 330 new Sherlock Holmes adventures, plus poems and forewords, from over 150 contributors, and along the way, through the very generous efforts of the participants, we've raised over $40,000 for the Stepping Stones School for special needs students at Undershaw, one of Sir Arthur Conan Doyle's former homes. Additionally, the books have raised awareness of the school around the world.

Back in 2015, when the initial hope for a single book of possibly a dozen new Holmes tales had grown and grown to three massive simultaneous volumes of 63 new stories, I sat down to write a foreword. In it, I referred to a phenomenon that I had observed during my previous four decades of collecting, reading, and chronologicizing literally thousands of traditional Holmes stories: All of these different narratives – the pitifully few original sixty of The Canon and all the rest from so many other later literary agents – fit together remarkably well as one wonderful whole. To describe it, I coined the term *The Great Holmes Tapestry*, and I've been proud since then to see it mentioned that way in other places when describing *The Big Picture* of all these stories, and not just Watson's initial sixty tales that crossed the *First* Literary Agent's desk.

As I've explained in other locations, this Tapestry consists of the overall and complete lives of Holmes and Watson from birth to death, filling in all those pieces of the picture that the original Canon does not. The Canon indisputably makes up the main fibers of the illustration, but there are so many other pieces to examine. Another way to look at this is to think of all the days in a life. I'm sure that someone somewhere has calculated the amount of time in Holmes and Watson's lives that are actually represented in The Canon. (There are always people who are carrying out these various scholarly tasks – counting the exact number of times a gasogene is used, for instance, or the total number of words uttered by Inspector Lestrade during all of his combined appearances. This

1

information is undoubtedly out there – *somewhere* – if one just knows where to look.)

The actual amount of on-stage time chronicled in The Canon adds up to just a limited number of days. In Holmes and Watson's full lifetimes – and as a deadly serious player of The Game, I emphatically declare that Holmes and Watson *had very full lifetimes!* – there were far more moments that have not been "officially" described than the little bit that is related within The Canon. Some would be satisfied with only ever knowing what's related in The Official Sixty Adventures, endlessly examining and re-examining these cases and preferring to think of Holmes spending the rest of his time between cases moping about the Baker Street sitting room in a brown study limbo for weeks on end. And that isn't correct at all. There is more to the complete lives of Holmes and Watson than the little time recorded in The Canon.

Even during those years when the First Literary Agent was still alive, before he had a chance to examine and evaluate first-hand his spiritualistic assertions, new stories from other directions were appearing to start filling in the missing pieces of these complete lives. Consider Vincent Starrett's "The Adventure of the Unique Hamlet", which was published in 1920. There are people who know much more about Starrett than I do, and they can probably relate what the First Literary Agent's reaction was to someone bringing forth one of Watson's manuscripts from a different source. What interests me is that someone so revered in the legendary Sherlockian Halls of Fame as Mr. Starrett chose to make public an extra-Canonical adventure – and such a well-regarded one to boot! – more than a decade before he produced his scholarly work, *The Private Life of Sherlock Holmes* (1933). In this regard, I like Starrett's priorities, and commend them to those who favor the more scholarly side of Holmesian Studies.

Some people – too many, actually – are satisfied only with The Canon, and go no further – either through ignorance or stubbornness. I'll admit that there is a certain completeness to the solid and wonderful Canon. I well remember the first time that I finished my reading of all sixty of the "official" adventures. I can only imagine how sad it must be for someone to reach that final story and mistakenly believe that there are no more. I was quite fortunate that I knew better from nearly my first encounter with Mr. Holmes. I discovered him in 1975, when I was ten years old, reading the abridged Whitman edition of *The Adventures* that only had eight of the twelve stories. I next found a tattered paperback copy of *The Return* – and I still have both of those very books on the shelves holding my collection. After obtaining *The Return*, I plunged into "The

Empty House" – thus learning how Holmes survived his encounter with Professor Moriarty at the Reichenbach Falls before I even knew that he was believed to have died – an incredibly valuable lesson in reading things in chronological order! And very soon after that, I discovered pastiches, and it became apparent that there was no need to feel sad when finishing The Canon, because it was simply a gateway to a much larger world, and not simply a closed and finite sixty-sided dead-end room.

Not long after my first introduction to Holmes, I received a copy of Nicholas Meyer's *The Seven-Per-Cent Solution* (1974). I recognized, even then, that some parts just didn't fit with the True Canon, and I was much more thrilled from beginning-to-end with Meyer's next book, *The West End Horror* (1976). In those early days, still before I'd even read all of The Canon, I was electrified by William S. Baring-Gould's biography *Sherlock Holmes of Baker Street* (1962 – and it's hard now to get my head around the fact that when I read Baring-Gould's incredibly influential masterpiece in the mid-1970's, it was only thirteen years old to my ten years.) And over the next few years, I occasionally found other Holmes books that thrilled me as well, including *Enter the Lion* by Sean M. Wright and Michael P. Hodel (1979) – which showed that a Holmes adventure doesn't have to come by way of Watson's pen to give a true account – and various books by the prolific and fun (and sadly deceased) Frank Thomas, such as *Sherlock Holmes and the Golden Bird* (1979) and *Sherlock Holmes and the Sacred Sword* (1980).

Through the years, I've been very fortunate to have the opportunity to track down and acquire literally thousands of traditional pastiches – as well as to read and study and chronologicize them. In the mid-1990's, I began to make notes as I re-read my favorites and also caught up on all those stories that I had acquired at that point but hadn't yet explored. In the years since, I've been constantly expanding and revising those original notes while acquiring many more pastiches, and now I have a massive Sherlockian Chronology of both Canon and pastiche, well over 800 dense pages, stretching from 1844 – with a story relating the meeting, courtship, and marriage of Holmes's parents – to January 1957, and Holmes's death, as shared by Baring-Gould. (I'm a staunch Baring-Gouldist, although I'll admit he didn't get everything right.) Through this entire Chronology, I've broken down traditional adventures in my collection – novels, short stories, radio and television episodes, movies and scripts, comics, fan-fiction, and unpublished manuscripts – by book, story, chapter, or paragraph into year, month, day, and even hour. And it never ceases to amaze me how well it all fits together.

As I've related elsewhere, all of the traditional Canonically-based Sherlock Holmes stories are linked together to that spark of imagination

3

that sets these narratives in motion, *The Great Watsonian Oversoul*. Although there are contradictions and incorrect statements at times – and usually the blame can be placed upon modern editors who foist their own agendas or unverified assumptions onto Watson's original notes – the overall consistency of this myriad of adventures is astonishing. For example, an obscure story brought forth by one later literary agent in the 1940's will fit perfectly – chronology-wise – with another written in the last year or so, and I'm almost certain that the more recent literary agent didn't have any clue about the earlier one when tapping into *The Oversoul* to bring forth the narrative. Somehow, as each of these little sparks from *The Oversoul* are revealed, their connection to the whole becomes apparent. And while editing these current three simultaneous volumes, *Parts XIII*, *XIV*, and *XV*, I saw this same thing happening yet again.

When I solicit and receive stories for these books, I only set out a very few requirements: The stories must be absolutely traditional. They have to be set in the correct time period, of equivalent Canonical length, and with no aspects of parody, anachronisms, or actual supernatural encounters. Sometimes participants will want to float an idea by me before beginning, or even send a draft of a story to get my input along the way, but I refuse to read it. I want the first version of a submission that I read to be the final version. But by doing it this way, I cannot say ahead of time if someone is going to submit something that has a relationship or connection to another entry. I'll leave it to perceptive readers to have fun spotting the overlaps in this new collection.

A few times through this amazing journey of over 330 stories (so far), there have some overlaps. In one volume, two of the contributors submitted stories that were both set within days of each other, and in one Holmes fools Watson with a false investigation, while in the next Watson fools Holmes (or tries to) in the same way. Rather than tell one of the contributors, "No," I happily used both of their stories, side-by-side, as to my mind they strengthened rather than diminished each other. On another occasion, one author was worried to discover that his story about a jewel theft had been placed chronologically in that particular book next to another story that was also about a jewel theft. However, the two narratives were so different, and diverged immediately into such varying directions, that I don't believe that anyone noticed or was bothered by it.

That's one of the thrills of reading a Holmes story – one never knows which way it will go. It may be a straight-forward narrative or convoluted, with international consequences, or of huge importance only to one person. It might be comedy or tragedy, or a procedural investigation, or gothic horror. It might have a London setting or take us to the countryside, or to the Continent or North America, Asia or Africa. It could cover just hours, or be spaced to relate connected incidents that occur years apart. We might find ourselves early or late in Holmes career. Holmes or Watson – or neither! – might not even appear at all. There may be a comfortable trope, such as Holmes and Watson hiding in a supposedly empty location waiting to trap the criminal, or something brand new.

Mysteries may range all the way from murder down to nothing more than a simple misunderstanding with a crime-free solution. The tale may involve great historical events or the tiniest of mysteries that only affect the lives of a few people. It might be Victorian or Edwardian, or possibly a little bit later. The story could be narrated by Watson or Holmes, or someone else. There may be a treasure hunt or a series of mysterious warnings, brought to Holmes from high-born clients or low. The majority of the story might consist of the client's strange tale, narrated while sitting in front of the fire in the Baker Street sitting room, or we may find Our Heroes in the foreground from start to finish.

To paraphrase Bilbo Baggins, who warned his nephew about the dangers of stepping onto the road: *"It's a [fascinating] business, [Watson]. You [start a new adventure], and . . . there's no knowing where you might be swept off to."*

It never gets old, and there are never enough.

I mentioned my requirements for a story to be included in these books, but I neglected to list perhaps the most important one of all: Holmes and Watson have to be *heroes*.

When I first dreamed of editing a Holmes back – specifically on January 22nd, 2015, as evidenced by the email that I still have proposing it to publisher Steve Emecz – the reason that I wanted to do so was simple: People were forgetting that Sherlock Holmes is a hero. More than just forgetting, actually – they were desperately going out of their way to actively destroy him. It has become fashionable to use the names of Holmes and his associates in ever-more lurid and demeaning and insulting representations – as if each iteration has to outdo the one before it in terms of just how outrageous and broken Holmes can be. He has to be absolutely hopeless and irredeemable, or a sociopath, or a murderer. He can only function if Watson serves as a caretaker at best, and Watson is given his own set of defects as well. A push-back was needed.

I'm so fortunate to have been able to find like-minded individuals who also want to support Holmes the Hero, and who write stories about the True Sherlock Holmes. In the four years since the idea first occurred to me, these 330-plus adventures have served as an alternative against those who would erase and replace the heroic Holmes of the Victorian and Edwardian years, instead trying to make him some sort of damaged goods, or Van Helsing, where "Ghosts can apply after all", or a Dr. Who-like character who regenerates in a multitude of decades or formats, or worst of all, as a morally defective creep. Playing The Game means that Holmes is not a Magic Man who lives forever, or someone whose spirit dances into different realities or even completely different personalities with the same name. There are still bulwarks that stand to defend the True Holmes – these books and others like them – and I cannot thank those enough who contribute to and support them for all that they have done and continue to do.

Luckily, the True Holmes has continued to burn like a beacon through all of the greasy fog that still threatens to obscure him. There are still legitimate adventures appearing – *almost daily, it sometimes seems, and thank God for that!* – that tell us more – *but never enough!* – about Mr. Sherlock Holmes of Baker Street.

As these anthologies continue – and there's no end in sight, as at this writing, as I'm already receiving stories for the next two collections! – what will *not* change is that Holmes and Watson will continue to be represented as *heroes*. You won't find a story where Holmes or Watson turn out to be murderers, or Holmes deduces that he's been created by a writer. (I regularly turn these down, along with many other stories with objectionable premises.) One thing that has changed, however, is an informal rule that I had for a long time with the earlier books – only one story per author per collection.

This seemed to make sense for a long time, as I didn't want to be appearing to favor someone over another, and also because initially space was limited. After all, the first collection had humble ambitions, although it grew over time. At first, Steve Emecz and I had many discussions about what to do as more stories arrived and the initial single book grew fatter. Keep making the font size smaller as more stories arrived? The contributors kept contributing, and I didn't want to keep any new Holmes adventures away from the public. Just when I thought that things were about to get locked into place in that spring of 2015, I had a sudden surge of new submissions. What to do? Why, expand to two volumes. And as that year progressed, what was two books then became three, containing 63 new Holmes adventures.

When we decided to continue beyond the initial record-breaking three-volume set as an ongoing series, the plan was to have modest one-volume editions. That worked for *Parts IV* and *V*, when we we had ended up having enough contributions to issue new collections in both the spring and the fall. Then came *Part VI: 2017 Annual*, which was huge and really should have been split into two books. After that, when the number of contributions pushed the boundaries, we decided to expand into multiple simultaneous volumes, as needed. (We were happy to discover that these multiple volumes were more popular anyway.) So the next sets have appeared in twos: *Parts VII* and *VIII, IX* and *X, XI* and *XII*. And now, with this new collection, I've again received so many stories that they can only be contained in three large books, and this time with more stories than the initial record-breaking 63 from *Parts I, II,* and *III* in 2015.

And part of this is due to allowing multiple contributions from authors. In *Parts XI* and *XII: Some Untold Cases*, I had two different stories from the great Mike Hogan that fit the collection's parameters, and I couldn't pick one or the other. Then I saw that one would go in the *Part XI* and the other *Part XII*. Problem solved. It wasn't my intention to make this a new accepted policy – it just worked out that way. Then, when I first began assembling and editing another anthology, *The New Adventures of Solar Pons* (2018), I was worried that I wouldn't have enough stories, so I also said that authors could contribute more than one. We ended up with a really great collection of 20 stories with some from multiple participants, so I needn't have worried. By then, my mind was open to additional contributions.

I was in the early days of preparing this set in mid-2018 when I received an email from reader Ed Enstrom. I'd never heard from him before, but he reached out through the email address shown at the end of this foreword to discuss errors that had slipped through and into the previous book. (I'm always mortified when this happens, but I have to point out – as I did to Ed – that sadly I can't devote a professional amount of effort to these books, as professionally I'm a licensed civil engineer, and my editorship is as an unpaid amateur who does this in his spare time. I look upon this work as that of a missionary of The Church of Holmes. I don't have any true publishing software, just the common version of Microsoft Word in which to assemble the book files.) I replied to Ed's email and, as a diligent amateur editor, I concluded – as I often do – by asking if he'd like to write a story.

He'd never considered such a thing, but he went away and, eight days later, he sent me his first-ever pastiche. I read it and saw that it was exactly what I'm always looking for, and promptly confirmed that I could use it. And then, soon after, Ed sent me a second story. And then a third. He had the fever.

Of course, just like in the case of Mike Hogan's two stories in the previous set, I hated to pick one over another when I could bring *all* of them to the public's attention. I was happy when this ended up being three volumes, because that way I could put one of Ed's stories in each book.

7

By then, some of the other much-treasured regular participants – Tracy Revels, Mark Mower, Roger Riccard, Arthur Hall, Dick Gillman, and Peter Coe Verbica – had sent more than one story as well, and I was very pleased to include all of them. And then, having written my own initial contribution, I decided to have a go at another, and then another – thus making me a multiple contributor to the books too. And that's how we reached *66* stories this time, beating the record of *63* set with *Parts I, II,* and *III* in 2015, way back at the beginning . . . .

> *"Of course, I could only stammer out my thanks."*
> – *The unhappy John Hector McFarlane,* "The Norwood Builder"

These last few years have been an amazing. I've been able to meet some incredible people, both in person and in the modern electronic way, and also I've been able to read several hundred new Holmes adventures, all to the benefit of the Stepping Stones School at Undershaw, one of Sir Arthur Conan Doyle's homes. The contributors to these MX anthologies donate their royalties to the school, and so far we've raised over $40,000 – maybe $50,000 by the time you read this! More importantly, thousands of people have been made aware of the Stepping Stones School, and this has been a wonderful and unexpected added benefit.

There are many people to thank. First and foremost, as with every one of these projects that I attempt, my amazing and incredibly wonderful wife (of thirty-one years by the time you read this!) Rebecca, and our truly awesome son and my friend, Dan. I love you both, and you are everything to me!

I have all the gratitude in the world for the contributors who have used their time, energy, and creativity to be part of this project. I'm so glad to have gotten to know all of you through the process. It's an undeniable fact that Sherlock Holmes authors are the *best* people!

I also must thank the people who buy these books and support them in so many ways. And don't forget – if you like reading them, considering joining the party and *writing* a story too! One of the things that makes me most proud of these books are the first-time authors who sent a story, and sometimes another for the next book, and so on, and now some of them have had enough for their own books to be published, and along the way they've learned about writing and publishing.

Next, I'd like to thank those who offer support, encouragement, and friendship, sometimes patiently waiting on me to reply as my time is pulled in so many other directions. We often go great amounts of time between communications, but I always enjoy our discussions. Many many thanks

8

to (in alphabetical order): Bob Byrne, Mark Mower, Denis Smith, Tom Turley, Dan Victor, and Marcia Wilson.

Additionally, I'd also like to especially thank:

- Steve Emecz – From idea to book, and then repeating the process, I've had a wonderful time ever since I first emailed Steve back in December 2012. Everything that has happened since then is amazing for me personally, and I owe so much of it to Steve, a great guy in every respect. Thank you for each opportunity!

- Will Thomas: I first heard of Will when I bought and read his first Barker and Llewelyn book, *Some Danger Involved* (2004) when it was initially published. I was thrilled. There are several authors who have taken Canonical characters and made them their own, filling in the details beyond the cursory Canonical descriptions – Marcia Wilson and the Scotland Yarders (especially Lestrade) for instance, Michael Kurland's Professor Moriarty, Carole Nelson Douglas and Irene Adler, Sean Wright and Michael Hodel's Mycroft Holmes, and Gerard Williams's Dr. Mortimer – and now we know the truth about Barker, Holmes's *"hated rival upon the Surrey shore"*. Others have written about Barker – he's been in one of my stories, and he appears in another by someone else in this very volume – but Will told us his first name ("Cyrus") and provided his background and a circle of friends and has given us so many amazing adventures.

  I've been able to make three Holmes Pilgrimages to London (so far), and while nearly everywhere that I went related to Holmes, I did work in a few other stops, such as the former homes of Solar Pons, Hercule Poirot, and James Bond. And several times I've stopped into Craig's Court in Whitehall – both because it was one of the locations of Watson's old bank, Cox and Company, and also because it was where Cyrus Barker's office was located. (As is the case with Mr. Holmes and several others, I also play *The Game* in regard to Barker and Llewelyn.) I'm only on one certain social media succubus to connect with other Sherlockians, and it was amazing fun to photograph myself and my ever-present

9

deerstalker in front of Barker's office on several occasions and post the photo, letting Will know in real time that I was right there right then, and then to see him immediately respond.

I'm very thankful that he both wrote a Holmes story for the first three-volume MX collection back in 2015 ("The Adventure of Urquhart Manse") and now that he's a part of this set too. Long may he continue to chronicle the adventures of Barker and Llewelyn!

- Roger Johnson – To one of the most knowledgeable Sherlockians and one of the most gracious and supportive people that I know! I'm incredibly grateful that Roger reviewed my first book, and then others after that. He and his wife Jean Upton have done so much to help promote these books, and they wonderfully hosted me for a few days during my Holmes Pilgrimage No. 2 in 2015, when the first MX anthologies were published. Since then, there have been many other projects – these books, and others – where Roger has stepped up and written scholarly forewords, no questions asked. I can't imagine these books without him.

- Derrick Belanger – Derrick and I started emailing in late 2014, and haven't stopped since. Soon after, I had the idea for the MX anthologies, and he was one of the initial group that I asked to join the party. (He recently reminded me that my invitation led him to write his first traditional pastiche.) Since then, he and his brother Brian have gone on to create Belanger Books, home of many successful projects – several of which I've been fortunate enough to edit – and Derrick has also written a great deal more new Holmesian material. Derrick: Thanks very much for your friendship, and for all of the additional Sherlockian opportunities.

- Brian Belanger – Although we've yet to meet in person, I've really enjoyed getting to know Brian over the last few years, both in connection to these projects, as well as those with Belanger Books. He's an incredibly talented graphic artist who continues to amaze me even more with each new project – and all of the people who have book

10

covers designed by him will certainly agree. Brian: Thank you so much for all that you do – it's appreciated by many people besides me!

- Sean M. Wright – Finding pastiches in my hometown was difficult when I was a kid, just starting out as a Sherlockian. As mentioned above, one of the first pastiches that I ever encountered was the Mycroft Holmes-narrated *Enter the Lion* (1979) by Sean M. Wright and Michael P. Hodel. It's still an amazing book forty years later, and it showed me that others besides Watson could provide narratives within The World of Sherlock Holmes. Others have written about Mycroft since then – Glen Petrie, Kareem Abdul-Jabbar and Anna Waterhouse – but for me the best and most definitive will always be *Enter the Lion* by Wright and Hodel. I was thrilled a few months ago to be put in touch with Mr. Wright and, as your diligent amateur author, be able to ask him for a new Mycroft Holmes story. Amazingly, he has several which he hopes to publish in the future, and more amazingly, he allowed me to use one of them here first. The boy Sherlockian in me, who back then had a Holmes collection on his shelf only about one-foot wide – including *Enter the Lion* – is thrilled, and so is the adult Sherlockian, and I cannot thank Mr. Wright enough!

- Ian Dickerson – In a couple of contributions to previous MX anthology volumes – "The Strange Adventure of the Doomed Sextette" in *Part IX (1879-1895)* and "The Giant Rat of Sumatra" in *Part XI: Some Untold Cases (1880-1891)*, Ian explained how he came to be responsible for a number of long-lost scripts from the 1944 season of the Holmes radio show, starring Basil Rathbone and Nigel Bruce, and written by Denis Green and Leslie Charteris (under the name Bruce Taylor).

  Since then, he's published two sets of the scripts – *Sherlock Holmes: The Lost Radio Scripts* (2017) and *Sherlock Holmes: More Lost Radio Scripts* (2018). There are still a few more of them that remain unpublished, and I'm very grateful to Ian for allowing "The Haunted Chateau" to appear here. When I first discovered Holmes as a boy, I quickly found a number of Rathbone and

11

Bruce broadcasts on records at the public library, and that was where I first "heard" Holmes. I can't express the thrill of getting to read these rediscovered lost treasures, having been tantalized by their titles for so long. Many thanks to Ian for making these available.

- *The Nashville Scholars of the Three Pipe Problem* – The area where I live in eastern Tennessee is not noted for Sherlockian activity, or even awareness of the great man. I've worn a deerstalker as my only hat year-round since I was nineteen in 1984, and no one ever seems to recognize who I'm honouring. The closest Sherlockian Scion is in Nashville, a nearly-four-hour drive each way. Understandably, I don't get there as often as I'd like, but I'm very grateful to be a member of The Nashville Scholars, now in its fortieth year, and to visit when I can. In particular, I'd like to thank four of the Scholars:

  o *Jim Hawkins*, who works tirelessly to promote the group, and with whom I was very glad to spend some time at the 2018 *From Gillette to Brett V* Conference in Bloomington, IN;
  o *Shannon Carlisle, BSI*: I met Shannon, an award-winning teacher, at my first Scholars meeting. She is noted for using Holmes as the basis for much in her classroom, and her students were particularly interested in Stepping Stones and Undershaw. I was able to provide some information, including descriptions of my visit there in 2016. I'm grateful for her friendship;
  o *Bill Mason, BSI*: I met Bill at *From Gillette to Brett III* in 2011, when someone mentioned that we were both from Tennessee. We exchanged copies of our first books and have stayed in touch ever since. He's very supportive, and I've enjoyed hearing much of his insight since then;
  o *Marino Alvarez, BSI*: I became aware of Marino when he published A Professor Reflects on Sherlock Holmes (2012 MX Publishing.) I met him at *A Gathering of Southern Sherlockians* in 2012, but I doubt if he remembers it. I next met him at my first Nashville Scholars meeting. And

then, to my great surprise and enjoyment, he unexpectedly submitted a Holmes story for this collection. I'm very happy and thankful that he's a part of this!

- Ray Betzner, noted Sherlockian and especially noted Vincent Starrett Scholar: Thanks for taking time to answer a Starrett question!

- Melissa Grigsby – Thank you for the incredible work that you do at the Stepping Stones School at Undershaw in Hindhead. I was both amazed and thrilled to visit the school on opening day in 2016, and I hope to get back there again some time. You are doing amazing things, and it's my honor, as well that of all the contributors to this project, to be able to help.

- Joel Senter and his wife Carolyn have been legends in the Sherlockian community. I personally got to know Joel through telephone conversations, starting in the late 1980's, when I would order items from their amazing *Classic Specialties*. Later, I would call Joel with product ideas or questions. When my first book was published by a publisher who didn't actually intend to sell it, Joel gave me great advice, and furthermore, he sold the book for me through *Classic Specialties*. I only met him and Carolyn once in person, at *A Gathering of Southern Sherlockians* in 2012, and they arranged for me to sell books at a vendor's table (shared with Tracy Revels, whom I also met there for the first time,) and at that same event, Joel made a point of presenting me with a check in front of everyone for the profits my books that had sold through their business. When I first thought of the MX anthology, Joel was an incredible supporter, and he and Carolyn wrote an amazing story, "The Adventure of the Avaricious Bookkeeper", which closed out the final of the first three volumes with a case set just before Watson's death. It was an amazing way to conclude those books. Joel and I continued to communicate by email until shortly before his death in July 2018, and I – like so many Sherlockians – was devastated to learn that he had passed. He helped so many people with his enthusiasm

13

and support, and this set of MX volumes is dedicated to him.

In addition those mentioned above, I'd also like to especially thank (in alphabetical order): Larry Albert, Hugh Ashton, Deanna Baran, Jayantika Ganguly, Paul Gilbert, Dick Gillman, Arthur Hall, Mike Hogan, Craig Janacek, Tracy Revels, Roger Riccard, Geri Schear, and Tim Symonds. From the very beginning, these special contributors have stepped up and supported this and other projects over and over again with their contributions. They are the best and I can't explain how valued they are.

Finally, last but certainly *not* least, **Sir Arthur Conan Doyle**: Author, doctor, adventurer, and the Founder of the Sherlockian Feast. Present in spirit, and honored by all of us here.

As always, this collection, like those before it, has been a labor of love by both the participants and myself. As I've explained before, once again everyone did their sincerest best to produce an anthology that truly represents why Holmes and Watson have been so popular for so long. These are just more tiny threads woven into the ongoing Great Holmes Tapestry, continuing to grow and grow, for there can *never* be enough stories about the man whom Watson described as *"the best and wisest . . . whom I have ever known."*

David Marcum
March 20th, 2019
The 122nd Anniversary of the
Radix pedis diabolic *experiment*

Questions, comments, and story submissions
may be addressed to David Marcum at
thepapersofsherlockholmes@gmail.com

"Take up and read!"
by Will Thomas

I cut my teeth on Sherlock Holmes. I still recall being enthralled by Basil Rathbone at ten, and reading *The Boy's Sherlock Holmes* a year later. When I was seventeen I joined a Holmes scion, The Afghanistan Perceivers, in which the average age was fifty. What does one do with a rambunctious seventeen-year-old? One makes him the book reviewer for the club journal, something that doesn't require attending actual meetings. I didn't mind – I was studying The Canon, the history of Victorian London, and the other great fiction of that golden age. I was giving myself an education of sorts. Then Nicholas Meyer came along with his *The Seven Per-Cent Solution* and rocked my world.

There is an itch many writers have to pen a Sherlock Holmes story. Twain had it. What is *Pygmalion* but an homage by George Bernard Shaw? It is an itch that begs to be scratched. Picture a bear upright against an old oak tree. I've never thought to myself, "You need to write a Hemingway story," or "A sequel to *The Catcher in the Rye*! Brilliant!" Yet countless times I have put pen to paper and scribbled "It was in the year 1894 that I first . . . ."

What is the fascination? I cannot explain it, but I feel it keenly. Many Sherlockians do as well. We want to create our own tale, or to read others' in the hope that for twenty minutes or so we can be transported back to when we read our very first Sherlock Holmes story.

Some cannot visualize a time when The Canon was so sacred one wrote a pastiche with trepidation. It would be like walking on Doyle's grave. Luckily, we live in more enlightened times now. The book in front of you, featuring stories from a slew of modern masters, is proof of that. The world of Holmes has become less stodgy, and a lot more fun, if such a thing is even possible.

I never wrote that Sherlockian novel I was planning. Another pair of fictional detectives . . . sorry, make that private enquiry agents . . . came along and demanded my time and attention. Yet I admire the attempts others have made to try on Doyle's slippers, if only for a brief while. Holmes fans are the better for it.

Rather than quote from Doyle, let me turn to St. Augustine, who said:

"Take up and read!"

The book lays in front of you, open and insistent. Shall you heed its siren call? Oh come, what are you waiting for? The game's afoot!

Oh, look. I quoted Doyle after all.

Will Thomas
February 2019

"When I Glance Over My Notes and Records . . ." *
by Roger Johnson

. . . I realise, with a certain surprise, that this remarkable series of books began only four years ago. And here we are in 2019, celebrating the 160th anniversary of the birth of Arthur Conan Doyle in an entirely appropriate manner by helping to maintain the house that he helped create for himself and his family.

But there are other anniversaries this year. On the 30th August 1889, for instance, J.M. Stoddart, who had come from Philadelphia to commission material from British authors for *Lippincott's Monthly Magazine*, gave a small dinner party at the Langham Hotel. His guests were Thomas Patrick Gill, Oscar Wilde (whose 165th birthday falls on the 16th October) and Arthur Conan Doyle. Gill may have been invited on the strength of his own editorial experience. If so, he can share the credit for the magazine's publication the following year of *The Picture of Dorian Gray* and *The Sign of the Four*.

Conan Doyle published no new Holmes stories in 1919. The masterly "His Last Bow" had appeared two years before in both *The Strand Magazine* and *Collier's*. "The Mazarin Stone", rather less inspiring, was published in 1921, adapted from Conan Doyle's one-act play *The Crown Diamond*, which had enjoyed a brief and unsuccessful run earlier in the year.

But if we look two decades further back, we see that *Sherlock Holmes: A Drama in Four Acts*, credited to Arthur Conan Doyle and William Gillette, had its copyright performance at The Duke of York's Theatre in London on the 12th June 1899, with Herbert Waring as Holmes. Gillette himself was the star, of course, when the play opened on the 23rd October in Buffalo, transferring to the Garrick Theatre in New York the following month. Its success, which owed much to Gillette's performance, certainly helped stimulate public demand for more adventures of the great detective – a demand that was shortly to be satisfied in part by the publication of *The Hound of the Baskervilles*. (Gillette's play was triumphantly revived by the Royal Shakespeare Company forty-five years ago, with John Wood magnificent as Holmes.)

1929 saw both the last silent Holmes film, *Der Hund von Baskerville* (now restored and made available *this year* for home viewing) and the first talkie, *The Return of Sherlock Holmes*, with Clive Brook in the lead. A print of the latter is held at the Library of Congress, but is apparently inaccessible to the public.

In 1939, however, there was a true cinematic landmark. Fox's lavish production of *The Hound of the Baskervilles* paired Basil Rathbone and Nigel Bruce for the first time as the detective and the doctor. Moreover, it was the first Holmes film to be set in the correct period. Late Victorian London was superbly re-created in Hollywood – and the sets were used again that same year for a similarly excellent production, *The Adventures of Sherlock Holmes*.

Twenty years later, Hammer's flawed but entertaining version of *The Hound of the Baskervilles* presented Sherlock Holmes in colour for the first time, and showed that a British studio could match Hollywood for action and suspense. In its sixtieth anniversary year, critical appreciation of this good-looking film, with its fine performances from a cast headed by Peter Cushing and Andre Morell, has grown. (I remember when the *Radio Times* critics gave it a rather harsh two-star ranking. Now it merits the full five stars. *Tempora mutantur . . . .*)

In 1954, while Carleton Hobbs and Norman Shelley were playing Holmes and Watson in a series for children on the BBC Home Service, the Light Programme transmitted twelve new dramatisations from the Canon, starring John Gielgud and Ralph Richardson. Unusually, these were produced by an independent company, and for some reason the BBC declined to broadcast the remaining four plays, though the whole series was eagerly taken up by stations in America and elsewhere. (Hobbs and Shelley remained British radio's definitive pairing for another fifteen years. 2019 marks the fiftieth anniversary of their final series as Holmes and Watson, which concluded, most appropriately, with *His Last Bow*.)

That same year, American audiences could see the great detective on television, in a light but very enjoyable series of short films with Ronald Howard and Howard Marion Crawford in the leading rôles. On this side of the Atlantic, we had to wait until video recordings were released some fifty years later, but meanwhile we had something rather better to look at. Fifty-five years ago, in an anthology series called *Detective*, BBC TV presented a superb, authentic Holmes and Watson. The actors were Douglas Wilmer and Nigel Stock, and the story was *The Speckled Band*. Its success led to a fondly remembered series the following year.

2019 also marks the thirty-fifth anniversary of Jeremy Brett's first appearance as Holmes, with David Burke as his Watson, in Michael Cox's series for Granada TV, *The Adventures of Sherlock Holmes*. It was the start of an extraordinary decade-long world-wide phenomenon, which at its best was unbeatable. In Burke we saw the true Watson, brave, intelligent, loyal and down-to-earth. Brett, for many, remains the ideal Holmes.

What else? Well, eighty-five years ago, The Baker Street Irregulars, which, in terms of its combined age and influence ranks as the world's senior Holmesian fellowship, was founded. Moreover, The Sherlock Holmes Society held its inaugural meeting in London at the same time as the BSI's first meeting in New York. Indeed, the two groups exchanged congratulatory telegrams! But while the Irregulars' sodality persisted through the hard times of the thirties and forties, the very differently constituted British society survived only until 1938, lying dormant until its revival as The Sherlock Holmes Society of London in 1951.

I can't conclude without mentioning the twentieth anniversary of two remarkable achievements. In 1999, thanks to the imagination and hard work of certain members of the SHSL – notably, of course, the sculptor John Doubleday – and the financial support of Abbey National plc, an imposing statue of the Great Detective was at last erected in London. Its unveiling on the 23rd September was the focal point of a week-long festival, which included an evening at the Cockpit Theatre to see *Sherlock Holmes: The Last Act!* written by David Stuart Davies for Roger Llewellyn, who had first staged it earlier in the year at the Salisbury Playhouse.

I doubt that even the author seriously believed that it would become an international success, but that's exactly what has happened. The play itself is first-rate, and even then Roger Llewellyn's interpretation was revelatory. Roger died last year, but his performance in *The Last Act* and its successor *Sherlock Holmes: The Death and Life* can still be enjoyed, as he recorded the two plays for Big Finish in 2010. (And as I write, we're less than a month away from the premiere of David's new play, *Sherlock Holmes: The Final Reckoning*, in which Michael Daviot and Mark Kydd play the detective and the doctor.)

I remember the explosion of interest in 1987, stimulated by the centenary of the first Holmes story, *A Study in Scarlet*. 2019 is another year peculiarly rich in significant anniversaries – *and opportunities*. David Marcum, MX Publishing, and the many contributors to this volume have created one of those opportunities. Let's make the most of it!

Roger Johnson, BSI, ASH
31st January, 2019

* "The Five Orange Pips"

An Ongoing Legacy
for Sherlock Holmes
by Steve Emecz

Undershaw
Circa 1900

As we enter the fourth year of *The MX Book of New Sherlock Holmes Stories*, we reach a staggering fifteen volumes – by far the largest collection of new Sherlock Holmes stories in the world. Through authors donating royalties and licensing, the series has raised over $40,000 for Stepping Stones School. With this money, the school has been able to fund projects that would be very difficult to organise otherwise – especially those to preserve the legacy of Sir Arthur Conan Doyle at Undershaw.

There are now over three-hundred-thirty stories and well over a hundred-fifty authors taking part – many MX authors, but many others including bestselling authors like Lee Child, Jonathan Kellerman, Lyndsay Faye, and Bonnie MacBird.

Volumes XI and XII continued the tradition of getting starred reviews from *Publishers Weekly*:

"Each of 17 Sherlock Holmes pastiches in Marcum's stellar 11th anthology (after Part X) is based on one of the teasing references that Conan Doyle made to cases that were never published. The end result is another triumph of ingenuity and faithfulness to the spirit of the canon . . . .This is an essential volume for Sherlock Holmes fans."

"Marcum continues to amaze with the number of high-quality pastiches that he has selected."

MX Publishing is a social enterprise – all the staff, including me, are volunteers with day jobs. The collection would not be possible without the creator and editor, David Marcum, who is rightly cited multiple times by *Publishers Weekly* and others as probably the most accomplished Sherlockian editor thus far. In addition to Stepping Stones School, our main program that we support is the Happy Life Children's Home in Kenya. My wife Sharon and I have recently returned from our 6th Christmas in a row at Happy Life and can report back that huge progress has been made and the lives of over 600 babies saved. You can read all about the project in the 2nd edition of the book *The Happy Life Story.*

Our support of both of these projects is possible through the publishing of Sherlock Holmes books, which we have now been doing for a decade.

You can find out more information about the Stepping Stones School at: *www.steppingstones.org.uk*

and Happy Life at: *www.happylifechildrenshomes.com.*

You can obtain more books from MX, both fiction and non-fiction, at: *www.sherlockholmesbooks.com.*

If you would like to become involved with these projects or help out in any way, please reach out to me via *LinkedIn.*

Steve Emecz
February 2019
Twitter: *@steveemecz*
LinkedIn: *https://www.linkedin.com/in/emecz/*

The Doyle Room at Stepping Stones, Undershaw
Partially funded through royalties from
The MX Book of New Sherlock Holmes Stories

A Word From the
Head Teacher of Stepping Stones
by Melissa Grigsby

Undershaw
September 9, 2016
Grand Opening of the Stepping Stones School
(Photograph courtesy of Roger Johnson)

"The world is full of obvious things
which nobody by any chance ever observes."
– Arthur Conan Doyle, *The Hound of the Baskervilles*

As we travel into the next journey of Stepping Stones School, the words of Arthur Conan Doyle ring so very true. Our developing outreach and employment support programs based at Undershaw focus on social mobility for young people with Special Educational Needs. Our work sits with Business and Companies that so often miss the obvious things and get caught up in practical barriers, rather than seeing the potential of the young people on our watch.

The funds gifted to us have allowed us to start developing a more sophisticated communication systems, which in turn will open doors to allow the world to observe the obvious things and look deeper at the skills and opportunities the young people of Undershaw bring to the community.

23

Dr. Mortimer looked strangely at us for an instant, and his voice sank almost to a whisper as he answered:

"Mr. Holmes, they were the footprints of a gigantic hound!"

The royalties we receive are the footprints in a gigantic story for Undershaw and the young people that learn under its roof.

Melissa Grigsby
Executive Head Teacher,
Stepping Stones, Undershaw
January 2019

Sherlock Holmes (1854-1957) was born in Yorkshire, England, on 6 January, 1854. In the mid-1870's, he moved to 24 Montague Street, London, where he established himself as the world's first Consulting Detective. After meeting Dr. John H. Watson in early 1881, he and Watson moved to rooms at 221b Baker Street, where his reputation as the world's greatest detective grew for several decades. He was presumed to have died battling noted criminal Professor James Moriarty on 4 May, 1891, but he returned to London on 5 April, 1894, resuming his consulting practice in Baker Street. Retiring to the Sussex coast near Beachy Head in October 1903, he continued to be associated in various private and government investigations while giving the impression of being a reclusive apiarist. He was very involved in the events encompassing World War I, and to a lesser degree those of World War II. He passed away peacefully upon the cliffs above his Sussex home on his 103rd birthday, 6 January, 1957.

Dr. John Hamish Watson (1852-1929) was born in Stranraer, Scotland on 7 August, 1852. In 1878, he took his Doctor of Medicine Degree from the University of London, and later joined the army as a surgeon. Wounded at the Battle of Maiwand in Afghanistan (27 July, 1880), he returned to London late that same year. On New Year's Day, 1881, he was introduced to Sherlock Holmes in the chemical laboratory at Barts. Agreeing to share rooms with Holmes in Baker Street, Watson became invaluable to Holmes's consulting detective practice. Watson was married and widowed three times, and from the late 1880's onward, in addition to his participation in Holmes's investigations and his medical practice, he chronicled Holmes's adventures, with the assistance of his literary agent, Sir Arthur Conan Doyle, in a series of popular narratives, most of which were first published in *The Strand* magazine. Watson's later years were spent preparing a vast number of his notes of Holmes's cases for future publication. Following a final important investigation with Holmes, Watson contracted pneumonia and passed away on 24 July, 1929.

Photos of Sherlock Holmes and Dr. John H. Watson courtesy of Roger Johnson

The MX Book
of
New Sherlock Holmes Stories
Part XIV:
2019 Annual
(1890-1897)

Skein of Tales
by Jacquelynn Morris

Steampunk or Victorian,
Past or present, future.
Japan and Russia, outer space,
New York and Londontown.
Male or female, old or young,
Puppet, canine, mouse.
In print, on page, in comic form,
On film, in AO3.
The depth of love
Was worth a wound
-Worth many wounds-
Of body, soul, and heart.
The world explodes with tales anew
Our two survive, intact.
The then and now
And what will be
The soul of what we love.
And friendship, always friendship,
Runs through this skein of tales,
The thread of scarlet connects us
To them,
And to each other.

The Adventure of
The Royal Albert Hall
by Charles Veley and Anna Elliott

It was March 4th, 1891, a cold Wednesday morning in Paddington, when I received the telegram that would begin this strange and harrowing adventure.

My dear wife Mary and I were comfortably enjoying our breakfast. Lily, our maid, then brought in the message.

"Beg pardon for interrupting, Doctor," she said, curtseying and handing me the tray with the yellow envelope. "The boy said it was urgent and needed a reply."

I opened the envelope and glanced at its contents. Mary was looking at me with evident curiosity, so I read it aloud:

> *If able, kindly attend Benefit Bazaar rehearsal at Albert Hall at four p.m. today. Then meet me at The Diogenes Club at five p.m. Pay particular attention to arrangements for Princess Beatrice. Reply Yes or No.*
>
> *Mycroft Holmes*

"Mycroft?" Mary asked, her expression puzzled.

"His brother Sherlock is in France," I replied. "The newspapers say he is occupied with some important matter for the French government."

"Then you absolutely must go!" she said. "Anstruther can take your patients today. Clearly you are needed, and besides, Cettie and Maude and I already have tickets for the Benefit Bazaar tomorrow! You can tell me all about it tonight."

"I don't quite understand – "

"You must pay particular attention to where Princess Beatrice will be standing during the ceremony. Then Cettie, Maude, and I will know just where we'll best be able to see her in the Hall."

I took out my pen and wrote "*YES*" at the bottom of the flimsy yellow paper, then handed it back to Lily. When she had departed, I poured coffee and looked across the table, gazing at Mary with the comfortable feeling of tenderness that has blessed me ever since our union. "What can you tell me about the Benefit Bazaar?" I asked.

35

She gave me a mischievous smile. "The whole Hall will be transformed, they say, into another and better world – the world of an advanced life form. There was a book about it when I was growing up."

"A book?"

"Yes, about people who can fly and do all sorts of wonderful things. I can't wait to see how they'll show it at the bazaar. I've heard there'll be trapeze artists and a brass band – the Coldstream Guards, I think. And lots of things to buy, because it's a bazaar. Tickets were five shillings each, and all the proceeds go to some worthy cause – a hospital of some sort."

She paused. "Tomorrow the Hall will be filled with society toffs, all costumed up and strutting about, showing off for Princess Beatrice. Great fun – my friends and I always love to laugh at that sort of thing, though not openly, of course. But today they'll just be getting everything hauled in and put up. So I'd expect chaos, actually."

I made a brief stop next door to ask Anstruther to take on the few patients that had made appointments for today and tomorrow. Fortunately, he was available to do so, and, returning to my office, I told my nurse of this new arrangement. Then I took a cab across Hyde Park.

Within an hour I was gazing at the gargantuan structure of The Royal Albert Hall, that world-famous and colossal monument to British architectural achievement. Its height alone inspires awe. I found myself marveling at the sheer mass of the structure. Then I reminded myself that I had come here on a mission.

I drew closer to the grand entrance, and, as Mary had predicted, I found chaos. I was surrounded by a river of humanity, a jumbled crowd that pressed forward like lemmings, determined to gain access to the building. Men and women jostled one another, carrying draped objects, framed pictures, posters, tables, and chairs. All were clamoring to get through the wide doorway.

Unencumbered and alone as I was, it was not difficult to make my way to the edge of the crowd closest to the door and squeeze through. Once inside, my ears were assaulted by the roar of the crowd. I felt I was in a museum of ancient history gone wild and magnified into a nightmare. Around me and above were architectural monuments and replicas such as I might have found in ancient Egypt, or India, or China, or Japan. All across the wide floor workmen were milling about, setting up booths, chairs, tables, and curtains.

At the center of this sprawling hive of activity was a great dark tower, shaped like an obelisk of the Egyptian variety. From a distance, the surface of the structure resembled carved brown sandstone. But closer inspection revealed it to be only painted cardboard. Its height was impressive, soaring nearly halfway to the great metal supporting bars that converged beneath the soaring glass dome one-hundred feet above me.

While I stood staring upward, I was startled by a large winged object, what might have been an enormous bat, dropping directly toward me from far above. I stepped sideways. Expecting it to crash into the floor, I watched, transfixed. The thing had the outlines of a human form. Without touching the ground, it bounced away from me and rebounded up in the air. Then I saw that wires connected it to the structural framework below the dome. As the human-like thing bounced once more, I saw its arms and legs were flexible, and I caught the scents of paint and India rubber. The thing had a face, but the features were blurred, like those of a mannequin in a shop window. I realized it was a gigantic human-size doll made of rubber, painted white, robed in purple with attached purple wings, and hung on thin wires.

A voice came from behind me. "Ah, Dr. Watson!"

I turned and saw a plump, round-faced, middle-aged man, well-dressed, his narrow beard carefully trimmed at the edges of his cheeks and chin. Behind rimless spectacles, his soft dark eyes regarded me with a mixture of amusement and gratitude. But he was perspiring, and his gaze also betrayed a note of wariness – or even, I thought, fear.

"How delighted I am to see you! How grateful! I see you are already making the acquaintance of one of our *Vril-ya*!"

"You have the advantage of me, sir," I said.

"I beg your pardon. A photograph of me is on the brochure for the exhibit, but I gather you have not had opportunity to review it. I am Dr. Herbert Tibbitts, and this bazaar is to benefit my hospital and school of massage and electricity. Probably you have not heard of those either, but I hope you not hold that against me. My research is in the formative stage – we have not yet proved our full potential to the general public. They laughed at Mr. Edison, too, I am told."

"How did you know I was coming?"

"Why, through Mr. Holmes."

"Mr. Holmes is in France, I believe."

"Quite so. I was told that by his landlady, Mrs. Hudson. So, I sent word to his brother Mycroft in Whitehall. Princess Beatrice facilitated the connection, I am sure of that. She is a friend of Mrs. Murchins, one of my patients and supporters, who told the Princess of my urgent need."

He drew me to one side, closer to the framework of the great cardboard obelisk, where we were out of the flow of passers-by. "It was somewhat a delicate matter for her to mention to the Princess, but I had no choice. I was duty bound, you see. I had been warned that there was a plot to disrupt this event. Well, *warned* would not quite be the word for it. *Threatened*, would be more accurate. Unless I pay over a huge sum, which I cannot possibly afford, my event will be somehow interfered with. That would be my ruin, for I have staked everything I own on the rental of the Hall and the creation of the decorative facilities you see around you."

I now understood Mycroft's purpose in sending me the telegram. "Surely the police can help," I said.

"I have enlisted their aid as well. And they of course will have men here attempting to prevent any harm coming to Princess Beatrice. But we both know that the ordinary police methods may fail to uncover hidden perils. I felt it wisest not to overlook the opportunity of gaining Mr. Holmes's insights. Or at least, now, the insights of your good self, since you have had the benefit of long experience with Mr. Holmes's methods."

"Thank you. I shall be happy to investigate and observe."

"Then please let me give you the abridged version of the program – the thing in a nutshell, so to speak. What you see around you is intended to represent an underground cavern city populated by an advanced race called the *Vril-ya*." Tibbitts gestured at the white, purple-robed winged mannequin that still dangled above us. "Readers of Mr. Bulwer-Lytton's book will be familiar with the vision. It connects wonderfully with the work we are attempting to accomplish – "

He broke off and peered at me through his spectacles as though seeing me for the first time. "You are familiar with the electric eel, are you not?"

I nodded, though inwardly I shook my head in bewilderment.

"Well, just as the electric eel is able to internalize electricity to defend itself, so too the advanced race of people imagined by Bulwer-Lytton are able to master and internalize the energy of life that permeates all things, and which we know to be related in some manner to electricity. Bulwer-Lytton named this energy *Vril*, and thus his people are called the *Vril-ya*. Their mastery of the energy also gives them the power to fly, and we here represent that power by this model that dropped upon you so suddenly."

Tibbitts gestured up to the rubber mannequin. "A clumsy imitation, of course, but with it we hope to provide inspiration to our attendees of the potential for scientific research into the use of electricity, coupled with massage. The curative potential, provided we have enough funding for sufficient research – "

He broke off again. "I can see the skepticism in your eyes, Dr. Watson. And you may be as skeptical as you like. But I hope you will nonetheless lend your powers to protecting this event."

"Of course," I replied politely. "Now can you tell me how you were threatened – how the demand for payment was made?"

"As I told the police. I received three telephone calls, each very brief, and the caller used a voice that I did not recognize. Also, I had three notes, the letters clipped from newspapers and pasted to form words. I turned those over to the police."

"When did you do this?"

"About a week ago, when the threats began. The last note came yesterday, and I turned that over as well. That was when I went to Baker Street, and then telephoned Mrs. Murchins. It was clear to me that matters were reaching the breaking point. And there was something else I told the police." He pressed closer to me and turned his head, facing toward the entrance. "Do you see that tall man over there?"

"The man with the eye-patch?"

"He is unmistakable, is he not? Such a giant! Well, this is the third occasion on which I have seen him. I call him 'Mr. Patch'. The first two times I saw him were not long after I received the notes demanding payment. He was strolling along Weymouth Street outside my office, quite deliberately. I told the police about it, of course, because he is such a menacing figure. But they would do nothing. He was free to be on the street then, just as he is free to be here now."

The man was indeed menacing in appearance, perhaps seven feet tall and weighing what could very well have been three-hundred pounds, all of it muscle. No one would want to provoke him.

I remembered the telegram from Mycroft, and his specific instructions. "I should like to see the rehearsal involving Princess Beatrice," I said.

"You are most welcome to do so. Preparation for the ceremony of the gifts will be at four o'clock. Fifteen minutes from now."

I utilized the interval to walk around the enormous hall where booths by the dozens were being set up. I saw vendors busily arranging their wares. In the booth closest to the entrance one could buy paintings that depicted scenes from Bulwer-Lytton's book. In another, one could purchase the music of "Princess Zee". The actual princess was not present, but the poster showed a bright-eyed woman dressed in black satin, her brunette hair adorned by a sparkling silver flower tiara. The actual tiara I saw in the hands of an attendant. It contained tiny glass bulbs and the attendant was attempting to connect it by wires to a pair of electric batteries.

Moving along the perimeter of the great hall I saw more booths, where workmen were arranging shelves and signs proclaiming that perfumes, dolls, petticoats, and even champagne would be on offer. Near the far end, a larger affair was being constructed, where, according to the sign that proclaimed it to be *"Krek's Plunder of the River"*, guests coming here tomorrow might catch fish in an artificial pond. And closer to the central monument there was another booth, entitled *"The Oon of Truth"*.

Below that sign another, smaller one, somewhat worn, had been pinned to the exterior of a purple velvet curtain. It read:

MADAME VADOMA IS IN

On an impulse, I pushed aside the curtain. Before me was a pleasant-faced woman of middle age, with coal black hair and a gypsy scarf, sitting before a round crystal ball. She wore heavy white theatrical makeup and eye shadow and was studying her reflection as she applied the finishing strokes of her crimson lip rouge with a small pointed brush.

"Open for customers?" I asked.

"Not till tomorrow, dear," she said with a smile. Her voice had the deeper tone some women develop over the years. It made her sound more authoritative, which I supposed was good for her business. "Come back tomorrow," she said, "and I'll tell your future."

"I don't know if I ought. I hear there's going to be trouble," I said, half-bantering, and half because I wondered if there had been rumors of the threats Dr. Tibbitts had received.

To my surprise, her face clouded over with worry. "I heard the same," she said. "But I need the money, and I've already paid my entry fee." Her eyes held mine for a moment. She asked, "Do you know what sort of trouble?"

"Only that the police will be here. Protecting the Princess."

She seemed relieved. "That's all right then. Are you with the police?"

"Just here on my own."

"Well, I hope you'll tell me what you learn." She smiled again. "And I hope I'll see you tomorrow."

I said I hoped I would too. She returned to studying her crystal ball and her reflection.

My next stop was a booth where attendants were unpacking boxes of small bulbous brown bottles that I recognized as Bovril, a beef bouillon tonic that I frequently recommended to those patients of mine who had anemia or digestive issues. I asked an attendant why the company, a reputable concern publicly floated on the London Exchange, had chosen to be here. "Oh, because of the name, of course," was the reply. At my blank look, he continued, with some emphasis, "Bo-*VRIL?*"

I felt somewhat abashed at having not made the connection more rapidly. "Of course. I see now," I replied. "Odd that I have recommended the product to my patients for some years, but I never thought about the name."

He gave me a knowing grin. "Tell your patients that they can buy their Bovril in bottles here tomorrow and the rest of the week. We'll have it available by the cup as well, all nice and hot."

He offered me a complimentary bottle then and there, but I declined. Dr. Tibbitts was nearby, ringing a large brass handbell to signal the crowd that the rehearsal was about to begin.

Fortunately for me, the rehearsal did not take long. I was mindful of my obligation to meet Mycroft at five o'clock, so I wanted to make my departure from the Hall without being delayed by a conversation with Dr. Tibbitts.

I successfully evaded the loquacious doctor. On my way out, I picked up a program book showing a map of the various booths in the Hall. As I did so, I also caught sight of the gigantic 'Mr. Patch', who towered head and shoulders over the remainder of the crowd. He appeared to be strolling, casually, without any purposeful intent, in the vicinity of the Bovril booth.

It was a two-mile cab ride from the Hall to the Diogenes Club, a setting familiar to me from when I had met there with Holmes, Mycroft, and the unfortunate Greek interpreter Melas. The doorman was expecting me. My watch showed the time to be just after five o'clock when I entered the Stranger's Room and found Mycroft seated in an upholstered armchair.

Holmes's older brother nodded as I entered, keeping his hands clasped atop the waistcoat that covered his capacious middle girth. "Please take a chair," he said. "Forgive me for not standing. My gout is acting up of late."

I was about to speak when he continued, "Pray, do not trouble yourself with chiding me about my diet, Doctor. I have embarked on the requisite abstinence and shall be quite myself in a few more days, though there will be less of me. We shall take tea in this room. Our waiter will be here presently."

"Did you call me in at the request of Princess Beatrice?"

"Ah yes, well, about that – " He looked up. "I see here is our waiter."

We waited as the fellow wheeled in the tea cart. On it was a quite respectable tea, with scones, clotted cream, small sandwiches, and caviar and biscuits. I served myself as the waiter stood by. Mycroft said to him, "Tea only, my good fellow. I have taken to heart my doctor's instructions to abstain from caloric intake."

41

When Mycroft's cup of tea had been poured, the waiter spoke for the first time.

"Now, Watson," he said.

I very nearly dropped my teacup. It was the voice of Sherlock Holmes.

I looked up and saw his hawk-like features crinkle with amusement. "You see, Mycroft?" He said. "No one pays attention to a uniformed waiter. Even Watson, who has heard that truism from me on numerous occasions, still falls into what I may postulate is a uniform pattern of human perception. Quite possibly the pattern derives from the very nature of the uniform. Whoever dons the garment is expected to behave in a certain prescribed manner, making study of the individual wearer unnecessary and irrelevant. But come, my good friend." He advanced toward me and clapped me on the shoulder. "Have you recovered yourself sufficiently?"

"I thought you were in France. The papers – "

"The papers said what we wished them to say. Mycroft is not without influence, and it is for the greater good, ultimately, that a small deception has been perpetrated on the British reading public. My assignment here is of greater importance to the Empire than anything I might accomplish in France. I am working on a complex matter, involving a criminal organization that derives its funds from a wide variety of sources."

"Protection gangs, for example?" I asked.

"Yes, Watson. You are as astute as ever, I am happy to note."

"The founder of the bazaar told me he had been threatened by anonymous notes and telephone calls."

"Indeed?"

"He pointed out a man he suspected but could prove nothing against. A giant of a fellow."

"With a patch over one eye?"

"That's him."

"The organization employs him as an enforcer. His name is Maurice Slag. I have just a few hours ago inspected his rooms, unbeknownst to him. Now, please tell us what you observed at the rehearsal today."

I told of the general layout of the Hall that had been set up for the bazaar. I told of the vendors. I recounted my conversation with Dr. Tibbitts, and with the gypsy Madame Vadoma, and with the man at the Bovril booth.

"Was there a booth showing the electric apparatus used by the massage school?"

"No, come to think of it." I showed him the program map of the bazaar. "And nothing on this diagram. Perhaps they did not want too close an inspection."

"I should also think that those who have paid for a booth would not want competition from the hospital and school," said Mycroft.

"And you saw the rehearsal?" Holmes asked.

"Yes, though it was more of a pantomime or dumb-show. The principals who will be present tomorrow were represented by staff employees."

"Please describe what happened, nonetheless."

"A woman impersonating Princess Beatrice came from the reception area – that is to the right of the hall here – " I showed them on the program map. " – and stood here, in front of the Bovril tent. Bovril is the principal sponsor of the bazaar and therefore has pride of place."

"What happened then?"

"The 'princess' stood and waited while eight other ladies came forward, each bearing small baskets."

"The 'princess' was carrying a large basket, I assume," Mycroft said.

"I forgot to mention that."

"Logic impels the conclusion. Please go on."

"Then each of the ladies – I gather they are the major committeewomen who are principal donors and board members to the hospital and school – each passed forward her basket in turn. Then the princess removed the envelopes contained in the smaller basket and placed them into the larger basket. Then Dr. Tibbitts announced that tomorrow at this stage of the proceedings the princess would be making a speech of acknowledgement and encouragement. All were admonished to maintain a respectful silence, staff members especially. After the speech, Dr. Tibbitts said, a poem would be read by Mrs. Wilde, the wife of the poet, and then would come a performance of the Coldstream Guards Brass Band."

"Tibbitts will have paid handsomely for that," Mycroft said.

"Now, Watson," Holmes said, "you mentioned that you saw the gigantic enforcer, Mr. Slag."

"Yes, twice. Once when I first arrived, and once when I was leaving. At that time, he was walking past the Bovril booth."

"What was he doing during the rehearsal of the ceremony?"

"I did not notice. My eyes were on the 'princess'."

"As one would expect," Mycroft said.

Holmes sat silent.

"Do you think there will be an attempt to steal the basket with the envelopes of contributions?" I asked.

"Not practicable," Mycroft said. "Cashing the cheques in itself would be a very difficult for the thief, even assuming he were nimble enough to somehow make his escape."

"What about a physical attack on the Princess?"

"The same difficulty applies. The person making the assault would be immediately seen and hundreds would crowd round to stop him or her."

"So what will happen?"

"We are not certain," Mycroft said. "Two weeks ago, Whitehall received intelligence that a foreign power has paid a substantial sum to disrupt the event, but as yet there is no indication of the form the disruption will take. Probably the perpetrators are making their plans based on today's observations."

A question occurred to me. "So why did you wait until this morning to send your telegram?

"Sherlock had planned to attend."

"In disguise, of course," said Holmes. "But this morning I learned that Slag had been seen waiting outside the Hall. So I took the opportunity to visit his rooms." He gave one of his small, quick smiles. "I am glad you are here," he said.

I had an idea. "An attacker might take the place of one of the winged mannequins – those effigies of the *Vril-ya* that I saw hanging from wires at the event. That attacker might have an accomplice, who would pull him upward to the building rafters after his attack, from which vantage point he would be able to make his escape."

Holmes looked thoughtful for a long moment. "Watson, you surpass yourself," he finally said. "Please cast your memory back to your departure from the Hall, and your subsequent arrival here. Were you followed?"

"I did not think to look."

"Then let us assume that you were. We must also assume that the someone who followed you is associated with the organization that has been paid to disrupt the event, that he knows that you have seen what there was to see at the Hall rehearsal, and that there was something important that would harm the plans of the organization if you were to disclose it. In short, you may be in danger."

"What am I to do?"

"A uniform," said Mycroft.

Thus it was that Holmes and I, both cloaked and hatted as Diogenes Club doormen, rode through the London dusk in a cab to my Paddington home and office. My nurse had gone for the day, but Mary was with the cook, preparing supper. Her face brightened into a welcoming smile when

I entered. But when she saw my uniform cloak, and my grim countenance, her face fell.

"You are on a case," she said. "When will you return?"

"Tomorrow morning."

"Good. You can tell me about the bazaar before my friends arrive. We are to share a carriage."

"If I do not return – "

"What?"

I tried to sound as reassuring as possible. "There is a possibility that I may be delayed. If I have not returned, under no circumstances are you or your friends to go to the Hall."

She shrugged. "When you read the telegram, I immediately thought there would be danger. Mycroft would not have called on you otherwise."

Outside by the cab, Holmes looked at me inquiringly. I patted my pocket where I now carried my service revolver, fully loaded.

"Satisfactory," Holmes said. "Cabman, please take us to the Royal Albert Hall."

A telegraph message from Mycroft had done its work, and the head of the Hall security staff awaited us as we approached the entrance. He handed over two large parcels wrapped with brown paper and twine. Holmes thanked him and said, "The ceremony begins at two o'clock tomorrow afternoon. Our arrival at one will give us ample time to inspect and observe."

"One o'clock, then," the man replied.

We returned to our cab. A half-hour later we were back in Whitehall. We paid our cabman and were inside the Diogenes Club once more, without incident.

"Now, Watson," said Holmes, before we had entered the lobby, "I have arranged a room for each of us upstairs. There we can change into our normal dress, resume our identities, and meet in the Stranger's Room to partake of a light supper."

Holmes declined to discuss the case during our meal. Nor would he speak of the matters he had been working on. Instead he chose as his topic the electrical nature of our own existence, and the legitimacy of the school owned by Mr. Tibbitts. "What is your opinion?" he asked politely.

"I try to keep an open mind about research," I replied. "But I fear Tibbitts's electrical hospital and school will prove to be as short-lived as his pasteboard structures."

45

I would have gone on, but Holmes held up his hand. "Pause for one moment, however, to reflect on the consequences for you and for me if the claims were to be verified."

"It depends on which one of us we are discussing," I said.

"Bravo, Watson!" He replied. "Please go on."

"The consequences to me and the medical profession – why, those would be adverse. Patients could be cured rapidly. Some might never get sick at all. The hospitals and my waiting-room would be empty – at least in comparison to the crowded state in which we see them today."

"Whereas for my business?"

"A universal electric cure would be an enormous boon for criminal investigators, at least temporarily. There would be more people, competing for scarcer and scarcer resources. More crime would be inevitable consequence, thus requiring more work to be done by those who are paid to contain it."

Holmes nodded. "But what of humanity in general? How would their lives be altered – for the better or the worse?"

"For the worse, eventually, given the overcrowding and competition for survival that I have described. Unless the electrical cure could change man's inner moral nature."

"A highly remote contingency."

I had an idea. "However, if we take a loftier, more generalized view of mankind as a whole, we might postulate that from among those additional minds, some other advance of science could arise. That advancement might provide humankind with additional food, clothing, and adequate shelter in far greater abundance."

Holmes was looking at me with that fixed and intense gaze that I knew so well.

Finally, he spoke. "Watson, you have done it once again." He set down his wine glass, folded his napkin, placed it on the table, and stood. "However, now we must change our plans. We must go."

"Where, Holmes?"

"First, I must send a message to Mycroft, for we will need him to work his magical influence and prepare our way for a second time. Then we must visit our respective rooms upstairs, to unwrap our parcels and change into new uniforms. Then, at one of my London bolt-holes, we must procure an item for which I ought to have foreseen the need. And finally, we must return to The Royal Albert Hall."

In the uniforms of Albert Hall stage technicians, we appeared at the rear entry door of the Hall just after midnight. Mycroft's influence had worked its magic once more. We were expected. Mr. Jennings, the night watchman, greeted us and led us to a doorway at the back of the Hall. We passed through the doorway to the narrow enclosed stairs that led upward to the great dome. As we climbed up the seemingly endless flights, Holmes gave instructions.

"When we reach the top, silence is essential," he said. "The dome will magnify every noise, however small, and carry it round within the perimeter to the other side. When we are in position we must wait in silence, lest we alarm our prey and lose the chance to stop his murderous attack before it begins."

"Who is our prey? Slag?"

"He may very well be. Do not rely on his supposed visual infirmity. He is known to be perfectly sighted in both eyes. He uses the patch only for distraction. He may bring an accomplice."

"Why do you suspect him?"

"Because he attended the rehearsal. And at his lair, I observed some items which I believe will prove dispositive."

I knew better than to press Holmes for details on what he had seen. I asked, "When will he come?"

"He must do his work before the workmen arrive to make the final preparations for the bazaar. He cannot afford to be seen by them when he is up here, for he is too large to pass for an ordinary stage technician. So he must make all his arrangements while the Hall is in darkness."

"Where will he come from?"

"I believe he will take the same stairway that we are climbing now. But there is another possibility."

From the stairwell, we emerged onto the narrow deck that encircles the great dome at its base, and from which the support structure of wrought iron-and-steel mesh radiates inward to the open corona at the centre. We were far above the lights of the street lamps. The only illumination came from a waning half-moon, which was just barely visible through glass of the great dome and the haze that perpetually envelops all of London. The effect of the moonlight was to place everything that surrounded us in a kind of shadowy fog, where it was difficult to ascertain anything more than the outlines of the objects that surrounded us.

Holmes gestured upward, to a short ladder beneath a small door. He spoke very softly and directly into my ear. "That door is the exit to the outside of the dome. Our adversary will doubtless be planning to use that route for his escape, and it is possible he may also use it to gain his entry. We shall have to watch in both directions."

He checked the dark-lantern that he had retrieved from his bolt-hole. It was still in readiness. "Now we must possess ourselves in silence," he said.

We waited in the strange half-light, suspended within the great artificial cavern. A dark void surrounded us in all directions, above and below as well as around us. The great expanse of physical emptiness seemed to magnify the uncertainty and the tension that I felt throughout my body. My thoughts went back to the equally tense wait in darkness that Holmes and I had endured eight years previously, in the closed bedroom at the estate of the villainous Doctor Roylott. Though shaken, we had come through that incident in triumph. I told myself that the same would occur in this instance.

Yet I found myself unnerved by the echoes within the great hall. The structure magnified even the slightest sound, from the occasional quiet footfall of the night watchman on the floor one-hundred feet below, to the chittering of a mouse or some other small creature on the opposite side of the narrow platform on which we crouched. I tried to take comfort in the knowledge that, being able to hear with such clarity, we would have abundant advance warning of the approach of our adversary. But the echoes, coming as they did from below as well as from the glass-paned dome above, also put me in mind of the physical danger in which we had placed ourselves. The wrong move, a careless slip, or a blow landing in a struggle could send either of us hurtling into the void, to be crushed by the impact of the fall.

The hours of our vigil crept by. There was not sufficient light for me to see the time on my watch, nor did I want to risk the sound I would assuredly make if I shifted my weight to remove it from my pocket. What I most feared was my own weakness – that, fatigued and dulled, I might make some blunder when the moment arose when I was most needed.

Then, with a thrill of anticipation, I heard a slow, creaking noise from above. The roof door was opening. There was a brief glow of additional moonlight through the doorway. Then a shadowy figure blocked the light. A silhouetted man stepped backward, noiselessly placing one foot and then the other on the topmost ladder rung. Then the door closed quietly. The man descended. From where we crouched, he looked extremely tall. In a moment or two he would be standing on the narrow platform ten feet away from where we waited.

I reached to my pocket to draw my gun, but Holmes's hand on my arm bade me stop. Clearly Holmes wished to wait and determine what the intruder was intending. We shrank back, pressing our bodies against the outside perimeter of the great hemisphere, and watched the shadowy figure take the final steps down the ladder. I caught the scent of something. Was it flowers? Chemicals of some sort? A familiar scent.

My attention returned to the shadowy figure. The giant turned for a moment, and I saw his craggy face. Though it was blurred in the half-light and the distinctive black eye patch was nowhere to be seen, the face was unmistakable. It was Slag. On his back he carried a rucksack, like that of a soldier.

He advanced toward the wrought iron framework that led from our perimeter walkway into the center. As he reached one of the beams he crouched down, and, kneeling, shuffled forward, hand over hand, until he had nearly crossed the distance between our platform and the central corona, a large circle of dark emptiness that lay just ahead of him.

He stopped, leaned to one side and reached down, and began to pull at something. I realized it was one of the wires from which hung the painted effigies of the *Vril-ya*. He began to haul on the wire. As one would pull up a great fish onto a boat, so he pulled up the rubber effigy, hauling it onto the metallic mesh that stretched between the iron rod on which he knelt and another, running parallel about a foot away. The two parallel rods and the mesh formed a narrow platform suitable for a workman to place small pieces of equipment, but not strong enough to reliably support the weight of a man.

The effigy flopped over the outside rod and lay on the metallic mesh.

Holmes's voice was barely a low murmur, close to my ear. "When he reaches into his rucksack, we shall take him."

Carefully I sat up, and as silently as I could manage, I drew out my revolver.

The man reached for his rucksack and unclasped the buckle.

"Now," said Holmes. He snapped open the dark lantern. His voice shattered the silence. "Slag! Raise both your hands or be shot!"

In the lantern's yellow light, the giant froze.

But then, from behind us, came a new voice, low and confident. "I think not, Mr. Holmes."

I had heard that voice before, in the gypsy fortuneteller's tent. It was the voice of the woman calling herself Madame Vadoma.

Holmes turned the dark lantern and cast its beam of light onto the person who had spoken. But instead of the gypsy woman I saw a hard-faced young man with close-cropped blonde hair, smirking with satisfaction.

Holmes said, "Ah, Caruthers. It is Caruthers, is it not? Known to the police as Mr. Slag's associate? The two of you share a suite of rooms, I believe."

Caruthers was apparently unarmed, but he seemed undisturbed by the light, or by Holmes's words. "Just like you and Dr. Watson used to do, before he married," he said. "But did you know Slag's big brother Victor lives with us? Well, I've got a bit of news for you, Doctor. And you'll put down your gun when you hear it."

I leveled my revolver at the leering face. "Go on," I said.

"Victor . . . at this moment . . . is with the lovely . . . Mrs. Watson," Caruthers said.

My heart dropped like a stone.

"He's waiting for a message from his brother and me that all is well. You don't want to disappoint him."

"A trickster's lie," said Holmes. "Watson, this man overheard your conversation with Dr. Tibbitts when the two of you stood at the central monument, just on the other side of the curtain behind his fortuneteller's booth. He heard enough to know your voice and identity when you entered. Then he saw your wedding ring. Now he has improvised this hollow threat."

The confident smile remained on Caruthers's face, and his voice took on a wheedling, insinuating tone. "I did see your wedding ring, Doctor. That's how I knew your weak spot. That's how I knew to send Victor along to your wife. If Victor doesn't get that message, he'll be very angry, won't he? Now hand over your gun."

"He wants to shoot us both." Holmes said.

I hesitated. For Mary, I knew I would sacrifice myself.

"You must trust me, Watson," Holmes continued. "Slag has no brother. His flat in Kensington is frequently under observation by the police. They saw him leave this morning. I was there at noon today, Caruthers. I saw your array of gypsy costumes and your cosmetics on your dressing table. I even saw what you recently used to remove your makeup. I say recently, because you reek of cold cream. The odor of cold cream is quite distinctive."

The smile on Caruthers's face turned to a snarl. Like an animal, he sprang forward at Holmes in a blind rage, hands outstretched like claws. He would have reached his target, but Holmes moved sideways, and then grasped the man's coat and pulled him along, so that his momentum carried him into me. I lashed out with the barrel of my gun, hitting him on the side of his leg. He staggered on past me and between two of the parallel rails that ran towards the centre of the great void below.

His right foot sank into the thin wire mesh and his ankle twisted. He nearly fell, going off balance, but he still lurched forward precariously, like a man about to fall off a high wire. "Help me!" he cried.

The giant Slag, crouched on the adjacent rails, stood and lunged to rescue his partner. But both men were now off balance. Their combined momentum bore them each sideways on their respective wrought iron bars. They converged. At the edge of the dark corona the giant Slag and his criminal companion staggered for a moment, each still clutching at the garment of the other, each trying to right himself.

But to no avail. In the next moment, both men had vanished from my sight.

Two seconds later, from one-hundred feet below us, came a great clattering metallic crash as two bodies and one rucksack hit the floor.

The echoes of the crash died away. Then we heard the sound of footfalls, and the voice of the night watchman.

"Are you up there, Mr. Holmes?"

"I am, Mr. Jennings. We shall be with you shortly. Please stay away from the rucksack. It contains canisters of phosgene gas. One or more of the canisters may have ruptured. Phosgene gas is a deadly poison."

"I owe the triumph to you, Watson," Holmes said, as the two of us began the long descent down the narrow stairs. "Your remark regarding the winged effigies first put me in mind of the stagehands required to manipulate those artificial creatures. In the uniforms of stagehands, attackers would be relatively innocuous, and yet be close enough to cause some spectacularly disruptive event, the kind of chaos that a foreign government would pay for so handsomely as Whitehall's intelligence had ascertained.

"Then when you suggested we needed to take a loftier view, I remembered having seen a chemical laboratory in the rooms shared by Slag and Caruthers. The shelves contained steel canisters of chlorine and carbon dioxide, as well as charcoal filters – the requisite materials for producing the deadly phosgene gas, which is colorless and odorless. On the shelves were also packets of a red powder used in theatrical demonstrations to simulate colored smoke. Taking the loftier view in my mind's eye as you suggested, I realized that the winged effigies hung from the upper framework of the dome could each support a phosgene gas grenade. Trailing red smoke and hung out of reach, the effigies would induce death – not only from the gas itself, but also from the chaotic stampede created by a panicked crowd attempting to escape. The result would not only kill the Princess, it would also besmirch the reputation of the Royal Albert Hall forever."

I shuddered. "Who would want such a horrible outcome?"

"Someone who was to have been paid well to achieve it. I believe this night's work of ours will cost that someone dearly."

"You are still determined to oppose that someone."

"I am, Watson. I must. I have no other choice. But I do not wish you or Mary to be drawn into danger."

Holmes was silent until we reached the bottom of the staircase, at the ground level. Then he extended his hand.

"I will stand at your side when you need me, Holmes," I said.

"I know, old friend. And when the time comes, so you shall."

Leaving Holmes to deal with the aftermath at the Hall, I went home directly, taking the first cab I could find at that hour and urging the driver to employ all possible speed.

I found Mary sleeping peacefully in our bedroom. At breakfast the next day, I described to her the decorations of the Hall and the best vantage point for her and her friends to see the princess during the ceremony.

I said nothing of our midnight encounter with the late Messrs. Slag and Caruthers.

NOTES

1. As we know from "The Final Problem," fewer than two months elapsed between March 5th, 1891 and that memorable afternoon when Professor Moriarty called on Holmes at 221b Baker Street. It may be that the Professor was thinking of his foiled attempt at the Albert Hall bazaar when he said, "At the end of March I was absolutely hampered in my plans."

2. From March 5th through March 9th, 1891 a bazaar themed on Bulwer-Lytton's underground realm of the *Vril-ya* was actually held at the Albert Hall to benefit The London School of Massage and Electricity. The first day was a success. The others were not. Dr. Herbert Tibbitts, the organizer and principal funder, declared bankruptcy soon after. More details are available via this link:

    https://observationdeck.kinja.com/the-ill-fated-sf-themed-coming-race-bazaar-of-1891-1554861334

3. Bovril has become an icon of British culture. Today the company is owned by Unilever UK. The product is fundamentally unchanged from Victorian times and is distributed worldwide.

The Tower of Fear
by Mark Sohn

It may well be that the year of 1891 is remembered for both the Great Blizzard of that March and the particularly savage weather that befell both England and Scotland in the December. Certainly, the snow that fell remorselessly was the cause of a great many injuries and deaths and it will be noted that the Thames partially froze. My friend Sherlock Holmes had been recently engaged in a matter of unparalleled importance concerning the government of France, but as yet with little success.

It was while returning from a rather more trivial case in the North of Scotland, however, that we found ourselves in contempt of the highest court – that of nature Herself. We had secured a compartment on the Highland Railway's pride, the renowned *Caledonian Flyer*, and had made impressive progress south from Inverness when, with a sudden lurch and squeal of brakes, we were thrown against each other, my case crashing down and bursting atop me, leaving me tangled in my own clothing.

Barely had I extricated myself from this mess, much to Holmes's amusement I might add, when the guard came rushing along the corridor. "Gentlemen, please do not be alarmed. We have come up to a snowdrift and shall have to halt here until the track can be cleared."

Raising an eyebrow, Holmes went out to the corridor where others were already congregating and, grabbing my winter cloak, I followed him to the door from which he had already jumped. "Watson, perhaps you would stay with our things. I shall return shortly."

Indeed, the way forward was impassable. The track vanished into a veritable wall of hard-packed snow that must have fallen in avalanche-fashion across the track. No sooner had Holmes ascertained this fact than a rumbling came from the area of the valley through which we had recently passed. Correctly surmising this to be a fresh fall, Holmes was soon back after a brief conversation with the train driver and fireman. It seemed that the stretch of rail that passed to the West of Cairn Gorm was notorious for snow drifting onto the track, and there was little for it but to seek shelter locally. The temperature was falling with every half-hour, and it would not be long before anyone foolhardy enough to try to remain on the train would soon begin to suffer the severe effects of the cold.

Under the command of both Holmes and another passenger, a retired Major of Cumbrians, a small party set out for help, seeking assistance from the nearest village which was reckoned to be some three miles away.

Wrapped and muffed against the bitter chill, Holmes gave a cheery wave and left me in charge of the remainder. I had some experience of cold from my Afghan days and knew all too well that unless help reached us soon, some of the weaker passengers would be at risk from exposure. With this in mind, I undertook a doctor's round of sorts, acquainting myself with my charges.

Aside from the train crew, the other passengers were a clergyman of advanced years with poor hearing and also a small party from America in one compartment, who treated the whole episode as an adventure and seemed unperturbed by our predicament. More ominously, one compartment was taken by a uniformed Sergeant of the Metropolitan Police, who sat impassively despite the wretch chained to his wrist. This was, I learned, the safe-breaker Carstairs, originally of good breeding, but who had fallen low in his acquaintances and had been apprehended in Inverness attempting to dynamite his way into a strongbox in the basement of the Culbraith and McNair Bank.

This mixed lot, then, were my charges, but no more than a few hours had passed when, with a cry of *"Hi-Hola Hup!"*, Holmes arrived in a spray of powdery snow, and in nothing less than a sledge! Pulled by two magnificent Clydesdales, the sledge was an open coach and, as Holmes vaulted down from the bench, a second, smaller sledge arrived. "The ingenuity of these people, Watson – you see there the fitments for wheels for summer use." Indeed I could see that these vehicles were adaptable to suit the weather, but where had he found such transport? The answer was, it transpired, a nearby estate, and it was to there that we were to travel.

With the fireman and driver volunteering to remain with the locomotive to keep the boiler lit, the guard would telegraph the train company from the post office and then the stores at Garry, returning with supplies for his crew to see them through while a work party could be summoned to clear the tracks. Holmes had already sent a telegram to the Highland Rail Company informing them of the blockage, and seemed in high fettle as we slithered and skidded along the track.

Garry Post Office and stores was little more than an outpost at the edge of the Highlands proper, but the postmaster and his wife were cheerful enough and we left the guard in their care, the sledge drivers being keen to press on so as to avoid being caught out after dusk. I was curious as to our destination, but Holmes seemed curiously reticent. Checking that the pensioner cleric was not unduly suffering, I contented myself with a fill of my pipe, glad for the bowl's warmth in my fingers. We swept on through a wood, the bare trees denuded of leaves, and came upon the shore of a narrow loch. No more than a hundred feet across, the loch swept away into the gathering haze that marked a fresh fall of snow.

54

It was then that we saw a pair of massive gates, an armorial and a design resembling a stag set into the ancient ironwork. At our approach, the gates were already being hauled open, and it took two large men to do it. A wide pathway curved from sight and, once around it, we could see we were in the grounds of a large establishment, perhaps a stately house or castle. It was the latter, as after a full five minutes we slid to a halt before the most imposing stonework I had ever seen, a central keep surmounted by a large round tower with a most wonderful clock and an imposing gothic door that must have stood nearly twenty feet high, the woodwork studded and banded as if built to withstand a siege. Two enormous cannon stood at either side as if preparing to defend the castle from attack. "Watson, look." Following Holmes's gaze, I perceived an undertaker's carriage, parked beyond the far corner of the castle, so as to be unobtrusive.

"Well, Holmes? What of this place? Why the secrecy?" Drawing me away with a sharp hiss of warning, my friend made as if to light a cigarette, ostentatiously patting his pockets as if seeking a light.

Taking the cue, I produced a match and lit first his then the one he proffered. "Watson, I can say little in our present company – Simply know that there may be people with dark motives amongst us. We are at Castle Cullen, ancestral home of the Lairds of Garrymore – although it may not be the warmest of welcomes, judging by the recent death of the Laird."

This was too much and I said so.

"Really, old friend," he replied, "after all my attempts to train your mind in observation and reasoning." Of course, he was correct. The footmen that had emerged to aid the passengers wore armbands of mourning and, as they brought us inside, we were informed by a solemn houseboy that indeed the Laird had passed the night before.

A massive stone staircase ran up from the hall to the upper floors, where we in the first group were shown to our rooms. Our maid was a nervous chatty young thing who told us some of the guests would have to share. Holmes and myself took a large chamber with two identical four poster beds, in which a fire was being lit by yet another of the castle's servants. "There is a bathroom along the hall, sirs and a pull for the maid. Dinner was to be served at eight, but I . . . there's been . . . ."

"That will be all, Molly." The man who had spoken was of stern countenance and clearly held a senior position within the staff. "Gentlemen. My name is Hobbs. I am the Head Butler. We had not expected more guests, so dinner will be delayed somewhat. Nonetheless, refreshments will be served in the library, and gentlemen may smoke in the card room."

Holmes was curious. "More guests? What guests had the Laird at the time of his unfortunate demise?"

With a look of impassive disdain, Hobbs paused before replying. "Why, his cousin Lord Seagrave and his sister, Lady Elizabeth, sir. They were here for the Laird's admission, though Lady Elizabeth has decided to take residence in the Hunting Lodge until the burial."

"You mentioned the word 'admission'?"

"Yes, sir. It is a family tradition that the new Laird be admitted to the tower seat, at which point he assumes the Laird's chain and takes up his duties."

I was curious. "Chain, you say?"

"Indeed, sir. The chain of the Lairds of Garrymore. I believe it was originally conferred on the second Laird in the Fourteenth Century. It is said to be cursed." With that, he departed.

"Extraordinary fellow, Holmes. What do you make of this?"

"Impossible to make anything of it, Watson – unless, that is, we can examine the body." Taking advantage of the hustle and bustle of the household, we made our way to the scullery and, finding a houseboy, Holmes was able to ascertain the Laird had been taken to the castle chapel to await burial. The chapel was guarded by two men of the Estate night and day, groundskeepers taking turns with the stable lads and footmen to stand watch over their fallen master.

With no other purpose, we took advantage of a hot bath and a change of clothes. I had my evening dress and the maid, Molly, had managed wonders with Holmes's shabby trousers and threadbare jacket, and we repaired to the card room to smoke. There was a rather good port and a creditable whisky from the castle cellars, and it was no hardship to sample these.

The mantel clock struck eight and we were joined by the men of the American party, as well as both the old Vicar and the Major. On introduction, I mentioned my time in Afghanistan and Simpson, the Major, became most voluble on the subject, regaling me with his own experiences at the Battle of Peiwar. Holmes wandered off and I saw him attempt conversation with the deaf clergyman, shouting into his ear trumpet to make himself heard.

From what I could hear of the Americans – and they were extremely boisterous – they had some interest in the export of Scottish Angus beef to the finer tables of their continent. Indeed, it was clear that they delighted in finding themselves in an authentic Scottish castle. The conversation soon turned to the Laird's death and the mysterious tower – which was barred to all but the sitting Laird by strict custom.

We were called to dinner by Hobbs at half-past-eight and filed into the dining hall. This was an impressive room, panelled in oak with arms and armour from centuries of wars long forgotten on the walls, interspersed with paintings of the castle and grounds, as well as a heavy tapestry depicting hunting scenes. We were seated at the long table, with a chair at the far end hung with black silk. A footman appeared and cleared his throat. "Gentlemen. The Lord Seagrave."

At this introduction, a rakish man in his late thirties swept into the room. He was exceptionally well dressed and groomed and had the appearance of a dandy, apart from the mourning band on his arm. He strode up to the covered chair, and for a moment it seemed he was considering seating himself there. Instead, he walked the entire length of the table to sit at the far end. Holmes and I exchanged a significant glance at this singular entrance.

A broth was served first, from large silver tureens. This was followed by collops – thinly sliced venison with toast and mashed potatoes. Dessert came in the unwelcome form of a mixed berry pie – I say unwelcome, as by this stage my waistband was under undue pressure! Finally, our glasses were refilled, and it became evident Lord Seagrave meant to take a toast. Somewhat to the general embarrassment of the assemblage, this consisted of a rather slurred reference to the departed Laird, and it was a relief when the meal was over.

Following the dinner, the clergyman bade us goodnight and retired for the evening. The rest of us made for the card room. Soon, I was embroiled in polite chatter with the others, but for his part Holmes seemed engrossed in the myriad of volumes arrayed on the shelves. The library itself was a curious affair, with a second tier of books accessible by a spiral wooden stair which curved around a statue of Atlas, the Greek god who supported the heavens, bent beneath his burden of the celestial sphere.

Suddenly there was a clatter and a hullabaloo from the great hall, which I and several of the others went to investigate. There, beneath the stairs, was a heavy door that I hadn't noticed before, locked securely by two oversized padlocks. Also there was Lord Seagrave, visibly the worse for drink and apparently attempting to hack the padlocks through with a large antique Claymore sword. Shouting curses to the Titans themselves as he swung the weapon, the Lord screamed that he was not afraid of any curse or ghost, and seemed to be challenging some unholy force to a duel.

"Restrain his Lordship at once!" At Holmes's call, Simpson, the retired Major of Cumbrians, marched forward and, assisted by myself and one of the burlier Americans, we managed to hold the Lord and disarm him. Hobbs had appeared, and I directed him to lead the way to his Lordship's chamber while I went for my medical bag, thankful – not for the first time – that I had thought it prudent to carry it outside of my normal practice. Although only a minute had passed, I found the Lord already in a state of exhaustion, having been half-carried to his bed. Quickly preparing a proprietary chloral sleeping draught, I made him drink it and, after noting his pulse and temperature, I ordered the light in his room to be dimmed and for Hobbs to summon a maid to act as a nurse for the night.

Before succumbing to the draughts effects, Lord Seagrave suddenly grasped my sleeve and spluttered some nonsense about the Laird being murdered by a phantasm. Turning from my patient, I saw Holmes, standing deep in thought. With a look of curious intensity, he turned on his heel and stalked off along the hallway.

Returning my bag to our chamber, I found Holmes sitting on the window ledge watching the moonlight on the loch. "Ah, Watson. Quite an evening, wouldn't you agree?"

I was in no mood for his whimsy, though, replying rather tersely. "Hardly an entertaining one, Holmes. The man was positively crazed with drink and no doubt afraid."

"Afraid. Yes, we concur. Indeed, he was afraid. But of what and why we shall not know until at least midnight."

"Midnight?"

"Yes, my friend. You should get some rest. We shall be going for a little exercise, and you will have more use of that bag of yours – though I dare say the next patient will be beyond any medical aid." Shaking my head at my companion, I plumped my pillows and stretched out to a light sleep.

I was shaken awake to find Holmes already dressed for a winter excursion. I donned my boots, cape, hat, and gloves and quickly checked my bag over. Following Holmes along the hall away from the main stairs, we came to a curtain, which he swept aside to reveal a narrow passageway that led to a spiral stairway and down to an annex that consisted of the servants' quarters, scullery, and kitchens. Here we had to tread carefully, as the sound of our footfalls bound to arouse interest at such an hour.

A shaft of light falling across the corridor had forced us to a halt, and one of the maids giggled. I froze, as did Holmes, as the girl appeared beneath a pile of laundry and turned towards us. I had prepared a feeble excuse about being lost, but thankfully the girl swept past no more than an inch from where we had pressed up against the stonework of the wall. How she didn't see us I shall always wonder . . . .

Careful to keep noise to a minimum, Holmes threw open the bolts on the door that opened out to reveal a courtyard, steam blowing from the stables on the opposite side where the horses stood in the shadows. Almost at once, a low growl sounded from the darkness, but Holmes quickly produced a piece of meat that he had secreted away from dinner, holding it in front of him to creep forward towards what revealed itself as a kennel of sorts.

At our approach a large, shaggy creature loomed, revealing itself in the moonlight to be a mastiff of some description, held by a length of chain. It seemed clear that this beast of a stable guard was easily bribed, however, as it took the meat and was soon nuzzling Holmes's hand. I, on the other hand had no meat on me save that on my bones and – reverting to the wild – the mastiff tried a bite of my rump as I passed. Holmes let out a quiet chuckle and pulled me away from the vicinity of the snapping jaws.

"My information was correct, old friend. See, the chapel is temporarily unguarded." It was thus. In the light, the large clock face showed half-past-midnight. The talkative Molly had told Holmes that refreshments were laid on every second hour in the scullery to avoid exposure, and the two men on watch were fairly frozen to the marrow. We had perhaps five minutes before they returned to complete their turn at vigil. Fortunately, the lock on the chapel door was of simple design and a poor match for my friend's legerdemain with skeleton keys. Slipping inside, we shut the door behind us and, as a precaution, Holmes relocked it from within. Producing his bullseye lamp, he lit it, taking care to keep the shutters folded over the lens to avoid any excess light that might betray our presence.

During the course of my career, I have conducted a number of *post mortem* examinations, but never under such conditions as that night. By the narrow beam from Holmes's lamp, I saw that the figure laid in the coffin was indeed a young man, and that he showed no sign of abnormality or congenital weakness of any kind. The cause of death hardly required an expert opinion, though, being a single deep circular wound that penetrated the heart and caused immediate death. Something about the lividity and the nature of the wound caused me to pause and, commanding Holmes to assist in rolling the body onto the side, I was able to observe that the spike – for indeed it must be such – had been driven completely through the Laird and even punctured the back of the shirt that he was still wearing – though oddly there was no tear at the front. Holmes seemed perturbed by the relative lack of blood, but I explained the force and manner in which the weapon had been used precluded a large amount of bleeding.

A quiet tramping sound grew louder and the glow of a lamp through the crack in the door told us we were no longer alone. Carefully replacing the coffin lid, we retreated to the altar and looked for any other way out. There was none, which obliged us to wait in the eerie stillness of the chapel until the Laird's men next relaxed their watchfulness two hours later. With a long, cold wait ahead of us, we made the best of it and wrapped ourselves up. Luckily, I had the foresight to bring a small flask of brandy, and

Holmes had some oatmeal biscuits that he had found cooling in the kitchen earlier. Silently, we toasted the fallen Laird and thanked him for his hospitality, however unwitting it had been or unforeseen the circumstance.

Breakfast, and with it news. The track would be cleared no sooner than Monday. This caused no small upheaval, but the train company had wired to promise recompense to the estate for any outlay in our upkeep. As for our nocturnal perambulation, we had escaped discovery – or so we had thought at the time. I decided to pay the Lord Seagrave a visit to ascertain his spirits and general health, leaving Holmes free to explore the castle and grounds. It was during this excursion that he came upon the criminal Carstairs, being exercised by his escort the Sergeant. Both men were being quartered in the servant's annex, an arrangement which evidently suited them well, judging by the rather portly Sergeant's florid complexion.

Lord Seagrave was a man transformed. Gone was the mania which had stricken him the previous night, and in its place an unfortunate arrogance which did nothing to commend the man to me. Disdainful of my services as a man of medicine, he seemed more interested in the disposition of the estate now that the Laird was deceased. I took my leave of him before my manners failed me and found Holmes in the great hall in a state of curious tension. The American party was leaving for an impromptu tour of the estate, having paid one of the ghillies rather more than was sufficient. Waving our boisterous colonial friends off, I accompanied Holmes to the library, where he had already laid a massive leather-bound tome on a reading stand. "Observe, Watson, *The Book of Cullen*. Within its pages lies the history of the castle and family for the past four-hundred years. It is unique, so we must handle it without the acids from our fingers staining the fibres of the paper." He pulled on a pair of white cotton dress gloves with a flourish and opened the volume with care.

The book was illustrated and illuminated, work clearly done by masters of the art. There was a chapter headed "*Et inventi sunt de catena*" – 'The list of the chain' – and this was indeed a roll of the Lairds of Garrymore, beginning with the second Laird and ending with the eighteenth – who had passed away fully nine months ago. "Why was there such a delay in the new Laird taking his seat?"

"It seems there was a delay in finding the unfortunate candidate, Watson." Holmes turned the pages again. "He was, in fact, in Canada."

"Canada! But why?"

"He was seemingly unaware of his inheritance and was working a claim in the new gold fields discovered in the high Yukon. Ah, yes, here we are. What do you make of this?"

My schoolboy Latin, so painfully learned, hadn't deserted me entirely. "'*Exigere aut pati necesse sit, specimen candidatus judicium ferri.*' 'The ritual must be exact or the candidate must suffer an ordeal of iron!' *Iron* . . . Holmes, the Laird's injuries . . . ."

"And what, may I ask, do you know of the Laird's injuries?"

It was Lord Seagrave, a sneer of disdain writ across his features. "Ah, Milord. You seem much recovered." Holmes sent a brief but significant glance in my direction before turning ostentatiously to welcome the Lord. "Tell me, what do you make of this unique volume my colleague Dr. Watson and I are examining?"

"I know it. I've tried to make sense of the damned book since I arrived. Still, I confess I am at a loss to explain the remarkable coincidence that brings Mister Sherlock Holmes and his pet physician to my birthright while my hapless cousin is barely departed."

"Coincidence? Yes, well . . . we shall see." Examining his fingernail as if it were an exotic insect, Holmes was icily cool. "I assume at some point you will attempt the ritual that saw the death of your, what was it, *hapless* cousin?"

"That is my business and mine alone."

"Perhaps. Perhaps not. I'm quite sure the Lady Elizabeth would have her own opinion on the matter." His expression one of bitterness and anger, Lord Seagrave turned on his heel and stormed out of the room, pausing at the door. "You are interfering, *Mister* Holmes. You and your friend had best be on that train when it departs."

"We intend to be. It might be safer for you if you were on it as well, *sir.*"

I have recounted before in moments of extreme concentration that there was in Holmes an air of barely suppressed tension, often released in bursts of energy. Such was the case now as I struggled to match him pace for pace as we strode down the treacherous icy driveway towards the main gates. "Tell me, Holmes, what good can come from this? I attempt study of your methods, yet confess myself unable to piece any of it together."

In reply, he reached into his inside pocket for a telegram and handed it to me with the air of a man producing a grand slam at whist. Earlier that day the eldest houseboy had taken a signal from Holmes and waited for the answer, which had arrived from none other than Mycroft Holmes, care of the Diogenes Club.

> *Delighted noisy morning at club interrupted. Steward enraptured. However vulgar enquiries made regards SL.*

Gambling wins reported at one club. Amount clear, believed negligible. Eastern Agencies disinterested with Nobel man.

"Holmes, this is nonsense – "

"Merely a rather childish affectation of my brother and myself. Whenever we communicate it is by form of reversal. Hence, hate becomes love, light becomes dark, and such like and so forth. Read it again."

I ascertained Mycroft had been discomfited at the upset to his routine at the Club – famous for its rule of silence – the steward also, but discrete enquiries were made (*SL* was obviously *LS*, as in Lord Seagrave), and he had made losses at the tables of several clubs, the amount unclear, but substantial . . . .

"Western Agencies, Holmes? Nobel man?"

"The Pinkerton Agency would be my guess, and Mycroft does not make errors of grammar, spelling, or punctuation. Nobel can only refer to the inventor of Dynamite – a backwards reference to a *user* of dynamite."

"Carstairs! But why would the Pinkertons be interested in a common dynamiter?"

"There the facts exhaust themselves, my stalwart Watson. But there is our destination." Holmes pointed to a wooded path, along which was barely visible a corner of a stone and brick building.

The Hunting Lodge was surprisingly charming after the austere nature of the castle. A maid showed us into to the sitting room, which was comfortably arranged with heavy rugs and a fire burning merrily in the large stone place. After a brief pause, we were joined by the Lady Elizabeth. No mean beauty, she wore a mourning veil over her fine profile, yet her dress was rather gay, being a rather fetching shade of deep blue. A brooch at her bosom held a mourning sash of jet silk and she wore black lace gloves.

"Mister Holmes and Doctor Watson? How good of you to pay me the respect of a visit."

Bowing, I took the hand that was proffered, yet Holmes rather rudely turned his back to the fire to warm himself. I was on the verge of cautioning him when he spoke. "There have been no others? Visitors, I mean. For example, hasn't Lord Seagrave had the decency to call on you?"

Something in his glance made me hold my tongue. Turning away, in obvious distress, Lady Elizabeth raised a beautifully embroidered handkerchief to her eye. Furious, my fists balled I rounded on Holmes, but the Lady spoke, her voice clear and resolute.

"He has not. Decency is not a word that fits him."

All of a sudden, Holmes was contrite, offering his sympathies and, thoroughly flummoxed, I could only wonder at the changing humour of the man.

From what Lady Elizabeth was able to impart, Lord Seagrave would stand to inherit the Lairdship from his unfortunate cousin, while as a woman, Lady Elizabeth could not hope to take the title whilst a suitable male was in line. It seemed an injustice that the next in line should be a man whose sole interest lay in servicing his gambling debts – no doubt intending to leave the estate to ruin. It seemed odd, to say the least, that the man who would shortly become entitled to a veritable fortune should seek to steal it, but so much about this business was odd. The manner of the Laird's death in the tower was, it seemed the most strange of all. The Lady told us one more thing: That a ritual had to be performed – this was surely the one mentioned in the Book – and that the nature of this ritual was the closest of all family secrets, being partially described to the candidate by the Laird *extant.*

Apparently, the remainder of the ritual was somehow laid out in the estate and only a true scion of Garrymore could hope to correctly establish the correct process by which to take his seat. The ritual itself could only be performed, she said, by the candidate alone. No others must be present in the chamber, to preserve the secret of the ritual. Another tradition. The new Laird was traditionally welcomed by the two castle cannon being fired. All most interesting, yet the mystery endured.

Taking our leave of the Lady Elizabeth – with a promise from her that she would endeavour to attend dinner that evening, Holmes and I parted company. He was going to the post office, but suggested I take a look around the estate in the hope of finding clues as to the ritual. The afternoon was cold, but the air bracing and I decided on a turn around the loch. It stretched on for a good mile or so, but one had only to walk through a patch of woodland to come upon the most enchanting scenes that made the distance seem trivial.

A delightful example was the Oriental garden upon which I stumbled, carven dragons rearing up either side of the pathway that forked off to a miniature temple of the pagoda type, through which the pathway drew up to a humped bridge leading to a tiny island laid out to resemble a Japanese forest, with a stone bench at the centre. Captivated, I took the fork and found myself inside the pagoda, which was lit by stained glass panels, each with an oriental glyph or symbol. Curiously, a lantern hung from the joist of the type used at sea, with green and red lenses to either side. Obviously, the temple could be illuminated at night, perhaps a relic of summer parties in happier times.

Nor was the temple all that I happened upon during that fortuitous walk. On the far side of the loch, as the watery sun began to fall behind the pale clouds, I came across the boundary wall of the estate and decided to follow it for awhile. Judging myself at the south-westerly extent of the grounds, I paused to fill my pipe and smoked while I admired the view across the loch to the castle. I could see the clock-face, but had to squint to read it at this distance. It struck me suddenly that there must be *two* clock-faces, as I was on the opposite side to the entrance from where I had first noticed the clock.

Resuming my perambulation, I headed along the far side of the loch. Here, in a clearing, was another fanciful construction, this being a quad of massive stones, one laid over the others to form a dolmen of the type spread across Europe. Looking inside, I found nothing of interest, save the carvings on the central stone. These were hard to decipher, but seemed to depict a Viking warrior or king being buried, at night to judge from the stars above and with runic shapes forming some illegible text. A sudden shiver reminded me of how quickly it became inhospitable this far north and I headed back to the comparative warmth of the castle.

Dinner that night was a sombre affair, dominated by the apparent enmity between Lord Seagrave and Lady Elizabeth, the latter now clad entirely in mourning black. Holmes was late returning, missing the first course and just in time for the main, a rather delicious beef cooked in claret with vegetables and some of the best potatoes that I have tasted. My friend was in good spirits as he took his place between one of the Americans and the old clergyman. "I hear you are interested in the Angus cattle."

The man dabbed at his moustaches with a napkin before answering, his voice a distinctive drawl. "We have an interest in establishing a herd in Chicago. There are some herds already, but there we feel is our best market for the beef. You are a detective, I am told."

"A consulting detective – amateur, naturally." Holmes was charm itself when needed.

"Why so? Why not take it up as a profession?"

"It is hardly a profession for a gentleman." Ignoring the flush of colour on the American's cheeks, Holmes moved the discussion back to cattle. "Have you any thought to the type of animal? Would you consider a Black Angus stock, or a white?"

"Why, Mister Holmes, you are misinformed – there are no white Angus cattle, only black or red. We intend to select a mixture of both, so as to provide some variety of pedigree."

The final course was a butterscotch and exceptionally well prepared. If nothing else, our sojourn here had been nourishing! With not a word exchanged between the Lady Elizabeth and Lord Seagrave, we repaired to the card room. Over a selection of rather roughly rolled cigars, a gift from the Americans, we discussed our relative days. I discovered the clergyman was rather senescent as well as deaf, but a pleasant fellow all the same. The Americans sat to play poker, and the stakes set in dollars being rather hard to follow, I lost interest. With a tap at my elbow and a nod of the head, Holmes moved to a window alcove and I followed after a moment's pause for discretion. "Watson, we must move quickly. There will almost certainly be an attempt at robbery and murder this weekend."

"Murder? Who is it – the intended victim?"

"Lord Seagrave."

"But . . . that's preposterous . . . ."

"Hardly. I cannot say much more here, but only the removal of a certain chain before the dawn rises on Monday will stay their hand." Tapping the ash from his cigar into a brass tray, Holmes looked around the room in a casual fashion. "You see the Americans? The man with his back to us is the Pinkerton man."

We walked around the room, skirting the card table. The man we were watching laid down his hand and one of his companions slapped the table in envy. "Dammit, Mac, you sure are lucky . . . ."

Speaking quietly, Holmes turned and smiled, as if enjoying a private joke. "Every time I have seen him, he has placed himself unobtrusively, yet firmly facing the door. Such might denote a military background, or the casual watchfulness of a skilled observer."

"Any of these men might have seen military service, Holmes."

"Quite. However, the man is of comparatively modest means. His boots are, as the others, of the western style. His are re-soled and with steel caps to preserve the soles and heels."

"Rather noisy for a detective, wouldn't you say?"

"Quite the opposite, Watson. Rubber heels would seem unusual on such boots and therefore mark him out. In all honesty I had narrowed it down to two men. You heard my accidental blunder regarding Angus cattle at dinner? The way he flushed crimson at my casual derogation of the professional detective?" I nodded. "My walk to the post office was well rewarded. The passenger list for the *Spirit of Boston* showed the four men had indeed sailed from New York to Glasgow, but a second cable to the American Aberdeen Angus Association (for there was indeed such an august body) revealed that of the four, only a certain L.S. McCormack was not on the register of members." I saw it at once. *McCormack – Mac!*

In the library, the Lady Elizabeth welcomed us warmly. In such sparkling company Holmes seemed loath to examine the book again, but his memory was not legendary for nothing and we left after a polite exchange. "Watson, old friend, would you care to join me in partaking of the night air?"

Shaking my head ruefully I let out a short laugh. "Somehow Holmes, an invitation from you has the ring of an official summons."

Quickly donning our winter apparel, we slipped out from a side door and straight into a fresh flurry of snow. Holmes seemed remarkably keen to see for himself the Oriental garden and the dolmen, though by now the grounds were in darkness. The only light came through the heavy clouds from the moon that was above us somewhere. Despite the conditions, Holmes refused to light his lamp, insisting on remaining furtive. Once I thought I heard a voice behind us, but it seemed we were alone on the path, the snow eddying and whirling about us.

At length we reached the temple. Holmes wasting no further time in lighting his bullseye, and had soon found the chain to lower the lantern. He quickly had this lit and I heaved on the chain to raise it to hang again between the stained glass panels I had noticed earlier.

It was only from the outside that we saw it, of course – what had seemed to be Chinese characters were actually cleverly disguised symbols. Even so, it took Holmes's chance discovery to see it. Wandering out over the bridge to the island he turned to see, reflected in the still water of the loch, the red-and-green panels. Spotting the bench, he sat there and looked again, suddenly calling out, "Watson – the lantern! Please turn it slowly."

I had a glimmer then of an idea, yet it seemed fanciful and even absurd. A clue to the ritual? Holmes himself described the exact moment when the green lens gave way to the red – a piece of the symbol was suddenly masked by the changing light and I include here an attempt at reproduction, firstly the original reflected image in outline, a pair of stylised dragonflies:

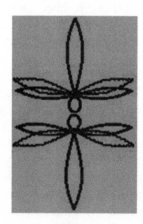

And here is what I saw after turning the lantern when I joined Holmes on the bench:

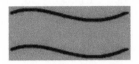

"Familiar, isn't it?" My companion had barely uttered the words when he grabbed my arm. "Unless I'm mistaken, we are about to be joined by someone who I'd rather didn't see this. Calmly and without fuss, turn the lantern around so as to show the green character again." Sauntering back to the pagoda, I quickly did as Holmes had asked and just had time to reach for my pipe when a figure emerged from the murk along the path. I was shocked at the identity of this interloper, yet apparently I was alone in my surprise, as Holmes called out a cheery greeting to the retired Major of Cumbrians.

"Ah, Major, there you are, and just in time to accompany us back."

"Back? Oh, yes, the castle. Whatever are you gentlemen doing out here in such godforsaken conditions?"

"Surely nothing compared to those at Peiwar, Major."

"What? Oh, no. Far colder. The mountains, you see." Holmes was breezily cheerful, and as such I suspected yet another of his machinations was underway.

Saying nothing, I lit my briar, and almost at once the Turkish blend I had been trying had proven a veritable tonic to the weather. My friend's eyes narrowed as he folded his arms purposefully. "The Cumbrians weren't at Peiwar, Major. I suggest you consider your response most carefully."

"Ah. I've been anticipating this moment since I learnt you were on the train, Mister Holmes." The "Major" sighed and asked for a cigarette, which Holmes provided. "I am indeed *not* a Major of the Cumbrians".

I was astounded at this development. "But your very bearing indicates officership."

He held his cigarette out in an expansive gesture. "It should. I was, in fact, a Major of the 117th Regiment of Foot."

"The Mallows?" I asked.

"The same. India, not Afghanistan."

"Why the need for duplicity?"

Holmes answered for the man. "Because the name Simpson, under which he travels, is less recognisable than that of Major Michael Shotton, retired, currently engaged at short notice on detached duties from his office at the Secret Intelligence Bureau, Whitehall."

Holmes had lit a cigarette by the time I had recovered from my shock. "No mystery I assure you, Watson. Mycroft has his finger on the very pulse

67

of the Empire. As I mentioned earlier, my sojourn to the post office more than repaid the effort. It was a simple mistake, yet I happened to read a most stirring account of the action at Peiwar, and the Cumbrians did not take part. I could only assume that such an error was due to a lack of preparation in the *déguisement de la guerre* – most uncharacteristic of the Bureau. Therefore, it follows that the Major was despatched to Scotland at the last moment. Since all the other parties had made their arrangements some time in advance, it could only be Carstairs that he was sent to watch."

Major Shotton was fulsome in his praise. "You are a testament to the art and science of observational reasoning, Mister Holmes. You will therefore already have concluded that Carstairs had other designs than the mere acquisition of currency at the Culbraith and McNair Bank."

"Indeed he did. None other than the Reykjavik Papers."

An expression of tension now showed the grievous burden Major Shotton had been compelled to endure. "Gentlemen, I ask you in the name of Her Majesty to swear this instant never to breathe a word of the theft of the Icelandic Trade Proposals."

We so swore, on our word as Gentlemen. "These papers were to have been our Nation's trump hand in the ongoing negotiations with the Nordic states regarding fishing and trade rights in the Arctic Regions. They are of the utmost importance and must be recovered before a certain meeting is convened in less than a fortnight's time."

Holmes was stillness itself for a full minute. "These waters run deep, and they are disturbed waters indeed. You think Carstairs has secreted the stolen papers somewhere on the estate?" The Major's silence was answer enough. "Very well. Watson, please extinguish that lantern." Taking the Major to one side, the great detective spoke, his words ringing with heartfelt sincerity. "Major. You may take it from me that Doctor John Watson is the very soul of discretion and trustworthiness. Further, I shall endeavour to find those papers and return them to your custody."

Waiting first for the Major to continue on his searches, we headed further into the night, around the silent waters of the loch to where the dolmen stood as if in mute expectation. Casting his light over the carvings, Holmes seemed absorbed in his study. Producing a piece of paper, and a ball of red wax, he handed me his bullseye and began making a rubbing of the inscription. Then with another piece of paper, he repeated the process with the image of the funeral of the Viking chief.

"What does this mean, Holmes?"

With a rueful look, Holmes shrugged his shoulders. "We have until dawn to find out. Now, we must return to the castle."

Consulting my watch, I found it was already close to eleven-thirty. It seemed hopeless. Even such a singular mind as Holmes's could not hope to solve two such separate problems and in such a short time. And yet . . . .

We hurried back, finding the door by which we had left mercifully still unsecured. However, we had hardly regained the relative warmth of the great hall when a cough sounded, a throat being discretely cleared. "Good night, Gentlemen. May I be of assistance?" It was, of course Hobbs, the Head Butler.

Holmes paused. "Yes. My friend Doctor Watson and I rather lost ourselves in the grounds. The snow makes finding direction hard to perceive. Perhaps you would be so kind as to attend the fire in the library for us and bring something to restore us to the living."

Hobbs seemed bemused by this request. "The library . . . very good, sir." With one of his almost-bows, he slid away to the servants' annex.

The fire was beginning to roar and I tipped the houseboy who had stoked it for waking him at such an unfriendly hour. I went for *The Book of Cullen*, but it was missing. Seemingly unsurprised, Holmes wasted no time, selecting several other volumes and laying them upon a table. A maid arrived with a steaming tray and I reached into my pocket once more, thanking her for her service.

Holmes shivered and clapped his hands together. "We have to fortify ourselves old friend, for I fear our beds will not see us tonight. What have we here?"

"Athol Brose, Holmes. Warmed slowly. It's a Scots oatmeal drink, with whisky and honey, and also cream." Holmes tried some and declared it was rather enervating. I found it to be a bit strong, but an excellent hand warmer and restorative. Then it was time to get to business.

The hidden symbol at the Chinese temple was, of course, an astrological symbol for *Aquarius*, the water bearer. Holmes had seen it at once, but for the thousandth time I felt a dullard in his presence. Fortunately for us, the library had books on many subjects, and one was found which contained an examination of the runiform language used by the Vikings and other Nordic races.

We pored over Holmes's rubbing to no avail, until suddenly I managed to redeem myself by pointing out what seemed an error. One of the symbols, an arrow known as the *Tyr*, was mis-drawn. Instead of being shown as the example on the left, the Tyr was shown as the other, slanted with a bar crossing the central. Again, a representation follows:

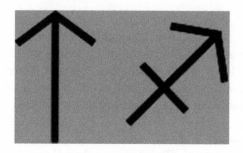

"*Sagittarius!*" Holmes slapped the table in delight. "*Aquarius* and now *Sagittarius.*"

"The Zodiac. Then the ritual is astrological by nature?"

Holmes grimaced. "But what meaning does it . . . ? Of course! We need to examine the history of the castle . . . at the time those follies were installed. Watson, fetch me that volume there from the second shelf – the blue-and-silver binding."

Doing as he asked, I handed over a heavy illustrated work on the history of the area in the preceding century. What emerged was a theory of Holmes's – that indeed the ritual was ancient, yet more recently there had been an attempt to set it into a physical form. One of the plates showed the drive to the castle had originally encircled an ornamental fountain, the illustration showing a bowl supported by a pair of nymphs. Identical in every respect, they were the very twin of each other. We both looked at each other: *Gemini.*

With three clues to the ritual, it was now near of one o'clock. At some whim, I began riffling through one of the volumes on the table, seeking anything of astrological nature. There was nothing. Finally, Holmes set aside the book that he had been examining and sat back with a heavy sigh. The drink we had been served was now cold and so it seemed were our chances. Replacing the books, I became aware of a presence and turned to see Hobbs standing by the doorway. "Gentlemen. It is late. I shall be turning in for the night, but if you have any requirements please feel free to avail yourselves of the bell for the kitchen."

"Thank you, Hobbs. You have been more than accommodating."

Holmes rose and stretched as if ready for bed. Something, however, was agitating at his mind, for suddenly he was off, back to the shelves, practically tearing at the blue-bound volume. I for one had had enough of this fruitless hunt. "What now?"

"Bell . . . bell . . . clocks have them . . . ." Looking up, Holmes waved at the doorway after the departed butler. "Hobbs mentioned the kitchen bell! A-ha! Here we are . . . ." Indeed we were. The illustration was of a clock-face being hauled up into place on the tower by block-and-tackle.

Clear as day, above our very heads, was the same ornate design, the Roman numerals and enamelled blue background more weathered, perhaps.

Turning the page, the next plate showed the clock completed, with a view of the workings. Unusually, it was operated by water. From the diagrams and descriptions in the book, it seemed a small channel ran from the loch and a pipework was arranged to turn a water-wheel of the kind found in water mills. A succession of gears contrived to turn a spindle that must have been as thick as a man's leg. This, then, was the means to wind the clockwork and keep the whole in operation. Turning the page back, my companion jabbed a finger at the image of the clock. "What do you see, Watson?"

"The clock, Holmes. There is no difference in the illustration, save perhaps it has the hands added."

Shaking his head, Holmes smiled thinly. "You see, but you do not observe." Another illustration, then, this one provided by Holmes himself:

With, of course, the pertinent detail isolated and rotated here:

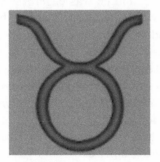

It was the missing sign! *Taurus*, the sign of the Bull . . . and time for bed. Even Holmes, with his iron will and constitution, was not an automaton, and he agreed to turn in. Not a moment too soon, I threw the heavy bedclothes over myself and was almost instantly asleep.

The next morning saw us up rather later than we had planned, and on account of this we eschewed breakfast in favour of prompt action. Finding the Police Sergeant in the kitchen, Holmes casually inquired after Carstairs. The dynamiter was under lock-and-key in the room that they shared. Naturally the name of Sherlock Holmes was well known to the

71

Sergeant and enough to admit us for a short while. Carstairs took the cigarette proffered to him and smoked. "To what do I owe the honour?"

"There seems to be a positive vogue for dynamite in Scotland these days. First the Culbraith and McNair Bank, and then the sudden avalanches that so conveniently blocked the tracks and led to us spending such a stimulating weekend . . . and in such estimable company as yourself."

"You know, then? About the tracks, I mean?"

"Yes, Mister Carstairs. I know that you were engaged to open a box here in this castle – that your employer hired some quarry men with knowledge of blasting to arrange and carry out the avalanches to stop the train."

I was curious as to several points, but confined myself to a single question. "What of the Police Sergeant, Holmes?"

With a gleam in his eye, my friend replied, "Rather a rosy complexion, wouldn't you say? Doubtless some whisky would be provided at the given hour, enough to ensure his watchfulness is suitably diminished. Some time tonight, by the way."

It was all so easily accomplished that I chide myself for not thinking of it. Carstairs was facing a lengthy sentence on his return to London, easily five years or more, and he was eagerness itself when Holmes put the scheme to him. He was to go through with it, but instead of exploding his dynamite, which had been sent here for him by his mysterious masters, he was to let us retrieve the chain and then, that very night we would present it to the rightful heir to the estate, with a word to the authorities to the effect that Carstairs had helped us of his own accord. That, of course, rather depended on us managing to enter the tower unseen and complete the ritual. To that end, Holmes and I announced we would be spending our last day in Scotland sketching the landscapes. This seemed rather a feeble excuse, yet it would have to suffice.

In reality, we would wait for nightfall and, at the hour Holmes had agreed, with the safe-breaker we would return and accompany him to the tower. With a hastily collected assemblage of what I hoped resembled artistic materials, plus some provisions that Holmes had had the foresight to beg from the kitchen, we set off as ostentatiously and noisily as we could.

We froze. All that day we froze, and with nothing to show for our suffering but a rather lacking attempt at the loch on my part and Holmes's own sweeping rendition of the valley beyond the estate. By dusk we were positively miserable. Even Holmes's cold meat pie and my ever-handy flask failed to keep our spirits high as a bitter wind began to keen and moan through the sparse trees and over the estate wall, behind which we had concealed ourselves on some stones. "Almost time, Watson."

"Thank heavens, Holmes. My wound is fairly killing me."

"Nonsense. If a Jezail musket couldn't finish you off, no mere Scottish breeze can."

"I almost forgot to ask you Holmes. What have you made of all the astrological gibberish?"

"I have a theory, but until I see inside the ritual chamber, I cannot hope to test it." Reaching for a piece of paper and a pencil, he rested it on a stone and wrote out the words *Gemini, Aquarius, Sagittarius*, and *Taurus* and handed me the paper. "There remain, of course, a number of possibilities, yet there is something rather suggestive here."

I couldn't see it, but Holmes was insistent that I persevere and I took up the pencil, writing out *Twins, Water, Archer*, and *Bull*, and scribbled out the appropriate symbols, my hand shaking from the hours spent in the open countryside. "I give up, Holmes, I really do." Without speaking another word, he reached across and ran the pencil across his words, striking out all but the initials. *G-A-S-T*... which is when I saw it! An anagram!

We had returned to the castle, loitering in the frozen half-light by one of the cannon. At length a low whistle came through the gloom, which Holmes answered with a sharp click of his fingers. Carstairs emerged from the darkness, with a cheeky grin on his face. "The Sergeant decided not to join us tonight, gents. He's sleeping off the whisky. Oh, here. This is yours Mister 'Olmes." The criminal handed Holmes a thin pick made of steel which my friend had loaned to him.

"How long?" Holmes asked.

"Oh, no more than fifteen seconds I'd reckon. Them police cuffs are alright for your common crooks, but not much cop for the likes of me." Ruefully I wondered what the sentence was for aiding a prisoner to escape.

Our odd little party made its way along the outside of the castle, stealing stealthily below the brightly lit windows to avoid detection from within. A low gurgle and gushing of water told us we were close, but when I saw what Holmes had planned, it took all my resolve not to turn back. A large water-wheel, all of twenty feet in diameter, was turning slowly, the stream of water from a lead-and-stone pipework running down onto the paddles. The water then flowed away down an ominous looking drain, an iron grille just visible in the foaming chasm. The noise here was alarming, a continuous assault on the eardrums. I could well understand why this contraption was on the remotest angle of the castle away from the living quarters.

"Holmes, are you mad? This will surely kill us! If any of us falls, we will assuredly be drowned or dashed to pieces beneath that infernal wheel."

"Calm, Watson. It is simply a mechanical problem. See the constant rate the wheel turns – it is actually turning at no more than a few revolutions per minute. Therefore, a well-timed leap from the bank *here*," – he indicated a piece of ground – "to the central spindle *there*, places you directly in front of that inspection hatch." He indicated a modest recess in the stonework, perhaps no more than a few feet square. "Carstairs is the smallest and nimblest of us all. Therefore he shall make the first attempt. Hopefully the hatch itself will be unfastened, or he will have to resort to the dynamite."

"Dynamite . . . ?" The question died away as Carstairs, grinning widely, walked past with a small hessian sack. Trailing the sack in the water, he held it there a full two minutes, all the time staring at the hatch behind the wheel as if it were his very nemesis. I stood, baffled at this odd display, but a pat on my shoulder from Holmes told me all would be explained soon enough.

And so it proved. The wiry safe-breaker leapt across to the spindle, then after an alarming moment when it seemed his footing was uncertain, he was over the wheel and into the darkened opening. Holmes had his dependable bullseye and shone a narrow beam into the depression to reveal Carstairs had wedged himself into a ridiculously small aperture no more than a few inches deep.

I shall confess my heart was fairly in my mouth, yet the cracksman was coolness itself as he extracted a small roll of cloth from his pocket and, hanging it around his neck by a cord, proceeded to chisel away at the stonework where it met the hatch. This was of solid oak and clearly quite impenetrable. After a tense few minutes though, he was able to place a small stick of dynamite in the cavity he had created and placed an ominously short fuse into the stick. The work was complete with his filling the wet hessian sack with water, the swollen fibres retaining the water quite adequately. This was placed over the stick to baffle and tamp the blast.

Cautiously, he wriggled his body around so he faced out towards the wheel which turned remorselessly below him. A flare from a match and he was out onto the wheel, but no sooner had he jumped down to the central spindle than he slipped, his feet shooting away from him as his body fell backwards . . . into the wheel. No sooner had this happened than he was submerged in the churning water and passed from sight.

"Watson, quick! Take the lamp." Holmes sprang across the gap onto the spindle, only to slip, perilously retaining his balance only with a supreme display of agility. "It is iced!" His warning rang out as I caught sight of poor Carstairs, now hanging limply in the wooden framework of

74

that diabolical wheel.

"There! Grab him, Holmes, for pity's sake." As Carstairs' body was borne aloft once more there was a flash and the loudest booming *"Thud"* I had heard since the war, the hatch splintering and cracking to hang from its mountings in a pall of smoke.

Holmes was up in a trice, heaving at the insensate burglar's lifeless body. "He's too heavy – damn it all!" That was enough – discarding the bullseye I took a step backwards and charged forwards into the chasm, vaulting upwards with every fibre in my legs straining. Seizing Carstair's sodden clothing I heaved at him with the last of my strength as the wheel turned and threw me backwards towards the drain.

At the very last conceivable moment, a hand flashed towards me and fingers that must have been made of steel clutched at my arm. Lurching forwards, I found myself running in the manner of a circus performer, until I was unceremoniously hauled into the passage and, with a sickening blow, everything receded into a grey darkness.

Slowly my surroundings came back to me. I was in the base of the tower with Holmes's face above me registering concern. "Holmes? What . . . ."

"Easy, old friend. I am afraid when I pulled you from that wheel you went head first into the stone. You have a magnificent swelling above your eye." I confirmed this for myself and groaned. Carstairs, happily, had made a recovery of sorts, though he was in a wretched condition.

Judging it safe enough, we risked a smoke, lucky that our tobacco and matches were dry enough, and confident no-one would venture near the tower to notice a few bedraggled burglars huddling in the dark. At length we pronounced ourselves warm enough to proceed – we were certainly nothing of the sort, but still we made our way to a circular staircase, the stone flags barely visible in the near total darkness.

I rued the impulsive way in which I had discarded the vital bullseye. Yet we had no choice but to proceed up to the next floor. Here, at last we had something by the way of luck. An ancient candelabra sat on a box which contained a single unlit candle and a forlorn stub. We took these and soon were examining a chamber, bare save the slowly turning spindle in the central boss and a pile of old furniture. Upwards to the next level, and here a heavy door barred with iron stood in our way.

Reaching for his lock-picking tools, Holmes attempted to tackle the lock, which was of an ancient, obscure design not commonly seen in these modern times. After several minutes of frustration, he triumphed, not a moment too soon as poor Carstairs was by now suffering badly from the effects of his drenching.

We found ourselves in a narrow, curving corridor that we presumed led to the great hall along one way and in the other to a circular chamber, this one slightly smaller due to the convergence of the tower. This new place had a fireplace, long disused and, of course, the spindle. As a doctor I couldn't allow a man to suffer, and after a quick inspection of the fireplace, I took the candle stub, lit it, and went back down for a piece of furniture that might suit a modest fire.

With just the thing, I returned and smashed it – it was a simple chair, already broken and mended many times – and soon, with some candle wax and the fluff from various pockets and suchlike we had the beginnings of a tiny fire. Reluctantly, Holmes agreed to a short halt to allow Carstairs – indeed, all three of us – to regain some warmth in our bones. It was a risk that the smoke might betray our presence – and yet, if a stick of dynamite exploding hadn't been noticed, it seemed worth the risk.

"Carstairs, I believe you were from a good family. How then came you to this life of crime?" My question was met with a blank stare.

Then, to my surprise a short laugh. "Ha! You are indeed the Doctor Watson I read about with such interest in the papers and that Christmas book that I pinched. Yes, Doctor, my family are the Virginia Water Carstairs, and I went to the finest prep school, and then onto tutelage with the best minds in Europe."

"Including Lambert of Bruges, the master of lock-picking, and Lupescu of Romania, the celebrated forger . . . ." Holmes's interjection was met with a wry smile.

"Yes, Mister 'Olmes, you have it right enough. Now – shall we crack on, gents? Time is, as Mister Franklin said, money." Throwing the rug over our modest fire, we soon had it extinguished, though not without some excessive smoke billowing forth. We went to the corridor, but had barely reached the stairs when a clanking of keys told us that the door to the hall was being unlocked. Swiftly, we turned back into the chamber and held our breaths as we heard a solitary pair of boots step past, footfalls echoing hollowly on the flags, the door being firmly shut behind. At length, Holmes risked a look and beckoned us to follow. He took the stairs with as much caution as prudence allowed. These stairs, however, seemed to go a full circle before the next level was reached.

We found a door, already unlocked, and beyond a chamber, in which stood Lord Seagrave, attired in full Highland garb, Garrymore tartan kilt, a black tam 'o-shanter, and a basket-hilted sword at his side. Clutched to his breast was *The Book of Cullen*. As if in a trance, he moved forwards and, from our vantage point, we saw he stood in a circular depression in the floor with an ancient stone throne facing him on the far side. At this moment, my foot slipped and I dropped the candelabra with a shocking clatter. Holmes seized the opportunity and strode forwards into the chamber, halting as the Lord drew his sword and held it to the detective's throat. "How dare you violate the sanctity of my birthright?"

"It is my understanding you intended to settle your debts with the Laird's chain and dispose of the estate. You seem to view your birthright as an expediency."

"I – yes, I had indeed intended . . . ." Sheathing his sword, the Lord waved at Carstairs and me, crouching on the steps, to enter. "You are right, Mister Holmes. My intention was to sell the chain, pay off my debts – but how did you know of them?"

"Do you have a brother? No? Well, I do, and he is everywhere. He sent me a telegram outlining a great deal indeed, including your predicament. Do not fear. This will not pass into the public sphere, you have my assurance."

Somehow Lord Seagrave had regained something of his nobility, and his countenance seemed somehow transformed, though perhaps it was his dress. "So," said Holmes "You intend to attempt the ritual."

"I do. It is my salvation – or my death. If I live, I intend to use the estate to pay my debts and remove the black mark over my family name that they have left. I will breed cattle – the Americans have given me the idea. I should think Garrymore beef would sell as well as any other."

I was seized with sudden admiration for this man, and felt I had judged him rashly. Holmes seemed to have considered the matter also, as his questioning took a gentler tone. "Lord Seagrave, it is my understanding that you were the one who discovered your cousin."

"I was outside. His wounds were severe, and yet he managed to reach the door and throw open the bolt before collapsing."

"An impressive act of will. Did he manage to say anything?"

"One word, but it is a secret word."

"The word *Atlas*?" At this, the Lord stood aghast. "This is impossible! You cannot know this! You simply cannot!" But, indeed he did know it. The ritual was traditionally a solitary business, but with the danger inherent, Holmes decreed that he would remain, whilst Carstairs and I would wait in the chamber below. What follows is, then Holmes's own account, in his own words . . . .

Watson and the safe-cracker Carstairs departed and I closed and barred the door after them. The ritual was, as the book had already revealed to me, almost definitely not a solitary one. Indeed, from the earliest days the practice was of Laird revealing the secret to first born son. The Laird would be seated on the throne with his son standing in the centre of the circle, on a worn brass compass. This was, as I had already observed, directly above the spindle below. Surrounding this were twelve stone flags

77

in sections forming the circle.

If I had reckoned correctly, there was a concealed level below us full of the workings of the tower clock – *and the mechanism for the double death trap on which I now sat!* Indeed, had the prospective Laird assumed his position on that compass without a second person – originally his father – seated on that throne, his death would have been identical to that of his predecessor. I had seen such diabolical mechanisms before, naturally, but this one was especially cruel in its cunning. A steel skewer, no more than the thickness of a man's finger, would be propelled from a concealment below the floor, through the back of the victim. I had wondered at the lack of tearing to the front of the deceased Laird's shirt, but now knew from the book that the aspirant must bear his chest to prove himself a man! Such is the stuff of ritual . . . .

The compass rose slowly dropped into the floor several feet until the Lord was visible only from the waist up, and at once, the flags around it turned, with an ominous scraping and grinding as the ancient mechanism shuddered into motion. The flags had rotated fully now, to reveal their undersides were set with inlaid brass depictions of the twelve signs of the zodiac. I had foreseen this, and yet I was still gripped by tension. I had every reason to be: If he failed to complete the sequence required of him, I would be alone in a room with a dead man, with questions to answer. If I had correctly calculated the energy stored in the mechanism, the lethal spike was under enormous tension with the slimmest of steel bars retaining it. Defying the cold, the sweat began to form at the base of my neck and brow.

It was now inescapable. My theorising had to be put to the final test. If I was correct, Castle Cullen would see a new Laird this very night. If not . . . if not . . . Dismissing the thought, my voice as firm as I could make it, I spoke. "Milord, are you ready?"

"Yes, if a man ever can be, I am – but I confess I am rather afraid."

"As am I. Now, listen extremely carefully, and do not waver from following my instructions to the letter." The Lord nodded, his jaw set. "Press down firmly upon the symbol for Sagittarius. Good." Indeed the symbol, once pressed, raised up an inch or so to stand proud of the stone. "Now, Taurus." Again, the symbol rose. "Aquarius. Gemini".

There was a second's pause then a shudder went through the very stonework as first the Lord was raised back to stand level with the floor as the flags turned back to display their bare faces. The sweat fairly pouring from my brow, I stood, half-convinced that at any second he would be impaled. As my weight left it, the throne seat slid aside and there was an aged bag of red velvet. "Milord, would you be so kind as to admit Doctor Watson and Carstairs. I feel this moment deserving of witnesses."

. . . I now resume my narrative with thanks to my estimable colleague Mister Sherlock Holmes. The bag, you will doubtless have guessed, contained the chain of the Lairds of Garrymore. With appropriate solemnity, Holmes bade the Lord take his ancestral throne and placed the chain around his neck. The chain itself was of heavy gold with a weird shimmer, as if it conveyed an uncanny power upon the wearer. "My Lord, it is my privilege to announce before these witnesses that you are now the Laird of Garrymore."

"Thank you, sir." Rising, the Laird clasped Holmes by the hand. "You have done me a great service, and you have rooms here as long as you shall live. All of you."

The door to the great hall was opened by Hobbs, who nodded to a houseboy, who ran to give the signal. With a twin booming that nearly shattered the windows, the mighty cannon fired in salutation and the guests who had been summoned to the hall bowed as the Laird strode forth. Addressing the assemblage, the Laird gave a speech of thanks and assured the staff their positions were more than assured.

The meal to which we were called was a jubilant affair, the mourning silk stripped from the head chair, and the repast was a gay one. We had been assured that Carstairs would be well looked-after his return to the rather bleary-eyed custody of his Sergeant. The Laird excused himself to replace the chain in its ancient hiding place, with Holmes's help to close it, and we decamped to the card room for a well-deserved cigar, Holmes taking the opportunity to slip away for a moment, though he kept his purpose to himself as so often.

"So, you haven't told me what this business about secret words all meant."

Smiling, he took a draw on his cigar and leant back in his chair. "Not the simplest of inferences, but the other night when the then-Lord Seagrave was in a state of delirium, he shouted out something about '*Titans*', issuing a challenge to them. My days at school were not all spent in the chemistry room. The Titans, I recalled included one who carried on his broad shoulders the very heavens themselves."

"Atlas!" I exclaimed.

"Somewhat of a thin thread of reasoning, but once the Lord confirmed that was indeed the word uttered by his dying predecessor, I had no doubt in my mind. This could not have been given to him by any true scion of Cullen. Only a murderer would have misled him so ruthlessly. Further it, would follow one who had no knowledge of the correct word, which, of course was . . . ."

"Stag?"

"You excel yourself, Watson! Indeed that is the word – formed, naturally from the first letters of the astrological signs involved." Leaning closer, he admonished me to remember that the word was not to be uttered again for fear it be discovered.

The new Laird entered and accepted port and a cigar from the Americans. A sudden murmur swept through the gentlemen present as the Lady Elizabeth swept in to the room. Having been absent at dinner, her sudden appearance was the more breathtaking for the lustrous green evening gown that daringly halted at her shoulders. Both Major Simpson/Shotton and the American party seemed particularly enraptured by her dazzling smile, and to a man we all rose. She went up to her brother and congratulated him on his ascendancy, though even from where we stood the antipathy was palpable.

Tapping his glass, the Laird addressed us as friends, explaining his plans for the estate and formally extending the invitation to the American party to form a business venture that would see Garrymore beef sold across the Atlantic. This, then, was the scene when a ghastly scream rang out from the great hall. A maid ran in to the library, sobbing and calling for a doctor. At once I sprang up and made my way to where a small crowd was already gathered.

There lay Carstairs, a rictus grin upon his features and blood on his lips. He had been run through in the same manner as the dead Laird. There was no aid I could give, save closing his eyes and laying my jacket over him. I turned to see Holmes, an expression of silent anger flashing across his features. Finally he spoke, each word clipped and tense as if spoken with a great effort of self-control. "It seems the Lady Elizabeth has another death on her account."

A veritable pandemonium ensued, during which at one point I was reduced to threatening the use of fisticuffs to restore order. Only a pistol shot brought us all to our senses, as the American, McCormack, had a small revolver aloft. "I think, Mister Holmes, you owe us an explanation of this accusation."

Brushing himself off, Holmes gave the Pinkerton agent a wry smile and nod of thanks. "I shall be happy to provide one. The former Laird had spent his time in the Yukon and wasn't in possession of the details of the arcane ritual of admission. He came here and was given what he believed was the vital word. It was false and he died horribly. Only Lord Seagrave or the Lady Elizabeth were in position to mislead him so cruelly. On the face of it, Lord Seagrave had the most to gain. He was, after all the next in line."

Holmes paused to re-light his cigar, before continuing. "My suspicion turned when Doctor Watson and I paid an unheralded visit to the Lady

Elizabeth at the Hunting Lodge. She wasn't in mourning, save for a veil, sash, and gloves – hasty adornments for our benefit." A stir of resentment went round the room, but Holmes was the epitome of coolness. "Further, the Lady misled us with a blatant lie in which she stated the ritual must be performed alone, with no others present. Discretion forbids a full explanation, save that the ritual is indeed impossible to complete alone."

The Lady Elizabeth was icily composed as she stood before us. "You have supposition, Mister Holmes. I hardly see myself fitted for the noose on mere guesswork and conjecture."

"I never guess, my Lady. I am sure the quarry-men can identify Hobbs as the man who paid them as I am sure Hobbs will confess himself, along with the name of his employer. He is at this moment in the handcuffs intended for the tragic Carstairs, though the Sergeant required a pail of icy water to revive him properly. It seems Carstairs merely waited until he was alone and extracted the Sergeant's key to make his bid for the chain."

"Whereas I myself have not even entered the tower, which surely I would have done had my intention been theft."

"There was no need. You knew at that time that your brother had no intention of remaining. Had he been killed, you would finally inherit all, but if he succeeded, it would have been simplicity itself to steal the chain during the long journey south. Doubtless his creditors include men who would not think twice about using brutal means on a debtor."

Taking a few halting steps forward, the Lady Elizabeth suddenly slapped Holmes across the face. "Damn you for an interfering swine, Holmes! You will not see me hang. I shall defend this charge and bring one of false accusation against you."

Just then, a booming voice rang out. "You shall not!"

The Pinkerton man, McCormack stepped forward and produced a silver badge. "My name is Donald McCormack, and I am a special agent of the Pinkerton agency. My purpose here can now be revealed, as the crook Carstairs, who I was sent to shadow, has expired." Waiting for the fresh ripple of excitement to subside, he continued. "We knew Carstairs had been involved in several of the most notorious cases of recent years. Then, in Scotland, he dynamited the strongbox at the Culbraith and McNair Bank." At the mention of that strongbox, Major Shotton stood bolt upright, yet need not have worried. "He was seen to swallow a jewel – an emerald which I have been detailed to return if only it can be recovered . . . ."

"It might be possible." Holmes interrupted the Pinkerton man there. "If my guess is correct, you were about to confirm the identity of Carstair's employer, were you not?"

"Indeed. It was the Lady Elizabeth. I visited Carstairs and he intimated as much to me, stating that the emerald was only the icing on the cake, and that his actual employment was to retrieve another item from that vault. Oddly, he stayed tight-lipped as to what it was. The chain was by way of a last-minute idea on the part of the Lady Elizabeth, having failed to secure it by other means." A glance of warning from the Major was enough for me. Coughing politely, I stepped across and whispered to Holmes, who agreed that the time had come to send for the Sergeant to make an arrest.

Monday morning and we assembled in the great hall to take our leave of the new Laird. After burying his ill-fated predecessor, he would begin the work of reviving the estate. We shook hands as friends and departed by the same sledges that had brought us here in what seemed to be an age ago. Happily, we found the train making steam and the tracks cleared. Holmes and I took the compartment previously occupied by Carstairs and the Metropolitan Sergeant, who took the next with Hobbs and, her head bowed, the Lady Elizabeth. These last were to be taken to Perth for trial. Soon the train blew its whistle and was moving, picking up speed until the frosted countryside was rolling past the window.

We had travelled perhaps five miles when Major Shotton and the Pinkerton man McCormack joined us at Holmes's request. My companion allowed himself the trace of a smile before proceeding. "Mister McCormack, I have followed the work of your fine agency with a growing regard. It would, therefore, be a sadness to see you return to Chicago with empty hands. Reach behind you, where the cushions meet."

Startled at this, the American did as he was asked, first to his right and then to his left where, after running his hand along the crease he stopped quite suddenly and froze. Slowly, as if unable to reconcile his senses, he withdrew a stone of the most radiant green I had ever beheld, an emerald quite the size of a duck egg. "How can you explain this, Mister Holmes?"

"Easily. Carstairs is – *was* – a regurgitator. He was trained to retain and then retrieve items by Lambert, the master lock-picker, with whom he studied. It is a common trick amongst stage conjurors wishing to secrete items such as keys without discovery. It follows then that, as he was arrested almost immediately, he would employ this trick and find a place he could be sure of re-visiting. This compartment was the obvious place."

Taking the emerald with his heartfelt thanks, the Pinkerton man left to rejoin his party. Major Shotton looked first to Holmes and then to myself with an air of expectancy that was followed by one of dejection. At last, when he could hold a straight face no more, Holmes let out that short laugh of his that signified triumph. Reaching across to the window, he pressed the bar that released it and slid it open, the sudden deafening rush of arctic air shocking to the senses. Reaching into his pocket, he produced a pencil which he slid down into the narrow gap between the glass and the door, pushing the pencil firmly against the glass with his thumb. With a smile, he pulled the window back up and, as the noise and buffeting of the outside air decreased, both myself and the Major let out gasps of incredulity. There, flat against the glass, was a fair-sized document: The missing papers! Carstairs was indeed a clever and imaginative man. Had his talents been turned to the public good, no doubt he would have risen far.

The Reykjavik Papers secured, we returned to London, I to my beloved Mary and my practice and Holmes to his own at Baker Street once more. With so many years having passed, I have taken the decision of including this case in the chronicles as the sensitive details therein have long since lost their capacity to cause harm. The Lady Elizabeth was sentenced to hang for murder and conspiracy, but there being some doubt in the minds of the jury, her sentence was commuted. The disgraced Head Butler, Hobbs, was sent down for two years' hard labour. That, it seemed, was the end of the affair.

There was, however something by way of a postscript. Some days after our return from Scotland, a parcel arrived for Holmes at Baker Street. The note accompanying it simply read *"In gratitude, a friend."* On opening the parcel, my friend discovered a magnificent engraving of a Highland stag, a beautiful fourteen-pointer. It hung in his bedroom at 221b for many years until his retirement.

The Carroun Document
by David Marcum

I regretted that it was too early in the day to decently adjourn to my club.

While certain members would doubtless already be in their fixed places – and indeed, many spent more time there in their favorite chairs than at their own hearths – I didn't want to cause undue comment, or start down that slippery slope wherein I, too, preferred to hide in that comfortable womb of favorite beverages and the latest periodicals and rounds of billiards rather than face the stark shades of reality.

But when Sherlock Holmes was in one of his moods, I was sorely tempted.

When my friend returned to London in April '94, after a three-year absence when he was believed to be dead, he found that he had become something of a mythological figure, in part because of my efforts to memorialize him by publishing a number of accounts of his adventures in a relatively new periodical. When he again took up the reins of his practice, those who had known him of old – either on the side of the law or otherwise – simply resumed their acquaintance in the previous manner. But those who had never encountered him except in the pages of a magazine now believed that he was someone larger-than-life – or worse, a fictional character.

Our rooms began to receive a certain amount of unwanted attention in the same manner that Dickens' homes had. Casual passers-by and tourists with much more specific (and dark) purposes of their own would stop and stare, standing upon the pavement across the way for varying lengths of time. And worse, we occasionally had visits from those simply wishing to get a look at the famous Sherlock Holmes, finding excuses to visit us on those routine mornings when Holmes's had his version of office hours.

That day, following visits ranging from that of a cabinet minister to a char-woman, there had been a few moments of silence while Holmes researched some fact or other in his scrapbooks. But soon the doorbell rang, and not long after Mrs. Hudson opened the door to reveal a mother and son. They appeared to be members of the comfortable middle class, with the woman sensibly dressed and the boy, about ten or twelve years of age, wearing some sort of school uniform. The woman introduced herself as Mrs. Burley and fumblingly apologized for taking up Holmes's time. I cringed inside, as I spotted what was held in the lad's hand: A dogged blue-covered journal – undoubtedly an issue of *The Strand.*

I realized why they were there, even as the woman explained that her son was quite taken by my stories – here she gave a cursory nod in my direction. But it was clear who they were here to see.

The young man simply looked at Holmes, his mouth slightly agape, and I couldn't tell if his expression denoted stunned amazement, satisfaction, or disappointment. His nose twitched, possibly from the pervasive smells of chemical experiments and pipe smoke.

Holmes listened politely for a few minutes, his lips becoming both tighter and straighter. It was when the woman asked if he might provide her son with some little souvenir, possibly one of his pipes, that the limit was reached. He rapidly led the way to the door, thanking them for dropping by while the woman attempted to keep talking, becoming louder and more ill-tempered as their visit ended. When the door was finally shut in their faces, Holmes stood glaring at it, listening first as the woman muttered darkly on the other side, and then as she and her son descended the stairs, closing the front door behind them. Only then did he begin that same litany that I'd heard so many times before.

"You see, Watson," he began, spinning in my direction, "why I was so reluctant to allow this foolishness? When you first cooked up the idea of 'publicly recognizing my merits', or however you phrased it, it was with the *caveat* – or should I say *threat*? – that if *I* didn't do it, *you* would. I rue the day that I didn't take charge of my own affairs then, instead of allowing you to do as you like."

"Really, Holmes – " I countered, all too familiar with these fits of pique regarding my writings. I made reference to how his practice had only increased following my efforts – particularly since he had returned from supposed death earlier that year. I pointed out that I had only written and published the majority of the narratives during that time when I believed him to be dead – and then I paused, withholding what else I was tempted to mention, related to my still-simmering resentment that he had allowed me to believe that he had died at the Reichenbach Falls.

Holmes continued to make point after point. It had all been discussed before: How my writings had degraded his serious work into a series of cheap tales. How he would lose any credibility if his reputation were to continue to be based on my inaccurate and romanticized scribbles. How he couldn't work as effectively if all of his methods were revealed as common knowledge. And of course he referenced Mrs. Burley and her son as the latest examples of how my efforts led directly to his valuable time being wasted.

It was at that point when I seriously considered bolting for my club. But before I could do so, there was a knock at the door, and Mrs. Hudson brought in a letter. While she handed it to Holmes, she gave me a look of sympathy. Clearly our discussion had carried beyond the sitting room.

Holmes thanked her shortly, took the envelope, and then examined it for a moment before slitting it open and withdrawing a single sheet. As he looked at it, I could see the tension of our recurring argument slough away as he became intrigued with the possibility of a new investigation. In a moment or two, he handed it my way as if there had been no rancor between us whatsoever. "This may interest you, Watson, if you wouldn't mind delaying the visit to your club."

I didn't bother to ask how he had divined my plans. No doubt my intention had been quite obvious. Rather, I glanced at the missive. It was a single sheet of ordinary paper. The script was formed from blue ink, rather thin and watery, using a pen with a worn nib. It was written by a right hand, at leisure, since the lines were evenly horizontal. There was nothing else that I observed of importance. It read:

Mrs. Raymond Oakshott
117 Brixton Road

Dear Mr. Holmes,

You may recall meeting my brother around Christmas-time several years ago. I don't mention his name here, but if I tell you that the matter involved a stone and a goose, you will certainly know of it.

As you know, after your leniency in the matter, my brother fled the country. Although we've corresponded since then, he hasn't been back to England. However, just this morning I received a letter threatening his life, and I don't know where else to turn. If you can visit me at my home – which I am unable to leave at present due to a family illness – it would be most appreciated, and I can provide any further details that you might require.

I look forward to seeing you very soon.

She concluded by again identifying herself as *Mrs. Raymond Oakshott.*

No. 117 Brixton Road was one of a row of very tidy houses on the east side of the street, three stories with dormer windows peeking from the attic above. I confessed to myself that it was quite different than I had imagined. I recalled several years earlier, when I had stopped in to visit Holmes on a cold morning two days after Christmas – and coincidentally deliver the first of my narratives of his cases to be published – only to find him studying a hat that had been found in the street. From that unlikely beginning, we had become involved in a matter of a stolen jewel – the stone to which Mrs. Oakshott had alluded in her letter – and a trek across London while evening fell around us. On the way, we had encountered Mrs. Oakshott's brother, James Ryder, and invited him back to Baker Street. He had accepted, thinking that we would provide knowledge regarding the stone, which he had stolen and subsequently lost. Instead, his guilt had been exposed, and he had promised to flee England, if only he was shown mercy. It being the Christmas season, Holmes had agreed.

I had later written up the story for *The Strand*, one of those cases that were published during Holmes's supposed death. But when doing so, I hadn't felt the need to visit some of the scenes mentioned in Ryder's tale – for instance, his sister's house, here in the Brixton Road, where he had surreptitiously carried the jewel stolen from the Countess of Morcar at the Hotel Cosmopolitan.

At the time he was telling us of his actions, and how, in order to hide it, he had forced the stone down the throat of one of the geese that his sister was raising in the back-yard, I had vaguely recalled the area. I knew that this house was just north of No. 3 Lauriston Gardens, where I had joined Holmes in early March 1881 on our first investigation together. When preparing Ryder's story for publication, I had spent time making sure that my recollections of the Alpha Inn and nearby Covent Garden Market were accurate, but I hadn't really given much thought to Mrs. Oakshott's house. I suppose that, knowing that she kept geese, I had pictured a dwelling that was conducive to raising fowl. The rather fine house before us seemed much too resplendent to have gaggles of geese in the back yard.

The door was answered by a young maid who took our coats and hats. She then led us through to a small parlor, modestly furnished. Standing to meet us was a middle-aged woman who introduced herself as our correspondent. She had iron-grey hair tucked tightly against her scalp, and a pursed mouth giving an expression of what must be perpetual perturbation. She directed us to seats and, when we had declined refreshments, dismissed the maid.

"Thank you for coming, Mr. Holmes. Doctor."

"Your note said something of an illness," I said, before Holmes could begin his interview with the woman. "May I offer my services?"

She seemed surprised, and a bit uncertain. "Why, thank you, Doctor, but it won't be necessary. One of the servants has a bad summer cold. She has been seen by my own family physician, and is now on the mend."

Holmes, seeing that this topic was apparently ended, asked, "How may we assist you?"

She blinked twice, and then said, "I didn't know where else to turn. My husband – he mustn't know of this!"

"And he is?" asked Holmes.

"He is one of the supervisory clerks at Barings Bank. He doesn't want anything to do with my poor brother – he won't want any complications in our lives. He managed to weather the Argentine bonds affair a few years ago, and he was doing well until you published that story, Doctor." She frowned my way. "I hadn't told him anything of my brother's sad transgression before then, and he only learned of it when one of his supervisors asked why his home and his wife were mentioned in the new Sherlock Holmes story."

From the corner of my eye, I saw Holmes frown my way, and could only imagine that this would be new grist for him to use when circumstances allowed another volley at my writings. "I apologize," I said to Mrs. Oakshott, taken aback that the story had caused her difficulties. "I had understood through conversations with the police that, in the intervening years, your brother's identity had become known to them, and that no action was contemplated toward seeking him out or prosecuting him."

She shook her head. "I had hoped that the matter would be forgotten. It is fortunate that my husband avoided gaining any such attention for as long as he did. For a while, he faced some ridicule, and speculation about our situation – his brother-in-law implicated in a jewel theft. And he was called in to explain the fact that we had at one time raised geese in the rear of the house."

"Indeed," said Holmes. "And how did that activity come about? It is rather unusual that residents of this neighborhood would be dabbling in such a rural pursuit."

She lowered her head. "We . . . we were guilty, for a period of time you see, of living beyond our means," she said. "My husband had obtained his promotion at the bank, and we felt that we needed to reflect his position and newfound prosperity with a house to match. We moved here, not quite realizing at first the extra expenses associated with maintaining a larger home than where we had lived previously. For a time, we were forced to economize, and at one point I had the idea to raise geese for market. I am a farmer's daughter, gentlemen, so hard work isn't new to me, and it is nothing of which to be ashamed. I raised the geese, and contracted with a man to sell them – a curious fellow who had stubbornly established his stall in the middle of a vegetable market. This unusual strategy did him well, and his prosperity was indirectly passed on to me. By the time my brother made use of my geese as a place to hide the stolen jewel, I had been associated with Mr. Breckinridge for three years.

"Since then, our situation has improved, and when questioned about my brother and your story, Doctor, my husband brushed off the association, and fortunately it never since been an issue. But now I've received this note threatening my brother's life, and my husband must not be involved in any way."

"Ah, yes. The note."

She looked at Holmes. "I wrote to you because I knew that you had been kind enough to help my brother several years ago."

"I don't know that we actively helped him," replied Holmes. "Rather, our response to his crime was passive, in that we allowed him to escape. I can assure you that, if events had played out differently and an innocent man were to be prosecuted for the crime rather than cleared, your brother would have arrested and tried, no matter where he ran."

Mrs. Oakshott's lips pressed together tightly, but she nodded. "I understand your position, Mr. Holmes. James was always weak, and we made allowances for it. Perhaps that is what turned him down the wrong path. I sometimes forget that others aren't as willing to give him the same allowances that we have."

"You said in your letter, and again just now, that there was a threat against his life?"

"Yes, and I don't know what to make of it." She reached to a side table, where a note had been lying throughout the conversation. Holmes took it from her and gave it his usual thorough examination inside and out before passing it my way. I noticed several facts, but kept them to myself, as long experience had taught me. What seemed to be most important was the message itself:

> Your brother James's life is forfeit. His crimes must be avenged. But you can pay the price instead. Be in Perham Down by sunset today for further instructions.

The message was written on common paper stock. The spelling and punctuation indicated someone reasonably educated. There was nothing else inscribed upon it, front or back. I returned it to Holmes, who set it aside on a small table by his chair. Mrs. Oakshott's eyes followed this movement, but she made no comment.

"Any envelope?" he asked.

"None. We found it pushed through the letter box this morning."

"Perham Down. A curious location. Do you know of any reason why it must be today, or why that chosen location?"

"No. I have never heard of the place."

"What crimes," asked Holmes, shifting his questioning, "– plural – do you believe this references?"

Her eyes widened. "I'm sure that I don't know. I had assumed that it was something to do with the jewel he stole while employed at the Hotel Cosmopolitan. Do you think that it could be related to something that has happened since?"

I thought it a rather naïve question, but before I could ponder, she continued. "Since James left England, we've barely stayed in contact with one another. I'm not even sure if he still uses his real name."

"Where did he go when he fled the country?"

"To France. In the south, I believe. After he – after you let him go that night, he came here. That's when he told me the truth – about how he had stolen the blue carbuncle, and then hidden it by forcing it down the throat of one of our geese. He explained how the goose was sold to Breckinridge's stall before he could retrieve it, and then how you became involved. He said that you had shown him mercy, and that he had to leave right away. I tried to make him stay – I didn't understand at first the seriousness of what he had done. But he made it clear that he might be facing a stretch in prison if he were to remain, and I saw the wisdom in letting him go. He is my baby brother, you see. I had to help keep him safe."

"Have you ever had any other messages like these? Demands to rescue him from some other trouble?"

"None at all."

"To your knowledge, has he *been* in any other trouble?"

"No. Or so I believe."

"Has he given any indication of how he is supporting himself in France?" I asked.

"Soon after he went there, he wrote that he had found work at a hotel on the southern coast. It was something that he knew how to do, you see. I've assumed that he continued in the same position."

"May I see some of his letters?"

At that, her open and frank expression changed suddenly, as if a candle had been extinguished. "Why?" she asked flatly.

Holmes's eyebrow raised in a most minute fashion, but it was likely unnoticed by anyone who didn't know him so well. "To see if I can gather any clues from them, of course. His whereabouts, for instance. Indications of how he spends his time, and with whom."

"There is nothing there. He has always been most careful to shield me from knowing too much."

"Why would he wish to do that?" I asked, becoming more curious by the minute.

She shifted a bit. "He is still a fugitive, you see. Possibly he doesn't want his whereabouts known."

"But you are his sister," I noted.

"The information might have been forced from me," she replied, as if that explained everything.

Holmes chose to let that assertion pass without comment, as if he were satisfied. "I would still like to see the letters."

She stood, clearly irritated. "I'll just be a moment." Then she walked from the room. We heard her go towards the back of the house.

I started to speak, but Holmes shook his head slightly and raised a finger to his lips. He had the barest hint of a smile, as if anticipating what would happen next. We didn't have to wait very long.

"I've misplaced them," said Mrs. Oakshott in tight voice. "In any case, I cannot see what they would have to do with this matter. Clearly whatever has happened to prompt that letter – " She glanced toward the table beside Holmes's chair, " – is here in England. At this Perham Down mentioned in the note."

"It is in Wiltshire," said Holmes, "on the edge of the Salisbury Plain."

"I didn't know," she said. "Is it a difficult journey?"

"Moderate," replied Holmes. "One must be rather lucky in terms of railway connections, but there is still time to be there by sunset."

"Then you'll go for me?" she said, with a hopeful and trusting tone in her voice, but – perhaps – also the slyest of casts to her expression. "I cannot go. I would be helpless in such a situation. And my husband must not know . . . ."

My surprise at her confident assumption of our willingness to make the journey was matched only by Holmes's response. "Of course, madam. I feel a certain responsibility for your brother, having taken it upon myself to rescue his soul. However, I must ask: Do you have the resources to pay what might be asked? I have a feeling that there is some sort of payment involved in this scheme. We know nothing of the reasons for these threats, or what crimes your brother may have committed. Are you prepared to meet the demands?"

"How can I answer that honestly, Mr. Holmes, knowing nothing about what you will discover? However, knowing is the first step."

Holmes nodded. "Will you be available throughout the day, should we have any questions?"

"I will remain at home, and instruct the servants to find me immediately with any message that you send."

"That is all that I could ask," he replied.

"Please," she added, taking a step toward him and laying a hand upon his arm. "Please start immediately. Every moment might matter."

As we stepped out to the street, Holmes began to look for a cab. Knowing that my back was to the house, I smiled and said in a low voice, "We're not going to Perham Down, are we?"

He looked at me. "No, we are not."

Something in the way he answered gave me an anxious start. "*We* aren't," I said, "but I hope that you aren't being exact, when you mean to say that *I* am going, while you stay here."

He shook his head. "My apologies, Watson. My exact response to your question was misunderstood. Neither of us needs to go on that wild goose chase."

I had expected so see some signs of amusement in his expression to match my own, but there was none. In fact, he appeared quite anxious – a trait that he had hidden quite well while still in Mrs. Oakshott's parlor.

"She was lying to us," I said.

"You saw it then?"

"Enough to be going on with," I nodded. "Besides the fact that the story of her servant's illness was suspect, it was the handwriting on the notes." I phrased it as a statement, but I was still marginally uncertain, realizing that Holmes had certainly seen more than I had.

"Exactly," he confirmed. "Although she had attempted to disguise the handwriting on the note, with the belief that using different and cheaper paper would be a distraction, it was clearly her own. I'm gratified to see that some of my little lessons on graphology haven't gone to waste. Whatever made her write both the note to summon us to today's appointment in her own name, and also the supposedly anonymous note purportedly threatening her brother in a badly disguised manner, is supposed to get us on a train to Wiltshire – which we will *not* do."

"But if we go there, forewarned as we are by perception of her deception, we can turn the tables on whatever awaits us."

Holmes managed to attract the attention of a west-bound hansom. It stopped by the curb, and we climbed in. Looking back, I could see Mrs. Oakshott, watching us from the parlor window. "Paddington Station!" Holmes called loudly for her benefit, and the cab did a smart turn and headed back toward cricket grounds.

"Nothing awaits us in Wiltshire but wasted time," said Holmes. When we were out of sight of Mrs. Oakshott's home, Holmes rapped on the ceiling and instructed the cabbie to make his way to Baker Street instead with all possible speed. The horse lurched into a respectable trot. "This seems to be an ill-conceived idea to take us off the London board. We have to ask ourselves why."

"It wouldn't be the first time someone has tried to distract you in this manner. There was the matter of the priest's hole in Piccotts End, for instance."

Holmes smiled. "Ah, Watson. It's kind of you to mention that – one of my little successes –and to refrain from reminding me of the matter of Moriarty's similar distraction and his attempted jewel theft at The Tower. That was a valuable lesson, and it took quite a bit to get back in Sir Ronald's good graces."

I wasn't being kind – That particular incident at The Tower had slipped my mind. There had been a number of instances when attempts had been made to decoy Holmes away from this or that affair. And those were greatly outnumbered by the times that someone had attempted the same thing with his clients – when Mr. Hall Pycroft was diverted to Birmingham, or the occasion when Miss Sarah Gaddesden had – against Holmes's express advice – used a railway ticket that had been delivered in an otherwise empty envelope to visit Caerphilly, where she encountered a figure from her past that left her reason destroyed forever.

"It isn't simply that Mrs. Oakshott wrote both letters," said Holmes. "There is also the fact that she wouldn't show us anything purporting to be from her brother and his new life."

"Why do you suppose she did that?" I asked. "The handwriting on the 'anonymous' notes was her own. It isn't as if we would have seen that it was her brother's."

"She couldn't show me his letters from France because she doesn't have any. I've kept my eye on Mr. James Ryder from the time he was allowed to flee, and while he did cross almost immediately to the Continent, he soon came back, taking the name of Bert Abel and settling in Margate. He's worked at a little seaside hotel there ever since, and has most gratifyingly stayed out of trouble. I believe that he's even married. It's possible that he knows nothing whatsoever about his invocation into this business."

"Then what could possibly have led Mrs. Oakshott to attempt such a trick?"

Holmes didn't answer, and we fell silent for a minutes. I came to myself as we turned northwest at the Camberwell New Road, suddenly wondering why we were returning to Baker Street. I assumed that Holmes wished to find some pertinent fact in his voluminous commonplace books, or perhaps change into a disguise before venturing out on some investigatory path which had suggested itself to him. I asked, and he shook his head. "Actually, Watson, I don't intend that we should enter the building at all – at least not yet. Rather, we shall observe for a bit – with the help of the Irregulars."

I raised an eyebrow, and he continued. "Consider: Someone who happened to have our rooms – as well as the inhabitants – under regular observation, would quickly identify the day-to-day habits of the household. Today is Wednesday. Does that suggest anything?"

It took me no time to realize it. "Mrs. Hudson and Mrs. Turner usually go to visit their sister, Mrs. Grimshaw, on the first Wednesday of the month – today."

"Exactly. And while that fact may be meaningless by itself, I have to consider it with the thought that someone went to a good deal of trouble – either Mrs. Oakshott herself, or at the behest of someone else – to direct us away from London on the very day that our good landlady is also away."

"Leaving Baker Street undefended."

"Indeed."

"But we've discussed this many times over the years – the perils of having a practice such as yours in a private dwelling, wherein your records, as well as various criminal relics and pieces of evidence, are relatively unsecured."

"Not only my records," Holmes replied. "Your accumulated notes now hold a number of dark secrets as well. However, what can we do? Should I rent an office with bars on the window and an iron safe? Should we convert our cellar, or the lumber room perhaps, into a strong-room? Would Mycroft provide me with a cubby in one of the Whitehall buildings in which to conduct interviews and hide my artifacts? The fact that his agents could root through my records at their leisure is as unsettling as the thought of having them rifled in Baker Street."

I smiled. "I propose a room for you in one of the turrets at Scotland Yard – one with a view of Westminster Pier. Surely they wouldn't mind if you displaced the current occupant."

Holmes snorted, but his amusement quickly faded as he fell to pondering why someone might want to lure us away. As we were crossing Vauxhall Bridge, he turned his head as a thought crossed his mind. "Perhaps," he said, almost speaking aloud to himself, "it's related to the Carroun murder. As you know, that case is coming to trial in a couple of weeks."

"It's possible, but why would anyone think that you have retained anything of importance? Gregson assembled all that he needed, at your direction, months ago."

94

"And yet, there is the note what, while having no direct effect on the matter, we suppressed. We suspected that the lawyer, Chartridge, overheard us discuss it."

"But what does that case have to do with Mrs. Oakshott? Or her brother for that matter."

Holmes settled back with a sigh. "Nothing. Or everything. We don't have enough data. This could all be a shot on my part in the wrong direction, wherein no attempt will be made to enter our rooms. Or if someone does want to get at our papers, it could relate to any number of cases going back more than twenty years."

"Perhaps," I said with sudden alarm, "someone wants to burn the place, as was attempted by the Professor. Or possibly they are trying to blow the place up, along the lines of the explosive package sent by the Baron in the Eye of Heka matter."

Holmes nodded. "I've considered that, but if someone had those inclinations, would they feel the need to decoy us away? It's possible, of course. Something quite complex could be rigged within the building to detonate when we return. But for now, I'm going forward with the simplest assumption that this is simply an arrangement for someone to enter unseen. With any luck, we'll be able to spot whomever goes in and then follow them. If they've already been and gone, we'll have to hope that we can identify what's missing."

I shook my head. "The opposite of looking for a needle in a haystack. It would be like trying to find the one piece of hay that has been pulled out of the rick and carried away."

"We can only take comfort in the fact that we were to be lured away for a full day or better. Hopefully that means the player on the other side doesn't want to enter the rooms in daylight and hasn't been there yet, and we'll be in place for his nighttime assault." He knocked his stick against the ceiling of the cab. "Faster!"

A few hours later, we were sitting in two straight-backed chairs and, although they were not as comfortable as one might have hoped, it was a considerably better situation than how we had waited in this very same room just a few months earlier.

That morning, we had crossed the river and threaded our way north through the area around the Palace, and then Mayfair. At Portman Square, Holmes had signaled to the cabbie to pull over. After settling the fare, we walked up Baker Street to the Bazaar, where it didn't take long to find one of the Irregulars, that informal band of lads who served as Holmes's eyes and ears. Instructed to gather as many of his comrades as he could find, the lad scampered and vanished into the crowds. Then we walked at a more sedate pace, belying Holmes's growing impatience, with the intention of meeting them in the Paddington Gardens.

Five minutes or so later, we gathered in the shade underneath one of the trees on the southeast side. There were a dozen or so of them, with one of the Wiggins brood taking nominal command, as was typical. Holmes explained that they were to form a net around our lodgings, remaining completely invisible while making certain to observe anyone entering the building – either by day or night. If someone did make his or her way inside, they were to be allowed free passage to both come and go. If an intruder was seen to be making away with something from inside, no hindrance would be offered.

Most imperative, Holmes explained, was that once the person left, he or she must be followed, and on no account could the trail be lost. "Recruit additional help as you see fit. There is a chance that the intruder has already been inside and gone, but I sense that the assault will come after dark. Watson and I will be across the street in Camden House. When you report, enter by the back way."

The boys dispersed, and Holmes and I walked through the side streets. A thought occurred to me. "Do you suppose that someone is at Paddington, waiting to see if we actually leave for Perham Down?"

"That had occurred to me. However, I felt that it was more important to get our forces in place here, rather than take the time to be seen boarding a train, and then departing a few stations down the line to return. If nothing comes of this, I'll think of something else."

We stopped and sent a wire to Mrs. Hudson at her sister's home, indicating that she should delay her return until she heard from us. "Of course," said Holmes, "there is the slightest chance that she has already returned early today – a change of plans, perhaps, or an unexpected illness. We'll only know if we see signs of her presence while we watch – stepping out on an errand perhaps, or if she lights the lamps tonight. We can't take a chance on approaching the house to deliver a message."

We reached the back of Camden House, and only then did I recall that it was now occupied, having been leased earlier in the summer. Holmes knocked, and the door was opened by the young mother whose family had recently taken possession of the place. She seemed surprised to see us, but we were quickly allowed inside. We followed her to the front of the building, taking care to stay back from the windows, where her husband sat in a comfortable-looking chair, looking puzzled.

We knew the couple slightly, and in our previous encounters, they had always seemed to be a bit in awe of my friend – not an uncommon occurrence. Holmes explained that we were expecting some sort of intrusion into our lodgings, most likely that night, and asked permission to wait and watch. He also related how we would be receiving messages by way of the back door from the Irregulars. They enthusiastically agreed, and soon we were seated in the very room where, just months before, we had captured the murderous Colonel Moran when he attempted to murder Holmes by shooting through the sitting room window directly across the street. Then, this room had been empty. Now it was fixed into a parlor of sorts, and felt much more crowded and small. I recalled Holmes's struggle with the murderous colonel, and how, as the man seized Holmes by the throat, I had struck him with great satisfaction across the head with the butt of my revolver. That spot was now filled with a filigree table.

Throughout the day, one or the other of us carefully kept an eye on the street below, confident that the rear of our lodgings, and even the unlikely route across the roof, was well-watched. It had become apparent that Mrs. Hudson was not in residence – a fact that gave us comfort, should an intruder actually appear. While we waited, our hostess made every effort to keep us more-than-well fed, and yet she also seemed to realize that we didn't with to be bothered. Holmes became increasingly tense as he muttered about various documents and objects that might be sought by an intruder.

It was the time of year when the sun normally set very late, but throughout the afternoon, clouds from the south began to build, and it was unnaturally dark by half-after-five. The wind picked up, and occasional spatters of rain hit the window like shot, although the storm took quite a while to actually break. When it did, the heavens opened, and I felt mightily guilty about the Irregulars who were out in it. It seemed as if the rains were approaching the level of a tempest, and I imagined the gutters overflowing as waterfalls and the ditches running like small rivers. Our view from the window was completely obscured by viscous-seeming water sliding across the glass. At one point, Holmes raised the sash to try and look through the narrow gap, but so much rain immediately forced itself inside to puddle on the floor that he was required to shut it again.

However, the initial heavy downpour did finally settle into a steadier soak, and we were once again able to peer across the street, although in a rather smeared way. As the shimmering lights resolved themselves, I was thrilled to see that, in our distant sitting room, a single lamp had been lit. Even as I spotted it, a shadow moved from the left window to the right, toward the chemical corner. Someone was there.

Holmes had seen it as well, of couse, but there was no need for conversation. Just a moment or so later, we heard the back door open and close, and then footsteps approaching along the hallway outside the room where we waited. One of the Irregulars slipped into the room, informing us that a man of indeterminate years, dressed in dark clothing, had made his way into our lodgings by way of the yard behind the building and through the back door, which he had apparently jimmied open. Assuming that the intruder would leave the same way, all routes from the back of the house had been more-than-adequately covered – including placing young Jim Byrne in the thickly-leaved branches of the solitary plane tree that grew in the yard – although the other possibilities of departure would also stay under surveillance until such time as the man's path was ascertained. Holmes made sure that the house would remain guarded even as we were led away.

It was a long wait, nearly an hour, before we saw the shifting shadows cease and the light in the sitting room vanish. Holmes and I stood, found our coats and hats, and made our way downstairs. The occupants of Camden House were still up, for it was not yet ten o'clock, and we thanked them profusely, with a promise to explain the outcome when we knew it ourselves. Then we let ourselves out into the mews to await a report as to which way we should travel.

Within moments, a little fellow named McGee skittered to a stop before us. "He left by the back," he panted. "He's circled 'round through Gloucester Place, and now he's headed down Marylebone Road, toward the Crescent." Holmes thanked him and we set out to follow.

The rains had nearly stopped, and the air was considerably cooler than it had been earlier in the day. Occasional puffs of breeze would buffet us unexpectedly, and I feared that another storm was following the first – and this time we wouldn't have the comforting protection of windows and walls. Yet, we were fortunate in that the winds seemed to take a different direction, and we had no further difficulties that night – at least with the weather.

We were lucky, I suppose, in that the fellow chose to walk rather than take a cab. Several passed by him along the way, and if he had wanted one, it would have been his for the asking. However, we would have been caught short if he had, for there wouldn't have been another anytime soon for us, and we would have been left standing in the street while he vanished into the darkness, trusting that the Irregulars would find a way to stay with him. I knew that this was on Holmes's mind, and once he muttered darkly when it looked as if our prey might choose to ride rather than walk. Fortunately, he stayed afoot, unaware that the silent pack of Holmes's juvenile agents were swarming silently all around him, dashing ahead on side streets and constantly anticipating his route, while we inexorably came along behind.

We stayed well back in the shadows but we needn't have bothered, for the fellow never looked behind him, or did anything to obscure his route. He kept to the well-lit main thoroughfares. As he passed beneath the streetlamps, we could see that he carried a case of some sort, first in one hand, and then in the other, as if he were simply a businessman returning home after an honest day's labors. He seemed to be a rather small fellow, and the weight of the bag pulled him to one side or the other as he progressed.

"It appears that I was wrong," Holmes said at one point. "Recognize him?"

"Surely it is James Ryder," I said. "Clearly whatever life he built in Margate is less important than involving himself in this business."

"Don't judge too hastily, Watson. He may have had no choice. This is a bigger scheme than his impulsive theft of the Countess' Blue Carbuncle. Somehow it involves his sister, and the plan to get us out of town is beyond Ryder's abilities. He reached the limit of his inspiration when he thought of using a goose as a temporary jewel box."

As our journey continued, we had traversed south and east before reaching New Oxford Street, and that was where we remained for quite a distance. In fact, if was only after that street became High Holborn, and we had passed the narrow entrance to Bloomsbury Court, that the object of our attentions began to look around him, scanning the house numbers. Then, he abruptly turned left into a door located just one building before reaching Southampton Street. We had time to see what had occurred and crossed the street accordingly before continuing in the same direction, but now we were across from where the man might possibly be waiting to see if he was being followed.

However, as we glanced to our left, there was no one hiding in the darkness of the doorway. We turned south at Newton Street, just across from the building in question, and then slipped into a convenient recess. In just a moment, Wiggins appeared at our sides and Holmes gave him instructions to have the building surrounded. "How many of you are there?" he asked.

"Seventeen now."

"Excellent. More than enough. Follow anyone who comes out."

As Wiggins slipped away, I looked around surreptitiously, noting that the structure in question, Number 130, was a narrow four-story building whose white color gleamed in the darkness in contrast to its darker-stoned neighbors. The ground floor was a closed and shuttered stationery shop, and beside it, to the left, was the plain door leading to the upper rooms where our subject had entered. The three windows across the first floor were lit, while the two floors above were dark. Even as I watched, a shadow passed across the illuminated drawn shades.

Holmes was quiet for a moment before reaching a decision. "I believe that we can force the question," he said preparing to step out. "The fact

99

that that our rooms were burgled with such confidence indicates that they are certain we are off the board entirely. Our arrival will be unexpected."

"Should we summon the police?" I questioned.

Holmes paused a moment and then shook his head. "If they are after something of a secret nature, then it should likely remain secret. No, we'll handle this ourselves."

He started to move from the doorway, but just as he did so, a hansom pulled to a stop in front of the building. Holmes gave an intake of breath and retreated backwards. I couldn't see what was happening without leaning past him, but fortunately Holmes narrated in a low whisper. "One man. Stout, with a stick. He's entering the building. Ah!" Then I heard the sound of horse's hooves carrying the hansom away.

He straightened. "I owe you thanks for that, Watson. If you hadn't slowed me by a second or two to ask about the police, we might have already been walking toward the intersection, possibly to be seen by our new arrival. It may interest you to know that we're somewhat acquainted with the man. It is Clarence Chartridge, the lawyer."

"Then this *is* about the Carroun paper. But – " I was still brought up short. "In what way could Ryder and Mrs. Oakshott be connected to that affair?"

"That's what we will now determine. You have your service revolver?"

"Never without it."

"Then quick-march to the north!" And he stepped out into the lane, slipping along the wall toward the white building before us.

The door was locked, certainly by Chartridge following his entry, but that simply meant a delay of a few seconds for someone with Holmes's practiced skills and specialized tools – specifically one that he favored and called "the smoker's companion". The door opened silently and we passed inside, quickly shutting it behind us. We took a moment to listen, determining whether our entrance had been detected. Apparently not, as the low murmur of voices we had heard upon stepping inside continued overhead. Holmes moved carefully toward the steps, faintly lit from a partly opened door at the top. My eyes adjusted and I was careful to place my feet on the outer edges of those same treads where Holmes had stepped, knowing that he had a cat-like gift for understanding how to avoid those which might creak or groan and reveal our presence.

We reached the top successfully and I indicated that my revolver was ready. With that, the door, already partly ajar, was pushed fully open and we stepped into the lit room.

Holmes immediately shifted to the left, while I moved in the opposite direction, keeping the three men facing us covered. One, in his fifties, was seated in a plush armchair, a small table beside him supporting a bottle of whisky and a half-filled glass. An attaché case was between his feet and a sheaf of papers was clutched in his hand. To his left was the elderly lawyer, Chartridge, dropping into a somewhat ludicrous defensive crouch while pulling a much-less humorous revolver from his pocket. And to our far left, apparently dismissed once his task as a housebreaker and courier was complete, was our old acquaintance, the cringing little white-faced James Ryder.

Before we had a chance to speak, Ryder bolted, turning and vanishing into an open doorway behind him. It was a darkened room, and before I could consider passing by Holmes and following after him, we heard a window slide open and a scrambling sound as someone climbed through and scampered down the side of the building, landing with a muffled cry.

"Let him go, Watson," said Holmes. "The Irregulars will trail him. We have bigger fish to fry." He stepped closer to the fireplace, where a pair of gas-lamps on the wall above provided a dim yellow glow. Reaching up, he adjusted the flames so that the room was better illuminated. Then he nodded toward an empty chair behind the lawyer. "Sit down, Mr. Chartridge. I'll feel much more comfortable with our discussion if I'm not worried that Watson will have to shoot you, should you try to flee."

The man straightened and gave a tight smile, glancing at the gun in my hand, very similar to his own. "I'm too old to run, Mr. Holmes. And I'm most curious to hear your explanation for staging an armed invasion of a private dwelling."

Holmes laughed – a short bark that never boded well. "Shall we summon the police, then? If so, I would ask that the papers on your lap, Mr. Elliot, remain there until they can be examined by the authorities to verify that they were recently extracted from our rooms."

"Certainly you don't want that," said Randolph Elliot, the man in the chair. We had met him during our consultation into the death of his daughter. "I call your bluff. After all, I only had these . . . *retrieved*, shall we say, by Chartridge's shabby little agent in order to make them public anyway, you know."

"I don't believe that you've thought the matter quite through," countered Holmes.

"Oh, but I have, you see," said Elliot, standing up, his anger giving him strength to master his enfeebled limbs. "It's obvious that our ruse to divert you to Wiltshire was a failure. What gave it away?"

"The handwriting on the anonymous note, though disguised, was clearly Mrs. Oakshott's."

Elliot shook his head and glared at Chartridge, as if it were somehow his fault.

"How is she involved?" Holmes asked.

The lawyer cleared his throat. "She is my step-sister," he explained. "And Ryder is my step-brother." His mouth tightened in distaste. "I was tasked with finding a way for someone to get into your rooms and retrieve the document we knew that you'd taken with you when . . . when you investigated the death of Mr. Elliot's daughter's. I conceived the idea of having my step-sister seek your help. We decided to send you to Perham Down. We looked for somewhere that you would be able to reach by our deadline, if you hurried."

"But why Mrs. Oakshott?" I asked. "Why draw her into this business? Surely when we realized that the trip was for nothing, we would return and question her further, and look deeper into the business."

"When you came back with further questions, she would have simply begged for you to drop it. I involved her and James in order to keep the circle of those involved quite close. She frequently speaks of her ill-will toward you both, and I knew that she would be a willing distraction. She has never forgiven you, Doctor, for mentioning her in your story, and bringing unwanted attention upon her family. She was quite willing to take this little revenge. And as for James . . . Let us say that I have a bit of leverage over him. He'll never be the sort to keep to the strictly legal side of the street, even in such a quiet little place as Margate. He's had a few scrapes in the last few years, and – related to his continued liberty – he owed me."

Nodding and speaking in a lower tone, lessening the tension in the room, Holmes turned from the lawyer to the other man and said, "Have you had a chance to read those yet?"

Elliot glanced toward the documents, still gripped in his hand. "No, of course not. Ryder just arrived with them – as you well know." He nudged the case with his foot. "He wasn't quite sure what he was looking for, so he brought a whole assortment of papers and notes. I'm confident that what I seek is here, but it will take some examination to find exactly what I want." His gaze darkened. "I won't return them until I find it," he threatened. "Dr. Watson will have to shoot me first."

"That won't be necessary," replied Holmes, stepping away and drawing out a straight-backed chair from underneath a side table. "No need for the gun, Watson," he said. "Pull up a seat while we wait."

Elliot and Chartridge both seemed surprised. Following Holmes's lead, I put away my revolver and located another chair behind me. Placing it where I could face the two men, with Holmes at my left, I sat down and awaited developments. After a moment, Elliot lowered himself back into his own chair.

"You may put away your revolver as well, Mr. Chartridge. I assure you that there will be no violence upon our part."

The lawyer glanced at Elliot, who kept his eyes directed our way. Then, with a shrug, he slipped the gun into his pocket and found a chair for himself.

"Assuming that Ryder did manage to find and bring the correct document," explained Holmes, pulling out a pipe and tobacco from his coat, "I must tell you that you most certainly do not want to read it." He opened the pouch and began to push shag into the pipe. "That being said, I doubt at this point you will be dissuaded. We have no wish to shoot you in order to get it back, as you likely realize, so that form of inducement is useless." He struck a match. "I won't attempt to wrest the papers from your hand as if we were boys in a schoolyard – although there is no doubt who would be the victor." A puff or two and the pipe was lit. "But I really cannot let you violate the confidentiality of others whose cases are referenced in those additional papers that have come into your possession."

Elliot smiled, not without some tension, and sank deeper into his own chair. Chartridge looked rather unnerved by the conversational turn the encounter had taken. "Surely," said Elliot, "you don't think that, after all this time and effort, I'll simply hand you these papers and ask you to look through them for me, naively trusting that in the end you won't shrug and smile and tell me that Ryder didn't get what he was sent for."

Holmes turned his head slightly. "It has only ever been for your sake, Mr. Elliot, that I chose to suppress the facts that Watson and I discovered in that paper. We knew that Mr. Chartridge likely suspected its existence, but I had no indication that you would go to these lengths."

"You say that you hid the paper for *my* sake," said Elliot. "Explain."

Holmes closed his eyes for a moment, as I've seen surgeons do before making the first cut. "Tell me the facts of the case as you understand them," he replied.

Elliot raised his eyebrows. Then he swallowed and took a deep breath. "My daughter, Elizabeth – my only dear child – was murdered by my ne'er-do-well son-in-law, Alexander Carroun. He apparently left so careless a trail that even the police could have followed it – if that idiotic inspector hadn't been assigned to the case and tried to claim that it was one of the servants that did it. However, I knew from the first time that I spoke with him that he was going in the wrong direction, and I hired you to oversee the matter. I don't need to repeat your steps in tracking him." He glanced my way. "I'm sure that the doctor has already written it up for publication," he snapped with acid in his tone.

103

I started to speak, but realized that anything said in my defense would sound thin. In any case, this wasn't the time. I also knew that Holmes would most likely reference these events at some point in the future when discussing my writings, and I didn't want to provide him with additional ammunition.

"In any event," said Elliot, "you *did* find him, although you betrayed my interests by concealing additional evidence that will help assure his execution. Beyond that, I don't need further explanation."

"I, however, would like to know more," said Chartridge. "I only became involved after the man had been caught and brought back to London."

Holmes nodded. "Carroun had been missing for several days before the murder," he said, "and it was later verified that he'd spent that time in an opium den near The Tower – not an unusual occurrence. He came to himself and made his way home, as was his usual way, whereupon he began to argue with his wife – your daughter, Mr. Elliot. The conflict escalated, and he strangled her. The marks upon her throat matched his hands, and his signet ring, which had become twisted during the crime, had turned palm-inward. Its distinctive pattern was graven into the flesh of your daughter's throat. The truth would have come out, in spite of Inspector Jones's misstep, and without my involvement. The police surgeon would have quickly seen the marks on her neck."

Holmes had recited these facts tonelessly and without mercy, and Elliot became progressively pale as he listened, although what he was hearing nothing new.

"Carroun fled, and as you know, Watson and I were able to make use of several individuals who serve as eyes and ears around the capital, enabling the police to surround his hotel Canterbury. Later, he confessed that, upon his arrival at home and during the subsequent argument with his wife, he had entered and departed unnoticed by the servants, which perhaps explained why he wasn't initially identified as the killer when the body was discovered. The police were called. Inspector Jones jumped to the unfortunate conclusion that the murder had been committed by the groomsman, Kevin Silsoe. This assumption was based solely on the knowledge that Silsoe had lied about his past, failing to admit a conviction in his youth for robbery. It didn't help his case that he seemed to have become rather protective of your daughter, to the point of it being gossiped about below-stairs."

Elliot nodded. "From what I understand, Silsoe had heard one of the earlier fights between Elizabeth and my . . . my son-in-law, and had lurked nearby to step in and protect her if needed, fearing that violence might ensue. I owe him a great debt . . . ."

"More than you know," I thought to myself as Elliot's voice drifted off. Holmes continued. "After you summoned Watson and me to the scene, I was able to piece together Mr. Carroun's presence in the room and discover the elementary evidence indicating the placement of his hands around your daughter's throat. As I mentioned, Watson and I quickly traced him to Canterbury, where he had most ineffectively gone to ground. We were on a following train, and were able to speak with him at some length in his hotel room. Following our discussion, he left with us, surrendered himself to the police, and was arrested. He then made his confession and is now awaiting sentencing."

"There is some talk," said Elliot, "that he will simply spend the rest of his life in prison, with the possibility of parole, instead of receiving what he deserves. Chartridge was around the corner the other day and overheard the two of you mention something about a letter that had been given to you by Alexander when you found him in Canterbury."

Chartridge had the decency to look ashamed. "I felt that it was my duty to continue to listen, gentlemen, even as I realized that I was eavesdropping. When you paused around the corner from me that day in the Old Bailey, I heard you mention a paper that Alexander Carroun had given to you when you met with him, and that it must not be revealed. I became . . . suspicious. I conveyed my thoughts to Mr. Elliot, and he became convinced that it might somehow provide an excuse for leniency at Carroun's sentencing. I don't entirely agree with him – after all, you are hiding it, and seem to wish to continue to do so, and if it would somehow mitigate Carroun's punishment, you are already preventing that from happening by concealing the existence of the paper. But . . . well, Mr. Elliot *is* my employer." He glanced at the older man, who kept his stony gaze upon my friend. "He fears that if the paper is allowed to continue to exist in any form, it still might come to light at a future time. He tasked me – "

"I told him," interrupted Elliot, "to come up with a scheme to find the paper, and bring it here so that I could destroy it. And here we are."

He glanced toward Chartridge, who continued. "I was able to learn fairly quickly about the habits of your household, Mr. Holmes, and the fact that you seem to keep materials like that close at hand. A ruse was required. I made use of my luckless step-siblings, one of which had been in your rooms once before, and – as Mr. Elliot has pointed out – here we are.

Holmes frowned but nodded. "This is a valuable lesson, and Watson and I will have to take more care in the future to prevent such indiscretions . . . and intrusions. In the meantime, I would urge you, Mr. Elliot, not to press forward on the nature of the paper. Would you instead accept my

105

solemn word that such a document does not serve to lessen your son-in-law's guilt in any way, and that it will never be made public, based upon a prior agreement that I have pledged? That, in fact, I have promised to destroy it myself, upon your son-in-law's death."

Elliot shook his head. "No, Mr. Holmes, I won't be satisfied with that. I must read it and destroy it myself." He shifted in the seat and raised the sheaf of papers that had never left his hand. "Watch them, Chartridge," he said.

The lawyer looked toward us uncomfortably, and with some embarrassment. Holmes nodded, and an understanding seemed to pass between them that we wouldn't prevent Elliot from making his examination. "It's the oversized cream-colored sheet – your daughter's personal stationary. I can see it there in your hand.

Elliot didn't seem to listen, as he proceeded to turn the sheets one by one, giving a brief glance at each. He didn't find what he sought after five or ten sheets, and so he set those pages aside, before continuing his journey through the clutch of papers in his hand. It was only a moment later that he reached the sheet described by Holmes, either unheard or ignored. Seeing his daughter's monogram, he gave a slight cry and teased out that single sheet from the stack, casting the others leaf-like to the floor.

It was just a page among many. The gaslight from over the mantel revealed where it had originally been folded thrice, to be placed in an envelope. Holmes had noticed that crumpled and torn envelope on the floor near the murdered woman's body, and had theorized that there was some document related to the case, most likely carried away by the murderer. In his cheap hotel room on a shabby Canterbury street between the Cathedral and the Great Stour, Carroun had reluctantly admitted this to be true while pulling the letter from his pocket.

It was a holographic document, unquestionably written by Elizabeth Carroun *née* Elliot, and dated from the morning of her murder, outlining to her husband why she'd grown to despise him, and listing in great and graphic detail every unfaithful and vengeful infidelity that she had committed against him over the years as her initial love turned to hatred. She spelled out names and dates of her illicit affairs, her handwriting sharp and jagged as she wrote with incredible anger, as if she were stabbing her husband with every word.

Possibly her most damaging thrust had been to inform Carroun that the young son whom he had believed to be his own had in fact been fathered by another – Kevin Silsoe, the young groom who had befriended her in the preceding months when her husband had drifted away into a life of drunkenness and debauchery.

Carroun hadn't denied that he killed his wife. He had shown us the letter – which Holmes had deduced had a better-than-even chance of already having been destroyed – to demonstrate what had driven him to a killing rage. He didn't use it as an excuse, but rather only as an explanation.

The man was broken when we found him, and had subsequently offered no defense, having sworn us to secrecy, as he did not want any further stain on the young boy whom he still considered to be his son, in spite of his wife's declarations. The one rock that he seemed to cling to was that she was lying to hurt him, and that the boy was really his. However, Holmes and I had met Kevin Silsoe when we first visited the house, and having seen both him and the child and their strong resemblance, coupled with Elizabeth Carroun's vicious letter, there was really no doubt. However, we chose to let Carroun hold onto his illusion, for what else did he have in the little time that remained for him?

Holmes and I had agreed to keep the secret, for the sake of the child. However, Holmes – who had a horror of destroying documents – had resisted my advice to burn it immediately. We had unfortunately, and carelessly, discussed the matter without making sure that we weren't overheard, thus inadvertently negating our joint conclusion that the child's grandfather, Randolph Elliot, should be prevented from learning the truth about the child's heritage. However, he had maneuvered around us, and now the truth was in his hands. We watched as he read the letter, his eyes moving from top to bottom and back again, until such time as his tears made reading impossible. Still, he continued to stare at the sheet until Chartridge leaned over and took it from him. Then he read it for himself.

At this point, Holmes rose, stepped forward, and gently took the rest of the papers from the man's hand, as well as gathering those still in the case and what had fluttered to the floor. Then, with a nod to Chartridge, we made our way downstairs.

The air in the street felt cool and clean, and I breathed deeply, as if to expel the grief we had just witnessed. I tried to formulate thoughts into words, but before I could do so, we heard footsteps coming rapidly down the stairs, and in seconds Chartridge burst onto the pavement. He seemed most surprised to find us so close.

"I thought that you would already be away," he explained. "I . . . I wanted to thank you. For your discretion. You must understand – " continued Chartridge. "Mr. Elliot is a hard man. He has many secrets."

"Such as the use of this dwelling?" Holmes asked, nodding toward the building behind us.

Chartridge nodded. "Yes. He maintains it for his . . . private business." He cleared his throat. "It's his nature to react toward a problem in this manner. Losing his daughter . . . that has been the hardest thing he's ever faced."

"And will he lose his grandchild as well?" I asked. "Will he abandon the boy because his father is of the wrong class?"

"No," said Chartridge firmly. "I will make sure of it. Sometimes Mr. Elliot reacts too quickly, but I won't allow him to make that mistake – to do something that can't be undone. He will have his grandson, and the boy will have his family. His birthright. I've been with Mr. Elliot for a long time. I owe him a great deal, and I'll make certain that he has this – that he doesn't ruin it."

"That's all that any of us can hope for," replied Holmes. An awkward silence fell then, and after a moment, Chartridge nodded and slipped back inside, pulling the door shut behind him.

After a moment or two of simply standing there, I became aware that Holmes was shaking his head. "We must be more careful, Watson. Both of us."

"Yes. It was indiscrete to discuss the matter in public, even if we did believe that no one was nearby."

"Not just that. Your publication of the Ryder affair, and the naming of Mrs. Oakshott, was irresponsible."

I felt my hackles rise defensively, but seeing that it was so, Holmes raised a placating hand. "It is not only you, my friend. I trusted in the sanctity of our rooms for the filing away of Elizabeth Carroun's last letter. You would think that I would have learned my lesson long ago, after Professor Moriarty's clever intrusions."

"There was no need to think – "

"There was every need to think so!" he snapped, but then the scowl drifted away from his face. "That can be discussed later. For now, we need to find Ryder before he jumps on a whaler and is lost to a normal life forever."

He put his fingers to his lips and gave a shrill whistle, as if signaling a dog to turn the sheep. Within a moment, young Peake, one of the more regular Irregulars, appeared from Bloomsbury Court. Motioning us to follow, he led us through into Silver Street and then the King's Yard Arms, where we passed into the mews behind Elliot's building. There we found Ryder, lying upon a mound of sacks. "He fell from there," said Peake, pointing to a first-floor window. "He tried to shin down the drain pipe but lost his grip. I think he broke his leg. We didn't have instructions, so we waited and made him as comfortable as possible. Wiggins went and found some whisky."

I leaned down and saw that Ryder's ankle was turned at an odd angle. I stabilized it while Holmes summoned assistance, and within an hour or so poor James Ryder had been treated at Barts. Holmes spoke to him calmly at his bedside, in low tones so as not to attract the attention of the other men on the ward, letting him know that what he had just been forced to do was resolved, and that he should return to Margate and stay on the straight and narrow. The little man wept and was still thanking us both as we walked out of the room. As we made our way home, we decided that it was up to Ryder whether to let Mrs. Oakshott know that the affair was at an end.

After what came to be known between us as "The Carroun Document", Holmes instituted a series of improvements in the way that he stored and protected his papers and evidence, along with making some substantial changes to prevent unwanted intrusions into our Baker Street rooms. And I have become more discrete in how I identify individuals within my notes, be they tobacco millionaires or geese-raising sisters – should that ever again be necessary. Carroun was not the name of the doomed husband and wife, and a search for Elliot or Chartridge or Silsoe, or attempts to find James Ryder in Margate, will only bring disappointment. But I can state that Elliot – whomever he really was – raised the child of his daughter and the groomsman as well as he could, and the lad grew to be a fine young man indeed. Just last week I was in attendance at the ceremony where he posthumously received the George Cross for his exemplary efforts and bravery during an incident at the front, when, due to his efforts, not a single life was lost – except, tragically, for his own.

The Threadneedle Street
Murder
by S. Subramanian

As I turn over the pages I see my notes upon the repulsive story
of the red leech and the terrible death of Crosby the banker.
– "The Golden Pince-Nez", The Return of Sherlock Holmes

The year 1894 must mark a water-shed in the career of Mr. Sherlock
Holmes, for this was the year that saw his dramatic return to the city of
London after three years of wandering the globe in refuge from the
murderous associates of his late, vanquished adversary Professor
Moriarty. These individuals were as determined to avenge their leader's
death at the hands of Sherlock Holmes as the latter was to complete the
task he had set in motion in 1891 – namely, the destruction of that entire
web of organised crime and violence, at the centre of which had been the
malignant controlling brain that Holmes had forever laid to rest in the
dreadful abyss of the Reichenbach Falls. That it was the superior will and
acumen of Europe's foremost consulting detective which prevailed in the
ensuing deadly contest is by now well known. Beginning with the arrest
of Colonel Sebastian Moran in the spring of 1894, the official force, under
the direction of Sherlock Holmes, made quick work of mopping up the
surviving remnants of Moriarty's empire and his most trusted lieutenants.

But quite apart from the triumphant return of Sherlock Holmes, the
year 1894 was also distinguished for the succession of quite extraordinary
forensic cases in which he was involved, not the least of which is
constituted by the violent death in a sealed room of Alistair Crosby, one
of London's most prosperous bankers. This mysterious affair, the details
of which I am at last at liberty to reveal years after the event, is as notable
for Holmes's unique insight into the solution of the case as for his refusal
to divulge his deductions to anyone, including the metropolitan police –
save only his oldest and most trusted confidant who now feels called upon
to share this knowledge with his large world of loyal readers.

The case was first brought to our notice in early November of 1894,
just a few weeks before the events I have chronicled elsewhere under the
heading of "The Golden Pince-Nez". It was one of the coldest and
stormiest of Novembers that I have known, and the third day of that month
was one on which the most sensible thing to do for anyone who did not
have some utterly compelling reason to believe otherwise was to remain

indoors in front of a large fire and warm one's hands in front of it. Without was a stormy blizzard of snow and sleet, while within was a warm fire in the grate, in the direction of which Holmes and I stretched out our legs gratefully while seated upon our respective armchairs, he busy with the papers of some old cases and I trying my best to interest myself in a *Lancet* article on the latest developments in the field of anaesthesiology.

Every now and then as he read his notes, Holmes's body would be racked with internal mirth, which would break out in an occasional chuckle. My curiosity, naturally, was properly aroused.

"Come, Holmes," said I. "You must not deny me a proper share of your enjoyment! What is it that is so amusing in that case from your past?"

"This was before the time of my Boswell . . . Tell me, Watson, would it bore you terribly to have an account of one of the most bizarre and macabre cases with which I have ever dealt – one which, nevertheless, had its moments of humour, however dark and sinister?"

"Bore me? Why, Holmes, nothing should please me better! Here – while you tell your story, permit me to arrange for some welcome fortification to our inner beings with the peerless luxury of a whisky-and-soda."

While I busied myself with the decanter and gasogene and a couple of glasses, Holmes drew his dressing gown tighter about himself and settled in more comfortably into his arm-chair. "Here then," said he, "is the singular case of Ebenezer Holloway, which was brought to my attention by the famous Harley Street alienist Dr. Moore Agar, whose introduction into my life is itself one of the more dramatic events of my career. What was brought to him as a problem for a nerve specialist he swiftly diagnosed as belonging more intimately to the province of the criminologist. Indeed, whether the matter lay in his or my domain of expertise itself proved to be a pretty problem."

"Why, what do you mean, Holmes?"

"Well, what would you say, Watson, if a woman complained that her husband insisted, every night, on smearing her face with a mixture of egg yolk and scented pomade, while pulling out three hairs from her head to the accompaniment of a spirited rendering, by himself, of '*God Save the Queen*'?

"I would say it is eccentric, at the very least – even disturbing. But criminal – ?"

"Ah, Watson! Yes, I am afraid so. You will be able to judge for yourself when once you have heard the details – "

That story, I am afraid, must remain forever untold, for just then there was a clang of the bell and the sound of steps upon the stairs, terminating with Mrs. Hudson opening the door and ushering Inspector Lestrade of Scotland Yard into our chamber.

"Thank you, Mrs. Hudson," cried Holmes. "Lestrade, your hat and coat! Watson, a glass of your stimulant should do our visitor a world of good on this wintry day! Come, Lestrade, pull up your chair toward the fire, and let us know what urgent mission – it could hardly be otherwise considering the inclemency of the weather – it is that brings you to our humble abode."

"Thank you, Dr. Watson," said Lestrade. "The whisky is a welcome relief, even if I am on duty. As for what fetches me here," he added sombrely, "murder is the word, Mr. Holmes."

"Ah!" said Holmes, rubbing the palms of his hands together. "Let us have the details."

"It strikes me as being pretty straightforward, but I thought I should nevertheless submit it to you for an opinion, having learnt from previous experience in your association that what appears to be a relatively open-and-shut case can actually have rather unexpected angles to it. Well, I will leave it to you to let me know what you make of it. Two hours ago I received this telegram, dispatched from the Moorgate Post Office near Threadneedle Street at three o'clock in the afternoon. As you can see, the message is cryptic and unsigned."

Here is the text of the telegraphic message which Lestrade shared with us:

> *Suspect foul play in Alistair Crosby's chamber 14 Threadneedle Street having just witnessed suspicious exit of theatrical managers Earnshaw and Thompson from building.*

"We receive many hoax messages at the Yard, Mr. Holmes," resumed Lestrade, "but we avoid taking chances. The local police station at Threadneedle Street was therefore immediately alerted, and a couple of constables were sent to inspect the large building in Threadneedle Street in which Alistair Crosby, the owner of the Crosby Mercantile Banking Enterprise, had a room. Here, we understand, he sometimes entertained his customers and business associates when it was not convenient for him to do so at the main bank premises located further down the Street. The local constabulary registered that Mr. Crosby had entered his office earlier in the morning but hadn't been seen leaving the building thereafter. Receiving no reply to their knocks upon his office door, they informed us at the Yard about the position of affairs. I immediately set out for Threadneedle Street with a contingent of my men, including the police

112

surgeon, after leaving behind instructions to track down the theatrical agents Earnshaw and Thompson."

"Are they not," I interposed, "the owners of the large and famous dramatic agency Earnshaw and Thompson?"

"Large, yes, Dr. Watson," said Lestrade, "and also, now, floundering. I shall come to their business fortunes in a moment, in the proper sequence. To resume my account. We found that 14 Threadneedle Street is a large, double-storied building which leases out office rooms to various professionals such as solicitors, stock-brokers, bankers, travel agents, and sundry financial intermediaries. The lobby of the building is presided over by a sleepy-eyed porter who maintains a visitors' log book in which people entering the building are required to sign their names with information on the time of their entry and whom they are visiting. There is a fairly constant stream of visitors and tenants in and out of the building, and the porter pays no particular attention to the traffic, except to make sure that all visitors sign the visitors' book.

"Alistair Crosby's office is on the first floor of the building. On our way in, we noted from the visitors' register that Earnshaw and Thompson had signed in at 2:25 p.m. to meet Crosby. We arrived at Crosby's office and, evoking no response to our calls upon the bell and knocks upon the door, we had no option but to break in. The office was a large room, dark, dingy, and poorly lighted by the illumination from a single low-wattage electric lamp suspended from the ceiling. On the wall across from the door were two windows, which we subsequently confirmed were barred, shuttered, and bolted from inside.

"On the side of the room facing the door was Crosby's desk, with the windows behind. In front of the desk, and for the benefit of his visitors, was a long sofa swathed in an ugly cloth-cover spilling over to the floor on all sides of it. These are items of information which I present to you for your consideration, Mr. Holmes, and which I recorded later, knowing as I do your passion for and insistence upon detail. They were certainly not the first things in the room that obtruded themselves upon the spectator's consciousness. Oh, no, sir, for what claimed the viewer's entire attention was the ghastly sight of Mr. Crosby sprawled on his chair at the desk. Closer examination revealed a mottled face, with the lips contorted in an evil, grinning rictus of fear and pain at the moment of death. The man had clearly been strangled by the pressure of another's fingers upon his neck, to the point where the Adam's apple had been broken. It is hard to survive a fractured larynx, gentlemen, and Alistair Crosby did not. Whitby, the police surgeon, estimated that the victim had expired not much before our arrival on the scene. Taking account of body temperature, lividity, and the absence of *rigor mortis*, he put the time of death at about an hour before.

113

In his estimation, it was very unlikely that death could have occurred after forty minutes past two in the afternoon.

"Entirely consistent with this surmise was a finding that must be regarded as crucial to the case. I refer to the discovery of Crosby's watch-chain upon the floor a little way away from his desk. It must have fallen from his pocket at the time of the assault upon him. Indeed, the watch seems to have smashed upon impact with the floor, and to have stopped at 2:36 p.m..

"Meanwhile, I received word that Messrs Earnshaw and Thompson had been picked up from their theatrical office in Leicester Square where they had apparently just returned, by their own admission, in a cab from Threadneedle Street. After a thorough inspection of Crosby's office room, I returned to the Yard where Earnshaw and Thompson had been brought in for questioning – "

"Before we come to that, Lestrade, a couple of matters of detail, if you will allow me. First, are there any other means of entry into or egress from the room apart from the door and the two windows?"

"No, Mr. Holmes. The door, which is equipped with a spring-latch and is self-locking, was, as I have said, locked, and the windows, as I have also said, were shuttered and barred and bolted."

"Nevertheless, was there any means by which a man might have climbed on to a perch near the windows – by way, for instance, of a drain-pipe giving on to a sun-shade beneath the windows?"

"No, none. From the windows to the pavement below is a sheer drop of around thirty feet."

"Was there anything in the nature of a cupboard or a cabin in the room?"

"No, The room was bare of furniture, save for the desk, chair, and sofa, as I have mentioned."

"Can you give me a physical description of Crosby?"

Lestrade allowed himself a smile, as he said, "The man wouldn't have won a beauty competition, Mr. Holmes – not even one in which you and I participated – "

"A touch, Lestrade, an indubitable touch! I note that you find that extraordinarily amusing, Watson! I must learn to be wary of both of you, for there is no telling from where you may pounce! I take it then that the late Alistair Crosby didn't have a particularly prepossessing appearance, but could you give me a more objective account?"

"Mr. Holmes, the man was very corpulent. He had a florid face, his teeth were in rather bad shape and colour, he had a mane of flowing, unkempt graying hair, and a completely unregulated and startlingly black

114

walrus moustache. To boot, I have been told that he had an unfortunate speech impediment, in the form of a pronounced lisp."

"I see your point about beauty competitions. Finally, I presume you will have examined the body. Is there any particular finding that you feel bears remarking upon?"

"Well, the man was not a particularly keen dresser, but it did strike me as odd to find, when we moved his body, that the back of his jacket was rather excessively dusty, with even a small segment of cob-web attached to it."

"Indeed?" murmured Holmes. "That is certainly suggestive. Very well, Lestrade, pray proceed with your account of your meeting with the theatrical agents. The firm of Earnshaw and Thompson, did you say? As a keen student of the less savoury aspects of our society's functioning, I find that one of the most effective ways of keeping one's finger upon the pulse of criminal life in the City is to be thoroughly *au courant* with the agony columns of the newspapers, and sundry scandal sheets. I seem to recall that, not very long ago, one of the young actresses in the repertory of Earnshaw and Thompson was involved in some unfortunate affair of the heart."

"That is quite correct, Holmes," said I. "You refer, I think, to the unhappy suicide of the beautiful actress Molly Paxton, who had been lured away from her own *fiancé* in the repertory by what turned out to be the false promises of some lecherous old money-bags occupying an important position in the commercial life of the City."

"Ah!" said Holmes. "Trust Watson to be well-informed in these matters. Pretty young things are, after all, his especial province!"

"That is unworthy of you, Holmes – " I began bitterly, when he interrupted me.

"Oh come now, Watson. One good turn deserves another, so you must not resent me my little retaliation in response to your uproarious endorsement of Lestrade's crack, at my expense, regarding beauty competitions. But come – let us move away from these distractions, and allow Lestrade to continue with his narrative."

"Before proceeding with an account of my interview with Messrs Earnshaw and Thompson at Scotland Yard, let me just confirm your recollections, Mr. Holmes and Dr. Watson, of the tragedy of the Paxton girl's suicide not long ago. As it happens, the 'lecherous old money-bags' alluded to by Dr. Watson was none other than our recently deceased banker, Crosby. It is widely believed that Earnshaw and Thompson themselves played a disreputable part in the affair, by leaning on the girl to propitiate the advances of the banker. It is a sad and wicked world we live in, gentlemen, and it was therefore in no sunny spirit of

115

accommodation that I addressed my interrogation of the two men I knew to have had a role in the poor girl's death, and who were now my prime suspects in a case of murder.

"To put matters as compactly as I know how: Earnshaw and Thompson had, by their own admission, gone to meet Crosby at his chamber this afternoon. The visitors' register at the Threadneedle Street building confirms this. The two men had signed in just before half-past-two to meet the banker. The object of the meeting was apparently to try and re-negotiate the terms of a loan they had borrowed to finance their latest theatrical venture, the farce *Billy Boy*, which however failed to find any favour with the theatre-going public. The show, in short, was a huge flop, and the firm of Earnshaw and Thompson found itself in a financial mess and unable to service its debt to the Crosby Mercantile Banking Enterprise.

"The two men expressed complete shock and disbelief when told about the murder of Crosby. They said they were unsuccessful in their effort to secure any accommodation from the banker, and it is my impression, though they tried to conceal the fact from me, that Crosby was both very short and very rude with them. From what they told me, the meeting with Crosby lasted no more than ten minutes, and they were back on their way to Leicester Square by a little after forty-minutes-past-two. This tallies with the time it would have taken them to reach their destination by cab when they did. Both men vouch for each other and vehemently deny any suggestion that they may have visited violence upon the person of Crosby.

"I cannot dismiss the contents of the anonymous telegram that was dispatched at three p.m. from the Moorgate Post Office, nor any of the evidence relating to probable time of death and the time of the theatrical agents' visit. I have retained Earnshaw and Thompson for further questioning, but I don't know for how much longer I can do that without concrete, as opposed to purely circumstantial, evidence to implicate them in the matter – even if the circumstantial evidence points to them as the chief suspects in the case. Before proceeding further, I thought I ought to consult you on my further course of action. What would you advise, Mr. Holmes?"

"Well, it is clear that you must produce the two men as quickly as you can before a magistrate, and seek their custody – or at least, if that is not granted, some reasonable restrictions on their mobility and a guarantee of their availability, at short notice, for further questioning."

"Will you not visit the scene of the crime, Mr. Holmes?"

"Unfortunately, I am detained at the present time in the matter of the Linlithgow succession case. However, before I let you go, permit me to satisfy myself on one point. Could you tell me who else, among the tenants of the building, have attended their offices today?"

"Today being a Saturday, Mr. Holmes, the building was sparsely populated at the time of which we speak. Only four of the chambers, apart from Crosby's, were occupied. These were the offices of the solicitors Seppings, Maybury, and Dodgson, the travel agencies London Tours, and William Butler and Sons, and the stock-broking firm of Peabody and Company. The stock-broker's client is an elderly gentleman, and the log book suggests that broker and client concluded their business and left together by a quarter-to-three. The two travel agencies' clients were both young ladies, one an American and the other a Swiss tourist – who also, judging from the sign-outs in the log book, concluded their business with their respective agents and left, along with them, by a quarter-to-three. Mr. Dodgson, the solicitor, seems to have entertained his client, a Mr. Gilbert Irving, between a quarter-to-two and a quarter-past-two, and himself to have left the premises by half-past-two. The log book confirms this, and also that Irving left the building at 2:20 p.m.. The porter's recollection, too, is that of a number of the building's tenants and visitors leaving roughly at the same time shortly after the exit of Messrs Earnshaw and Thompson. This is all that I am able to tell you at the present time."

"That was an admirably lucid account. For reasons I have mentioned, I am unable now to give this case my undivided attention, but I shall certainly mull over the problem, and follow up on it to the best of my ability. Should anything of significance occur to me, I'll get in touch with you. Thank you, Lestrade."

There was a long silence after Lestrade's exit, as Sherlock Holmes sat back in his armchair, eyes closed, and puffing at his pipe. Eventually, he stirred, and in response to my look of enquiry, he said, "Watson, if Lestrade does his job properly, he will investigate the antecedents of Mr. Gilbert Irving – and if I know anything of what is going on, he will discover that there is no Mr. Gilbert Irving – or if there should indeed turn out to be such a person, that he has no connection with Mr. Dodgson of Maybury, Seppings, and Dodgson, Solicitors. But I shall hold my peace until we have further developments. In so doing, I may well be abetting a felony, but there are occasions when one must consult not so much the provisions of the law as the command of one's conscience. Meanwhile, I shall apply to my old friend Shinwell 'Porky' Johnson for further information on some matters of interest in the case. No, not another word, now, Watson. My ideas are as yet tentative and ill-formed, and I need also to attend to the pending Linlithgow affair. Pray bear your legitimate quest for resolution patiently, and rest assured that I shall speak to you again on

117

this matter at the right juncture, even if that should take some time from now."

And there I had to leave the affair until further notice.

In the days that followed, Holmes brought his investigation into the Linlithgow case to a successful conclusion, as readers will remember who have any recollection of the arrest of the notorious forger and swindler Barrington. As for the Threadneedle Street murder, the Metropolitan Force charged Earnshaw and Thompson with colluding to murder Alistair Crosby. Holmes himself pleaded other commitments to avoid any further explicit involvement in the case. In due course, the case was brought to trial in the Crown Court. After a sequence of sittings at the Old Bailey, the presiding Judge passed a verdict of "Murder by person or persons unknown". Earnshaw and Thompson were relieved of the suspicion against them, the Judge holding that while the factors of motive and opportunity threw strong suspicion on the accused, the evidence against them was almost entirely circumstantial, and not material enough for conviction based on grounds that completely precluded reasonable doubt.

At this stage of the proceedings, Sherlock Holmes finally broke his silence on the subject – but only in private conversation with me.

"The Court did right, Watson," said he, "in acquitting Earnshaw and Thompson. Blackguards though they are, they are nevertheless guiltless of the murder of Crosby, which is the crime with which they were charged."

"But if not they," I said, "who then? And how?"

"Precisely," said Holmes. "Here, for what it is worth, is my reconstruction and resolution of the case. Mind you, I have no shred of evidence in support of my speculations. What I have to offer must remain a classic example of the method of armchair reasoning, but I daresay it possesses the virtue of pointing in the direction of the balance of probability, taking due note of motive, opportunity, means, the known facts of the case, and some others that have come to light in the course of further enquiry.

"I put it to you that the stage plays an important part in this mystery. Earnshaw and Thompson were theatrical agents – they seem to have had a disreputable role to play in the betrayal of one of the young actresses in their repertory, Molly Paxton, to the desires of Crosby the banker, who comes across in every way as a signally repugnant satyr. Remember also that Miss Paxton was affianced to a fellow-actor. Upon consultation with Shinwell Johnson, whose command over information regarding the City of London and its inhabitants is unrivalled, I learnt that the *fiancé*'s name is Harold Brewster, that he had been passionately devoted to Molly Paxton, and that he nearly went mad with grief over her tragic death by suicide. Who, more than him, would have a motive for the downfall of three men whom he justifiably regarded as villains of the deepest dye – Crosby, Earnshaw, and Thompson? What if he were to murder the first and frame the other two in the perpetration of the deed?

"It is significant that we have a sign of the stage in the very name 'Gilbert Irving' – the librettist W. S. Gilbert and the actor Henry Irving are two of the grandest names associated with the theatre in England today. You may recall my saying that if Lestrade were to investigate Gilbert Irving, he might discover that such a person does not exist! What if Earnshaw and Thompson were indeed innocent of the murder of Crosby? How might they nevertheless have been implicated in the murder if Harold Brewster were involved in it? This is the problem I set for myself, initially as a wholly academic alternative to the thesis of Earnshaw and Thompson's guilt, and subsequently as a possibility that converged more and more on the realm of probability. Consider then the following construction.

"Brewster is consumed with the desire for revenge upon Crosby, Earnshaw, and Thompson. Being himself a member of the troupe owned and managed by the latter two, he learns that they have defaulted on the loan borrowed from Crosby, and of their appointment to meet with him on that fateful afternoon at half-past-two. As an accomplished actor, it is a minor effort for him to disguise himself subtly so that he cannot be identified as Harold Brewster. Assuming the name Gilbert Irving, he arranges to meet the solicitor Dodgson at a quarter-to-two, and arrives, at the appointed hour, at the Threadneedle Street building where Dodgson has his chamber. For half-an-hour, from a quarter-to-two to a quarter-past, Brewster – that is, *Irving* – is in consultation with Dodgson – oh, on some manufactured problem – the drafting of a bogus will, shall we say, or any equally bogus rental agreement, or any one of a dozen other possible subterfuges.

"At a quarter-past-two, Brewster walks down the corridor from Dodgson's room to Crosby's, with whom he has arranged a meeting at twenty-past-two. I would not know in what connection, but would hazard the guess that it had to do with the arrangement of some vulgar assignation on Crosby's behalf, given the man's lascivious appetites. Brewster knocks on and is admitted to Crosby's room at twenty-past-two. He has a lot of work to do in the next ten minutes, which he accomplishes successfully by virtue of being both an immensely strong young man and one driven by the compulsions of rage as much as adrenaline.

"First he strangles Crosby and crushes his larynx. He then hauls the body out of the chair and dumps it behind the sofa where it is hidden from view by the over-flowing cloth-cover on it. No doubt Brewster has acquired an idea of the lie of the land from an earlier visit to Crosby's

119

room for some similar purpose aimed at propitiating the man's baser instincts. I have since examined the room myself, and the space behind the sofa would accommodate even such a grotesque man as Crosby.

"Let us say all of this takes him seven minutes. He then opens the brief-case which he has fetched with him, removes his outer garments and clothes himself in the standard black suit which is Crosby's trademark dress and which Brewster has packed in his brief-case, uses his own outer garments to pad out his stomach and chest, and proceeds to alter his appearance, with the help of a wig, a false moustache, and false dentures so as to resemble Crosby. This is no very difficult job for an accomplished actor to perform in quick time – and not least given that Crosby, from what we have heard, was a caricature of a man. Once he has affected the latter's lisp, the transformation of Brewster into Crosby is complete and perfect. The dim light of the room makes things even easier. At half-past-two, he is ready and waiting for Earnshaw and Thompson.

"We may imagine that for ten minutes thereafter, Brewster, in the persona of Crosby, gets the two men, who are sitting on the sofa behind which Crosby's corpse is resting, to supplicate themselves before him for an easing in the original terms of the loan. It is no doubt with considerable pleasure that 'Crosby' abuses and insults his debtors and throws them out of the room by thirty-eight minutes after two. Once the two men are out, it is a matter of a very short time for him to remove his wig and moustache and dentures, to divest himself of the black suit and stuff it into his brief-case, and to resume the persona of Mr. Gilbert Irving.

"He then hauls Crosby's body from behind the sofa back onto his chair, adjusts the time on Crosby's watch to 2:36, smashes the watch, and leaves the watch-chain lying on the floor. The dust on the back of Crosby's jacket should be explained by the dust which no doubt accumulated on the floor behind the unswept sofa. All this should take him just three minutes or so, so that, by a quarter-to-three, he has joined the stock-broker and his client, and the two travel agents and their respective clients out of the building. On the way out, he signs the visitors' log-book, and falsely enters the time of exit as 2:20. Here he is taking a chance, but hoping that the sleepy-eyed porter will not specifically pick him out from the general traffic exiting the building. All that is left for him to do, on his way back to his home, is to stop at the Moorgate Post Office and send that telegram off to Scotland Yard.

"Naturally, having accomplished what he had set himself to do, Harold Brewster could not afford to stay on in the country. I suspected that he would already have booked a passage on a steamer to Australia or South Africa or Canada. As it happens, I learnt where he lived from Shinwell Johnson and confronted him that same evening with my reconstruction of the crime. Brewster came completely clean. He did not appear to be particularly disconcerted by the possibility of being exposed by me. His primary emotion, it seemed to me, was one of a certain sense of fulfilment over the job done, a sense of having sought and found reparation for the loss of his loved one. He struck me as being true through and through. I told him his secret would be safe with me, provided Earnshaw and Thompson were not convicted of murder. If they were, I would have to go public on my version of the truth of the matter. Brewster agreed, and the last I saw of him was when I left him that evening. Later that night he boarded the *Toronto*, sailing from the Port of London to the Port of Halifax.

"I am glad that Earnshaw and Thompson have been let off by the court. It is right that they have not been convicted for a crime they did not commit, though perhaps it is also right, in terms of some notion of cosmic justice, that they have paid somewhat for their unforgiveable betrayal of that poor young actress and her steadfast lover. You know me, Watson. I am not one to be governed by the softer emotions. But neither am I unmoved by the power of true love. Yes, I have abetted a felony. But have I done wrong? What would *you* have done, Watson?"

"The same as you, my dear fellow," I replied warmly, "even it means, as it has meant for you, having to forego the accolades of an admiring public for yet another brilliantly accomplished forensic triumph."

"Thank you, thank you," said Holmes, turning away, and obviously moved in a manner that was alien to his usual cold and aloof nature. And then he observed. "Sometimes, Watson, the world and its complexities are too much. One yearns at such times for what is simple and true. Helen Lemmens-Sherrington sings this evening at the Royal Albert Hall – perhaps for the last time in public. Come. Let us take ourselves to the concert, and follow that up with a late supper at Simpson's."

The Collegiate Leprechaun
by Roger Riccard

Chapter I

It was the week after Christmas 1894. I was in Dublin, Ireland with my longtime friend, the consulting detective, Mr. Sherlock Holmes. We had just completed a case for the Baron of Swann[1] and were preparing to return to London.

It had been a life-changing excursion for me. This second Christmas after my dear Mary's passing made me believe I had nothing to celebrate. I was on a path to a bitter life. Holmes's encouragement and our attendance at a play performance of Dickens' novel, *A Christmas Carol*, had made me realize the folly of my ways. I vowed to be a better person to honor her memory.

On what was supposed to be our last evening in town, we were enjoying dinner in the hotel restaurant when we were approached by a middle-aged cleric. He was exceedingly thin of build, with a lean, clean-shaven face. He approached us in such a hesitant, bird-like manner, that I was reminded of the cranes that populated my favorite fishing spot as a lad.

His thick Irish brogue would be next to impossible to translate into print, so I shall endeavor to keep the vocabulary, if not the actual pronunciation.

"Excuse me, gentlemen, but would that be yourself, Mr. Sherlock Holmes, the London detective?"

Holmes gazed up and down at the man in that customary fashion of his, then rose and extended his hand, "I am, Father, and this is my esteemed colleague and friend, Dr. John Watson. Please, have a seat and tell us what brings a chemistry professor from Trinity College into our company on this chilly December evening?"

The man had settled down after shaking my hand across the table as Holmes completed his invitation.

"Your reputation is well-earned, sir," he smiled. "I am Professor of the Institutes of Medicine Chemistry Department at Trinity College. Though how you could have deduced that so quickly is beyond my ken."

Holmes waved off the question like a pestering insect, "Your watch fob indicates your affiliation and the stains on your fingers are well known to me from my own chemical experimentations."

While Holmes was making his statement of observations, I had made one of my own and offered, "May I order you something to drink, Father? A hot coffee or tea, perhaps, to dispel your chill?"

"Aye, a hot coffee would be most welcome. Thank you, Doctor. Though I fear even that could not completely alleviate the shaking you perceive, for 'tis not all brought on by the chill o' the night."

Holmes immediately responded to that, "You exhibit no other symptoms of disease, Father. Could it be a fear that fills your soul?"

"Not exactly, Mr. Holmes," he answered. "Let me start at the beginning, lest you think me a doddering old fool with a wild imagination. First of all, my name is Father O'Keefe and I have been at Trinity College, first as a student, then on the faculty, for twenty-nine years now.

"In all that time, I've seen many a prank and, of course, there's the superstition that any student who passes beneath the bell tower while the bells are tolling will fail their exams. But never has there been a hint of spirits or other supernatural creatures hanging about the campus."

I could see the frown form on my colleague's face as Holmes anticipated the direction this tale was taking. Apparently, Father O'Keefe noticed it as well.

"I know what you must be thinking, Mr. Holmes. I am sure there is an earthly explanation for what I'm about to tell you, which is why I'm coming to you instead of suggesting to the faculty that an exorcism is in order."

Holmes replied in a warning voice, "So long as it is understood that no one entertains the existence of ghosts, Father. I've clients enough in *this* world."

A wide smile split the lean face of the cleric, "Hardly ghosts, sir. In fact, 'tis not fear you perceive, but laughter at myself as I thought about voicing aloud my reason for consulting you. It seems absurd as I think on it, but something must be done. I believe your talents could prove most efficient in putting an end to the situation."

His smile was infectious and I chimed in, unable to contain my curiosity. "Whatever can it be that you find both humorous and disturbing, Father?"

"It appears, Doctor, Mr. Holmes, that we have been invaded by a Leprechaun."

"Really, Father . . . ." Holmes started to say, but O'Keefe held up his hand.

"Hear me out, Mr. Holmes. I don't believe in the Little People any more than you do. But I and several students have seen someone dressed in the typical garb associated with such creatures lurking about the campus at night. As you may know, the believed occupation of such persons is that

123

of a cobbler, and the odd mischief that this one is pulling is leaving pairs of women's shoes under the bell tower."

"Women's shoes?" I repeated.

"Aye, Doctor, and it's a mystery where they come from, for the college is not open to female students, nor are there any women on staff in any capacity."

"No cooks or housemaids?" I suggested.

"Nary a lass passes through our gates. All the work is done by the students or hired male help. Not even students' mothers or sisters are allowed to set foot on campus."

"Surely the solution is a simple one, Father," offered Holmes. "Merely post a guard to apprehend the culprit and expose him – or her – for the miscreant that they are."

O'Keefe shook his head and again I couldn't help thinking of the cranes who captured their meals in their beaks. "We have done exactly that, Mr. Holmes, just two nights ago. The men assigned to the task were subjected to a puff of smoke just as the creature appeared and were rendered unconscious for several minutes. When they awoke, a pair of emerald-green slippers lay directly in the center of the campanile and the being had disappeared."

"How often has this person appeared or left evidence of his coming?" asked the detective.

"It started three days after the holiday break began. There's been sightings or evidence at least once a week, sometimes as often as three times, but there's been no pattern, only that they've never shown up two days in a row. They haven't always left anything behind, but we've collected five pairs of shoes, so far. When I learned of your presence in Dublin, I thought it was a Godsend that you should be here in our hour of need."

"Hardly a Godsend," replied Holmes. "But I shall come take a look. What say you, Watson? Shall we go chasing rainbows?"

"A pleasant enough diversion." I agreed. We finished our coffee and accompanied the good Father by his carriage to the old college campus.

An apothecary named Thomas Smith, who was Lord Mayor of Dublin at the time, founded the University of Dublin in 1592. It was not until 1711, following the construction of the first Anatomy School Building, that the Trinity College Medical School was officially opened.

As we passed through the gates I noted, even by the gaslights, that both ancient and modern architecture competed for prominence among the campus buildings. After boarding the horse and retrieving lanterns to make our way across the dimly lit courtyard, we followed the chemistry professor to the central bell tower where these events had occurred. It was

124

founded on a tall archway of perhaps some thirty feet in height. Six round layers of stone stood on that, forming the base for several columns around arched windows with a handful of statuary saints guarding the points. A large dome ascended from there, and a smaller dome housing the bell topped that. The entire structure was overseen by a large cross reaching toward the heavens.

Holmes stopped us before we entered the archway. "Has anyone entered this area or cleaned it since the incident with the smoke?"

"No, Mr. Holmes," answered the cleric. "The students, what few have remained for the holidays, by tradition generally obey the superstition and avoid this area, and our groundskeeper only sweeps here when the wind has blown in an inordinate amount of dust, leaves, or snow."

"Then we are fortunate that there has been no recent snowfall," observed my companion. Motioning us to stay back, he knelt on one knee, slowly swung his lantern back and forth, and peered intently across the pavement. Spying what he sought, he walked carefully over to a specific spot and knelt down again. This time he bent over with his cheek almost touching the ground. Satisfied at what he found, he reached into his coat pocket and retrieved one of his ever-present envelopes he uses to collect evidence. With his penknife, he scraped up some substance off the pavement. When he was satisfied he had a sufficient quantity, he stuffed the envelope into his pocket and stood.

Addressing our client, he declared, "Our first order of business is to identify this powder. Let us repair to your laboratory, Professor, so that I may run some tests."

O'Keefe, seemingly pleased to be addressed by the academic title he had earned, eagerly led the way to the building which housed the science department. Showing Holmes where the supplies were kept, we then stood back and watched. Before retrieving any of the items he needed from the storage room, he carefully examined the door lock with his lens. Completing that task, he set about testing the powdery residue with various agents and noting the reaction to each.

As we waited off in a corner so as not to disturb my friend, Father O'Keefe and I engaged in conversation regarding some of the new medications and drugs being touted by the latest medical journals. We were particularly animated about a new drug that was all the rage, but was only good as a treatment for symptoms and not the root cause of the condition responsible. I lamented how drug companies seemed more concerned about the profits made off these types of medications rather than the research needed to find cures that would eliminate the need for such drugs in the first place.

Suddenly Holmes spoke up, "Gentlemen, we have our first clue."

We joined him at the lab table and noted the color of the vial before him. "First, Professor, let me assure you that this clever concoction did not come from your store of chemicals. You do not have all the substances required, and the storeroom lock appears not to have been molested. The unfortunate aspect of that discovery means that our suspect pool has increased to beyond the student body, whereas if it had been stolen from here, we could narrow the list considerably.

"Tell me: Of the people who have seen this culprit, did they notice anything unusual about the face? A prominent nose, perhaps, or an unusual pipe?"

"Now that you mention it," replied Father O'Keefe, "the face seemed to lack animation. It was almost as if it were frozen in place in a comical sort of grin, with a large curved pipe hanging from his mouth on the right side."

"Was there the glow of tobacco or any smoke coming from the pipe?"

"I don't recall, Mr. Holmes. His overall appearance was disturbing enough without looking at details."

"Yes, such is usually the case with the casual observer," sighed the detective. "Could you judge how tall he was?"

"He moved in an odd, bent over fashion. But I'd judge his overall height to be between three-and-one-half and four feet."

"Interesting. Could you demonstrate this unusual gait?"

The cleric shrugged, attempted to bend into the posture he was trying to remember, and walked across the room and back in a shuffling manner, which reminded me more of a monkey in a zoo than a human being – a thought I expressed aloud.

"Perhaps it was a trained monkey in a mask of some sort," I offered.

"An interesting thought, Doctor," replied my friend, off-handedly. Then he queried our client once again.

"Have there been any incidents involving women in connection with the college recently?"

Warily, O'Keefe asked, "What do you mean by 'incidents'?"

"Not a scandal, Professor. I was thinking more along the lines of protests against the college in general. Perhaps in its teachings about how doctors should treat women patients and their unique medical issues, or some such thing?"

Relieved, the cleric answered, "Nothing comes to mind, Mr. Holmes."

A thought occurred to me and I asked, "What *is* the college's stance on female doctors, Father?"

His eyes widened as if I'd accused the Pope of witchcraft. "Women as *doctors*, Dr. Watson? No, no, no. I mean, I'm sure Miss Nightingale's work has proven the advantages of female nurses, and their maternal instincts are certainly amenable to that sort of thing. Midwives, of course are a suitable work for their gender. But the intellect and calm, logical thinking required to be a doctor? No, I don't believe we'll ever see *that* day."

Holmes interjected, "So no woman has ever applied for admission to the college, even for a non-medical degree?"

O'Keefe shrugged his shoulders, "Once in a great while we'll receive such an application. One young lady even attempted to be admitted in disguise as a man with forged academic credentials. Of course, she broke down during the interview process and was revealed for her true identity."

Holmes cocked his head in interest, "Really? When did this occur?"

"Oh it was ages ago, Mr. Holmes. During my senior year as I recall."

"Nothing recent then?"

The Father shook his head in that crane-like fashion and declared, "None that I'm aware of, Mr. Holmes. But you could ask Chancellor Parsons, He'll be back tomorrow morning."

Holmes nodded as he strode over to the window and looked out upon the courtyard at the bell tower. As he stood there, his left arm draped across his waist supporting his right elbow which extended his hand to where his thumb curled under his chin and his forefinger extended over pursed lips. He held this pose for several moments. Then, without taking his eyes from the tower, he asked another question.

"I presume you have kept these shoes somewhere. I should like to examine them."

O'Keefe stammered in surprise, "The . . . the shoes, Mr. Holmes?"

My friend turned to him in a commanding pose, "Of course, the shoes, Professor. They could hold a vital clue. You *have* kept them, of course?"

Embarrassed, our client answered, "I know where they were, but I don't know if they're still here."

"Explain," ordered the detective.

"We did not consider any evidentiary value, Mr. Holmes. They were added to the goods we collect for the poor. They may still be here, but it's possible they've already been distributed."

Holmes shook his head and sighed in that way he usually reserved for the incompetent police who unwittingly destroy evidence.

Gathering his emotions, he forced himself to quietly ask, "Please take us to where they were. It may not yet be too late."

We crossed the campus to the chapel where an anteroom held some few boxes of clothing and other sundries for the poor. To our relief, one box held several pairs of shoes. We separated out the women's pairs which

O'Keefe identified as those left behind by the mysterious intruder and boxed them up separately to take back to the laboratory, where the lighting was more conducive to examination.

There were, indeed, five pairs of ladies footwear. They were all of the same size, but varied in style from the most fashionable to sturdy boots for outdoor work. The recent emerald slippers were the most ostentatious and achieved a luster from a great quantity of beadwork covering the upper leather.

Holmes thoroughly examined each pair from heel to toe and sole to laces, often going back to check one pair against another. His magnifying lens in constant use, he also manipulated the leather with his hands, checking for suppleness and even smelling the insoles, presumably to determine if they'd yet been worn.

At last he leaned back in his chair, hands folded behind his head as he gazed at the ceiling. He held this pose for nearly a minute before finally facing our client.

"The motive remains a mystery, Professor, but I believe we can track down your *Leprechaun* even so. There's no more for us tonight, but I shall make enquiries in the morning that may shed some light upon this mystery."

"You have hopes, then, Mr. Holmes?" said our cleric, with obvious relief in his voice.

"'Hopes' is indeed the word, sir. For now I think I shall return to town and smoke a pipe or two over this pretty little problem."

Chapter II

The next morning, we arose for an early breakfast. This surprised me, for Holmes often forgoes his meals when on a case. When I mentioned this fact, he replied, "There's little we can do before nine o'clock, Watson. I have made a request of our friend, Inspector Shanahan of the Dublin police, and I expect him momentarily."

His prediction soon came to pass, for within five minutes the inspector arrived and pulled up a chair at our table. Retrieving a sheet of paper from his breast pocket, he handed it over to the detective.

"Here's the list you requested, Mr. Holmes, but why you would need this is beyond me."

Holmes glanced at the paper and put it into his own pocket, "I'm just gathering some information for a private client, Inspector. Nothing serious enough for the police to be concerned about, I assure you."

"If you say so, Mr. Holmes. But should things take a turn toward criminal intentions, I'll appreciate a message."

"Thank you, Inspector," replied my friend with a smile and patting his coat pocket. "But I trust that will not be necessary. Good day to you, and thank you for this."

"Will you be staying in Dublin then?" the police agent asked as he stood to go.

Holmes tilted his head slightly and replied, "I fully expect to be back in London by the New Year, Inspector. Thank you for your hospitality."

After the gentleman was out of earshot, I asked my friend, "You really expect to solve this case in four days, Holmes?"

In answer, he pulled the list from his pocket, as well as a map of Dublin, and marked several locations with a pencil. Upon completion of this task, he held the map up like a newspaper to study and announced, "I should be surprised if our task was not complete in two, Doctor. Please finish your coffee and we'll get started."

Fortunately, the weather, while cold and crisp, did not deter our travels with rain or snow. Scattered white clouds broke up a bright blue sky and played peek-a-boo with a winter sun that shone brightly, but gave off little heat from its position so far to the south.

Our first stop was just down the street from the hotel, a shop specializing in ladies' clothing, including footwear. Upon entering, we were immediately approached by an attractive woman in her mid-thirties with long auburn hair framing a thin face. She was wearing a white blouse with puffed sleeves and green piping around a bib front with green buttons. A long, green, pleated skirt brushed the top of tan boots that increased her height by a good two inches, but still left her well below five-and-one-half feet, looking up into our faces with confidence.

"Good morning, gentlemen! I am Mrs. McCullough. How may I help you today?" she asked in a bright cheery voice and Irish brogue that only added to her charm.

Holmes, being equally charming, gave that disarming smile of his and replied, "Good morning, Mrs. McCullough. I should like to see your line of ladies shoes."

"Certainly, sir. Right this way." She turned and led the way to a side wall of the store where many styles of women's footwear were on display and several boxes lined the shelves below.

She raised her hand indicating the display wall and asked, "Is there any particular style that you're interested in, sir?"

The detective stepped forward, lifted one shoe from its display shelf, and began examining its sole. "I am more interested in their construction than their style, madam. Also, possibly, in your supplier."

She crossed her arms over her breast, tilted her head to one side with a suspicious look and, in a more demanding tone, responded, "I don't understand. Are you here to buy a pair of shoes or waste my time with a lot of silly questions?"

I felt the necessity to step in at this point and answered for my friend. "We are working with a charity, Mrs. McCullough, and should like to identify a shoe supplier who could assist us in our work for the poor. We shall be happy to purchase a pair of shoes in exchange for the information we seek."

Fortunately, with her eyes on me, she did not see the look that Holmes gave and her manner eased somewhat.

"Well, that's different then. I don't suppose you'll want my Paris supplier for the high fashion items. But I'll write down my local cobbler for you. He's a good man. Fair prices for quality work."

I took the paper from her as Holmes continued checking several other pairs. Finally he turned and stated, "He is indeed a quality craftsman. I think he'll do quite nicely if we can strike a good price. Pick out a fine pair, Doctor. They will be well worth it."

I chose a pair, which were of the latest style in a practical work shoe, explaining to the proprietress that they were for my landlady. She boxed them up and bid us goodbye and good luck.

"Well done, Doctor," Holmes said as he hailed a cab. "I was prepared to offer a different explanation, but your winning ways with the ladies is a great asset to me. Tell me, how did you know Mrs. Hudson's shoe size?"

I settled into my seat, setting the shoebox at my feet, and answered. "While you were gallivanting around the Continent as 'Sigerson'[2], I had occasion to treat the poor woman for a severely sprained ankle. Now tell me, did you learn anything from your examinations?"

"There is a unique stitching pattern to her cobbler's work," he stated, looking at the paper closely where she had written the name. "It is quite distinguishable and matches that found on the shoes at Trinity. I hardly think it would be duplicated by anyone, save those who work for him, this 'Conan Mulcahey'."

We arrived at Mulcahey's shop on Grafton Street in less than twenty minutes and found a grey stone building with a sign in broad strokes reading *Mulcahey Leather Goods.* There were no windows in front on the ground floor, just a bright green door. We entered and were greeted by the smells of machine oil and freshly tanned leather. A bell, hung above the doorway, announced our presence. A gentleman of about fifty came striding toward us from beyond a counter which separated the entry from the manufacturing area. As he wiped his hands with a rag from his back pocket, I noted that he stood about five-feet-six and was stocky, but by no means fat. His muscular arms were well-developed and his hands thick with callouses. Eyeglasses were propped up on his forehead where his black hair was beginning to recede and pick up streaks of grey. He was clean-shaven and greeted us with a ready smile.

"Top o' the mornin' to ye, gentlemen. What can I do for ye today?"

Holmes continued the ruse that I had established with Mrs. McCullough and informed the man, who turned out to be the owner himself, of our mission to explore shoe suppliers for our charity.

His grin faded slightly at that statement and he asked, rather warily, "Be there no shoe suppliers in England for that task, sir?"

Without missing a beat, Holmes replied, "Indeed, I'm sure there are. But we are working with Father O'Keefe at Trinity College and would prefer to give the business to a local establishment."

"*Charity* implies no profit, gentlemen. How would I pay me workers to make shoes that 'twill be given away?"

Holmes smiled in response and answered, "We realize that we cannot expect all our suppliers to be non-profiteers, Mr. Mulcahey. We would certainly come to some sort of payment arrangement with you through our philanthropic donors. But perhaps we can negotiate a price somewhere between your costs and your rate to wholesalers?"

"What made ye come to me?" the leather crafter asked, still suspicious.

"We had chance to speak with Mrs. McCullough, who recommended you quite highly after we noted the excellence of your product. We were particularly impressed by your stitching. Might we see how you accomplish such fine work?"

At the mention of the lady's name and praise of his craftsmanship, the gentleman seemed to warm up to us and opened a gate in the counter to allow us into the shop area, where he conducted a brief tour. One side of the shop seemed to be dedicated to things like horse's tack, saddles, and leather-covered furniture, whereas the other was strictly for items of clothing such as coats, jackets, gloves, hats, and shoes. I stopped and admired a particularly fine black leather saddle with white stitching, obviously meant for a show horse. Noting my interest, Mulcahey spoke.

"You've a good eye, sir. That saddle is meant for the Lord Mayor himself."

I praised his artistry, then I noted something unusual on a bench: A sheet of rubber-like material about a quarter-inch thick. As I felt it, I enquired, "What is this for?"

"We've been experimenting with that rubber as cushioning underneath our leather-covered furniture and for possible variations on the Wellington boot."

"Very interesting," Holmes noted, as he too felt the material. Then we moved on to where the shoes were being manufactured. Here we found a half-dozen workers in various stages of the shoe-making process, each hand-crafting a particular pair. We stopped by a bench where a young man, who couldn't have been more than fifteen or sixteen, was attaching uppers to soles on a short patent leather boot. The holes had been pre-punched and his fingers flew through the stitching process in that pattern that was unique to Mulcahey's brand. I didn't time it, but I'm sure it took him less than five minutes to complete the task on one boot and start on the other.

After several seconds of observation, Holmes turned to the proprietor and asked, "I noticed at Mrs. McCullough's that some of your ladies shoes involve intricate beadwork. As far as our charity work, I doubt we would request such luxury, but I am curious as to the process. Where might that be done?"

Mulcahey took us around to another bench. If Holmes was expecting a short person whom might be a suspect in the college sightings, he was sorely disappointed.

"This is my niece, Alma. It's her artistry that gives our beaded shoes their flair for the ladies."

Alma stood and curtsied to us. She had a pleasing face surrounded by chestnut curls, but must have been at least five-foot-five and pleasantly plump – hardly someone who could impersonate a Leprechaun. I judged her age to be around twenty and noted a modest engagement ring on her finger.

Holmes returned her curtsy with a bow and, in an ever gallant tone, spoke of her work. "A pleasure, Miss. I was telling your uncle of the fine beadwork I have noted in our examination of your products and he has given the credit to you. It must be quite a task to produce such intricate work in quantity."

"Thank you, sir. But I do have some help. My little sister comes in after school to assist me in the afternoons, though with school on break she comes in more often. She's just out today running errands for mother."

"Ah, a talent that runs in the family. I suppose she works there next to you?"

"Certainly."

Holmes tuned to Mulcahey, "You are a lucky man, sir, to have such skills run along your family lines. Well, we must be going, but we will report to our superiors what we have found and see if they wish to put a proposal together for your consideration in our cause. Good day to you, Mr. Mulcahey, and to you Miss Alma. Please pass our compliments on to your sister . . . ."

"Brigid, sir"

"Brigid. Very nice. Well to her as well, and thank you."

We left the establishment and faced the traffic on Grafton Street. I turned to my friend.

"Did you learn anything from that tour, Holmes?"

"Indeed, Doctor."

I waited for him to expound but, as he so often does, he kept his thoughts to himself and appeared to be searching up and down the street.

Not spying what he was hoping for, he sought out a constable on patrol and enquired as to a certain type of establishment and any nearby spot for lunch. We walked up the street and entered a café called Bewley's. According to the signage it had been established in 1840, but the interior décor was all of modern style and convenience.

Holmes requested a table near the entrance and all throughout our stay he unobtrusively, but thoroughly, observed every patron who passed through those doors. We were having coffee and awaiting our bill when his manner changed as he took a keen interest in a young man who entered.

This fine fellow was just under six feet in height and thin as a rail. A shock of orange hair flowed from under his flat cap. He was dressed much like a clerk in a modest suit which showed its age by being just a bit too short for his teen-aged growth spurt. He obtained a table in a somewhat secluded corner and seemed to be waiting for someone.

"I believe we have our man, Watson," he murmured to me from behind his coffee cup.

I took a surreptitious glance and, noting the details I have just described, replied to my friend, "Surely not, Holmes. That fellow is much too tall to play a Leprechaun."

"Nevertheless, he's worth watching. If my surmises are correct, our young sprite will be along shortly."

As predicted, within five minutes a young lady joined him, giving him a brief kiss on the cheek as he rose to greet her. He didn't have to rise far, for she couldn't have been even five feet tall. She was a pretty little thing and somehow seemed familiar. The searching look on my face must have been evident, for Holmes asked, "Remind you of anyone, Doctor?"

"I'm not sure. She nags at my mind, but I can't place her."

"We just met her older sister, Watson. The resemblance is obvious."

"Wait, you're saying that's Brigid? How could you possibly know that?"

The check arrived at that moment, interrupting our conversation. Holmes doled out the appropriate amount, with a little extra for our efficient waitress, and then went back to sipping his coffee.

"Pieces are coming together nicely," he commented, as we watched the young pair enjoy bowls of what appeared to be a steaming stew.

Exasperated I insisted, "Holmes, please answer my question. How do you know that's Brigid?"

He sighed and replied, "Other than the obvious family resemblance, I knew by the arrangement of her work station next to her sister that Brigid would be no more than five feet tall. The fact that she met our young man adds to that confirmation."

"What is it about him that convinces you he is involved?"

"What have I always told you about observing people? Their clothing style and fit are all most people see. But you must observe their shoes, trouser knees, cuffs, and sleeves. The fact that his coat does not quite cover his shirtsleeves make his occupation all the more easy to decipher. He is a clerk who works for either an apothecary or a chemist. The frayed cuffs indicate much note-taking, and the chemical stains he has unsuccessfully tried to cover are still evident."

Understanding now where Holmes's mind was heading, I asked the obvious, "So what now? Do we confront them or report them to Inspector Shanahan?"

"We've only conjecture at this point," he replied. "I would still prefer to ascertain motive before involving anyone official. When they leave, I suggest you follow Miss Brigid and I shall shadow the young man to his place of work. I will meet you back at the hotel no later than three o'clock.

Thus, we parted ways when our charges finished their brief lunch. I was able to casually keep the young lady in sight, as her stature made for an easy pace for even my old war-wounded leg to maintain. She did, indeed, turn in to Mulcahey's. As she did not leave right away, I concluded that she was reporting to work. I caught a convenient cab and was back at the hotel, warming myself by the lobby fire, before two o'clock.

Chapter III

I was starting to doze off from the effects of a full lunch and cozy fire when Holmes arrived back at the hotel shortly before three, bearing a sizable parcel.

"Rouse yourself, Doctor. Let us repair to my room to make plans."

Upstairs, Holmes threw his parcel on the bed and sat down in a green velvet wingback chair by the window. He gazed out at a sky that was growing more leaden as the day progressed and threatened snow before nightfall. I took up a place at the writing desk and awaited his report.

"Our young friend's name is Brian Hayes and he works at Power Chemical, just one block over from Mulcahey's, on Clarendon Street. So, now we have two possible players in our little game. Both work less than a quarter-mile from the college where the mischief is occurring."

134

I looked across at my friend as he withdrew his pipe from his pocket, filled it, and began smoking as he stared out in the direction of the River Liffey. When no further information came forth, I felt obliged to ask the question, "How do you see any connection between these two youngsters and Father O'Keefe's problem? I suppose I can see Brigid as the Leprechaun, but why? How does Hayes fit in? Why are they doing all this anyway?"

Suddenly, small hailstones began pelting the window. Holmes leaned forward and gazed toward the ever-darkening sky. "I can only theorize as to the '*why*', Watson, and you know I loathe to postulate without sufficient data, which we are not likely to receive tonight in this weather.

"As to our participants, I am convinced young Brigid is our spritely Leprechaun. Hayes' role, in addition to being a close friend and confidant, is that of protector."

He stood, walked over to the bed, and dumped the contents of his parcel onto the green plaid quilt which covered it.

I was startled and puzzled at first by what I saw. But after I approached and picked one of the objects up and examined it, I realized what Holmes had in mind. I gave him an understanding smile and commented, "These should indeed overpower Brigid's protection. And you're right, the storm will discourage any mischief this evening. How shall we pass the time?"

As the weather grew worse into the afternoon and evening, we decided to forgo any excursions into the Dublin music halls or theatres. We stayed in for a fine dinner, some quiet reading, and early to bed.

Dawn broke with scattered grey clouds in a cold blue sky. By the time I awoke, dressed, and descended to the dining room for breakfast, Holmes had already fortified himself with coffee and gone out, leaving me a message that he would return by lunchtime. I chose to eat a hearty meal at that point, for I knew that, weather permitting, this evening could prove to be a long one and it was likely that Holmes would want to be "on station" prior to the dinner hour.

Afterward, I decided to return to my room, reading a periodical I had purchased in the lobby, while I awaited my companion's return. It was nearly noon before his knock came to my door.

"Hello," I greeted him as I opened the door and he strode in to sit in one of the armchairs by the radiator to warm himself. "Any progress this morning?"

"Indeed," he replied, as he pulled out his pipe and charged it. "I'm convinced more than ever that the Celtic language had a heavy influence upon Vulgar Latin."

"What?"

"I've been to the Trinity College Library, Doctor, since I was there preparing for tonight. I had a chance to spend some hours with *The Book of Kells* [3] and other ancient Irish documents. The intermixture of Celtic and Latin influence upon each other is quite obvious. That combination may even be the founding root of the Romance languages."

I shook my head, "Fascinating I'm sure, Holmes. But what of our case? Have you made any headway?"

He blew out a smoke ring and punctuated it with the stem of his pipe. "I've made discreet enquiries. In addition to being a skilled leather-worker, Miss Brigid appears to have other talents she wishes to exploit."

"What would those be?" I asked.

"Let's just say they would make Father O'Keefe cringe."

From there, he went on to explain what his plans were for the evening, in anticipation of the "leprechaun's" return. We went over our respective roles and several variations, depending on how events unfolded. By late afternoon we were fairly convinced that we had planned for every contingency.

That evening, we were in Father O'Keefe's laboratory just at sunset. The weather had cleared, but there was no moon, for it was in its new phase. Once the sun descended, the darkness was complete. The few lamp lights of the bell tower courtyard threw limited circles of light on the ground. Underneath, the tower was utterly black, perfect for Holmes's purpose. He laid his trap and we took up positions out of sight to await the arrival of the mythical creature.

Bundled up as I was against the winter chill. I still fought shivering, afraid it might give away my position. It was fortunate that I was able to do so, for along about nine o'clock I was startled by the sound of an approaching figure, just on the other side of the bushes from where I was concealed. It stopped within ten feet of my position and hesitated. I could hear some movement, as if it were preparing itself for its dash to the tower.

Instead of the dash I anticipated, the creature crept along silently on tiptoe, staying midway between the lamps to avoid their meagre light. I could barely make it out. Bent over as it was, it seemed much shorter than our suspect, Miss Brigid. It carried what appeared to be shoes in its left hand and something else clutched in its right. As it got closer to the tower, it made a final quick dash for the protective darkness beneath, like a rabbit seeking the safety of its hole. That proved to be its undoing.

As prearranged, Holmes and I approached from the opposite side, donning our protective devices as we did so. There was a cry of surprise when the Leprechaun realized it had stepped onto a large tarp, treated with

136

the same glue used in fly paper. It dropped the shoes and tried to twist itself free. Before doing so, however, Holmes made our presence known and, in desperation, it threw a glass bulb on the ground which shattered and spilled out its contents. Fortunately, the glue absorbed most of the powder before it could rebound into the air. What little did escape was efficiently blocked by the firemen's respirators Holmes had procured earlier in the day. He and I were able to circle around behind the culprit before it could completely break free of the sticky compound which slowed its progress. Just when it managed to obtain the concrete again, we were upon it.

Finally, I was able to glean enough by the faint light of the courtyard to see the head of this Leprechaun was a rubber mask, obviously a protection against the debilitating powder it had flung in our direction. As I held its arms, Holmes pulled the mask away and revealed the pretty features of Miss Brigid herself. Suddenly, she yanked hard and I almost lost my grip just as a roar came from behind Holmes and he ducked, sweeping a leg under the attacking form of a young man. I repositioned my left arm around the young lady's throat and pulled my revolver from my right pocket, ordering the attacker to stop. Holmes, however, had already driven his knee into the fellow's back on the ground and quickly handcuffed him. At the sight of my gun, Brigid screamed and kicked fiercely backward into my shin. Her strength outclassed her weight, obviously enhanced by adrenaline. The kick threw me off balance, but I dragged her down with me and rolled her onto the ground where my nearly hundred pounds of weight advantage kept her pinned face down.

"That's enough, Brigid!" I yelled. "The game is up! The only chance you and Hayes have is to give up and explain your actions. If you try to escape, the police will track you down and bring scandal on your families."

Upon hearing herself and her companion identified, she stopped struggling. Hayes, under Holmes's control, was yelling, "Leave her alone! You've got me, let her go!"

We both pulled our prisoners to their feet and marched them off. Their surprise was evident when we escorted them into the nearby building and deposited them into seats within Father O'Keefe's laboratory.

The old professor was both pleased and surprised at our arrival.

"So, you've caught two birds in your flypaper trap, Holmes. I admit I had my doubts, but well done. Now who have we here?"

Before anyone responded, Holmes spoke up and overrode the priest's query.

"I am more concerned as to the '*why*', Professor." Turning to the girl he asked, "Young lady – " (I noted that he avoided using her name.) " – my name is Sherlock Holmes, and this is my colleague, Dr. Watson. You have caused quite a bit of consternation among these academics. I have a theory, but would like to confirm: Just what was the point of leaving pairs of ladies' shoes under the bell tower?"

Before she answered, Hayes spoke up, "Sherlock Holmes, the London detective? Of all the devil's own luck, that you should be in Dublin at this time." He bowed his head and shook it in disbelief.

Up to that point, Brigid had maintained a defiant look on her face. But Holmes, in that disarming manner and tone that has served him so well among the fair sex, had calmed her considerably.

Her face softened a bit and she replied, "My family has an ancient saying, Mr. Holmes, 'Where the shoes go forth, the feet shall follow'."

I gave her a quizzical look, and she shrugged and said, "It loses a bit in translation, Doctor. Generally, only the wealthy had proper shoes back then and they were the ones who led the way. The point is, the shoes I left were a symbolic gesture to prepare the way for women to be admitted to this school based on their intelligence, just as the men are, and not discriminated against merely because of their gender."

Professor O'Keefe spoke out at that. "The mere fact that you believe in such poppycock proves you lack the intellect to attend this institute of higher learning."

"Symbolism, Father," she replied, acknowledging his priest's collar, rather than the academic rank which Holmes had used, "can be a powerful cultural tool. Does the church not use statues and stained glass? Wine and wafers for communion? The crucifix and the sign of the cross?"

O'Keefe turned red and stepped toward her. I maneuvered into a position where I could intervene if necessary, but he stopped short and rose his voice in dismay.

"How dare you compare your cheap little shoes to the Sacraments of the Church!"

Hayes had also stood in protective mode. But with his hands still cuffed behind him, his actions were limited. Holmes acted in his stead and put a hand on the shoulder of our client.

"We are here for explanations, Professor. Judgement is yet to be determined. Go on, young lady."

"Symbolism fits the movement, Father," she continued. "I'm not campaigning for the souls of people and I don't need the gold and silver ornaments of the church. My shoes, which are of the highest quality available in Dublin, I might add, are meant to encourage a march toward women's equality for the opportunity to learn and contribute new ideas to the world."

"A woman's place is to keep house and bear and raise children for her husband," O'Keefe answered, with contempt.

She slowly shook her head, "I've read the King James version of the Bible, Father. There are a good many strong women – merchants, warriors, and queens among them – who have proven themselves more worthy than you would allow."

"Worthiness often comes at a cost, young woman. We'll see how much you're willing to pay with some jail time," the priest answered smugly.

My impression of our client had changed rapidly over the course of this exchange, and now his bird-like appearance was more vulture than anything else. Before I could respond with my opinion of his attitude, however, Holmes pulled him aside and ticked off some points on his fingers as he addressed him in tones too low for us to hear. When they rejoined us, O'Keefe was more subdued, yet tried to remain threatening.

"You are very fortunate, Miss. Mr. Holmes has appealed to my charitable side at this time of year and convinced me to let you and your companion go, under the condition that this behavior stops immediately. No more clandestine visits to this campus. If you are caught here again, you will be charged with trespassing and assault on the students who tried to stop you the other day. Is that understood?"

Brigid made as if to give a defiant reply, but a look from Holmes arrested her tongue and she merely agreed.

"There is one other condition," the professor added, as Holmes removed the handcuffs from Mr. Hayes. "You are to go with these gentlemen right now and answer all their questions, truthfully. If you fail to do so, I shall subside my charitable mood and see you spend the New Year in jail."

Chapter IV

We left with our charges, and all our equipment, and walked the few blocks to Bewley's Café, where Holmes ordered coffee all around to combat the chill of the evening.

Once settled into a quiet corner, Holmes began his questioning.

"Miss Brigid, I understand the symbolism of your actions, but I would be interested to hear what your overall plan was for getting the school to admit women. Surely you had more in mind than the steps you've taken thus far."

"Your reputation precedes you, Mr. Holmes," she answered in her lilting Irish brogue. "Though I am not sure if your presence in Ireland at this time is a run of bad luck or a blessing from St. Patrick himself."

"We were here on another case. But please, tell us your story," answered my companion. "I have surmised that there are more than the two of you involved in this activity and I'll not ask you to name names, but I am sympathetic, if you will trust me with the larger picture."

His statement caused me pause at first. Holmes opinion of women was not of the highest order, though certainly more liberal than Father O'Keefe's. Certain women had gained his respect over the years: My late wife, Mary Morstan, for instance. Miss Violet Hunter, and certainly *the* woman, Irene Adler. Overall though, he found the gender a challenge to his ordered brain and logical thought patterns. I wondered what it was about this girl that caught his attention.

The plucky young woman looked at her cohort, who merely shrugged indecisively. She gazed into her coffee cup momentarily, stared into Holmes's eyes and began her tale.

"All me life, I've seen women – strong, proud women – subject themselves to men. Often foolish simpletons or bullying egotists, just because society, or the church, or even the government, expects them to ignore their own God-given intelligence and talents and conform to the *status quo*.

"Me own sister shouldn't be making shoes for our uncle. She should be keeping his books and negotiating contracts with his suppliers. She's outstanding at mathematics and shrewd in her own shopping for our family. She should be taking classes in economics and contract law, instead of sewing leather. But the college is restricted to boys. Often stupid boys, who only get in because of their father's money."

"Yes," responded Holmes, "I've seen her efficiency at laying out patterns in leather hides to best utilize them with as little waste as possible. She shows an ordered mind that could develop in a variety of ways."

Brigid tilted her head at the detective, "You've been to Uncle Conan's shop?"

Holmes nodded, "The shoes you left behind were a clear trail back to Mulcahey's. But I perceive that there is more to this story. You, yourself, have a unique gift that would benefit from a college education. How did you discover your talent for chemistry?"

She reached over and took Mr. Hayes' hand. "Brian left one of his chemistry books at our house one evening. He's an apprentice at Power Chemical, though I have the feeling you already know that.'

Holmes nodded, raised his hand, and bade her go on.

"Well, I glanced through it before returning it to him the next day on my way to work."

Her demeanor grew animated. An excitement tinged her voice, like a child on Christmas morning.

"T'was so *fascinating*, Mr. Holmes! I couldn't put it down. I read into the wee hours until I fell to sleep. Everything fit so well together. The

Periodic Table was a wondrous thing to experiment with in me head, to see how different combinations might work. I'd never felt so . . . *alive*!

"Of course, studying books can only take one so far, you know. I ached for chances to experiment for real. Brian was able to get me some small batches of chemicals, but I really wanted to work in a laboratory and the college is my only chance, since businesses won't hire female chemists."

Remembering my own fascination with the medical sciences at her age, I understood her passion, but her methods still confused me and I said as much.

"Forgive me, young lady, but how do shoes and Leprechauns fit into your plans?"

She wrapped both hands around her coffee cup and took a sip as she formulated her answer. Setting it back down, she looked across the table at me.

"Being a Scotsman yourself, Dr. Watson, you know how your culture and mine differ so much from the English. There are deep-rooted superstitions and legends that are ingrained in our souls. I knew the learned men of the college would put no stock in Leprechauns. I also knew they would be against me and my cause anyway. I needed to stir up public opinion. Get people talking about the strange goings-on at the school. Then, once it was on everyone's mind, expand the conversation to debate over why women aren't allowed the same higher educational opportunities as men."

I nodded in understanding, but continued to question her.

"How were you planning on bringing the conversation into the public eye?"

Holmes, who had patiently put up with my interruption, chimed in again.

"If I may, Doctor. There are other persons involved in this movement beyond these two."

Brigid and Hayes looked at each other apprehensively. Even though they were caught, it was obvious they did not want anyone else to suffer consequences based on their actions.

Holmes stubbed out the cigarette he had been smoking and continued. "I've been to *one* of the local newspaper offices so far, although there may be others involved, and I noted a certain Mr. Lemon, who seems to be a likely ally to your cause."

Hayes leaned back in his chair, "Johnny would never have admitted that 'til we were ready. What did you do to him?"

Holmes arched his eyebrows in all innocence and replied, "Absolutely nothing, Mr. Hayes. In fact, he doesn't even know I was there, being away from his desk at the time. I gained access to the newspaper offices under an assumed name. On the pretext of offering them an article on the influence of the Celtic language on the Latin Vulgate, I was led through the writer's room and noted Lemon's workspace, which had papers addressed to him by name. On his desk, I saw what I was on the lookout for: Research material on prominent women in history, including Queen Victoria, Florence Nightingale, and Ada Lovelace. [4] It was obvious that he was preparing a defense of the same position you are proposing regarding women's place in society."

"How did you come to be looking at newspaper offices, Holmes?" I asked.

"It was elementary, old chap. At some point, this *Leprechaun* was going to need publicity for her cause. A connection to a sympathetic reporter was called for."

"You were quite sure the creature was a woman then?"

"Her size and the deposits of women's shoes were indicative of that probability. But please, Miss Brigid, continue your tale. How did you come up with that knockout compound?"

She folded her hands in front of her, tilted her head slightly so that her chestnut hair brushed her right shoulder, and replied, "The chemical mixture was obvious as I studied the various elements involved. Measuring the proper dilution took some time, as I only wanted a limited effect to cause loss of consciousness and not permanent harm. The other issue was to protect myself from its effects. Brian was able to help me with the respirators they use at the chemical plant, based on the Tyndall [5] design. It took a while, but I managed to combine it with rubber from my uncle's shop and make a mask that would appear as the Leprechaun's face. I certainly didn't count on someone like you, appearing with your own respirators, to counteract my defense."

The devices that Holmes and I had used that night, now in a bag at our feet, were, in fact, fireman's respirators Holmes had borrowed from a local firehouse. He nodded with just a hint of a smile of admiration for this young lady's ingenuity and spoke again.

"I believe I have all the information that I need. I know that tonight was due to be your last venture on to the campus – thus your promise to Professor O'Keefe was an empty one. Nevertheless, he is satisfied that these shenanigans will stop. I have convinced him that he does not want the publicity of having the college outwitted by a woman on so many occasions. I would suggest that you have your friend Lemon keep your name out of his story. He will be publishing it just before the school students' return from holiday, I take it?"

"That is the plan, Mr. Holmes. Tonight was going to be my last delivery. Then Johnny would publish his story just as the students were returning. We thought that would stir up the superstitious ones into talking about it and even have their parents concerned about the strange goings-on at the college. After a time, he'll then widen the topic from ladies shoes on campus to why ladies aren't admitted to the school."

"A sound campaign, Miss Brigid.," Holmes replied. "I wish you well. Although I fear bureaucracy and doctrine may not move swiftly enough for your own desires, you are planting seeds that will bloom for future generations. For now, may I have your address, in the event I am able to offer further assistance?"

I handed the girl my notebook and pencil and she swiftly wrote out her particulars and handed it back.

"Good night to you, Miss Brigid, Mr. Hayes. We shall take our leave of you and be returning to London on the morrow. Should the need arise, you can always telegraph me at 221b Baker Street. Come along, Watson, I believe our conspirators would like to be left alone."

True to his word, Holmes and I took the boat back to England the following afternoon, after he sent word to Inspector Shanahan that all was well. In the following days, I noted Holmes diligently experimenting with his own chemicals. He also shared with me a message he had sent to his brother, Mycroft, relaying the address of a certain young chemist who might do well working for the British government.

NOTES

Ten years later, in January 1904, the short notice that *"the Board of Trinity College have received a letter from the King authorising them to admit women to the degrees of Dublin University"* appeared in several Irish newspapers. This was the end-product of many years of debate among the Board of Trinity College Dublin and university society, more broadly speaking.

The first female student to enter the institution was Isabel Marion Weir Johnston. She hailed from the north of the country, and was the daughter of Sir John Johnston, who had been a prosperous businessman in Derry and was a former president of the "Londonderry Chamber of Commerce".

1. "The Seventh Swann" by Roger Riccard, as recorded in *Sherlock Holmes Adventures for the Twelve Days of Christmas* – Baker Street Studios (2015)
2. "Sigerson" was the alias Holmes used while hiding from Professor Moriarty's gang after the incident at Reichenbach Falls. See "The Empty House".
3. *The Book of Kells* (Trinity College Dublin MS 58) contains *The Four Gospels* in Latin based on the Vulgate text which St. Jerome completed in 384 AD, intermixed with readings from the earlier Old Latin translation.
4. Countess Lovelace (1815-1852) was the only daughter of Lord Byron, and was a renowned English mathematician known for her work on Charles Babbage's Analytical Machine. As the writer of the first algorithm for that machine, she has been called the first computer programmer.
5. John Tyndall (1820-1893) was the Irish physicist who invented the fireman's respirator.

A Malversation of Mummies
by Marcia Wilson

It was a chilly winter day. Crime was all but absent in the interests of staying warm and alive . . . and Sherlock Holmes was housebound, convalescing . . . and bored. Three words that only managed to strike terror when used together while in the same sentence as *"Sherlock Holmes"*.

Dr. Watson regretted that he would have to forego his own warmth in the interests of his lodger staying alive if he was forced to spend ten more minutes in his closest friend's company.

To do him credit, Holmes had not been consciously maddening.

Then again, Holmes rarely was. Watson could scarcely believe that he missed his chemical experiments.

"Holmes . . . I'm going out." Watson said at last, and rose to his feet.

Holmes blinked drowsily from his usual chair. The lassitude of his entire body should have screamed the presence of some infernal drug, but even morphine and cocaine could not compete with the great detective when he was falling into a black mood.

Three days of this while the storm raged about London. Holmes had fretted from his sickbed – a sickbed that was all his own doing. Ignore his body and pay the consequences, and was it truly that important to get the particulars about that French coiner so quickly? It wasn't as though anyone could travel the Channel back to the Continent with blizzard conditions over the waters . . .

Too late, Watson had realized Holmes's energy had been a frantic way of keeping his encroaching black mood at bay. There was nothing for it now but for the two of them to live with the consequences of hot soup, warm fires, and whatever mental activity that could keep Holmes's brain above the level of the lower orders of the animal kingdom.

Needless to say, Holmes had taken the lack of crime badly. Even Christmas was good for some imaginative forays into illegal intelligence, but this was just the plain ordinary sort of bad weather where it made more sense to burrow down and keep warm.

The detective was grossly unappreciative of the lull in murder, assault, kidnapping, theft, and blackmail.

Watson had been the reluctant audience to this since the beginning. He wavered between the wild hope that something would baffle the Yard and they would come . . . and the knowledge that Holmes's open glee at having a bloody mess to unravel would unravel a tenuous relationship with

145

the police. Police liked to solve crimes – they didn't like to have them. Gregson avoided 221b for months, sometimes years at a time. Hopkins was half-terrified of calling Holmes in on something frivolous. MacDonald was off on a case on the other side of the island – the worst side, in Watson's opinion as his war wounds were no lover of bitter Hebridonian north winds. Morton had been on extended recovery since his malicious wounding by anarchists, and after that, there weren't too many detectives left. Youghal, they'd heard, was undercover over the latest Fenian disaster. Poor man. He lived in England, not Ireland, by choice.

Lestrade still came by, both to visit and to share the news at the Yard – a sort of verbal telegraph station. Holmes wouldn't admit it, but he looked forward to knowing what was going on, even if he scolded the little man for telling his stories backwards, or forgetting important details. Lestrade took it all in stride, which was rather at odds with his general reputation at the Yard itself. Between the two men, the usual rules of conduct were suspended. Watson understood it on a deep level, but was at a loss to explain it.

If only someone could come by with a problem. A non-fatal problem – something bizarre, something out of the ordinary . . . something *urgent*. Something that Holmes could solve without taxing his system by going outside . . . .

Gnashing his teeth, Watson yanked the frozen door open with all his strength and found himself staring cross-eyed at a gloved fist that had just managed to stop from pounding the space where his face had replaced the dimensions of the door.

"Good heavens!" Inspector Lestrade gasped. His breath steamed in the cold. "What's wrong, Doctor? An emergency case?"

"Yes." Watson sighed. "Do come in, Inspector . . . ." He made room for the small man and made certain that the coat-rack had space. "I was about to go get a newspaper."

"I wouldn't bother." Lestrade grimaced. "The newspapers aren't going to be printing for another set of hours at least."

Watson stopped in his tracks. "I beg your pardon?" He stared. "The evening papers always come at . . . ." His voice trailed off. "Has something happened?" he asked at last. Lestrade was not looking his usual self, which was as dapper in demeanor to match his clothing. "And, err . . . ." A strange scent reminiscent of an abandoned leather factory hung ever so faintly about his clothing. "Lestrade . . . where have you been?"

"That's part of the reason why the papers are delayed." Lestrade answered. He seemed strangely undisturbed, but then, Lestrade always swore he never had the time to read the rags – especially the ones that talked much about the Yard in less-than-glowing terms. "Is Mr. Holmes in?"

Watson snorted. It was an automatic reaction. "Yes, I'm afraid so." He rubbed at the tight band at his temples. "I warn you he's in fine fettle, Inspector."

"Really." Lestrade's expression suddenly looked a great deal happier. That was a warning sign if there ever was one. "Is he on a case then?"

"No, quite the opposite. I thought a newspaper would distract him a bit before supper . . . ." For the second time, his voice trailed off. "And now there's a delay." He wondered what the pubs were like right now.

Lestrade only looked happier. "Has his Detective Doldrums? I just might have a cure for that."

"It doesn't involve chess games that turn into vicious scrums afterward, does it?"

"Tsk. Don't dignify what happened at Lord Beckett's as 'scrum', my good man. That was nothing less than total annihilation, and you ought to know – we were both in it." The little man flashed a grin at the doctor. It was the sort of grin that would come from a hard, working-class man who has been suddenly given an outlet for years of frustrations. Not every man would consider a brutal free-for-all with hired thugs a gift from the gods, but when it came to Lestrade . . . He didn't even take broken bones personally.

Watson caught himself smiling in return. "One of these days we'll have to tell Holmes about that." He confessed. "Do you suppose it would alleviate some of his mood?"

"No, let's save that story for when we really need it," Lestrade smirked. "And I'll use my day's story on our friend upstairs." He paused. "You might want to take notes for this one. It was a 'snorter', to use MacDonald's favourite word."

Instincts for trouble died hard. Watson pulled his coat back off to join Lestrade's and the two ascended the stairs.

Holmes had caught from the murmurs down the stairs that someone had come to visit, and that it was Lestrade. His evening visits were not an uncommon event – Holmes found himself looking forward to the distractions, although Watson was just content to have the company.

He was still frustrated at the man. Lestrade had some small talent for his work but he was resolutely blind and deaf to the world and its clues. He could recognize when something was amiss . . . but *why* it was amiss in the first place he couldn't say. It was maddening.

". . . bring up some tea," Watson was saying as he pushed the door open.

"Thank you," Lestrade breathed as he pulled his hat off. "Mr. Holmes. I'm afraid I have some bad news to deliver."

By the time Lestrade had finished speaking, Holmes had shot his eyes to his cuffs, collar, trouser-legs, and trouser-cuffs. For this time of year the detective was unusually clean – scrupulously so, which meant he hadn't been sent on one of his usual mud-spattered jobs.

Being clean in London was not an easy task. If there was a personable trait the two detectives shared, it was that they both would prefer to be as clean as cats given the choice . . . not that they often were. So there was something out of the ordinary already.

As the men moved closer into the room, Lestrade dallied by the fire with his outstretched hands. With that movement a peculiar odor emanated from his clothing. It was subtle, like cologne applied yesterday with only the base notes remaining. Holmes's eyes widened and he sat up. He did not know that odor. For the first time in years, he had encountered something new.

"By all means, Lestrade if you have bad news, best to get it over with." As he spoke, his eyes sought clues to the man's new strangeness. So far there were none – a case that had kept him indoors for most of the day. Lestrade was tired. He pressed his weight on his good foot. But he was clean of any traces of mischief. And that odor . . . .

"Well, as I was telling the Good Doctor, the papers will be delayed a few hours. It can't be helped, I'm afraid, and it's partly involved with the work I had to do today – " A memory crossed his face and he gulped hard, his diaphragm clenching for a moment in reflex. "Beg your pardon." Lestrade apologized. "I've had a day that I don't ever care to repeat ever again. Ever. It's been decades since I last dealt with a case of stolen mummies."

"'Mummies?'" Watson blurted – saving Holmes the reflex of repeating that last word. "Lestrade, did I hear you correctly?"

"Lord, yes." Lestrade sank down in the settee opposite from Holmes. "Just a moment . . . ." He fished in his pocket and pulled out two small objects. "Here, Mr. Holmes. What would you make of this?"

It was an instantaneous change. Holmes's grey eyes sparkled, for he had never been able to resist that question when it was posed to him.

Watson vanished from his spot at the table and re-materialized at his elbow. Lestrade thought the two men looked rather alike in moments like this – curiosity wasn't the only glue that bound them together, but it was a very powerful one.

The boxes were opened and arranged side by side in Holmes's lap. The contents were familiar to any doctor.

"Human bones," Watson exclaimed. "Fragments of the skull. But they appear to be two different skulls."

"They are stained differently." Holmes agreed. "I see that the one on the left is very black and shiny. Bitumen, perhaps? I would conduct a chemical test to be absolutely certain. The other is more ochrous in colour, softer in appearance and . . . ." He peered closer. "Would that be pitch?"

Lestrade had been smiling through this exchange, with the air of a man who has accomplished something. "Very good. Which one would you say is the genuine Egyptian mummy fragment, and which one would be the forgery?"

"Lestrade," Watson protested as Holmes promptly dived into the challenge. "Why would someone go through the trouble of forging a mummy? Surely the museum wouldn't pay so much for the genuine article."

"You're right, they do not. Museums will not pay for something they can get for pennies from their cousin living abroad who knows a nice grave-robber down the road." Lestrade's voice was somewhat sarcastic. "One of our former men in the Yard, Inspector Tomlinson – I don't know if you've ever met him – "

"Wounded in the line of duty at the wharfs by a man who did not know he was ambushing a policeman in the dark." Holmes interrupted. "1880. March, I believe . . . . Forced to take an early retirement from the Metro."

Lestrade nodded, respect tinged with regret at the memory. For someone who said so few good things about his professionals, Holmes had every incident committed to his memory. That was something even the Home Office didn't do.

"Quite so. But he was hale enough to find work as a commissionaire. He'd done some early service for the Queen before taking the badge . . . and he operates at the British Museum. They put him in the Natural History section, right enough. The stuffed sharks don't bother him like they do some of the other Johnnys, and soon enough he was trusted with the truly valuable exhibits."

Lestrade hesitated as Mrs. Hudson tapped on the door with the tea-tray. He shut his mouth with a loud click and waited on tenterhooks as Watson thanked her for her time. Holmes made no notice of his landlady. He was busy studying the bones.

"Do go on, Inspector."

"Well, it was a sordid enough little story. Someone entrusted with responsibility he didn't deserve had been taking advantage of his access within the vaults of the Museum. Research project, he said. What he was doing was taking advantage of what was lying forgotten in storage. Thank you." Lestrade took his tea gratefully. "Thank you very much. This is the first thing I've felt like ingesting all day."

That suggested un-pleasantries to Watson. He glanced at Holmes, who was thinking along the same lines. A loss of appetite . . . mummies . . . corruption. None of this appeared to be a savoury sort of stew.

"I hate cases that involve people who have been dead for more than three-thousand years," the little Yarder muttered into his cup. "It's all so dreadfully complicated. The paperwork alone . . . ."

Watson cleared his throat. He sympathized entirely. "Why were you picked for the case, then?" he wondered. "I understand you can turn down a few cases if you feel you're out of your depth."

"Depth had nothing to do with the mess, Doctor!" Lestrade cried indignantly. "I was the last one on the staff qualified to identify the mummies as forgeries. It isn't something you actually take a course in at the local Academy."

"I would imagine not, which is a shame." Holmes mused. "A little education never hurt anyone."

"You never met my parents." Lestrade answered gloomily. "They saw education ruin their first two children. They weren't going to repeat their mistakes a third time . . . ." He downed his cup. Watson was ready with the teapot – and something stronger to go with it.

"Who else, might I inquire, would be qualified to identify forged mummies – and for that matter, how does one add that experience to one's portfolio?" Holmes laced his long fingers together, leaning forward slightly in his interest.

"You have to rather be involved in previous mummy-forging cases to really get the experience." Lestrade shuddered. "I was a bobby on the beat back in 1871 when I had my time. Inspector Davids was the man on that case."

"Ah, The Wonderful Welshman," Holmes smiled, oblivious to the grimace on Lestrade's face. "One of the brightest minds of his generation."

"That he was. He needed help from the uniforms, and when there was time, he'd show us what he was doing. It was a shabby little business, with the ordinary sort of smuggling relics." Lestrade took a drink of "doctored" tea and visibly relaxed. "Every time I see a canopic jar, I have a bad start. Saw too many of them . . . with their original contents."

"Who else besides yourself has had experience with identifying mummies?" Watson wanted to know. That old curiosity gleamed in his eyes. He did love a good story, and this was threatening to be quite the tale.

"Normally there's enough of us around, but – well. This case . . . Gregson has a rotten sinus infection, Morton has some experience but he's

150

down with a bad case of the influenza, and Inspector Brown has the ordinary common cold. I'm the only one left on duty that can take Inspector Davids' training to all of this. I'd planned to show Hopkins and Youghal the ropes, but Inspector Brown gave them what he has, and that's that. I'm hoping these samples will be enough for when they recover. It's really better when you're dealing with a complete mummy, not just the bits and pieces left over."

Holmes tilted his head, peering sharply at the relics, and then back at Lestrade. "You have failed to mention why the mummies in the British Museum were of interest in the first place."

"Just a moment." Lestrade lifted a finger, reached around, and pulled his hip-flask out. "No offense, but I've been around enough things today that there's no sense in keeping any uninvited guests alive in my bloodstream," he warned. "All right, where was I? The mummies." He coughed slightly. "An even twelve in all. Some sort of minor priest's family – name's got a vowel in every other letter. At the risk of sounding sacrilegious, every generation had a priest in the family, and they went to their glory in style." He shrugged. "They'd been stripped of their gewgaws before any of us were ever born, but still, people convince themselves there's something left to steal if only they can find it. They'll make off with the whole thing and smash it open with hammers – looking for what, I don't know." Lestrade shuddered again. So did Watson.

"The bloomin' fool in charge of the department had come across something in the archives that was about as worthless as worthless gets – a crate of forged mummies that had been bought by the Museum years ago by a curator who had gone senile in stages."

"Oh, no." Watson's eyes were large as shooting marbles. "Lestrade, are you saying there was a case of switching the mummies?"

"Who was going to look at the embarrassment of a crate of fake mummies?" Lestrade shrugged practically. "One by one, they were switched out and, when there was time . . . well, that's when he started on his real work – selling the mummy parts in pieces." With a rather jaded flourish he pulled out his shorthand notebook. "Good thing Gregson's paperwork isn't affected by his sense of smell. He's putting together quite the little collection of cults and bizarre little clubs staffed by people with more money than sense. D'you have any idea what the little fools will pay for a skull? A week's wages for a constable. And they don't even know if they have the real article or not!"

Holmes chuckled. It would seem such thoughts had occurred to him in the past, and they still amused him. "The difficulties of being wealthy," he noted.

Lestrade snorted. "That's merely one particular headache I'll never have to nurse," he said with feeling. "By the time Tomlinson saw what was going on, about half the mummies had been switched, and half of those had been broken up. Do you want to know the good news?" He didn't wait for a response. "We couldn't press the man on selling the false mummies. Merely transferred it into a count of fraud – "

"Why, for heaven's sake?" Watson demanded.

Lestrade shook his head sadly. "Couldn't upset the Board," he told them. "The orders were down from the Home Secretary. One more delicate case that no one wants to touch." A sudden thought crossed his face, making it darken with a sour emotion. "I swear they're trying to get rid of me," he said under his breath. Watson mixed another cup of tea. "Thank you." Despite the already ingested amounts, Lestrade was barely flushed. It made Holmes wonder about the quality of Lestrade's day . . . .

"They were all in a box that was dropped – by accident, I was told."

"Do you believe it was an accident?" Holmes's eyebrows belied his own belief.

"Anything's possible. I wasn't there when it happened."

"Ah. Do go on."

"Not much more to tell." Lestrade suddenly cleared his throat again – that nauseated look was back in his eye. "I had to sort out the genuine mummies from the imitation mummies so we could have a better idea of how many charges of forgery, fraud, and theft we were dealing with."

Holmes studied the boxes a moment. Mrs. Hudson entered with the supper tray. With more optimism than the thrift borne of experience, she had put out a plate for Watson, Lestrade, and Holmes.

"Holmes, do try to eat something," Watson urged, at the risk of humiliating the man before Lestrade.

"You're assuming he'll want to eat after this," Lestrade said darkly. "It's been ten hours since I last had anything. I'm only just starting to feel human again."

Watson gave them both his best stern expression. "You both need to eat," he directed. "Holmes, because he is recovering. Lestrade, because you don't want to be where Holmes is right now."

"That's a devil of a bedside manner, Doctor."

"I learned it in Afghanistan."

"Well . . . ." Holmes lifted his head. "From the physical examination of the samples you have shown me, I would presume that a simple chemical test would determine if the mummy is genuine, for I would suspect the forgeries can be quite clever."

"Genuine mummies were full of bitumen," Lestrade agreed. "But that's only one of the tests. False mummies smelt of pitch when they were lit."

"Hmm, one could hardly test the British Museum's property by setting a flame to it," Holmes smiled. "And one could hardly test all the broken-up pieces as you described."

"But what's left?" Watson wondered. "If it isn't by sight . . . and it isn't by chemical test, how does one determine the false from the true?"

Lestrade winced. "I . . . are you certain you want to know, Doctor?"

"How bad can it be?" Watson wondered – just before he caught on to Holmes's expression. "Holmes?"

Without saying a word, Holmes rose gracefully to his feet, gently deposited the boxes on the chemistry-table, and went to the little drawer where his private stock was kept. Before his silent audience, he selected a bottle that Watson knew was only for the most strident of occasions, and wordlessly filled Lestrade's flask with it.

"Err . . . thank you." Lestrade said hesitantly. A two-hundred-year-old brandy was rather out of his usual league.

"Not at all." Holmes said firmly. "Have some supper. Mrs. Hudson has a way with curried chicken."

Watson was primed to explode.

Holmes tucked his hands inside the pockets of his mouse-coloured dressing gown and exhaled to the ceiling. "Our friend can tell us if I am correct in my deductions . . . but you said earlier that Gregson, who was qualified, had a sinus infection. Later on you said that Gregson's paperwork was not affected by his sense of smell – but I get ahead of myself. It merely reinforced the suspicions I began to gather when all the other inspectors you mentioned were either disqualified from identifying the mummies, or were un-trainable because they had common colds or something similar."

Horror dawned reluctantly upon Watson's face. "Lestrade," he croaked. "Did you have to . . . *smell the mummies*?"

Lestrade ran his finger around his collar. "It's the forgeries that have the bad odor," he admitted. "The real articles . . . they almost smell pleasant." He suddenly shrugged and took another drink. "Almost. It's not like you can forget what it is you've got in your nose."

"Oh . . . ." Watson spoke in a voice that was far too small for a man of his size.

"Sort of earthy, which is hardly surprising – Almost fresh. But there's a bit of an ammonia fume underneath it all. Those pitch-soaked imitations are the ones that take off your head."

153

Watson worked saliva into his mouth for a really good swallow. "I see." His voice cracked, just slightly. "I agree, Holmes. Supper is the least society can offer after a day like that."

Lestrade shrugged, pleased but not fully comfortable with being given something like food and sympathy all at once. "Don't feel sorry for me," he cautioned as they rose. "But you'll excuse me if I re-treat my hands with strong lye soap before I join you at the table."

Holmes lifted the cover off the nearest tray and sniffed. "Watson, you're rather quiet."

"I don't think Lestrade's finished telling his story, Holmes."

"Oh?" Holmes quirked an eyebrow as he portioned up equal amounts of chicken, rice, and whatever vegetables Mrs. Hudson had found on the market. A moment later he blinked. "By Jove, you're perfectly right. And you're perfectly right about my health. I deserve to be incarcerated in my rooms if I've overlooked something as simple as that."

"Simple as what, Mr. Holmes?" Lestrade had returned, with hands so clean they looked blistered. He'd given his face the same treatment, which was hardly surprising.

"The newspapers." Watson blurted. "What in the world did the mummies have to do with the newspapers? There wasn't a blackout of the press was there?"

"Goodness, no." Lestrade breathed out a quick prayer to whatever gods were sympathetic to the Yard. "It's just that . . . well . . . it's inevitable that we would find a few paper-trails to . . . the buyers of the mummy parts." He paid his plate a quick obeisance and took up a forkful of rice. "The majority of them, outside of the young geese who want a skull collection . . . well . . . there was the group or six that was into human ingredients for satanic cults . . . strange worship . . . And art forgers."

"Art forgers?" Watson repeated. He really was handy for that – he didn't worry about sounding idiotic when he was astonished.

"Art forgers. Powdered mummy was a vital ingredient for ink, and a form of water-colour back in the day." With a poise that would have impressed the most war-bitten regiment, the inspector went through a few enjoyable bites of his free meal. "Went out of favour when word got out what it was made of."

Holmes had lowered his forgotten fork. "Lestrade, you're telling the story but not in true storytelling fashion. What would art forgeries have to do with the newspapers that we read?"

They watched as the decision to just up and tell them flittered across his face. "One of the addresses turned out to be the leading supplier of printer's ink for the rags of London. As soon as we arrested him, he refused to tell us where his mummy ink was being kept. As we caught him in the

154

process of trying to destroy some rather decent Rembrandt copies, we have a suspicion he's buried some of his evidence in those rather large vats of ink in his factory." Lestrade smiled wryly as the reactions to his story ricocheted around the table. "Mr. Holmes, are you going to eat that?"

The Adventure of the Silent Witness

by Tracy J. Revels

My good friend Sherlock Holmes never accepted cases for publicity, and was often content to allow inept investigators to take credit for his virtuoso performances. Readers of the sensational press will perhaps recall the infamous crime that occurred in the village of St. Anthony some twenty years ago. At last, thanks to a visit from an individual most intimately associated with this harrowing event, I may reveal the true and astonishing details of how Sherlock Holmes brought one of the nation's most vicious murderers to justice.

It was a lovely spring morning and I was returning from a delightful stroll about Regent's Park when I saw a woman, swathed in black crepe and a heavy veil, standing across the street from our residence. She seemed hesitant, glancing up and down from the window to the door, all the while twisting a velvet bag in her gloved hands. I had been Holmes's friend long enough to recognize a potential client. I approached her and tipped my hat.

"Madame, perhaps I can assist you. Are you in search of Sherlock Holmes?"

My question drew an audible gasp. "Yes, I am. Are you Mr. Holmes?"

"No, but I am his friend and confidant. My name is – "

"Doctor Watson! The man who writes the stories!" Her voice, which had been low and fearful, suddenly lilted into earnest delight. "I am happy to make your acquaintance. My name is Margaret DuRant, and my late husband was your greatest admirer. He too was a doctor with literary ambitions." She gestured toward the building. "You are correct, I wish to consult with Mr. Holmes, but I fear that he will find my problem absurd."

I did my best to be reassuring. "Do believe me when I say that Mr. Holmes is receptive to conundrums of all varieties and would be very interested to hear your case."

There was just a hint of a smile beneath the black lace of her veil, and I realized that I had perhaps oversold my own curiosity as to her predicament. I felt my face grow warm as she reached out and shook my hand.

"Then I will trust you to be my advocate. If all else fails, I will at least have met the gentleman whose adventures gave my beloved husband so many happy hours."

With pleasure, I escorted her across the street and up to our sitting room. Holmes met us at the door, begging us to excuse the condition of the chamber. There was barely room to walk between the piles of newspapers and debris from various chemical experiments. Holmes had no doubt glanced us from the window and tried to tidy the place before we could climb the stairs.

"My deepest condolences on the recent loss of your husband," Holmes said, as introductions were made. "It is his death that brings you to me, I presume?"

The lady turned back her veil. She was truly magnificent woman, not above thirty, with a perfect milk-and-roses complexion, bright blue eyes, and a determined chin. Yet I could sense that self-possession was difficult for her, and that she was struggling with deep and painful emotions.

"No, Mr. Holmes, my husband's death was a tragic accident. Another problem brings me here, one that concerns my dear little ward, Laura Henley. She is the only surviving witness to a terrible crime. Surely you have heard of the murders at the village of St. Anthony?"

Holmes took his seat, nodding solemnly. "I was in Florence at the time, resolving a matter of some concern to the descendants of the Medici. There was, I read, an arrest made in the affair?"

"Yes, but the man is a harmless, deluded fellow who talks to trees. No one who knows him could truly believe that he would murder children in their beds!"

"Then justice has not been served," Holmes said. "If it is not too distressing for you, Madame, would you please review the facts in the case? It would be helpful to hear them from someone who is not a sensation-seeking reporter."

The lady opened her bag and pulled out a small notebook. "I knew you might ask me to do so, and I have written down everything that I can recall. I keep a diary – therefore I feel confident as to my chronology of the events."

"An ideal client," Holmes said. "Please proceed."

"The village of St. Anthony is very small and almost all of our people are simple farmers and artisans. There is only one significant street in our village, and along it lie the train station, the police office, and a few businesses. The center of sociability is the Black Sheep Pub, which also serves as our inn. There are more than a dozen homes in the village, but most people live in the countryside. The Tudor manor of Hawkhurst is just to our east, on a slight ridge, as if peering down upon us. Sir Henry Dunham lives there, and many of our people are his tenants and workers. Is this clear?"

"Exceedingly."

The lady looked back to her notes. "It was two years ago that these events were set into motion. Mr. Joseph Henley, the village blacksmith, went to Brighton for a holiday and returned with a wife and seven step-children, whom he soon adopted and gave his name. The Lonely Bachelors nearly all had apoplexy."

This strange statement struck me as needing explanation. "Lonely Bachelors?"

"A silly club, Doctor Watson, made up of unmarried fellows in the village. They meet every Thursday night at the Black Sheep. They were offended that Mr. Henley, who had been viewed as the staunchest of their tribe, fell from grace. It seems that he had met the widowed lady at a seaside concert and married her less than two days later."

"She was beautiful?" I asked.

"She was rich," Holmes snorted. Mrs. DuRant nodded in my friend's direction.

"Mr. Holmes has the heart of it – the lady was comfortable, having received a large insurance settlement upon her husband's passing. She was at least a decade older than poor Mr. Henley, and no sooner had they arrived than she insisted they rent the finest house in St. Anthony. She had pretensions of gentility that – to speak plainly, sir – soon made her an object of contempt. She had clearly come from humble stock, and her sudden wealth was not accompanied by good breeding. She wore silks and satins, but when angered had the vocabulary and lungs of a fishwife. None of the local women cared for her, and after she forced Mr. Henley to give up his shop, he became an object of derision to the men as well."

"And the children? Were they equally obnoxious?" Holmes asked.

"I was only beginning to know them when Julian – my late husband – resigned from the Lonely Bachelors Club and I likewise renounced my career as the village schoolteacher at the time of our marriage. They were not bad children at all. There were seven of them – my pupils were Louise, the twin boys Samuel and Stephen, Mary, Ellen, and Eddie. They had their share of naughtiness – especially the boys. Louise, who was sixteen, had an inflated opinion of her looks and marital prospects. She was breaking village lads' hearts by the score, but otherwise, they were normal, robust, and interesting children." The lady smiled and removed a small picture from her bag, handing it to me. It was a photograph of a diminutive girl dressed in a starched pinafore. "This is Laura, the youngest child. She was just five when the family took up residence, and six when the awful event occurred. I had not made her acquaintance at the time, but the local gossips said she was exceptionally shy."

The lady hesitated. The hand that gripped the notebook began to quiver.

"Now I will explain the tragedy. On the evening of the fourteenth of March, a year ago, someone entered the Henley home under cover of darkness. It would not have been difficult, for few people bother to lock their doors in St. Anthony. This unknown person murdered the family in their sleep. Laura, we believe, must have been awakened by a sound and crawled beneath the bed she shared with her sister Ellen. We think this is how she was overlooked by the killer. The rest of the family was bludgeoned, their heads quite . . . caved in . . . ."

The lady's composure slipped. I quickly fetched her a glass of water, which she accepted with whispered apologies. Holmes waved a hand.

"Perhaps I can summarize and you correct any error," he said. "The victims were killed in their beds with one notable exception, that being the oldest girl, Louise, whose body was found in the kitchen. She was not struck, but strangled to death. The tragedy was discovered around daybreak, by a constable who was making his morning rounds when he noticed that the front door was ajar. When he called out to the residents and received no answer, he stepped inside to investigate. He found the bodies, raised an alarm, and soon half the neighborhood had swarmed inside."

"Yes, you have it exactly. My husband served as coroner."

"Did he speculate as to a weapon?"

"He believed it was a smooth but heavy object, perhaps a cane or a club, wielded with considerable violence. No such item was found in the house, though a bowl of blood in the kitchen indicated that the murderer had taken time to wash his hands and clean his weapon before he departed."

Holmes closed his eyes. I knew he was working to picture the ugly scene in his mind as carefully as any painter might craft a beautiful masterpiece. "The oldest girl was the last to die. Surely her screams and struggles would have roused the others, had she been the initial target. That is instructive. There were no signs of any . . . outrages upon the poor lass?"

The lady blushed, but shook her head. "None. My husband's opinion was that the murderer killed her and dropped her to the floor, then went away." She slipped her notebook back into her bag. "And now I come to the crux of the matter, Mr. Holmes. The death of the entire Henley family left poor Laura without kith or kin in the world. My husband and I took her in, and a short time later our local magistrate ruled that she could stay with us. Her inheritance is now all in a trust, so that when she comes of age, she will have a comfortable start in the world. As much as her sad story grieves me relate, I will tell you that Laura has brought great happiness to my world. Julian and I had no children of our own, and from the very start Laura was kind, good, obedient, and loving toward us. Her only flaw was her silence – we could not induce her to speak. Julian found no physical reason for her muteness, nor did several specialists with whom we consulted. Laura can communicate her basic wants via hand signs, and I am working to teach her how to write, though her progress is painfully slow. However, I have no doubts as to her innate intelligence. And now, Mr. Holmes, my story becomes even more dark and fearful, for I must tell you about her dollhouse."

I sat straighter in my chair. Holmes's brows lifted. There was something in the lady's manner that made the simple word seem sinister.

"After Laura came to live with us, Julian gave her a large dollhouse with three floors and a half-dozen rooms, all of them furnished with tiny tables, chairs, and beds. The kitchen was so lifelike you could imagine a family of pixies pouring milk from a real glass pitcher and baking bread in the tiny cast iron oven. Laura was enthralled, and would spend all day playing with it. It had been in her nursery for almost a month before I noticed the changes she had made.

"Laura is genius at construction with scraps of paper, fabric, and yarn. At first I thought she was merely redecorating the house to her liking, but then I realized that she had transformed it to resemble, in every detail, the home in which her family had lived and died. Looking even closer, I saw, to my horror, that she had replicated the scene of the crime. She had manufactured little dolls out of clothespins and string, dressed them in tiny nightgowns, and used red ink to splatter on their faces and on the walls. I was so horrified I was about to snatch up the abomination and hurl it into the street, but Julian stopped me.

"'Don't you see?' he asked, "Laura is trying to tell us something about the crime she witnessed. She cannot speak or write, but she can build. Somewhere in this exhibit is, perhaps, a vital clue to the killer's identity.'"

"It was pointless to question Laura, or to argue with my husband. Once its construction was complete, Laura abandoned the dollhouse for her other toys, which allowed Julian to take his lens and inspect each room. He spent many evenings with it – Mr. Holmes, I feared he would go mad, so intense was his obsession. I urged him to walk away from the thing, to take some recreation. At last he agreed to go to the Black Sheep and share a pint with the Lonely Bachelors. He returned very late, and rather in his cups, but just as he was tumbling into bed he told me that he had shared his problem with his friends, and they would be around soon to see the grisly relic for themselves. He hoped they could help him make sense of the thing.

"That very night, only an hour after we had retired, there was a knock at the door. It was a lad with a note that one of the cottagers had suffered

160

a terrible seizure and medical help was required. Julian was none too steady on his feet when he rode out, warning me not to wait for him. Yet I could not sleep. A storm had come up, the lightning seemed determined to rip the sky to pieces. Poor Laura was equally alarmed. Julian had not returned by breakfast, and at mid-morning, Constable O'Shane arrived with the terrible news. My husband's body had been found in a quarry between the village and the cottage. Perhaps lightning had spooked the horse, which had slipped and tumbled down a ravine. My husband was crushed in the fall."

Holmes seized a pen and jotted some notes on his sleeve cuff. "This event occurred?"

"Three months ago – and we never learned who had summoned my husband. But my story has not reached its conclusion. My husband was well-loved in the community, and virtually everyone attended the wake for him. His friends the Bachelors, however, took me aside and asked if they might see the dollhouse. They had talked among themselves and wished to examine the thing that had mystified Julian. I showed it to them, and to a man they went pale. The Vicar mumbled a prayer, and Sir Henry demanded to know, from Constable O'Shane, if all the details were accurate to the morning he found the bodies. He swore that they were, and Mr. Darby, the solicitor, pondered whether the dollhouse should be turned over to some more experienced investigator. In the end, they left it in my care. I moved it to the back of the nursery and covered it with a curtain, for I could not bring myself to destroy it, nor could I bear to look upon it every day.

"A week later, I had to travel to Edinburgh to deal with some financial matters. I took Laura with me, but Mrs. Smith, my housekeeper, remained behind. The next morning, I received a telegram begging me to return, for during the night someone had broken into the house. Mrs. Smith had heard footsteps, but was too frightened to do more than cower beneath the sheets as a horrible smashing sound came from the nursery. When she gathered the courage to emerge from her room, she found the dollhouse broken into kindling!"

Holmes leaned forward. "What was the effect of its destruction on young Laura?"

"She looked sad but made no protest."

"Was the crime investigated?"

"Both of our constables came and examined the scene. They dismissed it as village mischief."

"Fools!" Holmes snapped. "Yet . . . this is not why you have come to me, is it? Something else remains."

"You are a wizard, sir. Indeed, there is one more act to this drama. A week ago, out of the blue, a large package arrived on our doorstep. It came with a note saying '*For a dear child – From a friend.*' Inside was a splendid dollhouse, the same size and shape as the one that had been destroyed. I have no idea who sent it to her, or why. I know only one thing – she has again reconstructed the scene of the crime, in every detail."

Early afternoon found us at the station, waiting to board the train for St. Anthony. Holmes had sent me out with our client, insisting that I treat her to a luncheon while he quickly conferred with his friends at Scotland Yard. Mrs. DuRant excused herself to the washroom, and Holmes hurriedly filled me in on his findings.

"The case was bungled from the start. Half the village wandered through the house, gawking at the corpses and collecting souvenirs. It was nearly a week before the locals decided they were out of their depth. Inspector Blaine was sent – he's a third-rate man at best – and he fixed the blame on the town lunatic. It is a disgrace to the nation, Watson. I must reconsider the wisdom of ever accepting another international inquiry!"

I could only smile at my friend's hubris. "Do you really think that you can solve this mystery, which is now more than a year old?"

Holmes scowled at me. "Give me proper evidence and I can solve a case that is three-hundred years old. Perhaps someday I will share with you my conclusions about the vanished princes in the Tower! But here comes the lady, and that whistle signals our train."

Our journey required more than an hour along the tracks. I found Mrs. DuRant to be the most pleasant of travelling companions. For a time, Holmes ignored our conversation on congenial subjects, but finally he roused himself from his study of the passing countryside and asked the lady to describe the individuals who composed the Lonely Bachelors society.

"I do not wish to seem a gossip, Mr. Holmes."

"You must be a gossip, Madame, if I am to make progress. What is each gentleman's name, age, employment, and general demeanor?"

"Very well. Vicar Richardson is the oldest of the gentlemen, about fifty or so, sweet and kind to all, but very easily confused and addled. Mr. Darby, who I would guess to be only in his late twenties, is a solicitor with clients in several communities. He is quite rotund, a friendly, jolly fellow. Constable O'Shane is about thirty-five, a quiet, stalwart man, burly and with a great scar on his right cheek, which was given to him by a felon back when he was a night watchman in Liverpool. And, well, as for Sir Henry . . . ." The lady pursed her lips. She spoke slowly, seeming to choose her words with great care. "He is cold and said to be cruel. He was married

162

in his youth, but his wife killed herself, and everyone believes he drove her to it. He is forty years of age and, except for the company of the Bachelors, he keeps to himself. He could do much more for the poor people of the village, but he eschews all but the most essential duties of his class."

"Would you describe any of the gentlemen as handsome?"

"What an awkward question! I suppose some girls would find the constable attractive, if not for his scar and his rather morose manner, but the vicar is old, Mr. Darby is shaped like a barrel, and Sir Henry – well – is Satan considered handsome? That is whom he most resembles!"

A short time later, we arrived at St. Anthony, a lovely and bucolic, tree-lined village that seemed frozen in time. I halfway expected to see barefoot peasants tending sheep, or a Tudor gallant riding by on a velvet-draped horse. Mrs. DuRant directed our attention to the only significant dwelling along the street, a house in a strange, early Georgian style, with three floors and many windows. It projected an aura of decay: Paint peeled from its walls and one chimney was crumbling. There was a rusted chain and padlock on the door. Much to my surprise, Holmes dismissed the lady's offer to ask for the key from the policeman on duty.

"There would be nothing to see there," Holmes announced. "I am far more interested in the miniature version."

He said this loudly, in a tone that rang across the cobblestones. I sensed, rather than saw, faces at windows. Strangers are always a novelty in an English village, and I knew that we were being observed as we made our way toward the lady's residence. Holmes made a striking figure in his long checkered coat and cloth hunting cap – not for the first time, I doubted my decision to put his cases before the public, making him a celebrity. He asked a number of questions about the village, inquiring as to the location of the Black Sheep Public House, as well as the police station and the proximity of Hawkhurst. By the time we reached the widow's modest little two-story home, the entire neighborhood had been alerted to our presence.

Once inside, we were greeted by a plump, matronly housekeeper and her charge. Young Laura was a winning child, small with long blonde braids and enormous, bright green eyes that made her seem like a doll brought to life. She dropped a proper curtsey to us, but said nothing, though when my title was stated she abruptly attempted to hide behind the housekeeper's skirts.

Holmes chuckled and knelt down to her level. "Miss Laura may have had her fill of doctors who wish to force her to speak. But perhaps, young lady, you will tolerate the company of a detective? I would like to see your remarkable dollhouse, if you are willing to show it to me."

My friend had a special magic with children. Nothing in his manner was threatening, nor was he patronizing or condescending in their presence. Instantly, the little girl clasped his hand and towed him toward the hall. He signaled for us to stay behind. Mrs. DuRant ordered tea, and afterward gave me a tour of her late husband's study and consulting room. I felt an instant connection to my fellow medical man, for along with all the necessary tools of his profession he had possessed a superb library of both classical and popular literature. Seeing the piles of yellow-backed novels told me that if had we ever met, we would have been friends.

"It has been almost an hour," Mrs. DuRant said. "Do you think we should see what they are doing?"

I agreed and we moved to the nursery. I tapped on the door, then eased it open. Much to my surprise, Holmes was not inspecting the dollhouse with his lens, but instead was lying prone on the floor across from Miss Laura, arranging tin soldiers in a rather fantastic formation.

"A-ha, rescue! We were recreating the battle of Waterloo, and I am afraid the Iron Duke was getting the worst of it this time!" He knocked over the Wellington figure as the little girl clapped her hands. She grinned with delight, but made no sound.

"Why, these are Julian's old playthings!" Mrs. DuRant said. "Laura, where ever did you find them? Mr. Holmes, I do apologize!"

"Do not scold her, Madame. I have rarely passed a more entertaining hour."

While Holmes helped the child pick up the scattered toys, I made my own inspection of the dollhouse, which had been pushed into a corner. It was a very large one, a cutaway style, with some twelve individual chambers. All were decorated with incredible detail, filled with furnishings such as chairs, beds, tables, and bureaus. While many of the pieces were clearly the work of a toymaker, others had sprung from the little girl's imagination. The dolls in the beds appeared splattered with blood, or rather red paint, and one doll was placed in the kitchen, lying beside a table that bore a bowl of fruit, a pitcher of water, and a bulls-eye lantern. I reached inside, careful not to disturb anything, and peeked beneath a bed. There, the smallest of all the dolls was confined, as if hiding under the covers.

"Watson!"

I jumped away from the dollhouse. Holmes was bidding his tiny hostess goodbye. Once we were in the hallway, he turned to Mrs. DuRant.

"I see there is a small building behind this house. Is it occupied?"

"No, though I am having it renovated to be a sewing room for Mrs. Smith."

"Do you think the three of you could shelter there tonight, without undue inconvenience?"

To the lady's credit, she did not balk at the odd request. "Of course, but why?"

"Because I have every reason to believe that this matter will resolve itself before dawn, provided I have a clear field for operation. You will not mind giving me a key to the back door? Excellent. You will need to retire to the outside room at sundown and extinguish all lights. You will do this?"

"Yes. Laura will think it a grand adventure."

We departed the house immediately. Holmes sent me to engage rooms for us at the Black Sheep while he made a detour to the telegraph office. On his return, we went into the pub and ordered our supper, along with two pints of ale. The small barroom quickly filled with locals, including sweat-drenched farmers, a few artisans still in their aprons, and the strange quartet which we recognized as the Lonely Bachelors. Holmes clinked his mug to mine.

"Here's to good fortune, Watson. Thursday is the traditional gathering night of this crew – there would have been more work in store for us had Mrs. DuRant arrived a day earlier. What would you say to another pint?"

"I'd say I have not finished – "

Holmes was suddenly on his feet, calling for a second round. Then, in a rare moment of clumsiness, he stumbled on the warped boards and spilled a good deal of his ale across the cassock of the village vicar. Holmes insisted on buying the man and all his friends a drink to make amends. The next thing I knew, he was calling me over, introducing me to the gentlemen who, suddenly, had become his closest mates. The vicar seemed truly amused by Holmes's antics, and the swarthy, bearded nobleman offered a thin, sour smile. The solicitor, who was clearly already in his cups, was happy to join my friend in a game of darts. Only the constable seemed unwilling to indulge in the new comradery.

"And what is your business here?" he asked, after Holmes had lost several matches to both the solicitor and the vicar. "Your name is certainly well-known."

"I would hope it would be, to a man in your profession," Holmes proclaimed. "And I am here to bring the murderer of the Henley family to justice."

The vicar nearly spat out his drink. "You can't mean it! You've solved the mystery?"

"Indeed I have," Holmes proclaimed. "As well as the murder of the good Doctor DuRant – for I am convinced he was killed by the same evil hand."

Sir Henry frowned. "What makes you say this? Our friend died in an accident."

"So his killer would have you believe. But what could be easier than driving a horse from a road on a dark and blustery night, especially when its rider was already intoxicated?"

The constable's face went pale. "Why would you think – "

"Because the silent witness has told me," Holmes said, draining the remainder of his drink and signaling the barmaid for another. "You gentleman saw the original dollhouse created by little Miss Henley. Though it was destroyed, another has taken its place, in even finer detail. It tells me everything I must know, and I will use it as evidence to convict a killer. Inspector Lestrade will be here in the morning to slap on the darbies. Now, if you gentlemen will excuse me . . . Sorry, Watson," he muttered, staggering against me as he rose from his seat. "My head is a bit light. Perhaps I should retire for the evening."

I felt my cheeks glow with embarrassment. Never had I seen Holmes in such a sorry state, as drunken as a sailor on shore leave after a year-long cruise! We struggled up the stairs to our room. The moment I slammed the door, Holmes bolted for the window.

"Quick, Watson, there may not be a moment to lose."

"Holmes? Good heavens, have you taken leave of your senses?"

"On the contrary, I have rarely felt the game this invigorating." He threw open the window. "Ah, a stout oak. Our job is easier. I doubt you would have enjoyed scampering down the drainpipe."

Before I could beg him to halt and give me time to digest these developments, he threw his leg over the sill and was out and into the heavy branches of the tree, agile as a monkey. With some trepidation, I followed. The moment we came to ground, Holmes grabbed my sleeve and tugged me through a series of inky pathways until we reached the rear of Mrs. DuRant's house. Holmes leapt the fence and admitted me with an exaggerated bow. Once we were inside, he paused only long enough to light a candle.

"Holmes, why in heaven's name did you make such a scene?"

"Because, Watson, I believe that our killer is as nervous as he is vicious. Now he knows the clock is ticking, and he has only one evening to destroy the evidence of his crime."

"So it is one of the Lonely Bachelors?"

"Yes. I have my man."

As he spoke, Holmes led me through the darkened house, into the nursery. He edged the dollhouse into a patch of moonlight, then motioned for me to take a spot behind a large chest of toys. He blew out the candle and slipped behind the curtains.

"Holmes, who – ?"

"Not a word, Watson! We must wait in silence."

I inwardly groaned, especially as I perceived that the post I had been assigned was none too comfortable. Fortunately, I did not have to endure the cramped position for more than an hour. The village clock had just struck midnight when there was a scraping at the glass. I risked a glance over the top of the chest and saw a shadowy figure standing outside, endeavoring to open the window. He pushed it up, then slithered inside. He was cloaked, his face covered with a velvet mask. There was something in his movements that suggested power and strength, as well as grim determination. I immediately regretted not having my trusty army revolver in my coat pocket.

The man rose to his feet and approached the dollhouse. He hesitated, as if listening for sounds in the dwelling, then removed something from his cape. It was a short, heavy stick, and with a sharp gasp he raised it above his head.

Holmes leapt forward, seizing the wrist that held the club. The man spat out a curse and spun around. My friend had the advantage of surprise, but his adversary was clearly stronger. For a horrible moment they twirled together, the other man bearing down as if eager to wrap a hand around Holmes's throat. I sprang from my spot, but before I could reach them Holmes twisted one leg around and tripped his opponent. The man fell, losing his grip upon the heavy club, but there was a flash of metal in the moonlight as he drew a snub-nosed pistol from his cape. In my rush to come to Holmes's aid, I seized the first likely weapon at hand and, without thinking, brought it down on the villain's head. He collapsed, unconscious.

"Bravo, Watson! I owe you my life," Holmes laughed. "And I see that you owe Miss Laura a new hobbyhorse!"

It did not seem to me a time for joviality. "Holmes, who is it?"

"The fiend of St. Anthony," Holmes replied, reaching down to rip away the man's mask. "Constable O'Shane."

"So you knew he was the murderer because of a . . . *toy*?"

Holmes had feigned drunkenness in the pub, but he had not deceived his audience as to his intentions. At daybreak, Inspector Lestrade was staring down at the prisoner, whom we had trussed up in DuRant's old consulting room after I cleaned and bandaged the rather ugly gash that I had made on his forehead.

Holmes settled into the doctor's chair, placing his palms together. "I suspected O'Shane from the start – after all, he was the town's night watchman and his presence around a home, even if detected by a sleepless neighbor, would not have raised an alarm. Then there was the murder weapon, described as a smooth object, much like a constable's Billy club, and wielded with considerable skill. The family was a large one, so it was easy for him to lose count and miss the smallest child, who had crawled under her bed. No doubt he was also in a hurry to confront his final victim, the one found in the kitchen . . . Miss Louise."

"But his motive?"

"A simple one. He was in love with the girl, who was a striking beauty. But she had social pretensions and elevated expectations. Watson, you recall Mrs. DuRant's words on the subject of her careless heart-breaking."

I watched our prisoner as Holmes spoke. His face drained of color and his bottom lip began to tremble. Whatever courage and nerve he had possessed had deserted him, and he rocked woefully back and forth within his bonds. Then, to my surprise he murmured a phrase – "She said they would never allow it."

Holmes gave a grim smile of satisfaction. "And so you killed them all, to clear the way to her. You woke her from her sleep, brought her to the kitchen, told her what you had done. Perhaps your hands were still bloody. Miss Louise reacted in horror. She began to scream. You had to stop her. So you put your brutish fingers on her tender throat and began to squeeze."

Constable O'Shane gave a rough, grief-stricken cry. If not for the sheer horror of what he had done, the magnitude of his crime, I could have taken pity on him. Holmes turned, addressing his comments to Lestrade.

"And so the girl died. Now O'Shane could do nothing except clean his weapon and slip away. The next morning, he 'found' the bodies. No doubt he was alarmed when he saw that he had left the youngest member of the family alive, but when it became clear that the little child was robbed of speech, and the detective from London pinned the crime on a local lunatic, O'Shane relaxed. Imagine his terror when his old friend DuRant later announced to the Lonely Bachelors that the Miss Laura had recreated the crime scene in perfect detail in her toy. O'Shane knew that a fatal clue remained and a keen eye might catch it."

"And what clue was that?" Lestrade asked.

Holmes motioned to the dollhouse, which he had carried into the room and placed upon the doctor's desk. "Here, in the kitchen. What do you see that strikes you?"

Lestrade frowned. Clearly he felt such an exercise was beneath his dignity. "A stove, a table, and chairs . . . is that a dolly on the floor?"

Holmes sighed. "Look at the table. What do you see on it?"

Lestrade squinted. "A bowl, a pitcher and . . . a lantern?"

"A bulls-eye lantern. Not a common item of housekeeping in a kitchen, but absolutely essential to a policeman. In his hurry to clean his weapon and exit the house, O'Shane forgot about it. The next morning, he retrieved it after 'finding' the tragic scene."

Lestrade frowned. "Wouldn't it have been easier to have just written out the name of the killer? Or even . . . made a dolly of him?"

"I doubt Miss Laura saw the constable clearly. Something woke her, and she hid beneath her sibling's bed, hearing the killer's actions as he snuffed out her sister's life. Frightened, she stayed in her hiding place until his footsteps faded away. On creeping out and wandering the house, everything she observed was burned into her memory, even as the horror of it took away her ability to speak." Holmes turned back to his prisoner. "The night DuRant informed his cronies about the dollhouse, you knew you could take no chances, as he felt certain that he could solve the case given just a few more days and the assistance of his friends. You waylaid him on the way to a patient –you contrived the false pretense to draw him from the house. But the Lonely Bachelors insisted on viewing the dollhouse at the doctor's wake. As long as it existed, you knew that you were in danger. So at the first opportunity, when Mrs. DuRant and Miss Laura were away, you destroyed it."

O'Shane had said nothing more, but he was so white I feared he would faint.

"Then where did this new dollhouse come from?" Lestrade asked.

"A friend," Holmes said, "one who knew of the mysterious creation that had been wrecked. That limits us to three potential donors. The vicar is too addled, and the solicitor hardly seems the type to be so generous. But Sir Henry . . . ." Holmes turned with a tight smile. "This dollhouse is a very pricey plaything, delivered from the finest store in London. I suspect that only the richest man in St. Anthony could afford such a gift."

"But why?"

"Because he wanted to know the truth. He wanted to avenge his friend – and perhaps," Holmes said, with a pointed look to me, "he wished to impress a beautiful young widow. He longed to change her hostile feelings toward him, and assisting in the solution of the crime would do so. He trusted in the child's talents and the widow's fears to bring a competent investigator onto the scene."

My jaw dropped. Holmes shrugged.

"To steal a phrase, '*The lady doth protest too much.*' There is an attraction, one that they each recognize and now will be free to pursue." Holmes pulled out his watch. "As it is almost seven, I would suggest, Lestrade, that you take your prisoner on to London, and allow Watson and me a few moments with the lady and her ward, to assure them that they are in no danger."

As readers will recall, Inspector Lestrade was hailed for his diligence in bringing a murderous monster to justice. Constable O'Shane, it was later revealed, was a Liverpool tough who had fled the city and, thanks to forged credentials, reinvented himself as an officer of the law. He committed suicide in his cell, leaving behind a note that confessed to his crimes. Sir Henry's influence spared Mrs. DuRant and little Laura any further notoriety.

Only yesterday, the case was recalled to me when I received a visit from Mrs. Laura Ellsworth, the former Miss Laura Henley, who was in London to open a gallery of her miniature palaces. She is a married lady now, and an artist of note, whose enchanted creations are found in royal nurseries across Europe. She told me of her happy life after Mrs. DuRant became Lady Margaret Dunham, and how, thanks to the love of her adoptive parents, she regained her voice. She was very disappointed to have missed a chance to reminiscence with Holmes, but she left a gift for him which is currently perched atop the breakfast table. I shall be much interested to see what he thinks of the replica of our Baker Street suite, so marvelously rendered in every detail.

The Second Whitechapel Murderer
by Arthur Hall

It was, as I recall, an unseasonably fine day at the beginning of the spring of 1895 when, returning to our Baker Street lodgings after an invigorating morning walk, my friend Mr. Sherlock Holmes and I had hardly closed our front door when a harsh rapping upon it surprised us. We glanced at each other and he turned back at once and opened it wide.

"Lestrade, my dear fellow," he cried with some astonishment. "What has brought you to us in such an excited state? I think it would be as well if you came in and took coffee with us, so that you can explain when you've recovered your composure." The little detective mumbled his thanks and took the stairs with us, and Holmes called to Mrs. Hudson before we entered our sitting room.

When we had settled ourselves, my friend looked at the inspector with some curiosity as we awaited the arrival of our coffee.

"I cannot recall seeing you in such an agitated frame of mind previously, Inspector. What can have transpired to induce this?"

Lestrade's bulldog-like countenance took on a look that I interpreted as near to despair. "Mr. Holmes, I thought we had finished with this dreadful business, though we were unable to get anywhere with it."

At that moment our good landlady entered with a tray of cups and a steaming coffee-pot, and so silence prevailed until she had left. I rose then and began to pour, as Holmes replied. "To what do you refer, Lestrade?"

"The Whitechapel murders, of a few years ago. As far as we know at the Yard, Mary Kelly was the final victim. There has been none other since November of 1888."

Holmes nodded as I handed both men their cups. "She was, as you say, the last known to be slain, although I am far from certain that we are aware even now of all the victims in that case. There were several other women of the streets murdered during the 'Reign of Terror'." He frowned. "But I understood that Scotland Yard had all but given up the investigation after so long, so why are you concerning yourself with it now?"

The inspector drank and put down his cup. "The Yard never closes a file until the culprit is behind bars, Mr. Holmes. What I am upset about is the new murder of last night."

My friend and I exchanged glances of unpleasant surprise, our coffee forgotten as we stared at Lestrade.

Holmes spoke first. "Was the body dismembered in the same fashion? Are there identical features to the crime?"

The inspector took out his notebook, turned to a page and read from it. "Lottie Burrows, aged about twenty-six. Found by a constable around midnight while on his beat in Whitechapel. She was lying in an alley with an immense gash, thought to be from a surgeon's knife, carved from her chest down to her stomach. Does that not sound familiar?"

Holmes's frown deepened. "There are certain characteristics in common with the previously known victims, such as the location of the murder and the fact that a scalpel was considered to be the murder weapon. This woman was a lady of the night, I presume?"

"You put it so delicately, Mr. Holmes, but of course you are right. What other sort of woman would be in such a place at that time?"

"Quite so. I should however remind you, Lestrade, that my intended investigation at the beginning of the original murders was halted by Scotland Yard. I endured the chastisement of yourself, Gregson, and Hopkins simultaneously in this very room, as I recall."

The inspector looked away, fixing his stare on the carpet for a few moments. "To this day, I swear I know not why we were ordered to come here and speak to you in such strong terms. I can only suspect that Commissioner Sir Charles Warren wanted only Edmund Reid and Abberline on the case." He hesitated, before adding. "I suspect that something you said was reported in the press and reached the wrong ears."

Holmes shrugged. "It was certainly featured in an article in *The Standard*, quite erroneously, that I had hinted at the involvement of royalty or freemasonry at the fringes of this affair. I suppose that suggestion would have been enough to exclude me from all further proceedings, if it were taken seriously in certain quarters. I do think, however, that a little discussion between us could have cleared this up, had you sought an explanation before acting on the strength of the assumptions of an over-enthusiastic young reporter."

"I can assure you that we were following orders, Mr. Holmes. It did not sit well with either my colleagues or myself."

"And so," Holmes smiled suddenly, leaning forward in his chair and clapping his hands, "we reach our present situation, which may or may not be connected. Tell me then, Lestrade, how do your superiors view this new outrage?"

There was a moment of silence in the room, when the only sound was from the passing hansoms and four-wheelers in Baker Street.

"When I suggested any connection to the previous murders, it was ignored – I know not why. It was as if I had never spoken. Someone is hiding something, I am sure. Perhaps after all, there is truth in that newspaper article."

"At any rate," my friend said then, "it can do no harm to look into this, since Scotland Yard appears to consider it a separate enquiry, as it may yet be. But as you say, it cannot completely be ruled out that the original Whitechapel murderer may be responsible. I feel that it would be churlish to turn my back on the situation, despite the Yard's previous attitude to me regarding the matter. If you are confident, Inspector, that you will not be subjected to the wrath of your superiors for involving Doctor Watson and myself, we will glad to accompany you to the mortuary, where I will make my own examination of the body of this unfortunate woman."

We travelled together in the four-wheeler that Lestrade had waiting. This was not the first time I had visited the Whitechapel Workhouse Mortuary, where the body of Lottie Burrows had been taken, and I was anticipating without pleasure renewing my acquaintance with the place. It was situated in a large yard off Old Montague Street, a small brick building that I would have described as little more than a shed. We entered through the gates at the end of a narrow alley known as Eagle Place, and from Holmes's expression I gathered that he had not seen the place before.

The windows were of insufficient size to admit much natural light, but a number of oil lamps aided visibility. A man wearing a stained leather apron over his morning suit emerged from the surrounding shadows and extended his hand to the inspector with a pleasantness that surprised me, for it is far more usual for those with such an occupation to be of a disposition that reflects it. Lestrade introduced him as "Doctor Phillips, the appointed Police Surgeon to H Division."

"I take it that you wish to examine the body of the woman Lottie Burrows, Doctor Watson?"

"Not I, but my friend."

Doctor Phillips regarded Holmes curiously. "Did you not state your profession as consulting detective, sir?"

"Indeed so. Be assured that I have acquired sufficient knowledge to conduct such an inspection."

The mortuary doctor glanced at Lestrade, who nodded.

"Very well. I will be nearby, if you need me."

"I would be grateful," Holmes said, "if you would remain."

"As you wish."

At that, Holmes proceeded to walk slowly around the table to which we had been led, his eyes half-closed in concentration as he mumbled to himself. He stopped suddenly and leaned closer to the body.

173

"Doctor Phillips, have you made further incisions during your examination?"

"I have not yet made my examination. I was preparing to do so when you arrived."

"Then this long gash, from the trachea almost to the abdominal area, was sustained during the attack?"

"Presumably. As I said, I have done little as yet, apart from conduct some preliminary observations."

"Did they reveal to you that the heart has been removed?"

I heard a sharp inhalation from Lestrade, and concealed my own surprise.

"Indeed they did. I was about to remark upon it."

Holmes looked up from the body. "Did anything else strike you?"

"I trust you are referring to the incision itself. This was carried out with considerable surgical skill. If there is one thing I can tell you with confidence, gentlemen, it is that whoever did this was no crude butcher."

Holmes nodded slowly. "My thanks to you, Doctor. Your information has been of immense assistance." He turned towards us. "I think there is little more to be learned here. Come gentlemen, we can now leave the good doctor to his work."

Outside, we crossed the yard and stood before the coach.

"Lestrade, have the newspapers any knowledge of this, any at all?"

The inspector shook his head. "No, Mr. Holmes. As I said earlier, my superiors wish to avoid any association of this with the other murders. The incident will be treated as a separate, unconnected crime. Also, a disclosure to the contrary would almost certainly cause panic."

"Quite. It is of paramount importance that no specific details are released of the things we have just learned, nor of the crime itself."

"I have already taken such steps, although the newspapers seem to have their own sources of information sometimes, as we know. For my part, the constable who found the body and all others involved since have been sworn to silence as to all but the most basic information."

"Excellent. While this is maintained, we have a good chance of early success."

Lestrade's expression lightened. "It appears as if I was right after all, don't you think – about the connection to the original Whitechapel killings? I'm sure we all remember that the murderer, although he was never found, was perceived to possess such skill as we have just heard Doctor Phillips state was used upon Lottie Burrows."

"That is still possible, although the removal of the heart alone suggests other motives – perhaps a different killer."

"There is little more to be done," said the inspector, "until I receive Doctor Phillips' report at the Yard. I expect it later today."

"One line of enquiry is open to us at once." Holmes disagreed. "You will recall that, before my 'interference' was forbidden by the Yard, I suggested that some effort should be made to establish whether the previous victims were known to each other. As far as I am aware, this was ignored. Perhaps now, Lestrade, you might care to ascertain if there is any connection between those women and our present subject, Lottie Burrows."

"I will most certainly look into that, on my return to the Yard."

"God forbid that there should be further victims," I interjected.

I caught a quick glance from Holmes. "Indeed, Watson. And now, Inspector, I am sure that you will want to continue your enquiries from Scotland Yard. No, our thanks to you, but Watson and I will walk for a while rather than share your conveyance again. I find that exercise often promotes constructive thought."

Holmes said little as we walked. Several times I made to speak, only to be dissuaded by his expression and the knowledge gained from experience: When he is deep in thought in the midst of a case, he is best left alone.

Eventually we came upon a hansom that had just delivered its fare, and so made our way back to Baker Street. I can recollect him making but one remark during the journey.

"There are similarities, Watson, yes. And yet, from a few years ago, there is something . . . ."

This new case was clearly playing upon his mind, haunting him. It did not surprise me therefore that he instructed Mrs. Hudson on our return that he would not be requiring luncheon, and scoured his index as I ate.

"That was a delicious kedgeree, Holmes. You really should eat."

"I have no time or energy to spare. If my hypothesis is in any way correct, then there is much to do. However, old fellow, I would be obliged if you would ask our good lady to bring a pot of strong coffee."

This I did, and as we drank together I asked if he had made progress.

"Some, I believe, although I am far from certain. If I am right, I fear that more blood will be spilled soon. Tell me, Watson – are you of the opinion that, for example, a man's severed arm or leg could somehow be reattached to his body to function as before?"

I smiled. "Holmes, this is quite impossible, although I believe it has been attempted many times before now. During my service in Afghanistan, I heard old legends of successes by mythical miracle-makers, but nothing as regards truth. No, I regret that medicine cannot achieve such things, and may never."

He nodded slowly. "As I thought. And yet . . . ."

Neither of us felt an inclination to leave our rooms that afternoon, as the first signs of a dense fog were already apparent in the street below. Holmes returned to his index while I read the mid-day edition of *The Standard*, but gave up after a short while. As we sat in our armchairs and smoked, he would not be drawn as to his discoveries, as was his custom until he was quite certain that his case was complete. Mrs. Hudson served an excellent steak-and-kidney pie that was more than sufficient for us both, but Holmes merely toyed with his before pushing away his plate.

As I rose from the table, I chanced to glance out of the window.

"Holmes, we are about to receive a further visit from Lestrade."

He closed his eyes for a moment. "I have feared this, since we left him earlier."

We heard Mrs. Hudson on the stairs, and then the policeman burst into the room. "Gentlemen, good evening. I fear I have some terrible news."

"Who is the latest victim?"

"Mr. Holmes, how could you have known? I have come straight from — "

"I expected it," my friend replied gloomily. "It was highly probable if my theory is correct, and yet I could do nothing to prevent it. Pray tell me what has happened, and of any similarities or common factors shared by the killing of Lottie Burrows."

The inspector sat at Holmes's bidding but refused a cigar or glass of porter.

"A young woman, younger than the first, met the same fate in Whitechapel, less than an hour ago. Her name was Jane Moulder."

"Was her heart also removed?" I enquired.

"It appears so, Doctor. The physician who was present saw this immediately, and I expect confirmation from Doctor Phillips before long."

"She was a lady of the night, as before?" Holmes asked.

"She was, starting her trade early this evening. Her killer must have been watching for her, no doubt using this accursed fog as concealment. We can hardly dismiss the evidence now – this is the Whitechapel Murderer again."

Holmes shook his head, slowly. "No, I cannot see that as likely, despite the similarities to the previous killings. Lestrade, have you given any thought to my suggestion of making comparisons with Lottie Burrows?"

176

"I saw from my notes, as soon as I added the entries for this evening," the inspector produced his notebook and turned over several pages, "that there are two things shared by both women."

"Enlighten us, pray."

"Both worked regularly out of the same tavern, The White Hart, at 89 Whitechapel High Street."

"I recall that place from the previous murders, Holmes," I remarked.

"Quite so, Watson," he agreed.

"Again, it points to the same killer," Lestrade insisted.

Holmes leaned back in his chair. "We shall see. What of the second feature that the women had in common?"

"They both attended, from time to time, the free clinic in Brick Lane, not far away. I understand that it is run by Doctor Lawson Venables, the Harley Street surgeon, as a charitable enterprise."

"Excellent, Inspector." Holmes expression lightened at once. "Well, unless you have anything else to tell us, I see that you're anxious to return to the Yard. I will, I assure you, keep in mind the most revealing similarities between this murder and the previous Whitechapel case that you have so astutely recognised. I'm quite certain that we both will know more soon."

With that Lestrade was dismissed, looking rather bemused. I myself experienced no surprise when my friend turned to me as the inspector descended the stairs.

"Watson, what do you say to an evening enjoying the company of the revellers in The White Hart in Whitechapel High Street?"

"I cannot say I relish the notion."

"Am I then, to pursue this alone?"

"You know me too well, Holmes."

"I was certain of it. Come, old fellow, let us retrieve our hats and coats and see if we can find a hansom in this thickening fog."

It proved difficult, but after a short walk we came upon a conveyance waiting nearby. The fog swirled about us and horse trod carefully, no doubt confused by the limited visibility, but we eventually arrived in a narrow and dismal street.

"I presume the tavern to be in that direction," Holmes said as the surrounding fog muffled the cab's retreat, "since it is there that the only lighted window is visible."

We walked across to the opposite pavement, twice narrowly missing figures that loomed suddenly before us. As we neared the pub, much raucous laughter and the sound of a singing voice strained to its limit reached our ears, as did the succession of jumbled notes of an attempted accompaniment on a badly-tuned piano.

Through the shifting haze, I saw that a series of arches bridged the badly-lit street as it continued on past the building. From that direction, I heard the cries of women who had lost their companions or who were plying their trade with difficulty. The drumming of horses' hooves came to us and immediately ceased. We entered into an uproar of sound and confusion, as the "entertainment" continued and customers jostled each other, not always good-naturedly, near and around the bar. I found the thick smoke-laden atmosphere oppressive, but was relieved to see that our appearance attracted no particular attention. I would have expected some initial scrutiny in a place unaccustomed to the patronage of gentlemen, but then I saw several fellows in evening clothes, one a local member of parliament, drinking heavily with (I assumed) local young women precariously balanced on their knees. I now knew the answer to an unspoken question: Why had Holmes not employed disguises for this venture?

My friend caught the eye of a young man, hardly more than a child, who served as a waiter. Shortly afterwards, we were sitting at a corner table with two pints of ale before us. The glasses were smudged, and neither of us drank.

For the next two hours or so we were engaged in an activity that I found acutely embarrassing, and so will not record in detail here. Suffice it to say that Holmes and I were approached, as he intended, by several women who worked in The White Hart, or from it. He was his most charming self, buying drinks and subtly introducing questions into the conversation. When he was satisfied and we were again alone at our table with our drinks untouched, he leaned towards me and spoke softly.

"There is nothing more to be learned here, Watson. Most of these women knew both Lottie Burrows and Jane Moulder, but can provide no useful information as to who might have had reason to wish them harm or bring about their deaths."

"A wasted evening then, and not one I would care to repeat."

He laughed quickly. "I must apologise for causing you such discomfort, old fellow, but our time may not have been so uselessly spent as you imagine."

"But you, yourself, said that we had learned little."

"True, but for the last hour or more I have been observing that fellow leaning against the bar. From both his and the barman's demeanour, it seems obvious that they are strangers to each other, and he is therefore unlikely to be found here regularly. What do you conclude then, when I tell you that since his arrival, which was not long after ours, he has been ensuring constantly that we have not moved from our seats? I imagine that his field of vision must be exceptionally wide, since he has hardly found it necessary to turn his head."

Through the heavy veil of smoke I saw that he referred to a short, sallow-faced man, wearing a black bowler.

"You believe he has followed us here?"

"I am certain of it."

"In the fog?"

"That explains why I was unaware of it."

"Do you know him, Holmes?"

My friend gave an almost imperceptible nod. "I do, of old. His name is Saul Naughton, a paid assassin by trade. He was certainly behind the disappearance of two witnesses in the Aquinas-Piper scandal. His involvement was never proven, but the case was dismissed. Had it been placed in my hands, the embezzlers would now be in Dartmoor and Naughton would have gone to the gallows."

Keeping my gaze away from the man, I asked: "But why is he pursuing us? Could he be the murderer of those two women?"

"That is of course possible, as things stand now, but unlikely since he works strictly for payment. As to how it came to be, I surmise that this new Whitechapel killer returned to the scene of one or other of his crimes and saw Lestrade there. Possibly out of curiosity, he then followed him to Baker Street and realised that we were conducting a parallel investigation. Seeing us as a threat to his purpose, whatever it may be, and not being skilled in any other form of murder but that which he has demonstrated, he hired a professional. Hence the presence of Naughton here tonight. There are, of course, other possible explanations, but that is the one that immediately suggests itself."

"If he is as competent as you imply, we are in great danger."

"But not for the first time. Do you have your service revolver with you?"

"My hand rests upon it in my pocket."

"Capital. I also am armed. We will, I think, make it difficult for our professional murderer to earn his pay."

He rose and I did likewise. "It may take some searching to find a cab on a night such as this," he said more loudly, "so it would be as well to be on our way."

As we neared the door, I noticed that Mr. Saul Naughton avoided looking in our direction. Outside, I felt immediately relieved to be free of the clamour in that place. Holmes took my arm and guided me to the shadows of a deep doorway across the street. A few moments passed before Naughton emerged, peering into the fog in both directions before setting off the way we had arrived. As the fog swirled around him and finally engulfed him, we stepped from concealment and my friend's voice sounded strange in the dull silence.

"We will see more of him soon, I think. This way, Watson."

He led us along the side of the building to where the street continued with periodic arched sections above and shiny cobbles underfoot. Lamps shed a meagre glow at intervals, penetrating the fog hardly at all, and Holmes paused to listen often.

"Why have we chosen this way?"

"To make it easier for our friend, Naughton. As soon as he concludes that he is no longer on our track, he will hurry along here to overtake us. Doubtlessly, he is thinking that the fog will aid in his concealment and that of his intended crime."

We stood very still, the silence and the heavy fog surrounding us.

"I hear nothing."

"Nor I, as yet. Patience."

We walked on, groping with the uncertainty of the blind and continuing to listen after every few yards. Once a cat ran out of the gloom, startling me, and the dripping of escaping water from an unseen source sounded loud because of the insulating properties of the fog, but we saw no sign of human habitation. Then Holmes listened again, for longer.

"I was right. We are being followed."

"I heard no footsteps."

I stood close enough to see him shake his head. "It is a coach that pursues us, at a frantic speed."

"How can you be sure that it's Naughton?"

"I cannot, and if it is some other, nothing amiss will occur as he passes us by. However, I can't imagine many of the residents hereabouts leaving their homes on a night such as this, so keep your weapon ready."

At that we kept to the narrow pavement, moving close against a whitewashed wall. I could now hear the drumming of horses' hooves on the cobblestones, getting louder with the passing of every instant. We waited.

Even with the muffling effect of the fog, the sound became deafening, before a brougham pulled by four black stallions burst into view beneath an arch a few yards behind us. In a moment of clarity, I recognised the silhouette of a man in a bowler hat whipping up the horses and cursing continuously before Holmes gripped my arm and shouted into my ear.

"Run!"

We took to our heels at once, the echoes of our footfalls like dull hammer-blows upon the cobbles. The street was too narrow for the coach to pass without striking us, and my friend had seen this and sought to

180

shelter us. The brougham was gaining on us with great speed and I was sure that the next moment would bring death to us both, for the doorways that presented themselves were far too shallow for our purpose. I could feel the horses' breath (perhaps only in my imagination) and the crack of the whip seemed near to my face while the hooves threatened to trample me to the ground, but Holmes gripped my arm once more and pushed me against two dilapidated gates that were loose enough on their hinges to allow us space.

The coach thundered on and I caught a glimpse of the driver looking back over his shoulder and pointing something towards us across an upraised arm.

"Down, Watson!"

We sank to the ground as a dull explosion erupted like cannon fire. I recognised the sound as a shotgun blast as we rose to our feet and discharged our revolvers several times. We were rewarded with a cry of pain as the fog closed around the brougham. The sound of hurrying hooves faded, and silence descended once more.

"After our small excitement, I think we should retrace our steps and attempt to procure a conveyance," Holmes said as he brushed dust from his coat.

Doing likewise, I glanced at the scarred and torn remains of the gate. The shotgun blast had all but shredded much of the wood. We made our way back to The White Hart with some difficulty to discover a scuffle taking place outside. We emerged from the fog to see two men, accompanied by ladies of doubtful repute, hammering away at each other while the innkeeper and other customers cheered them on. It became apparent that the cab standing nearby was the source of the disagreement, each party claiming it as his own because of the unlikelihood of finding another in this inclement weather.

An impatient cabby shouted down at the combatants as he gripped the reins impatiently. "Come on now, gentlemen. Hurry and settle this, will you? I could have taken half-a-dozen fares while I'm waiting here on a night like this."

We were on our way in an instant, Holmes having offered the fellow double if he took us at once. He said little during the journey, the attempt on our lives appearing to cause him no dismay. It was I who spoke first, when we were once again safely in our rooms.

"Are you all right?"

"Perfectly."

"You aren't perturbed by our experiences tonight?"

He smiled faintly. "Not at all. I foresaw something of the like at the appearance of Naughton."

"Is he dead, do you suppose?"

"I have no way of knowing. Doubtless we'll learn more when we relate our evening's work to Lestrade tomorrow morning. For now, Watson, I will wish you goodnight."

As the door of his room closed behind him, I wondered what it was that he had seen or remembered about these hideous crimes that had escaped me unnoticed. Was it, as Lestrade continually suggested, some common feature with the original murders, or some other similarity known only to him? The question haunted me as I lay searching for sleep, until it finally overcame me.

"Hurry, Watson! I can recommend the kippers." My friend seemed in unexpectedly good spirits as I descended from my room. His own breakfast plate was a scene of devastation, and he had already called for and received a second pot of coffee.

"You indicate that time is short, Holmes. We have a full day ahead, then?"

"Indeed. We must visit Scotland Yard first thing. After that, I think we will make the acquaintance of Doctor Lawson Venables."

I took my place at the table and Holmes rang the bell.

"As the physician serving both victims," I said, "perhaps he will throw some light on the matter."

"I have no doubt that he will furnish us with some most valuable information," Holmes replied as my breakfast was set before me, "whether is he aware of it or not."

The fog of last night had cleared completely. Mid-morning had arrived by the time we found ourselves seated in the familiar confines of Inspector Lestrade's office. We had been kept waiting, unavoidably, while he issued instructions to the latest shift of constables responsible for the Whitechapel area. Holmes had once mentioned that their beats were set out in such a way as to overlap every fifteen minutes. I hoped that local residents could draw some comfort from this.

"Well, gentlemen," Lestrade began as he seated himself behind his desk, "I do hope you've managed to discover something that might help us bring these outrages to an end. I am loath to admit it, but we at the Yard have made little progress, other than to increase the number of officers who will scour Whitechapel tonight in anticipation of another killing."

"If our enquiries of today bring the results that I am hoping for, Lestrade, there will be no more victims."

The inspector smiled, I thought disbelievingly. "Is this the good news you gentlemen have brought me this morning? That would be a weight off my mind, I can tell you."

"Not quite," Holmes said, "but I may be able to clarify a related incident that you will have heard of by now. I would speculate that you have received a report of a stolen coach in Whitechapel last night. The coachman will have been found murdered or badly injured, and the conveyance itself not far away with either a dead man holding the reins or traces of blood on the cabby's seat."

Lestrade's eyes narrowed suspiciously as he picked up a sheet of paper from a pile awaiting his attention. "We have had such a report, from a constable on the early beat thereabouts. A coachman was found strangled near the corner of Commercial Street and Wentworth Street and was identified from the contents of his pockets. A different officer discovered four wandering horses harnessed to a brougham in Hanbury Street, off Brick Lane, with a corpse leaning from the driver's seat. We later recognised him as Saul Naughton, a cove we've had our eye on for some time. But how did you come to know of this?"

Holmes related the events of the previous evening, while the inspector listened attentively.

"Thank you, Mister Holmes," he said at last. "That explains these incidents satisfactorily. I am pleased to see that Doctor Watson and yourself escaped unhurt." He stretched wearily in his chair. "We must be thankful for small mercies, I suppose – we can close the file on Naughton now, but we are no nearer to finding this murderer who cuts out women's hearts." A sudden thought struck him. "Mr. Holmes, could it be, since we are concerned with hearts here, that there is some sort of romantic intention involved. A suitor whose advances were spurned, perhaps?"

My friend raised his eyebrows. "That is certainly a new and interesting line of enquiry, Lestrade, and I wish you well with it. As for Watson and myself, our efforts may yet bear fruit before long and we will without fail inform you at once."

After an indifferent luncheon at a nearby coffee house, we eventually set foot in Brick Lane. It was a thoroughfare of no less depressing appearance than the rest of Whitechapel, and Doctor Venables free clinic for the underprivileged was situated on the corner of Brick Lane and Thrawl Street, almost opposite the Frying Pan Public House.

"Doubtlessly, these premises were formerly a shop of some description," said Holmes as we entered. A long queue of dirty urchins, impoverished women holding babies, and men in various bandaged or damaged states glared at us suspiciously as we strode past them. They thought, no doubt, that we sought to obtain treatment ahead of them, and the babble of conversation took on a sinister note.

Holmes seemed oblivious to this, and we quickly reached a battered desk where a well-dressed short grey-haired man sat. He held a stethoscope against the chest of a pitifully thin elderly beggar.

"There is perhaps some small improvement," the doctor observed. "but if you persist in this excessive use of tobacco, I can promise nothing but more difficulty with your respiration."

The patient grunted something which may have been thanks and stumbled away. The doctor turned to beckon the next ailing person, and saw us for the first time.

"To what do I owe this honour, gentlemen?"

I could not tell if there was a hint of sarcasm in his voice, nor if disapproval had entered his expression. He had the face of a kindly man, as suggested by his service here, but it was also the face of a man besieged by worry. He made no effort to shake our hands.

"My name is Sherlock Holmes," began my friend, "and this is my friend and colleague, Doctor John Watson."

Doctor Venables nodded. "I have heard of you, Mr. Holmes, but I fail to see anything to attract a consulting detective here."

"We are here because both victims in the recent Whitechapel murders regularly received treatment from you. It occurred to me that you may be able to furnish some information."

The stethoscope swung against the doctor's chest as he turned away, but not before I saw the alarm in his eyes, as Holmes would have done. "I cannot imagine that I could supply anything relevant. If I have, the official force will doubtlessly recognise it."

"We are working with Scotland Yard," I remarked.

His gaze met mine for an instant, almost contemptuously, before returning to Holmes. "I have read of these crimes in the newspapers but, I repeat, I can tell you nothing more. Those women were among the many unfortunate patients I administer to. Why, in any case, would anyone commit murders and remove the hearts of the victims? It is in the nature of some barbaric ritual."

"Why, indeed," Holmes agreed. He glanced at the small framed photographic portrait among the books and bottles on the desk. "I presume that lady to be your wife, Doctor?"

The alarm returned to Doctor Venables' eyes. "Are you of her acquaintance, sir?"

"I am unsure. She resembles greatly a nurse who cared for me in a Liverpool hospital."

"Then it cannot have been her. She has never been to Liverpool, nor was she ever employed as a nurse."

"Clearly I am mistaken. That quite settles it."

Doctor Venables glared at us impatiently. "And now I must ask you to excuse me. As you see, I have many patients waiting."

The glitter in Holmes's eyes told me he had been set upon a new scent. As he closed the clinic door behind us, I asked him how we were to proceed.

"The nearest telegraph office of course, Watson."

"To report to Lestrade?"

"To seek his confirmation on a vital point."

I thought back. "Holmes, I believe I have it. Doctor Venables mentioned that the victims were found with their hearts cut out, yet Lestrade told us previously that this information was to be withheld to avoid panic. Am I correct?"

My friend beamed at me. "You progress constantly, Watson. If the good inspector confirms that this information is still restricted, then we have our first solid indication that we are on the right track."

We turned a corner to discover a dusty little Post Office between a hardware shop and a cobbler's workplace. Holmes returned in minutes.

"I have instructed the Postmaster to look for us here. I do not think the reply will be long in coming."

We walked a few paces to where a bench was situated near a horse trough and seated ourselves.

"Holmes," I said, to break the silence of a few minutes, "why did you ask after Doctor Venables' wife? I see no connection with our enquiries."

"You have evidently realised that my remarks were a ruse, old fellow, and you are quite right. It was a long shot, but quite worthwhile."

"I am afraid you have confounded me."

"It is simplicity itself. I observed Doctor Venables' response to the mention of the Whitechapel victims, and became immediately convinced that he knew more of this affair than he was prepared to confide. A reference to his wife also brought a reaction. Once I had ascertained that the lady in the photograph was indeed his wife, I asked myself if she could have ceased to care for him, bearing in mind his usual kindly nature and obvious continuing affection for her. A glance at his shirt supplied the answer."

"I confess that I noticed nothing."

"That is because you were not seeking the signs that I was convinced were there. A wife does not neglect her husband to the extent that his collar

185

is worn in a soiled condition unless they are estranged, or unless she is unable to do otherwise."

"She could be ill. But you believe, I think, that she is restrained against her will?"

"I had expected something of the sort to explain Doctor Venables' reluctance to assist us. It is not he who is committing these murders in Whitechapel, but he is being forced to collude in some way."

I was about to ask a further question when a man appeared in the doorway of the Post Office. He looked up and down the street and, on seeing us, approached with a yellow envelope which he handed to Holmes.

My friend ripped it open as the man retreated, and drew out the form from within.

"Is it as you suspected, Holmes?"

His face was grim as he thrust the paper into his pocket. "Just so. I fear we will have to forego dinner for a few hours."

Darkness had begun to fall as we took refuge in a convenient doorway within sight of Doctor Venables' clinic. Every few minutes, and sometimes at longer intervals, a bedraggled figure would emerge and trudge away in one direction or another.

"This doctor cannot be a bad fellow, Holmes, since he keeps long hours at this place, in addition to his work in Harley Street."

"That has yet to be definitely determined. It is a matter, I think, of degree."

"What are you expecting to happen?" I asked.

"Very soon now, the last patient will leave. Then, if my theory is correct, Doctor Venables will visit the man who has enlisted his aid by force. There is but one such that I have heard of who, I am convinced, is behind these new murders. I believe I know his name from references in my index, but not his motives. I hope to learn these, and to bring an end to these crimes, before this night is out."

I knew it to be useless to question my friend further. As was always his custom, he would tell me that which he wished me to know at his chosen time after the case was concluded. I sensed the mounting excitement in him as full darkness set in.

"Ah!" He exclaimed. "The doctor is locking the shop. Now, let us see which direction he chooses."

The road had been mostly quiet until now. A succession of hansoms appeared, some of them slowing down in the hope of a fare from the walking doctor. He ignored all of them, his gaze fixed straight ahead and his stride brisk. A landau and a four-horse brougham passed by before Holmes spoke again.

"We must proceed with utmost care, Watson. At all costs he must not see us."

The darkness assisted us greatly. The streets were poorly lit, some of the lamps without light completely, and we were able to stay fairly close to the physician as he left street after street behind.

In Mile End Street, near Ducking Pond Lane, a black square structure loomed out of the darkness. Doctor Venables entered it unhesitatingly and Holmes put a hand on my shoulder.

"A warehouse, formerly for imported carpets. That smell is hessian, I think."

We held back for some minutes before approaching. As we drew nearer, it became apparent that the place was disused, but had not been so for long. The exterior, such as we could see, was uncared for, its timber warped.

"Careful, Watson."

Holmes gripped the handle, and to our surprise the door opened easily. We drew our weapons and entered a dark passage leading to a vast open space. Voices could be heard from far off.

We reached the end of the passage and I thought my heart would stop as I felt Holmes stiffen next to me. Hanging before us, seemingly suspended on nothing, was the body of a young woman. Her long hair swirled slowly about her head as if she were a mermaid beneath the sea.

"She is quite dead," Holmes whispered as our surprise passed. "Immersed in formaldehyde, or a similar preservative."

"You do not seem surprised," I said in an equally low voice.

"You see before you the reason for the resurgence of the Whitechapel murders. But look beyond."

"This is a laboratory, Holmes! I have seldom seen so much equipment used in such a manner."

"For what has been attempted here, nothing less would have sufficed."

Then the voices came again, that of Doctor Venables rising to a high pitch.

"But you promised! You fiend, you gave me your word!"

A figure bathed in shadow, facing the doctor, replied in tones that chilled my blood. "I cannot release her to you until I am sure. If the procedure fails, I will need you again. I can only trust you, Venables, while I have the power to compel you to obey me."

"But I went to great lengths to assure you, before I bought this place and the equipment, that this could never succeed. Medicine cannot do the work of God. If a life is taken, it cannot be retrieved. If there is any humanity left in you, let me take Marguerite and leave here. I have promised to keep silent."

The figure moved into the pool of light from the surrounding oil-lamps. I could make out a shock of light hair and a face that could have been hewn from stone. He was of average height and moved clumsily, but it was his voice that marked him as different. A pitiless drone, it held no emotion.

"And what if the first two attempts fail? What if Leonora remains in death? No, I must have fresh material to replace that which has failed her. I will continue until I succeed. She must live again."

In that vast space, I heard a sob escape Doctor Venables. Holmes and I moved slowly and silently around the perimeter until we stood close to both men, still unseen. My friend chose that moment to intervene.

"Good evening, Mister Tiberius Fell."

Both men went still with shock, but Fell recovered first.

"I know not who you are, sir, nor what your right is to be here, but you are addressing *Doctor* Fell."

"I think not. You were dismissed from the Medical Council, despite your considerable qualifications, for conducting experiments that are forbidden."

"I was discharged by unimaginative fools, men who have no vision."

"But you served the late Professor Moriarty well, I understand, by attending to his wounded henchmen on occasion, after battles with the police."

Fell looked as if he would explode with anger. "That man was a genius, almost such as myself! What do you know of him?"

"I was there at his death. My name is Sherlock Holmes."

"You are *Holmes*?" A pistol appeared in Fell's hand and he began firing as he shouted hysterically, "You will not prevent Leonora's return to me! I will place a new heart in her breast and she will live! She is the only woman I've ever loved!"

I had a glimpse of Doctor Venables scurrying for cover behind a tall cabinet. Sheltered by a wide pillar, Holmes and I prepared to return Fell's fire. I was convinced that the man was quite mad, for he raved in a maniacal voice as he discharged his weapon around him in random directions. His shouts had become incoherent, as a splintering of glass preceded a great deluge of liquid that washed across the floor behind us.

Fell went suddenly statue-still and dropped his pistol, and we continued to hold our fire. We watched in strange fascination as he ran towards the shattered glass case, kneeling among the fragments and the wetness of the floor to embrace the body that had fallen, forever lifeless, from it.

188

"Let him have a few moments," Holmes said as Doctor Venables emerged to join us. "There is a room back there where I think your wife has been held," my friend told him. "It would be as well to take her home. You may expect a visit from Inspector Lestrade later."

Without a word, Doctor Venables made off in the direction that Holmes had indicated. A terrible wailing, an inhuman sound, that had issued from Fell's mouth ceased. A look of sudden comprehension filled Holmes's face and he turned to me urgently.

"Quickly, Watson."

But it was to no avail. The instant that I saw Fell lying there, I knew it was too late.

"Prussic acid," I explained to my friend. "Concealed on his person, I imagine."

"Another file that Lestrade can safely close."

"I cannot believe that a man well versed in medicine would aspire to something so impossible," I retorted. "Medicine will not allow for the heart of one person to be extracted and placed in the body of another. Nor, I suspect will it ever. It seems to me, Holmes, closer to witchcraft than science."

"The achievements yet to come remain as yet unknown to us," he replied. "I first suspected that Fell was behind the new Whitechapel murders when I saw in my index that he was barred from his profession for conducting some quite bizarre procedures of his own invention. At one of the London hospitals, he was discovered trying to stitch the severed arm of a corpse to the body of some poor fellow whose own arm had recently been amputated. From there he eventually entered the service of the late Professor Moriarty, as you heard. After the professor's death, he fled to Germany, where he met, became obsessed with, and married Leonora von Buhler, the remains of whom you see before you. She died of an ailing heart shortly after the couple returned to this country, and that is when Fell must have sought out Doctor Venables, whom he knew from his training days at Oxford."

"In order to abduct the doctor's wife." I ventured.

"Precisely. Having accomplished this, he was able to prevail upon Venables for his equipment and everything else that he required. I presume that Fell had contracted some form of madness to have conducted himself in such a manner, and the similarity of the victims of the original Whitechapel murderer was a convenience for him."

"So Lestrade was wrong. There was no connection, other than that, to the former crimes?"

He nodded. "So we have discovered, although the inspector's conclusions were understandable. I suppose, Watson, that it is necessary to report to that good fellow before returning to Baker Street. But cheer up, old friend, I am sure that Mrs. Hudson has kept your dinner piping hot."

The Adventure of the Jeweled Falcon
by GC Rosenquist

Chapter I

The corpse lay on its back in the dark of the alley off of Wardour Street. It was just after dusk and a brisk April breeze cut through my coat, chilling my bones as I busily searched through the contents of an open briefcase that lay on the pavement near the dead man. The victim had been a tall, thin man in life, impeccably dressed and groomed. His long face betrayed the first signs of middle age around the mouth and forehead. His head was bald except for a wide shock of neatly trimmed brown hair that extended from the ears and around the back of his head. His arms and legs were splayed out, palms up, hands open, as if he'd been caught utterly by surprise by his attacker. A black bowler cap sat by his left foot, the top of which had been punched in.

A handful of constables guarded the two ends of the alley as Holmes, down on one knee, leaned over the corpse, his long slender fingers flitting through pockets, feeling along wrinkled folds of clothing, searching for any clue that would help solve the mystery of the murdered man's death. Inspector Lestrade stood beside him, holding a brightly lit lamp over the corpse, but remaining respectfully quiet as Holmes did his work.

"This man has been murdered twice," Holmes stated.

"*Murdered twice?*" Lestrade repeated in disbelief. "How can that be?"

"Look for yourself, Inspector," Holmes offered. "Shot once in the stomach with a small caliber weapon and then strangled so violently with a wire garrote that his head is nearly decapitated."

Lestrade stretched his own neck out, took in the bloody scene, then pulled himself back. "Seems excessive to me. Why would a man shoot and then strangle his victim?" he asked.

"Because a man didn't do this, Inspector," Holmes replied. "Two men did, working in concert with each other to make sure the job was done completely."

Lestrade scratched his chin. "Hmm. A powerful man who'd made powerful enemies, wouldn't you say, Mr. Holmes?"

"Perhaps, Lestrade," Holmes said. "We won't know for sure until Watson finishes going through the man's belongings."

"Yes," I said, picking up Holmes's subtle urging in his voice for me to hurry with my search. "It seems that this man's attackers were looking for something particular. They've left quite a mess all over the alley."

Discovering nothing of value during my inspection of the man's briefcase, I expanded my search to the papers that were scattered all around. Some were invoices and receipts for items such as children's dolls and gold tie-clips – nothing of such worth to incite murder. Others were business contracts written in French. The man was a salesman of some kind.

Apparently impatient with the pace of my thorough inspection concerning everything I'd discovered, Holmes joined me in raking over the alley. It wasn't long before he found something.

In a depression under a brick at the bottom of a wall on the east side of the alley, Holmes pulled out what looked like a leather billfold. It had obviously been thrown away and lost during the attack. Holmes held it up to Lestrade's lamp and opened it. "Excellent," he said victoriously. "No money, but I've found a business license. Our victim's name is Montague Caprice and he's a pawn shop owner in Paris, a place called *Bonne Affaires* – 'Good Bargains'. Here's his return ticket to France, aboard the British steamer *Reliant*. Caprice was supposed to be aboard at half-past-six." Holmes checked his pocket watch. "The ship has long since sailed."

"He must have had business to tend to here in London, but ended up murdered before he could get back to his ship," Lestrade mused aloud.

"Precisely, Inspector," Holmes agreed. "But that leaves two questions: Was Mr. Caprice buying or selling, and what exactly *was* he buying or selling?"

"Something worth his life, unfortunately," Lestrade said.

"And if it's worth one life, that means it's worth others," Holmes said worriedly. "We must find the object and those who stole it before more murders are committed."

Chapter II

Holmes, needing a detailed itinerary of Montague Caprice's business trip and a list of his buying and selling interests in London from whomever was in charge at Caprice's shop while he was away, asked Lestrade to send a cable across the Channel. Lestrade had a high-ranking contact in the Paris Police Prefecture who owed him a favor. As Lestrade went off to Scotland Yard, Holmes and I went back to our modest lodgings at 221b Baker Street to wait for the response.

We were met at the bottom of the stairs by Mrs. Hudson. "There's a lady here to see you, Mr. Holmes," she said. Then she leaned forward and whispered suspiciously, "She's an American."

"Do have her come up, Mrs. Hudson," Holmes said.

I had just finished pouring Holmes and myself a glass of brandy to warm our bones when into our sitting room stepped a woman unlike any that I'd ever seen before. She was uncommonly tall with skin the color of a pearl in the sunlight. Her black hair, shining in the flickering lamp light like a cannonball, was cut severely short and parted on the left, rather like a boy's haircut, revealing a long, slender neck that plunged into a surprisingly muscular set of shoulders. I'd wager that, given the chance, she could have easily wrestled me to victory.

Her oval face seemed carved out of a block of polished marble, and the bone structure underneath protruded boldly at sharp angles, exposing high cheek bones and a prominent chin. Her eyebrows were two thin black wisps hanging over a pair of large, deep-set topaz eyes. Her nose was strong yet delicate, her lips full and painted a dark shade of red. Dazzling diamond earrings hung from her earlobes and a rather unique necklace, razor thin and metallic, hung loosely around her neck. She wore a tight fitting, low-cut silk maroon dress that barely dropped past her knees and had a short slit on the left side, defiantly ignoring the current conservative fashion of the day. A pair of black, high-heeled, leather boots grounded her securely to the floor. For an American woman, she had an exotic, foreign beauty that was simply stunning. I couldn't take my eyes off of her.

She held her hand out for Holmes, whom seemed as taken by her visage as I was. "My name is Florence Mansfield," she said in a clear, low, unaccented voice, confirming her New World origin. "I left my coat and hat downstairs, I hope that's all right."

"Fine, fine, Miss Mansfield," Holmes said. "Would you care to join us in a glass of brandy?"

"That would be lovely."

As Holmes went to pour her a drink, I introduced myself and offered her a seat by the fire.

"I've heard so much about you, Mr. Holmes," she began as she crossed her long legs. Holmes handed her a glass and sat down across from her. "In America, you're quite the celebrity, you know?"

"I am?" Holmes said, genuinely surprised at her comment. "I had no idea."

193

"Yes," she continued. "In Chicago, where I'm from, we so look forward to reading your adventures in *The Strand*."

"I'm afraid the blame for that should fall upon my capable biographer, the good Doctor Watson, here," Holmes said, motioning towards me. "His blatant exaggerations and colorful prose often turn my most mundane cases into penny dreadfuls of the first order."

"Don't be so modest, Mr. Holmes," Miss Mansfield said through a fawning smile. "Those adventures are the reason I'm here. I desperately need your unique talents in a matter of utmost importance."

"I see. First, tell me, this is just for my curiosity . . . is it the current rage that American women go out without their fingernails painted?"

"My fingernails?" she repeated and looked at them.

The polish on her nails, a practice that some women had begun to follow, had mostly flaked away, and the nail on her left hand middle finger was cracked to the quick, a detail I'd failed to see earlier.

"Oh, I do apologize, Mr. Holmes. I've just arrived in London and I haven't had time to have them repaired."

This didn't ring true to me, as everything else on her was perfect: Her hair, her clothes, make-up, her jewelry.

"About my case – "

"I'm listening, Miss Mansfield."

She took a long sip of brandy from her cup then her eyes focused on Holmes. "Have you ever heard of the Jeweled Falcon of Malta, Mr. Holmes?"

"No. I can't say that I have."

Miss Mansfield took in a deep breath and continued. "In 1530, the fabulously wealthy Knights of Rhodes, a remnant of a Crusader army, talked Charles V, the King of Spain, into giving them Malta, Gozo, and Tripoli. In return, the Knights of Rhodes had to pay Charles a yearly tribute. The first of these tributes, ordered by Grand Master Villiers de L'Isle d'Adam to be made by Turkish slaves, was the sculpture of a glorious golden falcon, encrusted from crown to talon with the finest jewels in the Crusader's coffers. A foot tall, it proved to be one of the great artistic masterpieces in history. Countless fanciful rumors circulated at the time about the falcon's breathtaking beauty. One story told of how the jewels on the falcon's golden skin lit up so brightly in the sunlight that those who looked at it directly went blind."

Miss Mansfield stopped here to finish her brandy. Her eyes were wide and filled with the excitement of telling the story, and her hand

194

had a slight tremble as she brought the glass to her lips. As she began again, I found myself getting caught up in the tale.

"Well, as you can imagine, something that beautiful, that priceless, would have the thieves of the entire world chasing after it. So, when the falcon was put on a galley commanded by the one of the Order's members, a French knight named Cormier, for transport to Charles, it was stolen. A famous admiral of buccaneers sailing out of Algiers at the time, Barbarossa, took the knight's galley, and with it the falcon. Documents at the time record that it stayed in Algiers for the next hundred years. Then, in 1713, it somehow surfaced in Sicily, possessed by King Victor Amadeus II. From there it shows up in Turin. In 1734, it turned up in the possession of a Spanish soldier who was with the army that took Naples. But by then the falcon had been painted with a thick layer of black enamel by someone very clever in an effort to hide it's true worth, and this lowly Spanish soldier had no idea what it really was. Seventy years later, the Falcon somehow found its way to Paris, and for the next eighty-nine years, Mr. Holmes, it has been passed around Paris like a common cold, going from one antique dealer to another, finally spending as much as twenty years in the possession of a family-run junk resale shop on the banks of the Seine."

The story was starting to sound familiar to me now. My mind was starting to piece the puzzle together. Could our most recent murder victim, Montague Caprice, be the owner of this junk shop of which she spoke? I glanced at Holmes and he flashed me a quick, knowing nod. He was thinking the same thing.

She continued, "I first read about the jeweled falcon in a history book I took from my father's library when I was a child. I've been obsessed with it ever since, traveling the world and tracking its movements from one location to another until a few days ago, when I was given information from a trusted source that the falcon was now in London, in the hands of yet another man ignorant of what he truly had. Unfortunately, Mr. Holmes, the trail has suddenly gone cold and I need your help to find the falcon for me. I'm not in the least familiar with London or its underground black market. I will pay whatever retainer you demand and triple your usual fee."

Holmes, without removing his gaze from hers, finished his glass of brandy and then gingerly placed it on the end table.

"It's a fabulous story, Miss Mansfield," he said, puzzling his fingers together in his lap, "but I'm afraid you confuse me with a treasure hunter."

"You won't help me then?" she asked.

195

"Dozens of these treasure-hunt stories have come across my doorstep over the years, and each one of them has never had a satisfactory resolution. I've seen men waste away their whole lives in pursuit of these fantasies, only to die alone, penniless and miserable. I'm a man of evidence and fact and science, I cannot waste my time searching for a King of Spain's mythical treasure bird. I'm sorry."

Miss Florence Mansfield sighed heavily, uncrossed her legs and stood up. "Well, then, I can't say I'm not disappointed. But thank you for seeing me, Mr. Holmes," she said. "If you reconsider, I'm staying at the Regal Hotel on Regent Street."

This time, Holmes reached out first and they shook hands. "You are young, Miss Mansfield," he said. "Take my advice – don't end up like those men of whom I spoke. You have a long life ahead of you. Live it to the fullest. Don't waste it."

She nodded, turned, and then went out through the door.

"Do you think she'll take your advice, Holmes?" I asked.

"Of course not," Holmes answered. "She's been bitten by a snake and the poison is forever in her veins. It's too late for her. No matter. We'll see her again, I'm sure."

"But you refused to take her case," I reminded my friend.

"Yes, I know. But she is of interest to me in another case, the one concerning Montague Caprice. You see, she's one of his murderers."

"Then that would mean that this black falcon is the object over which Caprice was killed."

"Well deduced," Holmes said. "You're coming along."

Before I could squeeze more of this startling information out of him, Mrs. Hudson knocked on the door then came rushing in.

"My, you are popular today, Mr. Holmes! There's a man downstairs to see you," she said. "He mentioned something about finding a black bird."

Chapter III

The man sat in the same chair that Miss Mansfield had occupied a few minutes before. His name was Caesar Woodbine – a fidgety, boisterous middle-aged Frenchman who spoke English well, despite a heavy accent. He was a short, stout man with tightly curled black hair and side whiskers that crept down the wide, jowly contours of his face like ivy on a brick wall, melting into a graying beard that hid the fact that he didn't seem to possess a neck. His upper lip was shaved, his mouth small, and a thick bulbous nose hung over it like a reddish, weathered café awning. His eyebrows – thick, dark and also curly –

196

kept a pair of green, suspicious eyes permanently hidden in shadow, making it hard for me to read them. He wore a silly pink bowtie and a green velvet jacket with white carnation stuck in a black lapel. The jacket was a few sizes too small for him, barely disguising a small protruding belly. A pair of baggy, grey-pinstripe black pants covered a set of thick legs that didn't seem to bend at the knees when he walked. He reminded me of a traveling carnival barker.

"I'm a professional explorer, Mr. Holmes," he said, his voice resonating like the roll of a bass drum. "I need your help in locating a family heirloom that was stolen from the vault of my family home many decades ago. A black falcon, about a foot high. I've been traveling the world, chasing after it for thirty years – Spain, Italy, Russia, France, and now here, in soggy old England. Oh, please do forgive my rudeness at insulting your cherished homeland, I meant no disrespect. It's just that the cold and clammy climate of this island always pains the marrow in my old bones. Too long spent here and I find it very difficult to walk without the most excruciating discomfort."

"No offense taken, Mr. Woodbine," Holmes said through a light grin. "Now tell me about this black falcon of yours. Priceless, is it?"

Woodbine let out a laugh that sounded like a cough and shook his head. "Oh, no, no, no, Mr. Holmes! On the contrary! Its true value to me is found only in restoring it back to my family vault, where it belongs. You see . . . er . . . I grew up in Algiers where the most varied forms of avian predators in the world reside. My late mother, praise her innocent white soul, fancied herself an artist, carving countless representations of the birds in the area out of local soapstone until her last dying breath. Her final piece, the black falcon, was her finest work. It was displayed in the most notable museums on the continent for years until one day, when someone tried to steal it. My late father couldn't bear the thought of losing my mother's masterpiece, so he locked it up in the safety of our family vault. But alas, safety is a relative concept, wouldn't you say, Mr. Holmes? A month after locking the falcon up, someone broke into our home while we were away and took it. The theft broke my poor father's heart and he died soon after. I've been chasing after it, looking for revenge ever since."

"Remarkable, Mr. Woodbine," Holmes said. "So this has been a rather personal journey for you, getting the black falcon back?"

"Oh, Mr. Holmes, more than you can possibly know. I will pay you whatever you wish if you help me locate my cherished family heirloom and restore my mother's dignity back to its rightful place."

"My rabbit's foot appears to be working rather well today, Mr. Woodbine," Holmes said. "That's the second such offer I've had this evening."

"Wha – what do you mean, sir?"

"I mean, that not long before you arrived, I'd just concluded a meeting with a striking American woman named Florence Mansfield. She had a similar story to yours, only with an important detail changed – hers was about a priceless black falcon, a tribute to Charles V from the Knights of Rhodes."

The scaffolding underneath Woodbine's face seemed to collapse and his mood took a darker turn. "Florence Mansfield? So that's what she going by now," he muttered. Then he coughed into his fist, trying to recover his joviality. "See now, you can't believe a word she says, Mr. Holmes. She's a liar!"

"More so than you, Mr. Woodbine?"

"Her – her real name is Kiki Holiday," Woodbine stated, his voice rising. "She's nothing more than a prostitute from Chicago who'd heard the story of my falcon from one of her clients. All that dwaddle I'm sure she entertained you with, about the bird being encrusted with priceless jewels, is bunk, I tell you! She's been interfering with my securing the black falcon for years! And believe me, she's a scorpion with a sting that never misses! She – "

"What game are the two of you trying to play with me, Woodbine?" Holmes interrupted, leaning forward in his chair. "I should resent you trying to make me a pawn in this silly competition you have with this American woman!"

Woodbine's face turned red. He slammed his hands down against the armrests of the chair and shot up to his feet. "Game? I play no game with you, Mr. Holmes! I just want what's rightfully mine, and if you won't help me, I'm sure I can find someone else who will!" Woodbine finished with an angry nod, stormed out of the room, and down the stairs.

I was shocked that Holmes let Woodbine know that we talked to Miss Mansfield – or Miss Holiday, rather. Usually that was something Holmes kept close to the vest until the proper time. I let him know my feelings and he let out a jolly laugh.

"Don't fret, Watson. Now Woodbine will go directly to see Miss Holiday and they'll keep each other busy, giving us time to sort this adventure out properly."

"But what if they take the next steamer?"

"Do you honestly think they'll leave England without their precious black bird? Why, they've probably never been this close to procuring it before. They can feel the weight of it in their hands. They can see the bright glimmer of the jewels underneath the black enamel. They can smell the air of all the countries it has passed through over the years coming off of its skin. No, it would take the very hand of God to remove them from our misty shores at this point."

Just then, Mrs. Hudson came in and handed Holmes an envelope. He tore it open and pulled the missive out.

"Ah!" he ejaculated. "It's the return cable message from the French Police with Montague Caprice's London itinerary and his list of buying and selling targets." Holmes took a moment to read it. Then his eyes lit up, he folded the paper and put it in his coat pocket.

I couldn't stand the suspense, so I inquired impatiently what the missive said.

"All is well, Watson," Holmes cheerily answered. "It confirms everything I've suspected. Among the list of items Caprice was selling was the black falcon and – better yet – it gives three London shops that were interested in purchasing it. Hurry, man! Grab up your coat and your service revolver. We've some shopping to do!"

Chapter IV

Our first destination was a classy little trinket shop in Mayfair, on Hill Street. The placard over the door read "*Small Wonders*" in a highly decorative font. Peering through the lace-curtained window, I could see that the shop was filled with shelves of items ranging from complete sets of silver dining ware to ornate nutcrackers.

When we passed through the door, a tinny bell rang from somewhere above us and the air was scented with a mild, fruity perfume. A well-dressed and distinguished older gentleman and a plump woman of similar age came out through a curtained entrance behind a glass case and welcomed us warmly, they called themselves Mr. and Mrs. Whorley. Holmes went up to the glass case, while it was my job to search innocently among the shelves and racks for any sign of the black falcon.

"What can I do for you this evening, good sirs?" Mr. Whorley asked.

"I'm looking to purchase a gift for my mother," Holmes answered cleverly. "It's her birthday, and she's very fond of birds."

"Oh, how wonderful, sir," the plump Mrs. Whorley crooned. "We have a selection of bird items over here. Follow me." As she led Holmes over to a shelf near the front window, I could feel the focused gaze of her husband warming my spine. I tried to be as unsuspicious

199

and unthreatening as I could, even tipping my hat to him in a friendly gesture, but there was no doubt in my mind he thought I was a thief. Still, I went from wall to wall, even scanned the tables of merchandise in the middle of the room, and found no sign of a black falcon. Finally, I found myself standing next to Holmes as Mrs. Whorley showed him three shelves of tiny bird sculptures made of glass, crystal, and soapstone.

"These all seem to be a variety of small garden bird," Holmes said. "Would you happen to have anything in the way of predatory bird – say a hawk or a falcon? My mother used to be an ornithologist, you know? She preferred birds of prey."

"Very interesting, sir," she said. She scratched her chin a moment as she thought about it. "I can't think of anything we have like that in the store, I'm afraid. It's a shame you weren't here earlier today. A dealer came in offering to sell us a statue of a black falcon."

"How unfortunate for me," Holmes said.

"Yes," Mrs. Whorley agreed. "It was a beautiful piece of art with a proud face and strong talons. I think your mother would have loved it. The dealer was very nice, but he wanted an exorbitant amount of money for it – very much out of our range."

"Would you happen to have the dealer's card, madam?" Holmes asked.

Mr. Whorley, still behind the counter, interrupted. "I can give you his information if you wish, sir," he said.

"If you could, that would be a great favor to me. My mother would so appreciate it," Holmes said.

Mr. Whorley reached under the glass counter, pulled out a small red leather bound book, opened it, flipped through the pages, and then wrote the information down for us on a sheet of note paper.

"Our warmest well-wishes to your mother, sir. I'm so sorry we couldn't be of more help to you," Mrs. Whorley said sincerely.

"Quite all right, madam," Holmes said, shook her hand then we left the shop.

"Very accommodating, weren't they, Holmes?" I asked.

"Yes, very," Holmes replied. He handed me the paper, Caprice's information was on it. I put it into my pocket for safe keeping.

The next shop on the list we visited, Ye Royal Re-Gift Shoppe, was a few streets over to the south, in Charles Street. It was anything but "Royal". It was an old, run-down shop where the floorboards creaked, the used merchandise was damaged or well-worn, and the air smelled musty. I could hear rats scurrying in the walls. Holmes and I performed the same "mother's birthday" act for the owner of the shop, Mr. Goodwin was an unassuming man of slight build but with such a full head of silver hair, that looked as if a cat was sleeping on his head.

When Holmes questioned him about predatory birds, specifically a falcon, Goodwin shook his head impatiently. "We've never had anything like that in the store, sir," he said curtly, bordering on rudeness.

"Do you know of anyone who could help us?" Holmes asked.

Goodwin's eyes narrowed. "You could try Small Wonders, a shop a few blocks up. They stock things like what you're looking for."

"You don't have a dealer who supplies you with your merchandise?" I asked, trying to be a little more specific.

Goodwin swept his hand in a great arc, covering the whole room. "Does it look like I have a dealer, sir? All the merchandise I have in this room is from people coming in and selling me their old personal items. I couldn't afford it any other way."

"Well, thank you for your time, sir. We'll indeed follow your advice and visit this Small Wonders shop," Holmes said.

Once outside I made my opinion on the man's manners known.

"You think Goodwin was lying to us? You think he might have the black bird, Watson?" Holmes asked.

"I think he was a rather suspicious, unfriendly type," I answered. "The possession of a priceless treasure would certainly allow him to close that rat trap of a shop and send him to the beaches of the Mediterranean for the rest of his life."

"I see. Still, try to keep an open mind. We still have one more shop yet to visit," Holmes said.

The night had grown cooler, my feet were starting to hurt, and I was eager to get back to the comfortable, warm climate of our Baker Street parlor. Thankfully, Holmes insisted that we take a cab to our next destination. We arrived at the last shop around closing time.

The Artist's Mart was a large warehouse-like establishment located near the Thames on Maiden Lane. A young, attractive, dark-haired woman who wore spectacles on the tip of her nose was the only person in the shop when we entered. She was wiping smudges off the glass that protected a flowered watercolor painting with such concentration that she didn't hear us come in. Oil and pastel paintings filled almost every inch of every wall, each with a price well beyond my capabilities. The floor of the shop was littered with hundreds of granite, marble, and clay-fired sculptures. Some were in the classical Greek armless style, while others were depictions of fruit bowls, or trees, or animals. It seemed to me to be the perfect place to sell an object like the black falcon. I felt good about this shop immediately.

Holmes coughed into his fist, startling the young lady so terribly that she dropped her *chamois*. She flashed him a look of utter derision as she knelt down to pick it up.

"I'm afraid we're closing for the night, sir," she said sharply.

"I do apologize for the lateness of our entrance," Holmes said then continued on with the "mother" story, only he became more specific about what he was looking for, actually mentioning the black bird.

"I've never seen a black falcon statuette before, sir," she said rather quickly. "And none of my dealers would supply such a thing, as there doesn't seem to be a market for it. People prefer roosters, eagles, or ravens – not falcons. Now, if you don't mind, it's been a long day and I would like to go home."

After a sincere apology, Holmes and I left the shop and, as I jumped back into our waiting cab, Holmes gave the driver very detailed instructions, most of which was out of my hearing. When Holmes joined me in the cab, he slapped my knee and grinned.

"She has the jeweled falcon then?" I asked.

"That young girl in the shop? Don't be silly, Watson. But I do know who has it," he stated boldly. "Are your aching feet up to helping me secure it?"

"Of course," I said.

"Good," he said. "Then we're off!"

"But how do you know who has the bird?"

"Sit tight, my impatient friend. I'll explain on the way!"

Chapter V

"Mr. and Mrs. Whorley?" I asked in disbelief. "But they were as friendly as could be and were very forthcoming to us. They seemed so honest."

"Of course they did," Holmes said as the cab raced through the city streets. "A clever ploy. They told us just enough of the truth and then overcompensated for what they didn't tell us by drowning us in kindness – a kind of sleight of hand, if you will, to get rid of us and buy themselves time to run off with the falcon. If you recall, they were the only people of the three shops who admitted to even knowing Caprice, which means Caprice never made it to the two other shops on his list."

"Why? What stopped him? Were they involved in his murder?"

202

"No," Holmes replied. "You see, Caprice had no idea what he had, but the Whorleys immediately recognized the bird for what it was and eagerly purchased it from him at his ridiculously low asking price, knowing it's a priceless artifact and that it's the stolen legal property of Spain which, by international trade treaty, makes them dealers in illegal contraband. We must hurry back to Hill Street, as they'll do their best to get the bird out of the country and to more friendly shores, where they'll be able to sell it then disappear."

Holmes had the driver stop before we reached the alley behind the shop. When we approached on foot, there was a large black brougham parked behind the building under the foggy yellow light a single street lamp. Two large and powerfully muscled steeds were mounted in front. Holmes and I got out, paid the driver, and waited in the darkness of the alley across from the rear of the shop.

"Our luck has held, Watson. It appears that they haven't left yet," Holmes whispered.

The well-dressed coachman at the front of the brougham sat almost perfectly still, his back straight, his crop in one hand, his hat in the other. Then there was a crashing sound and out through the rear door of the shop exploded Mr. and Mrs. Whorley, but something wasn't right about the situation. They both had their hands on a tall, narrow box that was tied all around with string, and both were trying to yank the box from the other's grip. I had no doubt as to what was in it. Their low voices muttered curses so offensive that they would have made a sailor blush. They wrestled with each other, spinning in violent circles, legs kicking, feet stomping. Mrs. Whorley suddenly let go of the box, reared her right hand back, and slapped her husband across the cheek, the sound of which resembled a firecracker. Mr. Whorley's head jerked backwards and when it snapped forward again, it was with the momentum of his entire body. With a great shove of one hand, he threw his wife to the ground. She screamed out as she landed on her back and then rolled to her knees, but when she got to her feet she had a revolver in her hand. Mr. Whorley saw this and turned to jump into the brougham, but her shot landed square in his spine. He went down like a bag of bricks.

"Enough of this senselessness!" Holmes exclaimed and then took off across the alley. I followed him, my own revolver out and ready.

Mrs. Whorley must have heard our footsteps for she saw us coming. Her eyes were wide open as she fired off a quick shot, which caused Holmes and me to separate as we scrambled. Then she grabbed up the box from her husband's dead grip and jumped into the brougham. It took off down the alley at an alarming pace, sounding like the churning belly of an oncoming thunderstorm.

"Come, Watson! Hurry!" Holmes called, but I was already on his heels chasing after the carriage as it barreled its way towards the busy city streets.

Chapter VI

It appeared to a well-constructed vehicle, the best that money could buy. Made of the finest heaviest wood and iron, its profound weight was a great burden on the two mounts pulling it, and was the only reason Holmes and I managed to reach it before it made Davies Street and sure freedom. Holmes jumped on to the left rear spring iron and held fast to the roof irons with one hand as he reached out with his free hand to grab mine. I pocketed my revolver and then reached out. He pulled me up, positioned me on the right, and didn't let me go until my fingers had solid purchase.

"You take the woman and secure the falcon!" he shouted over the deafening noise of the wheels. "I'll face the coachman and see if I can persuade him to stop this juggernaut!"

I nodded and watched as Holmes pulled himself up and over the roof rails. In a split second he was across the roof and on top of the coachman.

On the left, Berkeley Square passed in a blur of motion. I pulled out my revolver, took in a deep breathe, and then threw myself around the side, my feet landing perfectly on the folding step beneath the door.

The large, uncurtained window in the door offered me a clear view of Mrs. Whorley sitting on the couch inside the coach. Unfortunately, it also gave her a perfect view of me, and she had the dangerous end of her own revolver aimed right at my stomach.

She pulled the trigger just as we passed Curzon Street and turned south. The speed in which it was traveling lifted the wheels on the right side completely off the street, throwing my body up safely away from the harm the woman's bullet could do.

The noise of the gunshot startled the already panicked horses and the ride became a violent battle against tremor, earthquake, and concussion. I bounced around like a hot potato, nearly losing my grip on both the roof iron and my own revolver.

In between, up and down, side-to-side, I managed to register brief glances at Holmes as he battled with the coachman. Punches and kicks were traded, the coachman's crop whipped at Holmes, who successfully parried the blows with his forearm.

Ahead of us, the wide, busy intersection of Park Lane approached quickly. Beyond that, an endless eternity of darkness, which could only be the wide environs of Hyde Park. Holmes and the coachman seemed to notice it just as I had and suspended their battle temporarily.

We burst out on to Park Lane like an unstoppable train engine, just missing the northbound path of a cabriolet, the driver cursing as we passed. Our coachman took the reins in hand again and pulled to the left. The horses responded quickly, nearly turning us over again.

The left side wheels came down hard, sending the brougham into a violent swerve. My feet slammed into the roof irons, left and right, right and left, but I still kept a solid grip on my service revolver. Ahead of me, Holmes and the coachman resumed their feud.

A hansom cab came up on our right. The driver seemed oblivious to the swerving menace we represented and didn't allow any room for safety. The brougham's rear end came out like a fist, hitting the hansom and sending it rolling into the dark recesses of Hyde Park.

That was when I heard another shot. I looked up just in time to see the coachman stiffen vertically, arch his neck, drop his crop, and then reach around for his back. He spun once, went limp, and fell off the footboard. The mad woman, in trying to kill Holmes, had shot the coachman instead!

If my count was correct, that was her fourth shot. She had two more left in the barrel, but it would only take one to kill Holmes or me. I had to do something. As Holmes tried to grapple with the reins and control the horses, I pushed myself over the side of the coach nearest to where she sat.

My feet completely shattered the window in the door on the way down and I slid through the opening, falling to both knees once inside the coach. My dramatic entrance startled Mrs. Whorley so efficiently that she screamed out and dropped her revolver to the floor.

I pressed the barrel of my gun to her cheek and cocked the hammer. "Don't move!" I shouted. Never taking my gaze from her, I reached down and picked up her revolver, feeling the hard edge of the box containing the falcon down there as I did so.

I pocketed her weapon, got up carefully, and reached the seat beside her. There were two flat windows facing outward, one of them was holed by the bullet that had killed the coachman. The brougham finally stopped swerving, but it was still traveling at a reckless speed.

I watched as Holmes desperately fought with the horses, hearing him shout commands, but they ignored him and thundered forward through the darkness, relentlessly. I'm not sure how, but we were suddenly heading east down Constitution Hill.

Buckingham Palace was on the right but barely noticeable in the dark and at the speed we were traveling. Somewhere inside the Queen was sleeping soundly, completely oblivious to the excitement going on right outside her front door. We came to the roundabout at the intersection of The Mall and Buckingham Palace Road. The horses ran through it, sending the brougham into the air then down again.

Mrs. Whorley and I smashed our heads against the ceiling of the coach, and we were thrown back down into the seat. She took this opportunity to grab the barrel of my revolver, trying to wrestle it from my grip.

The struggle caused me to let off a shot that went up through the roof. The brougham took to the air again, and when it came down, it was on brick pavement, causing Mrs. Whorley to hit her head again and release her hold on my revolver.

She fell back on the cushion, unconscious. I'd never felt more relieved about such a fate.

Outside, Holmes pulled and jerked the reins. We made a slight turn to the left, heading down Birdcage Walk, towards the brightly lit Westminster Bridge. Fear froze my spine as I imagined those crazed horses taking us over the edge, off the bridge, and then down into the Thames.

Another hansom was run off the road as we charged onwards, but thankfully, the time of night proved beneficial, and we didn't encounter the usual amount of traffic. The bridge entrance was only a few yards away when I felt a noticeable decline in our speed.

Still, we traversed the bridge at a formidable clip. I could see the shivering reflection of the moon on the face of the Thames as we raced across. The dim glow of the lamps flickered by, one after another. The brougham moaned and cried, protesting every turn of the wheel. Then it was over, just as quickly as it had started.

We finally jerked to a stop halfway across the bridge. Sighing in relief, I grabbed up the box, pushed the door open, got out of the coach, and stood on firm ground, thanking my good fortune that I was still alive. Holmes remained up in the coachman's seat, his hands still wrapped in the reins, his chest heaving for breath. The horses coughed and snorted in their exhaustion, probably as relieved as I was that it was all over.

'Well done," I breathed.

"It wasn't me, Watson," he said as he stood up then stepped down from his coachman's perch. He motioned towards the horses and, through heavy breaths, he continued. "It was them. They couldn't go on . . . any longer."

The slam of a door suddenly echoed through the night sky, the terse thudding of running footsteps followed. By the time Holmes and I realized what it was and made it around the brougham, Mrs. Whorley was climbing her way over the rail of the bridge.

Chapter VII

"Mrs. Whorley!" Holmes called. "Stop! Don't do it!"

She glanced back at us, her face a contorted, reddened mask of hate and anger. "It's a better fate than hanging, sir!" she spat.

Holmes and I didn't say another word. It was clear she meant to go through with her plan so we rushed her, as fast as we could, reaching the rail just as she threw herself over. I leaned over the edge and watched as Mrs. Whorley disappeared down into the darkness. She didn't make a sound as she fell, all was perfectly silent until she hit the water, and even then, the splash was quick and muted.

We scanned the surface of the Thames for many seconds, the only evidence that Mrs. Whorley ever existed was in the way the impact of her body had disturbed the river's serene black surface, causing silent, ever-expanding, silver-edged, moonlit ripples to dance away from us in near perfect circles. Finally, the floating outline of her body appeared below us.

I heard Holmes sigh in disgust. "Too many," he said.

"How's that, Holmes?" I asked, for clarification.

"Too many lives lost, Watson," he answered. "I'm curious to see this mysterious, priceless object that everyone is dying to own."

I still had the box tightly squeezed in the fold of my left elbow. The weight of it seemed heavier now than it had felt a few minutes ago. I looked down at it and realized I was curious too. We turned away from the edge and slowly walked back to the brougham. No one was on the bridge with us so I felt it was safe enough to satisfy our curiosity. I found a spot near a lamp that shed enough light for us to get a good look at the bird and then began untying the string that was wrapped around the box. Opening the top, I reached in and pulled it out. Holmes took it from me and held it up in the light with both hands.

As Holmes turned it around in his hands, I was stunned to silence.

The Whorleys had obviously spent significant time and effort removing the black enamel, probably using acetone and an old rag, but some of the lower part of the falcon was still covered. What had been stripped clean shined in the dim light like a crystal in the sun.

The bird stood upright, its head forward, the look on its face proud and fierce. Its wings were crossed in the back and clung tightly around its body like a suit of armor. It immediately commanded a feeling of awe. As if this wasn't amazing enough, I had to comprehend the fact that the entire bird was encrusted with the finest, most perfect jewels I'd ever seen. Its skin was pure gold, its oval-shaped eyes were inlaid with faultless red rubies ringed by expertly cut tiny diamond facets. The layers of the bird's breast feathers alternated between imperial topaz and fire opal all the way down to its dark amber sculpted legs, where a pair of pearl-and-opal manacles secured the bird's golden talons to the largest solid piece of square cut emerald I'd ever seen. The claws on the bird's talons were diamond. Its three-layered shoulder feathers went from white opal to jadeite and finished with onyx. The flight wings were finely sculpted out of cat's eye, and the tail feathers of onyx. It was crafted with such skill, a genuine miracle of human ingenuity and labor that I believed it could fly right out of Holmes's hands. The jeweled falcon turned out to be the masterpiece it was rumored to be.

"The one time the treasure turns out to be real, wouldn't you say?" Holmes asked, trying but failing to conceal his astonishment.

"My . . . my God, Holmes," I stammered. "If news ever got out that this thing actually exists, it could start a world war. What do we do with it?"

"We put it back into the box and then head to Scotland Yard," Holmes answered. "We'll need Lestrade's services if we are to write a final chapter to this adventure."

Chapter VIII

After Holmes explained the entire jeweled falcon affair to Lestrade, the inspector sent a boat crew to the Thames to fish Mrs. Whorley's body from its cold waters and a morgue wagon to pick up the bodies of the coachman and Mr. Whorley. Then he escorted us, with four constables, to the Regal Hotel on Regent Street.

The front desk manager gave us the room number of Miss Kiki Holiday, 308, and we all hurried up the steps. Still holding the heavy box containing the precious bird, I did my best to keep up. Immediately upon standing in front of Miss Holiday's door, we heard angry muffled voices and the sound of heavy stomping coming from inside. Then there was the unmistakable crack of a gunshot. Lestrade ordered one of his constables, Wilmot – a giant hulk of a man – to break the door in. The door came apart like splintered balsa wood under Wilmot's fury and we all rushed into the room, weapons out and ready.

Miss Holiday and Mr. Woodbine were in front of the window wrestling one another. Both had their hands wrapped around the grip handle of a small revolver. There was a single bullet hole in the ceiling and a high end table had been knocked over. A soiled glass ashtray and its ash-filled contents were spilled on the carpet.

Once the two of them saw us standing there, they froze.

"Miss Holiday and Mr. Woodbine. It's a pleasure to make your acquaintances again," Holmes said as he went over, reached up, and took the revolver from them. He turned, handing it over to Lestrade, and then instructed the two miscreants to have a seat. There were two high-backed sitting chairs in the middle of the room, across from a well-worn couch. They sat, their faces clearly alarmed at our sudden intrusion.

Lestrade stepped up, put his fists on his hips, and leaned forward. "Just what in the Queen's golden crown is going on in here?" he asked with such a flourish they were forced back into their chairs.

"It was just a . . . a misunderstanding," Miss Holiday said. She traded a quick, sneering glance with Woodbine. I had the distinct feeling that if we left, those two would eagerly resume their wrestling match, even without the revolver.

"The only misunderstanding we have here, Miss Holiday," Holmes began, "is which one of you killed Montague Caprice first."

"Montague Caprice?" Woodbine echoed, his wild eyebrows fluttering like the wings of a butterfly. "Never heard of him."

"Come now, Mr. Woodbine. We're well past the tired charade. We know both you and Miss Holiday were there in that alley earlier tonight with Mr. Caprice. I have no doubt that the bullet in the ceiling that came from the revolver I just confiscated from you will match the one taken out of Caprice."

"Bah!" Woodbine exclaimed.

"Quite. But our victim was also garroted," Holmes continued. "with a wire garrote used by someone very strong and very determined."

All eyes went to the American woman sitting quietly next to Woodbine. She saw this and reacted. "Why are you looking at me? I don't even know what a garrote is."

Holmes grinned and shook his head. "You've said before that you closely followed my adventures in *The Strand*, Miss Holiday. Can you recall in any of those stories when I made an inaccurate accusation?"

She didn't answer. She sat there like a Greek statue, her eyes forward, her mouth drawn tight.

"Neither can I," Holmes said. "I think you do know what a garrote is. The said murder weapon is, in fact, in plain sight on your person at this very moment."

Following Holmes train of thought, I scanned the woman with my own eyes. She didn't look any different than the last time I'd seen her. She wore that same thin, silver necklace, that same silky deep maroon dress that left little to the imagination, those same black leather boots, and a set of silver rings on her fingers. I'm sure everyone else in the room was doing the same thing as I.

Holmes let out a confident laugh. "No one else, it seems, can see what I see," he said as he calmly stepped around the back of Miss Woodbine's chair. He brought his hands up to her neck and quickly slipped off her necklace. He held it up for the rest of us to inspect. "Here's the garrote, Inspector – the very one that nearly took off poor Mr. Caprice's head. Note the large circular clasp locks at the end – large enough to slip a finger through. And the wire is quite sharp, I assure you."

"The blood in a woman that wears a murder weapon around her neck must run like ice, Mr. Holmes!" Lestrade said in disgust.

"Indeed, Inspector," Holmes agreed. "The only question left now is, why? Why kill the man who knows where the jeweled falcon is?"

"It was a mistake!" Woodbine blurted out. His face was red and seemed ready to implode.

"Shut up, you cretin!" Miss Holiday muttered.

"It was as you said, Mr. Holmes," Woodbine continued. "We'd followed Caprice from Paris, and then lost him as he disembarked in London. We managed to track him down a few hours later, cornered him in that alley, and forced him to tell us where he'd sold the falcon."

"Ah," Holmes interrupted. "But he lied to you."

"Yes, he told us he'd sold it to a little shop on Hill Street, Small Wonders, I think it was called. So we paid a visit to the proprietors, a Mr. and Mrs. Whorley. They told us Caprice tried to sell the bird to them, but that he wanted an exorbitant amount of money for it and they couldn't pay his price. They told us he'd left to sell it somewhere else, but there are hundreds of shops in London that would carry such an object. The job was too daunting, too big, and would take too much time. We'd already killed him to hide our tracks, and that's when I thought of hiring you to find the bird. Apparently, my sworn enemy here had the same idea and visited you on his own."

"Ha!" Holmes erupted. "Irony has laid itself thick this time, eh, Watson?"

"Thicker than can be believed, I'm afraid, Holmes," I replied.

"What do you mean?" Miss Holiday asked.

Holmes, through a wide, devious grin, answered. "I mean, dear lady, that Mr. and Mrs. Whorley did indeed possess the jeweled falcon at the time you visited them. Caprice didn't lie to you. The Whorley's did!"

"How do you know this?" Woodbine asked.

"Because, Mr. Woodbine, Watson and I have successfully retrieved the bird from them."

"You have it? In your possession?" Miss Holiday shrieked in disbelief.

"Of course," Holmes replied. "Watson is holding it as we speak. Didn't you see the box he was carrying when he came in?"

They both jumped up from their seats, but Lestrade was quick to have his constables cuff them before they took a step towards me.

"Please, please, Mr. Holmes!" Woodbine pleaded. "Let me see it! Please! Before I'm sent to the gallows! I must see it!"

Holmes and Lestrade traded glances then Holmes went over, righted the overturned table, and waved me over. I placed the box on the table and stepped back as Holmes reached in and pulled out the jeweled falcon. Carefully, gently, he placed it on the table.

It sparkled in the ceiling lamp light magnificently, even more brilliantly and beautiful than when we'd seen it on the bridge. I looked over at Woodbine. He was shaking, his face was pale, and his eyes had welled up with tears.

"All these years, all those miles, all the sacrifices," he whispered. "To finally see it . . . to know it's real . . . It's worth the gallows."

Miss Holiday's was a markedly different reaction. Her face resembled Medusa when Perseus cut off her head. She kept struggling to get at the bird, her teeth grinding together, but two constables held her back. She hissed and spat like an animal as they dragged her and Woodbine away.

Lestrade, Holmes, and I stayed behind, marveling at the bird's intense beauty.

"What happens to it now, Mr. Holmes?" Lestrade asked.

"Ask my brother, Inspector," Holmes replied, and through the door stomped Mycroft and two huge men in black hats and black coats.

"You knew that I would be here, Sherlock?" Mycroft asked as he approached.

"I knew your agents inside Scotland Yard would get word to you about what I've been doing," Holmes said. "I knew you wouldn't be long in arriving."

211

"Quite clever," Mycroft said. "As for the bird, it will become property of the Queen, and as such, will be protected with the utmost precaution."

"Added to the Crown Jewels, I assume?" Lestrade asked.

"You assume incorrectly, Inspector," Mycroft said as those men in the black hats and coats boxed the bird, picked it up, turned and left the room. "It's worth too much and would attract too much attention from foreign governments, like Spain. No, it'll be hidden in a secret room somewhere in Buckingham Palace, where it'll be safe and won't cause any trouble."

"So good to see you again, Mycroft," Holmes said, shaking his brother's hand.

Once Mycroft had left, Holmes turned to me.

"You know, Watson," he said. "I believe he is wrong about one thing."

"What's that?"

"I have a feeling that the story of the jeweled falcon isn't over," he explained. "Things as precious as that bird always have their fake counterparts. I'm sure one is out there and people are chasing it. Perhaps the falcon's story will someday make it to the shores of America, only to cause more trouble, murder, and mayhem."

"Dear God, Holmes," I said. "I hope that you're wrong."

The Adventure of the Crossbow
by Edwin A. Enstrom

As I look back over the notes of the adventures that I shared with my friend Sherlock Holmes, I realize that each one of them has its own distinct character. Some are tragic, such as the case of the Ambersons and their unfortunate puppy. Some are pleasant, almost comical, such as the case of the trained seal and the aubergine. Others are merely mundane. As important and consequential as they were for the people involved, they had no interesting features that would make them suitable for a literary explication. However, through all of these runs a common thread, that of *ratiocination*. No matter how convoluted and confusing the situation, Holmes's keen and logical mind was able to unravel the complexity and reveal the truth. One of the more confusing of these adventures involved a murder by crossbow . . . .

Holmes and I had just returned from a pleasant stroll in the park on a fine May afternoon and were settled in our easy chairs when we heard the peal of the doorbell. I glanced at Holmes and, as was his wont, he answered the question that was in my mind.

"No, Watson, I am not expecting anyone. I have no appointments for today. Perhaps it is someone calling on Mrs. Hudson."

He was soon shown to be in fault, for we heard footsteps on the stair, followed by a knock on the door, and Mrs. Hudson entered with a young woman behind her. We both rose to our feet.

"Miss Charlotte Saintsbury to see you, Mr. Holmes," said Mrs. Hudson, disappearing to her quarters below.

"How do you do, Miss Saintsbury. I am Sherlock Holmes," he said, gesturing to the basket chair. "And this is my trusted colleague, Dr. John Watson. Please sit down and make yourself comfortable."

Miss Saintsbury appeared to be about thirty years of age. She was dressed simply but elegantly in a gray dress with a matching small hat. Her chestnut hair fell in soft curls to her shoulders. She would have been very pretty had not her face showed every indication of distress.

"How may we help you?" inquired Holmes.

"Mr. Holmes, let me start by saying that it was recommended that I come to you by Mrs. Cyril Morton. You may not know that name. You

213

knew her has Violet Smith and she has recently married. She speaks very highly of you."

The name brought back many memories of an earlier adventure that I was privileged to share with Holmes. A conspiracy had attempted to forcibly marry Miss Smith and gain control of her fortune. Holmes was successful in discovering the scoundrels and freeing the lady. (I have published this case under the title "The Solitary Cyclist").

"Mr. Holmes, I am betrothed to Nigel Appleton, whose uncle was murdered yesterday. The police regard Nigel as a prime suspect. I know he has his faults, as any man does, but I also know that he would never murder anyone. Oh, can you help me?"

Holmes tented his fingers and stared at the ceiling for a few moments.

"Miss Saintsbury, no matter how well we think that we know someone, there are hidden depths in each of us that are never understood by those around us. I cannot commit to proving someone innocent or guilty. All I do is try to find the truth and let the chips fall where they may."

"Oh, sir, that is exactly what I want. The truth will prove Nigel innocent. Will you take my case?"

Holmes has always affected a disparaging attitude towards women and has called them deceitful and untrustworthy. However, those who knew him well were aware that he was very susceptible to the charms of a pretty woman. I knew he would take the case.

"Very well, Miss Saintsbury, I will investigate your case. Do you happen to know the name of the police officer who is in charge of the investigation?"

"Yes, Nigel told me that Inspector Lestrade is in charge."

A grimace crossed Holmes's face. We had crossed paths with Lestrade many times over the years, not always pleasantly. Lestrade was as tenacious as a bulldog when pursuing criminals, but he had as much imagination as a doorknob.

Miss Saintsbury took a calling card out of her handbag and wrote something on the back. Handing it to Holmes, she said, "Here is my address. Nigel is back living in his uncle's house and I have written his address on the back as well."

"I will begin my investigation at once and get in touch with you when I have something to report," said Holmes, ushering the young lady to the door. When she had gone, he asked me if I had the time to accompany him.

"Certainly. I have been acting as a *locum* for Anstruther for a few days, but that has come to an end."

"Capital. Let us pay a call on our friend Lestrade and see where the case stands."

We secured a cab and made our way to Scotland Yard. Fortunately, Lestrade was in his office and had time to see us.

"Mr. Holmes, Dr. Watson, to what do I owe the honor of this visit?" asked Lestrade, not very pleasantly. He was often antagonistic to non-policemen becoming involved in his cases.

Holmes explained that we were inquiring on behalf of Miss Saintsbury, the fiancée of Nigel Appleton. Lestrade's expression changed to one of relief.

"Mr. Holmes, I know we have had differences in the past, but this time I should very much like to work with you on this case. Quite frankly, we are stymied. What few clues there are lead nowhere, and there is no hard evidence."

Despite the soothing words, it was evident that Lestrade was mortified that he needed Holmes's help. Holmes affected not to notice. It was quite incomprehensible to me why Lestrade should take this attitude. Holmes had many times saved him from his own bungling and yet let Lestrade take the credit. Such are the imponderables of personality, I suppose.

"Mr. Holmes, here are the facts of the case. Yesterday morning, Mr. Alexander Forsyte was found dead in his office. The office was locked and his clerks had to break in. They found him behind his desk, slumped back in his chair with a crossbow arrow in his chest."

"Bolt," said Holmes.

"Bolt? No, the door was not bolted."

"What you referred to as a crossbow arrow is properly called a 'bolt'. If it is blunt and four-sided it is called a 'quarrel'," replied Holmes.

"I don't care what you call it. The missile from the crossbow was in his chest and had penetrated the heart. The desk faced an open window, which overlooked a small courtyard. Across the courtyard about thirty feet away was another building, with windows on the same level as Forsyte's office. We searched this other building and found a crossbow lying on the floor in an empty office. According to the landlord, this office had just been rented a week ago. He gave us a description of the renter and we have started a search for him, but it looks hopeless.

"Another piece of the puzzle is this," continued Lestrade, handing Holmes a piece of notepaper. On the paper was written:

OLD CRIMES ARE NEVER FORGOTTEN.
PREPARE TO DIE.

"Hmm," said Holmes. "Cheap notepaper, available at any stationers. Written with a broad-nib pen in crude block letters. Nothing to tell us here. Where did you find this?"

"We found it in the desk when my men searched the office. It may indicate that the murder was a revenge killing. We are investigating Forsyte's history to see if that is the case. It will be a hard slog. Another possibility is that it is meant to throw us off the track. Forsyte was a rich man and his nephew, Nigel Appleton, inherits everything. As you well know, financial gain is often a great motivator for a crime. In fact, Forsyte and his nephew seemed to have had an argument recently. And Appleton does not have an alibi for the time of the killing, so he is a prime suspect."

We took leave of Lestrade, first having procured a note from him to allow us to inspect Forsyte's office. When we were back on the street, Holmes asked me what I thought about the case.

"Well," I said, "using a crossbow seems like an outlandish way of killing someone. Seems more like amateur theatrics to me."

"I disagree. Suppose you wanted to kill someone and could not get close to him. How would you do it? A revolver or a rifle would make a loud report and would cause people to immediately start looking for its source. A thrown knife requires a great amount of skill and is inaccurate at best. Poison is very chancy and may be detected by the victim. No, a crossbow is a very good choice. Powerful and silent."

"I see your point," I replied, "but certainly a crossbow is hard to come by. One cannot just go the neighborhood ironmonger's and pick one up."

"True enough. Finding the source of the crossbow will be a major clue. Let us visit the scene of the crime and see what that tells us."

Forsyte's office was on the second floor of a nondescript building. We climbed the two flights of stairs and came to a hallway that ran along the front of the building. On the right wall were a series of windows that looked out onto the street. On the left were two doors. The first one showed *"Forsyte Imports"* in gilt lettering. The second one was guarded by a bored-looking constable. Holmes showed him the note from Lestrade and he stepped aside to let us enter.

Holmes first inspected the door. It had four rectangular panes of frosted glass, the bottom right-hand one of which had a hole broken in it, just above the doorknob. Evidently this was done by the clerks in order to gain admission. Holmes picked up a bowler hat that was lying on the floor and inspected it briefly. He handed it to me but I could see nothing unusual about it. The initials *"AF"* were inscribed on the headband, so I presumed it belonged to Alexander Forsyte.

Holmes then sat in the chair behind the desk and looked around. He leaned back and looked at the ceiling. He leaned forward and put his

216

elbows on the desk. He let his arms go limp and fell face forward onto the desk.

"Holmes, what in the world are you doing?" I cried.

"I am trying to reconstruct the crime, Watson. It is always a good idea to have a complete understanding of the physical constraints. There isn't much else for us here. Let us go speak to the clerks."

We went back to the other door, which led to a largish room containing two desks, assorted hard chairs, and many filing cabinets. At one of the desks was seated a smallish man with a dazed look on his face. He seemed to be staring into space when we entered. He started and turned to us.

"May I help you, sirs?" he faltered.

Holmes explained who we were and why we had come. He asked if the man would be willing to answer a few questions. The man said that he would.

"My name is Harold Calder and I am the junior clerk here. The senior clerk, Mr. Charles Bascombe, is away at our solicitor's trying to find out what is to become of the company . . . and us."

The poor man was a bundle of nerves, wringing his hands, fidgeting in his chair, and stammering in his speech. It made me nervous just watching him.

"See here, Mr. Calder," I said, "there is no need to be frightened. We mean you no harm. Just take it easy."

"Sirs, it is not you that frightens me. I have been a wreck for the past week, ever since Mr. Forsyte told us that he was going to sell the business and retire. I have a wife and child and I don't know what will become of us if I should lose my post. Now that Mr. Forsyte is dead, it is all the worse."

"Calm yourself, sir," broke in Holmes. "By all appearances this is a thriving business and whomever takes it over is sure to keep the employees who know it so well."

This seemed to ease him a bit and he gave us a wan smile.

"Now Mr. Calder, will you tell us exactly what happened yesterday? Start from first thing in the morning and leave nothing out, not even the smallest detail."

"Yes, sir. I came in at my usual time of nine o'clock. Mr. Bascombe was already here and Mr. Forsyte was in his office. I went right to my work. At ten o'clock, Mr. Bascombe went into Mr. Forsyte's office for his regular daily meeting. He came out about twenty minutes later. At quarter-to-eleven, I started preparations for our daily elevenses. We have a gas ring here, but no water, so I went down to the ground-floor kitchen, filled the teapot and brought it back upstairs, and put it on to boil. When the tea was ready, I poured out a cup for Mr. Bascombe and another for myself. I put the teapot, an empty cup, and a bowl of sugar on a tray and went to Mr. Forsyte's office. I knocked on the door and called to him but got no answer. I knocked again and called louder but still didn't get any response.

"I tried opening the door, but it was locked. It never had been before. I tried looking through the keyhole but couldn't see anything. The key must have been in the lock. Then Mr. Bascombe came and asked me what the matter was. I explained the situation to him. He also knocked and called and tried the keyhole. He said that we must break in. He looked around and saw the teapot on the tray. He grabbed the pot and, telling me to stand back, he took a mighty swing and broke the glass near the doorknob. He swung a few more times to break the shards that were sticking out. He handed me the teapot and I put it back on the tray, while he put his hand through the opening and fumbled with the key to unlock the door."

Here Calder looked like he was about to faint. I picked up the glass of water that was sitting on the corner of his desk and made him drink some. He took several deep breaths and appeared to be composing himself to continue.

"Well, sirs, when we opened the door, I almost swooned. We saw Mr. Forsyte slumped back in his chair with his head thrown back. An arrow was stuck in his chest, pointed straight up towards the ceiling. It was obvious that he was dead. I hope I shall never see such a sight again. Mr. Bascombe told me to run for a policeman, which I did. I found a constable on the next block and told him what we had discovered. He came back with me and made us go to our office and stay there. Some time later, an Inspector Lestrade came, along with several other policemen, and I told them this story that I have just told you. That's all I know, sirs."

Just before Calder finished his tale, another man had entered the office. While Calder was rather shabbily dressed, the newcomer was quite the opposite and well turned-out. He introduced himself as Charles Bascombe, the senior clerk. Holmes explained why we were there. Bascombe nodded and sat down at the other desk. He told us that, according to the solicitor who was the executor of the estate, Bascombe and Calder should just carry on business as usual until things were straightened out. Holmes asked Bascombe to give us the story of the previous morning. His story matched that of Calder almost exactly.

Holmes asked, "What was Mr. Forsyte's state of mind yesterday? Was it as normal, or was it tense or agitated?"

"Why, sir," replied Bascombe, "now that you mention it, he did seem on edge – almost frightened I should say. Maybe that is the reason that he locked the door."

"Do you know why he should be like that?"

"No, sir, not at all. He has always been of an equable temper."

"I looked through Mr. Forsyte's desk," said Holmes, "and didn't find a checkbook. Do you know where it is?

"Of course," said Bascombe. "I have it. I make out all of the company's checks and Mr. Forsyte signs them. I'll get it."

Bascombe went to one of the filing cabinets, took out a check register, and handed it to Holmes, who spent a few minutes looking through it.

"I see checks made out to tradesmen and to shipping companies and other businesses, but I also see monthly checks for fifty pounds made out to James Smithers. They were cashed at the Merchant Seamen's Bank. What are they for?"

"I don't know," said Bascombe. "When I asked Mr. Forsyte about it, he told me it was for services rendered. He wouldn't tell me anything more."

"Thank you for your time, gentlemen," said Holmes, 'If there are any further questions, we shall see you again."

Once we were out in the street again, I said to Holmes, "Those monthly payments to Smithers look very much like blackmail to me. What do you say?"

"Perhaps, Watson. If so, that is a very clever blackmailer. Most blackmailers will ask for a large sum at first. This creates panic and fear in the victim, who will be hard-pressed to raise the amount or maybe cannot raise it at all. He becomes more probable to go to the police, even if his indiscretion becomes a public scandal. When the blackmailer then asks for a modest sum, the victim is less apprehensive and thinks it is better just to pay the sum and stay quiet. The blackmailer is thus completely safe."

We had reached the neighboring building and found the landlord in his office on the ground floor. Holmes introduced us and explained our investigation.

"Now, sir, what can you tell us about the man who rented the room where the crossbow was found?" asked Holmes.

"Well, sir, he came about a week ago, looking for a room to use temporarily until his new office was completed. He said his name was Richard Morris. I had two offices available, one on the first floor and another on the second. They both had the same monthly rental fee and the first-floor one was much nicer, not to mention that there was one less staircase to climb. But he insisted on taking the one on the second floor. He paid one month's rent in advance and left."

"And have you seen him since?"

"Only once. Two days after he had rented the office, I met him on the stairs. He was carrying a largish flat box up to the office. That's the last I saw of him."

"I see," said Holmes. "Can you give us a description?"

"He was of medium height, with dark hair and a full beard. He wore thick eyeglasses and must have had very poor vision because he walked very slowly and kept one arm outstretched to keep from bumping into things. He spoke in a low, raspy voice. He seemed to me to be young, maybe around thirty years of age."

"Thank you, sir," said Holmes. "You have been very helpful."

It was now late afternoon. "Watson, I think we should call a halt now and continue tomorrow. We've gathered a lot of information and should take some time to digest it. Let us return to Baker Street."

The next morning, I had almost finished my breakfast when Holmes came out of his bedroom and sat down at the table. I had spent some time last night thinking about what we had learned and I had an idea that I wanted to share with Holmes.

"Holmes, I think I've made a connection. Forsyte was being blackmailed for something he did in the past, or the killer, Mr. *X*, murdered Forsyte in revenge for something he did in the past. Isn't it possible that these two things are the same one? Or that the blackmailer and Mr. *X* are the same person?"

"Perhaps, Watson. That is something I'm already considering, but I doubt that the blackmailer is Mr. *X*. Blackmailers don't kill the goose that lays the golden eggs."

After breakfast, we made our way to the address on the back of Miss Saintsbury's card. It turned out to be a late-Georgian mansion of white marble, with a portico and tall pillars around the front door. The door was opened by an imposing-looking butler, who might have come straight out of a Jane Austen novel. Holmes gave him his card and asked if we might see Mr. Nigel Appleton. The butler stood aside and ushered us into a lavish sitting room. A few minutes later, a young man entered, holding Holmes's card in his hand.

"How do you do, sirs," he said. "I have been expecting you. Charlotte told me that you have taken up my case. How may I help you?"

"First of all, "said Holmes, "we need as much information as possible about you and your relationship to your uncle. For example, Miss Saintsbury said that you were back living in this house. What did she mean by that?"

Appleton's face fell and I could see that he was debating what he should say.

"I can see that absolute honesty is the only path. I ask you that what I tell you here is not spread abroad. I was orphaned at five years of age and came to live with my uncle. Our relationship has always been cordial, if not loving. When I reached my majority, I found a post with an accounting firm and was soon able to have my own flat. I somehow got mixed up with a fast crowd and started to live beyond my means. A few months ago, I borrowed some money from a moneylender. I was paying it off, bit by bit, until two weeks ago, when he called for the entire remaining balance. As you can guess, I did not have it.

"At that time. A friend of mine gave me a tip on a horse running at long odds at Newmarket. He said he had inside information and it was a sure winner. I – er – borrowed ten pounds from the cash box at my employers and was going to replace it the next day after my horse had won. As you can guess, the horse did not win. The missing cash was discovered and I confessed what I had done. My employers did not prosecute, but I was asked to resign my post.

"I gave up my flat and moved in here. Naturally, I had to tell my uncle what the circumstances were and he was very angry. We had strong words about it – or rather, *he* had strong words and I just listened. He was kind enough to lend me the money to pay my debts, but he put me a probation of sorts. I have to find a new post and stay out of trouble for six months. I am looking for a post now."

"I see," said Holmes. "Are you the next of kin to your uncle?"

Appleton blushed to the roots of his hair. "Yes, I am. He had some very distant cousins whom he had never seen. I am the heir in his will. I know that makes it look very bad for me."

"Where were you two days ago between 10:30 and 11:00 a.m.?"

"I had finished an interview in Gresham Street and was walking to Cannon Street for a second one. I didn't take a cab because shillings are not so plentiful with me now."

"If memory serves, "said Holmes, "the direct route between those two streets passes close to your uncle's office."

"Yes, sir. The office is about halfway between the two streets. I passed it about two streets away."

"Very good. I should like to speak to your butler. What is his name?"

"His name is Symes."

Appleton led us out to the hall, introduced us to Symes, and then left us.

"Symes, how long have you been with Mr. Forsyte?" asked Holmes.

"Twenty years, sir."

"Good. Have you ever had any hint that your master was engaged in anything illegal or immoral? Maybe something in his youth before you came to him?"

Symes glowered at Holmes. "Certainly not. Mr. Forsyte was upright. He didn't have an immoral bone in his body. Even if he had done something in his youth, I should think that I would have had some inkling of it in twenty years."

We thanked Symes and returned to Baker Street. Now we had another possibility. Appleton was on bad terms with his uncle and was in the neighborhood of the office when the murder occurred. And a large inheritance is a powerful motive.

The next morning at breakfast, I told Holmes about another idea I had had during the night.

"Holmes, you have earlier said that you didn't think that the blackmailer and the assassin were the same person. I've had a thought. Supposing that Forsyte was about to expose the blackmailer to the police. That would give the blackmailer a motive to kill Forsyte. Does that make sense?"

"Yes, it does Watson, but it leads to other problems. Why would the blackmailer send the threatening letter informing Forsyte of his intent? Surely that would put Forsyte on his guard and make him more likely to go to the police."

"I don't know. This case has me very confused," I admitted.

Nothing new was learned for the next three days. Holmes and I were in our sitting room when a commissionaire arrived with a message from Symes, Forsyte's butler. It read: *"I have just found out what I think is important information. Please come as soon as possible. I have also notified Inspector Lestrade."*

We made our way back to Forsyte's mansion, where Symes ushered us into the sitting room. Lestrade and a maid were already there.

"Sirs," said Symes, "this is Susan Reilly, our maid. She has just told me something that seems to have a bearing on your investigation. First let me explain that the room at the end of the hall is what we call the 'gun room'. That is where Mr. Forsyte keeps his collection of medieval armaments: Swords, halberds, crossbows, maces, and such. The room is hardly ever used. Occasionally Mr. Forsyte would take his dinner guests there to show them his collection, but other than that, no one ever goes there. It is Susan's task to dust the room once or twice a week. Now, Susan, tell the gentlemen your story."

"Sirs, I dusted the room a week ago. I had the feeling that something was wrong. At first, I didn't know what it was. As I dusted the room, I realized that one of the crossbows was missing. I didn't think much of it. I thought the master had taken it for some reason."

"Why didn't you tell this to the police?" asked Lestrade.

"I did not know it was important. I was told that the master had been killed, but no one told me how. It was only this morning that cook told me that he had been shot with a crossbow arrow. I immediately told Symes what I had seen."

"A-ha!" exulted Lestrade. "Now I have him! Appleton had motive to gain the inheritance. He had opportunity to be close to the office, and he has means by taking the crossbow. I suspected him all along."

"One moment, Lestrade," interjected Holmes. "Possibilities are not certainties. What solid evidence do you have to make an arrest?"

"I may not have enough to make an arrest, but I have enough to drag him down to the Yard for a thorough grilling," answered Lestrade, leaving the room.

Holmes just shook his head. As Symes was ushering us to the front door, Holmes noticed a room to one side. "Symes, what is this?" he asked.

"That is the master's office, sir. He and Mr. Bascombe often worked at home, especially if he was working on something important and didn't want to be disturbed."

We had returned to Baker Street and had just finished our lunch when Wiggins appeared. He was the leader of the gang of street urchins who had been jocularly dubbed "The Baker Street Irregulars". Holmes used them occasionally because they could go everywhere and see everything without being noticed.

"Watson, while you were busy with your patients the other day, I gave Wiggins a task to perform. I can tell by his expression that he was successful. Isn't that right, Wiggins?"

"Yes, sir," replied the boy. "I waited outside the bank for three days. This noontime, a man appeared who answered to the description you gave me. He had a full beard, thick glasses, and he walked slowly. He went into the bank and I watched him through the window. He gave the teller a paper and the teller gave him money. After he left the bank, I ran in and asked the teller if that was James Smithers. He said it was."

"Excellent thinking, Wiggins," cried Holmes. "You will go far."

"Thank you, sir. I caught up with Smithers and followed him. He turned the corner and walked a couple of blocks to a tea shop. Through the window I saw him go into the cloakroom. Some minutes later he came out. And what do you suppose happened?"

"I can guess, Wiggins. No beard and no glasses?"

"Yes, sir. It was a disguise. He walked off briskly and I followed him again. But then he hailed a cab and was off. I wasn't close enough to hear the address he gave to the cabman."

"Don't feel badly about that," said Holmes, "I think I already know where he went. Here are three shillings for you. And I think I'll need you again, so stay close."

After Wiggins had left, Holmes said, "Watson, it is always good practice to have more than one string to your bow, which Lestrade should learn. I have been following several lines of investigation and this result narrows down the field considerably."

"But why is it so important that the blackmailer uses a disguise?"

"Think about the description Wiggins gave, Watson, and it will become clear."

At breakfast the next morning, Holmes asked me if I were free at eleven o'clock. I said I was and precisely at that time we were ringing the bell at Forsyte's mansion. Symes conducted us to the sitting room, where we found Lestrade, Harold Calder, Charles Bascombe, Nigel Appleton, and Charlotte Saintsbury. Symes stayed, and Wiggins was also present, hunched down in a chair in the corner. Holmes started right in.

"Thank you all for coming. I've asked you to attend so that you can hear the explanation of the murder of Alexander Forsyte. The case has been confusing from the start. There was the thread of blackmail for some unknown transgression in the past. There was the thread of revenge for some transgression – possibly the same one. And there was the thread of murder in order to gain an inheritance. The problem was to untangle these threads and ascertain which one was the actual motive for the crime. Wiggins, do you recognize anyone here?

Wiggins stood up went around the room, looking each person directly in the face. "Yes, I do, sir."

"Good. As I was saying, the problem was to untangle the threads. As it turns out, none of them was the reason for the murder. The true reason was embezzlement and – Grab him Lestrade!"

Bascombe had jumped up and run for the door. He threw it open and was promptly grabbed by a burly constable who was posted outside. Lestrade ran over and snapped on the handcuffs. He dragged Bascombe back into the room and forced him back into his chair.

"Mr. Holmes, are you quite sure?" said Lestrade uncertainly. "Mr. Bascombe was at his desk when Mr. Forsyte was shot."

"Ah, Lestrade, that was just one of the false scents laid down by Mr. Bascombe. He was very clever at it. Unfortunately, he didn't expect to be opposed by someone cleverer than he. Let me tell you the full story as I have reconstructed it, starting at the beginning.

"Mr. Bascombe had control of Forsyte's checkbook. Every month he wrote a check to James Smithers, a person who did not exist. He forged Forsyte's signature. Wearing a disguise, he opened an account as Smithers at the Merchant Seamen's Bank and cashed the checks there. Wiggins is a witness to that. Bascombe was so well-dressed that I suspected that he had a source of income other than that of his clerk's salary.

"A week or so ago, Forsyte notified his clerks that he was going to sell the business and retire. This was devastating news to Bascombe, since an audit would certainly show the embezzlement, leading to a long term in prison. He stole a crossbow and bolts from Forsyte's house one day when he was there working with Forsyte. Still using his disguise, but using a different name, he then rented an office in the adjoining building, making sure it was on the second floor directly opposite the window of Forsyte's office. A day or two before the murder, he left the crossbow in the empty office."

"But Mr. Holmes," cried Lestrade, "How could he be at his desk and fire the crossbow at the same time? It is impossible."

"It is not impossible. What makes you think that the bolt was fired from the crossbow? In fact, it was not. Forsyte was stabbed with the bolt. The fact that the bolt was not straight into the body proves it. A bolt would not turn down that much in a flight of forty feet or so. The bolt could have been at such an angle if Forsyte were bending forward, but then he would have fallen forward on the desk, not slumped backward in his chair.

"Bascombe stabbed Forsyte during his regular morning meeting. He put the bogus note of revenge in the desk. He hung Forsyte's bowler hat over the doorknob to cover the keyhole to make it seem as if the key were in the lock on the inside. He then locked the door from the outside, put the key in his pocket, and went back calmly to his desk.

"Later, he joined Calder at the locked door and broke the glass with the teapot. While Calder was putting the teapot back on the tray, Bascombe reached through the hole in the glass, threw the hat on the floor and unlocked the door with the key which he had hidden in his hand.

"When he was later interviewed, Bascombe told a pack of lies. Forsyte didn't know anything about Smithers' checks. Forsyte was not fearful that morning. He may have been disappointed in his nephew, but there is no indication that he meant to disinherit him. Do you have any questions?"

"Well, Mr. Holmes," said Lestrade, "that all makes great sense and I think I have enough to make an arrest." With that, he and the constable bundled Bascombe off to Scotland Yard.

"Mr. Holmes, however can I thank you?" asked Miss Saintsbury. "I knew that Nigel was innocent, but I don't think anyone else could have made sense of this."

"It was my pleasure, Miss Saintsbury. This case has been very rewarding."

On our way back to Baker Street, Holmes said that I should be sure to write up this case. "But be sure to stress the logic in it, and don't fill the story with your usual folderol."

The Adventure of the Delusional Wife
by Jayantika Ganguly

My friend Sherlock Holmes and I have had our fair share of dramatic clients and hysterical clients, but one in particular comes to mind, perhaps prompted by a news article I read earlier today. After all, it was unusual for even Holmes to be greeted with an intimate embrace by a fair lady at first sight.

It was some time during the summer of the year 1895. Holmes and I were taking a leisurely walk home rather late at night, returning from a concert by a young musician my friend favoured lately, and an excellent dinner at Simpson's. Holmes was explaining something about Mozart (at this point, I was unsure if this related to the evening's concert at all) while I was half-immersed in a guilty reverie featuring the decadent French dessert we had at dinner, a lovely new addition to Simpson's menu. Just as we turned the corner at Marylebone Road to enter Baker Street, a well-dressed young woman appeared, nearly colliding with us. We stopped just in time and she gaped at my friend, her eyes wide with shock.

Then she leapt forward and threw her arms around Holmes in an intimate embrace with a cry of, "*Mon mari!*"

Surprised, I glanced at my bewildered friend and controlled my urge to burst out laughing with great effort. Holmes's expression was extraordinarily comical – his usual impassive face caught between stupefaction, mortification, terror, and misery. It was a sight I will remember – and laugh at, much to Holmes's displeasure – for the rest of my life.

However, Holmes was nothing if not a well-bred, chivalrous gentleman. Gently, he extracted himself from the lady's arms, murmuring, "I'm afraid you have the wrong man, Madam."

The young woman – she was rather lovely, I observed – appeared outraged, and still somehow managed to cling to Holmes. "Is that the way you ought to speak to your wife, Mr. Sherlock Holmes?" she cried loudly. "How could you do such a thing to me? You abandoned me in Paris the day after we got married, and now, when I have finally found you, you pretend not to know me? What happened to your promises to love and cherish me till death do us part?"

Even Holmes would not be that callous, I thought, watching him struggle in vain to escape the woman's grasp. I looked around, and saw several curious faces peering at us.

"Shall we discuss this at home?" I suggested mildly.

Holmes looked at me with a face that said, "*Et tu, Brute?*"

Stung, I asked, "Do you wish for an audience?"

Before he could reply, the girl grabbed me by arm as well, and both of us were dragged to 221b Baker Street. The woman introduced herself to Mrs. Hudson as Holmes's wife, nearly causing her to faint with shock.

"Dear me, Mr. Holmes," our landlady said, with a hand upon her heart. "When on earth did you get married?"

"On the fifteenth of March this year," the girl declared.

I frowned. Holmes couldn't possibly have been in Paris on that date: He was in England, and I had accompanied him for a particularly vexing case brought by Mycroft Holmes. It was a clandestine affair, however, so we were statutorily bound to remain silent about our involvement in it. Nonetheless, I had to say something in my friend's defence.

"At *La Basilique du Sacré-Cœur de Montmartre*," she continued dreamily. "It was a most romantic day, the Ides of March."

Beware the Ides of March – the words flew unbidden to my mind. I couldn't remain silent any longer. "Impossible," I ejaculated. "Holmes was with me that day."

The woman rounded upon me, apoplectic with rage and pouring forth a string of vile epithets in French.

Holmes held up a hand. "Madam," he said coldly. "I have already said that I do not know you, and I will thank you to keep a civil tongue in your mouth. I will see to it that you receive the psychiatric aid you clearly require."

The woman froze. Her bright blue eyes shimmered with unshed tears as she turned to me and said softly, "My apologies, Dr. Watson. You are a dashing, attractive gentleman and my husband's best friend. I am sorry that I insulted you." She took my hands in her softer ones and stared at me with a miserable expression.

Helplessly, I glanced at Holmes, beseeching him for help. With a peculiar smile on his face, he turned away and strode up the stairs.

I wrenched my hands from the young lady's grasp and followed after my friend, murmuring an apology to Mrs. Hudson.

I found Holmes and his older brother glaring daggers at each other in our sitting room.

"This isn't a good time, Mycroft," Holmes snapped. "Go away."

"Nonsense," Mycroft Holmes said, seated in the most comfortable spot on our couch and leisurely sipping our best brandy. "It is a matter of national importance."

"It is always a matter of national importance with you," Holmes grumbled. "Nonetheless, I have pressing matters to attend."

"Well, then, if something troubles my little brother so, I shall offer you my assistance," Mycroft said gallantly, his grey eyes twinkling with mirth. "What unsettles you so, Sherlock? Could it be a lady?"

"How did you know?" I blurted out inadvertently.

"Elementary," Holmes spat.

Suddenly, I was roughly shoved aside, and the young lady rushed in, greeting Mycroft with a cheerful, *"Beau-frère!"*

I had never seen the mighty Mycroft Holmes so nonplussed before. He recoiled from the young lady's approaching hands with astonishing speed and stared at his brother in horror.

"According to her, we were married in Paris on the fifteenth of March," Holmes said flatly.

Mycroft's expression cleared. "Ah, I see. Is this your 'pressing matter'?"

Holmes nodded reluctantly.

Mycroft turned to the girl and offered her a seat and a drink. She accepted both with gratitude. I poured brandy for everyone and a refill for Mycroft.

"So, my dear girl," Mycroft said jovially. "Why don't you tell me about yourself?"

She frowned. "Sherlock has said nothing about me . . . nothing at all?"

"Ah, my brother is rather reticent – Surely, you must know."

She frowned again. "He was so passionate earlier, proclaiming his love at the *Jardin des Tuileries* and playing his violin for me and asking me to marry him . . . ." She looked at Holmes with brimming eyes.

"I do not know you, and I have never seen you before today," Holmes declared rather callously.

"Now, now, Sherlock," Mycroft chided mildly. "You should be courteous to the ladies."

Holmes leaned back in his seat, glaring silently at his brother.

"My name is Claudine Holmes, *née* de Gouges," the girl said. "I am pursuing medical studies at the *Faculté de Médecine* and currently working as an intern at the *Hôpital de la Pitié de Paris.*"

Mycroft's eyes widened. "Could you possibly be related to André de Gouges, of the *Conseil de Surveillance de l'Administration de l'Assistance Publique?*"

The girl – Claudine – smiled. *"Oui.* That's my Papa."

"What an extraordinary coincidence," Mycroft murmured.

"You know Papa?" Claudine asked.

"Indeed," Mycroft said with a smile. He glanced at his pocket-watch. "I am afraid I must take my leave, my dear. I have an appointment to keep."

The girl grabbed his hand immediately, and the portly man looked extremely uncomfortable. Holmes smiled slightly at his brother's distress.

"Must you?" she asked, turning damp, limpid eyes up at him. "Can't you stay a while and let me speak with you? Perhaps that will remind my husband of our marriage." She threw a glare at Holmes, the very picture of a righteously offended wife.

Mycroft sighed. "I suppose I could reschedule my meeting," he murmured. He turned to me. "Dr. Watson, may I request you to deliver an urgent letter for me to an acquaintance at the Langham? I might cause a diplomatic incident if I simply miss the appointment."

Before I could reply, Holmes interjected, "Watson's leg has been giving him trouble. Let me take it."

Mycroft nodded sympathetically. "Certainly. Thank you, Sherlock." He glanced at the young lady. "My dear girl, you do not mind if I send out my brother for an hour, do you?"

She looked apprehensive. "Will he return?"

"I give you my word that he will," Mycroft said seriously. "Dr. Watson and I will keep you company until then."

"*Bien*," she said, looking none too pleased, but clearly not wanting to offend Mycroft. Courteous as he was, Mycroft Holmes had the undeniable aura of authority that made it difficult to disobey him.

Holmes watched with an impassive face as his brother wrote a short note, but his glittering eyes betrayed his excitement. The game was afoot.

Holmes departed as soon as the note was handed to him. A look of silent understanding was exchanged between the brothers. At the doorway, Holmes paused and glanced at me. He nodded in Mycroft's direction and patted his pocket.

I understood immediately what he meant. *Protect my brother.*

Soon after Holmes's departure, Mycroft requested a refill of his brandy, providing me with an opportunity to retrieve my gun and pocket it.

I watched silently as Mycroft Holmes played the part of a charming, indulgent brother-in-law to perfection. Claudine narrated tales of her courting by Holmes, which involved such outrageously romantic gestures that no one who knew Holmes would believe them. Either this girl was a raging lunatic caught in up in the delusions of a spectacularly delirious mind, or she was an excellent actress with a nefarious purpose whose

230

target was one – or both – of the Holmes brothers. Is that why she had been loitering in Baker Street? If she had really intended to see Holmes, would it not have made more sense for her to introduce herself to Mrs. Hudson and wait for us to return? In any event, I knew I had to remain vigilant. Holmes would never forgive me if I let his brother come to harm on my watch.

I was jolted out of my musings by a loud noise. Claudine had set her glass down on the table with significant force. I was surprised that the glass was still intact.

"I did not mean to cause offence, my dear," Mycroft said mildly. "My brother, despite his cold exterior, has a rather sensitive heart. Given his determination to ignore your existence, I merely wondered if you parted on bad terms. Sherlock has never been very good with affection. I am sure Dr. Watson will agree."

I nodded. "Of course."

To our horror, Claudine burst into tears. "You don't believe me," she cried pitifully. "You think I am making up stories."

The older Holmes shot me a beseeching look. I sighed, wondering when dealing with hysterical women had become my role in the company of the Holmes brothers.

"It is difficult to believe you if the man you call your husband insists he has never seen you before," I said quietly. "Unless he has good reason for it. Holmes is an honourable man. He would not disgrace a lady, much less his wife, without justification."

Claudine sobbed louder. Mycroft and I shrugged helplessly at each other. I was worried that Mrs. Hudson would be brought upstairs by the commotion.

"Good heavens, woman," came Holmes's icy voice from the doorway. "Calm yourself."

"No one believes me!" she wailed.

"And for good reason," Holmes said. He strode in and threw himself upon his usual chair.

A moment later, an elderly gentleman entered the room. Mycroft stood up immediately and greeted him.

Claudine stared at him in shock. "Papa!" she cried. "Why are you here?"

The man frowned at her. "Who are you?"

"Is she not your daughter, Claudine?" Holmes asked.

The man shook his head violently. "*Non.*"

Claudine launched herself at the man, who stepped back, alarmed. "Papa! *Je suis tellement désolée*, Papa!" she said tearfully. "*Désolée, c'est ma faute, j'aurais dû y penser*! I should not have run away from home!"

231

"Where is my daughter?" the man – who I assumed to be André de Gouges, Mycroft's acquaintance – demanded. "What have you done with her?"

"But . . . but I *am* Claudine, Papa!"

Monsieur de Gouges clenched his fists. "As if I would not recognise my own daughter!"

With another wail, Claudine collapsed. Holmes leapt from his chair and caught her before she could hit the floor.

The next instant, the girl was pressing the muzzle of a small pistol to Holmes's temple. I pointed my revolver at her, but it was a stalemate. If she fired, she would kill Holmes before my bullet would hit her.

"You really are a rather chivalrous gentleman, aren't you, Mr. Sherlock Holmes?" the girl said, her voice cold and mocking. It was as if she had transformed into another person right before our eyes. "How I would love to blow your brains out."

There was challenge in Holmes's eyes, as if he was completely unbothered by the threat to his life. "Go ahead," he said calmly.

"Holmes!" I protested.

He waved a casual hand at me. "Not to worry, Watson. If her purpose was to murder me, she would have done so by now. Professional assassins will only kill their assigned targets. Why waste their skill on someone they haven't been paid to finish?"

The girl smiled. "Clever, clever Mr. Holmes," she said. "How did you know?"

"The strength of your grip belied your seemingly frail manner . . . and you clearly do not possess the demeanour of a doctor."

She huffed. "All doctors cannot be like your beloved Watson."

"No," Holmes said. "But all doctors have certain similarities that is a natural result of their training. Your hunting instincts are too strong to successfully affect that manner.

"I see," she said thoughtfully. "I shall certainly keep that in mind next time."

"Good luck," Holmes retorted.

She smiled at him, her eyes predatory. "You really are fascinating. Would you mind being mine for real?"

"I am afraid I must turn down your gracious offer," Holmes replied.

"Pity," she murmured. She looked up at Mycroft. "The bird has flown?"

"Indeed," he replied.

She clicked her tongue in annoyance. "Months of work, all ruined by two clever men," she grumbled. "I didn't want to do this, but you leave me no choice." She jabbed the gun harder against Holmes's temple. "Mycroft Holmes, tell me where to find the bird if you value your brother's life."

Mycroft sighed and remained silent.

"You are choosing a traitor over your brother's life?" she cried.

"The British Empire shall always of paramount importance to my brother," Holmes replied instead, his shoulders shaking with silent laughter. "You are wasting your time. If you wish to shoot me, you can do so."

"You will not make it out of this room alive if you shoot Holmes," I warned.

"What a valiant avenger you have, Sherlock," she drawled. "How on earth shall I make my daring escape?"

In a flash, she turned her gun upon Monsieur de Gouges and fired. The Holmes brothers reacted simultaneously. Mycroft pushed the Frenchman out of the way just as Holmes slapped her arm, changing the bullet's trajectory. Then Holmes knocked the gun out of her palm and pinned her down.

Holmes and I quickly tied her to a chair. For good measure, I injected her with an anaesthetic. We heard Mycroft request the Frenchman to go downstairs and fetch the patrolling policeman on duty.

"Excellent work, Sherlock, Dr. Watson," Mycroft said, as we finished securing the girl.

With a slight smile, Holmes and I looked up at him. It was then that we noticed the blood on Mycroft's arm.

Holmes went pale. "Mycroft? You are hurt?"

"Merely a flesh wound, Sherlock," Mycroft replied, his voice steady and reassuring. His face was white, however, and he was sweating. He staggered a little.

Holmes immediately threw an arm around his brother's waist and helped him to sit. I quickly fetched my medical bag, praying the older Holmes wasn't seriously injured. I examined Mycroft quickly and assured Holmes that it was only a flesh wound that would heal easily. Holmes nodded, but watched with piercing eyes until I finished dressing the wound and Mycroft shook his head at his damaged clothing.

"This was my favourite," he said sadly.

"I will buy you a replacement," Holmes offered.

Mycroft beamed at him. "Thank you, little brother. And don't fret so, Sherlock. I'm all right. You are making the Good Doctor worry."

"I'm sorry that you were shot."

"Merely because my ever-increasing girth proved to be a hindrance," Mycroft said, eyeing his protruding abdomen balefully. "Perhaps I should engage in some physical exercises occasionally."

That drew a strangled laugh from Holmes, much to my surprise – and Mycroft's as well, if the expression on his face was anything to go by.

"You and physical activity are antonyms, Mycroft," Holmes said.

Mycroft huffed. "May I remind you which one of us is the better swordsman?"

"That was years ago," Holmes protested.

"Polish your swords for the next time we meet, then, Sherlock," Mycroft challenged. "*En garde*, little brother."

Approaching footsteps halted their conversation. Holmes stood up and placed himself protectively in front of his brother, hiding the sight of Mycroft's torn sleeve.

Monsieur de Gouges had returned with Morgan, one of the sergeants of whom Holmes actually approved. We quickly summarised the events of the evening to the policeman, keeping Mycroft's involvement out of it except as a spectator. "What a mess," Morgan muttered. "Are you all right, Mr. Holmes?"

Holmes nodded, surprised at the sergeant's concern. "I am. Thank you, Morgan."

"What do we do next, Mr. Holmes?" Morgan asked. "I will arrange for this vicious woman to be taken into custody, but isn't it likely that she will end up in an asylum rather than gaol?"

"She isn't criminally insane," I protested. "She is just a clever criminal with excellent acting abilities."

"I understand, Dr. Watson, but the jury . . . ."

Holmes held up his hand to silence us. "Let her stand trial – we'll see what happens thereafter. Meanwhile, we need to locate the *real* Claudine de Gouges."

Morgan's expression turned sombre. "Do you think she is still alive?"

"I'm certain of it," Holmes replied confidently. "Keep an eye on your prisoner, Morgan."

Soon after, several policemen arrived, and Morgan took the girl away.

"Do you really think that my daughter is alive, Mr. Holmes?" the Frenchman asked once the policemen had left.

Holmes nodded.

Monsieur de Gouges brightened. "Please find her. I came to London to visit your brother for this purpose. Imagine my shock when I found this strange girl pretending to be my Claudine!"

Holmes fixed his raptor gaze upon the Frenchman. "May I enquire why it took you several months to seek aid to search for your daughter, Monsieur de Gouges? It appears to me that she has been missing since March."

"She has, Mr. Holmes," Monsieur de Gouges replied. "In fact, marriage records show that she married an Englishman named *S. Holmes* on the fifteenth of March! Claudine left a letter for us, saying that she was marrying a man but she was afraid I would disapprove of a foreigner, so she would be away for a while. She had already applied for a leave of absence at the university as well as the hospital. However, after six weeks, when there was still no sign of her, I contacted our *Sûreté*, and they found the marriage records and travel records showing the couple had departed for England on a boat from Dunkirk. However, there were no records of them arriving at Dover! Thus, I contacted your brother to ask if he could locate my daughter in England. Perhaps the couple used an alias . . . because if they boarded in Dunkirk, they must have landed in Dover!"

Holmes looked at Mycroft. "Is this your matter of national importance?"

The older Holmes smiled slightly. "Indeed. The description of this *S. Holmes* obtained by the *Sûreté* matches the description of one of the most wanted men on Scotland Yard's list. I fear the girl may have been abducted, and the fake Claudine may be an accomplice." His expression darkened. "There is espionage involved, Sherlock. You must find the girl quickly."

Holmes turned to the Frenchman. "Why would anyone abduct your daughter and keep her hidden for several months?"

The Frenchman and Mycroft Holmes exchanged a look.

"The entirety of this week," Mycroft told us, "we are to engage in confidential negotiations with a certain African dignitary, on behalf of the British government and the French government. Representatives from several other countries have also arrived in London for this purpose. The British and French governments have decided to present a joint proposal, which is likely to succeed compared to the others. Needless to say, one or perhaps more of the others do not wish to see us succeed. If this dignitary were to be assassinated – or even grievously injured – while in England, the consequences would be enormous,"

"This was your urgent appointment today?"

"Yes, but we rescheduled as soon as Monsieur de Gouges contacted me. Our schedule is completely different now, including the venue. The other representatives will continue their appointments as scheduled."

"Isn't that detrimental?" I asked.

"The protection of this person is of utmost importance, Dr. Watson," Mycroft said.

"How long have talks been ongoing about this?" Holmes asked.

"The dates and venue for this meeting were decided last December."

235

"Plenty of time to hire assassins and enquire into the background of the British and French representatives, then," I observed. "Is that why they used your name and abducted Claudine de Gouges?" I asked Holmes. "They even found a date upon which your whereabouts could not be accounted for."

Holmes nodded. "They have been very thorough."

Mycroft fixed his gaze upon his brother, and Holmes stared back. Their eyes were the same – grey, sharp, and cleverer than anyone else's.

"You can work in peace, Brother," Holmes said. "I will find the girl and bring her back safely within a day."

Mycroft smiled. "There you have it, Monsieur de Gouges. If Sherlock says he will do it, it is as good as done. We can return to work. Let us make our collaboration a success."

Monsieur de Gouges bowed. "*Merci*, Mr. Holmes. I will have the papers from the *Sûreté* delivered to you in a few hours."

"Thank you."

Monsieur de Gouges took his leave.

"It is nearly morning," Mycroft said ruefully. "My apologies for keeping you up this late, Dr. Watson

I assured him that it was perfectly all right and offered him an analgesic for his arm, which he refused. I noticed Holmes's face harden at the mention of his brother's injury yet again.

"Rest here, Mycroft," Holmes said. "There is no point in you going back home now, and I want you to remain under Watson's eye.

"Really, Sherlock, there is no need to be concerned," Mycroft grumbled. "It is a minor injury.

"The last time you said that, you nearly died," Holmes snapped. "For my peace of mind, if nothing else, let Watson care for you. At least you shall not terrify him into conceding your welfare.

Mycroft Holmes laughed heartily. "That is true. Dr. Watson is used to treating you, after all." He turned to me and said kindly, "Despite Sherlock's allegations, Dr. Watson, I assure you that I am a much better patient than him . . . unless you ask me to exercise.

It was only my years of medical practice and field experience that allowed me to keep my face neutral

Holmes sent his brother to his room to sleep, and settled in the sitting room with a pound of shag tobacco. I retired to my room to rest as well. Dealing with two Holmes brothers at once was rather tiring

When I woke up, it was already nine. Holmes had left, and Mycroft was enjoying his breakfast – which, I noticed, was far more extravagant than what Holmes and I normally received. Mrs. Hudson always favoured Mycroft, much to Holmes's dismay – but then, Mycroft could be even more charming than Holmes when he chose to be. She fawned over the older Holmes even more than usual – it appeared that before he left, Holmes had informed her that the girl who was pretending to be his wife yesterday was actually an assassin who shot Mycroft, and that his brother needed some care. She wasn't to let Mycroft out of the house, and no one was to be allowed into our quarters, either. Mrs. Hudson took to the task quite devotedly.

The older Holmes, on the other hand, seemed to be rather bored. I handed him a pile of unsolved cases which Holmes had put aside because they hadn't caught his interest, and it took him barely an hour to finish them all. I offered him my unpublished case-notes next, which he read through with great enthusiasm.

"Sherlock really is doing well," he commented. "You have my gratitude, Doctor."

I shot him a confused look.

Mycroft smiled indulgently and refused to explain, returning his eyes to the notes. He had read through all of them by the time his brother returned with a pale girl in tow.

Mycroft's eyes widened in recognition. "Mademoiselle Claudine?" he asked.

The girl nodded nervously.

"Where on earth has your father been hiding you? Your mother and uncle have been out of their minds with worry," Mycroft said.

"I was in a small convent in Surrey," she said quietly. "My . . . false husband . . . abandoned me there a few days after we arrived in England. I was put in seclusion and not even permitted to speak to anyone outside or send a letter home." She shuddered. "It was worse than prison. I thought I would lose my mind. Then Papa came to see me last week and I was so happy, but instead of taking me home, he told me I would have to stay there for a few more weeks. It was then that I knew he and Sherman had been in it together." Silent tears dripped down her face. "Why would he do that to me, to his own daughter . . . ?

"Man's greed knows no bounds," Holmes said.

"How did you know?" I asked Holmes.

"It was evident, Watson. Monsieur de Gouges was familiar with the girl we caught yesterday, and he was rather surprised to see her here. When I took Mycroft's letter to him yesterday and told him that his daughter was waiting for us at Baker Street, he was quite nervous – rather than relieved. The girl acted on her own – she wasn't supposed to contact us. I believe she was put on surveillance duty to look for Mycroft, but when she ran into us last night, she decided to have some fun. It upset the plan. Besides,

237

what father delays the search for his missing child, even if a letter is left behind?

"How did you find her?

"Well, my grand declaration made him anxious and he sent a lackey to the convent to ensure his daughter remained there. I merely followed the man, knocked him out, pretended to be the lackey, and retrieved her.

"Well done, Sherlock, well done," Mycroft said. "Your legwork is incomparable.

The subtle shift in Holmes's expression showed his pleasure. His brother's compliments always pleased him the most . . . perhaps because Mycroft was his only acknowledged superior.

"What will happen to Papa?" the real Claudine asked.

Mycroft sighed. "He will lose his position, in all likelihood, I am afraid," he said. "However, he has also served his country faithfully for many years, so his punishment shouldn't be too harsh, either. It will be up to your government, my dear.

Mycroft's words turned out to be true. The French government hushed up the matter and Monsieur de Gouges suddenly declared his retirement and moved to his ancestral house in the French Riviera for the rest of his days. Claudine, on the other hand, went on to become one of the best and most famous doctors in Paris. The man who had pretended to marry her was also soon caught, thanks to Holmes.

The false Claudine was sent to an asylum, as Morgan had feared, and was released on grounds of good behaviour in a few months. We heard no more of her, until, a few years later, an unsigned postcard from Egypt arrived, addressed to Holmes, with the words, *"You never did ask for my name, mon mari."* Holmes said nothing, and with a small smile, put the postcard away in his drawer.

Child's Play
by C.H. Dye

[The letters from the brassbound trunk are yellowed and tied together with the ribbon from a box of rock candy. Some of the pages are lacy with snipped out pieces, victims of the censor's scissors, and others are missives so short that it's clear that they were sent merely to indicate the continued existence of the author. Near the end of the packet is a thicker sheaf, and the top page bears a date in the spring of 1916.]

My dear Ann,

I know I have been a poor correspondent these past few weeks, but it is difficult to find things to tell you that the censor will not cut away. The war, like all wars, has its measures of tedium, and its bursts of madness, even here in the relative safety of the hospital, but I think the worst of the recent [Paragraph Removed]. *And I have time once again. I remember that in a letter last autumn you asked if I would ever write a story about me, and not my friend Mr. Sherlock Holmes – one in which I played a major part.*

To be honest with you, my dear, I might dream at night of the Afghan War, but I have no heart to compare it with the fresh horrors that surround me. The years when Holmes was "dead" are equally painful to recall, given the other losses that befell. But if you will consent to be my editor, I have thought of a tale which might be of interest to you, if no one else. Holmes is in it, of course, but in this case I truly contributed skills of my own.

It was in the hottest part of summer, in one of the busy years after his return, that Holmes and I were called in to act in an unofficial capacity in the matter of the kidnapping of the youngest son of a certain peer of the realm. I have hesitated to put pen to paper about this matter before, it is because at the time the utmost secrecy was required. Even in this letter to you, it is incumbent upon me to obscure the identity of the noble family involved by altering names, and more, for the matter was a delicate one. No whisper of the kidnapping reached the police or the newspapers at the time, although the boy was snatched from his nurse in broad daylight, right in front of his badly frightened sisters. Indeed, Holmes would not have been called in at all, had not the eldest of those sisters, a determined young lady in her ninth year, put her mother into an even greater panic by escaping her father's London house via the scullery and coming to Baker Street of her own volition.

"Lady Agatha Petherbridge," Mrs. Hudson announced our visitor with an amused light in her eye, presenting us with a visiting card that had been created from the side of a cardboard box, a sharp pencil, and great determination.

"Send her up, by all means," Holmes said, handing the card to me. I had cajoled Holmes into agreeing to a dinner at Simpson's, followed by a visit to the opera, and we were moments away from starting out, but I could hardly resent the delay. He had been skirting the edge of a black mood for days, and I welcomed any distraction which would keep his thoughts away from his dusty morocco case.

"Another missing cat, do you think?" he inquired brightly, referring to another case which had been brought to us by a child. But the moment that Lady Agatha stepped into the sitting room I saw his eyes darken with concern.

She looked from one of us to the other and settled quickly upon Holmes. "You don't look very like your picture in *The Strand Magazine*," she told him, in a voice that trembled.

"It would be disadvantageous if I did," Holmes said, quite seriously. "Even criminals do read those stories, after all."

Her lips pursed and her eyebrows drew down. "Does that mean the stories aren't true? That you aren't as clever as they make you out to be?"

I thought it best to intervene. "Mr. Holmes is every bit as clever as the stories make him out to be, my Lady. But even he cannot help you unless you tell him why you're here."

She twisted her hands together. "It's a secret. And I'm telling. And it may get Lammie killed, but I can't see any other way to get him back. We're not allowed to go to the police."

"Lammie is your brother?" Holmes asked.

"Yes. His name is Andrew, really, but we call him Lammie. He's just a baby, you see, so Nurse was calling him Lambkin, except Miggins – my sister, Margaret – she's a baby, only a bigger one, she started calling him Lammie and now we all do."

Her thin hands were still twisting relentlessly, and Holmes reached out to take them into his own.

"Did you see what happened? Were you there when your brother was taken?"

"Yes. And I know who took him. Well, one of them anyway. The little man from the corner. He had a scarf over his face, but I know it was

240

him. He had the same trousers on. There's a patch on the knee that's been put on crooked."

"You're very observant," Holmes said, and her shoulders straightened at the praise. "What else can you tell me about the man from the corner?"

"He isn't English. I heard him swearing at a stray dog the day before yesterday, and he didn't use any of the words that Father does, or even any of the ones that the grooms do when they've had a horse step on their toes. It didn't even sound like English."

"Could it have been German or French?" I asked. She shook her head. "No, the sounds were all wrong for either of those. And I don't think it was Russian." She tugged at Holmes's hands.

"Please. Come with me and you can see him for yourself. I had to climb out the scullery window and go through the mews to come here because he's watching our front door, or he was when I left. Please come. Mama's probably worried about me too by now."

Holmes and I returned with Lady Agatha by the same route as she had come to us, escaping a beating from two burly footmen only because our young client intervened. But we were hustled up the stairs roughly nonetheless, and into the presence of the Duchess, who was pale with fear, and heavy with the promise of another child to come. I will not recount the details of that discussion with the Duchess. I cannot, for even now there are parties whose lives and reputations would be at risk.

Suffice it to say that the Duke, at that very moment, was on the Continent, engaged upon a secret diplomatic mission, despite the fact that all England thought him to be recuperating from a lengthy illness at home, and the Duchess was certain that even if he were informed of the kidnapping, his honor would demand that he refuse to allow his son to be a hostage against that mission. Indeed, the kidnappers were pressing the Duchess not for money, but for her husband's true location, promising to deliver the child into his father's hands intact if she would only deliver them the opportunity of discovering the parties to the negotiations. It was clear that Holmes would not be able to consult with the police for assistance. Not even Mycroft Holmes – whose sympathies would be certain to lie with the diplomats – could be trusted. With a European war hanging in the balance, the sacrifice of one tiny boy was of little moment to anyone but his mother, his nurse, and his badly frightened sisters.

The man whom Lady Agatha had identified as one of the kidnappers was selling pinwheels at the entrance of the park across the street. He was small, and dark, and his clothing made me think of the Balkans. Holmes and the Duchess were still discussing how to go about rescuing the child when another man came up to speak to him. "That's his friend," Lady Agatha told me, pointing out the arrival. "I've seen him before, too."

"That's a messenger," I realized. "Holmes! We can follow him to the child!"

"So we can," Holmes agreed. "Your Grace, as you do not actually know the location of your husband at the moment, continue to tell the kidnappers the truth. They'll be watching for messages to arrive. I'll send you messages too, pretending to be him, to throw them off the track, always including the word 'because' as the beginning of a sentence. We must buy time."

"Yes. Yes," she agreed, as we hurried down to the scullery again to make our way out of the house. And so it was that when we began to follow the trail of the kidnappers, we did so with nothing more than the clothes upon our backs and the heavy money-belts which were thrust into our hands by the Duchess at the last moment.

"Bribe them if you think it will work, pay any ransom you must," she ordered Holmes, "but bring me back my lamb!"

We were just in time. The messenger was sauntering away, and we fell into place behind him, following as inconspicuously as we could. Thankfully, night was falling as we neared the docks, where our attire made us stand out far more than our prey.

He never hesitated, but leapt into a small boat tied amongst the others beside the quay and began to row out to a sloop which was anchored farther out in the river. He'd no sooner climbed aboard the sloop than we could see the men aboard it preparing to set sail.

"The boy must be aboard," Holmes said, pounding his fist against a piling in frustration. "If it weren't for the need for secrecy, we could have the river police stop them right now." He nodded to the familiar blue lights of a patrol boat further out on the water.

"If it weren't for the police," I countered, "we could take one of these boats and go out there to fetch the boy back ourselves."

Holmes shook his head. "I don't know how to sail a boat, in any case," he admitted. And at my incredulous look he shrugged. "I've never had the opportunity to learn."

"Holmes," I said patiently. "I know how to sail."

"You do?" he cocked his head at me and then nodded decisively, reaching for his purse. "Which one of these boats is big enough to sail across the Channel?"

> *[At this point the page is cut across and new pages of a different size, written in a different the color of ink, are appended with a straight pin . . . .]*

It may come as no surprise that Holmes and I were in the habit of always carrying our passports and papers. Still, the customs officials in Dieppe were openly curious as to why two English gentlemen had sailed to France in evening clothes and a rather ancient sailboat. Fortunately, the older man remembered Holmes's name from that business in Lyons long ago, and was more than pleased to find himself sworn to silence. He provided us with two heavy sailor's coats, and the direction of the doctor he had recommended to the party with the sick baby who had come ashore two hours before us, and from there the hunt began in earnest.

In theory, the chase was quite exciting – Holmes was at his brilliant best, and the kidnappers were suspicious enough of possible pursuit that we were hard put to keep them from vanishing from our ken – but in practice it was rather uncomfortable. We were seldom able to take a proper meal, and indeed seldom able to sleep in anything resembling a bed. Gradually we accrued the necessities. A razor here, clean stockings there, and eventually a carpetbag when our pockets grew too heavy. Our formal clothes were put into the bag as we acquired local attire, but even that precaution was insufficient. Holmes constantly traded our coats for coats of a different make or color, and I soon lost track of which hat was meant to be mine. Fortunately, the Duchess's largess was mostly in the form of gold coins, and they found a welcome everywhere we travelled. Our quarry moved constantly, and the child was handed over from one party to another whilst in France and again in Austria.

Ten days, and nearly as many countries later, the kidnappers finally went to ground in a decrepit neighborhood of Belgrade, affording Holmes and me the chance to rest and plan a rescue. Extracting young Lord Andrew from their clutches was not going to be simple, however, given that there was more than a little evidence that they had confederates among the officials of the city, and the need for secrecy was still paramount. We decided to take a leaf from the kidnappers' own book and simply take the boy back, rather than attempting to pay a ransom. Holmes would pose as an itinerant and insistent peddler of tinware at the front of the house whilst I crept in the back and retrieved the baby.

My instructions were specific. To collect the child, signal my success to Holmes, and immediately leave the city, taking passage up the Danube to Vienna, where I would resume my persona as respectable medical gentleman, hire a nursemaid to take care of the boy, and make my way by rail to the port of Hamburg. From there I would take ship to Newcastle, and thence to the Duke's country estate in Yorkshire. Holmes would draw pursuit in another direction, most likely by rail, and send telegrams to various places for me to call for as his itinerary became clearer. He would attempt to join me, but I wasn't to count on his assistance. There was no guarantee he could shake off pursuit soon enough to be of any use.

It was necessary to make several purchases to support my role, since I would be crossing borders and my luggage was certain to be inspected at some point along the way: Secondhand clothes, new collars, a medical kit from a pawnshop near the university, and a small stock of the remedies I thought I might need. But the most important of my preparations was the purchase of a medium-sized trunk. I stocked it with infant necessities – napkins and smallclothes, as well as the other sundries required for the care of a boy not quite eighteen months of age – and a supply of tinned milk, rusks, and jam to tide the child over until I could purchase better food. The trunk I sent with my newly acquired luggage to await my arrival at the dock. It was not, perhaps, the most ideal of cradles, but it would do once stuffed with cushions. I also acquired a bolster, which Holmes and I wrapped in a blanket and fashioned into a bundle of approximately the same size and shape as the bundle I hoped to be carrying after I had rescued Lord Andrew. As the rescue had to be made in the hour before nightfall, it wouldn't do for my appearance to alter noticeably.

The house where the boy was being held was at the end of the row, and my approach from the back had to be made under the eyes of several children and some young women who were out beating rugs. I paid them only as much mind as I might pay to the children of Baker Street – nonchalance being a better disguise than skulking. My ears were pricked for noises from the front. Holmes had promised me an excellent distraction. It came, right on cue, in a huge clatter of tin and a volley of shouts. The children immediately darted away to go watch what promised to be a fight, and the women weren't far behind them. That left me free to test the door handle of the house I wished to enter. Much to my relief, it turned, and I stepped quickly inside.

The kitchen passageway I entered was pleasantly cool in comparison to the heat of the low summer sun, and had my errand been less vital I might have lingered there. As it was, I paused only long enough to slip the felt covers over my shoes, to muffle the sound of my footsteps on the flagstones as I made my way deeper into the house. There was no telling in which room the kidnappers had the baby. He might be anywhere from the scullery to the attics. I searched as quickly as I dared, trying not to think too wistfully of my revolver, or the walking stick which waited with my luggage, for the only weapon I had to hand was a sand-filled sock. In any event, fortunately, neither weapon proved necessary. At the top of the stairs I found a door that had been left open and a glance through it showed me a cot in the corner of the room. I was beside it in a flash, and wasted no time in exchanging my bolster for the sleeping child. That he would

244

continue sleeping was guaranteed by a bottle of "mother's helper" still open on a small table near the window. I took a moment to tip a bit of it out and taste it, so that I could estimate the concentration of the opiates and alcohol in the mixture. It was a foul brew, despite the treacle that had been used to sweeten it, but I could only be glad of it at that moment. The child would raise no fuss to alert his kidnappers as I removed him.

Holmes and I had argued about the next step in the plan, but as I gazed on the flushed face of the child, I conceded the necessity. Out of a pocket I drew a small pot of henna, mixed with water and oil. I lay a glob of it on Lord Andrew's upturned cheek. His opium-induced slumber was so heavy that he never stirred to disturb the dye.

From my vantage point next to the window, I could look down upon the street. Holmes, in his guise as a tinker, was exchanging shrill unpleasantries and occasional blows with three men, who were baiting him like dogs with a bull from different corners. The noise had gathered a large crowd, and I took some comfort in the thought that so public a murder would be unlikely. But it galled me nonetheless to have to turn away, knowing that there was already blood on Holmes's shirt.

Down the stairs I went, then, the weight of the child in my arms as heavy as my duty, and back out into the alleyway. Once clear of the house I pulled a dog whistle from my pocket and blew upon it until every mongrel in the vicinity was howling, and half-a-dozen of the wretched beasts were trying to attach themselves to my ankles. The howling I approved – it would signal to Holmes that I had the child and he could break off the confrontation in the street. The dogs at my heels he had planned for, and I left them arguing over a string of sausages from my pocket. Four streets over I was able to attract the attention of a cab driver, and I settled gratefully onto the cushions. The trip was not a long one, but it gave me sufficient time to change my jacket and to check on the artificial birthmark which the henna had left on Lord Andrew's face. I had to admit that Holmes was correct. No one asked to describe me and the baby now would omit mention of that temporary disfigurement. It drew the eye away from blond curls and blue eyes, and made the small face seem older.

By sunset we were at the river. Holmes had negotiated my passage with a rapscallion Roumanian riverman named Ionescu, whose boat, the *Mirela*, was primarily devoted to freight of one sort or another, but which had a tiny cabin that could be turned to my use. "A smuggler, but an honest one," Holmes had told me, based on his observations, after he'd turned over the fare. "Just stay out of the cargo hold and you should have no trouble."

You can imagine my dismay when I realized that the launch which was drawn up against the side of the *Mirela* bore the markings of a customs official. There were uniformed men on the deck of the boat, along with the small crew, and it seemed that some sort of confrontation might be taking place. But Ionescu, seeing me hesitate on the dock, raised a lazy hand in greeting and signalled one of his men to take a small boat to fetch me.

Once aboard, I was ushered down to a tiny cabin by the crewman, half-filled already with my luggage. He demonstrated how to close the porthole and lit the lamp, all the while explaining in a mix of German and Roumanian and Turkish that I need only give the customs official the proper baksheesh and we would soon be on my way.

But the customs official, when he came down to speak with me, seemed far more concerned with the possibility of disease than of mischief. By that time I had begun my own examination of the child, and my stethoscope was hanging from my neck, but I think, in retrospect, that my own high color and perspiration must have made it seem as if I too were unwell. I said that the boy was suffering only from mismanagement of the usual "summer complaint", but it was not until we had, by thermometer, eliminated the possibility of fever in the boy and myself, that the man's scowl lessened.

"This boy is your son?" I was asked. while Ionescu watched from the doorway, his eyes glittering with curiosity.

"No. The son of a friend, whose wife has died in childbirth," I explained, the lie coming glibly to my lips. "I am taking him to his Aunt, where he can be cared for properly."

"And why do you go by river?" he persisted, drawing out a notebook. "Surely the train would be faster?"

"Faster, yes, and more comfortable," I agreed. "But no place to wash napkins if he soils them." I gestured at the porthole. "This way I have the entire river."

"Why not wait until tomorrow, and the regular steam packet? It will reach Vienna much sooner than the Mirela."

"Because the hotel where I slept last night has bedbugs. And because I do not mind if the journey is slow. I can use the rest."

Both answers were true, which is perhaps what made them convincing. In any case I have no doubt that my exhaustion from the long chase was evident upon my features. Ionescu thought them good enough, for he intervened. "You see, my friend," he said, clapping the customs man on the shoulder with one hand while he signalled to me by rubbing his thumb against his fingers with the other and then spreading his hand wide. "Everything is as I told you. And now you can finish your work and go home to your wife and supper." The official nodded and smiled stiffly, stamped my passport, accepted the five sovereigns I belatedly offered, and made his way above decks once more.

246

Once they were gone, I latched the door and lay the baby down on the narrow bunk before opening the trunk so as to ready it for the night. As I sorted through the clothes and cushions, looking for the oilcloth which I hoped would be sufficient protection for the rest of the contents, something crackled within one of the pillowcases. I stopped to draw it out. A sealed fold of parchment, addressed to the King of Bohemia in Holmes's most formal hand, lay on top, and beneath it, on rougher paper, ten dancing men scrawled in a single line. *"Just in case,"* I parsed out. I admit it unnerved me. That Holmes thought it worth the risk to leave the letter in my luggage was bad enough – what if that customs official had insisted upon checking through my things – but that he foresaw the possibility that I might find myself in a state of such *extremis* that I must seek help from his former client! And yet, already I had spent more than I planned on bribes. I tucked the letter into my breast pocket and resolved that I would use my money much more carefully, in the hopes of never needing it.

I finished preparing the trunk and settled my young charge in amongst its cushions as the boat began to make headway, and the gentle lap of the waves against the hull became a steady, soothing splashing. The hot breeze came in at the porthole, promising to cool as the night deepened.

All at once, the exertions and excitement and oppressive heat of the day combined to rob me of all my energy. I stripped off my coat and waistcoat and lay down on the bunk, hoping that a short nap might revive me. I'd taken several measures to prevent the lid of the trunk from closing, but I thought it best to reach over a hand and rest it beside the baby too. With that precaution in place, I let myself doze, but I soon fell into a heavy sleep. I dreamt of Mary, and of our daughter Rose, who had not lived to see her first birthday, and woke from the dream in a cold sweat when the boat's whistle sounded, anxiously lifting Lord Andrew out of the trunk to be certain that he was still breathing.

He frowned and blinked open his eyes, saw a stranger and began to wail his dissatisfaction. I found myself rocking him, and singing to him, as I had once sung to my own child, and after a time he settled his small head against my chest and stuffed his fingers into his mouth for comfort. It was well into the night, and the air off the river was damp and refreshingly cool. The lamp had failed, but the moonlight coming in at the porthole was sufficient for me to examine my situation and despair at the myriad of problems which were embodied by the child resting in my arms. Most pressingly, I had no notion of whether or not the lad's abductors had kept him on a reasonable sanitary schedule.

Common sense told me that I should immediately set about ensuring that he would stay clean and dry, but I hesitated, caught in memories of another tiny warm body tucked up against mine, and Mary smiling from

247

her chair. She had teased me – Oh yes, she had! – about how much I had fallen in love with our Rose. But it was she who died of grief not long after that terrible morning when we woke to find the baby cold and still. No minister of the church can explain to me why God calls back a child who went to bed smiling and healthy and playing peek-a-boo between her fingers. Cot deaths, we call them, we doctors, and blame mothers for somehow endangering the babes they love. I had no answer for Mary when she begged me for one – no logical reason why our Rose had suddenly become nothing more than a *memento mori*, a stiff, small bundle in a black-framed photograph, so clearly not merely asleep in her mother's arms. Not even Sherlock Holmes could have solved that mystery.

A spreading damp told me that I had lingered too long in contemplation, and I admit to being glad of it, for attending to the practicalities drew my attention inexorably to the present. Lord Andrew was older than Rose had ever been, and a boy, and the differences were all the more apparent as he argued the process of being changed into clean clothes with me in that astonishingly comprehensible infant language of tone and gesture. By the time I had finished, he had lectured me quite thoroughly.

He did have a few words of English, however, the most important of them the word "Up!" delivered as an imperious command once his buttons were buttoned.

"You'll have to wait a moment, my Lord," I told him. "Uncle John needs to change his shirt."

"Up!" he said again, and lifted his arms to me.

"I'm wet," I protested, pointing to the evidence.

He cocked his head at me, considering. "Weh?"

"Yes, Uncle John is wet." I pulled my shirt up over my head and removed my equally damp vest.

As I bent down to set my things aside, he grabbed for my hands and made his infant demand once again. This time I acceded to the request, and when he promptly began to investigate my face with his hands, went to sit where the moonlight would allow him to more easily study my features.

"No Don," he informed me, frowning.

"Yes, John," I said, realizing that he had hoped for some more familiar face. "I'm just a different John, Lammie. A new John." He wasn't sure whether or not to believe me, and studied me some more, as babies will, with touch as well as vision, tugging at my mustache and patting my bare shoulders. When his untrimmed fingernails found the scar on my chest, I flinched despite myself. The baby flinched in turn, freezing and watching me with trepidation. "It's all right," I reassured him, moving his

248

hand gently across the old scar. "I just wasn't expecting that. It's all right, Lammie. It doesn't hurt anymore."

A quiet tap at the door surprised me, but it was followed by a childish voice saying, "Awake? Want food?" in clear, if ungrammatical, English.

I got to my feet, carrying the baby, and went to unlatch the door. Ionescu's son – a lad of perhaps twelve years – stood there with a tray of bread and grapes and cheese. He smiled up at me. "You sleep for food. I bring you. Papa say baby want goat? We get for daytime."

"Why on earth would the baby want

[Here the page is torn, and there appears to be some part of the tale gone astray, for the ink and paper change once more. The next few pages show signs have having been water damaged and dried again before they were written upon.]

By the morning of the third day we were still south of Buda and Pesth, but I could only be grateful for the delays. His little Lordship threw off the lingering effects of the opiates he had been fed at last and proved to have a sunny disposition, and a great deal of energy and curiosity. Indeed, he was so much improved that had not Nicolae produced a sleeveless jerkin with a loop at the back to which we could attach a safety line, I would have felt less-than-safe allowing him out of my arms whenever we went on deck. I repaid Nicolae by furthering his English lessons at the same time that I played with Lord Andrew, drawing pictures on a slate with chalk for both of them to try to name. Nicolae in his turn offered to watch the baby whilst I did any errands ashore – an offer I gladly accepted. When at last we came to the great twin cities of Hungary that afternoon, I found a vendor with English books and newspapers near the post office and purchased a copy of *Treasure Island*, knowing that a good story would do more for the boy's grasp of English than a dozen dictionaries.

At the post office, I found two telegrams in my name from Holmes. The first had been sent from Sophia, and the second from Varna on the Black Sea, and neither included any information to the point. I sent an equally nonsensical reply for Holmes to find at Constanta on the Black Sea, knowing he would look only at the time and place, as I had done.

With a lighter heart, I returned to the Mirela, only to find Ionescu in a dangerous mood. He scowled from the foredeck all that evening, even while I read aloud from Nicolae's book to the fascination of more than one member of the crew. It wasn't until we were five miles further upriver that Ionescu approached me. By then, Lammie was asleep, and I was ready to take him below again.

249

"Captain," I said, recognizing that this was a moment to acknowledge his authority.

"Come with me," he ordered gruffly. "Nicolae, put the little one to bed and stay with him until the doctor comes."

"Yes, Papa."

I gave Lammie to Nicolae and followed Ionescu to his cabin. It was larger than mine, with a real bed and a large desk as well as space for chairs. He took one of the chairs and waved me into the other before spreading a newspaper out on his knee. "Can you read Serbian?" he asked.

"Not more than enough to ask for a hotel or my dinner," I said.

"Then I will tell you that on this page there is a reward posted worth more than five-hundred *lei* to find a kidnapped child. A boy, with blond hair and blue eyes, of just the age of the boy you brought aboard my boat. A boy who was stolen from his home in Belgrade three days ago."

"Lammie's home isn't Belgrade," I protested. "You can try speaking Serbian to him, if you like, to see what he understands."

"I did try. And you are right – he does not understand the language. Too, he has the mark on his face, which the description does not mention." He tapped the paper meaningfully. "But *I* have been to India. And I have looked in your cabin and found this." He pulled the pot of henna paste from his pocket and set it on the desk. "Five-hundred *lei* is a lot of money."

I rubbed my face with both hands while I made the calculation. He was right. It was a great deal of money. "I don't have the resources to pay you that much," I admitted. "But I doubt the people who placed that advertisement truly intend to pay." Holmes might have been able to think of a convincing tale, but I was going to have to resort to the truth. Holmes . . . . I felt for the letter in my jacket pocket and drew it out. It was still sealed, and addressed to the King of Bohemia, but surely Holmes had considered what to reveal and what to keep secret when he wrote it. "Can you read German or English?"

"German, of course. English?" He wobbled a hand. "Train schedules, bills of lading, that sort of thing."

"Well, I'm not sure which this is written in," I said, holding out the letter. "But it may explain everything. I was given it in case things became desperate."

Ionescu scowled again but accepted the letter and broke the seal after looking long and hard at the inscription. I caught a glimpse of a few words and took a deeper breath. It was in German, thank goodness, and by the way Ionescu's gaze was moving down the page, he was reading with ease. When he reached the signature, he blinked and threw his head up to look at me, mouth fallen open. "Sherlock Holmes?" he exclaimed. "The

250

Sherlock Holmes of London? You are *that* John Watson? They are *your* stories?"

"I thought you said you couldn't read English!" I exclaimed.

"I read them in German. But in the last one he fought with Moriarty and went over the waterfall, didn't he? But now you say he is alive? In the story you lied?"

"Yes, Sherlock Holmes is alive. You met him. He's the man who negotiated my passage," I said. "And no, I didn't lie in the story. I thought he was dead for three years, until he came back to London." I smiled ruefully. "Holmes thinks I'm a terrible liar."

"It's true, you are," Ionescu said genially. "Your ears, they go red."

Did they? "Well, there's not much a fellow can do about that," I mumbled into my mustache. Ionescu was reading the letter again, his expression flickering between pleasure and concern. At last he handed it back to me, shaking his head.

"We have a problem, my friend," he said. "The man who gave me this newspaper – he saw Nicolae playing with the baby, and I am a good liar, but I do not think he believed me when I said they were both my sons."

"You lied?"

Ionescu shrugged. "He lied to me, I lied to him. He said he was a riverman, looking for work, but he smelled of police stations."

"Oh, dear." I wanted to pace, but the cabin was too small to do it comfortably. "I could disembark at the next village. Buy a carriage or a cart and a horse, and take the boy on that way. I don't want to bring you trouble."

Ionescu dismissed the possibility of trouble with the sweep of one broad hand. "If he was police you are safer on the river, where the police must argue about whose turn it is to make arrests. And I do not think he wished to involve the Hungarians, and will want still less to involve the Austrians. No, if he comes it will be to steal away the child from us. And he may bring friends."

"Even more reason for me to go," I said. "What if Nicolae were to get hurt?"

"Nicolae knows where to hide if he must. He will not be hurt, and if he is, it must be on my head. No, you will stay with me, and when all is done and safe, you will find a way to make up for me those five-hundred *lei* I am not collecting."

"His mother will probably pay it," I agreed. "And gladly."

Ionescu chuckled. "I was thinking more of a story from you, a story of how your friend came to be alive. There should be more stories of Sherlock Holmes in the world."

I took the hand he offered. "And there shall be, if he ever gives me permission to publish them. But in the meantime I would be glad to tell you what I know."

The next two days were busy for me. Between Nicolae's pleas for more of *Treasure Island*, his father's hopes for more tales of Sherlock Holmes, and Lord Andrew's infant insistence that I spend his waking hours conversing with him about everything he saw or felt or heard or touched or smelt, I had little time to fret over the need to trust Ionescu and his crew for protection.

I could not, in conscience, ask Ionescu to alter his arrangements for cargo as we went along. Too much of what the Mirela carried from village to town was freshly harvested, and perishable. It was the man's livelihood, after all. But as we made our way west, on the final stretches to Vienna, I found myself watching every boat on the river with suspicion, and finding reasons to keep Lord Andrew in my arms or in our cabin whenever we were at a dock.

At last we reached the outskirts of Vienna, where there was far too much traffic on road and river for anyone to track it all. Lammie was excited by the trains that ran alongside the river, and Nicolae was eager to point out the buildings he knew, despite the glare of the setting sun. I was with them both at the rail, trying to divide my conversation between them, when a steam launch suddenly diverted from its path, coming straight towards us with the sun behind it.

I thrust the baby into Nicolae's arms. "Quick, hide him!" I ordered, digging into my pocket for a candy that the lad could use to muffle the startled wails. My walking stick was in my hand without a thought, and if I'd had my revolver, I think I would have fired a warning shot at the approaching vessel. Ionescu was shouting orders to his men, for all the world as if we were about to be boarded by Stevenson's buccaneers.

Suddenly the launch slowed and turned to parallel us twenty feet away. A tall figure stood near the prow and raised a megaphone. But instead of an order to heave to, I heard my own name, in a voice I knew as well as my own. "Watson!" It was Sherlock Holmes! "Watson, would you please ask Captain Ionescu if I may come aboard with a guest?"

[The bundle of letters ends here, as if the need for correspondence had ended. There is one more letter in the box, folded around the newspaper announcement of the death of a young officer. He is very young, and there is a daredevil air to his expression in the small photograph, despite the formality of the pose or the crispness of his new uniform. The letter itself is short, and sad.]

My dear Ann,

Will you forgive me if I never finish writing the kidnapping story? The exciting part is done with, after all, and I cannot consider polishing it for publication, now that the boy I called Lord Andrew has been taken from us at Passchendaele. I shall never forget him, nor his delight at discovering his father had joined us there on the river at Vienna. Nor shall I forget our parting in Paris, when we stepped down from the Orient Express to discover that the Duchess and her daughters had come from London to meet us. He gave me a kiss, as his mother bade him do, but I doubt he understood that we would never meet again in this life. Perhaps in the next I shall sit with him, and tell him the tale of those days on the river.

I'll write a different story for you to take to Doyle, one that has a surer chance of being published. It will be about Holmes, of course, but that will mean it will sell. Get a good price for it and you should be able to repair the roof before winter.

All my love to the children,

John

The Lancelot Connection
by Matthew Booth

Towards the end of the year 1895, a particular series of events of no significance to this narrative found Sherlock Holmes and myself once more in the greatest of our university towns. It was during our visit that a particular incident came to our attention and the subsequent chain of events brought us to the conclusion of one of the most instructive enquiries undertaken by my illustrious colleague. It is possible that I might have set the facts down at an earlier stage, but I had given my word to one of the major players in the drama that I would keep them to myself until such time as the effects of the tragedy at the heart of the matter had subsided. A few weeks ago, I received notification that the person to whom I had made the pledge has passed away, so I feel that my manacles of silence can now be unclasped and the full details of the case set down before the public.

We were staying in furnished lodgings which we had had occasion to use on previous occasions, Holmes and I, close to the famous circular scientific library which is so well known in that town. We had been in residence for a little over a week and, for myself, the blue skies and the sandstone buildings of the old town, with the distant chiming of the college bells on the quarter-hours, had been an invigorating and refreshing alternative to the dark recesses and fog-shrouded pockets of London. However, I could tell from his restless manner that Sherlock Holmes was eager to return to his natural habitat amongst those same vile alleys and dark corners of the streets of the capital, to be once more ensconced in those Baker Street rooms from which he operated his crusade against crime. As matters turned out, he was to be forced to wait another couple of days before he could return to the sanctum of his armchair and the cluttered comfort of his own rooms.

It was early in the morning, as I have cause to recall, that we were called upon by Professor Cavendish Fawcett, the noted literary academic. He was a small but lean man of nearer sixty years than fifty, and with the rounded shoulders of his profession, brought on by years of study. His suit was untidy rather than shabby, with traces of chalk dust around the lapels and the cuffs of his jacket. His hair was grizzled, grey, and somewhat unruly, and his dark, furtive eyes peered at us over the lenses of a pair of ancient *pince-nez*. He walked into the room with a severe limp, his right leg moving in a stiff and unnatural manner. He leaned heavily on a Penang lawyer cane, approaching us in a peculiar shuffling gait. He wrung my companion's hand with a feverish anxiety before settling down into the chair which I had offered to him. Some strong coffee brought a flush of colour to his pale, sunken cheeks, and when he spoke it was with a querulous, strident voice.

"I can only thank the providence which protects us all that you are in our midst, Mr. Holmes," said he, "for in all England you are the one man who can help me."

"I trust that I shall be able to do so," replied Holmes, "but I can make no judgment on the point until such time as I have the full facts of the matter before me."

The old professor nodded. "Of course, yes, I fully appreciate that fact. But, sir, you will come to understand the nervous anxiety in which I find myself all too clearly, once you have heard my story."

"Pray, be precise as to the details," said Holmes in that business-like tone which I knew so well.

"You may know my name, Mr. Holmes, in connection with the study of English literature. I think it is not unjust to say that I am one of the foremost authorities on Elizabethan and Jacobean drama, particularly on the subjects of Shakespeare, Marlowe, and Johnson. It is possible that you have read my learned and, if I may say so, rather daring dissertation on the religious intricacies of *Tamburlaine the Great*? Perhaps not – it is of no matter. Suffice it to say that there is no aspect of this period of English theatrical history which is unknown to me or upon which I do not have some opinion.

"In addition to my academic work, I am a trustee of the distinguished museum of this city and a close friend of Mr. Percival Warlock, the curator. At present, I am heavily involved with an exhibit of my own design, involving the evolution of drama, from the Ancient Greeks through to the morality plays of the medieval period, the Renaissance, up to our present notable works. It is a fascinating study, Mr. Holmes, and I would enjoy it for its own sake even if it did not, on occasion, produce some exciting and intriguing opportunities beyond simple academic interest.

"It was during the course of these various researches that I came to learn of what I can only describe as one of the most important and thrilling discoveries of recent years. It has long been suspected that the published works of Shakespeare which we know today are but a small snippet of the great man's total productivity. It is a theory, to which I happen to subscribe, that Shakespeare in fact produced far more than those plays which have survived, but these unknown works were either discarded as being unworthy of production or else they were destroyed by accident.

"Recently, proof of the theory came into my possession. I happened to make the acquaintance of an old woman of Italian descent who had

255

heard my name and knew of my reputation. She had something which had been passed down through generations of her family which she wished to hand to me, for she thought that I would be better placed to make the best use of it. How it came into her family originally is a matter which is lost to the mists of time, alas, but the important point is that she presented me with a small, slim package, which contained several sheets of fragile paper, scrawled over with that scribbled writing which seemed all too familiar to me as being the hand of William Shakespeare himself.

"It was the manuscript of a play entitled *Lancelot and the King*. It is, as the title suggests, a blank verse treatment of the Arthurian legend, told from the perspective of Lancelot. It is a love story above anything else, but it is as much about the love between Arthur and Lancelot as between both men and Queen Guinevere. Indeed, if there is a villain in the piece then it must be the queen herself, for she is painted as a woman not tormented by fate to betray her husband, but driven by her own carnal lust for two men. It is Lancelot who is the tragic hero of the piece, broken by a love which he cannot resist, whilst Arthur is in essence the fool, cursed by his own flaw of failing to recognize treachery in those closest to him.

"The play describes the breakdown of the friendship between the king and his best knight, and paints that disintegration as being the direct result of Guinevere's entirely selfish actions. It is a brave move to present the woman in such a fashion, but it makes for a devastating tale of the destruction of friendship which, in turn, leads to the breaking of the structure of Camelot itself and, in turn, the entire kingdom. I tell you, gentlemen, Tennyson's *Idylls* does not come close to the intricacies of this play, either in terms of being a history of Arthur's tragedy or in terms of poetic intelligence."

Sherlock Holmes had listened to this narrative with a mounting interest. "The piece sounds fascinating, Professor Fawcett, and no doubt such a manuscript would be of interest to any serious scholar."

"You say nothing more than the truth," said the academic, nodding his head. "It was my intention to display the manuscript in the exhibit of which I have spoken, where it would be the crown jewel of the collection, so I brought it back here and I wasted no time in showing it to my young assistant, Mr. Laurence Maguire. It was young Maguire who pointed out that the discovery of a lost Shakespeare would ensure the success and the profitability of our exhibition at the museum."

"Indeed!" remarked Sherlock Holmes. "The manuscript alone would be sufficient to draw attention to your collection, Professor. There is no doubt about its authenticity, I presume?"

Professor Fawcett's face paled at my companion's question. "I am in no doubt of it myself, Mr. Holmes, but a colleague of mine says he is somewhat cautious."

"May I enquire his name?"

"Mr. Zachariah Templeton, a lecturer at the university – although he is a student of the metaphysical poets rather than Elizabethan drama. Now, if I may, Mr. Holmes, I should like to proceed with my narrative, for I come to the darkest part of my own little drama. Of course, I would not be here if matters had moved along without some form of criminal activity.

"I had intended to have an early start to my work today at the museum, for there is much for me to do in preparation for the opening of our exhibition. I got to the museum a little after seven this morning and went straight to the antechamber in which our collection is to be displayed."

"One moment!" interjected Holmes. "Do you have a key to the museum itself?"

"I have, since I am a trustee. But this morning I was admitted by Percival Warlock, the curator. I was not surprised to find him there even at that hour. He is dedicated to his work." The professor took a moment to gather his thoughts. "Warlock's face forewarned me of disaster. He led me to the exhibits room and I could see that one of the windows in the far wall was broken. You can imagine my fear at this discovery, for I knew that the manuscript was in that very room in the glass display case which I had obtained for it. My fears became absolute when I saw that the case was empty."

Holmes's eyes glistened with anticipation. "The play had been stolen?"

"Just so."

"Was the door to the exhibits room locked when you arrived this morning?"

"No, it was open. But the thief must have entered and left by the window – otherwise he would have been locked in the museum for the night, for the outer doors were locked. Warlock said as much, for he had to open the main door to the building upon his arrival."

"A credible deduction, Professor. Who else has keys to the exhibits room and the display case?"

"Maguire and I have keys to both, as does Warlock. He and I have always had keys to the museum itself, and recently I had given Maguire a key to the museum, with Warlock's blessing, for Maguire was often cataloguing the collection in his own time."

Holmes's eyes glittered with interest. "And the glass of this display case had been smashed?"

"No. The door to the case was unlocked and Maguire's own key was in the lock."

Holmes put a finger to his lips. "That is suggestive."

"It is not unnatural for Maguire to have had cause to open the cabinet in order to make some examination of the manuscript," said Fawcett.

"Perhaps not, but it becomes a point of interest when that same manuscript is stolen soon afterwards."

The old professor shook his head with a growing disquiet. "No doubt – but Maguire was not responsible for the theft, Mr. Holmes, and my certainty stems from a darker cause than larceny."

Holmes leaned back in his chair and drew heavily on his pipe. "I apologize, Professor Fawcett, I had assumed that it was the theft of the manuscript of *Lancelot and the King* which you wished me to investigate. You have more to tell us, then?"

The academic rose from his chair and began to pace the room. "The display case in which the play was to be shown stands on a pedestal so that it is raised some three feet from the ground. It is at the far end of the room, directly under the very window which the intruder had broken in order to gain access. Do I make myself clear?"

"Perfectly."

"There, at the base of the pedestal and lying on its back, there was the body of a man, the victim of a vicious attack."

Holmes wriggled in his chair with excitement. "Did you approach it?"

"How I found the nerve to do so, I shall never know. The sight of his face staring up at me from under that terrible wound was too monstrous for me to bear."

"What sort of wound?"

"To the head. He had been battered to death."

"You say the body was on its back and the face visible to you. Did you recognize the man?"

Professor Fawcett stared curiously at my companion and I felt a sense of dark inevitability about his reply. "I did, sir. It was the broken body of young Laurence Maguire, my loyal assistant."

For some silent moments, Sherlock Holmes remained seated, his pipe clenched between his teeth and his austere grey eyes scrutinizing the anguished face of his new client. At last, he sprang from his chair and within seconds he had thrown on his hat and coat.

"Come, Professor Fawcett, you must show us to the place at once. Make haste, gentlemen!"

Within a quarter-of-an-hour, we were walking through the corridors of the famous museum. We were recognized and waved through by the police, and greeted by the curator, Percival Warlock, a man of advancing

258

age with flaxen hair and a neatly trimmed moustache. His manner was agitated and the hands which shook our in greeting were trembling with apprehension.

"A terrible deed, Mr. Holmes," said he. "It is a disaster for us all."

"We shall see whether we cannot throw some light on the matter," said my companion affably. "The time to speak of disasters will be if no progress can be made in the investigation, no sooner."

"Heaven bless you for saying so," said Mr. Cavendish Fawcett. "Ah! Here is the room."

He showed us into a large area filled with glass-fronted cabinets, some of which lined the walls and some of which were set out in a line down the centre of the room. Inside the cases were various folios and rare volumes throughout the ages of theatrical production, the treasure trove of Fawcett's exhibition, all of which might have been of more particular interest to us had it not been for the dark intrigue which had engulfed us. At the far end of the room was the pedestal of which we had heard, topped with the rectangular glass case whose door had been opened, a key inserted into the small lock at the base. The red velvet stand inside was empty, designating the place where this special manuscript had been displayed. Above, there were two broad windows, the glass of one smashed, its splinters scattered on the floor below.

Lying on the two steps which led to the pedestal was the body of a man. He was a tall, well-made man of perhaps thirty years of age. His arms were thrown out above his head, the fingers clenched in agony. His hair was dark and luxurious, but his handsome features had convulsed into a look of shock and fear, and his forehead had been terribly injured. We stared down at the savage ferocity of the blow which had inflicted the wound and Holmes, with a look of grim concentration upon his face, examined the indescribable wreck of the man's head.

"There is no sign of any weapon?"

"None."

"The police were been notified immediately?"

"Of course," said the curator, Warlock. "As you saw, they are interviewing the staff at this present moment."

"I fancy they shall have no luck there," muttered Holmes. "I shall introduce myself to the local inspector presently. This broken window is how the thief made his entrance, of course."

My companion moved and stood beneath it. He was perched on the tips of his toes, craning his neck, but he was unable to see through the glass. "What is immediately outside this window?"

"A balustrade, Mr. Holmes, and a small stone balcony," said Warlock. "All the windows have them."

"They look out onto the gardens?"

Warlock nodded. "There is a small pathway between the building and the lawns, but nothing more."

"The intruder will have used this balcony to climb up to the window, of course," mused Holmes. "He would not have been able to reach up to break the glass otherwise. It might be a risky climb, but an active man would be able to jump up to this balustrade and heave himself up onto the balcony. From there, he could break the window and attach a rope to one of the pillars of the balcony, then climb down it into the room. Naturally, he left by the same means and lowered himself down the ground using the balcony, having untied the rope. So much is obvious."

"How can you deduce the rope?" I asked. "There is no sign of one."

"Elementary. If the window is too high to be reached without the aid of the balcony, it is likewise too high to make the jump from the sill to the ground. Therefore, the thief could not merely jump from the window to the ground in order to carry out his crime. He would need some means of lowering himself into the room and pulling himself back out of it."

"That is simple enough," said Cavendish Fawcett. "But what can we glean from that?"

Holmes gave a shrug of his shoulders. "Perhaps nothing more than the certainty that he came prepared for his task."

"He must have been a fairly youthful man," I observed.

Holmes raised a cautionary finger. "We must not run away with ourselves, my dear Watson. A middle-aged man in good health might have been able to perform the deed. I am certain that I could do it myself. I think we may refine your observation to say merely that the intruder was an athletic fellow, but I do not think we can venture much further than that." He moved back to the centre of the room and allowed his eyes to drift around the area. "Hmm. There is much to be learned. I think it would be as well if I were to have five minutes alone in this room, if you do not mind, gentlemen."

He ushered the curator and Fawcett out of the exhibit room and closed the door on them. For some moments, he remained at the door in silence, his finger pressed to his lips. Then, he whipped out his magnifying lens and began pacing noiselessly around the room, sometimes stopping, on occasion kneeling, and once lying flat upon his face at the broken shards of glass from the window. I had witnessed similar displays before and I was accustomed to my presence being almost entirely ignored upon such occasions. Holmes gave a sharp gasp of satisfaction at one moment and I watched his long nervous fingers removed a torn fragment of cloth from a ragged piece of broken glass from the window. He performed the task with such delicacy that I was reminded of the careful touch of a surgeon performing some subtle operation. On his hands and knees, he crawled over to a small, white object which lay on the floor. Leaning over him, I saw that it was a candle, the wax of which had fallen to the ground and hardened. Holmes examined these traces of wax with the utmost care. At last, he rose to his feet and examined with his lens the empty case from where the manuscript had been stolen before turning to me with that look of exultation which showed that his mind was engaged fully on the matter.

"These are murky waters, my dear Watson, and the affair is a somewhat tangled one," said he. "What do you make of this piece of fabric which I recovered from the broken window?"

"A fragment of a plaid cloak, or some such garment."

"Exactly. Now, coupled with that dropped candle over there, does this piece of cloth suggest anything to your mind?"

"Nothing, beyond the fact that the burglar must have come dressed in the cloak and using a candle to light his way."

"Anything else?"

I gave it some thought. "If the criminal's source of light had been dropped, he would be more likely to stumble against the window and tear his cloak, as he would be moving in darkness."

Holmes heaved an impatient sigh at my comments. "Admirable, Watson, but this is not the time for a display of your blazing talent for observing the obvious. Why should this burglar come armed with a candle and proceed to drop it at the scene of his crime?"

"He had just murdered a man, Holmes. Perhaps he was fearful of his actions."

"Possibly," remarked my friend, "but, if so, it leads us to another problem – a problem which causes me much more puzzlement than anything else."

"What is that?"

"Well, now, if this burglar is so terrified of what he has done that he drops his only means of illuminating his escape from the room, why does he not drop everything associated with the crime?"

"I do not follow you."

Holmes leaned close to my ear. "The weapon, Watson! Where is the weapon which inflicted this terrible wound? Are we to believe that this criminal is so appalled by the murder of Laurence Maguire that he drops his candle, yet retains the very object with which he has committed that act which now so shocks him into panic? If so, he must be a very inconsistent fellow. No, it will not do. Is it not more likely that he would discard the weapon before his candle? One would remind him of his guilt far more strongly than the other, after all."

261

I conceded the point with a nod of my head. "Where does that take us?"

Holmes gave a shrug of his shoulders. "A little further, my dear doctor, but not as far as we need to go. The fact that Maguire had apparently opened the display case himself, using his own key, is suggestive. Did the thief come into the room and find the display cabinet conveniently open, thus allowing him to take his chance?"

A thought had struck me. "If Maguire were in this room when the burglar smashed the window, surely he would have heard the breaking of the glass and locked the manuscript away. He would not leave the case open in the face of such an obvious threat of theft."

"The alternative is that, for whatever reason, he had abandoned his post, leaving the case unlocked and the manuscript at risk of theft," observed Holmes.

"Why should he be so careless?"

Holmes eyes were fierce with excitement. "An admirable question, Watson, and one which must surely give some pause for thought! Whatever it was must have been of some importance to the young man. We shall see. For the present, however, how about Maguire himself? What secrets can he tell us?"

He leaned over the body of Laurence Maguire once more, but his attention was turned to the man's pockets. His nimble fingers flew around the body, feeling, pressing, unbuttoning, and examining, all with such swiftness that the thorough nature of the inspection would hardly be credited. At last, he examined the dead man's watch, a heavy Albert chain whose fob was a small pendant. "Ah, it would seem this watch has more secrets to tell us."

Holmes opened the pendant by prising apart the small clasp. Inside, there was a lock of golden hair and a brief inscription:

> *Doubt that the stars are fire,*
> *Doubt that the sun doth move his aides,*
> *Doubt truth to be a liar,*
> *But never doubt I love.*

"Shakespeare seems to figure prominently in this case, Watson," said Holmes. "You recognize Hamlet's assurances to Ophelia, of course. Who is the woman who must give such assurances of her love to this young man, Maguire? Well, Watson, we must remember this point, and docket it, for we may come upon something later which will bear upon it. For now, I think our work here is done."

We found Professor Fawcett and Mr. Warlock in conversation with the local police inspector. Holmes exchanged and few words with the dapper official and offered his assistance if and when it was considered necessary. The inspector didn't seem to be entirely appreciative of my companion's offer, however, and his nod of thanks was somewhat abrupt. Perhaps sensing the professional rivalry between this local detective and his esteemed amateur colleague, Professor Fawcett invited us to take some refreshment at his home and we made our way to his small but cosy abode on the outskirts of town.

As we approached the house, we saw a tall fellow racing towards us. He moved at such speed that he was obliged to hold his large-brimmed hat on his head with one hand, whilst the flaps of his overcoat billowed out behind him. His slim cheeks were flushed with the effort and his dark eyes were wild with emotion. He gripped Professor Cavendish Fawcett by the hand.

"My dear Cavendish, I have just heard the terrible news," said he. "If there is anything I can do to assist, you need only ask."

"Thank you," replied the old academic. "It is good of you to say so."

Sherlock Holmes shook the hand of this newcomer. "You are Mr. Zachariah Templeton, I perceive."

"How on earth do you know my name?" asked the man.

"It is simplicity itself," replied Sherlock Holmes. "Like the professor here, you have the bowed shoulders of the scholar and your manner of address shows that you are well known to him. The well-thumbed edition of Donne's collected poetry in your coat pocket suggests a mutual appreciation of English literature. It is no great leap of the imagination to combine those two inferences and deduce that you are a professional scholar of the subject."

"So I am. But my name . . . ?"

"You have made notes on your shirt cuff on a variety of topics connected to the metaphysical poets. The questions posed and the possible avenues of discussion which flow from them suggest some form of debate or essay subjects. Your age and your familiarity with the professor preclude you from being a student, so you must yourself be a lecturer. When he first consulted me, Professor Fawcett told me of a colleague of his who was a lecturer in metaphysical poetry and whose name was Zachariah Templeton."

"It is amazing!"

"But entirely superficial. There is nothing magical about using one's eyes and recalling specific facts from one's memory."

Professor Fawcett was smiling. "I must agree with Templeton, sir. Your gifts are remarkable. Templeton, this is Mr. Sherlock Holmes and his colleague, Dr. Watson."

Templeton shook my companion's hand. "I see that Cavendish has not wasted any time in calling in the best help he could wish to have."

"Our presence in your hospitable town was entirely fortuitous," said Sherlock Holmes. "I understand that you have some concerns regarding the validity of this lost play by Shakespeare on the Arthurian legend."

Templeton was obviously embarrassed by the topic being raised in the presence of his esteemed colleague. "I was simply expressing my opinion. A man as zealous on his subject as Cavendish Fawcett can be easily swayed by his own enthusiasm."

"Men of single minds are often blinded to the truth," agreed Holmes.

"I have no wish for a dear friend to be embarrassed in public if his opinion on the script is wrong. I had no other concern than that."

"You are a noble fellow, but you need not concern yourself with the authenticity," said the professor. "We were just going for some light refreshments, Templeton, if you would wish to join us."

"I shall be delighted. I would like to hear of any conclusions which Mr. Holmes has drawn on this affair of the stolen manuscript."

We went into the house and Fawcett led us into a cosy sitting room, modestly but tastefully furnished. A woman was sitting by the window and she rose as we entered. She was very beautiful, no more than thirty years of age, and her skin was of a gentle colour, although the cheeks were tinged with passion, and the bright eyes were dimmed with sadness. Her sensitive mouth was drawn and tight in an effort of self-command. And yet, despite her obvious emotion, there was a delicate charm about her, and her fair hair glowed like a summer meadow in the afternoon sun.

"This is my wife, Anna," said Fawcett, going to her and taking her hand in his. "This is Mr. Sherlock Holmes and his colleague, Dr. Watson, my dear."

"I cannot pretend to be ignorant of your purpose here, Mr. Holmes," declared Anna Fawcett. "I trust you will do all you can to throw some light on the mystery."

We looked across at Sherlock Holmes, for he had made no reply to the lady, and the room had fallen into silence. He seemed to be in another place, far removed from that quaint room in which we stood, for his eyes had developed an abstracted glare and his thin lips were slightly parted in astonishment. He seemed to be entirely captivated by Anna Fawcett, but it could not have been anything approaching an attraction with him. He was, I took it, a perfect reasoning machine and his brain had always governed his heart so that such emotions as love were nothing but an intrusion into his cold, balanced existence. And yet, he was staring at the woman as though the secrets of the universe were locked within her.

"Forgive me," said he at last, "for my mind was elsewhere. I hope to be able to say that I am worthy of your words, Mrs. Fawcett, but I fear that until this moment I have been nothing short of a fool. I wonder what has happened to any brains which God has given me but, as I have had cause to say before, it is better to learn wisdom late than never to learn it at all."

"You have some clue?" asked Cavendish Fawcett with eagerness.

"It is an indication, nothing more. There is still much to be learned." Holmes walked over to the professor's wife. "Tell me, madam, are you as passionate a reader of Shakespeare as your husband?"

She gave a slight shake of the head. "I am nothing of an expert on the plays, Mr. Holmes, but you cannot be married to a student of the Bard without being afflicted with something of his enthusiasm."

"Quite so. You have heard of your husband's obtaining of this lost play?"

"Naturally."

"Do you have any views on the subject?"

Mrs. Fawcett frowned in understandable confusion. "I think it is an exciting discovery, of course, but I am not in a position to speak intelligently about it."

"You can understand why someone might wish to steal it?"

"It is no doubt highly valuable."

Sherlock Holmes rose to his feet and walked over to Zachariah Templeton. "And you, sir. Do you consider monetary gain to be the motive for the theft?"

The tall academic gave a short laugh. "I would have thought that falls more within your expertise than mine, Mr. Holmes."

"There are any number of reasons, but I fancy I have grasped the correct one."

"Then for Heaven's sake, tell us!" cried the professor.

Holmes waved a finger at him. "My friend Watson will tell you that one of my defects is that I am loath to communicate my conclusions until I am sure they are complete. I do not agree that it is a failing on my part, however, but that is of no consequence."

"But you must be able to share something of the truth with us," protested Zachariah Templeton.

"Perhaps I am so able, Mr. Templeton," replied Holmes. "And perhaps the best place for me to do so would be in the exhibit room where the incident occurred. However, before we make our way back to the museum, Professor Fawcett, I wonder whether I might just have a brief word with your wife alone."

"If you wish, Mr. Holmes. We shall wait outside."

After the two men had left, Holmes turned to the lady. She had risen from her chair and was standing at the mantelpiece, her head in her hands, gently weeping. Holmes was capable of extreme gentleness with women when he desired, and now he walked towards the lady and laid his hands on her shoulders. With a soothing word, he led her back to her seat and sat down opposite her, a gentle smile on his face.

"I have the solution to this mystery, Mrs. Fawcett," said he, "but I must ask you to confirm one point for me."

"What point is that?"

"What were the relations between you and Mr. Laurence Maguire?"

"Mr. Holmes!"

"No, no. If you will trust me, and treat me as a friend, you will find that I shall justify that trust."

"Mr. Maguire was my husband's colleague. I knew him only in that capacity."

"Will you not tell me the truth?"

"I have done so."

Holmes gave a sigh of impatient rage. "Madam, I had hoped to spare you this by coercing you to give me the information voluntarily, but I see that I am in vain. I have opened Maguire's pendant and I have seen inside it."

Her eyes flashed a terrified fire at my companion and her lips trembled with uncertainty. She stammered some denial, but the grave expression on Sherlock Holmes's lean face was unrelenting.

"Your shade of hair is especially fair," said Holmes. "It matches the lock of hair I found in the pendant on Maguire's watch chain. The inscription from *Hamlet* offering an assurance of love – it was your means of telling Maguire that you loved him, despite your inability to be with him."

Mrs. Fawcett nodded her head and took my friend's hands in hers. "Oh, Mr. Holmes, I have been a happily married woman for so many years that I never thought anything could corrupt it. I was wrong – I had not foreseen Laurence Maguire's intrusion into my life. He was everything my husband was not, and the feelings he aroused within me were impossible to resist. Just as the tides are drawn to the moon, so I was drawn to Laurence."

"And he reciprocated your love?"

She nodded. "And yet, Laurence had grown impatient with me. He wanted the truth to come out and for me to leave Cavendish. He had begun to interpret my inability to do so as a sign of dying love on my part. The pendant had been my way of assuring him of how I felt whilst also giving

266

me time to summon the courage to do what my heart and Laurence begged me to do."

"To walk away from your marriage?"

She held her palms to her cheeks in mournful regret. "If I had not wasted time, might Laurence still be alive today? I fear that is the question which will curse me until I too pass. Laurence loved me as I loved him, but he was unable to wait any longer to declare his love publicly. He was an honest man, Mr. Holmes, and the duplicity of working with the very man whom he was betraying had begun to corrode his soul. I am ashamed that I was not able to claim the same nobility of spirit."

"Mr. Maguire threatened to divulge your secret to the professor?"

"He said it was best for the truth to be told."

"Did you go to the museum last night in order to convince him otherwise?"

"I went to beg him to reconsider. I had told him I would sneak out once Cavendish was asleep."

"You pleaded with him not to speak out. Did he agree?"

Between those choking sobs, Anna Fawcett forced out her words. "He did not. He could wait no longer, he said, and he was to tell Cavendish this very morning."

Holmes was silent for a moment, those austere eyes glaring at the woman. "What did you do?"

"I could do nothing. He was adamant that his course of action was the right one. I ran home, my eyes stinging with tears and my legs barely able to carry me."

"Did Mr. Maguire lock the main door after you had fled?"

She nodded. "I heard him do so. The closing of the door felt like the final toll of the bell for our love and my happiness. I ran faster, and when I got home, I cried myself to sleep, but I had resolved to tell my husband before Laurence had the opportunity. I could have that decency if nothing else."

"But when you awakened this morning, you found your husband had left the house already?"

"Later, he sent word to me, telling me what had happened. My eyes have not stopped weeping since that terrible revelation."

Holmes placed a finger to his lips. "And yet, it must be said, that the man's death has saved you the hardship of your confession. It has preserved your secret, perhaps."

She understood the veiled accusation. "Do you accuse me, Mr. Holmes? Do you think I murdered the man I loved to safeguard my own shame?"

Holmes shook his head and rose from his chair. With a gentleness which I have rarely seen, he touched her cheek and raised her gaze to his. "I do not, madam. I fancy the matter was taken out of your hands by another. From what I can ascertain, this cycle of death and forbidden love makes you more a Juliet than a Lady Macbeth."

In reply, Mrs. Fawcett simply lowered her head and sobbed into her hands. I touched Holmes on the arm and gestured to the door. He gave a last look at the woman, urging her to speak, before submitting to my entreaties to leave her in peace. It was not until we were in the hallway that he turned to me with that familiar look of exultation on his face which spoke of his assurance of success.

"A convoluted business, Watson, but not one devoid of interest," said he.

"You have solved it?"

"I have the threads in my hand. It is as clear to me as if I had been there. Come now, we must return to the museum."

The police had left when we arrived and the sinister occupant of the exhibit room had been removed to the mortuary. Holmes strode into the room and made his way to the pedestal which housed the glass case where *Lancelot and the King* had been displayed. I remained by his side, whilst Cavendish Fawcett, Mr. Warlock, and Zachariah Templeton sat before us like students in a criminological lecture in which Sherlock Holmes was the tutor.

"The misapprehension about this case was that the theft of the manuscript and the death of Laurence Maguire were cause and effect," declared Holmes. "It is not too much of a stretch of the imagination to forge a connection between a theft and a death which occur in close proximity, but in this instance the events were independent of each other.

"I shall deal with the theft first. I have already explained that the burglar must have gained access to this room through the window. Likewise, I have detailed how a rope must have been used in order to gain such an entry and how the intruder must have scaled the outer wall with the aid of the balcony which adorns the window. My friend Watson commented that only a young man could have carried out such a feat, but I was rather more cautious than the Good Doctor. I confined my deduction to the trespasser simply being active. Clearly Professor Fawcett could not have made that climb. His lameness would have prevented him from executing the athletic steps required to break into the room."

Fawcett held up his hand. "I am grateful to you, Mr. Holmes."

"What is more, Professor," said Holmes, "you had a key not only to the museum, but also the exhibition room, and the display case. Why would you need to break into a building to which you have unlimited access."

Mr. Warlock slapped his knee. "By Jove! That must surely apply to me, too, Mr. Holmes."

Holmes nodded his head. "Indeed, sir. The breaking of the window indicated an external culprit and it was not too much of a difficulty for me to name the thief as you, Mr. Zachariah Templeton."

All the eyes in the room turned to the tall academic, whose head was bowed and his cheeks flushed with shame. "Say what you must, Mr. Holmes."

"It was you who entered through the window, climbing down the rope into the room, with the intention of taking *Lancelot and the King* from its display case. I suspect you came prepared to break the glass of this case but you were fortunate enough to find that the door to the cabinet was open. I doubt you pondered this happenstance for a great deal of time – rather, I suspect you took the script and made your escape."

Fawcett had gripped his friend by the shoulder. "But why, Templeton? Why?"

Sherlock Holmes spoke before Templeton was able. "He had doubts about its authenticity, as he told us, but his alleged concern over fearing you might ruin your reputation was a blind. If the play were genuine, it would be highly valuable. I fancy he took it in order to confirm its veracity and then see about selling it. Academic work is fulfilling but hardly profitable."

Templeton nodded his head. "It is as you say, Mr. Holmes. I saw at once the significance of the play and I saw the opportunity to make money from it. It could be exhibited anywhere in the world. The price it had would be immense. I broke in as you say and I found this room empty but the case open. I grabbed the play and fled. It wasn't until I examined it at home that I discovered it was as I feared. I am sorry, Cavendish, but Shakespeare did not write that play. It is skilfully done, no doubt, but it is a forgery."

"I do not believe it!"

"I said earlier that you are a man who is blinded by his own enthusiasm," said Templeton. "And it is exceptionally well done, but some of the phrasing is off and in a few instances – not many, I grant you – the metre is wrong. It seems to be from the correct period, but whether it was a prank or the work of a lesser scribe seeking to use Shakespeare's name to further his own career, it is *not* a genuine Bard. Maguire must have known it too, so I cannot imagine why he did not tell you."

Fawcett's hands went to his temples and he gave a cry of despair. "I must form my own opinion. Where is the manuscript? What have you done with it, you fiend?"

"It is still in my house."

"It could be nowhere else," said Holmes. "Once you had discovered that your burglary had been for nothing, you returned at once to the museum in order to replace the manuscript. By doing so, you would leave a case of forced entry but no theft. There would be no investigation in all probability if nothing was stolen, and you were not allowing yourself to be the subject of a police enquiry for the sake of a forgery.

"When you got back into this room, however, you discovered a corpse. In your initial shock, you dropped your candle on the floor and, in your haste to escape, you tore the fabric of your plaid cloak on the broken glass of the window. You see, Watson, the importance of my deduction about the absence of any weapon? The answer to the problem is that the intruder did not drop the weapon of murder in his panic, because the intruder was not the murderer.

"But now Zachariah Templeton has a difficulty. He knows that the theft and the murder will be connected, and he has in his hands the manuscript itself. So flustered was he by discovering the body of Laurence Maguire that all thought of the play went out of his mind and, as a result, he departed before realizing that he still retained possession of the one piece of evidence which might implicate him in a murder which he had not committed. Later, he cannot get back into the museum to replace the manuscript for the police will be present."

Templeton raved in the air. "It was maddening to find myself in that position. I had been such a fool and my penance was to live in fear of losing my life for a murder in which I had no part."

He turned to Fawcett. "I shall return it," he said, "but my assessment of it is correct. It is a hoax. What is not a fraud, Mr. Holmes, is my innocence of the murder of that young man."

Holmes nodded. "I am aware of that. The murder was not connected to the play, save in the most indirect and ironic fashion."

"I do not understand," said Mr. Warlock.

"The play concerned the forbidden love of Lancelot and Guinevere," said Holmes. "At the centre of this mystery is a similarly forbidden love, one doomed to tragedy and death. Three points about this case struck me as vital: That Maguire had left the open display case unattended, that his watch bore an inscription offering an assurance of love, and that there was no sign of the murder weapon.

"The first of these points suggested very clearly that something of the utmost importance had prompted Maguire to leave the manuscript vulnerable in that careless fashion. The second suggested a romantic angle to the case – not least because of the nature of the quotation, but also because of the lock of golden hair which accompanied it. You will recall that I was silent for a few moments when I was introduced to Mrs. Anna Fawcett. I was marvelling at my own stupidity, for it was at that point that I realized that the murder and the theft were not connected. Her hair was of such a striking blonde that the lock of hair in the pendant on Maguire's watch chain could only have been from her head. Thus, I began to see that the reason for the man's death was his love for Mrs. Fawcett, and not his interruption of what can only be described as a clumsy burglary."

Fawcett was on his feet. "That is a monstrous accusation, Mr. Holmes."

Holmes remained at his authoritative best. "No doubt, but your wife has confessed, sir. She came to the museum last night to plead with Maguire not to say anything of the affair to you. Her arrival was the reason for his dereliction of duty in leaving the display case open and unguarded. His mind was occupied with more personal and important matters. Of course, you know this, because you followed her to the museum and witnessed their altercation on the doorstep."

The old man's eyes glared with spite. "That is a lie!"

"The lie is yours, Professor, not mine," said Sherlock Holmes. "The final point which interested me was the absence of any weapon, as I have said. Once I had identified you as the murderer, the question was answered. The weapon was removed simply because it had to be removed."

"What do you say?"

Holmes lowered his voice, pointing to the professor's Penang lawyer. "You require the weapon in order to aid you to walk."

"I have heard enough of this nonsense!" spat the old academic, making for the door.

"There are four men in this room who are innocent of murder, Professor Fawcett," declared Holmes. "Do not for a moment think that their combined efforts will not detain you here until the police arrive. Once it is proved that the theft and the killing are not related, the focus of the mystery shifts. The love affair between Maguire and your wife gives you a motive to dispose of him. Your possession of a key to the museum gives you the opportunity to enter the building after Maguire had locked it when your wife left him last night. There is no escape."

The old man remained at the door of the room, his eyes turned in hatred on Sherlock Holmes. "That young jackanapes stole everything from me, Holmes. Anna was the only girl I had ever truly loved. My curse was that I met her in my twilight years, whilst she was still blooming. I never hoped to be everything she needed, but I tried my best for her and she never complained. Not until that Romeo walked onto our stage. What you say is true. I did let myself back in and I came into this very room. I found

271

him, young Maguire, mad with fear and rage. Rage at Anna, no doubt, and fear that the play had been stolen."

"I think not," said Holmes. "I fancy that Templeton is right. I suspect Maguire had determined that the play was a forgery but had kept silent. If Anna would not leave you for him, even after he had exposed their infidelity to you, he might well have the opportunity to have revenge in your public humiliation at the unveiling of the fraudulent play."

Fawcett was nodding his head. "Perhaps you are right. It is something the little snake would think of, I am certain of that. Whether that is true or not, Mr. Holmes, the theft of the play was nothing to me in that isolated moment. All I could see was betrayal before me. All I could hear were mocking lies in my ears – and all I could smell was deceit. I did it, gentlemen. I struck him down like the coward he was, but I must tell you that I remember nothing of the deed. For that, at least, I am ashamed."

We said nothing after he had spoken. He eased himself into a chair in the corner of the room and he began to weep silently. After some moments, Holmes dispatched Mr. Warlock for the police inspector. The old academic made no movement – to his mind, he was alone in the room, save for his guilt and his shame.

"I have one last question, Mr. Holmes," said Templeton. "If he was guilty of murder, why did he consult you at all? He must have known that your investigation into my own crime would reveal his own sin."

Sherlock Holmes chuckled gently. "He found himself in a similarly invidious position as you, Mr. Templeton, in having circumstances force him into checkmate."

"I do not understand."

"He did not know where the manuscript was, and he would do anything to get it back – even take a chance on involving me in the investigation. Additionally, a theft and a murder had been committed, and here was none other than Sherlock Holmes on the doorstep. Fawcett could not possibly have ignored my presence without raising suspicions."

Templeton nodded. "Old Fawcett must have cursed you for being so nearby."

"Any failure to consult me in such circumstances would have aroused immediate suspicion," replied Holmes. "Perhaps I am being conceited in imagining it to be the answer, but I confess that I am a man who cannot agree with those who rank modesty amongst the virtues."

The Adventure of the Modern Guy Fawkes
by Stephen Herczeg

Most of the adventures that involve my companion Sherlock Holmes are of a rather mundane nature, involving a cross-section of the folk who live the bulk of their simple lives within the great metropolis of London.

Sometimes, however, Holmes is called upon to decipher mysteries that involve the upper echelon of modern society, and on rare occasions his investigations are tangled up with even the highest levels of Government. Such was the case when I opened the front door to the frantic tapping of a distraught young man dressed in a heavy woolen suit and bowler hat, the distinct attire of the civil service.

He handed me his card, which announced him to be *"Godfrey Jones, Under-secretary of the Committee of Imperial Defence"*. I held my hand out to shake his hand and introduce myself, but was greeted with his coat and hat. Though slightly taken aback, I took it in good humour, as his distress seemed to overwhelm him.

"Thank you, my good man, I'm here on orders from the secretariat to seek out the services of Mr. Sherlock Holmes. Is he at home?" he asked.

I pointed to the stairs and said, "If you follow me, I'll take you to him." I backed away and allowed him entry.

We found Holmes reclining in his favourite chair, smoking a pipe and reading the daily paper. "This would be the man you are after," I said to Jones as I placed his coat and hat on a nearby chair. I extended my hand again and finally introduced myself.

"I am Doctor John Watson, Mr. Holmes's associate," I said and indicated Holmes, "This is Mr. Sherlock Holmes."

His face dropped a little and his cheeks flushed red with embarrassment. He held out his hand and took mine. "Oh, I am sorry, sir, I didn't realise."

I smiled and let go of his hand. "Never mind," I said and indicated a free chair. I handed Holmes the card and turned to leave to ask Mrs. Hudson for tea, but was greeted at the door by our landlady with a laden tray containing tea, three cups, and biscuits.

I smiled and remarked quietly, "You are a wonder, Mrs. Hudson."

She placed the tray on the side table and turned back towards me, a slight smile on her lips. "Yes, I am," she agreed as she moved past me.

While the tea steeped, I took a seat a little way from Jones and watched the proceedings.

Holmes carefully folded his paper and placed it to the side. I noticed that he had left a specific article on the top to continue reading later. I took note of the strange headline, *"Robbery at Woolwich Artillery Base"*. He read the business card and then looked up and studied Jones for a moment, I presumed that he was gathering data and forming an opinion about the man. I smiled to myself as I also observed Jones's agitation at Holmes's silence.

Finally, Holmes looked up into the young man's eyes and spoke. "Well, Mr. Godfrey Jones of Her Majesty's Civil Service, it is a pleasure to make your acquaintance." He rose and shook the young man's hand. "If I'm not wrong, you are a clerk, having been in the service for some six years after leaving Rugby Public School at the requisite age of seventeen. You once played rugby as well, but since moving to London have relinquished your sport. You are also married with a small child."

Jones's mouth dropped open. "How? How?"

A smile developed on my face, I'd seen this time and time again, but was a little perplexed at how Holmes had gleaned such details in such a short time. "Yes," I said. "How did you work all that out?"

"Quite simply, Watson." He indicated our guest. "Mr. Jones here is about twenty-two or twenty-three years of age. He sports a dark blue tie, with light blue-and-green diagonal stripes – the traditional colours of Rugby college. Plus I cheated. You are wearing your school's pin on your lapel."

Jones looked down at his lapel. Holmes smiled at the last remark, and I winced internally for missing that obvious detail.

"Mr. Jones here is also wearing a suit that is of a slightly out-of-date style, possibly purchased on his promotion from clerk two or three years ago. It is now heading towards retirement itself. He is quite well built, which suggests a history of sporting endeavours, but is sporting a slightly pronounced belly which indicates those days are over. He has a simple gold band on his left ring finger, and there is a small crusted stain on the right shoulder of his coat, which indicates spittle from an infant nestled there. Am I correct?"

Jones was still staggered in amazement.

"Yes. Yes, sir, you are correct on every detail. No wonder they wanted me to come and fetch you."

He sat down heavily, his brain whirring at a frantic rate, trying to take all of Holmes's abilities on board. I passed around cups of tea to break the tension.

274

Holmes sat back and sipped, his steely gaze still locked onto young Jones. "Who told you to come fetch me?" he asked.

Jones sipped his tea to steady his nerves and answered, "The Secretary, through his assistant, asked me to bring you immediately." He looked at the cup of tea in shock and placed it down a little unsteadily.

"He said immediately. I . . . I . . . must bring you back," he said standing up and taking us both a little by surprise.

Holmes smiled, "I'm sure it's not so urgent that we can't finish our tea."

Jones looked at the both of us and realised we weren't going to move. After a moment, he sat down again and picked up his cup.

"I – I have a hansom waiting outside," he said.

"Good, good. That will save time, and you can tell us all about why you are here," said Holmes.

Jones looked surprised again. "I'm sorry to say that I have been sworn to secrecy and was told to simply fetch you and bring you to the Houses of Parliament. Once there, all will become clear," he said.

Holmes's face showed a wide grin.

"Oh, really, how very intriguing. Someone was relying on your innocence to stir my curiosity. Very good," he said as he drained his cup and placed it on the side table. He stood. "Well Watson, shall we prepare ourselves and go with young Mr. Jones *here to see if there is* some game to be had in this little adventure?" He smiled to himself and added, "I feel that my brother is mixed up in this somewhere."

The hansom pulled up on Great George Street, about fifty yards from Westminster Bridge and across the road from the clock tower. Luckily for us, Big Ben was silent, as it was a good twenty minutes to the hour. The sound of that great bell is fixed in the minds of Londoners, but at that close distance it tends to have a dire effect on one's hearing.

We followed Godfrey across the street towards the magnificent site that is the Houses of Parliament. I looked up and down Great George Street and was surprised by the number of uniformed constables milling about. Usually one would see the odd bobby walking near the houses, but on that day, I spied a good half-dozen.

I thought to myself, "Something must be afoot."

Jones led us around the lush grass of the Speaker's Green, below a small arch in the side of the building, and up to a wooden door set back from the pathway.

He rapped twice on the door and announced himself. A heavy lock was turned and a bolt drawn before the door swung back into the building. A large cloud of smoke blew out of the open doorway, causing all three of us to cough. It slowly dissipated, revealing a heavy-set man with a ruddy complexion who eyed all three of us suspiciously whilst chomping on his cigar.

"Ah, Mr. Parsons," said Jones, evidently aware of the man's identity, "This is Mr. Sherlock Holmes and his associate, Dr. John Watson. The Secretary asked me to fetch them to investigate the, ah, the little problem."

The ruddy faced man looked Holmes and me up and down then drew on his cigar again before *harrumph*-ing and stepping back from the doorway to allow us passage. He peered out through the entrance once more before slamming the door behind us and bolting it shut.

"This is highly unusual, but I've orders from upstairs, so follow me, please," he said, letting the last word hang in the air before walking off along the long dark corridor leading away from the door.

I could detect a small grin on Holmes's face as he turned and followed Parsons, looking around from time to time to discern any details that might prove useful.

Jones walked next to me and spoke. "Please excuse Christopher. He was formerly in the Army and takes a lot of pride in maintaining the security here," he said.

"I was in the Army myself," I replied, "and I can quite understand. I can also see that he wouldn't like the idea of civilians simply waltzing in."

"Quite so," said Jones.

The corridor was a long, painted brick affair with no decorations of any kind. Every twenty yards or so, a small gaslight provided the only illumination. The barren nature told me that it was a service tunnel, used mostly by the cleaning staff or tradesmen who needed to access the underbelly of the Parliament buildings. Every so often we crossed another corridor and passed by dull, grey doors that were firmly shut. The only sounds were our footsteps on the ancient tiled floor.

Parsons stopped and opened one of the doors, revealing a set of stone stairs leading further down into the bowels under the building. A single gaslight shone on the ancient stone steps and allowed us to safely descend. The exit door led to another dimly lit passageway that headed off at a right angle to the one above.

We traversed this next narrow passage for about fifty yards before Parsons stopped, bent down, and picked up a small paraffin lamp. He lit it from his cigar and indicated an open archway leading into another passage perpendicular to the one in which we stood.

"I don't generally let civilians into this area," Parsons said. "Not within protocol, but . . . ."

Holmes finished his sentence for him, "You have your orders," and stepped through the arch.

276

We all followed and found a wide room with a doorway at the far end, along with a multitude of pipes running across the ceiling.

Parsons stepped up to a nearby gaslight and brought more illumination into the room by lighting it with his cigar. I noticed the pipes were a mix of dull brass and ceramic. I assumed they carried both water and sewage, and hoped they were watertight, as the thought of any leaks down here filled me with dread.

It was then I looked down and saw several small barrels, sitting in a neat pile, nestled against one wall.

Holmes spoke up, "I take it that this is either a store room or the source of your little problem."

"These appeared last night. One of the guards was doing a routine check, before I started, and found them. He reported to the duty clerk, then suddenly some shiny-bottom starts yelling 'Guy Fawkes!' and all hell breaks loose," said Parsons.

Holmes stepped up to the barrels and brought his lamp closer. Suddenly, he stepped back again and handed the lamp to me. "Keep this at a distance, will you Watson? I need to examine these barrels, but don't want the flame to get too close," he said. He turned to Parsons and said, "Do your protocols mention anything about smoking near explosives?"

Parsons looked sheepish and stepped back a couple of yards.

I approached Holmes and held the lamp at a suitable distance. Even from there, I could see traces of a black substance on the lid of one of the barrels. My rudimentary knowledge of explosives came to the fore.

"Is that - ?" I asked.

"I think so," Holmes answered.

He looked toward a brightly lit room through the door at the far end. He picked up a barrel and marched off towards the doorway. I started after him, but he held up a hand to stop me.

"No need for us both to be in danger, Watson," he said.

I stood, mouth agape, as he strode away.

"In danger?" I said to myself.

I watched from afar as Holmes placed the barrel on the ground just inside the room and pulled off the lid. He stared at the contents for a moment before dipping a hand into the barrel and bringing it out, full of black powder. He let it spill through his fingers and then rubbed two together with the remnants of the powder on their tips. I could see a smile play on his face and realised something was up. I hoped to be privy to it soon.

Holmes dipped his hand again, replaced the lid on the barrel and poured a small pile of the powder onto the lid. He picked up the barrel and turned back towards us.

Something just inside the other room grabbed his attention. He examined it for a moment before returning to us.

"Good news?" I asked.

"Interesting news, I think," he replied.

He placed the barrel on the floor, away from the others. I spied the small pile of black powder on top.

"Gunpowder, I presume," I said.

Holmes smiled and said, "That's what our perpetrator would lead us to believe."

He turned, plucked Parsons's cigar from his mouth, and rammed it into the little pile of powder.

We all reared back in terror.

The cigar simply sizzled slightly and let out a small stream of smoke. The powder remained inert.

"What in blazes?" said Parsons.

"It's sand. Fine, black sand, and ground up charcoal with a small amount of black powder," Holmes said.

"Good Lord," said Jones.

"Why?" I asked.

"I'm not sure at this point," said Holmes. "But something of this nature would be to sew discontent and terror, or to distract attention from another act." He turned towards Parsons, who was fishing out another cigar. "As you have said, the public isn't allowed into this area, so who would have access?" he asked.

"Guards," he said. "Cleaners. Maintenance crew. Why?"

Holmes pointed to the next room and said, "There is a cleaners' trolley sitting in the adjoining room. There are traces of the same black powder, so I am assuming it was used to transport these barrels. You would also have noticed that there is no fuse leading away from the barrels."

All three of us looked at the base of the pile. I felt ashamed that I had missed such an obvious clew.

"The only way to ignite this lot would be to set fire to a barrel itself, which would leave no time for the perpetrator to escape," said Holmes. He looked to the ceiling and posed another question. "And the room above?"

"That would be the House of Commons," said Jones, who had been silent for quite some time. "It's the main reason this was elevated beyond internal security and kept on the quiet."

"So the whole Guy Fawkes analogy is quite within reason," I said.

Holmes grinned then stepped towards the wall at the end of the room. He looked to the ceiling and through the doorway, then paced out the distance between the wall and the barrels.

"Twenty paces," he said pointing at the wall behind the barrels, "And this wall would be in the centre of the room to provide support for the chamber floor above."

He pointed to the ceiling and continued, "I propose that whoever sits on the Government benches above this point is the subject of this plot."

We re-assembled in the chamber of the House of Commons, several feet above the barrels of weakened black powder we had examined minutes previously.

The House was luckily empty as Parliament wasn't sitting that week. Holmes stated that this fact indicated that the barrels were merely a distraction from the true nature of this conundrum.

Parsons stood near the entrance with his arms folded and a scowl on his face. "I don't know why you need to be in 'ere," he said. "It's very out of the ordinary for Johnny public to be allowed access to the chamber. But – "

I finished his sentence, more in desperation at the man's insistence on protocol than anything. "You have your orders."

He nodded, grim faced. At least he had disposed of his foul-smelling cigar. I assumed even he wouldn't deign to smoke in the chamber – much to my relief.

Holmes was indifferent to Parsons's complaints. He was busy taking in the grandeur that is the chamber of the House of Commons. He paced the floor of the room between the two rows of benches, stepping up to the beautiful wood panelled walls at either end and examining them in detail. He knocked a couple of times, eliciting a shocked response from Parsons. "'Ere, what you doing?"

Holmes looked over at him and replied, "Ensuring that I'm correct in my assumption that the solid stone wall below us is in fact the same wall that this wood panelling hides from view."

Content in his deduction, he proceeded to pace out his measurements from below. He repeated the process a couple of times then turned to face the Government benches.

"Whomever sits in this area would have been the most affected by the blast from below," he said pointing at the green leather-upholstered bench, "*if* it were true gunpowder."

Godfrey Jones strode over and checked the location. He pointed to Holmes's right. "The Prime Minister sits there. To his left is the Chancellor," he said, pointing out each imprint in the leather as he turned. "Then the Foreign Secretary, the Home Secretary, and the Secretary for Defence,"

279

"Any of those last three," said Holmes, "could have been sitting directly above the bomb."

"But you said it wouldn't work," commented Parsons, "so it doesn't matter who it was,"

"As I said," added Holmes, "I think it is a distraction, aimed at sending a message, rather than inflicting any wholesale damage."

"Speaking of messages," interrupted Jones, "I think that brings us to the next piece of information that you should see."

Holmes and I both turned to look at him with slight surprise on our faces.

Jones brought us to the outer office of Sir Nigel Attleby, the Home Secretary. We entered and found a rather attractive woman sitting behind a desk looking extremely frazzled. She looked up as we entered, and her face dropped even further. "What is it now?" she asked.

Jones answered her with a calming voice, "I'm so sorry to disturb you, Miss Plumb, but these are the men that are helping us with the little problem downstairs. Sir Nigel also requested that they be brought to him when appropriate."

Her demeanour changed as she realised why we were there. "Ah, yes, I understand," she said, rising from her seat and stepping up to the padded leather door. "I'll see if he's free then," She knocked and waited until a muffled reply came from within. Opening the door, she entered and shut it before we could see inside.

Jones turned to us. "Please forgive Miss Plumb's mood. In addition to the barrels downstairs, we have a visit from King Alfonso of Spain next month, plus the Queen will be spending the summer at Balmoral. The Prime Minister has asked for an increase of security on both fronts due to this incident. Sir Nigel has been tasked with coordinating it all, which means it falls to Miss Plumb, his secretary."

I raised an eyebrow. It was quite unusual for a woman to hold such a position. Miss Plumb's reappearance broke me from my thoughts. She opened the door and stepped into her office, allowing us to file into the Secretary's room.

Holmes was at the end of the queue and stopped briefly next to the young lady. "Does your husband work in the Home Office as well?"

The woman's face dropped in shock. I turned in time to see it and assumed that my good friend had once again performed one of his miraculous observations.

"But, how – how could you know?" she stammered. "I've never seen you before in my life, sir."

Holmes simply smiled and nodded towards her hand. "You disguise it well, but your wedding bands have left a light mark on your ring finger. Perhaps you should leave them off for an extended time to allow the skin to darken in line with the rest of your hand," he said.

"I couldn't do that," she answered. "My husband would become enraged if he caught me without them. I only leave them off here to keep the peace amongst the other girls."

"I understand," he answered and tapped the side of his nose. "Your secret is safe with me."

"Thank you, sir. Sir Nigel signed a waiver for me when I married. David wanted me to resign, but then he left the Army and the money dried up, so I asked Sir Nigel if I could stay until David found employment. Really, I didn't think I'd be here this long. Poor David. He hasn't been himself since . . . ." Tears quickly formed in her eyes. She excused herself and fled from her office.

I walked over to a surprised Holmes and asked, "Something you said?"

"I think, perhaps, Watson, that there may be some deeper emotional strife within young Miss Plumb's marital circumstances," he said.

Inside Sir Nigel's office, the Home Secretary was a far different man than I had imagined. One tends to form an image of members of the upper levels of the civil service as stocky men tending to fat from their desk-bound lifestyle, and with the ruddy complexion of those who indulge in the demon drink a little too much.

The man who stood up and moved out from behind his desk was nothing like my cerebral musings. Sir Nigel Attleby was an athletic man in his early fifties. He was tall – even taller than Holmes – with chiselled features that would have had many a young lady swooning from his attentive gaze. He raised his hand and thrust it towards Holmes. "Mr. Holmes, I presume. A pleasure to meet you. Your brother has spoken well of you on many occasions," he said. "He and members of his department have worked closely with my own people at numerous times over the years." He turned in my direction. "And you would be Doctor John Watson, yes?" he asked.

I took his hand and shook, letting go before replying, "Yes. That I am, Sir Nigel."

"I've heard that you're the chronicler of Mr. Holmes's cases," he said, smiling again. "I don't think you'll find much to write about from this little nuisance."

"Interestingly enough," I said, "it is usually the seemingly mundane adventures that prove to be the most fascinating."

"Well, let's hope this remains as mundane as it seems." He leaned back against his desk and held out a hand to the three chairs before him and then looked up Parsons. "You'll be fine standing, won't you?"

Parsons scowled at the suggestion but nodded his head. Holmes, Godfrey Jones, and I took the proffered seats.

Sir Nigel studied each of us in turn. "Now, I know that Parsons has shown you the little display downstairs."

We nodded, and I noted, "You seem to be very calm, given that there's a large pile of gunpowder-filled barrels sitting below the House of Commons as we speak."

His expression remained calm. "Yes, but no one will be in there for another two weeks. So whoever put it there either didn't realise or didn't care. There was no way the barrels would go unnoticed for that period of time, and if ignited, they wouldn't have hurt anyone, and would have just been a nuisance. They're safe enough now, until we determine what's going on. So, yes, I am calm."

I peered at Holmes, who was studying Sir Nigel. "And you are correct," said Holmes, "The bomb, as it has been called, is merely a diversion. The powder in the barrels is not explosive, and there was no method to detonate it anyway. I'm still trying to discern what the person's motivation was in planting the barrels."

"I may have a clew as to the motivation," Sir Nigel said. He reached behind him and picked up a small handwritten parchment from a pile of paperwork. He turned and handed it to Holmes, who quickly read it. I noticed his eyebrows raise and a wry smile cross his lips. Then he then handed the page to me. It read:

> *We, the members of the Sudanese Mahdist Revolutionary Army, demand the immediate full-scale withdrawal of all Anglo forces from our country. If our demands are not met, we will unleash terror and hell upon the Parliament of Great Britain the likes of which have never been seen."*

It was signed "*Mahdi Muhammad Ahmed Bin Abd Allah*".

I turned towards Jones and offered the page to him. He waved it away which told me that he'd already seen it. I gave it back to Sir Nigel. "Is this real?" I asked.

Sir Nigel peered at the page whilst answering, "Her Majesty's troops are currently engaged with Egyptian, Italian, and Ethiopian forces in the Sudan, fighting against this Mahdi Muhammad Ahmed's army of militiamen."

282

"Would they have the resources to undertake an operation of this kind on British soil?" asked Holmes.

Sir Nigel thought for a moment then stared into Holmes's eyes, his expression had turned serious. "No, no, I don't think they would, but that's not to say that some other nation, or group of people, has provided them with the resources. I'm still not overly worried as I prefer to think that this – " He waved the page about. " – is another diversion, as you call it. But I don't know what the true objective is."

At that moment, Sir Nigel's now-composed secretary popped her head in through the connecting door and spoke. "Sorry to disturb you, sir, but the Prime Minister would like an update on the incident downstairs."

"Very good. I'll be with him shortly."

The woman withdrew and shut the door quietly. I noticed Sir Nigel's gaze lingered on the doorframe for a few moments before he turned back to us. I put it down to the stress of the situation, but I found out later that Holmes had other ideas which proved to be correct.

"I would think," Holmes said, "that you can assure the Prime Minister that the barrels are relatively inert and may be removed without incident. As to what is behind all of this, I will return to my rooms and cogitate upon it further. I believe that it will be a one or two pipe problem."

Sir Nigel looked a little perplexed by the last comment. "He simply means," I explained, "that he will need to sit back and smoke one or two pipes and think."

Sir Nigel's eyebrows raised. "Oh, an interesting way of approaching a problem."

"Quite so," I said.

"Well, gentlemen," he said as he ushered us out of his office and into the outer office, "I do hope to hear your solution quickly, but as you are aware, my presence has been requested, so I shall have to leave you."

He turned to his secretary. "Please give Mr. Holmes my home address, in case they have any information and need to contact me after hours. I'll be with the Prime Minister for a good while, but we will need to discuss the Balmoral arrangements when I return." The woman nodded and took down a small note to that affect. Sir Nigel then bid us *adieu* and left quickly.

I noticed the woman watch him leave, her gaze staying on the doorway in much the same as Sir Nigel's had earlier. I also observed that Holmes had seen the same thing.

We said thank you and goodbye and left her office. Parsons escorted us to a side door that led out onto Great George Street. As he started to leave, Holmes stopped him. "Mr. Parsons, if I might offer a suggestion." Parsons stopped and looked back a poorly hidden look of contempt on his face. "It might be worth your while to undertake an investigation of the residential premises of the Home and Foreign Secretaries, and anyone else that may have been in the supposed blast radius of the gunpowder bomb," he said.

Parson's expression relaxed slightly. "You think these idiots would try to get them at home?" he asked.

"If they have received local help, enough to get them into the Houses of Parliament, then they might be able to set up a similar bomb, or worse, a *real* bomb, at the home of one of our politicians,"

Parson's eyes grew wide. Holmes's suggestion had hit at the heart of his world. He disappeared quickly, leaving us alone with Godfrey Jones.

"Thank you, Mr. Holmes," he said. "I must admit that I am astounded at your ability to look at the simplest situation and determine so much detail. I can only hope to learn the art of deduction and follow in your footsteps. It would be a much more interesting than a life in the civil service."

I smiled a little at this confession, and a wry grin crossed Holmes's face. He answered, "If I were you, I would agitate to be moved to my brother Mycroft's department. Although he doesn't undertake the level of deductive reasoning that I do, he is much more adept at the art than I, and would be a worthy case study for someone in a position such as yourself."

Holmes held out his hand and shook Jones's before continuing, "If I might ask one favour of you: Could you have one of the barrels of black powder delivered to my abode this afternoon. I'd like to examine the barrel further. I believe it will assist in my deductions."

"Of course," Jones said, beaming widely, "Anything to help." He turned, shook my hand, and quickly disappeared back inside.

"A young lad full of admirable qualities, I think," I said.

"Yes, Watson, indeed," Holmes agreed. "I do hope he finds his mark before that place strips him of all ambition."

True to his word, young Godfrey Jones arranged for one of the barrels to be delivered to Baker Street later that same day. Holmes was elated and carried it to his chemical corner and then set about his work. I relied on the initial fact that the black powder had been heavily mixed with sand to allay any fears that Holmes's investigations would lead to any explosive result. With that in mind, I decided to leave him to his experimentation and occupy myself elsewhere. He wasn't home when I returned later that evening.

It was late the next morning, whilst I was enjoying some morning tea, that Holmes emerged from his bedroom, looking refreshed and exhilarated.

284

"Good news?" I asked.

He stretched his arms, smiled and said, "Why, yes, thoroughly good news." He sat down and helped himself to coffee and biscuits.

"Well?" I asked with a touch of impatience.

He smiled, took a sip of coffee and began to explain. "I have found out many interesting facts," he began. "The black powder, as I surmised is a mix of gun powder, sand, and ground charcoal. It will burn, but it isn't explosive in any way. Its purpose was to give the illusion of being an explosive, rather than having any destructive power." He took another sip of coffee, then continued. "The powder itself is interesting. It's the type that was used by the British military up until a couple of years ago, when they changed all formulations to cordite, which isn't as explosive but diffuses much more gas-per-weight, thereby creating a greater propellant effect. The original gunpowder burnt too hot and caused damage to the barrels and firing chambers of many of our guns."

He placed his cup down, rose, and walked over to our sitting chairs. He rooted around the discarded newspapers for a moment and brought out the object of his attention. "A-ha, here it is," he said, brandishing the article that I had spied on the day young Godfrey Jones had come to our door. Holmes read aloud: "*Two weeks ago, there was a break-in at the Royal Artillery Barracks in Woolwich. The stores were raided, but all that was stolen were twenty barrels of gunpowder destined for destruction. The Army has advised the local constabulary in case any local criminal gangs were involved.*'"

He looked up at me and smiled.

"Sounds as if we may have found the source of the black powder," he said, placing the paper down and re-joining me at the dining table, "although the quantity stolen doesn't equate with the amounts that would be in the barrels found under Parliament. I would estimate that only about two barrels-worth of powder was mixed across those we discovered."

"Now, the next question I needed to answer was about the barrels themselves."

"They aren't the same barrels?" I asked.

"No, surprisingly not. The stolen powder kegs themselves would have been much smaller, around nine inches tall and seven inches across, plus the strapping bands would have been made of reed or rope to avoid sparks."

I turned and spied the barrel sitting on Holmes's work bench. It was a hefty size, around two feet tall and one foot across, with distinctly metal banding.

"Yes, exactly, Watson. Those barrels are not the originals. In fact, they were built by a cooper down at the Port of London. I wired him last night and confirmed an order by an unknown buyer two weeks ago. Sadly, he only dealt with the delivery driver, whom he described as a balding man of about forty. He said that he'd never seen the man before, and believed that he would never see him again. I suppose that's the problem with cash payments. A business-man is only concerned with the money, not the details of the transaction."

"Where does that leave us?" I asked.

He took a final sip of coffee, placed his cup down, and looked at me over steepled fingers ."Well, we still have eighteen unused barrels of black powder. We are led to believe that a Sudanese organisation is behind all of this, but the powder was stolen on British soil and the perpetrators procured items from a London-based business and used a local to undertake the exchange. I dropped in on Lestrade to see if there has been any known activity amongst the local Sudanese population, but according to Scotland Yard, the only known Sudanese in London are a single family that lives in Canning Town. They've been monitored since before the war in the Sudan started and, according to Lestrade, are simple dockworkers who escaped from Northern Africa in the early 1880's."

"It's all a front then?" I said.

"Yes," said Holmes, "And – "

We were suddenly disturbed by an insistent thumping on the front door downstairs. Soon, we heard Mrs. Hudson unlatching the door before letting out a surprised cry. Loud footfalls proceeded up the stairwell, causing us both to stand in readiness.

The door to our apartments was flung open and there stood a very flustered Godfrey Jones. He took one look at the both of us and, through a series of strained inhalations, gasped, "Please come quickly. There's been a horrible accident."

Jones remained tight-lipped throughout our trip in the hansom. I could see he was fidgety and extremely anxious. I tried in numerous occasions to talk to him, but he fobbed me off with mumblings about secrecy.

It was as we pulled out of Pall Mall and into Carlton Gardens that I realised we were heading towards the secretarial residences. The Crown owned several properties in the area which were made available to members of the Cabinet whilst they were in London. The Home Secretary's address was amongst them.

My concerns grew grave as we passed through a small police cordon that blocked off the end of the street. Inspector Lestrade stood by a young constable and peered into the hansom. "Mr. Holmes? What the devil is going on? I have orders to let you and only you through," he said.

"All will become clear, Inspector," Holmes answered. "I will inform you as soon as I have finished my investigations."

"Blast!" Lestrade said as the hansom pulled away.

I was still wondering which Secretary was involved when we pulled up outside of Number Three. As I looked out of the cab I became shocked. Holmes even made a small murmur when he viewed the devastation. We quickly exited the hansom to survey the scene.

Carlton Gardens are generally a wonderfully kept set of Georgian Terraced apartments. Each is four stories high, and my understanding is that they contain several bedrooms for residents and staff, with a full-sized catering kitchen, a large dining room for state affairs, and everything that Cabinet ministers might require. They back onto St. James Gardens so that even families with young children had ample room for play and exercise.

On this day, however, the outside of Number Three was a site of utter desolation. The entrance-way appeared to have been blown apart from below. The front door was missing and the short staircase leading up to the door was simply a smouldering hole with broken masonry and brickwork strewn in a wide arc around the front of the building.

"Good Lord," I said.

"Indeed," said Holmes. "I think we have found the rest of our missing gunpowder – or what remains of it anyway,"

Once the hansom had driven off, Godfrey Jones joined us and simply stared at the hole in the ground at the front of the residence.

"They told me what happened," he said, "but I didn't think it would be this bad."

I turned to him and asked, "Can you tell us which Cabinet minister's residence this is?"

"Yes, it's Sir Nigel's house. The explosion occurred only an hour ago. I was at work at Parliament when I was commanded to fetch you and bring you here," he said.

"The Secretary? Is he . . . ?" I hesitated to finish the question.

Jones shook his head. "No, he's fine," he said.

"I'm afraid that can't be said for some other poor unfortunate," said Holmes from a few feet away.

I looked around. He was looking at some dark stains on the cobbles. I knew straight away what those stains meant.

"Oh, my," I said and turned back to Jones. "Who was it?"

His face bore a look of shock. He stared for a moment then dropped his head. "It was Parsons."

"Parsons? Why in blazes was he here?" Then I realised. He came on our insistence to check up on the members of the cabinet.

Holmes had wandered over to the very front of the house and was peering down into the void left by the explosion. I joined him to gain a better view. The house had a lower basement level, where I presumed the help lived. A small courtyard was visible below the street, probably available to the staff for their use. Previously it would have been a cosy place to sit and possibly smoke or take tea. Now all the furniture was destroyed, and the plants burnt to cinders.

Holmes stood at the edge of the courtyard wall and was peering with great intent at the blackened vegetation below. "Hmm," he said, "I need to gain access to the courtyard." He turned to Jones. "Is there a way that we can enter the house?"

A voice answered from within the house itself. "Yes, Mr. Holmes. Yes there is," it said.

We turned to find Sir Nigel standing in the ruins of his entranceway wearing a smoking jacket over a pair of silk pyjamas. A stern look crossed his face. "I will give you all the help you need to find this culprit," he said.

Sir Nigel met us at the rear door of the property. His sombre mood persisted, and he quietly led us through to the front of the house where a small staircase led down to the servants' quarters. He remained behind with Godfrey Jones as Holmes and I made our way down the stairs and out into the small courtyard.

It looked more of a mess up close than before. Holmes immediately set about viewing the entire scene and taking in as many minute details as he could. I watched as he surveyed the wreckage, dropped to his knee from time to time, and pulled out his glass to examine the clews, such as they were.

I scanned the area myself. The two longer walls consisted of the front of the house, with two windows that looked into the servants' sitting room and the solid retaining wall that lined the street side. At one end, a small under-croft appeared to lie beneath the front stair case. It must have been in there that the barrels of powder had been placed. The explosion brought down the staircase and virtually buried the evidence from view. At the other end, two trees had been planted amidst a once-lovely garden bed. A line of planter boxes bordered the bed which had a small sitting area in the centre, the furniture now blasted into pieces. The far wall had a gate that led into the neighbouring courtyard. The gate had been blown off its hinges and could be seen lying beyond.

As I walked over to the garden bed to lessen my view of the devastation, I noticed something completely out of place. More dark stains were spread out across the grass that had been protected from the brunt of the blast by the planter boxes. The blood stains radiated away from the blast and towards the small gate.

"Holmes, I think I've found something," I said over my shoulder. As I turned, I found him standing right behind me, holding a small item of interest in his hand. It was the stub end of a cigar. Burnt – but still relatively whole.

"Parson?" I asked.

He nodded then said, "What have you found then, Watson?"

I pointed to the blood stains and suggested we follow them into the next yard. He agreed, and I led the way.

I was astonished at what we found, but I believe Holmes had already deduced this eventuality. Lying just inside the courtyard and hidden from view was a body. He was covered in blood and had received horrendous burns from the explosion. I checked his pulse and found that he was well and truly dead. I managed to turn him over and we discovered that he was a balding man about forty years of age. The evidence suggested that he was the delivery man that had bought the barrels from the cooper.

"Our culprit?" I asked.

"I would think so," said Holmes, "The evidence is adding up." He returned to the adjoining courtyard and studied the scene once more.

I joined him and asked, "Do you know what happened yet?"

"I can surmise from the existence of the dead man and this cigar, that our poor Mr. Parsons, by pure accident, thwarted the plan to kill Sir Nigel, and inadvertently took his place." He pointed to the staircase. "I presume that Mr. Parsons came to the house early this morning, smoking a cigar as was his habit. He stopped on the entrance stairs to finish it off and casually tossed the remnants into the courtyard rather than the street."

He stepped over to where he found the cigar and pointed out the under croft and then the line of planter boxes. "Mr. Parsons just happened along at the same moment that our assailant had managed to set up his explosives and was waiting for an opportune time to ignite them. He may have known that Sir Nigel likes to retrieve the daily papers himself of a morning."

I interjected at that point, "How do you know that?" Then I promptly answered my own question in my head just as Holmes confirmed it.

"I had Sir Nigel watched," he said. "Now, Parsons tossed his cigar into the courtyard and was most unfortunate to have it land on the line of gunpowder that our assailant had laid down to act as a fuse."

He pointed to a smudged line of dark black powder which I had taken to be ash or charred detritus from the blast. "The fuse lit and quickly raced towards the black powder. The result is evident." He pointed to the planter boxes. "Our bomber was hiding behind those planters, which are good and heavy and would have provided adequate protection. When he heard the fuse ignite, however, he stood in surprise, thereby becoming the second victim in this little fiasco."

"The fool," I said.

"Quite so," agreed Holmes.

"Who was he then?" I asked.

"For that, I think it is time to head inside. There is a little more to this story, yet."

We found Godfrey and Sir Nigel seated around a small table in the parlour. Coffee had been served for all four of us, and the two of them had poured for themselves while they awaited our return. Sir Nigel was the first to see us and placed his cup down in preparation for our arrival.

"Gentlemen, I ordered some refreshments – although I'll admit, at the moment, I don't quite have the stomach for food. Devilish time," he said.

"Thank you, Sir Nigel," said Holmes in a rather stern voice, "but I think it best if we move forward as quickly as possible,"

I was taken aback by Holmes's mood. He seemed annoyed at the events that had occurred, and I was a little afraid that he would overstep the mark and damage the relationship we'd built with the Home Secretary.

I assumed he was about to rebuke Sir Nigel for something, but he spoke to Godfrey Jones instead.

"We have found the body of a poor unfortunate in the neighbouring courtyard. The police must have missed it on their first investigation. Sloppy if you ask me, but is does me no good to dwell on it. Would you be so kind as to go out and inform the constables outside, so they can deal with it? Tell them I have investigated and will update Inspector Lestrade in due time," he said.

Jones put down his own cup and rose. "Of course, Mr. Holmes. Do you think it was the man we are after, or just an innocent victim?"

"I'm still trying to determine that, but with Sir Nigel's help, I believe I will have a solution before you return," he said.

"Very good," Jones said and rushed off.

Once he was gone and out of earshot, Holmes turned to Sir Nigel. "That was mostly for your benefit," he said. "I think it would be prudent to bring Mrs. Button out so that we can put this despicable affair to bed, so to speak."

Sir Nigel's face dropped in shock for a moment but relaxed into a slight grin. "How the devil did you know?"

"Well, to be honest," he replied, "there was no deduction necessary. I had an inkling as to what has been going on and asked a few discrete questions. My informant apprised me of the affair. Don't worry," he added, "your secret is safe with me for as long as you require it to be. That was the main reason I sent young Jones away."

Sir Nigel rose and said, "Very good. I thank you for your discretion."

After Sir Nigel left, I turned to Holmes as I just had to ask: "Who is Mrs. Button?"

"Ah, yes. I used some of that time away from Baker Street last night to initiate further investigations. Plus, I called on the services of my irregulars to conduct low level surveillance, not only of Sir Nigel, but his personal assistant, one Mrs. Angela Button," he said. "You know her as Miss Plumb."

"Why would you need to have his secretary observed? What does she have to do with all of this?" I asked.

Holmes smiled. "Oh, I think we'll find that she has everything to do with this," he said in that slightly irritating but knowledgeable way of his.

It was at that point that Sir Nigel returned and stood aside to let the young lady in question into the room. We both nodded in deference to her.

"Mr. Holmes, you wished to see me," she said retaining as much dignity as she could muster, given her presence in Sir Nigel's home.

"Mrs. Button," Holmes began.

She cut him off by saying, "Angela, if you please," a hint of aversion at the use of her married name crossing her face.

"Firstly," Holmes continued, "let me apologise to both yourself and Sir Nigel, but I employed the use of my associates to have you followed last night."

Both began to protest, but Holmes held up his hands. "I also had my people follow the Chancellor, the Defence Secretary, and both of their assistants as well. The main object was to detect if there were any agents of foreign interest doing the same."

Mrs. Button found some inner courage and spoke up, "I know what you see before you must seem like some sordid little affair, but you would be wrong. Sir Nigel and I have a simple platonic friendship, that's all. I've been his assistant for over ten years, well before I was married, and well before he held the position of Home Secretary. I came to him late last night after David, my husband, and I had a row. He was drunk again and accused me of all manner of ills. Frankly, I'd had enough, and stormed out. At that time of night, I had nowhere to turn but here."

Holmes paused for a moment to gather his thoughts before continuing, "Now, Mrs. – ah – Angela, could you describe your husband to us."

A slight look of surprise flitted across her face before she spoke. "A typical Englishman if you like. Just turned forty years old. Keeps his hair very short, in fact shaves it bald on occasions. Tall. Has started to become a little stocky due to the drink. Why?" she asked.

As the description continued, my face dropped in realisation. I looked across at Holmes who remained stoic. "I was a little afraid of that," he said.

"What do you mean, sir?" asked Sir Nigel, "What does Angela's husband have to do with any of this?"

"Sadly, everything," said Holmes. He indicated the settee and continued, "Madam I think it would be best if you were to take a seat. My explanation may be a little long and, for you, a little disturbing."

Mrs. Button sat down with Sir Nigel standing behind her. Both retained concerned looks on their faces.

Holmes waited until they were settled, and for a little dramatic effect, before he began. "I'm afraid that your husband, ex-Corporal David Button, was the sole perpetrator behind this whole affair. My inquiries have indicated that he served at the Royal Artillery Depot at Woolwich up until six months ago, when he was dishonourably discharged for theft."

Tears formed in Angela's eyes and she dropped her head forward. "He wanted to set us up in a little country estate. I was ashamed of his actions, but we'd just married and I've always been told to support your husband no matter what. Foolish man." She looked up, a trail of tears running down each cheek. "I pleaded with Sir Nigel to help out, and he managed to have the charges dropped, but they had to discharge him as a matter of protocol."

Sir Nigel nodded. His face showed sorrow. I wasn't sure if it was for Angela or for himself.

"I managed to get him a job on the cleaning staff not long afterwards, but he showed up intoxicated on several occasions, and even I couldn't protect him," he said.

Mrs. Button nodded, turned, and looked up into Sir Nigel's eyes. He patted her shoulder and she placed a hand on his for a moment before turning back to Holmes.

"David kept blaming me for all his troubles. He said I was having an affair. He said I was making him less of a man because I kept working. Last night was the first time I became scared. He threatened to kill Sir Nigel, and then he threatened me," she said.

"The black powder was from a robbery at the Woolwich depot," explained Holmes. "Several barrels of old stock. The fake bomb under the House of Commons was probably an attempt to scare you, Sir Nigel. It was never going to work, but he must have used what he learned from his cleaning job to get back into the House and plant the bomb. I found a disused cleaner's trolley nearby. Last night, I presume, a combination of drink and his temper caused him to act. He must have arrived very early this morning and brought the powder in via the next-door courtyard."

"Yes," said Sir Nigel, "That's the Foreign Secretary's residence. He lives in Newcastle when Parliament is in recess. A caretaker comes in a couple of times a week."

"Quite so. Now, I am surmising that Mr. Button finished his work. Placed a trail of powder to the barrels in the under-croft to act as a fuse, then waited behind the row of planter boxes for Sir Nigel to retrieve the morning paper. He fell asleep instead and the unfortunate Mr. Parsons arrived early, looked around the front of the house, and lit up a morning cigar. Once finished, he was either about to leave or to knock on the door to ensure all was fine. He flicked the remains of his cigar into the courtyard, where it ignited the trail of powder. Mr. Button awoke to see the powder alight. He stood up just at the same time as the barrels ignited and exploded," Holmes said.

Mrs. Button reacted in surprise. "How do you know he was down in the courtyard?" she asked.

We all realised that she was the only one who didn't know about the body. "Oh, I'm so sorry dear," said Sir Nigel, "I afraid that Mr. Holmes and Dr. Watson found a dead body in the garden next door."

"And it fits the description that you gave of your husband," said Holmes.

A hand shot up to her face as she gasped, her face a mask of horror.

"I am so sorry to break it to you like this," Holmes said. "In your husband's defence, there's no indication that he intended to light the fuse. I believe it may have still been a ruse to scare Sir Nigel away from you."

"No. I loved my husband," Mrs. Button replied, "but of late his delirium over our supposed affair has escalated. The last thing he said as I fled from own house was that he was going to kill Sir Nigel and he had the means to do it. At the time, I took it as another set of his drunken ravings, but it seems . . . ."

She stopped abruptly as tears streamed from her eyes.

I took that moment to begin our excuses. "I don't know if there's much more we can achieve here," I said as I stood.

Sir Nigel nodded as he reached down and comforted the sobbing woman.

We quickly found ourselves out in the street and were approached by Inspector Lestrade, his face a mass of questions. "What is going on, Mr. Holmes?" he asked. "I have a bomb going off in a Government minister's residence. I have two dead bodies, and I've been kept away from the scene of the crime all morning."

Holmes held up a hand to quieten the policeman. "All will be explained, Inspector, I assure you. At this stage, you have the perpetrator, a Mr. David Button, the second corpse found on the scene. What started out as an act against the Houses of Parliament – " Lestrade's face dropped in shock at this revelation. " – has turned out to be a domestic issue with tragic results. For now, please be so kind as to allow Sir Nigel and his house guest a little privacy for a couple of hours. They have had a major shock. I still need to tidy up one or two loose ends myself, but I assure you I will come by later and explain the full details to you."

Lestrade huffed and stormed off. Waiting was not one of his favourite hobbies.

Holmes took a deep breath and stared up into the clear blue sky.

"Do you think Angela will be alright?" I asked.

Holmes smiled and turned towards me, "I think that after the shock of this tragedy subsides, Mrs. Button may end up acquiring a new wedding ring that she will be more than proud to display, and a new title that will allow her to cease her duties in the civil service for good."

I smiled at his assumptions. "But she said that there was nothing to Button's insinuation of their affair," I said.

"Ah, yes," he said, "but the affairs of the heart aren't always so easy to deduce, even for those directly involved."

He looked down the street towards the devastation in front of the Home Secretary's residence. "I won't be holding my breath waiting for our wedding invitations, but I think it will be a nice surprise when they arrive," he said.

I chuckled to myself and we walked off to fetch a hansom back to Baker Street.

Mr. Clever, Baker Street
by Geri Schear

As my friend Mr. Sherlock Holmes and I sat down to breakfast one Friday morning in April 1896, our landlady Mrs. Hudson placed the morning's post on the table before us. In addition to the usual assortment of letters, bills, and requests for my friend's services, the morning's collection included a parcel. This was wrapped in heavy butcher's paper and twine, and the address, written in purple ink, was, "*Mr. Clever, Baker Street*".

"The postman said he couldn't think where else to send it, and so he brought it here," Mrs. Hudson explained in response to my friend's quizzical look.

"It seems a reasonable assumption," I said.

Sherlock Holmes was too busy studying the object to reply. He held it in his long thin fingers and rotated it slowly, his kippers and coffee completely forgotten.

"Butcher's paper, cheap ink . . . The address was written by a man with limited education. I am surprised it arrived – assuming it has, in fact, reached the correct destination. There are other Baker Streets in Great Britain, after all, and *Clever* is, I believe, a proper surname. Still, the odour and stain suggest I am the intended recipient. Therefore, I think I am justified in opening it, and seeing what may be learned from the contents."

"The odour?" I asked.

He handed the object to me. "What do you make of it, Watson?"

I took the item from him and immediately noticed the stench. "Perhaps it is meat," I said.

"If so, it is rotten," he replied.

I proceeded to rotate the parcel, even as he had done. "Well, as you said, Holmes, the address specifies nothing more than Baker Street. It was posted in Great Portland Street, so it hasn't travelled far."

I turned the parcel over and examined the base.

"Ah, there is the stain . . . Something within may be leaking, or perhaps the parcel was set upon something . . . Why don't you simply open it?" I said, as I returned it to him.

My friend's eyes flickered towards our curious landlady. "There is no need for haste. Thank you, Mrs. Hudson."

The woman wiped her hands in her apron and reluctantly departed. Only when her footsteps faded down the stairs did Holmes carefully open the package.

I covered my mouth and sprang back.

"A head!" I cried. "Good God, it's a head!"

The parcel contained the head of a man. He looked about forty to fifty years of age with drooping eyes, a bashed-in nose, and a sagging, thin-lipped mouth. His grey hair was thick and curled around the forehead and ears. The skin was course and heavily wrinkled. The face was deeply tanned, suggesting a man who had known a great deal of hardship.

The neck ended in a jagged line of bloody clotting where the head had been severed from the body. All this I perceived from several feet away. Only my years of medical service and my time spent in combat enabled me to maintain my composure. The sight of that ghastly thing – a severed head, sitting amid our breakfast things – was one of the most grotesque things I have ever seen.

"From the degree of putrefaction, I'd put time of death around twenty-four to forty-eight hours ago. There has been no attempt at preservation," Holmes said, unperturbed.

As he focused his considerable energies on the foul, stinking thing, I opened all the windows and doors and held a handkerchief to my nose and mouth. Thus fortified, I joined my friend back at the table and watched as, using his magnifying glass, he studied the line of butchery closely.

"Yes, undoubtedly the instrument of death was an axe, a four-inch blade with a notch some two-and-a-half inches along. That may help us identify our killer."

"He was no physician," I observed.

"Nor butcher," Holmes said. "This head was hacked off in a most crude manner. This is your province, Watson. What say you: Was the fellow alive when he was decapitated?"

"I fear so. The blood vessels very much suggest it. I wonder he sat still long enough for the killer to complete his grisly task."

"From the angle of the cuts, I surmise he was lying down during the beheading and, from the odour, I believe he was rendered unconscious with the aid of a considerable amount of alcohol."

"A small mercy."

"Very small."

"I would further deduce from his complexion that this fellow was a heavy drinker." Holmes sat back from the head and looked at me.

"Given these grotesque contents, I am sure you would concur, Watson, that I *am* the intended recipient of the parcel?"

"Without doubt."

"Thank you. From his appearance, we can deduce our friend here worked outdoors. You observe the tan? It fades around the forehead, suggesting he wore a flat cap."

He turned the head around and examined the back. "Yes, even the neck is deeply tanned. The executioner was considerate enough to leave us several inches of spine and we can see this fellow's tan extends the entire distance. Now, what sort of man works outside to the extent that even the back of his neck is exposed to the sun to such a degree?"

"A sailor?"

"Not a bad suggestion," he said, "but the sailor's cap would leave a clear demarcation along the brow, rather than the subtle fading we see here. No, this was clearly a flat cap. Also, this fellow was not, despite his other vices, a smoker, nor did he chew tobacco. It's rare to find a sailor who does not indulge in such habits. No, I suspect we have here a groundskeeper or gardener of some sort."

"I see, yes. And the poor fellow seems to have been clumsy, too."

"Clumsy?"

"He has a broken nose."

"To break his nose once may be clumsy," Holmes replied with a chuckle. "This fellow has done so at least three times. You see the breaks here, here, and here? That suggests ill temper. He might, I suppose, be a pugilist, but I think not. No, I believe our unfortunate friend here to be a quarrelsome sort, possibly due to his fondness for alcohol."

Holmes continued to scrutinize the head closely. Using the kitchen knife and a torch, he examined the mouth.

I recoiled as he sniffed at the unfortunate corpus's oral cavity.

"The fellow's teeth are in a shocking state," he declared. "His diet consisted of the poorest quality bread and fat, some of which are still present. I can still smell the alcohol. A cheap whisky, I'd wager."

"How does this help us identify the poor fellow?" I asked.

"A gardener in London, a heavy drinker, given to fighting . . . As the package was sent from Great Portland Street, I think we can reasonably deduce he worked within that vicinity. Well, Watson, let us finish our breakfast, and then we can start at Regent's Park and see what we can learn."

"Regent's Park? Not a private home?"

"With his history of fisticuffs? Unlikely. A big park is our best bet. We shall start there and see what we can learn."

"Shouldn't we go to Scotland Yard first?"

He frowned. "That will mean an unnecessary delay. Let us at least make a start on the case to give them some leads. It will save them infinite pains, my dear fellow. Come, an hour in the park, surrounded by the trees and flowers, just what we need after this stench. Or would you prefer a morning in a stuffy police station?"

"We should at least send word to the authorities regarding this delivery," I insisted.

"Oh, very well, I shall send a note with one of the Irregulars." He sat and wrote, adding impatiently as he did so, Then, after hiding the box in his room, he said, "Hurry along, Watson. We shall leave as soon as you have finished your breakfast."

"Let us go now," I said. "I find I have no appetite at present."

Mr. Augustus Tripe, the head gardener at Regent's Park, met us cordially.

"Mr. Sherlock Holmes?" he said, shaking my friend's hand. "Doctor Watson. Yes, I have heard of you both. My wife loves your tales, Doctor. Total fantasy, I am sure, but great fun. How can I help you?"

With a bark of annoyance, Holmes said, "We are looking for some information regarding one of your employees. He is aged around forty to fifty years, has grey hair, a broken nose, and is a heavy drinker. I believe he has a choleric temperament and frequently engages in fisticuffs."

"Oh, you mean Reggie Longbottom. What's he done now?"

"He's got himself murdered," Holmes replied. "His head was delivered to my apartment this morning."

"I'm sorry. Did you say his *head*?"

"Yes. Someone decapitated him and sent the head to me. Not what one expects to find over the morning kippers."

"Uh, quite."

"Perhaps you could tell us something about Mr. Longbottom?" I asked.

Tripe led us to his office and poured himself a generous measure of brandy. Holmes and I waved our refusal to his offer. "How did you know he worked here?" he asked, in an obvious effort to calm himself.

"I deduced it from his neck," Holmes replied.

"His neck?"

"Yes," I said, at Mr. Tripe's astonished expression. "There is nothing exaggerated about my tales, or Mr. Holmes's skills, I assure you."

"What can you tell us about Mr. Longbottom?" Holmes asked.

"Uh . . . well, as you said, Mr. Holmes, he was a real son of . . . an angry sort of fellow."

"Had he a family?"

"Yes, Mr. Holmes. They live in Gosfield Street. One moment, and I will find the address for you."

"Gosfield Street," Holmes said, glancing at me with a satisfied look. "Rather less than half-a-mile."

"As I recall," said Mr. Tripe, "Longbottom's wife takes in laundry, and the oldest lad is an apprentice for Mr. Remington, the baker in Langham Street."

"We are exceedingly obliged to you, Mr. Tripe. Tell me, did Mr. Longbottom have any particular enemies?"

"Not anyone in particular. It seemed to me that everyone took exception to the fellow. He was a difficult chap to get along with. A good gardener, mind. Odd that he could be so gentle with a geranium and so bloody-minded with his fellow man, but there you are. I hope you find the man who killed him."

"Thank you," Holmes said, as he took the address. "Tell me, when did he work last?"

He checked his records. "Wednesday. He worked the morning shift from six to three."

"Did you see him leave?"

"I did, yes. He passed me on his way out. I was by the gate discussing herbaceous borders with a visitor."

"He was alone?"

"Yes. That was his way. Not a popular man, I'm afraid."

We thanked Mr. Tripe and took our leave. As Gosfield Street was no more than a few minutes' walk away, and as it was a bright and sunny day, I agreed we should visit Mrs. Longbottom before going to Scotland Yard.

The Longbottoms dwelt in the top floor of a squalid little flat. We trudged up the narrow, unsavoury staircase to the top floor. From behind the many closed doors, we heard cries and bangs, and smelled odours I preferred not to contemplate.

The woman who answered our knock seemed weary and washed out, as if life had drained all the colour from her.

"Mrs. Longbottom?" Holmes said. "I am Sherlock Holmes, and this is my colleague, Dr. Watson. We need to speak with you on a matter of some urgency. May we come in?"

She had barely opened the door a crack and kept her body as a shield against our entry.

"We ain't buying nothing," she said.

"We are not salesmen," I said. "We are here concerning your husband, Reginald."

"Reggie ain't here. I ain't seen him these two days."

"Yes, we know. I am afraid we have some bad news for you. May we come in? It will only be for a moment."

She let us into the one-room flat and heard us. She took the news of her husband's death in silence.

Did Mr. Longbottom have any enemies?

Oh, Lord, yes. Hundreds.

"He were a combative bastard," she said, without blushing. "Always in a fight with someone. It's the drink, like. He takes a few and then he's off, shouting and swinging his fists. Half of London probably wants a piece of him. Other half would if they had a chance to meet him. Met him," she corrected.

"When did you last see him?" Holmes asked.

She frowned, trying to remember. "Don't really remember," she said. "I work, see. And Reggie, he works the early shift. He had to be at the park at six o'clock."

"What day was that?"

"Tuesday. Yes, that's right. Tuesday it were."

"Naw, ma, it were Wednesday," a young lad aged about twelve years interjected. "You told 'im to stop and pick up them trotters at the market on the way home, remember?"

"That's right. I were that mad he never showed. Reckoned he met someone and went off to the pub. You're right, young Tom. Wednesday, it were."

We thanked her for her assistance prepared to take our leave. As she escorted us to the door, she said, "Sirs, he were a useless lump of a husband to be sure, but he were all I had. Tell me he didn't suffer."

"No, indeed," I said. "It was very quick. I'm sure he never felt a thing."

As we left the unpleasant building I comforted myself that the Almighty must surely forgive a lie told with a generous purpose.

Inspector Gregson, though not in the normal course of events an emotional man, reacted with distaste to the package that Holmes placed on his desk.

"Mr. Holmes," he protested. "You might warn a man!" He fumbled in his pocket for a handkerchief and held it to his mouth.

"I did send you a note," Holmes said.

"I thought it was a joke."

The inspector reluctantly approached the parcel and managed to turn his grimace into a wry smirk. "Mr. Clever, eh?" he said.

"The killer's idea of provocation, I think, Inspector," Holmes replied. "It seems perfectly that clear this . . . *object* was sent to me as a clear message: He expects me to solve the mystery."

"What mystery?"

"The identification of the dead man, and who he, the killer, is."

"Well, I can't see how we can accomplish either of those things with nothing more than a head."

"Oh, we have already made considerable headway," Sherlock Holmes replied with gallows humour. "To wit, we have identified the owner of the head as one Reginald Longbottom. We have spoken to his employer, and to his wife. We know Longbottom was last seen on Wednesday afternoon at Regent's Park, where he was employed as a gardener. He left at his usual time of three o'clock. It should not prove too difficult to trace his steps after that, but Watson insisted we deliver the parcel to you before we went any further."

"I should think so, indeed." The inspector took the details of Longbottom's name, address, and other particulars that Holmes gave him. "Did the wife identify him?"

"Inspector, really!" I exclaimed.

Gregson had, at least, the grace to blush. "Uh, I suppose that might be a little . . . yes. Still, it is mere supposition on your part, Mr. Holmes. This identification, I mean. I don't say you're wrong, but we can't be sure, can we?"

"I assure you, I am correct," Holmes protested.

"Perhaps, but we have procedure," Gregson replied. "Don't worry, Doctor. We can be discreet."

The following morning a second parcel arrived, chillingly similar to the first. As before, Holmes waited until Mrs. Hudson left the room before opening it. In response to my protest – my *request* – my friend opened the grotesque thing at his desk. This parcel contained, not a head, but a heart.

"Human, if I haven't forgotten my anatomy lessons," he said.

"Human, indeed," I agreed. "Small and the vessels are sclerosed, so I would attribute the owner to be an older female, fifty years at least."

"Considerably more difficult to identify." Holmes said.

"There may be a connection between the victims," I suggested.

"Perhaps."

Again, we skipped breakfast and merely had coffee. We then took the grisly package to Scotland Yard.

"What, another one?" Gregson exclaimed.

With equal parts care and revulsion, he undid the brown paper and gagged when he beheld the heart. "Is it human?"

"That of a middle-aged woman, according to my learned friend," Holmes said, with a slight bow in my direction.

"That's heinous," Gregson exclaimed. "We must find this monster, Mr. Holmes. Have you learned anything about this killer?"

"Not very much. After we left you yesterday, Watson and I traced Longbottom's path from Regent's Park. He stopped at the market to pick up some pig's trotters for his wife, as he had promised. However, while there, he met a man who offered to take him for a drink. That was the last anyone saw of him. There seems to be no connection between killer and victim. Speaking of the latter, I trust you have confirmed his identification?"

"Yes, it was unquestionably Longbottom. His employer at Regent's Park identified him from a photograph. This is another Ripper case, isn't it?"

"Rather worse, I fear. This fellow shows considerably more cunning than the Ripper ever did. He seems to see me as his opponent in a game."

"Bizarre sort of game. What's the heart supposed to mean?"

"I suppose it means the head was too easy a clue," Holmes said. "It was a comparatively simple matter to identify the victim. The dead woman, on the other hand . . . ."

"Yes." Gregson rubbed his eyes and stared at the heart.

"Watson," Holmes said, "What can you tell us about this organ? I perceive that, unlike the head, it was removed with a knife and not an axe."

"Quite right, Holmes. Most likely a common kitchen knife, although a very sharp one. Also, the victim was dead before the heart was removed. The condition of the vessels indicates as much."

"Recently deceased?"

"Probably within minutes, but I cannot be exact."

"So she had not been embalmed?"

"It does not appear so."

"How does this help us, Mr. Holmes?" Gregson said.

"It tells us the killer most likely took the woman's life by some other means and then removed her heart," Holmes said. "That suggests she either lived alone, or he managed to get her from her home to wherever he is performing these grisly tasks. He did not steal the organ from a morgue."

Using a magnifying glass I peered closely at the vessels. "This is interesting. See here, Holmes. There is evidence of advanced *mesaortitis*."

"Of what?" Gregson said.

"It suggests syphilis," Holmes said. "I am correct, Watson?"

"Quite correct. Of course, a woman may contract that illness in any number of ways. Congenitally, for instance, or from her spouse, but it is possible she was a prostitute."

"It might explain why she was alone in a man's rooms."

"It might," Gregson replied.

"Have you discovered any mutilated bodies within the last twenty-four hours, Inspector?"

"No."

"Well, our friend may have other means of disposing the rest of the bodies. They may yet show up, but possibly not."

"But why?" I asked. "What does he hope to accomplish?"

"He wants to test me," he replied. "He sees himself as a rival, as a chess player. What the end game may be, who can say at this juncture? I must assume he is observing me."

"If he is following you, we can assign a team to watch, and we will be sure to catch him."

"A good thought, Gregson, but it won't work. If he were following me, I would have already spotted him. No, I am afraid he's too canny for that. He doesn't need to follow me. He knows where I live."

Holmes and I returned to Baker Street, and my friend spent the evening sitting in silent contemplation. Our room filled with the noxious odour of his tobacco, but I was loathe to remonstrate with him. I shared his sense of unease. A little before midnight I retired. Holmes stayed up, his silent form a statue in the armchair by the fire.

In the morning, Holmes hadn't moved. The post brought the usual motley collection of bills, appeals, and one letter, addressed in the now-familiar purple ink.

"At least it's not a parcel," I said.

Holmes made no reply, but his nimble fingers carefully opened the envelope and slid the enclosed sheet of paper onto the table.

Dear Mr. Clever, (Holmes read)

Again, you disappoint me. I expected to be in bracelets by now. At least you should be on my street, talking to my neighbours, looking for my door. Not so clever, though, are you? I know the truth.

Expect an extra special little treat in the next day or two. It makes me proper chuckle to think how much you'll weep.

Yours,
The Open Eye

"The Open Eye?" I asked. "Who is this fellow? Why does he describe himself, thus?"

Holmes was silent for a moment. "That is the question, is it not, my dear fellow? It seems this fellow sees himself as the only one who

303

perceives the truth . . . but what truth? Well, at least we have a day or two – if we can believe him – before he will strike again."

He sat on the armchair, his head sunk low on his breast, and not another word did he speak for some time. Around noon I rose and yawned and declared my intention of going for a walk. He made no reply for several moments, until I was at the door, and then he suddenly leapt to his feet and exclaimed, "What are you about, Watson? You are not going out?"

"I thought I might. Did you need me to run an errand?"

"No . . . I am not sanguine about you going out on your own, my dear fellow."

"Oh, really, Holmes, I've been going about on my own for many a long day. What is your objection?"

"This fellow, this killer . . . He implies his next victim will be known to me. I would be grieved to lose you, my friend."

My bark of laughter died in the face of his utter sincerity. "I shall carry my revolver, if it will ease your mind."

"Thank you, it would. And I beg of you, be alert every moment, and keep to the main roads."

"I will be very cautious, I assure you."

Rather than ramble around the streets as I had planned, I took a cab to Oxford Street. I thought I should be safe enough as part of the great crowd of shoppers who hurried along that splendid thoroughfare. The air was unusually clear, and the light was bright and sharp. However, despite the general cheer that surrounded me, I could not shake my sense of unease. I felt that I was watched, and I constantly looked over my shoulder. I saw nothing untoward. The streets and the shops were very busy, full of bustling shoppers and traffic. I tried to focus my attention on the purchase of a new umbrella.

That task completed, I made my way up the road, weaving through the jostling crowd. As I neared New Bond Street, a sense of danger suddenly overwhelmed me, and my hand sought the revolver in my pocket. I couldn't say what it was that made my blood pulse so wildly and my mouth turn dry. All I could say, all I knew, was I was in danger. A hand grabbed me by the arm and pulled me into a doorway.

Muttering an oath, I struggled. A soft, familiar voice muttered, "Be still, Watson, for pity sake!"

"Holmes!" I cried.

"Shh! There goes our villain. Hush now. He will linger and hope to pick up your trail. He will not be happy to have lost you."

I peered out the window of the haberdasher through the display, and observed the villain, a small, nondescript fellow, standing on the corner of

New Bond Street, his back turned to me. Even though I could not see his face, his choler was evident. The man was fairly hopping with rage. He tugged at the unfortunate passers-by and swore, confounded by my disappearance. I stepped back into the safety of the shop.

Holmes, unrecognisable in the guise of a retired naval commander with heavy white whiskers and eyebrows, said, "Mr. Mortimore will hide you safely in the stock room until this fellow has left. I will follow our prey and see where he leads."

"I should come with you, Holmes," I protested. "This fellow is dangerous. You need someone to see to your protection."

His grey eyes glinted beneath the wiry brows. "You can best help me at present, my dear Watson, by removing yourself from peril so that I may focus on the task at hand. I need stealth, and that is something best achieved alone. Be assured, however, I will do nothing of significance without my biographer. Return to Baker Street as soon as it is safe to do so, and stay there. When I am ready, I will send you an address. I will sign the message *Tyr*."

With deep reluctance and, it must be said, no small amount of resentment, I cooled my heels in Mr. Mortimore's stock room for some fifteen minutes, and then I slipped out the rear entrance and took a cab back to Baker Street.

The day wore on in a mixture of stultifying boredom and extreme anxiety. As evening fell, I drew the curtains and lit the lamp, mindful of the street below and the houses opposite. I remembered the incident "The Empty House", and how Mrs. Hudson had taken such a terrible risk in moving a wax likeness of Holmes to draw an assassin's bullet. Could this killer be lying in wait, ready to fire when he caught sight of his prey? It did not seem his usual behaviour, but perhaps fury might drive him to extremes. I tried to apply Holmes's reasoning to my analysis, but I did not proceed very far.

Deciding I had, as Holmes would say, insufficient data to reach a conclusion, I gave up. I turned my attention, instead, to looking up "Tyr" in the *American Encyclopaedia*, and learned he was the Norse god of justice. Of course.

Just as I sat down to supper, I was interrupted by Mrs. Hudson. "Excuse me, Doctor," she said. "There is a man below who wants you to accompany him to Cavendish Mews. Mr. Holmes is in need of your assistance, he says."

"Is there a letter? A note of some sort?"

"No, Doctor, nothing of the sort."

"What manner of fellow is he?"

"A common worker, but well-mannered enough."

"Describe him."

She sighed heavily but, being used to my friend's ways, did a reasonable job of describing a young man, aged about twenty, with ginger hair and a slight Scots brogue. Not the fellow who had given me several unpleasant moments in New Bond Street, then.

"Send him up, Mrs. Hudson," I said.

A few moments later, the young man appeared. He was a navvy, I thought, from his clothing.

"I am Dr. Watson," I said. "You have a message for me?"

"Yes, sir," he said. "I'm to tell you t'chum me tae a house in Cavendish Mews North to meet Mr. Holmes. A matter of some urgency, he said."

"What did he look like, this Mr. Holmes?" I asked.

The fellow hesitated. "Well, I didn't get to talk to him direct. Word were passed on by a bobby."

This seemed plausible. Still, Holmes had made a point of saying he would sign the message with the identifier *Tyr*.

"Well," I said, "Give me the address, and I shall be along after supper."

"I am supposed to bring you," the fellow persisted. "I were told it's dangerous for you out alone and I am not to leave you."

"Really? Well, you'll have to wait until I've eaten."

"It's an emergency," the fellow protested. "You don't understand – I don't get paid if I don't deliver you."

"Indeed? And how much am I worth?"

"Six-pence."

"Six-pence, by Jove. Not even thirty pieces of silver?" I asked.

The youth stared at me with a blank expression, and I wondered at the quality of religious education in the nation's schools.

"What is your name?" I asked.

"Andy. Andrew Campbell."

I fished a three-penny bit out of my pocket and said, "Well, Andy, I will give you three-pence now, and another tomorrow."

The fellow bit the coin to convince himself of its worth, pocketed it, and said, "Fair enough, gov. What time?"

"Six o'clock, if you would be so good."

"And you'll give me another three-pence?"

"You have my word – on one condition."

"What's that, then?"

"That you do not return to the address where you were to deliver me."

"Nae danger of that, man," he said. "Out of my way, innit? See you tomorrow."

He skipped off down the stairs, and I hoped with all fervour I had not made an egregious error.

I tried to eat and failed. I pushed the plate away and sat in the armchair by the fire and waited. Less than an hour later, a cable was delivered: *"Come at once to 4 Cavendish Mews South. Tyr."*

My heart heaved with relief. Immediately I donned my coat and hat and set off for the address named. *South*, not *north*, as Andy Campbell had said.

When I arrived, I found the narrow street crammed with policemen, vehicles, and newshounds. I was recognised by several of the latter, and they barraged me with their questions. I ignored them and continued on up the steps to the decrepit building. Around me, police officers bustled. A few nodded, but none stopped me.

"Do you know where Mr. Holmes is?" I asked a young constable I recognised.

"Top floor, Doctor," he said. "You may want to keep your hands to yourself. I wouldn't touch a blessed thing in this place."

With that advice, I buried my hands deep in my pockets and climbed the creaking, sticky staircase upwards. By the time I reached the third floor, I could hear Holmes's voice from somewhere above me.

I found him in the dingy kitchen at the top of the building. He stood with his back to the grimy window, facing the man who had given me those unpleasant moments in New Bond Street. He sat at a rough-hewn table, his hands in manacles before him. Inspector Gregson stood by the door. He nodded at me as I entered.

The scene had a macabre look. The room was lit only by one flickering lamp, and the table was stained with what could only be blood and human matter. From the gouges hacked into the thick oak, I wondered if this was where the unfortunate Reginald Longbottom had been beheaded. The entire building seemed alive with crawling things, and fetid with the stench of decaying flesh.

"Ah, here you are at last, Doctor," the prisoner said, cheerfully. "Sorry I missed you."

"Watson," Holmes said, "I am glad to see you safe and well. I would offer you a seat, but you would be ill-advised to accept one in this house of horrors."

"Thank you, but I should rather stand. And yes, I was glad to receive your message. Our friend here tried to lure me with a false message an hour ago. The fellow he sent will return to Baker Street tomorrow and give you a full account. You may be glad of his evidence, Inspector."

"I will be pleased to hear it," Gregson replied, "though there is no lack of evidence throughout this wretched place. The hangman will have this creature, and no mistake."

"What do we have here?" I asked, unable to phrase the many questions that sprang to my mind.

"Murder, Watson," Holmes replied. "Murder on a grand, grotesque, and barbaric scale."

The little man in the manacles met my eye and tittered.

"He is, of course, quite mad," Holmes said.

"You caught me at last, Mr. Clever," the little man said, giggling, "after I sent you all the clues. You can't say I didn't help you."

"Who is he?" I asked, trying to ignore the fellow's ramblings.

"His name is Albert Huggins," Gregson answered. "He is works in the post office."

"Great Portland Street," I said.

"Exactly so."

"He looks so ordinary."

"That is his weapon," Holmes said. "With such an ordinary face, this man, if the evidence is to be believed, enticed at least six men and three women to their deaths."

"Good God. You know that for a fact?"

"We found their remains scattered about the building. Likely, there are more."

"Does he own the building?"

"He appears to be the manager. However, he seems to have dispatched the other tenants, as well as the unfortunate Longbottom. Most of the butchery took place in this room, at this very table. The constables are gathering up the evidence."

"But why his obsession with you, Holmes?" I asked.

"He's a fake!" the man suddenly screamed. "Holmes the liar! Holmes the fraud!"

"I think you have all you need from me at present, Gregson," my friend said, suppressing a shudder. "If you will stop by Baker Street tomorrow evening, we can offer you some supper and perhaps Watson's additional witness."

The following evening, Andy Campbell returned at precisely six o'clock and told us how Albert Huggins had promised him six-pence if he would deliver one John Watson of Baker Street to his door. The fellow had thought nothing of it, except it was a chance to earn some easy money. Gregson heard him in near silence, and then sent him away with a constable to take his statement.

"Superfluous, given the amount of evidence we already have," he said. "We found five more bodies in the basement after you left, Mr. Holmes. These were intact. The oldest had been there five years, at least. The remains of an older woman were in the room on the second floor. We think she was Mrs. McCardle, a tenant who had lived there for three months. She was missing a heart."

"Ah, the second parcel."

"Quite. We're still searching. I have no doubt we'll find many more bodies, probably going back years, before we're done."

"But why did Huggins send those body parts to you, Holmes?" I said. "It seems baffling. Do you not think so?"

"Madness is baffling, Watson. However, I have met Mr. Huggins before. I thought the name seemed familiar, and I found him in my chronicles last night. He was introduced to me by an acquaintance at Barts in December 1880, not long before you and I met.

"Huggins' daughter had vanished, and he engaged me to find her. I learned that she had eloped to Scotland with a young man. Huggins refused to believe my evidence and insisted she had been kidnapped or murdered. No amount of reasoning could convince him. He insisted I bring her back. I refused, of course.

"He then convinced himself I was a charlatan. I suspect my later success and fame must have rankled. He saw himself as the only one who knew the truth." He sat back in his chair and sipped his coffee.

"When we received the letter, I surmised the killer was someone I had encountered during my career, someone whose case I had failed to resolve. I spent the night ruminating over my past failures – never a happy task. There were rather more of them than you might be pleased to acknowledge, my dear Watson. I was sure our killer was one of these. You will recall the singular case of 'The Yellow Face', for instance, and I need hardly remind you how I was bested by Miss Irene Adler. There are others. I did not consider Huggins, because I had successfully resolved that case, at least to my own satisfaction. I did not remember him until I saw him following you. By-the-by, my dear Watson, I owe you a most sincere apology."

"You do? Why so?"

"I took a decided risk when I allowed you to go out alone yesterday afternoon, knowing that Huggins had you in his sights."

"Oh come, Holmes. If a grown man, a retired soldier no less, and armed, cannot travel the streets of the busiest city in the world alone, I do not know what we are coming to."

"All the same, it was a gamble, and I am very sorry for it."

"You followed me, Holmes, and kept me safe. In the end, my little expedition helped catch that dreadful fellow."

"True. Still, I would never have forgiven myself if harm had befallen you. It was evident from his letter that Huggins planned for his next victim to be someone close to me. Almost certainly it had to be you. I assumed a disguise and hurried after you. Well, the rest you know."

"It's true you took a chance," I said, "but you really had no choice. It all worked out for the best, my dear fellow. Inspector, is it possible Huggins will escape the noose because of his madness?"

"I doubt it," Gregson said. "The nature of his crimes are just too abhorrent. We have discovered a dozen bodies so far, and it's likely the number is far greater. No, the public will demand blood, and he will hang."

He rose and shook our hands. "Thank you for supper, gentlemen. Mr. Holmes, this was as fine a service as you have ever performed for your country. We are in your debt."

"Thank you, Inspector," Holmes replied. "You know I am always ready to be of assistance."

The search in Cavendish Mews continued for several weeks. The number of bodies, or, rather, body parts recovered, belonged to eighteen victims in all. In most cases, only small fragments were recovered. A skull, a hand . . . What had happened to the rest of the bodies we never learned, and Huggins refused to tell. "Ask Holmes, he knows everything," he replied, and laughed.

He laughed when the judge donned the black cap, and he laughed when he ascended the gallows. He was still laughing when the door dropped and the rope silenced him forever.

The Adventure of the
Scarlet Rosebud
by Liz Hedgecock

Chapter I

I arrived at 221b Baker Street to find Sherlock Holmes pacing the sitting room like a man possessed. "Thank heavens you're here, Watson," he said, stopping in the middle of the room. "I was beginning to think my wire had miscarried."

"I came as soon as I could, Holmes," I replied, feeling aggrieved. "I was at Barts in the middle of a consultation with a patient – "

"Capital, capital. Sit down, and I shall acquaint you with the circumstances of the case."

"But I thought – "

"Do sit, Watson."

I took a seat in the armchair, but Holmes remained standing. "Tell me, have you ever heard of a woman called Marcia Le Fanu?"

I considered. "The name is somehow familiar, but I cannot recall how."

"You may be thinking of Le Fanu, the Gothic novelist and ghost story writer," Holmes said, impatiently. "If you are, it is quite apt." He crossed to the bookshelf, drew out a volume of his index, and put it in my hand. "For now, I wish you to read about Miss Le Fanu."

I looked up at him. "You wish me to sit here and read?"

"*Yes*, Watson." Holmes began to pace again.

I found the right page, and obeyed.

Marcia Mary Le Fanu. Born 1856, Ireland, to parents of Huguenot ancestry. Father a draper with his own shop. From the age of fourteen, Marcia claimed to see visions, which were at first attributed to religious fervour. Marcia's grandmother died when she was sixteen, and Marcia insisted she was receiving messages from beyond the grave. This was dismissed as hysteria until Marcia led her parents to a bag of money stored under the floorboards, saying that her grandmother had told her exactly where to find it. Her parents, completely convinced, decided Marcia should be allowed to use her gifts to help others.

In Marcia's early twenties, the family moved to Dublin, where she earned a reputation of renown as a spiritualist medium. She acquired a patron, Sir Geoffrey Carlton, who brought her to London in 1884 and set her up in a small house in Grosvenor Terrace. While Marcia did not ask for payment during her consultations, gifts from well-wishers and grateful clients soon made her a wealthy woman in her own right.

A note re: Fakery. Several people have tried to prove that Miss Le Fanu is a fraud, going so far as to attend her séances and request to speak to deceased relatives. However, no one has ever managed to prove anything against her, and some of these sceptics, following a consultation, have pronounced themselves convinced that Miss Le Fanu is indeed a true medium. There is no evidence of criminal activity on Miss Le Fanu's part. While outwardly extremely respectable, though, she remains a part of that shadowy world of supernaturalists which is reputed to exploit the public. She therefore remains a person of interest.

Miss Le Fanu is unmarried and still resides in Grosvenor Terrace, alone but for a small staff of servants. She holds a séance once a week on Thursday evenings, and also takes private appointments. Net worth: Unknown, but substantial.

I closed the book and looked up to find Holmes watching me. "She sounds like a most interesting person," I said. "For what sort of case has she called you?"

"She has not," said Holmes. "In fact, the entry you have just read is incomplete."

I frowned. "How so? What has happened?"

Holmes took the book from me and replaced it on the shelf before replying. "I received a wire from Gregson less than an hour ago. Marcia Le Fanu was found dead this morning."

Chapter II

The knocker on the front door of the house in Grosvenor Terrace had already been muffled in crape when we arrived. The door was opened almost immediately by a frightened-looking parlourmaid, her cap streamers quivering even in the still atmosphere. "Yessir?"

"I am Sherlock Holmes, and this is my associate, Dr. Watson. Inspector Gregson is expecting us."

312

The parlourmaid bobbed an awkward curtsey and the door opened wider. "They are in Madame's boudoir, sir, I will take you up." She was already on the stairs before we had both entered the hall.

We ascended the stairs behind her and I took in our surroundings. It was a narrow house, and a bare one. A plain stair-carpet, no pictures on the walls, no clutter. At the top of the stairs the parlourmaid paused. "It is that door," she said, indicating it with her hand but not, I saw, touching the wood. "You'll excuse me not going in, sirs." She was backing towards the stairs as she spoke.

Holmes and I exchanged glances. He shrugged and knocked.

"That you, Mr. Holmes?" shouted the familiar voice of the inspector.

"It is." Holmes turned the handle, but the door did not move.

"Wait a minute." We heard footsteps, then the snick of a key, and the inspector stood in the doorway, framed in bright autumn light. "Sorry about that. Just have to be careful. We've had all sorts around today."

"Really?" Holmes's eyes moved past Gregson to a huddled pale shape on the carpet.

"Oh yes. Anyway, nothing's been moved. I thought it best to let you and Dr. Watson take a look first." He stood aside to let us pass.

Marcia Le Fanu lay as if she were sleeping, save that her pale-grey eyes were fixed and glassy. She was a slender woman, of perhaps middle-height, with dark hair and regular, unremarkable features save for those grey eyes, which must have been impressive in life. Her nightgown was high-necked and of plain white cotton, as unornamented as her home. Her slippers, however, were of red satin, and contrasted oddly with the rest of her appearance. Holmes touched her slim wrist briefly, then withdrew his hand. "I take it a doctor has already called," he said.

"First thing Sir Geoffrey did," said the inspector.

Holmes raised his eyebrows. "Go on."

Inspector Gregson leaned on the mantelpiece. "The story, as I have it," he said, "is that Sir Geoffrey Carlton, Miss Le Fanu's patron – "

"I know who he is," said Holmes, tersely.

"Quite. Sir Geoffrey arrived at Miss Le Fanu's house at ten o'clock, as he does every Friday. The parlourmaid, Sarah, tells me that her mistress always receives him in the drawing room, but when she showed him in, Miss Le Fanu wasn't there. She went to look for her, and Sir Geoffrey followed."

"He has the run of the house, then," observed Holmes. The inspector's eyes rested on Holmes for a moment before continuing.

"They found her lying as you see her now. At first they thought she might have fallen into a trance – she was occasionally prone to such things.

313

Sir Geoffrey summoned his doctor, who pronounced her dead within minutes of his arrival."

"Hmm." Holmes knelt beside the body. "Where is Sir Geoffrey?"

"In the drawing room. He is overcome, as you can imagine. I asked him to remain at least until you had seen him."

"Did the doctor give a cause of death?" asked Holmes. His voice was casual, but the look he gave the inspector was not.

Inspector Gregson shook his head. "He thought it might be a heart attack."

"He did, did he?" Holmes straightened. "Watson, I would value your professional opinion. When do you think this lady died?"

I took off my coat, rolled up my shirt-sleeves, and knelt next to the body. Miss Le Fanu's arm was still limp – neither stiff nor difficult to move, as I would have expected. "When did you get here, Gregson?"

The inspector considered. "At about a quarter-past-eleven."

"I do not think she has been dead for more than six hours. Less, probably. When was she last known to be alive?"

"This morning at eight, when the maid came to draw her curtains. She said she didn't want breakfast."

"Wait," I said. "What's in her hand?" While one hand was open in front of her, the other, by her side, was oddly closed tight. "May I . . . ?"

Inspector Gregson knelt beside me as I worked on the stiffening fingers, careful not to bruise them. I saw a glimpse of red. "I almost have it." I went to my doctor's bag and found some tweezers, with which I gently drew the object from her grasp.

A scarlet rosebud.

Chapter III

We found Sir Geoffrey Carlton sprawled elegantly across a drawing-room sofa which looked as if it had been designed for straight-backed sitting only. A tea-trolley stood at his elbow, with tea and a choice of biscuits, but Sir Geoffrey stared into the unlit fireplace. He was perhaps fifty, handsome and well-preserved, with a touch of grey at his temples, and dressed in a fashionable style perhaps more suited to a younger man.

"Good afternoon, Sir Geoffrey," said Holmes. "Would you mind if we joined you?"

He continued to stare at the bare grate. "As you wish. It is all the same to me." His tone conveyed the utmost sadness.

Holmes and I perched at opposite ends of the other sofa. "I am sorry for your loss, Sir Geoffrey," I ventured.

He turned to me. "What is being said upstairs? What does Gregson say?"

"Dr. Watson has performed a brief examination of Miss Le Fanu," said Holmes. "No cause of death is immediately apparent. As I believe the doctor you summoned was of the same opinion, there will have to be a *post mortem*."

Sir Geoffrey gaped. "A *post mortem*?" His look of distaste was almost comical in its suddenness. "Oh, how frightful. What a thought."

"It is necessary in cases such as these, Sir Geoffrey," I said gently.

"'Cases such as these'." His tone was mocking. "Marcia Le Fanu was incomparable. The spiritualist world will not know her like again. In a sphere filled with tricksters and scam artists, she was the one true medium." He sighed. "I had sought to peer beyond the veil for some years. I had consulted mediums and seers all over London before finding the true vision through an artless Irish girl. I have seen the mountebankery that goes on – "

"I am sorry to interrupt," Holmes said smoothly. "Could you give a brief account of your movements from yesterday evening to your arrival here today, Sir Geoffrey?"

"What are you saying?" Sir Geoffrey demanded.

"I do not wish to imply anything," Holmes replied. "It is for the completeness of the record."

"I've already told Gregson." The man's mouth clamped shut.

"It isn't a request," remarked Holmes, rising and pouring himself a cup of tea. "Watson?" He paused, teapot in hand.

"If you would."

"Sir Geoffrey?"

A curt nod.

Holmes handed the cups, and resumed his seat. "Your movements, please."

Sir Geoffrey picked up his cup and saucer. "I dined at the Savoy with an old friend of mine."

"Who?"

"Freddy Metcalfe, if you must know. We were there until half-past-nine, when I went on to my club." Holmes raised his eyebrows. "The Athenaeum," Sir Geoffrey added wearily.

"And can you give me the name of someone who can confirm you were there?"

"The doorman, the waiters . . . I had a conversation with Bass the financier, if that's any use to you. And no, I can't remember what time that was." His eyes glinted.

"That will do," said Holmes. "When did you leave?"

315

"At eleven. I signed the book and tipped the doorman on my way out. He'll remember me. I found a cab home."

"You didn't take your carriage?"

"I did not." Sir Geoffrey sipped his tea. "I don't like having to leave anywhere at a particular time. I would much rather take a cab."

"You went straight home?"

"Yes, I did. 47 Portman Square, since I suppose that will be your next question." He allowed himself a small smile. "Then I went to bed. Will that do?"

"It will, thank you." Holmes drank from his own cup. "Sir Geoffrey, you knew Miss Le Fanu perhaps better than anyone else. Do you have any idea of what might have happened?"

Sir Geoffrey leaned forward and put down his cup. He sat straighter than before. "My honest opinion?"

"Your honest opinion."

"Assuming this wasn't a natural death – which I assume it isn't as you're asking me these questions – I think it was a rival."

"A rival?"

"Yes, a rival medium," he said, somewhat impatiently. "In fact, if I had to point the finger, I'd say it was Madame Paretski. She has accused Marcia of fakery, and she has scheduled séances at the same time to try and freeze her out. She has even advertised in the newspapers. She grew up in a circus, and she probably knows all sorts of questionable types who would think nothing of such a thing. She might – " He shuddered. "She might even have used some sort of *curse* on Marcia."

Chapter IV

Miss Le Fanu's body had been removed from the boudoir, and we had taken the chance to inspect her bedroom – another sparsely-furnished room, brightened only by an incongruous vase of red roses.

"Have you spoken to the parlourmaid?" Holmes looked enquiringly at Inspector Gregson.

The inspector grimaced. "I have. She's all we've got, pretty much – the cook lives out, and there's a jobbing handyman who comes once in a blue moon. The parlourmaid takes the discretion of the servant a little too far, though. It was like getting blood from a stone."

Holmes's glance was keen. "Do you think she knows something?"

"It's hard to tell. See what you can do."

Holmes surveyed the room. "I shall, but – downstairs."

He rang the drawing-room bell, and presently the housemaid appeared, wringing the edge of her apron. "Now – is it Sarah?"

"It is, sir."

"Sarah, I would like you to tell me about your mistress."

Sarah stood at the edge of the hearthrug, and a flush crept over her cheeks. "I – er – I – "

"Suppose you start with her routine – how she organised her day, where she went habitually, who her friends were."

The crease between Sarah's eyebrows smoothed a little. "Well, Madame was regular in her habits. I woke her at eight in the morning, and she breakfasted at half-past-eight, usually downstairs. If she was indisposed, I might bring it to her room."

"Was she often indisposed?"

"Oh no, that's not what I meant."

"But she must sometimes have been indisposed, or you wouldn't have mentioned it."

"Sometimes she was wakeful in the night, and then she slept in." Sarah closed her mouth, looking a little mulish.

Holmes sighed. "And after breakfast?"

"After breakfast, she conducted the business of the household, or answered letters. In the afternoons she might drive out, or read a novel, or do fancy work."

"Did she call on friends?"

"I don't think so. She was – not friendless, but she liked her own company." Sarah's mouth twisted suddenly. "I don't like thinking of her as someone who *was*."

Holmes led her to a chair. "I know it is difficult, but to get to the truth of the matter it is necessary." He paused. "What did she do in the evenings?"

"The evenings could be quite different. If Madame had no appointments, she dined alone at seven, and continued with quiet pursuits till perhaps ten o'clock, when she would retire."

"And that was her routine yesterday evening?"

"No, Thursday was the evening when she always conducted a séance. She was occupied until a quarter-to-nine, when everyone left. Then she had a light supper – soup and toast – read for a while in the drawing room, and retired to bed at half-past-nine."

"And that was her usual routine?"

"Yes, sir."

"Did the séance go well?"

Sarah frowned. "I think so. I don't attend, I just stay by the door in case Madame wants me. It was quiet – only two people came."

"Did she ever go out in the evening, for amusement? The theatre perhaps, or dinner with friends?"

"I can't say she did, sir."

"So, what happened on the evenings when Miss Le Fanu was conducting a séance?"

Sarah considered. "On those nights she dined early – at six or half-past. She would direct me to make sure the drawing room was ready, with the appropriate number of chairs set out, and inspect me to make sure I was ready to receive our guests. Her callers usually arrived at half-past-seven or eight o'clock – never later – and the session finished by nine. Madame always said that any more would injure her nerves."

"And how many additional appointments did Miss Le Fanu make in a week?"

Sarah thought. "Usually two or three, and as many as four, in a busy time. However lately –" She raised her hand to her mouth and gave Mr. Holmes a frightened look, as if she had spoken out of turn.

"Lately . . . ?" Holmes prompted.

Sarah bit her lip. "Lately . . . there had not been so many."

"Did Miss Le Fanu keep a record of her sessions?"

Sarah looked relieved, as if the responsibility had been taken away from her. "Why yes, yes she did. It was in a black book. I saw it if I had occasion to wait on her in the morning." She went to a small desk in the corner of the drawing room and drew out a slim black volume, which she handed to Holmes.

Holmes opened it and I saw a diary, a week to each page. On each leaf were dotted, in neat, regular writing, annotations of Miss Le Fanu's appointments. The parlourmaid was right. Within the last two months the entries had dwindled to no more than two sessions a week, and sometimes only one. "Hmm," said Holmes. "This interests me."

"Can you make anything of it?" I said.

"I can make something of anything," said Holmes. "But it needs to be the *right* something." He turned to the parlourmaid. "Do you know anything about Madame Paretski?"

It was as if a shutter had gone down. "No," said Sarah, looking straight ahead. "We do not speak that name in this house."

Chapter V

"I'm afraid Madame Paretski is not at home," said the butler, eyeing Holmes and me with disdain.

Holmes put a long, narrow foot in the door before the servant could close it. "When you say 'not at home' . . . ." He reached into his trouser pocket and spun a sovereign in his hand.

The butler raised his head to look further down his nose at us. "I mean, sir, that Madame Paretski is away from home at present, visiting her sister. She has been absent for three days and will return tonight, and if you wish I shall inform her that you have called."

Holmes assumed a contrite expression and handed over his card. The butler took it and glanced reprovingly at Holmes's foot. It was removed, and the door closed silently.

"Well, that was a wild-goose chase," I remarked, as we hailed a cab.

Holmes said nothing until we were safely embarked and rattling towards Baker Street. "Was it, though?" he remarked, gazing out of the window.

I huffed. "I should say so. She probably has a perfect alibi. An utter waste of time, if you ask me."

Holmes turned from the window and regarded me. One corner of his mouth turned up a fraction. "Madame Paretski may have the perfect alibi. She also has a large and well-appointed house, with a sagacious butler, and what I believe to be a genuine Canaletto in the hall."

I frowned. "What are you saying?"

The other corner of Holmes's mouth quirked up. "That Madame Paretski is, presumably, doing well." His hand shot out for his cane, and he rapped on the partition. "Cabbie! Can you take us to Drury Lane, please?"

"Right, sir," came the phlegmatic reply. The cab took a sharp left, and gathered speed.

"It's the wrong day for a matinee, Holmes," I said, feeling discombobulated.

"That is correct," said Holmes. "However, I am looking for rather a particular entertainment."

At Drury Lane, Holmes surprised me again by darting off the main path into the side streets, questing this way and that like a hound on the scent. "What on earth are you doing?" I asked, standing bewildered.

"Ha!" Holmes pointed at a peeling handbill, stuck over several more. I craned to read the wrinkled lettering. It screamed:

THRILL TO THE AMAZING TALENTS
OF MADAME PARETSKI!
AT THE KING'S THEATRE, SOHO
EVERY FRIDAY AND SATURDAY.
ADMISSION – 6d standing, 1s for circle.
DOORS OPEN 8 p.m.

I looked at Holmes. "Today is Friday," I said, smiling.

"Indeed it is," said Holmes. "We have just about enough time to get ready."

Chapter VI

"I feel ridiculous," I said, stomping beside Holmes in a worn pair of boots and a shiny suit a size too small.

"You look just right," said Holmes in an undertone, eyeing me beneath his cloth cap.

"'E looks wonderful," said my companion, squeezing my arm. "Don't 'e, Sukey?"

Sukey, an overblown buxom blonde whose dress was also a size too small, nodded in agreement.

"I still don't see why this is necessary," I said, perhaps rather grumpily.

"Oh, do put on your thinking cap, Watson," said Holmes, stopping short and directing us into an alleyway. "If Madame Paretski knows that two gentlemen came calling earlier, she is likely to be watching for two men of our description. She will not be perusing the couples. To be fair, I imagine most of Madame Paretski's admirers are not men. Hence I invited these two ladies, who are currently out of a theatre situation, to join us. And we can hardly turn up in evening dress at a sixpenny establishment. Now come along." He set off again, and I had to hurry to keep up with his long strides.

There was already a line outside the King's Theatre, though the doors would not open for another ten minutes. "She's popular, at any rate," I observed.

"Keep your voice down, Watson," Holmes said out of the side of his mouth.

"She is popular," said my escort, who had introduced herself as Blanche. (I suspected that was her stage name). "I've been a few times, and it's always a packed 'ouse."

The doors opened at – well, I could not tell exactly when, as I did not particularly wish to display my gold watch in such a place. I gathered from the grumbling around me, however, that it was past the advertised time. "Buck up!" called the doorman, sweeping us in. "Seats to the right, standing to the left."

I raised an eyebrow at Holmes, who nodded to the left. "We can see more that way," he muttered.

The King's Theatre had a steeply-raked auditorium which made me wonder if we could observe better from the circle, but Holmes elbowed a path through the indignant crowd until we were at the front. The raised

320

stage was dark save for one spotlight, trained on a plain table and three chairs. "I expected more frippery," I whispered, nudging Holmes. "Or at least a tablecloth."

"That's to show she ain't a faker," said Blanche. "Not one of them smoke-an'-mirrors types." I thought of Sir Geoffrey and couldn't help smiling.

"What does she do?" I asked.

"You'll see," she replied, darkly. "Ssh! 'Ere she comes!"

The babble behind us ceased so abruptly that a stray cough rang out like a gunshot. We waited, eyes fixed on the stage.

Out walked a small, round, grey-haired woman dressed in black, who reminded me of no-one so much as a slightly younger Queen Victoria. "Good evening, everyone," she said, gliding towards the centre. Her voice was well-modulated, and carried well even though she did not seem to raise it. "I hope you are all well. I will not say happy, for it is as plain as day that some of you are not. I shall see what I can do." She walked to the table and sat in the middle chair, facing into the audience.

"'Ere we go," said Sukey, and was immediately shushed by everyone in the vicinity.

"Someone here has lost a brother," said Madame Paretski. Her voice was sympathetic in its tone. "This loss is recent, I believe." She gaze around the room, and when I turned several people were waving their hands. Madame Paretski stood. "He says his sister is a young woman . . . who often wears blue."

Several hands were grudgingly lowered. Madame Paretski shaded her eyes and peered into the audience, then held out her right hand as if in invitation. "My dear, you should join me."

The crowd parted like a wave to allow a tall, awkward young woman in black to pass through. She hesitated, looking for the way to the stage. "The steps are at the side, my dear," said Madame Paretski, patiently.

Eventually she found her way and Madame Paretski invited her to the left-hand chair, then sat opposite. "Take my hand, my dear," she said, removing a glove and extending her own chubby one. The young woman fumbled off her black glove and took the medium's hand.

"Excellent. Now, let me concentrate." She fixed the young woman with a stare. "Your poor brother . . . ."

"Oh, he was!" exclaimed the young woman. "It happened so suddenly – "

"Pneumonia can be like that," said Madame Paretski.

The young woman gaped at her. "However did you know?"

"Your brother tells me," said the medium placidly. "He was your younger brother?"

"That's right." The young woman appeared to have gone into a trance. "William was my youngest brother. He was only eleven . . . ." She drew out an almost-clean pocket handkerchief and dabbed at her eyes.

"What a tragedy . . . " Madame Paretski squeezed her hand. "But William is at peace. He is in Heaven, and now he can run and play with no lessons to worry him."

The young woman sniffed loudly.

"But he says you must all take care of yourselves. Especially you – " Madame Paretski put her free hand to her temple and frowned. "Is it Mary?"

The young woman forgot to cry, such was her wonderment. "It is!" she whispered.

Madame Paretski smiled. "Yes. Mary, William says he can see much more clearly in Heaven than he ever could on earth. There is a young man who admires you. He worries about you, too, though he has given you no sign. You must keep well, Mary, and make sure your siblings do too, or he will never have the chance to declare himself. William says you should move out of those damp rooms."

Mary nodded until her head might fall off. "I'll talk to Mother." Her cheeks were pink.

"Good. And William says you shouldn't fret over him. He is in a better place, and has found happiness. He wants you to be happy too."

"I'll try. Thank you." Mary stood and made her way to the steps, and already she looked less awkward, and held her head higher.

Madame Paretski sat motionless for a moment, then moved back to the centre chair and put her hands to her temples. "I feel vibrations . . . another spirit wishes to contact me." Her gaze roamed the crowd. "From one Mary . . . to another."

A chill ran down my spine, and the room seemed to tilt a little. I closed my eyes for a second. When I opened them Madame Paretski was looking directly at me.

"Your wife is well and happy – now," she said, and her tone was matter-of-fact. "Mary says that she has found peace, and acceptance." Her eyes bored into me. "In a way she never could in *this* life." She regarded me silently, and as she opened her mouth to speak I could bear no more. I shouldered my way through the crowd and fled.

Chapter VII

Sherlock Holmes caught up with me as I was climbing into a cab. "Stop that at once, Watson," he said. "Get out. Please."

322

I shook my head. "I want no part of this." I slammed the door. "Baker Street please, driver."

"Wait, cabbie." Holmes opened the door and got in beside me. "All right." As the cab started to move he leaned back, closed his eyes and sighed. "I suppose it was only to be expected."

"*What?*" I stared at Holmes, and heat rushed through me until I expected fire to burst from my fingertips. "You – you – " I punched the upholstery as the next best thing to do.

Holmes opened his eyes. "That medium had obviously found us out, and decided to give you a little scare."

"But how could she?"

Holmes sighed again and heaved himself up in the seat to face me. "That would be far easier than the trick she played with that poor young woman. Although the advice she gave was actually sound."

I shook my head. "How could she possibly have known all that?"

"In London, how many young women have lost a brother?"

I opened my mouth to speak but Holmes held up a finger. "Exactly. The young woman was obviously in mourning. Her face was flushed and her breathing when she passed us was quick and shallow. Her hand was pale, and trembled. Her younger brother had died suddenly, she told us. Would that not suggest a possible diagnosis of pneumonia?"

"But the name?"

"The young woman herself gave us the name William. As for *her* name . . . did you not see the *M* on her handkerchief? The oldest daughter is most likely to be called after her mother, and Mary is a common name. Her hand was ringless, and she was an ungainly young thing, so an intimation that a young man was interested in her would be flattering. Her clothes, and breathing, indicated that the family – a largish family, since there are at least two brothers and maybe more – have none too much to spend on rooms, and have probably settled for damp ones as a way to save expense."

I shook my head. "When you explain it . . . ."

"It is nothing but a parlour game," said Holmes. "A most effective one, in the right hands." He leaned back again. "Short as our entertainment was, it has shown me one thing."

"What, Holmes?"

"We can discount Madame Paretski. I estimate that perhaps several hundred people were packed into that theatre tonight. Two shows a week, plus however many private clients she has, would be more than enough to keep Madame in the style to which she is accustomed."

"But the people we saw tonight could never afford a private consultation."

Holmes snorted. "You and I were not the only wolves in sheep's clothing there, Watson. I recognised several scions from noble families, some of whom are documented in my biographical index. I must remember to add that little detail in – it could be useful in the future."

"So Madame Paretski is no longer a suspect?"

Holmes shook his head.

"Then who is?"

Holmes smiled provokingly and closed his eyes. "That, Watson, remains to be seen. But as you know, I have my methods." And he would say no more on the subject that evening.

Chapter VIII

"I have been looking in the wrong place," said Holmes the next morning, as he gently raised the crape-muffled knocker of the house in Grosvenor Terrace.

I stared at him. "Have you?"

Holmes nodded. "I was looking *outside*, and I should have been looking *in*."

"What do you mean?"

Holmes faced the door as it opened. "Ah, hello Sarah. May we come in?"

Sarah opened the door wider to admit us, but her face remained closed. "The inspector's in the drawing room."

"I see. Please show us in."

The inspector was standing in front of the unlit fireplace when we entered. "Thought you two would arrive round about now," he said, his moustache twitching. "Want to hear the news?"

"Of course," said Holmes. I followed his gaze to the yellow envelope in the inspector's hand.

"He's a good man, McIlvanney. Wired as soon as he got a result." The inspector held up the envelope. "Chloral hydrate. A sleeping draught when taken properly – but easy to take too much. It was in the dregs of the glass by her bed . . . ." His eyes gleamed, and he leaned closer and lowered his voice. "I think the poor woman did away with herself," he said.

"Hmm." I considered. "That would fit with the decrease in her bookings. She was worried that her business was failing. It makes perfect sense. She was alive at eight o'clock in the morning, when she spoke to Sarah, but dead by ten."

"How convenient," said Holmes. "That wraps it up nicely."

"It does, rather," said Inspector Gregson, pocketing the telegram and rubbing his hands. He stopped when he glanced at Holmes. "What?"

"It's too convenient," said Holmes. "Too obvious and neat."

The inspector sighed. "Sometimes people do away with themselves, Mr. Holmes, it's a known fact. We can call it a 'misadventure' if you like — "

"There's more to this," said Holmes. "I know there is." He went upstairs.

"Shouldn't you ask?" I said, as Holmes opened the boudoir door.

"No," said Holmes, and went in.

The room looked much as it had the day before. Holmes crossed to the bureau and opened the hinged flap. "Now, Miss Le Fanu did her business work downstairs. So what shall we find in here?" He put down the flap and drew a writing-case from the left-hand cubbyhole. The others were empty. "No letters, sadly – just headed notepaper. Although . . . ." He opened the case to reveal the blotter, criss-crossed with line after line of Miss Le Fanu's neat writing, reversed. "Let us see." He scanned the room, then walked with the case to the mirror over the mantel, and held the blotter to the glass, turning it this way and that. "Look, Watson."

I joined him, and followed the reflection of his pointing finger. "There."

. . . felt such a passion . . .

"And there."

. . . I had resigned myself to a . . .

"And again, there."

. . . I shall come to you very soon . . .

"These lines are recent, and not faded," said Holmes. "They do not read like the words of someone disposed to kill herself."

I frowned. "He might have broken things off. Or disappointed her in some way . . . ."

Holmes stared at me.

"Have I said something stupid?"

Holmes grinned and clapped me on the back. "Watson, as always, you have said exactly the right thing! Now I just need to fathom how it was done."

"But if Marcia Le Fanu was alive at eight o'clock, when the servants were about, how could anyone – "

"Was she, though?" Holmes closed the bureau and crossed to the bell-pull.

Sarah appeared two minutes later, seeming calmer than she had the previous day. "Yes, sir?"

"I recall Miss Le Fanu was wearing a fine pair of red satin slippers when she was found," said Holmes. "Could you tell me where they came from, Sarah?"

325

Sarah was silent, and a flush crept over her face. "They were a gift from a well-wisher, sir."

"I see. An anonymous well-wisher?"

Sarah's expression took on a tragic air. "She made me promise not to tell!" She put her face in her hands and her shoulders heaved with sobs.

"There, there. It's quite all right." Holmes led the parlourmaid to a chair and gave her his handkerchief.

"Just when she had a chance of happiness!" exclaimed Sarah, between gasps. "She died just like that, when she'd spoken to me not two hours before!" She mopped her eyes, but the sight of the hearthrug set her off again.

Holmes knelt by the chair. "When she spoke to you, how did she seem?"

"She was a bit hoarse, but I didn't think anything of it. I thought she had a cold, as she said not to bother with breakfast."

"How did she look?"

Sarah was silent. "I – I couldn't say, sir."

"Why not? Was it dark?"

Sarah swallowed. "No . . . ."

Holmes waited, and Sarah's hands crept towards the edge of her apron.

"You didn't go into the bedroom, did you?"

Her glance flicked up, then down to the floor. "No, sir."

"Did you go into the boudoir?"

A slow shake of the head. "No. I tapped at the door and she called out, quick as a flash. 'Don't come in. Don't want breakfast.'"

"And she sounded hoarse."

Another almost convulsive swallow. "Yes, sir."

"Not like herself, in fact."

Sarah covered her face and moaned.

Holmes stood, and put a kindly hand on her shoulder. "Go and calm yourself, Sarah. That is the best way to help us get to the bottom of this."

Sarah stumbled from the room, and as her footsteps clattered away we heard a howl like a wounded animal.

Chapter IX

"So," said Holmes. "That changes things."

Inspector Gregson sighed. "An easy case once in a while, that's all I ask." He shot a sharp look at Holmes. "Care to tell me how it was done?"

Holmes pondered. "The maid said she was often wakeful. I imagine it could have been a few more drops than usual in the dose, or perhaps a further large dose in the glass of water by her bed."

"Yes, but done by whom?"

"That is the question," said Holmes. "I am getting closer to the answer. Watson, I have a fancy to examine Miss Le Fanu's bureau again."

We trooped upstairs and watched Holmes unpack the bureau: The writing-case, an empty letter-case, the pens and ink-bottles, the stationery in the drawers, and bundles of letters tied with white ribbon, all from family or female friends.

"There's nothing here," said Gregson at last, snorting and dropping the last bundle into the drawer.

"No," said Holmes. "That's exactly the problem. Given the phrases Marcia Le Fanu used in writing to this person, she would have treasured those letters." He rang the bell and Sarah reappeared, with a wary look on her face. Her glance fell on the open bureau, and her eyes widened.

"Sarah, did you dust in here?"

She nodded. "Usually it's a housemaid's job, or a lady's maid's, but as Madame had neither – "

"It fell to you."

"She was very neat," said Sarah hurriedly.

"I can see that. Did you dust the bureau?"

"Yes sir, but not inside. It was kept locked."

"And your mistress had the key."

Sarah's gaze settled on the bureau again.

"So you have never seen it open, until now."

"No, not unless I surprised Madame writing, and she would always cover up her things."

Holmes gave her a stern look. "Do you know who Miss Le Fanu's admirer was? Did he call at the house?"

Sarah gazed at Holmes with large, frightened eyes. "He did call, sir, once or twice a week. He was tallish, heavily-built, dark-haired with some grey in it, and he wore a moustache. He was a gentleman, sir, or I wouldn't have let him in, because he always told me to say 'Mr. Nobody' was at the door."

"Mr. Nobody, eh?" said Gregson.

Holmes's eyes narrowed. "I suspect Mr. Nobody is a client of Miss Le Fanu who originally came for a séance, and found something quite different. With the aid of Miss Le Fanu's black book, I suspect we can track him down easily. About these letters . . . ." He went to the fireplace and, picking up the poker, raked through the ashes.

"I'm sorry, sir, I haven't had time to sweep it out, what with – everything," quavered Sarah. "I usually do it every day."

"I'm sure you do," said Holmes. "Quite a lot of ash for one day, isn't there? Paper ash, too, and burnt to dust." He poked through it again. "Enough to signify that several letters have been burnt since it was last cleaned." He turned to Sarah. "How many people came on Thursday evening?"

Sarah frowned. "Well one came early, I remember, and Madame said to show him into the drawing room. The second came ten minutes later, at half-past-seven, and then there was ever such a wait for the third. He didn't come till ten to eight and one of the others must have become bored because he'd gone – " She clapped her hand to her mouth. "It was him, wasn't it? It was him!"

Holmes jumped up and steadied her. "I very much fear that it was," he said. "Let us examine the hallway." He took the unresisting maid's arm and guided her downstairs.

"Oh!" wailed Sarah, and pointed. She walked as if pulled by an invisible rope, until she was at a door set in the back of the stairs. She flung it open, and we stared at the assortment of coats and umbrellas and galoshes within.

"More than enough room," said Gregson, making a note. "Who was it, though? I mean, he won't have given his real name."

"No," said Holmes. "But after a few more calls I shall be able to tell you."

Chapter X

We had arrived at Portman Square at one o'clock to be told that Sir Geoffrey Carlton was at his club.

"I dread to think what this case is costing in cab fares," said Holmes. "We've ranged all over London this morning." But he was smiling.

The flunky at the Athenaeum showed us into the dining room, where we found Sir Geoffrey holding forth to a florid grey-haired man, waving his empty fork as if he were conducting an orchestra. He saw us, and the fork froze.

"Ah, Sir Geoffrey," said Holmes as he approached. "Do you mind if we join you?"

Sir Geoffrey's expression reminded me of a peevish child. "I am lunching with a friend," he said, laying down his fork. "Are you members?" His eyes moved past Holmes and I saw a waiter approaching.

"We have news about Miss Le Fanu," said Holmes.

"Oh!" Sir Geoffrey removed the napkin from his shirt collar. "Why didn't you say?"

He motioned to the waiter and murmured in his ear. "Of course, sir," said the waiter, and stood while Sir Geoffrey took a sip of his wine, apologised to his dining companion, and eventually got to his feet. The waiter led us to an anteroom, containing four easy chairs and a low table, and withdrew.

"So," said Sir Geoffrey, settling himself in a chair, "what do you have to tell me? I assume it is important, as you have come to find me." He leaned forward, waiting.

"Yes," said Holmes, taking the chair opposite. "We have learnt the cause of Miss Le Fanu's death."

"And?" Sir Geoffrey's eyes were alert, watchful.

"She died of an overdose of chloral."

"A sleeping draught?" Sir Geoffrey passed his hand over his brow. "Oh no. How sad." He looked up. "What a terrible waste." His eyes moved from Holmes to me, and back. "I don't suppose she meant – "

"We believe someone administered it to her," said Holmes.

Sir Geoffrey's shoulders stiffened. "What – a servant?" He half-rose from his chair, then sat down. "I've never trusted that parlourmaid. She has a furtive air."

"It wasn't the parlourmaid, Sir Geoffrey. What would she have to gain, save the loss of her situation?"

"Then who?" snapped Sir Geoffrey.

"As you know, Marcia Le Fanu holds a séance on Thursday evenings. Three guests came, but only two attended the séance. Sarah assumed the other guest had left, but he took advantage of a delay to slip away and conceal himself in the hall cupboard. He waited until Miss Le Fanu was taking supper, then went to her bedroom and carried out his orders. He put a generous dose of chloral in her water glass, topping it up with water. He waited in the adjacent bedroom until the cook had left for the day, and Sarah had gone to bed. He re-entered Miss Le Fanu's bedroom and checked she was asleep, and that her water glass was empty. Then he crept downstairs and let himself out."

"But – but who would do such a thing?" blustered Sir Geoffrey.

"Who, indeed," said Holmes, uncrossing his legs. "Yet the story does not end there."

"No, it does not! Who gave him a key? Are you sure it wasn't the parlourmaid? This story makes no sense!"

"No, it doesn't, does it?" remarked Holmes. "But there is more to come. We haven't got to *your* part of the story yet."

329

"My part of the story? Have you gone mad?" Sir Geoffrey made to rise.

"Don't move, Sir Geoffrey. Inspector Gregson is outside, and I shall bring him into the club if I must."

Sir Geoffrey lowered himself back into the chair. "I had nothing to do with it. My evening is fully accounted for."

"It is, isn't it? Dinner with a friend, showing yourself at your club, talking to a crony, taking a cab, and no doubt making a noisy return home. That gets us to what – half-past-eleven?"

"When I went to bed."

"Yes, and got up again later, put on the same clothes, strolled round the corner, and hailed a cab. You could have left well-enough alone. You could have let your accomplice do his job, but it wasn't enough. You had to see for yourself."

"Rubbish." Sir Geoffrey folded his arms.

"We found Miss Le Fanu not dead in bed, as you would expect, but collapsed on the hearthrug in the boudoir. How did she get there?"

Sir Geoffrey shrugged. "Perhaps she heard a noise and fell."

"Perhaps. Or perhaps she stirred because she felt you removing the chain round her neck which held the key to the bureau." Sir Geoffrey started. "Ah yes, I saw the faint red line on the side of Miss Le Fanu's neck, a light chafing, when I examined her. It probably took a while, but eventually she woke, no doubt dazed from the sleeping draught, heard a noise in the boudoir, and went to investigate. And there you were, reading and burning her love letters."

"Love letters?" Sir Geoffrey snorted. "Who would write love letters to Marcia?"

"A man who attended one of her séances out of curiosity, and fell in love. Miss Le Fanu reciprocated his feelings, and was planning to abandon her clients – and her patron – to begin a new life with him. You had noticed her change in attitude, her refusal to commit to more sessions with you, or anyone – "

"That doesn't mean I'd kill her!" shouted Sir Geoffrey. "Mediums are ten-a-penny. I could find one at the next gimcrack theatre."

"Ah, but Marcia Le Fanu was your pet, your *protégée*, your seer. She was your *property*. So when you became suspicious, you got an associate to sneak in and drug Miss Le Fanu. He could have taken the letters with him easily – but you wanted to learn the truth, and take revenge, yourself."

"So how did I get in, eh?" Sir Geoffrey looked almost cocksure. "I suppose I floated through the window."

"The front door was unbolted, courtesy of your accomplice. When you filched a key on a previous visit to Miss Le Fanu, you had two copies

330

made: One for him, and one for you. You entered the house in the dead of night. If Sarah heard you on the stairs, she would probably assume you were her mistress roaming the house, unable to find sleep. You went upstairs, took the bureau key, and were working your way through the letters when Miss Le Fanu surprised you. You whispered that she was dreaming, took her back to bed, and gave her another sleeping draught – one which you were sure would finish the job. She drank it – but due to the tolerance she had acquired, even that could not quieten her, for she came into the boudoir again. I don't know what you said to her, nor how you got her to sleep, but I suspect she drifted to her death believing that she was in the arms of her lover. Finally she was still, and cold."

"I couldn't hurt her," whispered Sir Geoffrey, as if confiding a secret. "I couldn't even bear the thought of someone else hurting Marcia."

"So you poisoned her instead. And it took so long for the chloral to do its job that when Sarah knocked at the door, you were caught unawares. What could you do? You answered for Miss Le Fanu, and bought yourself some more time. Once she had gone, you tidied yourself as best you could and waited for an opportune moment – for you know the movements of the household – you slipped out, threw away your key and Miss Le Fanu's chain, and rang the bell punctually at ten o'clock."

"You have no proof," stammered Sir Geoffrey, his eyes darting round the room.

"Oh, I do. It has been a busy morning for me. We went through Miss Le Fanu's little black book, and when we matched up the names and physical descriptions of the people who attended her last séance, the guest who went missing corresponded almost exactly to Madame Paretski's butler, who is under arrest.

"Ah! Though you try to hide it, I see that we have our man. Madame Paretski's butler, I confess, confused me - Why use him? - until I considered it from your point of view. As Miss Le Fanu's patron, you would naturally be asked questions if she died unexpectedly. Therefore you would need a solid alibi and an accomplice to carry out the first part of your plan. None of your clubbable companions would do . . . and who would be more appropriate, a greater twist of the knife in Miss Le Fanu's back, than the servant of a rival that Marcia despised?

"You had visited Madame Paretski years ago on your quest for a medium, and you were unimpressed. Her butler, however, was another matter: A smart man with *gravitas*, so much more respectable than Miss Le Fanu's harried parlourmaid. He would assist you for cash and, more importantly, the benefit of his mistress and himself. From the butler's point of view, he is a man with fingers in countless pies, running a complex book of favours owing and favours returned in his head, as all good servants do.

331

He no doubt saw this as a very useful contact for the future, if it paid off. And if it did not, he could always stick to the line that he was only administering a sleeping-draught, and knew none of the rest – which is exactly what he is doing. In fact, you tried to make him believe that he had caused Miss le Fanu's death by giving her too much chloral hydrate – guaranteed to ensure his silence.

"A daring double bluff on your part, Sir Geoffrey, to point me in the direction of a rival medium. However, while Madame Paretski's alibi was watertight, she will also be questioned. We also sought and found 'Mr. Nobody'. He has been informed of Miss Le Fanu's death and is currently under police guard, since one death is more than enough. Oh, and one more thing. We called on your friend Metcalfe, and Bass the financier, and stopped in at the Savoy, and came here earlier today, and everyone is in agreement."

"About what?" asked Sir Geoffrey, in the flat tone of a defeated man.

"Your acquaintances and the staff are prepared to swear that on the evening Miss Le Fanu died, you had a scarlet rosebud as your buttonhole, and described your clothes quite accurately. Now Miss Le Fanu had a vase of red roses in her bedroom – but they were in full bloom. When we met you yesterday morning, your clothes were as everyone had described the evening before, save that you wore no flower in your buttonhole. You had left it clasped in Miss Le Fanu's hand."

"A parting gift," said Sir Geoffrey, and his mouth twitched convulsively. "I am the last of my line, you know. Marcia was my only link to my family, and – "

"Indeed," said Holmes. "Now if you don't mind, it is time to hand you over to Inspector Gregson."

Sir Geoffrey rose and, moving as if walking in his sleep, accompanied us out of the anteroom, out of the club, and into the plain black carriage where Gregson sat, waiting.

Chapter XI

We arrived back at 221b Baker Street at six o'clock that evening following an afternoon of statements, interviews, and explanations.

Holmes was quiet on the way home, and when I looked across at him, his mouth was set firm and his posture rigid. Beneath that calm exterior, I suspected that his pulse was racing, though he would never admit it.

"We have time before dinner," I said. "Would you play something for me?"

"Of course," said Holmes. He retrieved his violin from its case and launched into a whirling Spanish dance.

332

"Sarasate?" I asked when the last chord had died away.

He nodded, and began another. His bow danced and his fingers flew, barely pausing between pieces. After the fifth he stopped. His breathing was fast and shallow, his bow dangled from his fingers, and a sheen of sweat stood on his brow.

"You don't believe in the supernatural, Watson, do you?" he said, looking at me.

I remembered Madame Paretski's eyes on me, and her cold revelation. "No, Holmes. I do not." He continued to regard me. "Do you?"

Holmes shook his head. "I despise such fakery, particularly where it does additional harm. I do not know whether Marcia Le Fanu was a fraud, or whether she truly believed she had a gift. But she did not deserve to die." He tucked the violin under his chin and this time the music was slower, with the rhythm of a rocking cradle. I recognised the "Barcarolle" from *The Tales of Hoffman*.

The piece drew to a close, and this time Holmes lowered his violin and stood, eyes closed. Then he opened them and smiled, and it was as if a storm had passed.

"The worst is over," he said, laying his violin in its case. "Let us change for dinner, Watson." And we spoke of the case no more that evening.

The Poisoned Regiment
by Carl Heifetz

I had anticipated no visitors and thought that I could spend the afternoon in quiet solitude with my thoughts, pursuing my reading. Unexpectedly, there was a gentle tapping at my bedroom door. Mrs. Hudson quietly called my name. "Dr. Watson, you have a visitor. He's downstairs waiting for you with Mr. Holmes. Should I tell him that you'll be down? I've already served them coffee and biscuits."

I had previously escaped to my room to avoid the noxious fumes from Holmes's pipe and chemistry experiments, and was leisurely glancing through an article on mental diseases in *The Lancet*. I hated to be disturbed, but I was pleased to assist in any way possible. I replied, "Tell them that I'll be there soon."

"Before coming down," said Mrs. Hudson, "the army officer has requested that you don this military uniform."

After I heard her steps leave the area, I opened the door and saw a uniform lying on a chair outside. It would suit the most elegant medical officer. The insignia indicated a substantial elevation in rank. Prior to retiring from the service, I had only been a junior surgeon. Thus, it appeared that – for the time at least – I had been promoted to a more senior position. The khaki outfit was clean, starched, and pressed. There was even a baton and a shoulder strap.

I was somewhat confused by this turn of events, but knew that the answer to my queries, as well as a fresh cup of coffee, were only a few steps away. I welcomed the intrusion, since I assumed that the presence of a guest had required Holmes to open the windows and put away his chemicals. The fresh breezes of a clear spring day would serve that purpose very well.

As I took the steps down from my room and entered the sitting room, a tall thin man of military bearing arose from the table, turned, and briskly walked in my direction. I shook hands with Colonel Thomas, my old medical commander from my original regiment, the 66th Berkshires. After all these years, he retained his erect figure and strength. Even his mustache still had its firm black bristles.

As we seated ourselves at the dining table, I poured some coffee. Lifting my cup, I said, "Colonel, what would bring you all the way from Reading to confer with a retired Army surgeon, and why have I apparently been promoted?"

"As I've just been discussing with Mr. Holmes, we have a serious problem at the regiment," he replied. "Our training has been terribly disrupted by a mysterious illness, just when we are slated to depart for action. Based on some of your background – your medical skills and your discretion – we believe that you can determine the cause. Additionally, for reasons of security, this must be investigated by an outside man – or *men* in this case. As a colonel, I'm entitled to award field commissions to medical staff – thus your recall to duty and your promotion. It's essential that you and Mr. Holmes accompany me to our headquarters as soon as possible. Your elevation in position will enable you to get appropriate support from the men as needed and also give you complete access to our facilities. It's urgent that our medical difficulties not be bandied about in the press, who are presently critical of our military incursions. We know that you and Mr. Holmes can be trusted to keep a confidence."

After we nodded our heads in the affirmative, the colonel continued, "More hot coffee and pastries are available in my coach. I'll fill you in as we journey to the rail station."

Energized by the prospect of an investigation to serve my nation, I put down my mug. Forgetting the pains that were residuals of my military wounds, I quickly joined Holmes in gathering what we would need for our investigation. When we were ready, we followed Colonel Thomas down to the front door. We climbed into a commodious military four-wheeler and, as I sat in the comfort of the cushioned seats and enjoyed the excellent coffee and Danish pastries, Colonel Thomas further described the situation.

"We are in the process of preparing for an attack against one of our Asian colonies, which is in revolt. Time is of the essence since we ship out within two weeks. However, we've been delayed by a mysterious illness. Unfortunately, most of the men have been hit with a recurring fever. It has the hallmarks of an infection, but resembles no illness that we've ever experienced. It's also possible that it might be a poisoning of some sort. We desperately need your investigation, since we do not have expertise in this area. I've seen government reports indicating that you and Mr. Holmes have solved several cases in the past involving mysterious diseases."

Holmes spoke then for the first time that I'd heard since descending from my bedroom. "Of course we will be pleased to render any assistance possible." Then he settled back in thought – although not for long, as we had one stop to make. Holmes was in the shop for only a few minutes. Upon his return, the colonel looked with shock at his purchase, but withheld any comment.

Within a few moments, we had arrived at Paddington Station, where a special train was awaiting us. During the journey in a very comfortable first-class cabin, Colonel Thomas elaborated further.

"For the last three weeks, many of my men have taken sick – none with symptoms with which I'm familiar. I have seen tetanus, enteric fever, influenza, and unfortunately many injuries and bullet wounds. The effects of this recent illness are very uniform and unlike any that we've ever experienced."

"What are the major aspects that led you to believe that it is an infection?" Holmes asked.

The colonel replied, "Here is a list of symptoms supplied by my medical staff: All of the men suffered a high fever, sweating, muscle pain, malaise, weakness, anorexia, headaches, myalgia, and back pain. The most unusual sign is the recurrence of the febrile condition. Just when the men seem to have recovered, the fever returns. Nothing is getting done and we aren't prepared for combat."

Holmes blandly asked, "Do you have any sick cows in your facility?"

I nodded to myself. Holmes had instantly perceived the same idea that crossed my mind, although I didn't understand how he could have known. More importantly, I could only wonder that the army's physicians hadn't suspected it as well. Of course, further investigation would be needed to confirm Holmes's implied hypothesis.

"No, sir," replied the colonel, somewhat puzzled. We receive all of our meat from local butchers who acquire it from surrounding farmers."

"Then we will need to examine the various farms in the area. Can you supply us with horses for transportation to the countryside after we determine where the local vendors where they get their supplies? Also, have you received any new supplies of veal or fresh milk lately?"

"Now that you ask, it has occurred to me that we haven't been served veal for several days. And we've found a new supplier for milk. Why do you ask?"

Holmes gave a brisk smile but instead of answering countered, "When we arrive, can you show us the direction of the kitchen? We'll need to ask some more questions. Then, you can go about your duties while Watson gets the lay of the land and I gather whatever evidence is available."

Upon arriving at the station, we were quickly transported by dog-cart to the gates leading to the regimental facility. The road was smooth, no doubt maintained in that condition by the military. We alighted and followed the colonel for a brisk walk. Approaching a building with several small smokestacks emitting fragrant fumes, I noted that the camp grounds were littered with paper. Apparently they hadn't recently been policed –

evidence of a shortage of available troops. Also, we saw no soldiers conducting training. All was still and quiet.

The colonel directed us to a low building where we would be quartered. After pointing out various landmarks, including the base kitchen, he took his leave.

While I set out those materials that we had brought with us from London, Holmes departed to explore the camp. He was gone no more than half-an-hour before returning, summoning me to follow him to the camp kitchen.

Holmes greeted the bustling cooks with, "Good day, gentlemen. I am Sherlock Holmes and this is my colleague, Dr. Watson. May we have your attention for a few moments? It's about the sickness that has overcome some of your comrades."

An older fellow with sergeant's stripes signaled the other five cooks to continue with their work while he stepped around the counter, walking in our direction to address us while wiping sweat off of his brow. He removed his chef's tall hat and toweled off his bald head as well.

He indicated the direction of a set of double doors leading to the cooler outside air, inviting us to follow him to a source of shade near the next the building.

"How may I help you, gents? If you're investigating, please do not blame me or my men. We run a very clean kitchen to the highest military standards."

Holmes smiled in his gracious way and said, "Sergeant, I'm certain that you are very astute in how you prepare the food for your men, and I look forward to sampling your output. We are merely after some background information."

"I would be honored," the sergeant responded, "to answer any of your questions. We've been troubled by the lack of soldiers coming to the mess hall, and are very concerned for them."

"Then please tell us why you haven't served veal for several days," said Holmes.

The sergeant appeared to be surprised by this query, responding, "It's true that we haven't served veal. It's been on the menu schedule, but our supplier hasn't delivered it to our butcher. We'll have to find another source of the meat. Right now we're substituting chicken from our coops. The source of veal hasn't been able to supply milk either."

"May I ask you who was supposed to deliver the veal and milk?"

"Macgregor's farm. About five miles from here. His veal is the best around. We're sad to see that he hasn't been around for several days. Do you think there's some connection between – "

337

"Thank you very much, sir," interrupted Holmes, turning in the direction of the brick headquarters building. "We'll take no more of your time."

Suspecting what the next step was likely to be, I followed Holmes into the regiment's headquarters and through an oak-paneled door without knocking into an office. Holmes seemed to know instinctively where to go. The colonel was sitting at his massive desk addressing his officers while the trio examined a large map with outlines of India. Seeing us enter, he quickly folded the map and invited us to sit in a divan against the far wall. He frowned but waved his hand towards the other men, who quickly left the premises.

Facing us, the colonel asked, "Gentlemen, would you care to join me in some sherry while we discuss any further action?"

I was parched and quickly assented with a nod of my head, and Holmes responded "Yes, thank you. I need to ask for a favor."

"Of course, Mr. Holmes," he replied. "I'll provide any assistance that you require." He gently poured three glasses of sherry from an engraved glass decanter.

"Thank you, Colonel. I will need directions to Macgregor's farm, a cart with digging tools, and two healthy men in mufti."

He glanced at me, and I added, "We also need several pairs of surgical gloves and gowns."

Looking quizzically at both of us, the colonel said. "Everything will be provided. It will require about twenty minutes."

With that, the colonel stepped out of his building and motioned to one of the sentries. The young soldier ran off quickly and in a few minutes returned with a military cart pulled by two horses. As we boarded the vehicle, we saw a pair of burly solders approaching, carrying several shovels, trowels, hoes, and pitchforks. The younger of the two, a non-commissioned officer who appeared to be in charge, directed the other to load the implements in the cart. Holmes made sure that the tools were covered by a tarp.

Riding in a large military van pulled by two sturdy stallions, we bumped over a rutted trail. A gust of wind blew dust over our clothing and into our mouths and noses. The young officer directed our route, and we eventually arrived at a farm featuring a wooden fence and several barns. Close by was a white three-story house, and several outbuildings were in the distance. The facility appeared to be well kept. The grass was neatly mown and several young cows wandered slowly between bales of hay.

In a low voice, Holmes asked me, "Do you notice anything unusual?"

"Not that I can see."

338

"There are no older milk cows in sight, nor are there calves. It appears that they have restocked the cattle. No doubt they are not producing milk yet because none of the cows are old enough to have borne calves. This will explain why there has been no veal or milk recently."

As we opened the gate, we were approached by two men on horseback.

The older one, a bearded man, asked, "What are you doing on our farm? We do not permit strangers upon our grounds. Some of our cattle have taken sick and we're trying to protect them."

Holmes smiled and responded genially, "Good afternoon, gentlemen. My friend here is a doctor. We'll be careful of your stock. We understand that you've been looking for a breed bull. We're here to do business. We have a bull that is just waiting to provide you with calves and return you to the milk and veal business."

The younger man said, "I don't know how you knew this, since we haven't advertised. But if your bull is healthy, we want to take a look at it."

Holmes said, "The bull is at the regimental base being raised for a show. I suggest that you ride over there right away before his services are used. I see you're already on horseback so there should be no difficulty. We'll be happy to watch over your farm. We're from the army base and can warn away any interlopers."

The two men looked at one another, and after a bit of silent communication, they seemed to reach a decision. They saluted, waved their hats, and smilingly rode off to the base.

"Is there a bull at the base?" I asked softly.

Holmes nodded. "The signs were there, Watson, if only you had observed them. I'm surprised that you didn't notice the animal in the pasture as we approached the base. He pawing at the ground with his forelimbs, indicating a desire to mate."

After the two men had disappeared, Holmes hopped down, opened the gate, and then led us on a tour of the grounds. In the distance we saw several buzzards circling. After ten minutes or so we arrived at the site. Holmes shooed away the birds and then walked over to where they had been focused. He got down on hands and knees to examine several mounds. He then yelled, "Come over here. Bring the shovels and pitchforks. We need to examine these small hills."

The soldiers warily approached the elevations and began to dig. The grass and dirt were loose, and an odor of decaying flesh soon surrounded us. The soldiers easily revealed several large rotting carcasses.

"Look here, Watson. What do you see?" Holmes enunciated.

I replied in a clipped tone, "Cows that may have succumbed to a fatal illness." I stepped closer. "The white material is lime that has been placed to obviate the smell of the carcasses. Some of these bodies are very young – newborns, or even aborted." I coughed at the odor. "They're trying to hide the fact that they were harboring animals with infective disease." I glanced at Holmes. "This explains the lack of veal and fresh milk deliveries."

"Obviously," he replied.

"We'll need to bring one of the carcasses back for examination."

Holmes said, "It would be pointless to retrieve and then subject these dead animals to bacteriological examination. The process of crepitation would obfuscate our ability to define the species of bacteria that might be the cause of this disease. Perhaps in the future, someone will produce a selective growth medium that can separate the species of microbe in the infection. However, such is currently not the case. We will leave the bodies behind."

The soldiers seemed relieved that we would not be transporting one of the foul bodies in the cart, and set too with enthusiasm to rebury the remains. We were waiting at the gate when a cloud of dust became visible in the distance, approaching our location.

As the farmers approached, large smiles were present on their faces. "Sir, thank you very much for recommending the bull. He fits our purposes exactly. We have a mating arranged for next Wednesday."

Holmes winked at me and smiled. He then waved as we set the cart in motion and drove off. He said, "Everyone is happy. The farmers are happy, the bull will be happy, and the cows will be happy."

The journey back to the base was without incident. The wind had diminished, alleviating the potential for dust blowing in our faces. The weather was still fair with a refreshing breeze, although there were few wispy clouds on the horizon. The military encampment was quiet. There was no marching. However, a few men could now be seen policing the grounds. That signaled a possibility that recovery from the disease was imminent. However, we still needed to prevent further cases.

The colonel came out meet us while his men unloaded the tools from the back of the cart. "So, are you any closer to determining the cause of the fever?"

I nodded. "As suspected, the cows that supply meat and milk for the base had become diseased. The symptoms may recur, but we can being preventive actions immediately."

"My earlier investigations," added Holmes, "revealed that there are no infected cattle or horses within the encampment. None of the men, as far as I can superficially tell, are still contagious. But the disease may still lurk somewhere in the camp."

The colonel nodded. "We must still remove any possible sources. What do you gentlemen suggest?"

Holmes replied, "There is still one area to pursue. Let us return to the kitchen."

After finishing our restorative fluids, Holmes led the way. Approaching the sergeant in charge, he asked, "Do you have any milk left from Macgregor's farm?"

"Well, Mr. Holmes," replied the man, continuously mopping sweat off of his broad brow, "we still have some in the cold room souring for pudding. We expect to use it for dessert tomorrow. That is the last of it that that we received from them. "

Holmes said, "Do not use the milk. We will need to evaluate its safety."

The sergeant nodded his head in agreement, but it was obvious from the expression on his face that he felt the suggestion ludicrous. "We need to retrieve it," added Holmes. The sergeant nodded and led us down into the cold cellar where the perishable items were stored. Electric bulbs illuminated our steps. The odor of vegetables and fish filled the atmosphere. We spotted the location of the milk on a table next to the dirt wall. Holmes lifted the glass jug and carried it upstairs. The rest of us followed.

Outside, the colonel summoned a cart to carry us to the base's medical facility. I asked that it detour by our quarters, where I quickly went inside and retrieved our bags, including Holmes's purchase, made that morning before we caught our train.

Returning to the cart, I explained, "We can provide a bacteriological exam to determine if the soured milk can be used." The colonel nodded, but a puzzled look was on his face.

In the base hospital's small laboratory, Holmes spotted a number of hanging lab coats, which he distributed for all of us to wear. After putting on his garb, he handed each of us a pair of cotton gloves to protect our hands. Then he reached for the item purchased that morning: A small cage containing five white mice.

The colonel leaned in with great interest as I prepared several syringes with oral needles and then administered a tiny amount of the milk to each mouse. I then handed each one to Holmes so that he could deposit it back the wire cage that he had purchased, along with a water bottle and food pellets.

He then looked at me expectantly. "Now," I said, "I'll attempt to cultivate the microbes in a broth made from milk protein and beef extract."

341

The sergeant summoned a small amount of beef broth from the kitchen. Using a sterilized Pasteur pipette, I placed several droplets of milk in each of five tubes. "I'll now let them warm up a bit in the ambient air. I'd perform a direct microscopic analysis of the milk, but I'm certain that the presence of fermenting microbes, likely yeasts, would overwhelm the view. Now, it's time to rest until the specimens are ready for our observation. At that time, we'll all need to wear our lab coats and gloves once again."

With that being said, Holmes and I were returned to our commodious private quarters to prepare ourselves for dinner. In the sitting room attached to our bedrooms, we found a bottle of Scotch whisky, a siphon of soda, and several glasses. We knew just what to do.

The following day, I arose to find myself abandoned. Holmes wasn't in the dining area. I wandered over to the medical facility, where I found him sterilizing a wire and allowing it to cool. He then smeared a droplet of some substance on a glass microscopic slide. He repeated this procedure five times, with each droplet being taken from one of the five tubes that we had prepared the previous day. After this was done, he then gently flamed the bottom of each slide above an alcohol fire. After they had cooled, my colleague delicately performed a staining procedure known as the Gram Stain. As the slides dried, I was directed to observe the mice for evidence of infection, such as fever and lethargy. Since each of the animals appeared to be febrile, we sampled blood from their hearts, smearing the droplets blood onto glass slides, spreading it into a thin film, and then gently drying the specimens over a flame. We repeated the staining procedure and, leaving the slides to dry, left for the officer's mess for a substantial repast.

After a hearty breakfast, we returned to our *ad hoc* laboratory. Holmes looked around until he located a very fine microscope. We took turns viewing the slide through an oil of immersion lens. The bacteria that we saw were quite different from those that we had previously encountered. The cells were Gram Negative, clustered together, and were shaped between rods and cocci.

Finally Holmes said, "I've seen these bacteria described as *coccobacilli*. These microbes are unique. I have some other slides that I prepared earlier before you awoke, Watson."

I noted that the bacteria on the additional slides were identical to those associated with the milk.

"This second set of slides," Holmes explained after a moment, "was obtained from the blood of the last soldiers residing in the sick room. I collected it this morning. I'm happy to say that the men appear to have

342

recovered from their illness and will soon return to duty. However, we still must declare the source of the infection – although the matter now seems to be moot, as the Macgregor's cows have died, and the disease with it."

"Holmes," I said, "I recognized the possibility of the outbreak's source almost immediately, based on my medical experience and training. How did you simultaneously reach the same conclusion?"

My friend lifted his head with an apparent lack of interest in the discussion, now that the matter was completed. "As you are aware, Watson, my family were country squires. As a result, I had a great deal of contact with animals and their diseases during my youth. The symptoms described by the colonel reminded me of Undulant Fever, a disease in cattle.

"I determined that we would need to locate and remove the source of the infection. My first query to the colonel was do you have any sick cows in your facility. Then I hypothesized that the infection sprang from a nearby farm. The lack of fresh veal indicated the cows had been infected with an abortive disease. Since the cattle had aborted, their milk production had ceased, and as we saw, the famers had recently replaced their sick cows. Fortunately, they will be providing veal and milk in the future, should their association with the camp's bull be successful. Now that our job has been completed, we must inform the colonel of our findings

"What I find more curious is why this couldn't have been investigated without our help. The army has no end of talented medical professionals. Perhaps I'll ask brother Mycroft the reasons for the secrecy – if he'll agree to tell me."

And he did – but that's another matter entirely.

The Case of the
Persecuted Poacher
by Gayle Lange Puhl

It was high summer and Sherlock Holmes and I had just finished a grueling case. It had taken twelve days. We tracked down the culprit of the arson of the Wholen Bucket factory and the slaughter of the company's mascot, a fallow deer. Pet of the company's founder, Sir Henry Wholen, the animal's body had been found in the smoking ashes of the fire set to ravage the production floor. A bizarre tale of rage and revenge had unfolded as Holmes investigated the crime. Sir Henry said at the police station, as the arsonist was thrust into a cell, that he had never seen such clever work in his life and, frankly, I could not determine if he was referring to the criminal or to Holmes.

When we arrived back in Baker Street, Mrs. Hudson stopped Holmes at the door as I trudged up the steps to our sitting room. She seemed to be upset with him. I was myself exhausted. As I lay slumped down in my armchair in front of the empty fireplace, I could hear footsteps sounding from the lumber room overhead. A few minutes later, Holmes astonished me by coming in with rods and reels and other fishing equipment in his arms, dumping it all on the carpet at my feet.

"What is this?" I exclaimed.

My friend was smiling, but behind his eyes I could see concern. He, too, had extended himself physically in the handling of the last mystery. A slight clumsiness, a certain fumbling of his pipe and matches – these were the only signs he gave of his exhaustion. Otherwise his stern, cold exterior remained intact. I knew how he worked to present such a front to the world, even to me, and I worried that one day the control would slip and the man I knew would break down. Now he had some scheme in mind, and I realized I would have to humour him for his own sake.

"This time I must play the physician, Watson. Do you think that I haven't noticed the effort you put in these past two weeks as we searched for the arsonist? You have become a shadow of your normal self. Mrs. Hudson has taken me to task about your health. I cannot not have her worrying me about your welfare every time I bring you back from one of these little escapades."

"You are sending me away!"

"No, my friend. I am proposing a little trip for the two of us to the banks of some chalk stream, where the fish linger in rocky coves and the cool shadows of the overhanging trees play among the burbling pools of clear water. A week of catching our own suppers and trekking over verdant hills back to a comfortable inn should restore the sparkle to your eyes and the vigor to your step."

This behavior was very out of character for Sherlock Holmes. I looked into his eyes closely. I realized that he was fighting the very demons that both of us feared and that could be calmed only by the use of the contents of a morocco case and small bottle of liquid that resided in a locked drawer from within in his desk. I needed to help him from reaching for the key that could plunge him into the desperate existence from which I had worked so hard to rescue him years ago. I knew what part I had to play in this drama, but I also knew I couldn't allow Holmes and his pride to *know* that I knew.

"I could say the same about your step, Holmes, but I'm too tired to argue. Where shall we go?"

"All that can be determined in the morning. I've asked Mrs. Hudson to prepare a nourishing supper for us both. After a good night's sleep, arrangements will be made. Leave it all to me."

I came down to breakfast the next morning still very tired. A cup of hot coffee and a good breakfast did little to revive me, and I was ready for a nap. Holmes had been busy, however. He was dressed for travel and had already picked through and set in order the rods and other fishing gear he had brought in the night before. Now he was consulting railway timetables and looking up inns from a collection of guidebooks that he kept in his bedroom.

I awoke from a doze in my chair to find him standing at our sitting room door, murmuring instructions to a uniformed commissionaire from the messenger office down the street. Money exchanged hands, and Holmes turned to find me upright and blinking, fumbling with the teapot.

"A fresh pot of tea, Mrs. Hudson!" he called down the stairwell. "That tea is cold, Watson," he said, taking the pot out of my hands. "I have completed the arrangements, and when Willard returns with our tickets, we can leave. I've already packed both your bag and mine. Ah, Mrs. Hudson is ahead of me. Here is the tea and some biscuits. Let us refresh ourselves. Our train leaves from Euston Station at noon."

"Where are we going?" I asked.

"A charming place called Shottery, one mile from Stratford-Upon-Avon, the birthplace of William Shakespeare. I've booked rooms at a local guest house, and there are several trout streams within walking distance."

This all sounded wonderful, I had to admit. Holmes seemed invigorated and bustled about the room, putting the finishing touches on our luggage and even consenting to drink a cup of tea. I went upstairs and changed into my country tweeds. As a last-minute thought, almost a reflex action, I slipped my service revolver into my pocket. When our tickets arrived, Mrs. Hudson put a package of sandwiches into my hand as we entered the cab. Once at the station, it was the work of a moment to find our carriage. The train left London for Warwickshire soon after.

The crowded streets and polluted skies of that great city were quickly left behind. Our view out the windows gradually changed to green fields and tidy little farms. Halfway through the journey, I unwrapped the sandwiches and Holmes and I had lunch, assisted by the flask from his pocket.

We departed our first-class carriage at the station. Holmes had arranged for us to be met by a hired trap, driven by a local man. It was only a mile to Shottery, and with our bags and fishing tackle in the back, it was a pleasant drive through country lanes, shaded by over-arching trees. There were many spots of green dotting the landscape, both at the fields' borders and lining the roads. The sky was cloudless, and a bright sun laid dappled light over lanes and fields alike. We passed thatched houses, some half-timbered and others brick, accented by banks of flowering shrubs and neat stone walls. Off in the distance but not too far ran a twisty little stream, reflecting the light with multiple sparkles off the water.

The driver drew up to a sturdy brick building with the sign "*The Green Bush*" hanging over the door. It was a riot of what the Americans called "Steamboat Gothic". There were turrets, balconies, multiple stories, steep roof lines, ornate stained glass windows, and a veranda that twisted around the entire ground floor like a wide ribbon. A section of it had been glassed-in. On every level, elaborate gimcrack wooden trim was hung and draped, gleaming white against the rosy red brick of the structure. The sweep up to the front door was crushed gravel, and as we descended from the trap the large oak double doors opened onto the porch. A rotund man, about forty and obviously the owner, came out and shook both Holmes and me by the hand. He was my height and, along with his girth, he was notable for his snapping black eyes, flashing out from over red, bulbous cheeks. A young boy scurried past us and carried our bags and fishing tackle into the house.

I surveyed the front of the guest house. "What an unusual building, Mr. Flynn."

He smiled at us both. "I'm a lucky man, sir," he responded. "My wife brought this into the marriage. It has proven to be a nice little property, with the added advantage of letting us meet interesting people like yourselves, gentlemen."

We turned from the welcoming smiles of our host, Mr. Hyram Flagg, to the view from The Green Bush veranda. The clumped and gleaming spires and roofs of Stratford-Upon-Avon shone bright in the distance, nearly hidden by the greenery of tree and shrub. To the south was the flash of the rails of the train line that had carried us here, and to the north, the rising ground displayed trees and dry stone walls encasing fields of barley and wheat.

As we turned to enter the guesthouse, Mr. Flagg cleared his throat. "If you gentlemen find the charms of fishing and hiking starting to fade, I could recommend some other activities," he said confidentiality. "We have no theatre in town, but the shows and opportunities offered by the 'As You Like It Club' have entertained many gentlemen from London in times past." His sly grin and wink left no doubt as to the landlord's meaning.

I was not shocked by his words, but I felt a wave of revulsion. I was well aware of the existence of such "houses" in London. I had been introduced to one when I was a young medical student by a trio of enthusiastic fellows from my college. After a trip as an observer, my common sense and my newly-found knowledge of certain diseases that could be found in those places decided me to swear off such "amusements". Suddenly the green innocence of the countryside was tainted. Sherlock Holmes brushed past the man with a set face and I hastened to follow him into the lobby.

Inside The Green Bush, the ceiling and the wainscoting echoed the outside decor. Doors led away to other rooms and an ornate set of stairs twisted to the upper floors. We followed our luggage upstairs to a comfortable suite consisting of a tidy sitting room and two small bedrooms. There was a community bathroom down the hall.

The sitting room was furnished with a fireplace and filled with potted flowers, comfortable armchairs, a table with four wooden chairs around it, and a gas lamp hanging from the ceiling. The view out of the sitting room window matched that of the one we saw from the front porch. Outside the pane of glass, we could see the window opened to a tiny balcony hung with more "wooden lace", the hallmark of The Green Bush.

I suggested that a nap was in order after our train ride. Holmes agreed and we retired to our respective bedrooms. Within fifteen minutes I was asleep. When I awoke, the afternoon was long advanced and Holmes had left the rooms. I took the opportunity to do a hasty search of his luggage. I was dismayed to find the morocco case tucked into a corner of his bag, along with the little bottle. The bottle was full, its contents as yet untouched. I heard a footstep in the hall and rushed back to the sitting

347

room, where I dropped into a chair and picked up a newspaper lying on the table. A moment later Holmes, followed by the young boy from our arrival carrying a tea tray, entered the room. My friend dismissed the boy and handed me a cup from the tray.

"Have some tea, my dear Watson," he said. "I think we have enough time for a walk before dinner. Mr. Flagg informs me that there are several trout streams within two miles of the inn, and his other guests have given good accounts of the fishing. Mrs. Flagg is in charge of the dining room and posted a toothsome menu on the notice board downstairs."

"That sounds fine," I replied, and in a little while we were out of The Green Bush.

Shottery was a tiny village, decorated mainly in a half-timbered style. It's most famous claim to fame was as the home of Anne Hathaway, who married William Shakespeare of nearby Stratford-Upon-Avon. We passed her home on our walk, tucked off the road with a thatched roof and plastered sides. Surrounded by flowers and a few trees, it was a charming sight in the summer afternoon.

We strolled down the High Street. It was remarkable for the number of businesses named out of the works of the Bard. At the edge of town were a few buildings that appeared smaller and more shabby than the rest of the neat little community. I noticed a public house with the sign "*The Rose and Thorn*" hanging over its door. Next came some shops carrying second-hand clothing and a boarded-up restaurant. Beyond was a pleasant path that wound through a field or two before returning us to our guesthouse.

We returned with good appetite. The dining room was situated just off the lobby. It was half-full, and we had no trouble finding a table for two in a corner. Our fellow guests appeared to consist of middle-aged couples and groups of young people on walking trips. There was one table of fishermen. Holmes preferred not to mingle. Instead, he amused me all through dinner by murmuring his observations and deductions of our fellow travelers' occupations and points of origin by what he saw as they ate at their own tables. Mrs. Flagg, a plump, pleasant woman, directed the waitresses while the young boy who had carried in our bags cleared the plates and brought glasses of water. After a satisfying meal of roast beef and mashed potatoes, we returned to our rooms and turned in for the night. Holmes made arrangements with Mrs. Flagg before we went upstairs to have an early breakfast served in the morning. He also asked that a picnic hamper be prepared for our lunch the next day.

By noon of the next day, Holmes and I were casting our lines into a quiet corner of a secluded stream nearly two miles from Shottery. I had watched his manner carefully when we got up that morning and again checked the bottle when he was in the bathroom. There were no signs it had been touched. Reassured, I had given myself up to enjoyment of the day, including our walk through the countryside and our successful haul of fish. A fat trout lay in Holmes's creel atop a bed of fresh green grass. I had reeled in another trout and was setting my eye and hook on a promising bit of cover under a fallen tree in an eddy when Holmes called for a break. I took in my line as Holmes uncovered the picnic basket from the cool shade of a nearby tree and pulled two bottles of beer out of the water below it.

We had just repacked the sandwich wrappings and the empty bottles into the basket when our solitude was interrupted by the appearance of the young boy from our guest house. He obviously had run all the way through the fields, and was panting for breath as he handed Holmes a note.

"It is from our landlord, Watson," said Holmes. "He tells us there has been a tragedy on the grounds of Drinkwater Hall, the estate of Sir William Singer, the local lord of the manor. Sir William has learned of our presence here and asks that we attend him at his home. He fears that this matter is beyond the resources of the Stratford police."

"What can have happened?" I asked.

The young boy piped up. "It's murder, sir. I heard Strom talking to Mr. Flagg. Old Woods, Sir William's gamekeeper, was murdered."

"Who is Strom, son?"

"Sir William's butler, sir. Mr. Flagg said it was urgent. Shall I carry your fishing tackle and the basket, sir?"

"Yes, take them back to The Green Bush. First direct us to the Hall." Holmes was poised to leave, his formerly languid manner gone. I was sorry for the death of an unknown man, but inwardly I rejoiced at the bright look in my friend's eye, the snap in his voice, and the energy with which he moved. With a case of possible murder at hand, he no longer needed the stimulation contained in the little bottle secreted in his bag. All thoughts of fishing evaporated. The boy went off one way to return our belongings to the guest house and I followed Sherlock Holmes to Drinkwater Hall.

It was a large Portland stone building, complete with a west tower and a crenelated roof line. A porch, adorned with stone pillars and a crest carved in the keystone over the front door, offered entry. I discovered later that the estate was nearly two-thousand acres, although it had formerly encompassed nearly twenty-thousand acres when it was first founded by Sir Titus Singer back in the 1400's. We had followed the stream as instructed and then walked up the gravel lane that stopped at the wide steps of the entrance. Beyond the stately home, the brook continued in a curve

349

around the side of the mansion. To the right was a rose garden and a grove of ancient trees. A wide swath of gravel surrounded the building. Manicured grass and tasteful shrubbery completed the look. An ancient stone bridge arched over the stream and linked the road from the Hall to the rest of the world.

Holmes knocked on the massive front door. A tall, thin man with slicked hair smoothed back over his ears, obviously the butler, responded. He took our names and led us down a wide hall to what appeared to be a sitting room. We were announced and the door closed behind us. We were face-to-face with Sir William Singer and his wife, Lady Singer.

I had expected a man and woman to match the grandeur of the building, a pair august and austere, aristocratic, with faces out of a medieval tapestry. Instead, Sir William and his wife sat on an overstuffed couch together. She held some needlework and Sir William fingered an old book. I was suddenly reminded of the elderly couple who kept the sweet shop and post office in my hometown when I was a young boy. Lady Singer was dressed in a lavender afternoon dress and Sir William wore an elaborately quilted dressing gown with slippers on his feet. Both smiled up at us, their faces maps of wrinkles and their hands dotted with age spots. Their white hair and their mannerisms told the story of a long relationship. It was obvious that Sir William was an invalid, with a bath chair parked outside in the hall. Lady Singer's mild eyes strayed often to her husband, her hand always ready to smooth his robe or tuck back a bit of wayward hair.

I recognized Sir William as the hero of Odessa Harbour in the Crimean War. As a Naval officer, he had assisted in the defense of the *HMS Furious* when it was shelled by Russian forces just outside the Dardanelles. Although wounded, he had continued at his post, and had also dragged three injured men to safety during the battle. Later he was knighted by the Queen and retired to Drinkwater Hall, where his family had resided for generations. I did quick calculations in my head. Sir William had to be nearly one-hundred years old, and his wife just a bit younger.

We were to learn that much of the estate had been sold off in the eighteenth century. The Singers had no children, but lived a quiet life, cared for by the faithful Strom, who managed a small group of servants.

"Welcome, Mr. Holmes, welcome," said the knight. "And Dr. Watson. You must excuse me for not rising. Age and my past have conspired to anchor me to my seat. I really fear my dancing days are behind me."

Sherlock Holmes smiled at Sir William's words as he greeted the knight and his lady. I followed his actions as Lady Singer waved us to chairs and rang a little bell on the low table before her. A moment later Strom entered, a loaded tea tray in his hands. He placed it on the table and left.

"We are just having our lunch," said Lady Singer. "We dine lightly at our age, but you are welcome to join us."

Both Holmes and I accepted a cup of tea. The tray was removed after a few minutes and Sir William became serious.

"You must understand why I called you here, Mr. Holmes. Your talents are well-known in this neighborhood, thanks to Dr. Watson, and news travels quickly in a small community. Early this morning, about seven o'clock, one of my men found Donald Woods' body on the bank under the ash trees. Woods is . . . was . . . my gamekeeper. He has been with us for over fifty years, coming to Drinkwater with his widowed father as a lad of ten when the father took up the position of gamekeeper. The estate has grown so small that the gamekeeper's position is less important than back in the day, but my people are loyal to me and I to them. I kept him on and he was very useful on the estate.

"I'm told his head was bashed in and a bloody tree limb lay next to his body. I called the police and I understand they are still down there. I asked for Scotland Yard's help. The Commissioner's grandfather was at school with me. An Inspector O'Reilly was sent at once. He has questioned me and my wife. Unfortunately we had little to tell him. Woods was last seen after supper last night by Strom, walking across the lawn to his quarters near the stables. He was known as a sober man, hard-working, who has not taken a vacation in years. His family, a sister and brother-in-law, live in Lancaster. Woods never married. Strom said he was tight with a dollar, which is better than being free with his money."

"What do you wish of me, Sir William?" Holmes inquired.

The old man stirred in his seat. "I used to be athletic, sir. I played Rugby when I was a youth, and cricket. I traveled the world in service to my country. But now I cannot do such things, and I need someone to go where I cannot go and do what I cannot do. Investigate this murder, Mr. Holmes, and report back to me. Find the killer of my employee. Do not allow me to leave this sphere with this uncertainty hanging over my head. My people are my family, Mr. Holmes, and it is my job to take care of my family." He looked at Holmes with a steady eye, his military bearing giving him a dignity one would not expect from a man sitting on a couch.

"I would be glad to look into this for you, sir," said my friend. "Since Inspector O'Reilly has done the groundwork, I shall start with him. Excuse us, Sir William." We bowed ourselves out, found Strom waiting in the hallway, and were directed to the Scotland Yard man.

We found him at the scene of the crime, a quarter-mile beyond the mansion beside the banks of the stream. The body was about to be taken up and moved to the local morgue. Inspector O'Reilly stood by the wagon, a short, slender man, nattily dressed in a city suit quite out of place in that rural landscape. His brown hair was thinning on top and a pair of round silver spectacles rode on his stubby nose. A sturdy sergeant, tall, broad, and silent, stood by his side. Inspector O'Reilly thrust out a hand.

"How do you do, Mr. Holmes? I am proud to meet you. You are almost a legend at the Yard. Inspector Lestrade speaks of you often, and of you, Dr. Watson. I was glad to hear that Sir William was going to ask for your advice. I have no hesitation in saying that I am baffled. No footprints on this hard ground, no witnesses, and the rough bark of that club yields no clues. All I can say with certainty is that Donald Woods is dead, his skull beaten in by that branch, recently ripped from the young ash tree over there. Splinters of wood were found embedded in his scalp and strands of hair and blood cling to the discarded weapon. Here, see for yourself"

The inspector led us over to a sheet-draped figure lying on the grass near the trout stream. He pulled back the cloth to disclose the battered head and upper torso of a man. Sir William had said that he was over sixty, and his white hair, now clotted with dried blood, confirmed that fact. Holmes asked for the sheet to be removed. Wood was huddled on his left side with his right hand thrown over his body and his left arm wedged beneath his side. The victim was dressed in worn tweeds, brown gaiters, and stout boots. Blood had dried on the features and the skull was battered and broken. Holmes knelt down and with his lens gave the body a thorough examination. He paid particular attention to the hands, boots, and the head wound. When he had finished, he turned to the murder weapon. It was a leafy limb with a thick base, the raw wood coated with blood and gore where it had been beaten against the gamekeeper's head.

"Watson," he murmured, and I also examined the body. As I rose to my feet I saw him at the ash tree, running his magnifying glass over the gash where fresh wood showed that the branch had been torn from the trunk.

"You are correct, Inspector. The ground is too hard to take foot marks. Yet here there are signs of a slight scuffle, and there in the grass are splashes of blood flung out by the attack. What did you find, Doctor?"

"Put simply, the right side of Wood's skull has been beaten repeatedly with that branch. Here are the ash splinters Inspector O'Reilly mentioned, and I see several strands of hair matching the victim's stuck in the blood of the limb. Hit on the right side of the head, I would conclude that the killer was a left-handed man."

"Thank you, Watson. I am always interested in your observations. However, by the splashes of blood on the grass here and here, and by the way his body fell, I believe the victim was attacked from behind by a right-handed person. Inspector O'Reilly, I would now like to see Wood's quarters."

Dismayed by Holmes's comment about my analysis of the case, I followed the two men and the constable to a tiny cottage set back in the trees on the other side of Sir William's mansion. It was a weathered building, plastered and with a shingled roof, surrounded by pheasant pens and rabbit hutches. Inside there were no signs of a woman's touch. The few bits of furniture were old and utilitarian. The rooms were cluttered with discarded clothing and old boots. Apparently Woods took all his meals at the servant's hall at the mansion. The only signs of organization were the neatly-kept guns and well-oiled traps of various sizes hung in up the second bedroom. Holmes poked around Woods' desk. He sifted through the old clothing and counted the number of bottles in the trash. He was inside for over an hour but emerged with a long face. He walked around the pens and checked the fences and cages but found nothing of interest.

Holmes bid goodbye to the inspector and we began our walk back to The Green Bush. He was silent as we left Drinkwater Hall behind us. Therefore I was surprised when, after we had walked nearly a mile, he paused on the path, leaned against a handy tree, and pulled out his pipe and tobacco pouch. He chuckled.

"What is so amusing, Holmes?" I demanded.

"How did you find the gamekeeper's cottage, Watson?" he drawled.

"It was a disorganized mess, Holmes. Hardly fit for human habitation at all."

"Yet there was one room where order and cleanliness reigned. One room where the tools of a man's trade were kept in excellent condition, ready to serve their purpose at a moment's notice."

"The second bedroom!"

"Exactly. Did you notice the small desk in the corner of that room?"

"Well, yes, but it was the display of guns and traps that drew my eye."

"Fortunately I have trained myself to look for the gold among the dross to which others are attracted. I searched that desk and found the ledgers and journals which make up a gamekeeper's working records. Several books held accounts, breeding records, and reports of the migration of various animals and birds across the estate. I also found these few pages, torn from a book, pressed in the back pages of one of the account books. The inspector glanced at them, decided they were unimportant, and allowed me to take them away."

Holmes drew three sheets of what appeared to be notepaper from his pocket and handed them to me. There were three typeset pages, torn and dirty, much folded and refolded, and with tears and holes on each sheet. There were hand-scrawled dates on each, and the contents referred to hawthorn trees. I looked at Holmes in confusion.

"What do these papers have to do with Woods' death?"

"That is what I plan to devote my evening to discovering. Let us go on our way. The sun is low, and I'm sure a good dinner awaits us at The Green Bush."

There seemed to be more excitement than usual as we entered the lobby of our lodging-place. Several guests were clustered around the admitting desk listening to Mr. Flagg, our host. He turned to us as we entered, his dark eyes glittering, and motioned us to approach.

"Here is Mr. Holmes now. He is sure to know. After all, Sir William sent for him himself. Mr. Holmes, is it true? Has Donald Woods been found murdered on Sir William's own doorstep?"

My friend was displeased at being so publicly questioned, so his normal stiff demeanor became even more reserved. "Donald Woods was found dead, Mr. Flagg, but not on the doorstep of Drinkwater Hall. You understand that, being called in to consult with Scotland Yard, I am not at liberty to comment on the case."

"Of course not, of course not," said Mr. Flagg with a twisted smile, "but I am a betting man, Mr. Holmes, and I am willing to wager that it was that Tom Fisher who had something to do with it."

"Who is he?" I asked.

"He is the local poacher, Dr. Watson, and as slippery a character as you are ever likely to meet. He came of good family, but his folks died when he was young and he took to the woods soon after. He lives here and there, said to have some shelters set up in the lands around Shottery and Stratford-Upon-Avon, and lives on the rabbits he can trap and the fish that he pulls out of other men's waters. He's had a running feud with Woods." His face was eager and wide-eyed as he waited for Holmes's response.

At this point, Holmes was handed a note by the ubiquitous young lad who had carried home our fishing gear. He glanced at it and then coldly announced to the whole lobby, "I am sorry, but I never comment on a case in which I am involved. Come, Watson, I see the dining room is open and I am hungry."

We took the table where we had eaten at the previous night and the crowd, seeing that they would learn no more from the renowned detective, went off to find their own dinners. The two trout that we had caught that morning were presented to us *a la* almondine, and I dug into my share. Holmes, for all his protestation of hunger, merely picked at his. Although strawberry shortcake was offered as the pudding, Holmes refused it and led me back up to our suite as soon as possible.

Night had fully fallen. Outside the windows, a sliver of moon hung behind the trees and darkness enveloped the view like a fog of black.

As soon as we stepped through the door, he handed me the note he had received in the lobby.

> *Anonymous source identifies Thomas Fisher, well-known poacher and troublemaker, as attacker in Woods' murder case. Please meet with me at 10 a.m. tomorrow morning at Drinkwater Hall to discuss plans on questioning same.*
>
> *O'Reilly*

"Well, that seems to wrap it all up, don't you think, Holmes? This poacher tangles with Donald Woods, probably about some game that Woods caught him making off with, and Fisher clubs him down, then disappears."

"It is precisely because I can think, Watson, that I find this easy explanation suspect. Who is the anonymous source? Are a few rabbits or a couple of fish enough to serve as a motive for murder? What about those odd pages we found in Woods' desk? They must be important, because Woods kept them so carefully. One was dated yesterday. No, there is more to be found that what information has been presented to us and the police. For a beginning, what about these pages concerning hawthorns?"

Holmes took the chair by the table and turned up the hanging gas lamp. I sat in the chair opposite him, my back to the window. He removed the pages from his notebook and examined them carefully with his magnifying glass.

"Nothing," he muttered. "Nothing! Confounded pages! The left sides show that all three have been ripped from a small book, the size to carry in one's pocket. Very handy for consultation in the field. Consecutive pages! My, my."

He ran his lens over each sheet, front and back. He held them up to the light. To my great surprise Holmes first smelled each page, then licked them one by one on both sides. At my expression of amazement he glanced at me, then smiled.

"A good detective must have many tools easy at hand, and ready to use them under unusual circumstances. I do not always have access to my supply of chemicals or the laboratory at St. Barts. Invisible inks have their own odors and tastes, as do poisons and other liquids. It behooves a detective to have extensive knowledge of such things. I once wrote a small monograph on the subject."

He stood and carefully held the sheets to the gas flame one after another. "Not lemon juice or milk, then," he said. He sat down and spread the three sheets out on the desk.

"Dated in pencil yesterday, two days before that and one week ago. Standard information on *Crataegus*, or hawthorn. Flowers, fruit, habitat, useful in hedges, found all over the Northern Hemisphere, and so on. Yet these must be important! Why, why? I am baffled, Watson. Sherlock Holmes baffled by three torn, filthy pages about hawthorns!" He slid back in his chair and stared at the mysterious papers with a disgusted look on his face.

I had seldom seen my friend so frustrated. I put it down to the exhaustion from which we were both suffering from our hard work on the Wholen Bucket case.

I picked up one of the pages from the desk and stared at it, hopelessly looking to see some fact the great detective had missed. Could I aspire to do such an impossible feat? Could I, in my ordinary, blundering way, find a clue that Holmes had missed, despite all the knowledge and experience he had accumulated in his career?

"These papers reminds me of Mr. Poe's story about 'The Purloined Letter'," I mused. "The letter in question turned out to be so dirty and torn that it was dismissed as unimportant, and therefore invisible to those searching for an important document."

Holmes slowly straightened in his chair. He turned to me and said, "Watson! Again you have pointed the way to light when all around me was darkness. I am really very, very grateful!"

I was flattered but bewildered. "I don't understand, Holmes. What did I say?"

Holmes had taken back the page I was holding and was arranging it with the other papers on the table. He again lifted each up to the light of the gas lamp. "The rips, smears, and holes disguise the true purpose of these pages. It is hard to see, but on certain letters on each line are tiny pinpricks. Write these down, Watson."

I scrambled for my notebook and pen as Sherlock Holmes began reciting letters from the page dated one week before. As he continued with the other pages a message slowly became clear.

Warning keep your nose out of my business or you will regret it.

Stop talking you will pay.

Meet me at bend in stream tonight midnight your place will make it worth your time.

"The bend in the stream was where Woods' body was found!" I cried. "Holmes, these warnings are most sinister!"

"Yes, the messages demonstrate a clear escalation of threats against the gamekeeper over the space of a week. One can deduce that Woods had some knowledge the murderer wanted kept secret. Woods was either talking about something illegal that he knew about, or he was planning to talk to the police or his employer, Sir William, about whatever it was."

"The last message sounds like the murderer wanted to pay Woods off in return for his silence."

"Yes," said Holmes. "Or it could be a way of luring Woods to a place where he could be attacked without witnesses."

My friend fell silent, still stretched out in his chair, hands resting on the tabletop, eyelids drooping, and his face aimed toward the balcony window behind me. I also sat quietly, so as to not disturb his thoughts, until I began to wonder at his immobility. When I opened my mouth to speak about it, he motioned toward me with a slight movement of one finger, and rose from his chair. He turned down the gaslight and sighed.

"It is late, Watson, and time all honest men were asleep. We will return to this problem in the morning. Good night to you."

He slipped his hand into his pocket as he turned away to his bedroom door. I was instantly on the alert. It was a simple little gesture he had used before, in a dangerous situation on another case, and I understood his meaning. I too rose and walked to my own room, but once inside I removed my coat, waited a few minutes, then doused my own light. I secured my revolver and stood behind the bedroom door. I held it open a crack and listened carefully.

At first there were no sounds in the sitting room or from Holmes's room beyond it. But after five minutes or so, there was a slight scrabbling on the tiny balcony that hung outside our sitting room. I heard the window sash being raised and a few faint noises from someone crawling in through the opening. There were soft footsteps, a match flared, and then I heard Sherlock Holmes's voice commanding the intruder to raise his hands.

Instantly I flung open the door and strode in, my weapon at the ready. Holmes had entered before me and was pressing the stem of his pipe into the back of a shabbily dressed man standing by the table with his hands up. In one hand a wooden match was still glowing. Holmes took it from the man's fingers and used it to light the lamp. I showed our visitor my very real revolver and searched him for weapons. Outside of a well-worn

357

hunting knife in a sheath at his belt, he was unarmed. I tossed the knife on the table and Holmes motioned him to one of the wooden chairs.

As he took his seat, I looked him over carefully. He was thin but wiry, his hands and face well-browned by exposure to the elements. He wore his brown hair long and shaggy, and he was dressed in a ragged old coat and crudely-patched trousers. His worn gray shirt had no collar, there were cracks and scrapes on his thick-soled shoes, and the battered old hat he twisted in his hands was simply unspeakable. His nose appeared odd, as if it had been flattened some years ago, and his eyes, green and sharp, betrayed an intelligent gleam as he stared back at us.

Holmes picked up the knife and examined it swiftly, the lens from his magnifying glass reflecting the flaring gaslight. When he was finished he flung it at the table where it stuck upright and quivering, the blade tip buried into the wood.

"To what do we owe the honour of this visit, Mr. Fisher?" he said, in a surprisingly mild voice.

"I've come to consult you," the brown man said. He blinked at the sound of his name but did not ask how Holmes knew.

"On what matter?"

"Why, on the murder of Donald Woods, sir."

"For which, I have been informed, the police suspect you."

"That is just it, Mr. Holmes. I didn't do it!" The flood gates opened. "I had nothing to do with it. I didn't like Donald Woods, it's true, I thought him a hard, tough old man, but I didn't kill him. His 'Sir William said this' and 'Sir William said that' was enough to drive a man to drink, but he was doing his job, I guess. It made a bit of fun to outsmart him and get away with the fat rabbit or pheasant on occasion, and he never knew how many fish saw my dinner plate and not Sir William's. No, it was not me that did for Donald Woods. Yet I am the hunted man, while the real murderer gets away."

"Where were you last night?"

"I cooked my dinner next to the Avon, on the west side of the river. I can show you the campsite. After that, I walked about a bit and spent an hour at the public house, The Rose and Thorn. I was asleep in my crib before eleven."

"Can you bring any witnesses to support your story?"

"Yes, a number of people at The Rose."

"After The Rose?"

"Well, none after that."

"You wish to consult me?"

"Aye. Everyone knows you two are here and that old Sir William called you in, along with that London copper. But I need you more. For them, it's the answer to a question. For myself it's the rope. I heard you pride yourself for standing up for justice and wouldn't let an innocent man go to the gallows. Prove me innocent, Mr. Holmes."

"You realize that it is most difficult to prove a negative, Mr. Fisher. To clear you, I would have to find the real killer. Sir William has already engaged me to do that. I cannot have two clients. Sir William is my client."

Fisher shifted his shrewd eyes from Holmes to me and back again. "I know that, sir. I want you to know that I didn't do it. But I have a suggestion. Have Dr. Watson here – " and he gave me an amused glance, " – spend some time with one of the hostesses at the As You Like It Club. He might come out with a few bits of information that a gentleman like yourself would never be told."

Holmes's lips turned up a bit at the corners at this suggestion and I felt my face getting red. "Holmes," I said sternly, "this man is a murder suspect. Shall I send for Inspector O'Reilly?"

The poacher was halfway to the window, his blade in his sheath, before I finished my sentence. Holmes raised his hand. "I don't believe our business is concluded, Mr. Fisher. As I said, I already have a client. However, I also don't believe you attacked Donald Woods. Therefore, I can treat you as a source of information rather than a suspect."

"How can you decide that, Holmes?" I said. "He sneaked in here and he is armed!"

"With a knife, Watson, not a tree branch. If an attacker possesses a knife, would he choose to use another weapon, one that takes time and effort to prepare for use? There were no signs of blade work on either the young ash tree or the limb ripped from it. The dead man had not been stabbed. I believe our friend here. Are there any other leads that you can give us, Mr. Fisher?"

"Not now, Mr. Holmes. I'll keep my ear to the ground. Goodbye, Dr. Watson. Ask for Muriel. She's a real chatterbox." With a wave and another grin, Fisher was out the window and enveloped by the darkness of the night before I could stand up.

Holmes then explained to me that earlier over my shoulder he had seen faint movement on the balcony outside which had prompted him to set the trap that caught our intruder. Finally, I was allowed to take to my bed just a few hours before dawn.

The next morning we met with Inspector O'Reilly on the steps outside Drinkwater Hall. Holmes informed the Scotland Yard man the details of his interview with Thomas Fisher the evening before. O'Reilly showed Holmes the smudged note accusing Fisher that had been shoved under the door at the local police station. Holmes examined it with his lens.

359

Aside from the note being written in block letters with a dull pencil on a scrap of paper torn from the back of an old envelope with no other markings, he could find nothing. Leaving the huge constable to guard the steps to the mansion, we went in and were shown by Strom to Sir William Singer. He was in the sitting room alone, explaining that his wife was upstairs with a headache. He was able to tell us little more about his gamekeeper, Donald Woods. At last, Holmes asked him who were Woods' friends.

"As far as I knew, Strom was the man closest to Woods," said Sir William. "I would suggest that you talk to him next."

Holmes decided not to do that in the presence of the butler's employer. We found Strom in his room in the back of the house. The tall, thin man sat impassively as the questioning began.

"How long have you worked for Sir William?"

"I was first hired nearly twenty-five years ago as his steward. He had managed his own estate before that, but his health finally demanded that he get help. After a few years, Zale, the old butler, died, and he asked me to take over his duties. As you can see, the estate is not that extensive, so I agreed."

"How large is the staff?"

"The inside staff consists of myself, the cook and housekeeper, Mrs. Smith, Rosie and Maggie, two housemaids that come in from town daily, Maggie's younger sister June, who acts as scullery maid, Brenton and Andrews, two men that serve in the mansion and do work outside, a stable man named Timothy and his young son who helps him, Woods as gamekeeper, and old Blake, who is head groundskeeper. Blake suffers from arthritis and rarely leaves his armchair these days, but he has a great memory, knows every inch of the estate, and instructs Brenton and Andrews about work that needs to be done."

Inspector O'Reilly made note of the names. "I'll arrange interviews for all those people later today," he murmured.

Holmes concentrated on Strom. "Donald Woods was here when you first arrived."

"That is correct."

"What sort of man was he?"

Bertram Strom fiddled with the salt-and-pepper pots on the table before him. "Dour. He was faithful to his duties, but seemed to have little joy in his life. As steward, I worked closely with him. He was village-educated, knew a great deal about the animals, birds, and fish in the area, and could name every tree on the estate. But he never married, seemingly talked to no one but old Blake and me, and had no family around here. He idolized Sir William and his wife, always speaking of them with great reverence and respect." Strom kept his eyes focused on the landscape outside the window, as if he was trying to recall details of a man's life that were already fading from his memory.

"Did he attend church?"

"No. Most of the help are members of the Church of England and attend services with Sir William and Lady Singer every Sunday. Woods would disappear Saturday nights and not be seen again until Monday mornings at breakfast in the servants' hall."

"Interesting. Did he mention where he went Saturday nights?"

"Never. His demeanor was such that it was not the sort of question that anyone felt comfortable asking him."

"Do you have any ideas about places Woods would visit on his time off?" asked Sherlock Holmes.

"None."

"Tell of the last day you saw him."

"That would have been Saturday. Today is Monday. He ate breakfast at the servants' hall. I asked him what he planned on for the day, and he told me he was going to check some rabbit warrens near the stream a mile up from the mansion. Later that evening, he ate supper with us, and I watched as he walked out the servants' entrance and made his way toward his house. That is the last time any of us saw him alive."

"Mr. Strom, I want you to gather all of the servants and bring them to the kitchen. Inspector O'Reilly, with your permission, I would like to sit in while you question them."

"Of course, Mr. Holmes." The butler nodded and left the room.

"I'll come with you," I said.

"That isn't necessary. The constable can take notes. I have another task for you. I want you to investigate how Woods spent his time off from work. Canvass both Stratford-Upon-Avon and Shottery. No shop is too humble, no church is too grand. Question everyone. At the railway station, inquire as to anyone who has arrived and departed in the last forty-eight hours."

Sir William's carriage took me to the station, where I tracked down the official in charge, a short, peppery man in his fifties, ex-military, and punctilious to his duties.

I established my credentials and, it being between trains, he took me back to his private office and offered me tea.

"Helping Sir William and Scotland Yard with Donald Woods' death, eh? Well, sir, I am glad to be of assistance. Passengers in and out of this station for the last two days? Why, man, that's impossible without a detailed description! This is the summer season! Hundreds pass through every week. Some are daytrippers, some come for a month, others for a few days, like Mr. Holmes and yourself."

"Well, can you at least tell me if Donald Woods was a customer of yours? Was he ever in the habit of taking the train to another town or city on Saturdays or Sundays?"

The stationmaster was thoughtful. He had seen Woods many times over the years, particularly when he came to the station to pick up shipments relating to his job on the Drinkwater estate. He couldn't remember the gamekeeper ever buying a ticket to another destination in all those years, much less every Saturday or Sunday.

I thanked him for his time and stood on the platform for a few minutes, smoking a cigarette. I was perplexed. If the murderer came on the railway from another location, it was impossible to trace him through the station. Each passenger carried a ticket, but those were turned in after the passenger left the carriages. No ticket carried a name, only a number, and since the tickets were usually paid for in cash, there was no way to track the purchases. Woods, the stationmaster insisted, had never left the area by rail. How then, indeed, had he spent his hours away from Drinkwater Hall? Did the answer lay in the people and buildings on the High Street before me? I was in Stratford. Could the answer be in Shottery?

Clearly I had a long day before me. Rather than march into every shop, restaurant, and public house available and announce my purpose, I decided to be more subtle. I would pose as a customer and deftly extract information from the clerks and serving staff of each establishment. I could see no flaw in this plan, so I started with the small restaurant next to the station.

The small eating place proved of no help. No one knew Donald Wood or had ever served him. The results remained the same all down the High Street. I methodically stepped into each place and asked about the weather, their goods, and finally about the Drinkwater Hall gamekeeper. Despite purchases of cups of tea, sweets, tobacco, and even measures of lace, a pamphlet on the beauties of the River Avon, and other things useless to me, although some might be utilized by Mrs. Hudson, I learned nothing. I was perplexed. Holmes made it look so easy. He could walk into any public house in the land and leave with enough facts to write a history of the locals, including their great-grandparents and every dog and cat in the area. I would leave with only the taste of the local beer in my mouth.

Perhaps my plan would work better in Shottery. It was a pleasant stroll through leafy paths to that village so close to Stratford-Upon-Avon. On the High Street I realized how hungry I had become and stopped in the first restaurant I saw. It was called the "Falstaff Arms" and advertised a hot lunch and friendly service.

362

The house stew was hot and even tasty. The service was friendly, personified by the perky red-headed waitress who brought me my meal and coffee. Since it was after the normal luncheon hour, the dining room was empty except for the two of us. She gave me a smile when I expressed surprise on her employment in such a small town. Surely she was made for more than dishes and scrubbing flagstone floors?

"Thank you, sir, but I am quite happy here. My father is the owner and my betrothed is a young farmer from just outside of town. Oh, but I do see all sorts of people, sir. Lots come here interested in William Shakespeare or Anne Hathaway. I imagine you are one yourself, sir."

She laid a serving of warm sliced homemade bread next to my plate. She was so young and pretty. Her answer to my next question caught me by surprise.

"Why, yes, sir, I did see Mr. Woods frequently. I was sorry to hear of the murder. My Harold doesn't like me to speak of it, sir, being that I am a respectable girl and engaged, but Mr. Woods used to come in here every Sunday night and get his dinner, rather late. He didn't drink much here, but I believe he always had his fill and more before he showed up. He would try to give me a squeeze or snatch a kiss, but I am a respectable girl, sir, and he never succeeded."

"What did your young man think of that?"

"Oh, he was not very pleased, sir, as you might imagine. The last time I told him about it, he offered to punch Mr. Woods' eye if he ever met him on the street."

"When was that, may I ask?"

"Let's see, it must have been a week ago, sir. Yes, a week ago exactly. I wasn't working here this past Sunday because my aunt had invited me to go to Cambridge on Saturday to select my wedding dress as her gift to me. She married a professor at St. John's College and has always been fond of me, sir."

"How did your fiancé spend his time while you were gone?"

"Oh, he had plenty to do on the farm, sir. When we got engaged he told me, 'Kate, you must understand, on a farm there are always plenty of chores. What with the animals and the sowing and the harvest and the upkeep on the buildings and fences, there is always plenty of work.' I laughed and said, 'Oh, Harold, I'm not afraid of hard work. I've worked in The Falstaff since I was a little girl and learned everything about running a house from my mother. You'll be getting a willing helpmate when we are married, Harold Prince!'"

"Was anyone helping him last weekend?"

"Yes. The hired man was with him, fixing the stone wall and working with the animals. Some of the cows got out and into the corn and they had to chase them back and repair the damage. Harold said they worked all afternoon and into the night."

I sipped my newly-filled coffee cup and sat in thought. It sounded as if while Harold was upset about Donald Woods annoying his girl, he wasn't upset enough to kill him. Plus, he had spent the entire day doing hard physical work on the farm. Would he have been energetic enough after all that to trek out to Drinkwater Hall and beat the gamekeeper to death with a tree branch? As a farmer, he would know of the hawthorn tree and all its uses. Kate was an attractive young woman. Had she told me the entire story about Donald Woods and herself? Had she told Harold?

Another customer walked in the door. Kate turned to show him to a table and I managed to ask one last question. "Did Donald Woods ever talk about how he spent his free time away from Drinkwater Hall?"

"No, I'm sorry. I think he must have had a lady friend, though. He did mention someone named Honoria."

With that she was gone. I finished my coffee and went out to continue my mission.

I started down Shottery's High Street, using the same plan I had used in Stratford-Upon-Avon. Again I accumulated a varied collection of items, including more tobacco, a card of buttons, a packet of tacks, and two different booklets about Anne Hathaway's cottage. By the late afternoon I had worked my way down to the edge of town and stood before the door of The Rose and Thorn.

I was reaching for the handle when a strong, thin hand grabbed my wrist and restrained me. I looked up in astonishment to find Sherlock Holmes at my side, pulling me back. He spun me around, matched me across the cobblestone street, and into an alley that led away from the shabby public house.

I started to protest such treatment, but Holmes shushed me and hurried me onward until we were well away from the town and strolling down a path through a meadow in the direction of The Green Bush. I recognized the place as the path we had taken after exploring Shottery the first evening we had arrived.

"I think we have missed tea," he finally said. "But we shall have plenty of time to get ready for dinner."

"Holmes! You startled me!"

He smiled and pulled out his pipe. We were walking down the gravel path, rich pasturage around us and some dull-eyed sheep staring from a small knoll close by. Wisps of raw wool, pulled from their coats, fluttered on a few prickly plants near the path. Overhead the sky sported some low clouds and the light was slowly fading as the sun neared the horizon.

"What have you discovered during your little walk?" asked Holmes.

364

Little walk, indeed! I had tramped up and down the High Streets of two towns in a vain effort to discover how Donald Woods spent his day off work. I decided to give Holmes a full report, putting in every little detail I could remember, including the conversation with the waitress Kate at The Falstaff Arms, and every mention she made about her fiancé, Harold. I would overwhelmed him with each boring fact available.

Unfortunately for my feelings, he didn't appear bored at all. He listened quietly to my report and even asked a few questions about Harold. By the time we approached the porch of The Green Bush, I was torn between irritation at his calm attitude and flattery at the close attention he was giving me.

"How was your day?" I finally asked, a touch sarcastically.

"Interviewing the servants was not very productive, I fear. I did discover one lead with promise. I must admit your efforts have been most useful to our case. Now I suggest we get an early dinner and a little rest. We have a big night before us."

"Whatever do you mean?'

"Later. It will all keep until after dark."

Holmes had the bad habit, as I saw it, of never explaining his plans during the course of solving a case. I knew it was futile to continue asking questions. My feet hurt from all the walking that I'd done, and actually an early dinner was attractive. There was baked chicken for dinner, and cake.

But it was not to happen that night. We got a pleasant surprise after we returned to the guest house. Mr. Flagg handed over an envelope bearing the monogram of Sir William Singer. He watched with snappy little black eyes as Holmes opened it. We had been invited to dinner that evening at Drinkwater Hall. The carriage would be sent. Holmes sent back his compliments and accepted for both of us.

We were the only guests. The meal was expertly served by Strom. When Sir William asked about the case, Holmes replied that he never explained during the progression of his cases, only at the conclusion. He did entertain Sir William and Lady Singer with stories of previous investigations, including the Bobby Shafto disappearance and the Doctor Faustus's Dancing School scandal. Sir William and Lady Singer loved listening to Holmes's stories.

After dinner, our hosts took us on a tour of the Main Gallery. It was a long handsome hall with a parquet floor and lofty ceilings. Hung along the walls were tier after tier of family portraits and paintings of royalty and nobility, dating back generations. They were all done by the fashionable artists of their times. Finally we stopped before a detailed oil of Sir William, painted in his younger years, wearing his military uniform and medals. When I commented on how life-like it was, Sir William grinned broadly and said, "You compliment my wife, Dr. Watson."

"You painted this portrait, Lady Singer? It is wonderful," said I.

"I had a talented governess who taught me well. I have sketchbook after sketchbook filled with little studies in charcoal and watercolors. I went through a phase of oil painting many years ago. I suggested that Sir William pose for me as my gift to him for our anniversary. He agreed and then insisted that it be hung in the Gallery. I have always wondered if I should have chosen a darker background colour . . . ."

"Nonsense! It is perfect just the way it is," said Sir William. He leaned out of his bath chair and reached for her hand. They smiled at each other and I felt a pang that such a perfect decades-long love should still exist in such a troubled world as ours.

Our night was not over. We arrived back at The Green Bush in Sir William's carriage by eleven o'clock. Instead of going to bed, Holmes told me to change to my fishing clothes while he did the same. Then he led me away from our guest house along the path to Shottery. The sky was clear and there was enough starlight to get along without a lantern. Holmes had excellent eyesight and guided me through the darkness. It was just before midnight when we both approached the front door of the closed Rose and Thorn. It was locked and the building appeared deserted.

The street was empty, and the windows of the public house black behind the limp and dirty curtains. Faint streetlamps glowed from down at the cross street. Holmes stood poised on the steps, his impassive face held high, as if he were sniffing the air. He left the front and started to circle the building. It was a one-story brick detached construction with windows at shoulder height. On the sides were other windows low to the foundation, nearly covered with rank weeds. No light emanated from them and, upon closer inspection, I could see there were dark curtains hung behind the glass.

The alley behind The Rose and Thorn was narrow. The blank backs of old buildings looked down on us. It was obvious that most of them were either warehouses or abandoned. A back door was secured tightly. Holmes knelt at the lock and pulled out a set of pick locks from his coat.

Suddenly I heard footsteps coming up the street. A light flashed down the gap between the pub and the building to our right. We froze. A man's voice called out and was answered by another from our left. After a few minutes it was clear that the two old friends were not going to move from the front steps of The Rose and Thorn. From their conversation, it was easy to deduce that one had a bottle. They sat on the steps to share the contents.

To continue on our mission was futile. We could be discovered at any minute. Holmes motioned silently and we picked our way down the alley toward the path that led back to The Green Bush.

Less than half-an-hour later, we were back in our suite. Without explaining anything, Holmes retired to his room. I also went directly to my room. I thought about ordering a pan of hot water for my feet, but the house was silent, all the occupants having gone to bed. I was reluctant to awaken anyone, so I went to bed myself.

By breakfast I had several questions and I was not in a mood to be denied answers.

I attacked my morning egg while Holmes spread marmalade on his toast. He munched away calmly as I gathered my courage to question him.

"Holmes," said I, "I think I deserve some explanation for last night."

"Do you?"

"Yes. To begin, I hope all the work I put in going door to door gathering information for you yesterday was helpful."

"Very helpful. Thank you, Watson."

I waited for him to elaborate. He didn't. I persisted.

"Why did you prevent me from canvasing The Rose and Thorn?"

"I didn't want you to become known to the denizens of that establishment at that time. My own investigations had shown that The Rose and Thorn is the front for another, more shady business, the As You Like It Club."

"The house of ill-repute mentioned by Thomas Fisher!" I cried.

"Yes, and also mentioned by our host, Mr. Hyram Flagg. Discreet inquiries of the older men in Sir William's employment led me to believe that Donald Woods frequently visited the club. In fact, he had become a regular guest during his days off. I determined that an excursion to the place would be edifying. Our dinner at Drinkwater Hall last night extended the evening into my timeline. I had been told the pub was closed only one night a week – last night. That would have been the best time to examine the premises and perhaps get a look at the books. We could confirm Woods' involvement and perhaps even establish the reason for his murder."

"The waitress at The Falstaff Arms spoke of a possible romantic interest, a woman called Honoria."

"That is a very valuable piece of information. Honoria was one of the names given as a soiled dove working at the club. Unfortunately, we were interrupted last night. We'll have to infiltrate the place in another fashion."

"What other fashion?" I asked.

Holmes sipped his coffee and ignored my question. "Inspector O'Reilly has gone back to London, but will return at a moment's notice. I must send him a coded message this morning, letting him know of our adventure last night. My investigation isn't yet complete, so we'll resume our fishing so as to throw off suspicion by the murderer."

We did just that. By the early afternoon, Holmes and I were back in our vacation pose. That day and the next, we spent all our time tramping up and down the stream where we had caught our first fishes. Each time we returned to The Green Bush, our landlord greeted us warmly, but I could feel him following our movements with his sharp eyes. The excitement of Donald Woods' death died down as Scotland Yard let it be known that they believed the murder was done by a passing stranger.

Thursday was the day of Donald Woods' funeral. We were picked up by the Drinkwater Hall carriage and attended with Strom as Drinkwater Hall's representatives. Afterwards, we were invited back to have dinner with Sir William and his wife.

Again the meal was delicious. Afterwards, Sir William suggested another tour, this time of the Drinkwater Hall library.

It was a large room, lined with oak bookcases and cabinets containing curios and rare manuscripts. The books were obviously the loving labour of generations, ranging from an ancient hand-illustrated Bible from an Irish monastery to a shelf of the latest mysteries that Lady Singer confessed she read aloud to Sir William in the evenings. There were some volumes bound in limp red Morocco leather. Others were hardbound with stamped covers and touches of gilt. Long shelves of volumes were devoted to British war histories, the law, architecture, public and domestic health, popular novels of the last century, classic plays, agriculture, and nature.

In that section there was a series of six small books with blue pasteboard covers, sized to fit in one's pocket. Holmes picked up one and flipped the pages casually. I glimpsed the title, *Nature's Gifts*, Volume Two.

"Sir William, these little books seem an odd addition to this magnificent collection. Did you purchase them?"

The knight turned the pages of another of the little books. "Yes, I remember. There was a door-to-door salesman. He told me he had knocked on every door in three counties around. I examined them, found the information sound and well-written. I ordered a set. I know that Strom ordered a set, and some other people in the area also ordered them."

"Do you know if Donald Woods ordered them?"

"I do not."

"What other books have you added to this wonderful collection?"

Sir William, with prompting from his wife, proceeded to pull out volumes and tell Holmes little stories about their acquisitions: A bargain here, a lucky find there, a presentation copy from the author, a gift from an old shipmate. Holmes seemed to be listening closely, but from long experience I could tell he was not. Instead, his mind was working on another level. Something had clicked a piece into the puzzle he was assembling, and he was endeavoring to understand its significance. Finally Sir William and Lady Singer bid us farewell and, in the carriage riding back to The Green Bush, Holmes sat quietly, his fingertips pressed together and his thick brows drawn together over his gray eyes.

Holmes wasn't there in the morning for breakfast, having gone out an hour before I awoke. The skies outside our window were crowded with dark grey clouds. The wind had picked up and the trees were rustling loudly, promising a storm. I decided to stay in our suite to wait rather than tramp out into the countryside. My friend came back in the middle of the morning and paced the sitting room as I lounged in an armchair, a yellow-back novel I had brought from London in my hand.

"Today is Friday, Watson. I believe that this case could be wrapped up by tomorrow morning, just in time for us to catch our train home."

"Where did you go so early this morning?"

"I went back to Drinkwater Hall. I'm sure that you noticed my interest in that little set of books in Sir William's library. Paging through the one on trees, I saw that the relevant pages of *Nature's Gifts* matched the pages sent to Donald Woods as threats. They didn't come from that book, of course. Its pages were intact. Further investigation was necessary. Thus I rose early this morning and hiked over to Sir William's. I didn't remember seeing those books in Woods' house. I looked again. The set wasn't there, and there were no signs of it ever having been there.

"I called on Strom and was invited to breakfast. I told him I was doing one last saunter around the neighborhood before leaving tomorrow. During the meal, I was able to examine his bookcase and determined that he did indeed have a set of the books. I found all the pages of the relevant volume were intact. His books were not involved in this murder."

"So that clue is worthless."

"I wouldn't say that yet. I have more investigating to do. Do you have any plans for dinner?"

I was surprised by the question. Holmes didn't normally concern himself with food in the middle of a case. "Dinner? I thought we were eating here at The Green Bush."

"No. I am bored with their cuisine. I think we'll eat in Shottery instead. The threatened storm is about to break. Today is a good day to stay inside with a book."

A few minutes later, a cloudburst settled the question. The rain came down in sheets and coated the window panes. Holmes went into his room.

I sat, irresolute, wondering if he was lured there by the small morocco case and the little bottle hidden in his valise. I couldn't open the door and ask him what he was doing. That was not the action of a gentleman or a friend. Yet how could I just sit here, my mind teeming with visions of him pulling out the case, holding up the vial, adjusting the minuscule plunger?

I was about to jump to my feet, to do what I knew not, when the door opened and Sherlock Holmes stepped out.

"Watson, this rain has made me restless. I need something to read. I was not as fore-sighted as you were to bring a book or two."

I looked into his eyes and saw no sign of the demon. Holmes left to visit the reading room downstairs, urging me to stay where I was. I didn't listen. I made a brief search of his valise, found his case and bottle undisturbed, and went back to my book. The muted sounds of the rain outside provided a calm background to the absorbing story I was reading.

I didn't notice how much time passed until Holmes returned, carrying a couple of books in his hand. Instead of joining me in the sitting room, he went back into his own room and firmly shut the door. At lunch he came out and we took our meal in the small glassed-in porch just off the main dining room. The rain was coming down more moderately now, but the skies were overcast, and all outside was wet.

My friend had something on his mind, for he spoke little and picked at his food. After the waiter had brought our coffee and the last of the other diners had left the room, he turned to me with a wry twist to his mouth.

"I suggest, my dear Watson, that you take a nap this afternoon, for the investigation bids fair to keep us out late."

"What do you mean?"

"We'll leave here at eight o'clock tonight. We're going out for dinner. I've ordered the trap that met us at the rail station. On the way to our destination I will explain all."

That was all I could get out of him. I've mentioned Holmes's exasperating habit of never disclosing his plans beforehand, for the man loved drama and lived to astonish friend and foe alike. After several attempts to get him to talk, I gave up and followed his advice.

By eight o'clock, our trap arrived and the young lad stood outside in the slop, holding the horse's head. We came out onto the front porch. I had dressed in what passed for my best clothing and Holmes was garbed the same. The horse trotted along for a few minutes, but as soon as we were well away from The Green Bush, Holmes called to the driver and the trap pulled off the road and into a copse of concealing trees.

Sherlock Holmes spoke softly so that the driver couldn't hear us.

"My search for reading material today bore welcomed fruit. I checked The Green Bush reading room for a set of *Nature's Gifts* and found it." He pulled volume two out of his pocket and opened it. "See here. Three pages have been ripped from the relevant chapter. Note the ragged edges of the missing pages between the leaves."

"What does it mean?"

"It means our host is involved in some fashion with the blackmail of Donald Woods. As for the murder, we must have more information. But I cannot discover that information without your help."

"I'm always happy to serve."

"Excellent! I knew you would not falter. Tonight, you will visit the As You Like It Club."

I sat silently. What was there to say? I found the task distasteful, but if it was necessary to solving the case then my duty was clear. Holmes briefly explained what he required of me and told the driver to continue on.

The trap dropped Holmes off two blocks away from The Rose and Thorn. I was delivered in solitary grandeur to the front door. As I entered the public house, I was surprised by the decor. Somehow I had anticipated something lush and vaguely erotic. Instead, I saw the ordinary walls and seatings of an old English pub. There were few patrons in the dim yellow light. Scuffed furniture, plastered surroundings, a soot-blacken stone fireplace, and a small curved bar guarding a rack of brandies and wine faced me. Behind the bar, a door with a frosted glass window interrupted the row of bottles. A tall whipcord of a man sporting a twisted nose stood there, running a cloth over the surface. He asked me what I would have.

I ordered a beer. He bent down to draw it from a cask beneath the bar top. As he placed it before me, I leaned forward and said the phrase Holmes had given me: "I see this drink is just as I like it."

He gave me a wink from his heavy-lidded eye. He removed the glass of beer. Then he came out from behind the bar and led me gently by the elbow to a door on the right of the fireplace. He nodded to one of the loungers sitting by the bar and the man nodded back. When he opened the door, I saw stairs going down into darkness. I hesitated, but he urged me forward. Together we stumbled down the steps and along a black corridor. In a few seconds we were mounting another set of steps. When the handle of the door at the top was turned and the gap widened, it was as if a jewel box had been opened.

The large room was brightly lit by electric lamps. Overhead were two elaborate chandeliers, hung with crystals and glowing with white bulbs. The ceiling and the walls were draped in red velvet. Scattered over the parquet floor were lavender overstuffed chairs, little tables, blue chaise lounges, chintz sofas, and many, many thick soft cushions. In one corner was a gilded iron spiral staircase that led to the upper floor and in another

371

was a fully-equipped bar. Next to that was a player piano. Everywhere were flashes of gold and silver. The air was thick with incense. Yet all that paled before the other feature that came into focus as my eyes adjusted from the darkness of the passageway.

There were women there. Thomas Fisher had referred to them as "hostesses", but these were like no other hostesses I had ever met. They were wearing very little clothing. Their bare arms and legs gleamed soft pink in the overhead lights. I counted at least three of them, draped over the furniture and standing in provocative poses by the bar. I saw feathers and flashes of white satin and black or red lace. There was no safe place to look. I stood stock still, trying to hide my discomfort. One of the women, younger than me and heavily painted, detached herself from the others and approached me.

"Hello," she said brightly. "My name is Muriel. What's yours?"

"John," I replied. She was very close to me and her breath was sweet. A soft hand tugged on my sleeve and I found myself sitting in one of the armchairs with Muriel on my lap. She was blonde and wearing what appeared to be a short black-lace satin shift and pink feathered mules. The neckline was cut very low and I could see her rounded breasts through the thin material. She giggled and wriggled, and asked me if I didn't want to buy her a drink.

My purpose there was to divert the inhabitants and buy Sherlock Holmes time. I motioned to the tall man and asked Muriel what she would like.

"I only drink champagne, love," she said, stroking my cheek with a manicured nail. The man stepped behind the bar and produced a bottle and two glasses.

I felt something was expected of me, so I took her hand and squeezed it. She responded with another giggle and snuggled into my arms. Then she straightened up and accepted the glasses. She barely sipped at her own, but insisted on feeding me the entire contents of mine It was refilled and the bottle was left on a convenient table by the chair.

I must admit that all her moving around in the chair was having an effect on me. Desperately I tried to think of some way to get her off of my lap. Unfortunately she mistook my efforts as eagerness on my part and began to whisper in my ear of all the delights I could find up the spiral stairs as she fiddled with my tie and ruffled my hair.

I was given more champagne. The bottle was drained and another one ordered. Finally she slid off my lap and I was drawn to my feet. Before I could understand what was happening my foot was on the lowest step of the stair and she was guiding me upwards.

I couldn't resist or make a disturbance because the owner was watching me. I fumbled my way up a few more steps, Muriel delightfully encouraging me, and then salvation came with the distant cry of "Fire!"

The door by which the owner and I had entered burst open and the man who had been sitting by the bar popped in, his face a mask of urgency. "Frank! There's a fire in the bar!" As if to prove his words, a thick wisp of smoke swirled past him into the room from the passageway behind.

Instantly the others in the room ran for a tapestry hung behind the piano. I followed. Shoving the instrument aside and tearing down the wall-hanging revealed a door. The tall man flung it open and we all tumbled out into a dirty alley. We had been in one of the seemingly abandoned warehouses situated in the street behind The Rose and Thorn.

To my amazement, two other women ran out behind me, followed by two men. One was a beardless youth who took to his heels down the street and vanished into the night. The other man was fat and came out pulling on a coat, his tie flung over his shoulder. He was shoeless and his trouser braces were swinging around his hips. When he turned away from the rather overweight woman who came out with him, I saw his face.

At that instant, my arm was seized in an official grip. Everyone who had escaped from the building except for the beardless young man found themselves in the unyielding custody of the local constabulary. Inspector O'Reilly, his sergeant and one of his constables were there, too, so Scotland Yard was well-represented.

"The fire! My bar!" cried the tall man as he struggled to escape the law's clutches.

"Don't worry," said a familiar voice. "A small fire in the office in a metal wastebasket and a couple added smoke bombs create a very effective illusion. The important papers, like the double set of books and the daily work journals, are quite safe.

"Easy, Officer, if you please! That is Doctor Watson and despite his untidy hair and disorderly appearance, he is on our side. Are you all right, old man?" At my nod, Holmes turned to the last man out the door.

"I thought I would find you here, Mr. Flagg!"

Indeed, it was our host of The Green Bush. He was hastily rearranging his clothing while glaring at Holmes and the police officers. He looked almost comical, with his shirt half-tucked into his pants and his bare toes digging into the dirt of the alley cobblestones. But his black eyes were mean and the scowl on his face twisted his round red cheeks into a caricature of his normal smiling face.

The woman who had come out with him was trying to keep her flimsy robe on her shoulders. Even under the lights of the police's torches, clear evidence of multiple bruises and scratches on her smooth pink skin, especially her neck and arms, was visible.

"Your name is Honoria," declared Holmes.

"That's right, ducky," she said. "And who are you?"

"My name is Sherlock Holmes," he responded. "As you see, your co-workers and your . . . ah . . . *employer* are about to be put up on charges relating to this house. Everything about it will become known. If you and these other ladies will answer our questions, I'll use my influence with the local authorities and Scotland Yard to lessen charges raised against you. Rest assured, however, that Mr. Potter here and his lackey are not included in this offer."

Honoria gave Holmes a shrewd look. She looked to the other women, who all looked frightened, and then to the tall man called Potter. He gave her a fierce scowl and shook his head. She glanced at Hyram Flagg who had balled up both fists. He tried to take a step toward her but was yanked back by the big Scotland Yard sergeant who held his arms. The formerly affable host of The Green Bush now looked as if he could tear her apart like a sheet of paper.

She spat at both men. "You shouldn't have tried to cheat me, Frank. I know you've been pocketing the girls' tips and skimming off the top." The tall man turned white. "I've got plenty on Mr. Frank Potter and I'll be glad to tell it to the coppers, Mr. Holmes. That pal of his there was assigned to keep us in line and not go to the authorities. He had some pretty crude methods to insure our obedience.

"As for you, Hyram Flagg, if all is to become known, then I will get my revenge. He beat me every time, Mr. Holmes, and never listened to my cries for mercy. Frank let him do it because he paid so well. Donald Woods was one of my regulars. When that poor, sweet, lonely man found out, objected, and said he would tell his wife, Flagg attacked him with a tree branch. He bragged about it to me three days ago and said he would do the same to me if I ever grassed."

Flagg called her a filthy name and broke away from the policeman. He lunged at her, his fingers clawing at her throat, yelling he would kill her. It took three of us to bring him to the cobblestones and two policemen to put shackles on him, Honoria screamed that she would tell all and encouraged the other women to do the same. Holmes stood over him when he was finally secured, and held the blue-backed volume two of *Nature's Gifts* aloft triumphantly.

"You left a wide trail, Mr. Flagg, and tonight has supplied the final bits of information I needed. Inspector O'Reilly, I think this is now your concern. I'm satisfied, however, that the person accused, Thomas Fisher, had nothing to do with Donald Woods' murder."

At that we heard a whoop and looked up to see the scarecrow figure of Thomas Fisher waving at us from a rooftop across the alley. Obviously he had heard his vindication from Sherlock Holmes and was gesturing enthusiastically. I saw him take a step backwards and with a final happy shout he disappeared.

O'Reilly stepped forward and gave Hyram Flagg the usual cautions. The Scotland Yard sergeant and the constable hustled him away. The women were taken away to get their statements, Muriel already giving great indications of Thomas Fisher's prediction for talking. Frank Potter and his cohort were arrested and left to the tender mercies of the local police. The local fire brigade arrived and, as they tended to the dousing of the small fire, the inspector turned to my friend.

"That was a good night's work, if you ask me." he said. "When I got your wire, Mr. Holmes, I dropped everything to catch the next train. Sir William put us up when I was here before and he offered me a room anytime I needed it. Even though it is late, Strom will let us in."

Strom did welcome us. He ushered us to Sir William's sitting room. O'Reilly requested a drop of his employer's brandy as a nightcap, and as Strom poured out the portions the doors opened and Sir William rolled in, clad in pajamas and his robe, a maid pushing the bath chair and his hastily dressed wife behind him

"I couldn't miss all the excitement!" said our client. Strom got them settled and gave them their share of the refreshments. I simply toyed with mine, for I was still feeling the effects of all the champagne I had been forced to drink earlier. Sherlock Holmes stood in his favorite pose before the fireplace, filled his pipe with Lady Singer's permission, and when he had it drawing properly, began his report.

"When we were called in to this case, I saw at once that it wasn't going to be easy to solve. I had no equipment here, I didn't know the local scene, and Donald Woods seemed to be a man so devoted to his work as to have little or no private life. I did determine that the murderer had to be strong in order to be able to rip that branch off the living tree.

"In an examination of Woods' home, I found three printed pages hidden in his desk. With Watson's help, I recovered the coded messages Woods had been receiving. He had been ready to give someone special knowledge that would injure the miscreant. The person offered to pay him off during a meeting on Sunday night. Instead Woods was murdered, struck down by a desperate man.

"We had a visitor in our rooms that night. It was Thomas Fisher, local poacher, who had been accused of the crime. He protested his innocence and I believed him."

"Why?" asked Sir William.

375

"Because he was armed with a hunting knife and your gamekeeper was killed by a tree branch. Who would disdain such a handy weapon as a knife for a crude tree branch that had to be broken from a nearby tree? I sent Watson out the next day to discover what Woods did during his days off. He came back with one important fact: Donald Woods had mentioned a woman's name, *Honoria*, as his 'lady friend'.

"While Watson was doing that, I tracked down Thomas Fisher. He had mentioned something that intrigued me. He had spoken of the As You Like It Club. As a patron of The Rose and Thorn, he was well aware of its existence. He gave me all the particulars he knew. There had been similar cases in San Francisco in '58 and Lyons in '64. When Inspector O'Reilly and I had questioned the Drinkwater servants earlier, two of the older men had acknowledged that they knew of the club, although they denied ever having visited it. I planned out my next move and stopped Watson from knocking on the door of the public house.

"That night I tried to pick the lock of The Rose and Thorn, but was interrupted. I sent Inspector O'Reilly regular reports of what was happening, holding him ready at a moment's notice to return to Stratford-Upon-Avon as needed.

"In an effort to disarm the murderer's fears of discovery, whoever he was, Watson and I continued our vacation. Scotland Yard assisted by declaring that they believed the attack had been random and the attacker had left the area. Then, Sir William, you invited us to visit your library.

"In your magnificent collection of books, I found the series of little blue-backed volumes of *Nature's Gifts*. The printing of three consecutive pages of the second book in the series matched the information given on the threatening notes sent to your gamekeeper. I immediately vowed to find the volume from which were torn the pages sent to Donald Woods.

"The salesman had told you he had knocked on every door in three counties. I didn't have time for that, so I concentrated on Stratford-Upon-Avon and Shottery, and the people who were closest to Donald Woods. Time was running out as I methodically eliminated everyone I had on my list of suspects."

Holmes glanced at the mantel clock, which was just chiming midnight. "Then yesterday it rained. The storm was too violent to allow fishing. Watson, clever man, had brought reading material from London, but I had not. I decided to check out The Green Bush reading room.

"There it was! A complete set of *Nature's Gifts*. The books were tucked on a lower shelf in a corner. I examined the second volume and the relevant pages had been removed – here, just as I found it."

Holmes brought forth the blue-backed book opened to the correct chapter. Sir William and Inspector O'Reilly passed it back and forth with exclamations of wonder and surprise. His audience waited eagerly to hear the rest of Holmes's story.

Holmes cleaned and filled his pipe again and held a match to it. "The rest was simple. I had merely to establish motive and to seek witnesses. A casual mention by Mrs. Flagg of her husband's intention to be absent that evening made me decide to put my plan into practice at once. Accordingly, I told her we would eat elsewhere, informed Watson what he needed to do, and put the plan into effect.

"Watson left me a few blocks away and entered The Rose and Thorn alone. When he didn't quickly return, I waited a few minutes. Then I managed to enter the bar through the window in the office behind the bar. No one in the pub suspected a thing.

"I searched the desk and bookshelves of the office. I found the first and second set of financial records and the day-to-day journals. It was obvious at a glance that there was enough skullduggery there that Inland Revenue, if not other agencies, were going to bring the owner, Frank Potter, to the dock. I couldn't be sure how long Watson could hold out against a bevy of eager females, so I set a small fire in the metal wastebasket and tossed a couple plumber's rockets in after I crawled out the window.

"One of Potter's employees raised the alarm. I gathered up Inspector O'Reilly and his army of police, whom I had arranged to have outside the pub waiting for my signal.

"All went according to plan, and the miscreants were arrested. Mr. Flagg tipped his hand, and I understand the women involved are very willing to give evidence about the entire enterprise. Mr. Flagg will greet no more guests at the door of The Green Bush."

The next morning, as our bags were loaded onto the same carriage that had brought us to the guest house from the station, I saw Holmes pull aside the young lad who had carried our luggage when we first arrived. They conversed briefly and Holmes pressed a sum of money into his hand.

Soon after that, Holmes and I mounted the steps to the train from Stratford-Upon-Avon back to London. As it pulled out of the town and gathered speed, I caught a glimpse of the fanciful outline of The Green Bush roof line over the fields.

There had been much disarray at the guest house that morning when we paid our bill and left. Mrs. Flagg had sat behind the desk in the lobby, alternately crying and calmly toting up bills and collecting money. As we took one last look at the Steamboat Gothic building, I said something about her changing moods to my friend, and Holmes shook his head.

"Undoubtedly she knew of his predilections, Watson, but I'm certain she knew nothing of the murder. It was fear that she would divorce him if she learned about his connection to the As You Like It Club that motivated Hyram Flagg's actions. She has been badly used and I pity her. Flagg, a known ne'er-do-well, married her because she inherited The Green Bush from her first husband and he saw an easy living. He enjoyed playing mine host at a successful guest house, and he also enjoyed the dubious entertainments in which he could indulge at the As You Like It Club. Remember, Watson, no man is a hero to his valet . . . or in this case, his errand boy."

It's Time!
by Harry DeMaio

Chapter I

London was undergoing an unusual burst of fair weather for October 1896 and, as I stepped from a hansom cab at 221 Baker Street, I took a moment to look about me. A small but steady stream of semi-fashionable ladies navigated their way around the impertinent young sprouts who were intent on hampering their progress. Several workmen carrying bags of tools on their backs were unloading a wagon full of building materials. The ubiquitous horses drawing carriages, growlers, and the occasional dog-cart clopped their way along the cobblestones. Oddly enough, the sun was actually shining through a very thin noonday haze. All in all, a fine day. Except for me.

I stepped to the front door and drew the bell pull several times. A simply dressed lady of uncertain years but clear eye, pleasant mien, and steady gaze opened the door. "Yes, sir?"

"Good day, madam, I am Mr. Fenton Church. I have an appointment with Mr. Sherlock Holmes. Would you kindly announce me?"

I handed her my card and she bade me come inside as she made her way, in a sprightlier manner than I would have expected, up a flight of stairs. *(Seventeen in all, as I was to discover.)*

She rapped upon the door to a first-floor apartment and no doubt, hearing from within, opened it and announced, "A Mr. Fenton Church to see you, Mr. Holmes."

"Please show him in. Mrs. Hudson. Thank you."

The voice did not bear out the image I had of the great Sherlock Holmes based on Watson's verbal images in *The Strand* and infrequent pictures in the London press.

The landlady beckoned to me and I passed in front of her and entered a chamber that screamed "eccentricity". Papers and files were piled on every horizontal surface, including the floor. No two pieces of furniture matched. There was a redolent and acrid chemical odor that caused my eyes to water. A table with scientific instruments and mysterious bottles and vials took up a corner of the room. Mismatched folders and books filled two walls of shelves. Newspapers were dropped in no apparent order.

Rising to greet me was the source of the voice. Not the famous consulting detective but his amanuensis, biographer, right-hand man, and lap dog, Dr. John H. Watson.

He extended his hand, his face wreathed in a smile. "Good morning, sir. Please come in and be seated." He took my hat and cane. "I am Dr. John Watson, and this is Mr. Sherlock Holmes."

Holmes waved languidly in my general direction but made no effort to extend his hand in greeting. He was dressed, if I may call it that, in a disreputable dressing gown, slippers, poorly matched trousers, and a collarless shirt. Clamped in his mouth was a briar pipe that seemed to have gone out. His hair was disheveled.

I thanked the doctor and looked at Holmes. "As Mrs. Hudson has already told you, I am Mr. Fenton Church, of Church and Smallwood, Insurance Specialists."

The man briefly came to life and half-murmured, half-slurred, "Yes, we have received your note. How may we be of assistance?"

I wondered if he might not be under the belated influence of alcohol or some drug. I looked at a somewhat sheepish Dr. Watson, but he said nothing.

"Over the past weeks, our firm has become liable for a substantial financial loss, and now I seem to have also lost a partner."

The doctor intervened. "Has your partner passed away?"

"I'm not sure. That is one of the reasons I've come to you."

Holmes spent a moment searching the ceiling and then muttered, "Have you approached the police? It would seem to be a case for them."

"No, I have not. Until I have more certain evidence that Gerald Smallwood and £20,000 have disappeared together, I don't want to chance going public with what may well be a scandal that will crush our firm and me with it. We are Insurance Specialists. We underwrite shipments of high-value goods while they are in transit. Trust, stability, and liquidity are our bedrock standards. If I go to the police, I may as well also go directly to the press. I need help from someone who has a proven record of discretion and success in solving thorny problems. I believe that is you."

"How have your relations been with Mr. Smallwood?"

"We've been business partners for over ten years, but Gerald and I led quite separate lives. I'm a widower with no offspring. I reside alone with no live-in servants and am not given to excessive social life. He, on the other hand, is married with two young girls, a son at Cambridge, and a resident domestic staff. He has often commented on how much of a drain on his finances they all are. His wife insists on frequent trips to Europe, especially Paris, and his two daughters are coming of an age where balls, cotillions, and non-stop social events are a basic requirement. Gerald

Junior is not leading an abstemious college life. Gerald is hardly bankrupt, but he isn't as monetarily comfortable as he might like."

"How did you discover the £20,000 [1] liability?"

"I did not. We are a small firm with just a few employees, even though we underwrite substantial transactions. Our senior clerk was pursuing the circumstances surrounding a shipping loss of a substantial quantity of refined silver coins from Bolivia intended for Canada. The shipment never reached its destination. Further research revealed that much of the paperwork associated with the shipment was confusing or missing. It isn't clear at this moment from the records whether the shipment even existed. However, we are saddled with providing restitution to a Bolivian combine that acts on behalf of the National Mint and insists that it has behaved honestly and will take legal action unless we make them whole for the lost shipment."

"I despair of theories not based on facts, but what is your opinion on this matter."

"I don't know. I wish to secure your services to do several things. One: Find Gerald Smallwood. Two: Pursue the silver transaction and determine if we are indeed liable for the loss of that substantial sum. Three: Determine if Gerald's disappearance is connected to the loss."

Wonder of wonders! The almost dissolute character slouched in front of me took on a totally different aspect. He looked alert, wrapped his hands together, and stared at Watson.

"Doctor, I believe we may be of some service to Mr. Church. I could use your assistance in this, if you're available." Watson nodded. "Mr. Church, what does his wife think has happened to her husband?"

"She is in a quandary. She is reluctant to approach the police. Three days is not a long time for an absence, but she insists she knows nothing about any travel plans made by him. His usual travel baggage is still in the house and only one suit is gone from his wardrobe. There may be foul play involved. I think you should interview her as soon as possible."

We spent a few minutes negotiating fees. Then, I gave him the address of the Smallwoods and said I would send a messenger immediately to inform the lady of their impending arrival. He in turn, informed me that he would also be paying a visit to our establishment later in the day, primarily to interview my senior clerk.

I told him we would assemble the relevant shipping documents and our firm's history with the Casa Nacional de la Moneda, the mint at Cerro Rico de Potosi, Bolivia, and also *Señor* Augusto, their appointed agent at the London Consulate.

I took my hat and cane and turned to the door. I saw Mrs. Hudson at the foot of the stairs and nodded to her as I passed and went in search of a cab. So I was now a client of the great Sherlock Holmes. The seeds had been planted.

Chapter II

At four o'clock, our junior clerk knocked on my office door and announced the arrival of Holmes and Watson. The detective was now appropriately dressed in business attire, as was his companion.

"Gentlemen, please come in. Would a tot of brandy not go amiss?"

"Thank you, no, Mr. Church. We have just come from the Smallwood residence. We interviewed Mrs. Smallwood and her daughters. She has heard nothing from her husband. She was unusually upset because they had planned a trip to Paris at the end of this week."

"The last time she saw him, he was in his study going over some papers. He told her he had some important business to attend to and left hurriedly, carrying some of the papers with him. This was in the evening after dinner. He didn't tell her where he was going or whom he was to meet. This behavior seems to be normal. Mr. Smallwood didn't share his business activities with her and apparently she was less than interested. The two girls had been out at a dinner party that evening and could add nothing of value."

Dr. Watson said, "I spoke to the butler who remembered summoning a cab for Mr. Smallwood, but he didn't hear the destination. He was still dressed in his business clothes, and wore a bowler and a light outer coat. He had a dispatch case with him but nothing else. Since Mr. Smallwood always carried a key to the premises, the butler went about his usual late evening duties and locked up the windows and doors as usual after admitting the young ladies, who were returning from their party."

"Thank you, Watson," said Holmes, "I asked to see the study, but found little that would indicate what had caused Mr. Smallwood to leave in such a hurry. There were several files on the desk dealing with what appeared to be consignments that had been successfully consummated. Was it usual for Mr. Smallwood to take business papers home with him?"

I replied, "Gerald has a negative feeling about our two clerks' competence and often felt he needed to check up on them. I have no such concerns. I believe they have both served us well for a long time. Nevertheless, it would not have been out of character for him to be reviewing transactions away from the office. I objected to him carrying files away from our premises when they should have been locked up in our safe, but he chose to ignore my concerns."

"To your knowledge, Mr. Church, are there any important files missing from the office at this time?"

382

"I don't know. I'll ask O'Shea when we bring him in here. Shall we do that now, or is there more you wish to tell me?"

"No, I believe we should spend a little time with your senior clerk. I would also like to speak to the junior as well."

"Very well, I'll call in O'Shea. Let us see if he can shed any further light on the Bolivian silver shipment and answer your question about missing files."

The senior clerk responded nervously when I introduced Holmes and Watson. A typical reaction, no doubt, in the august presence of the world's greatest detective.

"O'Shea, I have secured the services of Mr. Holmes and his associate to determine the whereabouts of Mr. Smallwood and to look into the irregular nature of our Bolivian silver liability. Please give them your fullest cooperation."

"Of course, sir. Neither Parkins nor I have seen Mr. Smallwood in the last several days."

Dr. Watson asked, somewhat unnecessarily, "Parkins is your junior clerk?"

"Yes, Doctor. He and I manage the firm's transactions after the partners have negotiated the initial contracts. We also maintain our banking activity, although here again, the two partners are the only approved signatories for payments and withdrawals."

"We believe Mr. Smallwood had taken some files from this office on the last day you saw him."

"That's correct, Mr. Holmes. He did that periodically. He said it was to keep himself abreast of the firm's business, but I believe he was checking on Parkins and me."

He looked at me and shook his head, "Sorry, sir, but it is most disturbing when he does that. He simply takes them without informing us."

"I understand, O'Shea. I've spoken to him about it, but he chooses to ignore my advice."

The detective said, "We visited the Smallwood home earlier today. There were several files lying on his desk. They should still be there. I asked Mrs. Smallwood and the butler to leave the office undisturbed. Do you know which ones he had taken?"

"As best we can tell, Mr. Holmes, there were five in all. Three dealing with successful transfers of bullion by the Scottish mint to various banks, one dealing with a long-term contract for shipping armaments for the Navy, and then the Bolivian silver documents."

"There were four on his desk. The Scottish and Navy files. There was no Bolivian file. Are you sure he had it?"

383

"No, Mr. Holmes, I'm not sure. All we know is it's not here. *Señor* Augusto at the Bolivian Consul very likely has a complete set of copies. It is he who is insisting that we promptly pay for the loss of the silver *bolivianos* which he believes were stolen while being transported to a ship at Portobelo."

I looked at my clerk and then the detectives. "Well, that puts the cat among the pigeons. Mr. Holmes, do you want to speak with Parkins?"

"Yes, if I would. You may stay here, O'Shea if you wish, after you call Parkins in."

Parkins is a first-class introvert. It is difficult to get him to expound on anything and his replies to questions are usually monosyllables. However, he is skilled at treating documents, sums, and transactions with infinite accuracy and attention to detail. Gerald Smallwood never seems to appreciate his value. I suspect he would like to replace him with a comely young lady. Parkins was even more nervous in Holmes's presence than O'Shea.

I looked at him and said, "Parkins, Mr. Sherlock Holmes and Dr. John Watson are investigating the absence of Mr. Smallwood and also looking into the Bolivian silver issue. O'Shea has already told us that you have not seen Mr. Smallwood for several days. Is that correct?"

Without raising his head, he mumbled, "Yes sir."

Holmes asked, "When was that?"

"Monday."

"Morning, afternoon, or evening?"

"Early evening."

"He had some files with him when you saw him?"

"Yes."

"Did you ask him which files he had?"

"Not my place."

O'Shea interrupted, "Mr. Smallwood had given us to understand that it was his prerogative to remove files from the safe and review them. What he also did, however, was take them to his home. We both found that very distressing."

"So, neither of you have any idea where the Bolivian file might be at this moment."

Both shook their heads. O'Shea raised his hands helplessly. Parkins stood mute.

"When you last had access to the file, was there anything that caught your attention?"

"Several of the usual shipping documents and bills of lading were missing or incomplete. There were no customs seals. *Señor* Augusto insists that these were mere oversights and that he has more than adequate certification to show that the *bolivianos* were in transit by land but never reached the ship."

Holmes nodded, "I believe we should interview this *Señor* Augusto. Is he a member of the Bolivian Consular staff?"

"Actually, he works for the Bolivian Mint, but is quartered here in London at the Consular office. The mint does substantial business with British banks."

"And yet, did you not say the missing consignment was destined for Canada?"

"Yes, Mr. Holmes, that was unusual. Was is not, O'Shea?"

"As I understand it, sir, there is a complex financial arrangement involving a Canadian mining syndicate that is proposing developing new silver veins. As you know, much of Potosi's silver deposits are assumed to be depleted. Tin is replacing silver as the primary metal from the Bolivian mines. This Canadian group seems to think there are still sufficient workable silver veins to make additional mining worthwhile. *Señor* Augusto says they were going to use the *boliviano* shipment as evidence to encourage new North American investment in the venture. It is all rather speculative, but of great interest to the Bolivian government."

Dr. Watson looked at me. "Which of the partners negotiated this contract?"

"We both did." I said. "It was quite routine in all respects, except for the destination and the insured amount. This is not the first insurance agreement we have written for Bolivian silver. But now, both the Bolivians and the Canadians are without their silver and we are caught in the middle."

O'Shea shook his head. "I'm afraid that is so, sir."

"I shall have to seek legal advice, but I share your pessimistic reaction. When does *Señor* Augusto expect his compensation?"

"Immediately, sir."

"Well, he can jolly well wait until we get this all sorted out. Never did like the man. He is a Spaniard, not a Bolivian, and I don't think he's particularly trustworthy."

Holmes raised an eyebrow. "All the more reason for us to interview him as soon as possible. O'Shea, will you set up an appointment for tomorrow morning?"

"Indeed, Mr. Holmes. I shall send you a message of confirmation."

"Thank you both. I still have some things to discuss with Mr. Church, but I believe we can let you get back to your labours."

After they had left, the detective raised a finger and said, "I believe the time has come to involve the police in the matter of your missing partner. I would like to call in Inspector Tobias Gregson of Scotland Yard.

We must convince Mrs. Smallwood that the intervention of the constabulary is now necessary. Inspector Gregson is highly intelligent, flexible for a policeman, and diplomatic. He has at his command far more resources for searching out missing persons than I have. However, the press will no doubt become involved."

I sighed, "I was afraid of this, but I see how you've come to this conclusion. All right, I will send an immediate message to Agatha Smallwood to meet with us first thing in the morning. Please invite this Inspector Gregson to join us. I suppose if something criminal has happened, she will have no choice in the matter. Neither do I."

And I didn't!

Chapter III

The next morning, we met at the Smallwood residence. Inspector Tobias Gregson of Scotland Yard joined us. He is as tall as Holmes, fair-haired, of a muscular build and robust voice. I found myself looking up at both detectives. I am of the same stature as Watson, with dark hair and – I am told – a pleasing voice. I wear a short goatee, while all three of them are beardless. Dr. Watson alone has a brisk moustache.

The Smallwood butler, Gates, received us and, after taking our outerwear, hats, and sticks, led us into a spacious receiving room where Mrs. Smallwood was already seated. There were no signs of the two daughters.

She nodded in our direction as she knotted and unknotted a handkerchief in her fingers. She is a petite woman with dark hair, wide blue eyes, and a startling fair complexion. She has retained an attractive figure which I am sure is the partial result of numerous visits to Parisian fashion ateliers. Her voice, however, is most unattractive – midway between a whine and a gasp.

"Good morning, Fenton. Good Morning, Mr. Holmes and Dr. Watson. Do you have any news for me?" She ignored Gregson.

"No, Mrs. Smallwood. I am afraid we do not. May I introduce Inspector Tobias Gregson of Scotland Yard? We believe the time has come, or may be past due, to introduce the police into the situation of your missing husband."

She gasped. "Oh, do you suspect something awful has happened to Gerald? Has he been abducted?"

Gregson spoke up. "Good morning, Mrs. Smallwood. It is far too early to jump to any such conclusions. However, since several days have passed and you haven't had any contact with Mr. Smallwood, we feel we should initiate a formal search. Mr. Church agrees with us. He too wishes to see the rapid return of his partner. I assume you haven't heard from anyone demanding ransom."

She shook her head and dabbed her eyes with the well-knotted handkerchief.

Gregson continued, "We'll be as discreet as possible, but I'm afraid the press may become involved."

Her eyes widened even further. "Oh, dear," she whined, "What will our friends say? Whatever shall I tell my daughters? They will be so embarrassed when their acquaintances discover that we're involved with the police. They may even be shunned. I don't know what could have gotten into Gerald. We were prepared to leave for Paris this weekend. I suppose I must cancel that trip." A sigh "What a bother! Well, gentlemen, if you say you must, you must, but please be sensitive to my situation."

Holmes had absorbed this conversation and said, "Mrs. Smallwood, we would like to conduct another search of your premises with the inspector. I assume you and Gates have left your husband's office untouched since Dr. Watson and I last were here."

"I certainly have. I never go in there. You'll have to ask Gates. I shall be with my daughters."

She rose and slowly left the room, heading for the elegant stairway that led to the upper floor.

Holmes turned to Watson and said, "See if you can find Gates, will you, old chap?"

It wasn't necessary, for the butler appeared at the door to the reception room. "May I be of assistance, gentlemen?"

I replied, "Yes, Gates. You've met Mr. Sherlock Holmes and Dr. Watson. Let me introduce Inspector Gregson of Scotland Yard. He will be initiating a formal police search for Mr. Smallwood."

The butler blinked but said nothing, except to give a short peremptory bow to the inspector.

Gregson said, "I understand that you were asked by Mr. Holmes to leave Mr. Smallwood's office exactly as he found it when he was last here."

"Yes, sir. I've locked the room, and no one has been in there since Mr. Holmes made his request. I've forbidden the maids to venture anywhere near there."

"Well, let's start there, shall we? But I shall need access to the rest of the house as well."

"Even the ladies' quarters, sir?"

"I'm afraid so. Please do not warn them."

I looked at Gregson, "Oh, I say. Is it necessary to treat the ladies as suspects? I doubt if they will go about hiding anything."

"It is a matter of procedure, Mr. Church. We want this search to be beyond any reproach."

I shook my head. "Very well. Gates, if the ladies protest, they may blame me for bringing detectives into the house. Let us go to the office."

We proceeded up the same staircase and down a hall, passing the bedrooms of the daughters. The doors were closed, but we could hear a loud female voice shouting, "The police? Oh Mother, what a disgrace! Whatever shall we tell our friends when they hear about it?"

Mrs. Smallwood's reply couldn't be heard. Gates unlocked the door to the study and we entered. Holmes seemed satisfied that nothing had been moved or removed. The Naval and Scottish Bank files were still laid out on the desk.

"Inspector, after you have examined those files, may I take them back to our office? They are proprietary business information and should be back in the firm's safe."

Gregson looked at Holmes and then nodded. While Holmes and Watson made another circuit of the room – Holmes on his hands and knees – Gregson had Gates repeat what he had told the detectives about Gerald's departure.

"You don't know what was in the dispatch case he was carrying?"

"I assume that it was papers, sir. There was nothing bulky or outsized in it."

"Was it customary for Mr. Smallwood to leave of an evening without saying where he was going?"

"Mr. Smallwood belongs to the Brokers' Club. It wasn't exceptional for him to go there, especially after he and his wife or one of his daughters might have participated in a minor altercation, if you take my meaning."

"Do you think that's what he did that evening?"

"I can't say, sir."

"Mr. Church, do you belong to the same club?"

"No, Inspector, I do not. I long ago abandoned any club memberships. Bit anti-social, I'm afraid."

"Well, Mr. Holmes, have you made any new discoveries?"

"Nothing of consequence, Inspector. Shall we invade the ladies' domain? I've already examined Mr. Smallwood's bedroom and closets. As Gates has told you, nothing is missing except the clothing he was wearing when he left the house. Perhaps, Watson, you would like to take a look in the kitchen, dining room, and storage room. As the inspector says, 'in the interest of complete procedure'."

I picked up the files on the desk and followed them out, and was treated to screams of protest from the mother and daughters as the inspector and Holmes knocked and entered the bedrooms.

388

Mrs. Smallwood was aghast and turned to me. "Fenton, I strongly object to this indignity. A lady's boudoir should be secure from prying eyes."

I replied, "Agatha, I understand your feelings, but the law doesn't stand on social niceties. I'm sure these detectives are the souls of discretion."

"Nevertheless, I shall speak to our solicitor about this. My girls are mortified."

And so it went.

Our next appointment was with *Señor* Augusto at the Bolivian Consulate. I wanted to stop at the firm's offices first and return the Naval and Scottish files. When we arrived there, O'Shea greeted us and said, "Mr. Church, there is a very peculiar letter here addressed to you. I believe it is of a personal nature and I haven't opened it."

He handed me an envelope with my name and the firm's address made up of cut-out letters from periodicals. Holmes took it from me and examined it. He was wearing gloves. I wasn't. "Low cost stationery, available at any local miscellany shoppe. Let's see what's inside."

I carefully cut open the envelope with a knife and brought out a single sheet of paper, on which similar cutouts read, "*If you wish to find your partner, drain the Thames.*"

"Oh, God!"

Gregson reached for the letter but was stopped by Holmes. "Let us see if we can deduce anything about the sender by using Sir Francis Galton's fingerprint identification system. Your fingermarks are already on the letter and envelope, Mr. Church, but we may be able to find others as well. It is a bit of a stretch, since there are only a few collections of fingermarks currently available at Scotland Yard, but it is still worth the effort."

The letter was posted at Oxford Street yesterday.

Gregson shook his head and said, "I guess we must take the warning seriously. I'll notify the River Police and have them commence a search."

"Watson," said Holmes, "will you return to the Smallwood residence and see if they have received a similar missive? Speak only to Gates. Let us not upset Mrs. Smallwood further. Please rejoin us at the Bolivian Consulate. We are due to meet with *Señor* Augusto there at ten. Do you wish to join us, Gregson?"

"No, I'll return to the Yard and have this letter analyzed and get the River Police hopping on a body search. The Thames is a long and wide body of water. Perhaps we can meet for dinner, Mr. Holmes, and you can bring me abreast of your dealings with the Bolivians."

I looked at O'Shea. "You and Parkins are to keep this development secret until you are told otherwise. Is that understood?"

"Yes, sir."

"Have you had any further insights into the Bolivian question since we last talked?"

"There was a brief article in the *Financial Times* citing the Canadian mining venture in Bolivia. It seems they intend to go on with their plans. There was no mention of the missing *bolivianos*. It cites several major North American companies and individuals who are supporting the effort."

Holmes raised an eyebrow. "Well, that should give us something further to discuss with *Señor* Augusto. Shall we go? Dinner tonight at Marcini's, Gregson. You'll join us, of course, Mr. Church."

I will probably end up footing the bill.

Chapter IV

The Bolivian Consulate is a modest three-storey building which may be replaced by a full-scale embassy in the not too far distant future. We shall see. Meanwhile, in addition to normal consular duties, the government of Bolivia and some private Bolivian companies conduct a variety of business activities there as well. It is not unusual to find representatives of commercial ventures, shipping companies – *Bolivia is landlocked* – mining interests, and a diversity of governmental departments in residence. Bolivia has no major military forces to speak of. Some cultural and entertainment events also work through the consulate and, of course, visits by government and select private (famous, wealthy, or both) individuals are facilitated. It is not surprising then to find *Señor* Enrico Augusto in a small but well-equipped office.

He is the official representative of the Potosi Bolivian Mint to Britain, but I have strong suspicions that his activities are scarcely limited to that function. I do not like the man.

"Ah, *Señor* Church. Welcome to my humble office. And who is this gentleman?"

"*Señor* Augusto, allow me to introduce Mr. Sherlock Holmes."

Augusto interrupted. "Surely not the *molto famoso* detective. I have read many of the stories about him."

Holmes countered. "Yes, I am afraid my reputation has been grossly overstated by my associate, Doctor Watson, in the pages of *The Strand*."

"I find that difficult to believe, *Señor* Holmes. And where is your biographer? I should like to meet him, as well."

"Doctor Watson will be joining us shortly. He is pursuing an inquiry at the moment which he should be completing as we speak."

"And *Señor* Church, how is your partner, *Señor* Smallwood?"

"That is one of the reasons that Mr. Holmes and I are here this morning. Mr. Smallwood has been missing since Monday evening, and we have reason to believe his absence may be connected to our issue about the 'lost' *bolivianos*."

"Surely you don't believe that I or my government bear any responsibility for his disappearance."

"No, no! It is just that we have reason to think that he was examining the documentation associated with the silver shipment when he left his home that evening. He hasn't been heard from since. I assume you've had no contact with him."

"None at all. I seldom deal with him. I usually conduct our business with you or your man, O'Shea, although we must have the signatures of both partners on any transactions we conduct."

"O'Shea has informed me that several documents were missing from our files, and that some of the paperwork on the shipment was incomplete."

"My files are available for your scrutiny. You will find that the shipment left Potosi by a carefully guarded wagon on its way through Colombia to Portobelo in Panama. There it was to be loaded on a ship that would make its way to Vancouver, Canada. Then it would be turned over to a Canadian syndicate and our responsibility and your liability would end. Somewhere *en route* or at the port itself, the shipment disappeared. The Bolivian and Republic of Colombia authorities, in association with the local Panamanian police, have conducted extensive searches to no avail. Their reports are in the file. My client, Casa Nacional de la Moneda, feels that sufficient time and effort has passed and insists that your firm provide indemnification according to our contract – £20,000."

Holmes asked, "May we examine the file, *Señor*?"

"*Ciertamente.* You will find everything is in order up to the disappearance. Bills of lading for the wagon, customs border documents at Colombia – but of course, nothing beyond that."

I looked at Augusto. "The Mint shall get its money only after we determine the situation with my partner, Mr. Smallwood. It is necessary that both partners sign for the release of the funds. I shall have to consult our solicitor on how to deal with his absence."

"I sincerely hope you can make a rapid exception, *Señor*. We have been dealing with you in good faith and have paid a significant premium for your services. We would like to continue the relationship. The Canadians intend to continue their mining venture in spite of the loss."

Holmes, in the meantime, was examining the contents of the file. He looked over at me and nodded meaningfully. "I'm not an insurance specialist nor a solicitor. What I see here is a chain of paper, much of it in Spanish, a language with which I have a passing acquaintance. It seems to support the claim that the shipment actually left Potosi and disappeared on its way to Panama. There is also an agreement signed by the partners of Church and Smallwood and *Señor* Augusto on behalf of the Bolivian Mint. Do you recognize Mr. Smallwood's signature, Mr. Church?"

"Yes, it is his and that is mine."

"And *Señor* Augusto, would you humour me by signing your name for comparison."

Augusto seemed nettled but took up a piece of foolscap and a steel pen and scrawled his name. To my inexpert eyes, there was a match.

"Without submitting this to handwriting analysis, are you willing to accept the validity of this document as the insurance agreement?"

Both Augusto and I nodded our heads. "Yes!"

"Well then, so shall I. I believe you should contact your solicitor, Mr. Church."

Just then, Dr. Watson arrived. He looked at Holmes and me and shook his head negatively. No letter had been sent to the Smallwood residence. Holmes introduced Watson to Augusto who gushed with admiration at meeting the *"autor famoso"*. We left.

Chapter V

Dinner at Marcini's. Inspector Gregson, Holmes, and Watson were already seated and working their way through flutes of champagne when I arrived. The two detectives seemed to be engaged in deep and serious conversation. Watson just sat listening.

"Good evening, gentlemen. That champagne looks very tempting." I signaled the waiter, pointed at their glasses and raised my hand. In a moment, I, too, was enjoying the sparkling bubbles of the French concoction. "Shall we order?"

Holmes and Gregson closed off their conversation and we all spent time perusing the menu. After we sent the waiter about his tasks, I questioned Holmes. "What did you conclude from our interview with *Señor* Augusto?"

"He is a sharp individual. Of course, most of those documents were flagrant forgeries. He was relying on the fact that they were in Spanish to hide the fact that there never was any shipment. If you had examined the official consignment notices, you would have noticed that the dates did not correspond. I suspect they came from the files of previous transactions.

However, I assume the contract that he, you, and Mr. Smallwood signed, if it indeed is his signature, is legitimate. Otherwise, the meticulous eyes of O'Shea and Parkins would have seized upon it. This whole transaction is a swindle and Mr. Smallwood discovered it. I do believe our *Señor* Augusto, when paid, will take your £20,000 and make haste back to Bolivia or some other country from which he cannot be extradited. The Bolivian Mint will see none of it, for none of their assets are missing. I do not believe the Canadians were ever expecting the shipment."

I stared at Holmes in disbelief. "That's incredible. I shall see my solicitor immediately in the morning. I suppose that since he did not receive our monies, he cannot be prosecuted."

Gregson intervened. "Attempted fraud is a punishable crime. I believe we'll have sufficient evidence to bring him in – provided he is still in the country."

The soup arrived, cutting off further serious discourse. Watson prattled on about his meeting with Gates, the Smallwood's butler. It seems Mrs. Smallwood has taken to her bed in anticipation of receiving further bad news about her husband. The young ladies were not so seriously distressed as to forego a cotillion under the watchful eye of their housekeeper. It also seems that Agatha Smallwood has a modest fortune of her own which she may be forced to use.

By this time, the entrees had been devoured and Holmes suggested we adjourn to a small side room for brandy and cigars.

I hadn't yet queried Inspector Gregson about his searches and the bizarre letter that I had received. He said he had temporarily called off the exploration of the river while they pursued a more likely objective.

"What was that?" I asked.

"Your home, Mr. Church."

"What? Have you all gone mad?"

"We think not," said Holmes. "You have overplayed your hand, Mr. Church. This afternoon, the inspector and I analyzed the letter and envelope for fingermarks. There were several different ones on the envelope, as you might expect from movement through the postal system. The letter itself was a different story. You sent it to yourself. We know your marks were on the sheet because we saw you handle it. What we also discovered was a second and separate set of fingermarks that matched your own. There were no other marks on the page. They were slightly smudged, no doubt the result of assembling and pasting the letters in the message. The inspector took out a warrant and at this moment, a crew of Scotland Yard constables are searching your home. We are waiting to hear from them now."

I rose from my seat and headed for the doorway. I had not counted on how swift the burly Gregson could be. As he towered over me, I recoiled and was grasped by Holmes and Watson. They sat me down and Gregson produced a set of handcuffs which he laid on the table. "We won't use these yet until we hear from the sergeant."

The moments ticked by and the three of them twirled their brandy snifters. A small disturbance broke out in the main dining room as a handsome police sergeant made his way to the room in which we were sitting. He entered, saluted Gregson, and nodded respectfully to Holmes and Watson. "Your directions were correct, Inspector. We found the body of a man we believe to be Mr. Gerald Smallwood under the floorboards of the storm cellar in Mr. Church's home. There was nothing on the body to definitely identify him. We believe he has been dead for several days. We have summoned the coroner and he will give us a more definitive conclusion. Unless you say otherwise, we'll remove the body to the morgue."

"No," said Holmes. "Please leave it there until the inspector, Dr. Watson, and I can examine it and the surroundings. We shall have to bring the clerk O'Shea and the butler Gates to the scene and have them identify the body, Inspector. Then we can formally notify Mrs. Smallwood and her family. "

Gregson reached over and took up the handcuffs. "I guess we'll need these after all. Sergeant, will you accompany Mr. Church to the Yard. Take the back exit here. We don't want to disturb the diners. Marcini's would never forgive us."

As I walked or staggered out of the room, I heard Holmes say, "Too clever by half, Mr. Church. I shall call on you in the morning."

Chapter VI

I am sitting in a detention cell at Scotland Yard. Oddly enough, I slept through the night. My conscience doesn't seem to be disturbing me. What is disturbing is the passing parade of law enforcement officials, recorders, jailers, and porters bringing me food and coffee. I've been allowed to contact my solicitor and he'll be looking in later in the morning.

Inspector Gregson was the first official to appear at my cell. He was full of news, all of it bad. "Well, Church. *(Note the absence of "Mr.")* We managed to catch up with Augusto as he was getting ready to leave the country. It seems he had stopped by your office to arrange the transfer of funds and O'Shea informed him that you had been arrested. He left immediately. What he didn't know was that O'Shea had also been called upon to identify the body we found in your home and while there, he told us of Augusto's visit. He is in a cell near you. We haven't had a chance to interview him yet. Sherlock Holmes wants a shot at him."

I chuckled. I never did like Augusto. It was he who originally came up with the scheme for me to defraud our firm and invest the embezzled proceeds in the Canadian silver mining venture. He, of course, would deduct what he considered an appropriate fee. I stupidly became convinced that a lot of money could be made with little risk. The firm itself carries fraud insurance. Unfortunately, the partners individually are not covered. Anyway, I doubt the Bolivian government or mint will lift a finger to save his skin.

Gregson was about to carry on when Sherlock Holmes and the ever-faithful Watson arrived on the scene. "Good morning, Mr. Church. *(Polite to the end.)* There are several items we should like to clear up. Is your solicitor here? No? Then, let me play out a scenario for you and you can respond or not as you see fit. First, we are convinced that you and *Señor* Augusto created a complex plot to defraud your firm of £20,000.

"Second, we are also convinced that Mr. Smallwood, while reviewing the Bolivian silver file, discovered some of the same inconsistencies that I did when inspecting Augusto's version of the documents. O'Shea and Parkins, not knowing Spanish, were unable to detect the discrepancies. Mr. Smallwood, fluent in the language, was able to reconstruct the plot and in a fury, ran from his house with the incriminating material. He came to your home, accused you of fraud and embezzlement, and demanded that you admit it in a court of law. He may have even threatened you with his cane. You responded violently and struck him several times with a blunt object sufficient to cause his death, whether intending to or not."

"After an initial bout of panic, you decided to hide the body under the floor of your cellar, intending to dispose of it after the investigation into Mr. Smallwood's disappearance died down."

"Now, here is where you outsmarted yourself. You decided you needed someone to assist you in diverting attention from yourself when it became apparent that Mr. Smallwood's absence would be discovered to be permanent. Who better than the greatest detective in Britain? By invoking my aid and pretending to be oh, so solicitous of your missing partner and his family, you hoped to rise above any suspicion involving you. You even subtly suggested that Mr. Smallwood might have been involved in financial chicanery. You doubted that anyone would tie you back to a fraudulent attempt to pay insurance for a non-existent shipment of silver. You protested loudly at having to pay for the liability."

"But you couldn't leave well enough alone. Trying to further mislead the authorities, you constructed and sent the infamous letter to yourself. If this had been a few years earlier, Sir Francis Galton's work in fingermark identification would not have yet been implemented by Scotland Yard. But it was. And we caught you. I'm afraid you are going to hang."

I stared at the three of them and said, "I shall await my solicitor."

Epilogue

My trial was brief and as the press would have it "conclusive". I'm sitting here in a cell in Exeter Prison awaiting the ministrations of the hangman. Augusto was also found guilty of fraud and sentenced to a long period as a ward of Her Majesty's penitentiary system. I did manage to sell the assets of the partnership to an insurance syndicate, thus preserving the jobs of O'Shea and Parkins. Since a convicted felon is not permitted to profit from his misdeeds, after the government took its share, I transferred the remaining proceeds of the sale to O'Shea and Parkins and a portion to Agatha Smallwood and her daughters. She is probably on her way to Paris to spend her way through it at the fashion houses and *modistes*.

Sherlock Bloody Holmes and that fool Watson! I rue the day I ever entered into that pigsty they call their "rooms". I sincerely pity the redoubtable Mrs. Hudson who deserves far better roomers than those two.

Ah, here comes the warden of Exeter.

"Good morning, Mr. Church. Do you have any last requests or communications you wish to send?"

"No, thank you, Warden."

"What would you like for your final meal?"

"Feeding a man who is about to be hanged is a colossal waste of food. Give it to one of the other prisoners.

"Would you like to speak with the prison chaplain and end your life on a prayerful note?"

"Warden, in spite of my name, I have never been in a church during my entire adult life. I'm sure that God, if there is one, would immediately see through my hypocrisy if I invoked Him now."

"Very well. I shall just check on the preparations and summon you to your fate."

(A lengthy pause.)

"Mr. Church . . . it's time."

NOTE

1 – £20,000 in 1896 is roughly equivalent to £2,520,000 today.

The Case of the
Fourpenny Coffin
by I.A. Watson

The gallery was filled with row upon row of wooden boxes, each five-feet seven-inches long by two-feet six-inches wide and deep, lined in rows with narrow walkways between them. Every one contained a sleeping man, cramped into the uncomfortable confines, laid on a straw-stuffed mattress, covered by a thin oilcloth sheet and whatever clothing they had added atop it. I immediately understood the slang term for the overnight accommodation, the *"fourpenny coffin"*.

The Superintendent who held aside a flap of the access door gestured me inside. "This way, Doctor Watson," he requested in a hushed voice.

I followed him along the central aisle, past tattered derelicts – ruined old men and emaciated boys who lay on their backs like corpses. Only the slow rise of their chests and the occasional snore or cough betrayed that they yet lived.

The destitute of London lay about us, confined in parade formation in their hideous cribs. The air was pungent with unwashed sweat and dirty laundry. I shuddered because I knew that for many of the sleepers this was luxury accommodation. [1]

We reached the end of the balcony, where we could overlook the hall below. There were seventy-two homeless sleepers behind us, but thrice that number on the floor below. A few wall-lamps remained lit to show the way down the connecting stairway and to reveal the extent of the long, crowded hostel.

"The Examination Room is at the back," the Superintendent whispered. He wore a peaked cap and a uniform jacket with brass buttons, a sign of his authority. There were also a pair of male orderlies on duty and two dour matrons patrolling the roped-off women's section on the lower level.

"Is it always this full?" I asked, trying not to allow my horror to show. London is a crowded place and it can be brutal on the poor.

"It's worse when the cold snap comes," I was told. "Year before last, when the great cold came, [2] we ran out of places. Even the rope-lines and the sitting rooms were overfull."

My visit had included peeks into the other mission rooms where even less fortunate souls were housed. Four-pence won the homeless a coffin-box where they could lay relatively straight under covers, with bread and

397

tea for supper and breakfast. Those who only had tuppence suffered on plain hard benches where they must sit upright, supported only by a rope strung for them to hook their arms over in order to prop them up – a line that was cut each morning at six a.m. as an unwelcome alarm call. [3] Those with but a single penny were allowed to sit but not slumber, bereft even of sleeping on a rope.

Yet even those men, women, and children were fortunate, for they had shelter from weather in a clean, vermin-free sanctuary, enjoyed what warmth hot water pipes running the perimeter of the room might offer, and safety from the violence that might befall a rough-sleeper at the hands of yet more desperate human predators. London is the richest city in the world, but there were poor souls for whom it might as well have been Tartarus. [4]

At the end of the lower floor were three doors. The largest double door led down a short corridor to the commissary where guests would be sent on their way tomorrow morning with a hot drink and a third-of-a-loaf. The other rooms were labelled "*Chapel*" and "*Examination Room*", and the latter was our destination.

The small tiled clinic was unremarkable, containing a padded metal inspection couch, a doctor's desk, a quartet of cheap wooden chairs, a preparation table, and locked cabinets of pharmaceuticals and bandages. The only atypical contents were an umbrella stand filled with second-hand crutches and a plumbed shower-bath with hosepipe in one corner for sluicing off patients.

The resident physician rose quickly from his seat, closing a ledger he had been studying and hastening to meet us. "Doctor Watson," he identified me. "You need not have come."

"The Trustee Board thinks differently, Dr. Manfred," Superintendent Hoker answered the worried-looking medical man. "They are concerned about our recent . . . problems. They are concerned about scandal, about the broadsheets, about – "

"I have already told the Trustees that further investigation can be conducted internally, discreetly," Manfred interrupted. "The parish coroner has indicated that he does not expect there to be any fuss."

Manfred was a somewhat seedy-looking fellow of middle years, with a growing paunch that stressed his waistcoat buttons and the dark bags under his eyes that suggested too little sleep or too much dissolution. I did not approve of his appearance – a doctor should maintain certain standards of character and dress – or of his attitude.

"Three deaths, sir!" I barked to halt the fellow's bleating. "Three men found deceased over four nights. If the local coroner does not consider that remarkable, then he is a duffer who should be replaced. And if you do not consider three such events costing three human lives to be worthy of every attention, then you are also worthy of dismissal!"

The doctor stepped back as if I had struck him. I admit to temptation. "There was no need to bring in people whose notoriety is . . . notable," he tried to rally.

"Your Board of Trustees believes differently. And a good thing too, if this is the standard of your professional behaviour. No, don't bother chelping your excuses, sir! My colleague will be joining us shortly, and I promise that he will have less tolerance for your misplaced priorities than I."

The Superintendent looked nervous. He was a man of humble class whose authority over even an inferior physician was severely lacking. "Mr. Holmes will be along soon?" he ventured hopefully.

The Examination Room door opened and a shabby chap slouched in without invitation.

"You cannot come in here," Superintendent Hoker told him brusquely. "Return to your bed or you'll be put outside!"

The intruder was a gaunt, crooked-shouldered chap with scraggly greying sideburns and a bulbous drink-reddened nose. I sighed.

"Let him through, Superintendent," I instructed. "Sherlock Holmes has arrived."

The interloper stood upright then, casting off the odd spinal twist that had so effectively conveyed his deformity and reduced his apparent height. He snorted in amusement and pulled away the spirit-gum glued whiskers, false nose, and yellowed dentures. "There was a time when I could surprise you with such transformations, Watson."

"I have studied you as you have studied me, Holmes. After your twentieth surprise appearance, even I begin to suspect. Besides, you asked me to meet you here at this hour. Who else would burst in on our conference so punctually at exactly the scheduled moment?"

Hoker and Manfred were less sanguine about their sudden guest's arrival and mutation. "This is Mr. Holmes?" the Superintendent frowned.

Holmes waved him a small greeting, still holding one peeled-off whisker like a giant hairy caterpillar. The world's greatest detective can sometimes betray a very boyish enthusiasm for deception and disguise. "Forgive the concealed appearance," he tried to salvage something of his reputation and credibility. "Given the recent occurrences at the Bell Lane Mission, I decided that a first-hand experience of residency might prove of consequence."

"You came in disguise to see what happens here for yourself," I understood.

"I did, Watson. I idled in with the crowd who came for their seven o-clock supper, rendered my four-pence to the steward at the door, sang 'All Things Bright and Beautiful' [5] and 'All People That On Earth Do Dwell' to the tune of 'Old One-Hundredth', crammed down my bread and mashed tea, and found my assigned place in the common hall. Except of course I slipped the fellow who was due to sleep in Box 133 a wallet of shag to swap places with me so I could have his coffin."

"Box 133?" Dr. Manfred frowned. "Why that particular place?"

Now it was Superintendent Hoker who looked somewhat disconcerted.

"That 'coffin' was the place where three men died on successive nights, Watson," Holmes instructed me.

"Not so," Manfred denied. "The first itinerant died in bed eighty-nine, the second in fifty-four, and the third in one-hundred-sixteen."

"Actually . . . ." Hoker ventured. "Well, that is technically true."

"The boxes are identified by the little metal numberplate screwed on to their ends," Holmes explained. "The plates have all been in place for a long time, enough to have become slightly corroded, fixed in place. Only four plates have shining screws denoting that they were recently exchanged – swapped over, in fact, to disguise the fact that one box has been site to three consecutive deaths."

Hoker glared at the ground, pale and unhappy. "Our visitors are superstitious and ignorant folk," he argued. "If word got about of a 'death cot', then they would shy away, would go back to the ruin and violence of the gutters rather than take Godly refuge here. If one of our visitors passes away, we customarily take the box for cleaning and then place it back in a different position, swapping it out with the one that formerly occupied that place. I switch the identification numbers to keep the rows in consecutive order."

This detail of procedure was evidently new to Manfred. "You mean to say that all three incidents took place in the same bed?" He glanced at me. "If I had known that then, I would have looked more carefully at the events."

I suggested that the Trustees had been right to call upon Holmes to review the "incidents".

My friend was more interested in uncovering additional data for his implacable mind to process. "Since the present Box 116 is currently vacated by its rightful occupant – me – I suggest you send your orderlies to haul it in here," he told Hoker. "It requires an inspection that is best conducted in better light, without the need for circumspection."

Hoker assented and dispatched the two male attendants about the work.

"What information have you on the dead men?" I demanded of him. "All the Trustees relayed to us were their names."

"Those would be from the ledger," Dr. Manfred said.

"The signing-in book where every visitor writes their name or leaves their mark," Holmes supplied. He must have scribed some pseudonym in that way himself earlier in the evening. "The clerk appends the name given by those men and women who are not literate."

"And not all our guests offer their real names," Hoker admitted. "But I can speak for the first man to die, Will Hosketh. He was a regular, here every night when he could afford it. A very kind old man. I was saddened to find he had passed in his sleep."

"You discovered him?" I checked.

The Superintendent nodded. "We wake the guests at seven. At this time of year we light the lamps because it is still dark out. They vacate their beds, fold their sheets, and make their way to the chapel for a brief prayer before breakfast. They are usually on their way by half-past-seven. One of my duties is to check the vacated boxes. You understand that occasionally our visitors are incontinent or otherwise unclean, and in that case we would need to change the mattress. And there are slow risers who need chivvying out of their beds."

"You took Hosketh for such a recalcitrant?"

"He could be a heavy sleeper, and an occasional drinker. We do not allow guests to come in if they are inebriated, but sometimes they will sneak a flask in and imbibe in the night. I thought Will might have been deeply asleep to ignore the bell, or else perhaps a little unwell. He was a man of advanced years, probably as old as seventy."

"But he was dead," Holmes prompted.

"Yessir. Even as I shook him I could tell. His lips were pale and there was a stiffness about him. I knew at once that he was gone."

"What is the procedure then?" I wondered.

"I inform Dr. Manfred," Hoker explained, and glanced at Manfred to take up the explanation.

"We bring the man and his bed in here to the examination room," the resident physician answered curtly. "I confirm the death and summon a colleague to countersign the death certificate. A notice is sent to the local coroner and a judicial decision is made whether to convene an inquest. The body is removed to St. Barts morgue pending funeral arrangements. [6] If there is no known next of kin, then a pauper's burial is arranged in a common plot."

Holmes turned back to Hoker. "When you discovered the man, did you observe any details that might actually be of aid? Any sign of struggle,

401

of convulsion?" He appealed to Manfred. "Any effusion of fluids? The condition of the sclera?"

Neither man had much useful information about the condition of the late Will Hosketh. Hoker must have read Holmes's disappointment and disdain because he added, "The old fellow had no family left. His son died out on the British Gold Coast with Wolseley back in '74. [7] After that he took to the bottle and into destitution. He made what living he could as a pavement artist, with chalks and charcoal. He was quite good. He once did me a drawing of my littlest girl, Effie. I still have it today."

"The other deceased?"

"Signed in as Benjamin Crewe, Labourer, and Hosiah Swinnart, Porter. I didn't know either of them. I took Crewe to be a tramping man. We get a lot of them passing through, looking for work or avoiding the law. Swinnart had a twisted leg that he said was from an accident. He was a Londoner by his accent. I checked the books and he'd been here four times before in the last eight weeks, but I'd not noted him."

Manfred evidently felt the need to keep up with the Superintendent. "Crewe was a crude, fit fellow, with labourer's hands. I took his death to be heart failure. These big types can go suddenly, you know. Swinnart was in his fifties, and he showed some signs of dropsy, so that may have killed him."

I dislike a doctor who does not clearly determine a cause of death. "What sort of examination did you give these dead men in your Examination Room?" I demanded.

"Enough to determine that they were beyond revival," Manfred argued. "I do not have the time nor the facilities here for autopsies. It is not my job. Determination of final cause is the coroner's province."

"Informed by your findings, sir! Did you do anything more than check for a pulse and make some likely guess?"

Holmes intervened before I lost my temper. It is not often that he must calm me down. "These corpses – what became of their possessions?"

Hoker answered quickly. "We have them here, sir, pending determination of ownership." He gestured towards a wall cupboard. "None of them had very much."

Under Holmes's imperious eye, he produced three parcelled bundles and untied the string that held the brown paper in place.

The first package to hand was the effects of Hosiah Swinnart. Holmes's long fingers raked through the humble pile, halting a moment to sniff and correctly identify the tobacco in the fellow's pouch, but otherwise finding little of value and less of interest in the crippled porter's property.

Benjamin Crewe's parcel included a browned, crumpled daguerreotype of some young woman, with the name *"Amy"* inscribed upon the reverse in faded ink. Any frame had long since been sold off. His possessions included a second shirt, the front half of a *New Testament*, and a used handkerchief of particular grubbiness.

Will Hosketh's assemblage included a tin of chalks, the tools of his trade, and a strip of leads and charcoals. He also carried three-dozen scraps of paper, clearly hoarded for sketching purposes. Most of them bore vignette images. I thought his work rather good, with an eye for faces and expressions, and said so.

"He had a bit of a talent, old Will," Hoker agreed. "When he could afford it, he bought a bit of decent paper and would do sketches of the ladies and gents promenading along Mayfair or the Mall maybe, then try and sell them pictures of themselves. Sometimes it paid off. He'd get nine-pence or a shilling for a quick portrait he did right then and there. But he'd always drink his fee away by the next day, poor fellow."

The Superintendent's rueful remembrance was interrupted by the bustle of his orderlies arriving with the dead men's box. They heaved it onto Manfred's examination table and left it for our inspection.

There didn't seem much to see. The wood was cheap plain varnished ash, jointed with tenon-and-mortice into that coffin-like bed. A thin canvas mattress roll about two inches deep was stuffed with straw. Buttons sealed in the stuffing, which could be replaced after the cover was washed. The stamped number-plate betrayed the evidence of exchange that had alerted Holmes to the case's oddest feature.

"I don't see what agency could kill three men in this same box, Holmes," I confessed. "I have checked it carefully for poison needles and hidden traps. The fellows who died ate the common fare served from a common pot. From the little we know of them, they had no acquaintance with each other or any other circumstance in common except for their reduced positions in society."

Manfred tried to object when Holmes eviscerated the mattress in his Examination Room, but his complaints were in vain. The canvass sheath was unbuttoned and the entire contents laid out across the surgery floor. "When each man died, was the mattress exchanged? Cleaned?" Holmes pressed the Superintendent.

"There was no need," Hoker answered defensively. "None of the dead men soiled himself or left any other mess. We swapped the beds but no more was required."

Holmes raked through the pale brittle hay that he had liberated from the bedding. He dropped to the floor to conduct a closer inspection through his magnifying lens, halting to examine each jack of straw before passing

403

on. Manfred and Hoker exchanged uncomfortable looks, surely wondering what the eccentric detective was searching for – or finding?

"Look here," Holmes called, gesturing me down to where he now held a little clump of matted straw, seven or eight strands stuck together. He parted the stalks that were adhered with a brown sticky substance.

"What is it?" I asked, not entirely sure I wished to know.

Holmes smelled the evidence but did not answer. He carefully folded the clumped wad into a paper, frowning.

He turned back to the parcels. "That was the entirety of the mens' possessions?"

"Apart from the clothes they were wearing when they went to the morgue," Manfred insisted. "Even their boots are here."

"Their pockets were checked?"

"Yes," Hoker promised. "There was some loose coin – not much for two of them, but old Will had the best part of five bob in change. What cash there was is in the vestry safe."

"Five shillings?" I echoed. That was a lot for a destitute beggar to carry. After all, a common dock labourer expects only two shillings a day wages. [8] "Pavement drawing is more lucrative than I had supposed."

"He could have bought a proper bed for the night if he'd wanted. I expect this was what he knew, had become used to."

Holmes counted Hosketh's treasury. "Four shillings and eight-pence," he observed, "That and four-pence for his coffin would come to exactly a crown. Did he by any chance pay for his final accommodation with a five shilling coin?"

"I'd have to ask the clerk," Hoker admitted. "If he did, then it would have been noticed. Nobody here ever produces an Oxford." [9]

"Someone did, the night of the first death," Dr. Manfred broke in. "It was almost as soon as the doors opened, before there was much in the cash box. Fairbody had to come through here to me for change to break a crown. I remarked it at the time."

"Do you still have the coin?" Holmes asked urgently.

The doctor shrugged. "Probably not. I don't keep track of loose change. Do you? I do recall it was new-minted, though, still shiny. One of the modern ones with the altered picture of Her Majesty, and St. George on the tail. [10]

"What of the other two men?" Holmes went back to the Superintendent. "Did you note anything about them when you discovered their bodies?"

"I was surprised to find Crewe like that," Hoker conceded. "And two men in two nights – we haven't had that before. I was worried that we'd have the press and the courts, like that business with Annie Knight. But as

404

it was, the coroner took a sensible view and we were spared. Until this third one, I suppose and . . . ." He broke off before he finished by saying, "you."

The Knight case loomed over our entire investigation. In January 1895, a sixty-five year old woman named Anne Clifford, alias Knight, was discovered dead in her "bunk" at a shelter on Hanbury Street, Spitalfields. An investigation and case went to court against the Salvation Army, who operated the hostel, but a jury ruled that Knight died from natural causes brought on by old age and debility. [11]

The Bell Lane Trustees were very shy of the notoriety and difficulties – another such action might bring down upon their mission. They evidently hoped that Sherlock Holmes might resolve matters before the coroner instructed the police.

"And Swinnart's discovery?"

"I'm not sure, sir," Superintendent Hoker explained apologetically. "That being Tuesday night, which is one of my times off, that and Sunday. It was Chaffinch, my deputy, who had the duty on Wednesday morning. By the time I arrived at eight o'clock sharp, the incident was dealt with. Swinnart was already carried into this Examination Room, awaiting Dr. Manfred's attention."

"You were not here?" I asked the medical man. I had understood the fellow to be present on-call during the hours that the hostel was in use.

"I had stepped out for a brief time," he told me defensively. He must have known that he had erred by his delinquency. Hoker's expression betrayed some satisfaction that the doctor's error was noted by someone of a station to comment on it. I suppose that a humble mission like Bell Lane, sequestered in a back-street between Spitalfields and Petticoat Lane Markets, would not be able to afford the best of physicians.

Holmes sorted through Hosketh's sketches, picking out the largest of them, on the best paper. It had clearly been intended as a portrait to sell, but was only half completed. It depicted a gay young lady in fashionable dress and hat, looking over her shoulder, laughing. So vivid was the charcoal etching that I could almost hear her merry voice – a most engaging woman, she seemed to me. But splatters of mud, probably thrown up by carriage wheels or horses' hooves, besmirched the sheet, rendering it unsaleable. "Do either of you know what lady this image portrays?" he asked Hoker and Manfred.

Neither man could say. Holmes lost interest in the doctor and the Superintendent.

"We must make further enquiries, Watson," my friend insisted. "Would you oblige me by speaking with the parish coroner whose inattention has so far been notable, and procuring for me whatever case files he may have assembled? If there haven't been proper autopsies then have them set in hand. You know the methods."

"Is that necessary?" Manfred interrupted. "After all, these are men of no consequence, who likely . . . ."

"I shall be rendering to the Trustees my account of events so far," Holmes continued implacably, "and expressing my poor opinion of the medical attention so far brought to bear." As the resident physician blanched then reddened, Holmes continued speaking to me. "I would also appreciate you tracking down our associate, Langdale Pike. You know where to find him. If anyone can identify at sight a young society beauty, then it is he."

I scowled but assented. Pike is not my favourite companion, but I will own that the fellow knows his seedy business. [12]

Holmes reached for his discarded whiskers. "I must one again don my guise of out-of-luck teamster and blend in with the breakfast crowd. I shall be asking about the rumours of deaths, and by name about the three deceased. A humble itinerant may learn more in that mission hall than might a consulting detective."

Hoker and Manfred may have had more questions, but my friend resumed the slouch, demeanour, and character of the tramp whom he portrayed, and nothing could then budge him from it.

I did not approach St. James's Street in the best of moods. London was damp, foggy, and cold. Since tonight would be Bonfire Night, the streets were filled with portuning children requesting "a Farthing for the Guy". [13]

My visit to the coroner had been difficult and lengthy. The fellow was one of the old-style appointees, a solicitor rather than a physician, with more interest in administrative process than in the discharge of professional medical duties. I now understood how three deaths over four nights in the same hostel might go unremarked and uninvestigated. By the end of it, I had delivered a piece of my mind that shocked the fellow out of his complacency and triggered orders for some competent pathologist to examine the three corpses. Hosketh would need to be exhumed from his pauper's plot.

I had such notes as existed for the cursory examinations that had been conducted on Hosketh, Crewe, and Swinnart. Manfred had fallen back on the old standby cause of death as "heart failure", which is not so much a determination as a description of lack of life. Every death results in heart failure. I also mentioned that to the coroner, somewhat forcefully.

It did seem from what paltry *post mortem* check had been made that Crewe at least was in good health. I was sufficiently disturbed by my reception at the coroner's office to make a side-trip to take a brief first-hand look at the two bodies still held at Barts morgue.

I don't pretend to have Holmes's almost supernatural ability to read the people he encounters as if they had their professions and circumstances inked upon their foreheads. However, in a long lifetime of medical and military service and as Holmes's companion on innumerable investigations, I have picked up some small capacity for noting relevant detail. I observed that Crewe had the sort of calluses any hard-working manual labourer might have, and that his back bore signs of a military flogging at some time in his past. Swinnart's leg had been broken and badly reset, perhaps six or nine months ago, which had presumably led to his difficulty in retaining employment and lodgings. The man did present some symptoms of *oedema* as Manfred has indicated, and that can cause sudden heart or liver failure, but without cutting the chap open I could not discover more.

Hence to Clubland, and the *louche* Langdale Pike's St. James's hideout. I found him sprawled along his customary bow window, watching the carriages pass outside. A box of Turkish delight lay on his lap and he offered me a piece of the gooey confectionary. I declined.

"Is this about the tragic Mrs. Ronder?" he asked me, anticipating, or at least hoping for some scandal or gossip regarding Mrs. Merrilow's mysterious veiled lodger, whom Holmes had but lately investigated. [14] I have no idea how Pike might have come to hear of the matter.

"It is not," I replied brusquely. "Holmes asks if you can supply the name and any detail about the young lady in this portrait." I handed across the mud-smeared image.

"And I don't suppose you will reveal to me what you and your great friend were doing this last year, when all was silence?" Pike probed.

"Those matters are none of your concern." [15]

"Mrs. Cawdore-Farrington was not involved?"

"Who?"

Pike swept the back of his hand towards the sketch. "The Honourable Alicia Sophie Victoria Cawdore-Farrington, of *those* Hampshire Farringtons, spouse of Major Sir Albert Cawdore, DSO, DL. [16] She looks uncharacteristically happy."

"You can identify her, then," I recognised. "Why is her merriment not typical?"

"Why, because she has the most miserable marriage in London, old spot," Pike answered me. "Everyone knows it. Nothing else is talked of. The beauteous Alicia was bought-in by the Cawdores for their stud book – the noble Farringtons are stony broke these days, they say, and desperate to fix their wagon to some name and fortune that can keep them solvent and respectable."

"The alliance between Major and Mrs. Cawdore-Farrington was primarily a marriage of negotiation," I understood.

Pike smirked. "What else? She is beautiful, talented, bright, and popular. He is a craggy Highlander thirty-two years her senior – dour, mean-spirited, and jealous. It could hardly be a match made in heaven. One almost expects to her of the notice of divorce as soon as the lawyers have finished drafting their causes."

"Divorce?" That was a serious matter, requiring significant evidence and substantial scandal. I had no idea what the judicial outcome of such a case might be, especially if there was no evidence of infidelity or spousal neglect or cruelty to convince a jury.

"Divorce." Langdale Pike sounded as if he might relish the long-drawn-out, gory business. I suppose it was fodder for his newspaper columns. "But not soon, I deem. If sweet Alicia tears herself from her dear lawful husband in an inuxorial display of independence, then she will forfeit all the allowance made by her husband's clan, and doubtless incur severe, even ruinous, penalties for breaking her marriage contract. Only with clear evidence of the Major's wrongdoing would she ever stand a chance in court of extricating herself to anywhere but the poorhouse."

"But this is certainly she?" I checked, indicating Hosketh's half-done picture.

"Unmistakably. And a rather nice sketch, I must say. I wonder to whom she was turning to speak? A shame the artist never filled in the second character."

Now that Pike had drawn my attention, it was clear that there was intended to be a second figure sketched in beside the first. The placement on the paper allowed for it, to depict the companion at whom she smiled to engagingly. Holmes had undoubtedly noted it, but I saw it only now. "Have you any idea who that person might be?"

"Speculation only, alas," the gossipmonger mourned. "A pity. Had this drawing been completed, then it might have been dynamite. If it was a man with Mrs. Cawdore-Farrington, a man other than the husband at whom she would never smile like that, then the Major might take any action he pleased to discipline her and to ruin her lover. It would not be incontrovertible evidence of infidelity, but it would probably sway a courtroom – juries love pictures, you know. It would certainly be enough to chain her to old Cawdore for life, or for such long miserable years as his remaining tenure on Earth can spawn."

Pike wanted to know more about the portraitist and the circumstances of the image being made. I had to admit something of the old pavement artist and his possibly-untimely passing.

The scandal columnist was unexpectedly helpful. "This was sketched very recently on Rotten Row," he opined. "Alicia is wearing the very latest fashion, and she is dressed for public riding, which means she was in Hyde Park. [17] Sketch-artists often go there and pencil hasty portraits of fashionable couples in hopes of selling them as souvenirs."

"How much might such a sketch earn them?" I wondered, thinking of the crown in Hosketh's pocket.

"Oh, six-pence or a bob, perhaps, if it takes the lady's fancy. Or a clip on the ear for cheek if her swain is feeling irritable."

"Not five shillings, then?"

"For a charcoal outline on cheap linen paper? Not likely. Besides, this picture is marred with mud. If the artist wanted to sell something to Alicia and her beau, assuming there *was* a beau and not a female friend, then he would need to start again on a fresh leaf."

"Perhaps he did?" I wondered. Theories began to assemble in my head.

I retrieved the sketch, though Pike was reluctant to part with it, eschewed another proffered lump of mawkish Turkish delight, and headed back to the mission to discover how Holmes's breakfast had suited him.

The sleeping hall and gallery of the Bell Lane Hostel seemed as eerie empty as when filled with shadowed, sleeping bodies. Now the long rows of stark wooden boxes were lit by watery rays of daylight through the high leaded windows. The sleeping crates did indeed resemble coffins, prepared for the influx of an army of exhausted and hopeless half-dead.

The halls smelled strongly of bleach, carbolic, and boiled cabbage. Three volunteers were sanitising the mission after its nightly hosting while others clattered in the kitchen preparing soup and rolls for a lunch-time charity run to the tramps under the railway arches. Despite the strong odours, I was still able to locate Sherlock Holmes from the chemical smells permeating from the Examination Room.

He has abandoned his disguise once more, and now stood in waistcoat and shirt-sleeves at Dr. Manfred's workbench. The resident physician, though he had technically discharged his shift, hovered anxiously and watched the detective at work.

I regarded the row of glass tubes and dishes on display, and the bottles of nitric acid and ammonia. "You are testing for poison," I recognised. "Atropa Belladonna?"

"Very good, Doctor," my friend greeted me. "You will excuse us, Manfred, while my colleague and I catch up on our respective investigations."

Manfred, singularly unhappy at being thrown out of his own surgery, slouched away to make whatever complaint he could to the Trustees who had imposed us upon his fiefdom. Holmes added a measure of silver nitrate to the sample in his test tube and watched in satisfaction as a yellowish-white precipitate formed.

"If this proves soluble in dilute ammonia but insoluble in *aqua fortis*, then deadly nightshade was present in my test sample," he told me. Then, after a glance at me, he noted, "You stepped into a puddle outside the coroner's office, and from the splatter pattern upon your left trouser leg you were stamping at the time. Did your visit anger you so much? I presume you have now set the legal representative upon a proper course?"

"I wonder whether I need ever speak to you at all to detail my researches," I admitted, slightly grumpily and unfairly. It had been a long night for both of us, but Holmes had managed less sleep than I.

"It is my incurable habit to read the people whom I encounter, and you are an open book, Watson. That is a compliment. There is no deception, malice, or dishonourable intent about you. Now come, tell me what Pike had to offer and what you observed of the corpses at Barts."

I surrendered and recounted my expedition. Holmes asked a few pertinent questions about the conditions of the cadavers, but was most interested in the identity of Mrs. Cawdore-Farrington. He followed my own line of reasoning but extended it further.

"I'm beginning to understand what happened here," he admitted. "There is one thing missing, but . . . No, let us begin with what we have. The talented but destitute Will Hosketh decided to venture his luck in drawing portraits on Rotten Row or Horseguards Parade. It is a little late in the year for such enterprise, but he had evidently had a sufficient windfall to invest in new charcoals and some few sheets of bonded paper. He sketched a likely candidate, the beautiful and fashionable Alicia Cawdore-Farrington, in her happy expedition with a companion. He never got to complete his vignette with that companion's image because some mishap befell his drawing paper, which was besmirched with splashed mud."

"Do you agree that he likely persisted and drew a second picture?" I ventured.

"I suspect so. But he did not complete it in time to sell it to the Hyde Park revellers." Holmes indicated the patched, holed work boots that had once belonged to the down-and-out pavement artist. "That granular orange soil testifies to a recent trip to Bedford Park, well west of Hosketh's usual

410

stamping ground. Let us suppose that Old Will, having completed his second work too late, enquires of some other person present the identity and address of either Mrs. Cawdore-Farrington or her companion, and then trudges out to call upon his subject at home. He still hopes to sell the picture of such a happy meeting. And so he did."

"His shiny new crown. Pike said it was far too much to pay for any street-sketch, but if it secured ownership of evidence that might be used against the lady . . . ."

"Then the payment might be cheaper than opening the way to blackmail," Holmes agreed. "I do not suggest that Hosketh had any such intent. Nothing I heard of him when I talked with the other guests at breakfast suggested about him any ingenuity of that kind. But I did speak with one acquaintance of his who offered a useful nugget of information."

It was time to hear Holmes's account of his undercover exploits. "My witness identified himself only as 'Snuffy'. He was on speaking terms with Hosketh and was stood in line behind him when Hosketh proffered his five-shilling coin for his night's lodgings. It was a matter of comment, when the clerk Fairbody had to go find sufficient change. Hosketh told Snuffy that he had sold a picture for the most money his work had ever bought, and had been 'sweetly rewarded and all'. Those particular words, Watson, which prove to be most relevant."

"How so?"

Holmes held up a delaying finger. "We shall get to that. First . . . ah, yes, the test is positive. Our sample contains not one but two dangerous concentrations of toxins, Watson. This test demonstrates the presence of belladonna. My previous experiment confirmed the inclusion of laudanum."

I frowned. "Nightshade vitiates the effects of tincture of opium," I objected.

"Not in the concentrations present in our sticky residue. The effects of ingestion of any substantial sample would have been to induce first catalepsy from the opiate and then tachycardia leading to heart failure from the belladonna." [18]

He set the dishes aside for now and returned to his account. "Nobody whom I was able to interview at the common table this morning knew aught of Benjamin Crewe. He was a true itinerant, a rough man whose demeanour suggested a violent disposition. The other visitors shunned him. Hosiah Swinnart was somewhat known and his death was a common topic. Of particular interest was the account of one of his close neighbours in a nearby bed the night that he died, who claims he heard Swinnart giggle, just once, as if pleased with himself. It may have been the last sound that Swinnart made. You see how helpful that is?"

411

"Not immediately," I responded. "Can you explain how three men were poisoned in their 'coffins', in different parts of the hostel hall, over four nights, under the watch of the Superintendent and his orderlies? Or even why?"

"I think I am ready to assay a possibility, Watson. Let us have Dr. Manfred and Superintendent Hoker back in here, and I will put it to them."

It was easy to find the men, since Manfred was in the hall berating the Superintendent for Holmes's interference. They fell silent when I appeared, and followed me back into the Examination Room with guarded expressions.

"The key was identifying the sticky substance that matted the straw from the coffin's bedding," Holmes told them without preamble. "The compound was of molasses, brown sugar, butter, and baking soda. And a strong dose of tranquilliser to mask the working of an equal dose of lethal poison."

Hoker did not follow. "Are you saying that the mattress was poisoned?"

"No," Holmes snorted at the suggestion. "Here is my hypothesis, based upon the data so far: Will Hosketh drew, then delivered and sold, a picture that depicted two people together who should not have met. He was paid well for his work by one or both of the subjects and sent on his way, but one or other of them determined to discourage the artist from attempting any other such portrait, or from speaking of his sale.

"In addition to his fee, one new crown, Hosketh was given a special treat, a luxury to be relished by a man in such impecunious circumstance as he suffered. He was given a confection made of the elements I identified. A seasonal confection, in fact."

I thought of the time of year, and of the hard sweetmeat baked to celebrate Guy Fawkes Night. "Bonfire toffee!" I cried. "Treacle toffee! Surely those are the ingredients?" [19]

"They are," Holmes confirmed. "Furthermore, the strong taste of black treacle is ideal for masking the bitterness of belladonna. The hardness of the confectionary – such toughness as to require a baked sheet of bonfire toffee to be shattered with a hammer before consumption – means that the sweet must be slowly sucked – It is too tough to chew. It is the ideal delivery mechanism for a slow-acting poison."

"Hosketh was given a bag of toffee to silence him," I understood. "But the others? Crewe and Swinnart?"

"Elementary. Remember, this is a rough lodging, for all the mission's precautions. I am informed that it is customary for guests to secure whatever valuables they have in the mattress on which they sleep, to prevent pilfering in the night. The buttoned covers offer easy access to

412

conceal humble treasures in the straw, items that can be retrieved come wake-up."

"Unless one does not wake up," I recognised.

"Indeed. And if the mattress is not changed, as the Superintendent has indicated it was not in this case, then the next occupant might find that same paper bag of treats and claim them for himself. The third box occupant clearly missed finding it, but the fourth, Swinnart, again availed himself of a discovery he doubtless thought providential."

"You searched the mattress," Manfred objected. "You scattered its contents all over my floor. There was no . . . bonfire toffee."

"Not then," Holmes agreed. "Only the seepage from its earlier presence, the sticky residue that allowed me to identify it had been there. After the third death, the bag itself was discovered and removed."

"By who?" Hoker demanded.

"By your substitute, of course. You said it was your deputy, Chaffinch, who had the duty that morning? Let's have him in and hear how he disposed of his find."

"Chaffinch? He's not in today. He has the day off, to spend with his wife and children and to celebrate . . . Bonfire Night."

I followed the horrified Superintendent's thinking. "Your deputy came across the toffee in the dead man's mattress. He reasoned that Swinnart had no more use for it, but Chaffinch's children . . . ." I stared in dismay at Holmes.

"Yes, Watson," he agreed. "We must go! At once!"

Four urgent men tumbled out of a growler in the cobbled terrace backroad of Tenter Street, between Tower Bridge and Aldgate. A long monotonous row of London brick terraces presented one door and three windows each to the narrow thoroughfare. Holmes led us not to the seldom-used front door of Jerome Chaffinch's address, [20] but rather through the arched passageway to the rears of the properties, where small vegetable plots backed on to waste ground belonging to the Catholic School Board.

I do not know whether the Roman Church would have approved of the use of its land to host a neighbourhood bonfire to celebrate the capture and execution of Catholic protestors, but I doubt anyone had enquired. A horde of excited children and a few indulgent parents were building a nine-foot high cone of rotten wood and stuffed newspapers ready for the event to come.

"There he is!" Superintendent Hoker pointed, identifying his deputy. Chaffinch was by the growing unlit pyre, supervising the addition of some broken packing crates. The fellow looked up in surprise that turned to alarm as he saw his superior and the mission's medical man closing upon him.

"Sir?" he managed. "Sirs?"

"The treacle toffee," Holmes required urgently. "Where is it?"

"The . . . the what, sir?"

"It's poisoned, man," I told him shortly. "It's what killed those three guests of yours."

Chaffinch went even more pale. He produced a grubby paper bag from his pocket and handed it to Holmes, like a guilty schoolboy caught smuggling treats into class. But his next words destroyed that cosy allusion. "Our Effie grazed 'er knee. I gave 'er a lump early for being a good girl."

The luxury had been reserved for the night's revels, then, but one lethal piece had already been distributed.

"The child," I called sharply. "Where is she?"

Chaffinch shouted his other children to locate their little sister. The urgent call alerted neighbours and other boys and girls to the crisis and the search became general.

Effie Chaffinch was found unconscious by the perimeter fence, half-hidden in a patch of dock leaves. She did not respond to calls to wake up or to shaking.

I took charge of the patient. There was no time to send for emetics so I simply forced my fingers down her throat to make her gag. I kept doing it, messy as it was, until she had vomited up as much of her stomach contents as I could get out of her.

"Brandy! Or whisky!" Holmes called to Dr. Manfred. There is no cure for belladonna poisoning, so treatment is by emetic and then continual stimulation. While Manfred raced for a spirits shop I applied artificial respiration.

"I didn't know!" Chaffinch gabbled to Hoker. "How could I know? I thought no 'arm! I'd never, sir, never . . . ."

"Your part in this was but minor, Mr. Chaffinch," Holmes assured the distraught father. "The author of this is the person who mixed this hellacious confection with such deadly intent. And, tellingly, had it ready to use before the pavement artist called."

Effie Chaffinch lived. With proper care and time she made a full recovery. The Bell Lane Mission Board of Trustees decided not to take disciplinary action against Chaffinch for his benevolently-intended theft, but Dr. Manfred's contract of service was not renewed when it expired.

Coroners' inquests confirmed Holmes's already-established conclusions about the presence of deadly nightshade and laudanum in the victims' stomachs. The verdicts were amended to murder by person or persons unknown. But of course Sherlock Holmes would not allow the matter to end at that.

He later estimated that he was one day too late in identifying the Bedford Park home of Mrs. Cawdore-Farrington's lover. By then Major Sir Albert Cawdore was in the obituary columns, reported as having died in his sleep of heart problems. A police investigation that the Cawdore household had not expected discovered that the Major's last meal had included a desert of his favourite treacle toffee, and a court-mandated *post mortem* discovered the poison that had killed him.

I need not revisit the scandal of the murderer's confession, nor his public instance that he acted alone without the aid, knowledge, or consent of the Honourable Alicia Sophie Victoria Cawdore-Farrington. In any case the salacious reportage of Langdale Pike and others can supply details for the ghoulish. I understand that the widow has emigrated to Mentone and no longer receives callers.

For the thousands of destitute men, women, and children in our Empire's very capital there seems no solution, except that steady march of civilisation by which we must preserve the best of what we have created and improve the rest. That there is no easy answer does not excuse us from tackling a hard one.

"Good old Watson!" Holmes exclaimed when I expressed this view to him. "In a city of unscrupulous employers and venal landlords there is a Bell Lane Trust and a Salvation Army. Where evil men plot crimes, then are also the well-meaning bumblers of Scotland Yard. And where adulterous murderers stain our national character there is John H. Watson – and therein lies our hope for redemption. We shall hold the line a little longer, my friend. Indeed, you know we must!"

NOTES

1. One description of such a venue appears in *The Quiver: An Illustrated Magazine for Sunday and General Reading* (1872), page 554:

    "I entered a long, narrow room, upon the floor of which were rows of what at first sight appeared to be coffins. On closer inspection, however, I found they were simply wooden bunks, in which the homeless people slept. These bunks were about forty in number, and were placed endways against the walls, leaving a free passage down the centre of the room. They contained neither mattress nor covers – a necessary arrangement . . . both on the score of cleanliness and economy."

    Gruesome as the accommodation may sound, at the time it was actually appreciated by some of its patrons, as attested by homeless food vendor John Fosh, interviewed in *Northern Whig*, "The Sorrows of a Sandwich Man" (January 23rd, 1891), page 7:

    "Four-pence for a doss. Salvation Army, Horseferry Road, a coffin bed and a leather blanket; but it's warm enough; the room is with steam pipes. At seven at night you goes in and gets some coffee and a bit of bread. When you goes out at seven in the morning you gets some more coffee and a bit more bread. Them and the doss is four-pence – and very good for the money."

    These and other useful period sources are assembled in an online article by Geri Walton, "Victorian Four Penny Coffins or Penny Beds, Homelessness, and More", at:

    https://www.geriwalton.com/victorian-four-penny-coffins-penny-beds-homelessness/

2. The winter of 1894-1895 was the coldest in London since 1881-1882 and was unmatched again until 1940-1941. The weather was worsened by global ash pollution from the eruption of Mount Krakatoa in the Dutch East Indies (now Indonesia) in 1883, and many climatologists mark 1894-1895 as the last great event of the "Little Ice Age" that had affected Europe since the 13th century. January 1885 was also notable for the appearance of thundersnow over Britain, a rare form of lightning storm in which snow or sleet – not rain – pelts from the sky.

3. Charles Dickens references such an establishment in *The Pickwick Papers*, as follows:

416

"And pray Sam, what is the two-penny rope?" inquired Mr. Pickwick.

"The two-penny rope, sir," replied Mr. Weller, "is just a cheap lodgin' house where the beds is two-pence a night!"

"What do they call a bed a rope for?" said Mr. Pickwick.

"Well the advantage o' the plan's obvious. At six o'clock every mornin', they lets go the ropes at one end, and down falls all the lodgers. Consequence is that, being thoroughly waked, they get up very quickly, and walk away."

4. A London census taken in January and February 1904 discovered 1,797 people without any accommodation – *"Of these 168 were sleeping on staircases, in doorways, or under arches, and the rest were walking the streets,"* – but also noted *"inmates of casual wards in London numbered 1,139. In addition, there were the vagrants in common, lodging-houses, including shelters; on the night in question there were 23,381 inmates of these houses . . . ."* (*Committee Report for the Departmental Committee on Vagrancy*, 1906).

It is troubling the London Assembly and the Mayor of London's office estimate there to be around three times this number of homeless in modern London, with less shelter accommodation.

5. This famous 1848 hymn by Cecil Frances Alexander would still include the now-omitted third verse:

> *The rich man in his castle,*
> *The poor man at his gate,*
> *God made them, high and lowly,*
> *And order'd their estate.*

6. St. Bartholomews Hospital, Smithfield, London, was founded in 1123. It is Watson's *alma mater* and the venue for his initial meeting with Sherlock Holmes in *A Study in Scarlet*. Threatened with closure in 1993, the institution was rescued by a "Save Barts Campaign" which included activities and a donation from the Tokyo Sherlock Holmes Appreciation Society.

7. The Third Anglo-Ashanti War took place in 1873-1874, in what is now Ghana, where 2,500 British troops and several thousand West Indian and African troops under General Garnet Wolseley repelled an Ashanti invasion. British casualties were light, with more dying from disease than enemy action.

8. Victorian incomes changed over the period of Holmes and Watson's adventures, but *Down East and Up West* by Montague Williams (1894)

gives an example of a sandwich-board advertising man receiving 1/- to 1/8 per day, for a full time annual income of £12 – £20. On the other hand, a young middle-class civil service clerk might earn £80 per year, rising to £200 over time ("Tempted London – Young Men", a series of anonymous articles in the *British Weekly*, 1887-1888), a butler could expect between £40 and £100 per annum (*Dickens's Dictionary of London*, 1879), and a general practitioner doctor such as John H. Watson might expect to enjoy around £1,300 per year on average ("The Wealth of Distinguished Doctors: Retrospective Survey", I. C. McManus, *British Medical Journal*, December 2005).

Arthur Sherwell's *Life in West London* (1897) offers an actual weekly budget for a poor family that shows them failing to meet all their debts on £1 13s. 7½d weekly. A. L. Bowley in *Wages in the United Kingdom in the 19th Century* (Cambridge: University Press, 1900) estimated the cost of living for an unmarried professional man, including rent, taxes, and maintaining two servants as £487 per year, allowing £10 for wine.

9.   "Oxford" was a colloquial name for a crown or five shilling piece. "Oxford scholar", shortened to "Oxford", was Cockney rhyming slang for "dollar", since Victorian exchange rates were roughly four U.S. dollars to one pound sterling – the dollar therefore being valued at around five shillings.

10.   Three different portraits of Queen Victoria appeared on British coinage during her long reign. Her "Young Head" image was imprinted from 1838-1887, then changed at her Golden Jubilee for the "Jubilee Head" picture that she so disliked, and then again in 1893-1901 for the "Widow Head" or "Old Head" portrait, with St. George slaying his dragon on the obverse. All the five-shilling coins were of Sterling silver.

11.   The *Sheffield Evening Telegraph*'s January 2nd, 1895 article, "Death in a Salvation Army Shelter", offers the following account of court proceedings:

> *"Agnes Braid, night officer in charge of the shelter, stated [that the] . . . witness did not see the deceased on Saturday night, but on going to wake her on Sunday morning found her dead. — The Corner: Are they in beds or bunks? — Witness: Bunks, sir. — The Coroner: I supposed there is something for warmth? – Witness: They put their own clothes over them [later this was amended to oil cloths being used for warmth]. The place is heated by hot water. — The Coroner: Kept at an even temperature? – Witness: No. . . . The Coroner: How many come in every night? — Witness: From 200 to 300. . . . A Juror: A more important question is that such a number of persons should be allowed to sleep in one room. The Coroner: A certain cubic measure is required or it would not be allowed . . . In the*

418

meantime, hundreds willingly go there; otherwise they would be sitting about on doorsteps. "

12.   The celebrated gossipmonger makes the briefest of appearances to assist Holmes in identifying a suspect in "The Adventure of the Three Gables" from *The Case-Book of Sherlock Holmes*. Secondary sources have fleshed out his background significantly but never authoritatively. Watson writes of him:

> *"This strange, languid creature spent his waking hours in the bow window of a St. James's Street club and was the receiving station as well as the transmitter for all the gossip of the metropolis. He made, it was said, a four-figure income by the paragraphs which he contributed every week to the garbage papers which cater to an inquisitive public. If ever, far down in the turbid depths of London life, there was some strange swirl or eddy, it was marked with automatic exactness by this human dial upon the surface. "*

It is generally accepted that Langdale Pike is a literary pseudonym. Langdale Pike is actually a prominent geological feature in the Cumbrian Lake District.

13.   The custom of fashioning a rag mannequin to burn on *Guy Fawkes Night* or *Bonfire Night*, November 5th, is still observed by the youth of Great Britain, in remembrance of the thwarted Catholic 'Gunpowder Plot' to blow up the Houses of Parliament on that day in 1605. Prior to immolation, this "guy" is displayed in a public place by children hoping to collect money for treats or fireworks.

14.   Watson includes an account as "The Adventure of the Veiled Lodger" in *The Case-Book of Sherlock Holmes*. The events therein are customarily dated to October 1896, which places Watson's meeting with Pike on Thursday, 5th November of that year and the three deaths on the 31st ult. and the 1st and 3rd inst.

15.   Holmesian debate is never more speculative than in accounting for the "missing year" in Dr. Watson's reports between the conclusion of "The Adventure of the Bruce-Partington Plans" on 23rd November, 1895 (recorded in *His Last Bow*, 1908) and "The Adventure of the Veiled Lodger" around eleven months later. No definitive story of Holmes's exploits in that time has yet been unearthed.

16.   That is, *Distinguished Service Order*, then quite a new award for *"meritorious or distinguished service by officers of the armed forces during wartime, typically in actual combat"*, and *Deputy Lieutenant*, a Crown

419

appointment as one of several deputies to the Lord Lieutenant of a ceremonial county.

17. Rotten Row is a wide track running almost a mile along the southern edge of Hyde Park. Originally established by King William III as a safe route between Kensington Palace and St. James's Palace through the then-robber haunted park, in 1690 it became the first artificially-lit highway in Britain. By the 18th century, the *Route de Roi* was known by its corrupted name, "Rotten Row", and it and the adjacent South Carriage Drive had become *the* fashionable place for noble and wealthy Londoners and handsome military officers to ride, to see and be seen. To facilitate Rotten Row's popular use, the road was converted into a "modern" bridleway in 1876 with a brick base covered in sand. Its popularity as an elite social venue continued well into the 20th Century, and Rotten Row remains open to the public to ride their horses along even today.

18. This is the combination of drugs that medical historians suspect was used to poison Solomon Northup, the free Black man who was kidnapped and sold into slavery in 1841 and whose story is told in *Twelve Years a Slave* by Solomon Northup, Sue L. Eakin, and Joseph Logsdon (Baton Rouge: Louisiana State University Press, 1975).

19. Variously called *bonfire toffee, treacle toffee, plot toffee*, or *Tom Trot* in England, *claggum* or *clack* in Scotland, or *loshin du* or *taffi triog* in Wales, the molasses-based confection is a hard, brittle toffee associated with Hallowe'en and Guy Fawkes Night in the same was that mince pies go with Christmas. Its flavour is similar to that of butterscotch. It was a home-made or commercially-branded staple treat in Victorian homes, an affordable but luxury item for the poorest classes.

20. In many humble terraced homes, the front door that led to the "sitting parlour" was reserved for important or "official" visitors such as a clergyman or landlord. All other access and regular domestic use came through the back door. This is why "back-to-back" terraces and their occupants, which had but a single door because each side of the building was a separate house, were considered inferior in status to regular terraces and their humble dwellers. Author I.A. Watson can attest that this practice and the prejudices that went with it were still observed by elderly residents of Yorkshire as late as the 1990's.

The Horror in King Street
by Thomas A. Burns, Jr.

As a general rule, I take great pleasure in writing these chronicles of the cases of my good friend and companion, Mr. Sherlock Holmes, but not this one. As soon as I have finished writing it, I will carry it straight to Cox and Company at Charing Cross and bury it in the depths of my battered tin dispatch box where it will never again see the light of day. The other parties who were officially involved in the affair, Inspector Athelney Jones and his superiors at the Metropolitan Police Force, are of a similar sentiment. Writing this account is purely cathartic – I am trying to make sense of that which makes no sense, but merely serves to illustrate the depths of depravity to which so-called civilized men can sink. No good purpose will be served by putting the facts of the case before the public, but perhaps the act of thrusting the manuscript into the dispatch box will erase my memories of the horror. I hope it will be so.

It was early in the evening of Saturday, January 30th, in the year 1897, a week to the day since Holmes and I had brought the matter of the Abbey Grange to a satisfactory conclusion. The weather was still frigid. Baker Street was well-nigh deserted except for the hansom cab which bore me home from an afternoon of billiards with Thurston at my club. A peculiar tranquility that often accompanies very cold weather embraced the city, muting all but the most propinquant sounds, such as the tattoo of the carriage horse's hooves, which were perversely magnified in the chilled air. The cab came to a halt across from 221b and I steeled myself against the anticipated blast of cold, then shoved the door open and slid out onto the cobblestones. My feet nearly went from under me as the soles of my boots touched the street rime and I had to grab the door of the cab for support lest I find myself sprawled on the pavement. When I had righted myself, I handed the driver a florin and waved him away when he essayed to make change – he deserved a few extra pence for simply being out in such weather.

I was making for the door of my lodgings with the help of my stick when a woman suddenly emerged from an adjacent doorway, blocking my path. She was youngish, probably in her twenties, but the grime and syphilitic sores on her face revealed her to be of lower class, likely a prostitute. A dirty, brown, hooded woollen cloak shielded her from the freezing cold and she was shod in heavy, lace-up boots. What was her likes doing in this genteel neighbourhood? I moved to avoid her, but she shifted

421

in tandem to oppose me. Her voluminous skirts fluttered and the face of a ragamuffin peered out from their folds. Now all of my nerves became instantly alert – it was a common ploy for some low-class women to use their children as accomplices for robbery. The urchin would rush out from under the woman's clothes and grasp the victim around the knees, taking scurrilous advantage of the natural reluctance of a gentleman to harm a child, while the parent rifled his pockets for a purse, a watch, or jewellery. I brandished my stick at the pair, shouting, "Away with you riff-raff, or I shall call for a constable!"

The woman replied, "Oh, please don't do that, Mr. 'Olmes! Not after I've come all this way to see ye!"

Of course. What else would such a woman be doing in Baker Street but desiring to consult my famous companion?

"I am not Mr. Holmes. I am Dr. Watson." I hesitated, then continued, "And you must come upstairs out of this beastly cold." I unlocked the door to the flat and held it for her, then preceded her up the stairs. Once in the sitting room, I turned up the gas and bade her and the boy to sit. "Why did you linger outside with a child in this terrible weather, Madam?" I asked her. "Did Mrs. Hudson refuse to let you in?" Our landlady should have known better than that, given all of the strange characters who have visited Holmes in these rooms over the years.

She gave a short dry cough. "Oh no, sir. I could see that yer rooms was dark, like nobody wasn't 'ere. So I waited for Mr. 'Olmes to come 'ome." She certainly had the Cockney's proclivity for the double negative and disrespect for the letter "*H*".

During this conversation, the child simply stood next to his mother, clutching her skirts. Now he began coughing as well, more severely than his mother. My blood went cold. I had heard that particular dry cough many times, and it never boded well.

"What is your name, lad?" He looked at the floor.

"Come on! Tell the gennleman your name."

The boy mumbled words that I could barely hear, then began that dry, hacking cough again.

"We calls 'im Lit'l Cedric," she said, "On account of 'is father is a Cedric too."

"Madam, I don't wish to alarm you, but have you and the boy ever been assessed for consumption?"

"Yes, Doctor, we 'ave. We've both got it," she said matter-of-factly.

Consumption was a scourge of poverty and ran rampant among the lower classes in London. It was almost always mortal in one so young. Treatment was painful and problematic. An infected lung was collapsed by injecting air into the chest cavity and increasing the pressure. The treatment deprived the bacillus of life-giving air, which sometimes eradicated it. Long term rest in a sanitarium was also effective, but sadly out of the reach of people such as these.

I heard a clatter on the stairs and the door to the flat opened to admit Sherlock Holmes, still in full morning dress. "I say, Watson, that sometimes my brother Mycroft can be such a pompous ass . . . . Hello! We have visitors."

I began to introduce our guests, when I realized to my chagrin that I hadn't even asked the woman her name. My concern for hers and her boy's condition had superseded formal niceties.

"That's all right, Doctor, I can klat for meself. I'm Mabel Copley, but folk call me Rosey."

"Pleased," said Holmes. "I can see, Madam, that you are the wife of a costermonger, reside in or near the Haymarket, a consumptive, and that you are recently bereaved. I also perceive that you have not as yet resorted to that ancient profession taken up by so many of your sisters."

"All of that is as 'urt as lepsog, Mr. 'Olmes, but I do not see how you have come to know it."

"Simplicity itself, Madam. Your familiarity with back slang labels you a costermonger, and anyone with more than a passing acquaintance with London knows that members of that profession make their home in or near the Haymarket. I am sure that Doctor Watson has already discussed your medical condition with you after hearing that cough, and the state of your eyes provides ample evidence of your recent grief. The fact that you care enough for your missing husband to retain your wedding ring is a good indication that you have not yet forsaken your marriage vows."

"And 'ow did ye know I am missing me Ced?"

"Why your boy is here with you, so who else would you grieve for but his father?"

"Yer fegir as nair, Mr. 'Olmes. It's ta help me find me Ced that I've come t'ye for. And I can pay ye!" She reached into the folds of her cloak and produced a leather money bag the size of a cricket ball, swinging it by the drawstring.

"Before we discuss remuneration, Mrs. Copley, pray give me the facts of the case so I may decide if I can be of aid to you. And I'm sure Dr. Watson will appreciate it if you eschew . . . er, avoid the back slang."

"I'll try, Mr. 'Olmes, but it's become an 'abit, ye know. What would ye like t'know?"

"When did your Ced go missing? What were the circumstances?"

"Me Ced is a coster and sells in the 'Aymarket, as ye've guessed." I saw Holmes wince at the word *guessed*. "Times is been 'ard of late 'cause winter is no time t'find veg t'sell. Poor Ced 'as been sellin' shif from the

Thames, but so many is doin' the same it's 'ard to make a yennep. We knowed Lit'l Cedric is sick and we been trying to get 'im in the work 'ouse, but they want papers and neither me nor Ced 'as much letters. Ced swore 'e would raise enow gelt to get Lit'l Cedrick a cure. Two days ago, 'e come 'ome wit' a proper toff, an 'e gimme a sack wit' an 'unnert guineas to pay for treatment for Lit'l Cedric. Then 'e said that 'e'd 'ave to go away with the gennleman for a while. I thot e'd 'av t'do summat agin the law to get that much yenom. Ced seemed real sad when he left, like I was never gonna see 'im a'gin on this airth. And I ain't seen 'im since. Ye gotta he'p me find 'im, Mr. 'Olmes! 'E's all I got!"

I couldn't believe my ears. "You have a hundred guineas in that bag?" That was more money than many a poor woman saw in her entire lifetime.

She clutched the bag fiercely to her breast. "I do that, and I'll gi'e ye summat, if ye'll 'elp me find me Ced, Mr. 'Olmes."

"Your problem is not without singular features of interest, Mrs. Copley. Now about this toff. Had you ever seen him before in the vicinity of the Haymarket?"

"No, Mr. 'Olmes, but there's so many folk comes to the 'Aymarket that I wouldn't notice 'im if'n 'e did."

"Would you recognize him if you saw him again?"

"I b'lieve so."

Holmes fetched a sketch pad from the shelf, along with a piece of drawing charcoal and a soft rubber eraser from a drawer, then bade Mrs. Copley to sit on the sofa and took his place next to her. "Now, did this toff have a narrow face like mine, or a broad one like Dr. Watson's?"

"More like yers, I fink."

Holmes drew a wide ellipse on the paper with the charcoal.

"Now, his nose, was it angular like mine, or broad like Watson's?" Thus, he prompted Mrs. Copley for over an hour about each of the man's features, deftly wielding the charcoal and the eraser according to her instructions, to construct on paper the face of the man she remembered.

Finally, she exclaimed, "Well, I never! That's 'im Mr. 'Olmes, that's 'im! By Gawd, yer a magician, y'are!"

"My grandmother was a Vernet," Holmes said smugly, "so I have some small skill as an artist."

I peered over Holmes's shoulder to view the visage of a youngish fellow with a fine head of hair that framed a cruel-looking face with narrow lips and beady eyes.

"Do you know the fellow, Watson?"

"Can't say as I do."

"Well, this sketch should bring us much forrader in locating the chap. My dear Mrs. Copley, please allow me the privilege of having you and your son to dine with Watson and me before you return home on this frosty night. I'm sure Mrs. Hudson can accommodate all of us."

She brandished the money bag like a weapon. "I can pay fer it, Mr. 'Olmes."

"I know you can, but this evening you are a guest in my home. Please do me the honour of accepting my hospitality."

Mrs. Hudson did indeed accommodate us with a fine mutton stew that had been simmering on the back of the stove all day, with bread, pickles, and the redoubtable Double Gloucester known as Cotswold, which had been supplemented with onions and chives. Little Cedric's eyes became as wide as saucers when Mrs. Hudson placed his very own egg custard tart before him after dinner. However, conversation at the table was subdued, with Mrs. Copley continually lamenting the loss of her husband.

After we had seen the pair off into the freezing darkness, secure in the knowledge that they were fuelled against the cold for one night at least, Holmes turned to me and said, "Watson, I'm off in the morning for the Haymarket to see if I can locate our elusive toff."

"I have an errand as well, Holmes. I'm going to Gray's Inn Road to the Royal Free Hospital to see if I can find a place there for Little Cedric. I fear he will not last the winter if I cannot."

Holmes had already departed by the time I arose on Sunday morning to the pealing of the bells of nearby St. Cyprian's. I would not be in attendance that morning, but I was secure in the knowledge that I would be doing the Lord's work that day.

William Marsden's Royal Free Hospital was the only institution in London that provided proper medical care to the indigent on a regular basis, and as one might expect, it was generally difficult or impossible to secure a place there because of the multitude that sought its services, even though yet another new wing was opened only two years ago. I did not know if I could obtain treatment for Little Cedric there, but I knew that I would not be able to sleep at night lest I tried. Alas, it was as I feared – despite much cajoling and pleading, I came away empty-handed, largely because the treatment for consumption was so protracted. One doctor did offer to collapse the lung *pro bono*, but I feared that would do little good without a proper place for the boy to rest and recuperate.

Darkness was already falling by the time I returned to Baker Street in early evening. As I approached the door to the flat, my ears were assailed by the cry of *"Freessh Fish!"*, and I turned to see a man in a battered coat and hat approaching, wearing a wooden tray over his shoulders that had several fish tails protruding from it at all angles.

The fish stink nearly overwhelmed me as he stopped a few feet away.

"Buy some fish, guvna? Fresh from de Thames dis mornin', they are."

425

"If you'll go 'round to the back gate, Holmes, I'll bring your dressing gown down to you so you can leave those reeking vestments in the yard."

He straightened up and said, "Very well, Watson. I suppose I can't go on fooling you with my disguises forever. I will accept your kind offer, and provide these fellows to Mrs. Hudson for our dinner, because they have remained surprisingly fresh in this beastly cold."

After Holmes had disrobed and scrubbed the fishiness from his body, we sat around the table in our rooms, sipping whisky-sodas and trading tales of our respective, dismal endeavours.

"The Haymarket costermonger community is a close-knit group and most of its members are acquainted with each other, so I had to convince a fellow whom I had kept out of the dock for burglary to claim me as a poor cousin from the provinces. I was still the subject of some rancour however, because as Mrs. Copley implied, times are hard for the costers in winter, and I therefore represented just one more mouth for limited resources to feed. I was unsuccessful in identifying our toff, although a couple of fellows admitted seeing him about. However, I did hear a rumour about a posting in the agony column concerning money to be had if a poor man was willing to work for it. Ha! That will be Billy now, with the papers. Come in!"

The door opened to admit our page Billy, staggering under the load of London's Sunday papers, a prodigious lot indeed. Holmes told him to put them on the table but I intervened, because there would surely be no room for our dinner if he did so. He put them on the sofa instead.

"It is well that you said so, Watson, as I neglected to tell you we are having a guest for dinner. I've asked Langdale Pike, my old school chum, to drop by."

Langdale Pike was a gossip-monger who published columns in several of the city's more disreputable rags. Holmes found him an invaluable source about the goings-on in so-called polite society, but I didn't like the fellow at all. Pike was languorous to the point of disconsolateness – I suspected he was no stranger to the opium pipe and I did not care for Holmes to spend much time in his company, given my friend's predilections in that direction. He usually dressed in what he referred to as "the latest fashions", but which seemed to be outlandishly bad taste to me, and he had an annoying habit of peering at people who spoke to him through a monocle which I doubt that he needed. Pike arrived just as Mrs. Hudson was bringing Holmes's late charges in as covered dishes.

"Thanks awfully, Holmes," he said when Holmes offered him a plate, "but I never eat fish unless it's fresh caught from the sea. A fish from the Thames may have eaten someone I once knew, y'know. I will have one of those whisky-sodas though, just to keep you gentlemen company while you dine."

Holmes poured a tot of single-malt into a glass, followed it with a spritz from the gasogene, and handed it to Pike, who took it to the sofa and proceeded to sprawl himself out on the stacks of papers there.

Since Mrs. Hudson had dinner on the table, we made desultory conversation while eating, helped along by Pike's tendency to jump randomly from one subject to another with no apparent stimulus. The Thames fish proved surprisingly palatable, although Pike's ill-timed earlier comment kept resurfacing in my mind. When the plates were cleared, the brandy poured, and the cigars lit, Holmes got down to the purpose of Pike's visit.

"I have a drawing of a fellow who may be important in one of my cases, Pike. I'd like you to look at it and tell me if you recognize him. However, if you do, I must ask you to make no allusion of this in your columns until I authorize it."

Pike assumed an affronted demeanour. "You wound me, Holmes. When have I ever betrayed your confidence?"

"Well, there was that time when we were at University . . . ."

"Is that the picture you have in your hand?"

Holmes unrolled the sketch and held it out to Pike, who didn't even take it.

"Whyn't you give me something difficult to do? That is a picture of Shrevvy Anston-Smythe."

"That is a name with which I am not familiar," said Holmes.

"I don't wonder. Shreeve, as they call him, is the fifth son of a fourth son and no one who is anyone, although I'll bet he'd like to be."

"So how do you know him?"

"Because he's a hanger-on of someone a bit more famous." Pike looked at us expectantly, waiting for someone to ask him.

Holmes obliged. "Who?"

"Teddy Grenville."

"Grenville. Now *there* is a noble name. Watson, I'll trouble you for my *Burke's* from the shelf." Holmes riffled through the great tome until he found the proper page. "Here 'tis. Richard Grenville, 6th Duke of Hereford. Eldest son is also Richard. Ha! Teddy is a fourth son too, it seems. Joined the Hereford Regiment of Foot – of course he did. Saw service in Africa. Now Watson, I'll trouble you again for my index. The *G*-box, please."

I retrieved the box of Holmes's criminal index that contained the miscreants whose names began with the letter *G*.

427

Holmes flipped through the cards. "Hmm. The *G*'s are not nearly as eminent as the *M*'s, but here's Gaston, the assassin, Gates, the poisoner and Gilhooley the Irish bomber. And of course, Mr. Teddy Grenville. Seems he was accused of luring a young woman of a fine family into a compromising position last year. It also seems that the patriarchs of the two families were able to come to a satisfactory arrangement, doubtless involving a sum of money from the Duke, sufficient to recompense the girl's father for the loss of her virtue. And young Grenville's name has been mentioned in other scandals as well." Holmes looked at our guest. "Anything to add, Pike?"

"Only that there's been a rumour that Master Teddy's been recruiting young rakes into a new social club he's forming – The Tiberian."

I raised my eyebrows at that. "A social club? For fourth sons?"

"Apparently. Rumour has it that they've already conducted some fairly scandalous *soirees*. Teddy seems to think he's the reincarnation of Sir Francis Dashwood."

"I'm not familiar with the name," I said.

"You shouldn't be," said Holmes. "Sir Francis Dashwood was a well-known scalawag in the last century who formed an association known by various names, one of which was 'The Hellfire Club', because of the impious activities in which the members engaged. While ostensibly of a religious nature, the organisation seemed to largely be an excuse to conduct orgies. There were allegations that some of the women involved had not consented to participate, but nothing was ever proven. It seems Master Teddy's group has a similar disposition."

"But why would such men give a large sum of money to a costermonger to take care of his sick son?" I asked.

"That is the question we must answer, Watson," Holmes replied. "They obviously wanted something from the fellow. We have to determine what that was."

I was roused from sleep by a rude hand shaking me by the shoulder. I opened my eyes to see Holmes's angular face wreathed in shadows from the light of the candle in his other hand.

"Holmes! What is it?"

"It's murder, Watson! Murder most foul! And I am an ass!"

I quickly dressed then found myself in a hansom cab. The clip-clop of the horse's hooves echoed from the buildings in the frigid dawn as Holmes and I made for a sordid alley off of the Haymarket, where Scotland Yard Inspector Athelney Jones presided over a corpse.

The alley in question was too narrow for the cab to enter, so the driver stopped in front of the uniformed constable that marked its location and

Holmes led the way as we walked in single-file along the side of the alley closest to the wall of the adjacent building. He directed the yellow beam of the bullseye lantern he carried toward the cobblestones in the middle of the passage, and I heard him mutter something about "a herd of elephants" under his breath. We soon identified the pachyderms at fault – two men standing in an undersized courtyard formed where the alley opened out at the end. Another constable was stationed there, along with a large stout man wearing a tan greatcoat, a woolen toque with earflaps, and a yellow scarf wound tightly around his lower face so that only a pair of small black eyes could be seen surveying the tragedy. Even though I couldn't see his face, I identified the man as Inspector Athelney Jones of Scotland Yard by his girth alone.

The beam of Holmes's lantern illuminated a heap of rags laying in a pool of blood – a closer looked revealed the body of a woman among the cloths, lying face down. She was also clad in a hat and scarf against the cold. Holmes reached down and turned her face to the light. Although her features looked different in death, there was no doubt that the woman was Mabel Copley.

Jones was obviously surprised at our arrival. "Mr. 'Olmes! 'Ow did you 'ear of this?"

"I have my methods, Inspector." In this case, those methods doubtless comprised a few well-placed agents at Scotland Yard.

"Hmmph," Jones snorted. "Well, we'll be needin' none of yer theories 'ere, Mr. 'Olmes. It's as plain as a pikestaff wot's 'appened. The gel tried to get out o' the wind by walkin' down this alley, when she was waylaid by robbers. She should 'av known better t'keep t'the main streets at so late an 'our."

Holmes shined his lantern about as Jones was speaking. "You may be correct, Inspector. It seems that she entered the alley from the Haymarket and got only this far before she was struck down. If you and the constable hadn't obliterated her tracks in the rime on your way in here, I might have been able to determine whether she knew that she was pursued and the height of her assailant." Holmes shined his light again upon the unfortunate Mrs. Copley, and then said, "Watson, be a good fellow and hold this light for me. Constable, help me turn her over."

I took the lantern and shined it on the body as he requested. The constable looked at Jones, who nodded reluctantly, then did as Holmes asked. Holmes squatted down next to the corpse and began undoing her clothes.

"'Ere, now!" said Jones. "Can't that wait until we get 'er back to the morgue?"

Not pausing in his work, Holmes said over his shoulder, "No Inspector Jones, it cannot wait. I am not accompanying the body to the morgue."

By this time, he had the woman's outer garments opened and was attacking the buttons on her blouse. He spread that apart and began on the under-bodice. When he had that opened he said, "Constable, help me pick her up so I can get these clothes off her."

The constable raised the upper part of her torso off the pavement, getting his hands full of blood in the process while Holmes slid her clothing off so she was naked to the waist.

"Hold her a moment, constable. Watson, shine your light on her back. Ha! Here is the blow that did her in, I'll be bound." He pointed to a vertical gash about five inches long just beneath her left shoulder. "Severed the pulmonary artery, from the look of it. She wouldn't have been conscious long. This killing was done with a curious blade, much broader in the middle than at the tip. Just look at difference in the size of the stab wounds, which depend on their depth." Indeed, it looked as if the killer had indulged in a frenzy of stabbing after she went down, with numerous wounds covering her back. "Lay her back down, Constable."

Holmes began going through her clothing, also getting much blood on his hands. "It is not here, Watson," he said. "The bounder has taken his money back."

"What money?" said Jones. Holmes ignored him.

"I'm afraid that is all we're going to glean from the crime scene," said Holmes. "Inspector, you can take her now."

"Well, thanks awfully," said Jones sarcastically.

"Watson, it is imperative we locate Little Cedric as soon as possible," said Holmes. "He is now likely an orphan."

The dawn sky was blushed with crimson as we followed the alley back out to the Haymarket. The lamplighter was extinguishing the flames in the lamps that ran down the centre of the broad boulevard as a few optimistic costermongers already circulated with carts or trays of fish. Holmes retrieved a half-crown from a pocket and began making inquiries, and it was not long before he returned triumphant. He bade me follow him to a vile back court off the Haymarket not far from the murder scene, which was strewn with garbage and nondescript urban effluvia. For once I was grateful for the cold, for it suppressed the odour of the decaying trash. We made our way to a basement door, which Holmes pushed open, and we entered a disgusting little black room that reeked of peat smoke and excrement. We found Little Cedric sleeping the sleep of the innocent under a pile of filthy blankets on a pallet next to a stove vented out a broken window. He woke as I picked him up but went back to sleep with his head on my shoulder after I shushed him.

Holmes went off to find a hansom and returned in it. As he exited the cab, he said, "Watson, the boy is in your charge. Find him a place where he will receive proper care. I have something else to do."

Finding him a place where he would receive proper care was obviously much easier to say than to do. The orphanages of London were horribly overcrowded, which was the reason that so many children without families lived on the streets. Nevertheless, I had to try. On our arrival back at Baker Street, I asked the cabman to wait, knocked up Mrs. Hudson, and delivered Little Cedric into her care. Then I got back into the cab and asked the driver to take me to the London Foundling Hospital in Guilford Street, which had been founded by the sea captain and philanthropist Thomas Coram. The hospital originally accepted only infants, but the problem of homeless orphans in London was so acute that the policy was changed to accept illegitimate children as old as twelve. Most of the children were not housed there. Rather, places were found for them in the provinces where they could be raised to an age at which they could be apprenticed and repay some of the expenses of their rearing. By and large it was a good system, as the child, now an adult, came out of the apprenticeship with a trade.

My initial experience at the Foundling Hospital was much like that at the Royal Free Hospital – everyone was apologetic, but the hospital was overcrowded and places were simply not to be had. I was about to give up in disgust and go back to Baker Street when I heard "Ho! Doctor Watson!" and I turned to see Dr. Moore Agar walking towards me.

Both Holmes and I had consulted Agar as a personal physician, although it had been some time since either of us had need of him. After exchanging ritual greetings, I asked him if he still had his practice in Harley Street.

"Yes I do, Doctor, and it is doing quite well. What brings you to the Foundling Hospital?"

I explained my plight.

"I see," Agar said. "Well, the hospital would not accept a child with an active case of consumption in any case. However, I have some friends in the administration of Sick Children's Hospital 'round the corner in Great Ormond Street. Let me discuss this with them and I'll get back to you this afternoon or in the morning. Are you still in Baker Street?"

I assured that I was and left in much better spirits.

I returned to Baker Street to find Holmes lounging on the sofa amongst the piles of newspapers from last night.

"I have had an interesting afternoon," said Holmes. I raised an eyebrow to encourage him to continue. "I thought it might be profitable to

431

surveil The Tiberian Club to see if there was any indication of criminal activity, so I spent the afternoon as a beggar in King Street. Unfortunately, there was no traffic of persons going in or out, but there was one curious incident." He paused for dramatic effect.

I indulged him. "And the curious incident was?"

"They accepted a rather large delivery of ice around four o'clock."

"Ice?" I was incredulous! "Ice, in this weather?"

"Precisely."

"What do you make of it?"

"I have told you previously that it is a capital mistake to theorize in advance of the data. So I propose to get data. I have also previously remarked to you that one cannot gain greater knowledge of the popular culture of London by an activity other than the perusal of the agony column." He handed me a copy of last night's edition of *The London Evening Standard,* in which an advertisement had been circled.

> *AN OPPORTUNITY is available* [it ran] *for any hard-working Englishman who seeks funds to improve his situation. Reply with the basis for yr. need. Will reply in this column with a meeting place in two days if yr. reason is acceptable.*

"If this is targeting the poor," I remarked, "it seems remarkably inefficient. Most of the members of that class are illiterate, are they not?"

"Yes Watson – most, but not all. Some of the literate poor make a decent living serving as modern-day town criers, if you will, bringing the attention of their illiterate brethren to advertisements such as this one and serving as a go-between for replies. I have sent a reply, so we shall see if it bears fruit on Wednesday evening."

The next day, Tuesday, I received the following in the noon post:

> *Dear Dr. Watson,*
>
> *You will be happy to learn that the Sick Children's Hospital will accept the boy you found as a patient as long as someone will be responsible for his expenses, which they estimate as approximately £300. I have been doing rather well of late, so I will pick up half of the cost if you and Holmes can shoulder the other half. If this is agreeable to you, you may bring the boy around to them this afternoon.*
>
> *Yrs. truly,*
> *M. Agar, M.D.*

432

Neither Holmes nor I were wealthy men, but I felt sure that between the two of us, we could bear the burden, especially in the light of Agar's generous offer. So, I informed Mrs. Hudson that she should make her charge presentable for transportation the following day, and I then took Little Cedric on his "first ever ride in a hansom cab". (Actually, it was his second, but he was asleep during his first.) After delivering him into the care of the good doctors of Great Ormond Street, I repaired back to 221b.

I found Holmes in a fine humour, so I took the opportunity to inform him that he was £75 poorer as the result of my afternoon's activities.

"Ah, it is well, then, that I took in five shillings and six-pence in alms yesterday." was his philosophical response. "But look here! I have received a reply from our scoundrels." He handed me a folded copy of today's paper.

> *Poorboy,* (it ran) *We agree your need is great. Pls meet our rep. in the Bear and Staff, Leicester Sq. at 7 sharp, tonight. Wear a red ribbon on your coat.*

"I have just enough time to don my disguise," said Holmes.

"Aren't you just a bit worried that you may be putting your head in the lion's mouth?" I asked somewhat testily.

"Not at all, dear fellow, when I will have you and your trusty revolver by my side. You will be sampling the pubkeeper's best in the Bear and Staff when this meeting occurs, and I will trust in you not to let me out of your sight until this affair is brought to a successful conclusion."

So it was that I found myself in that venerable old watering hole that Wednesday evening with my foot on the rail, inhaling the aroma of pipe smoke, hops, and old wood. An excellent pint of ale stood before me on the bar. I savoured it slowly, having no wish to dull my reflexes, given my imminent duty. A bit later, Holmes entered in his costermonger's garb with an incongruous crimson ribbon on his coat pocket and sauntered up to the bar.

"I'll 'av me a pint o' bitter, barman."

"Oh, youse will, will youse?" The barman replied in an unkind tone. "Let's see yer dosh, mate."

Holmes glared at the barman. "I've a good mind t'take me custom elsewhere." He reached in a pocket and flung tuppence onto the bar.

"A pint's thruppence and a hae'," said the barman. Holmes was digging in his pockets for more coins when another voice said, "Here's a bob, Steve. Give my friend a pint o' bitter and me the same." A shilling rang on the bar.

433

Shreeve must have been sitting in the shadows in the corner, as I didn't see him when I came in. But he was here now, standing behind Holmes. The barman instantly became contrite. "Sorry, yer ludship. I dinna know 'e was wit' you."

The barman poured two pints from the pitcher on the bar and gave Shreeve his change, which he ignored. Holmes snatched it up greedily. They retired to a corner table across the room. Since there was no need for me to know the details of their conversation, I did not try to hear. Rather, I simply observed them out of the corner of my eye so I could follow them if and when they left.

About fifteen minutes later, the pints were finished and Holmes and Shreeve exited the pub. I waited a moment, finished my drink, and followed. When I emerged onto Bear Street, I saw them just rounding the corner into Leicester Square. I followed, and when I arrived at the corner I spied them walking diagonally across the green. I tried to keep a consistent distance between us to avoid observation, but they seemed to be engaged in an animated conversation and Shreeve appeared to be paying little attention to his back trail. As I passed the statue of the Bard in the centre of the square, they were entering Spur Street, which was much darker than the square due to a dearth of streetlights. It was also more deserted, so I allowed them get a little further ahead of me before following them into Panton Street, which they traversed before turning south on the Haymarket. The Haymarket was much more crowded than the side streets even at this hour, and a chill went up my spine, as I had difficulty identifying the pair amongst the crowd. However, I was fairly certain that they were making for The Tiberian Club, so I hurried down to Charles Street, ignoring the entreaties of the ladies of the evening on the way, and spotted the pair halfway down, heading toward St. James Square. I waited until they reached Regent Street, then followed again, keeping a full block between us.

They crossed St. James Square and turned into King Street, so now I was sure they were going to The Tiberian. I gave them time to get there, then hurried down and stationed myself near the old Junior Army and Navy Club building, across the street from the fine old Georgian townhouse that housed The Tiberian.

By this time Holmes and Shreeve had vanished, so I was forced to conclude that they had gone inside. I reckoned to give Holmes about an hour before taking any action. I hunkered down inside my greatcoat, wrapped my scarf tightly around my face, pulled the flaps of my cap over my ears, and waited.

After a time, the lights in the first-floor windows overlooking King Street came on. The floor-to-ceiling windows were easily ten feet above street level, much too high for me to peer inside from the street, but I had taken the precaution of bringing one of Holmes's powerful monoculars along in my pocket. I focused on the window and looked into a dining room where I saw Holmes at the table with Shreeve, Teddy Grenville, and a third man whom I did not recognize. Holmes, Shreeve and Teddy sat down then the unknown man left the room. He returned a few moments later carrying a covered tray which he placed on the table, then he removed the cover and passed out plates of food. He then procured a bottle of wine and served the others before he sat down to partake of the meal along with them.

Deuced generous of Teddy to wine and dine a costermonger who answered an advertisement from the agony column, I thought.

The men, including Holmes, ate and drank with seeming relish. Teddy was holding forth in a seeming diatribe when Holmes suddenly collapsed face first onto the table. Teddy and Shreeve jumped up as if they were waiting for this and hustled Holmes's limp body out of the room, one on either side of him.

I knew that I had no time to go for aid. I drew my Webley Bull Dog, hurried across the street, and rattled the front door knob. It was locked, of course. A single strike with my shoulder convinced me that the door was stout enough to resist entry by that means, so I placed the barrel of the pistol next to the lock and fired two shots that reverberated loudly throughout the stony cavern of King Street. I sincerely hoped that someone would report the noise to the authorities. Another shoulder strike was enough to breech the door.

I rushed inside, shouting "Holmes! Holmes!" If any of the occupants had shown themselves I would have shot them down without a thought. But none did, so I raced through the house, throwing open doors looking for my friend. I found myself in the dining room in which I saw Holmes fall. The remnants of the night's dinner were still on the plates – beefsteak, mash, vegetables. A dark red stain marked Holmes place, where his wine glass had overturned. I pushed through the swinging doors into the kitchen where I was confronted with an anomalous sight. A man sitting at the counter, weeping uncontrollably, looked up as I entered. It was not Shreeve or Teddy, but the third man, the fellow whom I did not know. He did not seem to notice the revolver I pointed at him.

"I can't do it anymore," he said.

"Do what? Where's Holmes, man! What have you done with him?"

"I can't do it anymore!" he shouted. Now his eyes fixed on the revolver in my hand, then glowed with a malevolent light. He snatched a knife from the counter and the stool on which he sat overturned with a

435

clatter as he charged me. I had no choice. I shot twice and brought him down.

My physician's instincts commanded me to render aid as a rapidly spreading crimson pool appeared beneath him, but my reason told me I had no time. Instead, I broke my revolver and extracted the empty shells, then reloaded the cylinder with cartridges from my pocket. I felt that Holmes was in deadly danger somewhere in this house. I had to find him!

I found myself back at the front door. A staircase led to the upper floors of the townhouse, and a door under the stairs likely concealed steps to the basement. Up or down? Down, I decided. Nefarious activities were best conducted in the depths of the earth.

There was indeed a flight of stone steps behind the heavy door, but the downward passage was as black as sin beyond a small area illuminated by the light in the hallway. I glanced around and saw a candle in a stand on a side table. I seized it and lit it from the gas, then cautiously made my way down the stony staircase with the candle in one hand and the pistol in the other. At the bottom of the stairs was a dank stone passage that stank of sewer gas. Light blazed from an open doorway at the end.

Even now, sitting in my warm, safe rooms in Baker Street, I hesitate to describe what I saw in that horrible chamber. But I must, if I am to exorcize the demons that possess me!

I blew out my candle and set it down on the floor of the passage, then crept silently down the passage towards the door. I heard metal rattle against stone, then voices from within.

"Pick 'is feet up, will yer? That's it! He's a big 'un, so the chain needs t'be tight."

I peered around the corner into the room and the sight froze my blood.

Yellow light from a lantern on the stone floor revealed a man – Teddy it was – who, stripped to the waist, was wrapping a chain about the ankles of another man who was prostrate on the floor. Holmes! Shreeve, in a similar state of *déshabillé*, held Holmes's legs so Teddy could do the deed. The chain ran upward to a block hanging from the ceiling, allowing a body to be hoisted aloft.

The lantern light also glinted off a metal surgeon's table, a rack of wicked knives mounted on the wall, and several copper tubs on the opposite side of the room. Arms, legs and heads protruded from the gleaming chunks of ice that filled them. The bodies of men! The realization of what the meat on the plates in the dining room must have been washed over me like an icy wave. I stepped into the doorway, and as the two scoundrels turned to face me with wide eyes and their mouths forming shocked *O*'s, I fired deliberately four times, two bullets for each of them. I examined the bodies and determined that the final bullet in the cylinder was unnecessary.

The next evening, I sat in Baker Street with Holmes and Athelney Jones. The former looked distinctly unwell in his mouse grey dressing gown and slippers. He was out of bed against my express orders, but he insisted that he wanted to bring this affair to a close as quickly as possible. I could not blame him.

". . . and the Captain said that no charges will be brought against you, Dr. Watson, for shooting those rogues in King Street. I doubt there won't be any trouble from the Duke neither, as he would have no wish to see any of this in the papers."

"Not one of my better efforts, I am afraid," Holmes admitted. "During my meeting with Shreeve, he intimated that I was being recruited for a party of thugs who were going to 'teach a lesson' to another nobleman who had disparaged him in public. He invited me to The Tiberian for dinner as a show of good faith before giving me the money. Naturally, I suspected some kind of double-cross was in the offing."

"I knew that either Shreeve or Teddy – I suspect the latter – had murdered poor Rosey to get the money back. My suspicions were confirmed when I saw this hanging on the wall of the dining room." Holmes picked up a curious, lozenge-shaped blade of beaten bronze with a sharp point and a broad middle about a foot long. "I should think that the coroner will find that this fits the wounds on Mabel Copley's corpse very well. After I noticed it, I was contriving a means to absent myself from the premises without alarming my hosts when dinner was served. I noticed the meat had an unusual appearance, so I didn't eat any. The only reason to secure large quantities of ice, especially in the winter time, would be to preserve something, and I was beginning to get an inkling of just what might have happened to Cedric Copley. I did, however, sip the wine, so as not to arouse their apprehension that I was on to them.

"My suspicions were confirmed when Teddy began to brag. After poor Copley responded to the post in the agony column and informed the blackguards of Little Cedric's plight, they offered him a hundred guineas for his left arm! They assured him it would be removed by a competent surgeon for scientific purposes and that his chances of survival were high. Copley wisely demanded payment in advance and gave the money to Rosey. Of course, when he reported to The Tiberian Club to fulfil his part of the bargain, the bounders killed him out of hand and butchered him in that hellish abattoir in the basement. By this time, I knew I was in trouble, but unfortunately, I did not forsee the laudanum in the wine. I shudder to think of my fate had the Good Doctor not arrived when he did. I must

437

confess this was one time that my powers failed me – I did not deduce that I was destined to become part of the bill of fare at The Tiberian myself."

"How could you have?" I said. "Cannibalism is associated with primitive areas, not with the greatest city in the modern world."

"That is not entirely true," Holmes said. "While most documented cases of contemporary cannibalism have been so-called cases of survival cannibalism, such as that documented by Chase among the survivors of the ill-fated American whale-ship *Essex* and with the Donner party and Alfred Packer in the United States, cannibalism has also been associated with several killing sprees, the most notable being that of our own Saucy Jack in 1888. The repulsive Bean family of Galloway in the 1400's also comes to mind – the Newgate Calendar documents they had 'the legs, hands, arms, and feet of men, women, and children suspended in rows like dried beef' when their caverns were raided by a party in command of a personage no less than James I. And just three years ago, the infamous parliamentarian Henry Labouchere was acquitted of libel after accusing the Duc de Vallombrasa of feeding the French Army on the corpses of its own dead."

Holmes paused to take a drink of his brandy and soda – I noticed he was drinking quite a bit more than usual since his rescue from The Tiberian – and then continued. "Given the state of some of the more impoverished communities in London, I suspect cannibalism occurs here more often than the authorities would like to admit, especially in winter. It has also been reported in several tribes in the Natal where Teddy Grenville was stationed, and he likely acquired his taste for human flesh during that time. Besides, the practice would have appealed to that perverse instinct of his to flout society's taboos.

"There is a particular variety of lordling," Holmes went on, "who – whether as a consequence of *ennui*, privilege, or simply a general disdain for the rules of civilized society – takes a perverse delight in violating those rules whenever the occasion offers. Such defiance tends to breed on itself, so the rebellious behaviour becomes increasingly egregious with time. We English like to think that heredity is a significant determinant of a man's character, and in most cases I believe that it is, but just as when endeavouring to produce pure-bred animals from good stock, throwbacks arise that have none of the desirable characteristics that breeder is trying to attain. In the case of a dog or a bull, the throwback would be culled so the undesirable traits do not sully the line. When this occurs in a man, the situation becomes more complex. Social ostracism can be effectively employed to isolate miscreants and remove them from polite society, but that often results in an association of pariahs such as the one we saw in this case."

An uncomfortable silence descended on the room. Athelney Jones and I had an unspoken agreement not to discuss what Holmes had faced at The Tiberian, and my friend seemed grateful for our discretion. Afterwards, he had look drained and ashen-faced, and he had gone to consult with Dr. Agar the following afternoon. I haven't told Holmes as yet, but I've been investigating some rural areas that might be appropriate for a little holiday as soon as the weather breaks and I've nearly settled on a place in Cornwall. I'm sure I can co-opt Dr. Agar into my little scheme to get Holmes some much needed rest.

As I wrote at the outset, I think that no good can come of releasing the details of this distressing affair to the public, so I am off to Charing Cross in the morning to bury it in one of the deepest vaults in London. May it remain there until the One who lords over all of us makes his triumphant return!

About the Contributors

The following contributions appear in this volume:
The MX Book of New Sherlock Holmes Stories
Part XIV – 2019 Annual (1891-1897)

Brian Belanger is a publisher and editor, but is best known for his freelance illustration and cover design work. His distinctive style can be seen on several MX Publishing covers, including *Silent Meridian* by Elizabeth Crowen, *Sherlock Holmes and the Menacing Melbournian* by Allan Mitchell, *Sherlock Holmes and A Quantity of Debt* by David Marcum, *Welcome to Undershaw* by Luke Benjamen Kuhns, and many more. Brian is the co-founder of Belanger Books LLC, where he illustrates the popular *MacDougall Twins with Sherlock Holmes* young reader series (#1 bestsellers on Amazon.com UK). A prolific creator, he also designs t-shirts, mugs, stickers, and other merchandise on his personal art site: *www.redbubble.com/people/zhahadun.*

Matthew Booth is the author of *Sherlock Holmes and the Giant's Hand*, published by Breese Books and the co-author of *The Further Exploits of Sherlock Holmes*, a collection of new stories, commissioned by Sparkling Books in 2016. He contributed two original Holmes stories to *The Game is Afoot*, a collection of Sherlock Holmes short stories published in 2008 by Wordsworth Editions and contributed a story to Wordsworth Editions' collection of original crime tales, *Crime Scenes*. He is the creator of Anthony Rathe, a disgraced former barrister seeking redemption by solving those crimes which come his way. The character first appeared in a series of radio plays produced and syndicated by *Imagination Theatre* in America. Rathe now appears in Matthew's latest book, *When Anthony Rathe Investigates* published by Sparkling Books. A lifelong devotee of crime and supernatural fiction, Matthew has provided a number of academic talks on such subjects as Sherlock Holmes, the works of Agatha Christie, crime fiction, Count Dracula, and the facts and theories concerning the crimes of Jack the Ripper. He is also a member of the *Crime Writers Association* and a contributor to their monthly newsletter, *Red Herrings.*

Thomas A. Burns, Jr. is the author of the *Natalie McMasters Mysteries*. He was born and grew up in New Jersey, attended Xavier High School in Manhattan, earned B.S degrees in Zoology and Microbiology at Michigan State University, and a M.S. in Microbiology at North Carolina State University. He currently resides in Wendell, North Carolina. As a kid, Tom started reading mysteries with The Hardy Boys, Ken Holt and Rick Brant, and graduated to the classic stories by authors such as A. Conan Doyle, Dorothy Sayers, John Dickson Carr, Erle Stanley Gardner, and Rex Stout, to name a few. Tom has written fiction as a hobby all of his life, starting with The Man from U.N.C.L.E. stories in marble-backed copybooks in grade school. He built a career as technical, science, and medical writer and editor for nearly thirty years in industry and government. Now that he's truly on his own as a novelist, he's excited to publish his own mystery series, as well as to contribute stories about his second-most-favorite detective, Sherlock Holmes, to *The MX anthology of New Sherlock Holmes Stories.*

Harry DeMaio is a *nom de plume* of Harry B. DeMaio, successful author of several books on Information Security and Business Networks, as well as the ten-volume *Casebooks of Octavius Bear – Alternative Universe Mysteries for Adult Animal Lovers.* Octavius Bear is

443

loosely based on Sherlock Holmes and Nero Wolfe in a world in which *homo sapiens* died out long ago in a global disaster, but most animals have advanced to a twenty-first century anthropomorphic state. "It's Time" is Harry's first offering treating Holmes and Watson in their original human condition. A retired business executive, consultant, information security specialist, former pilot, and graduate school adjunct professor, he whiles away his time traveling and writing preposterous articles and stories. He has appeared on many radio and TV shows and is an accomplished, frequent public speaker. Former New York City natives, he and his extremely patient and helpful wife, Virginia, and their Bichon Frisé, Woof, live in Cincinnati (and several other parallel universes.) They have two sons living in Scottsdale, Arizona and Cortlandt Manor, New York, both of whom are quite successful and quite normal – thus putting the lie to the theory that insanity is hereditary.

Sir Arthur Conan Doyle (1859-1930) *Holmes Chronicler Emeritus*. If not for him, this anthology would not exist. Author, physician, patriot, sportsman, spiritualist, husband and father, and advocate for the oppressed. He is remembered and honored for the purposes of this collection by being the man who introduced Sherlock Holmes to the world. Through fifty-six Holmes short stories, four novels, and additional Apocryphal entries, Doyle revolutionized mystery stories and also greatly influenced and improved police forensic methods and techniques for the betterment of all. *Steel True Blade Straight.*

C.H. Dye first discovered Sherlock Holmes when she was eleven, in a collection that ended at the Reichenbach Falls. It was another six months before she discovered *The Hound of the Baskervilles*, and two weeks after that before a librarian handed her *The Return.* She has loved the stories ever since. She has written fan-fiction, and her first published pastiche, "The Tale of the Forty Thieves", was included in *The MX Book of New Sherlock Holmes Stories – Part I: 1881-1889.* Her story "A Christmas Goose" was in *The MX Book of New Sherlock Holmes Stories – Part V: Christmas Adventures*, and "The Mysterious Mourner" in *The MX Book of New Sherlock Holmes Stories – Part VIII – Eliminate the Impossible: 1892-1905*

Anna Elliott is an author of historical fiction and fantasy. Her first series, *The Twilight of Avalon* trilogy, is a retelling of the Trystan and Isolde legend. She wrote her second series, *The Pride and Prejudice Chronicles*, chiefly to satisfy her own curiosity about what might have happened to Elizabeth Bennet, Mr. Darcy, and all the other wonderful cast of characters after the official end of Jane Austen's classic work. She enjoys stories about strong women, and loves exploring the multitude of ways women can find their unique strengths. She was delighted to lend a hand with the "Sherlock and Lucy" series, and this story, firstly because she loves Sherlock Holmes as much as her father, co-author Charles Veley, does, and second because it almost never happens that someone with a dilemma shouts, "Quick, we need an author of historical fiction!" Anna lives in the Washington, D.C .area with her husband and three children.

Steve Emecz's main field is technology, in which he has been working for about twenty years. Following multiple senior roles at Xerox, where he grew their European eCommerce from $6m to $200m, Steve joined platform provider Venda, and moved across to Powa in 2010. Today, Steve is Chief Revenue Officer at CloudTrade, a company that digitises large companies' accounts payables. Steve is a regular trade show speaker on the subject of eCommerce, and his tech career has taken him to more than fifty countries – so he's no stranger to planes and airports. He wrote two novels (one a bestseller) in the 1990's, and a screenplay in 2001. Shortly after, he set up MX Publishing, specialising in NLP books. In 2008, MX published its first Sherlock Holmes book, and MX has gone on to become the largest specialist Holmes publisher in the world. MX is a social enterprise and supports three main causes. The first is Happy Life, a children's rescue project in Nairobi, Kenya, where he and his wife, Sharon, spend every Christmas at the rescue centre in Kasarani. In 2014, they wrote a short book about the project, *The Happy Life Story*. The second is the Stepping Stones School, of which Steve is a patron. Stepping Stones is located at Undershaw, Sir Arthur Conan Doyle's former home. Steve has been a mentor for the World Food Programme for the last two years, supporting their innovation bootcamps and giving 1-2-1 mentoring to several projects.

Edwin A. Enstrom is a budding pasticheurs and an Army veteran who spent one year in Vietnam. Now retired, he worked for forty-plus years for one company in various capacities, mostly within Information Technology. He is an avid reader, especially of fair-play detective mysteries. He is a puzzle lover, especially cryptic crosswords. Additionally, he's an internet junkie, spending several hours daily surfing the web, but with no smart phone, no television, and no Facebook or social media.

Mark A. Gagen BSI is co-founder of Wessex Press, sponsor of the popular *From Gillette to Brett* conferences, and publisher of *The Sherlock Holmes Reference Library* and many other fine Sherlockian titles. A life-long Holmes enthusiast, he is a member of *The Baker Street Irregulars* and *The Illustrious Clients of Indianapolis*. A graphic artist by profession, his work is often seen on the covers of *The Baker Street Journal* and various BSI books.

Jayantika Ganguly BSI is the General Secretary and Editor of the *Sherlock Holmes Society of India*, a member of the *Sherlock Holmes Society of London*, and the *Czech Sherlock Holmes Society*. She is the author of *The Holmes Sutra* (MX 2014). She is a corporate lawyer working with one of the Big Six law firms.

Melissa Grigsby, Executive Head Teacher of Stepping Stones School, is driven by a passion to open the doors to learners with complex and layered special needs that just make society feel two steps too far away. Based on the Surrey/Hampshire border in England, her time is spent between relocating a great school into the prestigious home of Conan Doyle, and her two children, dogs, and horses, so there never a dull moment.

John Atkinson Grimshaw (1836-1893) was born in Leeds, England. His amazing paintings, usually featuring twilight or night scenes illuminated by gas-lamps or moonlight, are easily recognizable, and are often used on the covers of books about The Great Detective to set the mood, as shadowy figures move in the distance through misty mysterious settings and over rain-slicked streets.

Arthur Hall was born in Aston, Birmingham, UK, in 1944. He discovered his interest in writing during his schooldays, along with a love of fictional adventure and suspense. His first novel, *Sole Contact*, was an espionage story about an ultra-secret government department known as "Sector Three", and was followed, to date, by three sequels. Other works include five Sherlock Holmes novels, *The Demon of the Dusk, The One Hundred Percent Society, The Secret Assassin, The Phantom Killer*, and *In Pursuite of the Dead*, as well as a collection of short stories, and a modern detective novel. He lives in the West Midlands, United Kingdom.

Liz Hedgecock grew up in London, England, did an English degree, and then took forever to start writing. Now Liz travels between the nineteenth and twenty-first centuries, murdering people. To be fair, she does usually clean up after herself. Liz's reimaginings of

445

Sherlock Holmes, her Pippa Parker cozy mystery series, and the Caster & Fleet mystery series (written with Paula Harmon) are available in ebook and paperback. Liz lives in Cheshire with her husband and two sons, and when she's not writing or child-wrangling, you can usually find her reading, messing about on Twitter, or cooing over stuff in museums and art galleries. That's her story, anyway, and she's sticking to it.

Carl L. Heifetz Over thirty years of inquiry as a research microbiologist have prepared Carl Heifetz to explore new horizons in science. As an author, he has published numerous articles and short stories for fan magazines and other publications. In 2013, he published a book entitled *Voyage of the Blue Carbuncle* that is based on the works of Sir Arthur Conan Doyle and Gene Roddenberry. *Voyage of the Blue Carbuncle* is a fun and exciting spoof, sure to please science fiction fans as well as those who love the stories of Sherlock Holmes and *Star Trek*. Carl and his wife have two grown children and live in Trinity, Florida.

Stephen Herczeg is an IT Geek, writer, actor, and film-maker based in Canberra Australia. He has been writing for over twenty years and has completed a couple of dodgy novels, sixteen feature-length screenplays, and numerous short stories and scripts. Stephen was very successful in 2017's International Horror Hotel screenplay competition, with his scripts *TITAN* winning the Sci-Fi category and *Dark are the Woods* placing second in the horror category. His work has featured in *Sproutlings – A Compendium of Little Fictions* from Hunter Anthologies, the *Hells Bells* Christmas horror anthology published by the Australasian Horror Writers Association, and the *Below the Stairs, Trickster's Treats, Shades of Santa, Behind the Mask*, and *Beyond the Infinite* anthologies from OzHorror.Con, *The Body Horror Book, Anemone Enemy*, and *Petrified Punks* from Oscillate Wildly Press, and *Sherlock Holmes In the Realms of H.G. Wells* and *Sherlock Holmes: Adventures Beyond the Canon* from Belanger Books.

Roger Johnson BSI, ASH is a retired librarian, now working as a volunteer assistant at the Essex Police Museum. In his spare time, he is commissioning editor of *The Sherlock Holmes Journal*, an occasional lecturer, and a frequent contributor to The Writings About the Writings. His sole work of Holmesian pastiche was published in 1997 in Mike Ashley's anthology *The Mammoth Book of New Sherlock Holmes Adventures*, and he has the greatest respect for the many authors who have contributed new tales to the present mighty trilogy. Like his wife, Jean Upton, he is a member of both *The Baker Street Irregulars* and *The Adventuresses of Sherlock Holmes.*

David Marcum plays *The Game* with deadly seriousness. He first discovered Sherlock Holmes in 1975, at the age of ten, when he received an abridged version of *The Adventures* during a trade. Since that time, David has collected literally thousands of traditional Holmes pastiches in the form of novels, short stories, radio and television episodes, movies and scripts, comics, fan-fiction, and unpublished manuscripts. He is the author of *The Papers of Sherlock Holmes Vol.'s I* and *II* (2011, 2013), *Sherlock Holmes and A Quantity of Debt* (2013), *Sherlock Holmes – Tangled Skeins* (2015), and *The Papers of Solar Pons* (2017). He is the editor of *Sherlock Holmes in Montague Street* (2014) *Holmes Away From Home* (2016), *Sherlock Holmes: Before Baker Street* (2017), *Imagination Theatre's Sherlock Holmes* (2017), *Sherlock Holmes: Adventures Beyond the Canon,* (2018) and *The New Adventures of Solar Pons* (2018). He edited the authorized reissues of the *Solar Pons* stories, and is currently editing *The Complete Dr. Thorndyke*. Additionally, he is the creator and editor of the ongoing collection, *The MX Book of New Sherlock Holmes Stories* (2015-Present), now at fifteen volumes, with more in preparation as of this writing. He has contributed stories, essays, and scripts to a variety of Sherlockian anthologies, *The Baker*

Street Journal, *The Strand Magazine*, *The Watsonian*, *Beyond Watson*, *Sherlock Holmes Mystery Magazine*, *About Sixty*, *About Being a Sherlockian*, *Sherlock Holmes is Like*, *The Solar Pons Gazette*, *Imagination Theater*, *The Art of Sherlock Holmes*, *The Proceedings of the Pondicherry Lodge*, and *The Gazette*, the journal of the Nero Wolfe *Wolfe Pack*. He began his adult work life as a Federal Investigator for an obscure U.S. Government agency. When the organization was eliminated, he returned to school for a second degree and is now a licensed Civil Engineer, living in Tennessee with his wife and son. He is a member of *The Sherlock Holmes Society of London*, *The Nashville Scholars of the Three Pipe Problem* ("The Engineer's Thumb"), *The Occupants of the Full House*, *The Diogenes Club of Washington, D.C.*, *The Tankerville Club* (all Scions of *The Baker Street Irregulars*), *The Sherlock Holmes Society of India* (as a Patron), *The John H. Watson Society* ("Marker"), *The Praed Street Irregulars* ("The Obrisset Snuff Box"), *The Solar Pons Society of London*, and *The Diogenes Club West (East Tennessee Annex)*, a curious and unofficial Scion of one. Since the age of nineteen, he has worn a deerstalker as his regular-and-only hat. In 2013, he and his deerstalker were finally able make his first trip-of-a-lifetime Holmes Pilgrimage to England, with return Pilgrimages in 2015 and 2016, where you may have spotted him. If you ever run into him and his deerstalker out and about, feel free to say hello!

Jacquelynn Morris, ASH, BSI, JHWS, is a member of several Sherlock Holmes societies in the Mid-Atlantic area of the U.S.A., but her home group is Watson's Tin Box in Maryland. She is the founder of *A Scintillation of Scions*, an annual Sherlock Holmes symposium. She has been published in the BSI Manuscript Series, *The Wrong Passage*, as well as in *About Sixty* and *About Being a Sherlockian* (Wildside Press). Jacquelynn was the U.S. liaison for the Undershaw Preservation Trust for several years, until Undershaw was purchased to become part of Stepping Stones School.

Sidney Paget (1860-1908), a few of whose illustrations are used within this anthology, was born in London, and like his two older brothers, became a famed illustrator and painter. He completed over three-hundred-and-fifty drawings for the Sherlock Holmes stories that were first published in *The Strand* magazine, defining Holmes's image forever after in the public mind.

Gayle Lange Puhl has been a Sherlockian since Christmas of 1965. She has had articles published in *The Devon County Chronicle*, *The Baker Street Journal*, and *The Serpentine Muse*, plus her local newspaper. She has created Sherlockian jewelry, a 2006 calendar entitled "If Watson Wrote For TV", and has painted a limited series of Holmes-related nesting dolls. She co-founded the scion *Friends of the Great Grimpen Mire* and the Janesville, Wisconsin-based *The Original Tree Worshipers*. In January 2016, she was awarded the "Outstanding Creative Writer" award by the Janesville Art Alliance for her first book *Sherlock Holmes and the Folk Tale Mysteries*. She is semi-retired and lives in Evansville, Wisconsin. Ms. Puhl has one daughter, Gayla, and four grandchildren.

Tracy J. Revels, a Sherlockian from the age of eleven, is a professor of history at Wofford College in Spartanburg, South Carolina. She is a member of *The Survivors of the Gloria Scott* and *The Studious Scarlets Society*, and is a past recipient of the Beacon Society Award. Almost every semester, she teaches a class that covers The Canon, either to college students or to senior citizens. She is also the author of three supernatural Sherlockian pastiches with MX (*Shadowfall*, *Shadowblood*, and *Shadowwraith*), and a regular contributor to her scion's newsletter. She also has some notoriety as an author of very silly skits: For proof, see "The Adventure of the Adversarial Adventuress" and "Occupy Baker

Street" on YouTube. When not studying Sherlock, she can be found researching the history of her native state, and has written books on Florida in the Civil War and on the development of Florida's tourism industry.

Roger Riccard of Los Angeles, California, U.S.A., is a descendant of the Roses of Kilravock in Highland Scotland. He is the author of two previous Sherlock Holmes novels, *The Case of the Poisoned Lilly* and *The Case of the Twain Papers*, a series of short stories in two volumes, *Sherlock Holmes: Adventures for the Twelve Days of Christmas* and *Further Adventures for the Twelve Days of Christmas*, and the new series *A Sherlock Holmes Alphabet of Cases*, all of which are published by Baker Street Studios. He has another novel and a non-fiction Holmes reference work in various stages of completion. He became a Sherlock Holmes enthusiast as a teenager (many, many years ago), and, like all fans of The Great Detective, yearned for more stories after reading The Canon over and over. It was the Granada Television performances of Jeremy Brett and Edward Hardwicke, and the encouragement of his wife, Rosilyn, that at last inspired him to write his own Holmes adventures, using the Granada actor portrayals as his guide. He has been called "The best pastiche writer since Val Andrews" by the *Sherlockian E-Times*.

GC Rosenquist was born in Chicago, Illinois and has been writing since he was ten years old. His interests are very eclectic. His eleven previously published books include literary fiction, horror, poetry, a comedic memoir, and lots of science fiction. His latest published work for MX Books is *Sherlock Holmes: The Pearl of Death and Other Stories* (April 2015). He has had his work published in *Sherlock Holmes Mystery Magazine*. He works professionally as a graphic artist. He has studied writing and poetry at the College of Lake County in Grayslake, Illinois, and currently resides in Lindenhurst, Illinois. For more information on GC Rosenquist, you can go to his website at *www.gcrosenquist.com*

Geri Schear is a novelist and short story writer. Her work has been published in literary journals in the U.S. and Ireland. Her first novel, *A Biased Judgement: The Diaries of Sherlock Holmes 1897* was released to critical acclaim in 2014. The sequel, *Sherlock Holmes and the Other Woman* was published in 2015, and *Return to Reichenbach* in 2016. She lives in Kells, Ireland.

Mark Sohn was born in Brighton, England in 1967. After a hectic life and many dubious and varied careers, he settled down in Sussex with his wife, Angie. His first novel, *Sherlock Holmes and the Whitechapel Murders* was published in 2017. His second, *The Absentee Detective* is out now. Both are available from Amazon.com.
https://sherlockholmesof221b.blogspot.co.uk/
https://volcanocat.blogspot.co.uk/

S. Subramanian is a retired professor of Economics from Chennai, India. Apart from a small book titled *Economic Offences: A Compendium of Crimes in Prose and Verse* (Oxford University Press Delhi, 2012), his Holmes pastiches are the only serious things he has written. His other work runs largely to whimsical stuff on fuzzy logic and social measurement, on which he writes with much precision and little understanding, being an economist. He is otherwise mainly harmless, as his wife and daughter might concede with a little persuasion.

Will Thomas is the author of ten books in the Barker and Llewelyn Victorian mystery series, including *Some Danger Involved, Fatal Enquiry*, and most recently *Blood is Blood.*

He was nominated for a *Barry* and a *Shamus*. He lives in Oklahoma, where he studies Victorian martial arts and models British railways.

Charles Veley has loved Sherlock Holmes since boyhood. As a father, he read the entire Canon to his then-ten-year-old daughter at evening story time. Now, this very same daughter, grown up to become acclaimed historical novelist Anna Elliott, has worked with him to develop new adventures in the *Sherlock Holmes and Lucy James Mystery Series*. Charles is also a fan of Gilbert & Sullivan, and wrote *The Pirates of Finance*, a new musical in the G&S tradition that won an award at the New York Musical Theatre Festival in 2013. Other than the Sherlock and Lucy series, all of the books on his Amazon Author Page were written when he was a full-time author during the late Seventies and early Eighties. He currently works for United Technologies Corporation, where his main focus is on creating sustainability and value for the company's large real estate development projects.

I.A. Watson is a novelist and jobbing writer from Yorkshire who cut his teeth on writing Sherlock Holmes stories and has even won an award for one. His works include *Holmes and Houdini*, *Labours of Hercules*, *St. George and the Dragon* Volumes 1 and 2, and *Women of Myth*, and the non-fiction essay book *Where Stories Dwell*. He pens short detective stories as a means of avoiding writing things that pay better. A full list of his sixty-plus published works appears at:
http://www.chillwater.org.uk/writing/iawatsonhome.htm

Marcia Wilson is a freelance researcher and illustrator who likes to work in a style compatible for the color blind and visually impaired. She is Canon-centric, and her first MX offering, *You Buy Bones*, uses the point-of-view of Scotland Yard to show the unique talents of Dr. Watson. This continued with the publication of *Test of the Professionals: The Adventure of the Flying Blue Pidgeon* and *The Peaceful Night Poisonings*. She can be contacted at: *gravelgirty.deviantart.com*

The following have also contributed to the companion volumes
Part XIII – 2019 Annual (1881-1890)
and
Part XV– 2019 Annual (1898-1918)

Marino C. Alvarez, Ed.D., BSI, is professor *emeritus* at Tennessee State University. His book, *A Professor Reflects on Sherlock Holmes*, and other Sherlockian articles appear in the *Baker Street Journal*, *Canadian Holmes*, and *Saturday Review of Literature*, among others.

Hugh Ashton was born in the U.K., and moved to Japan in 1988, where he remained until 2016, living with his wife Yoshiko in the historic city of Kamakura, a little to the south of Yokohama. He and Yoshiko have now moved to Lichfield, a small cathedral city in the Midlands of the U.K., the birthplace of Samuel Johnson, and one-time home of Erasmus Darwin. In the past, he has worked in the technology and financial services industries, which have provided him with material for some of his books set in the 21st century. He currently works as a writer: Novelist, freelance editor, and copywriter, (his work for large Japanese corporations has appeared in international business journals), and journalist, as well as producing industry reports on various aspects of the financial services industry. Recently, however, his lifelong interest in Sherlock Holmes has developed into an acclaimed series of adventures featuring the world's most famous detective, written in the style of the originals. In addition to these, he has also published historical and alternate historical novels, short stories, and thrillers. Together with artist Andy Boerger, he has produced the *Sherlock Ferret* series of stories for children, featuring the world's cutest detective.

Maurice Barkley lives with his wife Marie in a suburb of Rochester, New York. Retired from a career as a commercial artist and builder of tree houses, he is writing and busy reinforcing the stereotype of a pesky househusband. His other Sherlock Holmes stories can be found on Amazon. *https://www.amazon.com/author/mauricebarkleys*

Derrick Belanger is an educator and also the author of the #1 bestselling book in its category, *Sherlock Holmes: The Adventure of the Peculiar Provenance*, which was in the top 200 bestselling books on Amazon. He also is the author of *The MacDougall Twins with Sherlock Holmes* books, and he edited the Sir Arthur Conan Doyle horror anthology *A Study in Terror: Sir Arthur Conan Doyle's Revolutionary Stories of Fear and the Supernatural*. Mr. Belanger co-owns the publishing company Belanger Books, which released the Sherlock Holmes anthologies *Beyond Watson, Holmes Away From Home: Adventures from the Great Hiatus* Volumes 1 and 2, *Sherlock Holmes: Before Baker Street*, and *Sherlock Holmes: Adventures in the Realms of H.G. Wells* Volumes I and 2. Derrick resides in Colorado and continues compiling unpublished works by Dr. John H. Watson.

S.F. Bennett was born and raised in London, studying History at Queen Mary and Westfield College, and Journalism at City University at the Postgraduate level, before moving to Devon in 2013. The author lectures on Conan Doyle, Sherlock Holmes, and 19th century detective fiction, and has had articles on various aspects from The Canon published in *The Journal of the Sherlock Holmes Society of London* and *The Torr*, the journal of *The Poor Folk Upon The Moors*, the Sherlock Holmes Society of the South West of England. Her first published novel is *The Secret Diary of Mycroft Holmes: The Thoughts and Reminiscences of Sherlock Holmes's Elder Brother, 1880-1888* (2017).

Andrew Bryant was born in Bridgend, Wales, and now lives in Burlington, Ontario. His previous publications include *Prism International, On Spec, The Dalhousie Review*, and second place in the 2015 *Toronto Star* short story contest. "The Shackled Man" is his first Sherlock Holmes story, written after visiting 221b Baker Street.

Nick Cardillo has been a devotee of Sherlock Holmes since the age of six. His first published short story, "The Adventure of the Traveling Corpse" appeared in *The MX Book of New Sherlock Holmes Stories – Part VI: 2017 Annual*, and he has written subsequent stories for both MX Publishing and Belanger Books. In 2018, Nick completed his first anthology of new Sherlock Holmes adventures entitled *The Feats of Sherlock Holmes*. Nick is a fan of The Golden Age of Detective Fiction, Hammer Horror, and Doctor Who. He writes film reviews and analyses at *Sacred-Celluloid.blogspot.com*. He is a student at Susquehanna University in Selinsgrove, PA.

Leslie Charteris was born in Singapore on May 12th, 1907. With his mother and brother, he moved to England in 1919 and attended Rossall School in Lancashire before moving on to Cambridge University to study law. His studies there came to a halt when a publisher accepted his first novel. His third one, entitled *Meet the Tiger*, was written when he was twenty years old and published in September 1928. It introduced the world to Simon Templar, *aka* The Saint. He continued to write about The Saint until 1983 when the last book, *Salvage for The Saint*, was published. The books, which have been translated into over thirty languages, number nearly a hundred and have sold over forty-million copies around the world. They've inspired, to date, fifteen feature films, three television series, ten radio series, and a comic strip that was written by Charteris and syndicated around the world for over a decade. He enjoyed travelling, but settled for long periods in Hollywood, Florida, and finally in Surrey, England. He was awarded the Cartier Diamond Dagger by the *Crime Writers' Association* in 1992, in recognition of a lifetime of achievement. He died the following year.

Ian Dickerson was just nine years old when he discovered The Saint. Shortly after that, he discovered Sherlock Holmes. The Saint won, for a while anyway. He struck up a friendship with The Saint's creator, Leslie Charteris, and his family. With their permission, he spent six weeks studying the Leslie Charteris collection at Boston University and went on to write, direct, and produce documentaries on the making of *The Saint* and *Return of The Saint,* which have been released on DVD. He oversaw the recent reprints of almost fifty of the original Saint books in both the US and UK, and was a co-producer on the 2017 TV movie of *The Saint.* When he discovered that Charteris had written Sherlock Holmes stories as well – well, there was the excuse he needed to revisit The Canon. He's consequently written and edited three books on Holmes' radio adventures. For the sake of what little sanity he has, Ian has also written about a wide range of subjects, none of which come with a halo, including talking mashed potatoes, Lord Grade, and satellite links. Ian lives in Hampshire with his wife and two children. And an awful lot of books by Leslie Charteris. Not quite so many by Conan Doyle, though.

Edwin A. Enstrom *– In addition to a story in this volume, Ed also has stories in Parts XIII and XV of this set.*

Thomas Fortenberry is an American author, editor, and reviewer. Founder of Mind Fire Press and a Pushcart Prize-nominated writer, he has also judged many literary contests, including the Georgia Author of the Year Awards and the Robert Penn Warren Prize for Fiction. His Sherlock Holmes stories have appeared in such works as *An Improbable Truth* and various volumes of *The MX Book of New Sherlock Holmes Stories.*

James R. "Jim" French became a morning Disc Jockey on KIRO (AM) in Seattle in 1959. He later founded *Imagination Theatre,* a syndicated program that broadcast to over one-hundred-and-twenty stations in the U.S. and Canada, and also on the XM Satellite Radio system all over North America. Actors in French's dramas included John Patrick Lowrie, Larry Albert, Patty Duke, Russell Johnson, Tom Smothers, Keenan Wynn, Roddy MacDowall, Ruta Lee, John Astin, Cynthia Lauren Tewes, and Richard Sanders. Mr. French stated, "To me, the characters of Sherlock Holmes and Doctor Watson always seemed to be figures Doyle created as a challenge to lesser writers. He gave us two interesting characters – different from each other in their histories, talents, and experience, but complimentary as a team – who have been applied to a variety of situations and plots far beyond the times and places in The Canon. In the hands of different writers, Holmes and Watson have lent their identities to different times, ages, and even genders. But I wanted to break no new ground. I feel Sir Arthur provided us with enough references to locations, landmarks, and the social conditions of his time, to give a pretty large canvas on which to paint our own images and actions to animate Holmes and Watson." Mr. French passed away at the age of eighty-nine on December 20th, 2017.

David Friend lives in Wales, Great Britain, where he divides his time between watching old detective films and thinking about old detective films. Now thirty, he's been scribbling

451

out stories for twenty years and hopes, some day, to write something half-decent. Most of what he pens is set in an old-timey world of non-stop adventure with debonair sleuths, kick-ass damsels, criminal masterminds, and narrow escapes, and he wishes he could live there.

Tim Gambrell lives in Exeter, Devon with his wife, two young sons, two cats, and seven chickens. He has had short stories published in *Lethbridge-Stewart: The HAVOC Files 3* and *The Lethbridge-Stewart Quiz Book* (both Candy Jar books, 2017), *Bernice Summerfield: True Stories* (Big Finish, 2017) and *Relics . . . An Anthology* (Red Ted Books, 2018). Tim has written a novella, *The Way of The Bry'hunee*, for the Erimem Range from Thebes Publishing (due 2019), and his first full novel, *Lucy Wilson and The Bledoe Cadets*, will be published by Candy Jar Books in 2019 as part of the *Lethbridge-Stewart: The Laughing Gnome* series. Tim has contributed to a number of charity publications, including *A Time Lord For Change* (2016) and *Whoblique Strategies* (2017) from Chinbeard Books, and *You and 42 & Blake's Legacy: 40 Years of Rebellion* from Who Dares Publishing (both 2018).

Dick Gillman is an English writer and acrylic artist living in Brittany, France with his wife Alex, Truffle, their Black Labrador, and Jean-Claude, their Breton cat. During his retirement from teaching, he has written over twenty Sherlock Holmes short stories which are published as both e-books and paperbacks. His contribution to the superb MX Sherlock Holmes collection, published in October 2015, was entitled "The Man on Westminster Bridge" and had the privilege of being chosen as the anchor story in *The MX Book of New Sherlock Holmes Stories – Part II (1890-1895)*.

Denis Green was born in London, England in April 1905. He grew up mostly in London's Savoy Theatre where his father, Richard Green, was a principal in many Gilbert and Sullivan productions, A Flying Officer with RAF until 1924, he then spent four years managing a tea estate in North India before making his stage debut in *Hamlet* with Leslie Howard in 1928. He made his first visit to America in 1931 and established a respectable stage career before appearing in films – including minor roles in the first two Rathbone and Bruce Holmes films – and developing a career in front of and behind the microphone during the Golden Age of radio. Green and Leslie Charteris met in 1938 and struck up a lifelong friendship. Always busy, be it on stage, radio, film or television, Green passed away at the age of fifty in New York.

Jack Grochot is a retired investigative newspaper journalist and a former federal law enforcement agent specializing in mail fraud cases. He has written three books of Sherlock Holmes pastiches and a fourth nonfiction book, *Saga of a Latter-Day Saddle Tramp*, a memoir of his five-year horseback journey across twelve states. Grochot lives on a small farm in southwestern Pennsylvania, where he writes and oversees a horse-boarding stable.

Arthur Hall – *In addition to a story in this volume, Arthur also has stories in Parts XIII and XV of this set.*

Paul Hiscock is an author of crime, fantasy, and science fiction tales. His short stories have appeared in several anthologies and include a seventeenth century whodunnit, a science fiction western, and a steampunk Sherlock Holmes story. Paul lives with his family in Kent, England, and spends his days chasing a toddler with more energy than the Duracell Bunny. He mainly does his writing in coffee shops with members of the local NaNoWriMo group, or in the middle of the night when his family has gone to sleep. Consequently, his stories tend to be fuelled by large amounts of black coffee. You can find out more about his writing at *www.detectivesanddragons.uk.*

Mike Hogan writes mostly historical novels and short stories, many set in Victorian London and featuring Sherlock Holmes and Doctor Watson. He read the Conan Doyle stories at school with great enjoyment, but hadn't thought much about Sherlock Holmes until, having missed the Granada/Jeremy Brett TV series when it was originally shown in the eighties, he came across a box set of videos in a street market and was hooked on Holmes again. He started writing Sherlock Holmes pastiches several years ago, having great fun re-imagining situations for the Conan Doyle characters to act in. The relationship between Holmes and Watson fascinates him as one of the great literary friendships. (He's also a huge admirer of Patrick O'Brian's Aubrey-Maturin novels). Like Captain Aubrey and Doctor Maturin, Holmes and Watson are an odd couple, differing in almost every facet of their characters, but sharing a common sense of decency and a common humanity. Living with Sherlock Holmes can't have been easy, and Mike enjoys adding a stronger vein of "pawky humour" into the Conan Doyle mix, even letting Watson have the second-to-last word on occasions. His books include *Sherlock Holmes and the Scottish Question,* the forthcoming *The Gory Season – Sherlock Holmes, Jack the Ripper and the Thames Torso Murders,* and the Sherlock Holmes & Young Winston 1887 Trilogy (*The Deadwood Stage, The Jubilee Plot,* and *The Giant Moles*), He has also written the following short story collections: *Sherlock Holmes: Murder at the Savoy and Other Stories, Sherlock Holmes: The Skull of Kohada Koheiji and Other Stories,* and *Sherlock Holmes: Murder on the Brighton Line and Other Stories. www.mikehoganbooks.com*

Christopher James was born in 1975 in Paisley, Scotland. Educated at Newcastle and UEA, he was a winner of the UK's National Poetry Competition in 2008. He has written two full length Sherlock Holmes novels, *The Adventure of the Ruby Elephant* and *The Jeweller of Florence,* both published by MX, and is working on a third.

Kelvin I. Jones is the author of six books about Sherlock Holmes and the definitive biography of Conan Doyle as a spiritualist, *Conan Doyle and The Spirits.* A member of *The Sherlock Holmes Society of London,* he has published numerous short occult and ghost stories in British anthologies over the last thirty years. His work has appeared on BBC Radio, and in 1984 he won the Mason Hall Literary Award for his poem cycle about the survivors of Hiroshima and Nagasaki, recently reprinted as "Omega". (Oakmagic Publications) A one-time teacher of creative writing at the University of East Anglia, he is also the author of four crime novels featuring his ex-Met sleuth John Bottrell, who first appeared in *Stone Dead.* He has over fifty titles on Kindle, and is also the author of several novellas and short story collections featuring a Norwich-based detective, DCI Ketch, an intrepid sleuth who investigates East Anglian murder cases. He also published a series of short stories about an Edwardian psychic detective, Dr. John Carter (*Carter's Occult Casebook*). Ramsey Campbell, the British horror writer, and Francis King, the renowned novelist, have both compared his supernatural stories to those of M. R. James. He has also published children's fiction, namely *Odin's Eye,* and, in collaboration with his wife Debbie, *The Dark Entry.* Since 1995, he has been the proprietor of Oakmagic Publications, publishers of British folklore and of his fiction titles. He lives in Norfolk. (See *www.oakmagicpublications.co.uk*)

David Marcum *– In addition to a story in this volume, David also has stories in Parts XIII and XV of this set.*

Jacquelynn Morris – *In addition to a poem in this volume, Jacquelynn also has a poem in Part XIII of this set.*

Mark Mower is a member of the *Crime Writers' Association, The Sherlock Holmes Society of London*, and *The Solar Pons Society of London*. He writes true crime stories and fictional mysteries. His first two volumes of Holmes pastiches were entitled *A Farewell to Baker Street* and *Sherlock Holmes: The Baker Street Case-Files* (both with MX Publishing) and, to date, he has contributed chapters to six parts of the ongoing *The MX Book of New Sherlock Holmes Stories*. He has also had stories in two anthologies by Belanger Books: *Holmes Away From Home: Adventures from the Great Hiatus – Volume II – 1893-1894* (2016) and *Sherlock Holmes: Before Baker Street* (2017). More are bound to follow. Mark's non-fiction works include *Bloody British History: Norwich* (The History Press, 2014), *Suffolk Murders* (The History Press, 2011) and *Zeppelin Over Suffolk* (Pen & Sword Books, 2008).

Will Murray is the author of over seventy novels, including forty *Destroyer* novels and seven posthumous *Doc Savage* collaborations with Lester Dent, under the name Kenneth Robeson, for Bantam Books in the 1990's. Since 2011, he has written a number of additional Doc Savage adventures for Altus Press, two of which co-starred The Shadow, as well as a solo Pat Savage novel. His 2015 Tarzan novel, *Return to Pal-Ul-Don*, was followed by *King Kong vs. Tarzan* in 2016. Murray has written short stories featuring such classic characters as Batman, Superman, Wonder Woman, Spider-Man, Ant-Man, the Hulk, Honey West, the Spider, the Avenger, the Green Hornet, the Phantom, and Cthulhu. A previous Murray Sherlock Holmes story appeared in Moonstone's *Sherlock Holmes: The Crossovers Casebook*, and another is forthcoming in *Sherlock Holmes and Doctor Was Not*, involving H. P. Lovecraft's Dr. Herbert West. Additionally, his Sherlock Holmes stories have appeared in *The MX Book of New Sherlock Holmes Stories*.

Robert Perret is a writer, librarian, and devout Sherlockian living on the Palouse. His Sherlockian publications include "The Canaries of Clee Hills Mine" in *An Improbable Truth: The Paranormal Adventures of Sherlock Holmes*, "For King and Country" in *The Science of Deduction*, and "How Hope Learned the Trick" in *NonBinary Review*. He considers himself to be a pan-Sherlockian and a one-man Scion out on the lonely moors of Idaho. Robert has recently authored a yet-unpublished scholarly article tentatively entitled "A Study in Scholarship: The Case of the *Baker Street Journal*'. More information is available at *www.robertperret.com*

Tracy J. Revels – *In addition to a story in this volume, Tracy also has stories in Parts XIII and XV of this set.*

Roger Riccard – *In addition to a story in this volume, Roger also has a story in Part XV of this set.*

Brenda Seabrooke's stories have been published in sixteen reviews, journals, and anthologies. She has received grants from the National Endowment for the Arts and Emerson College's Robbie Macauley Award. She is the author of twenty-three books for young readers including *Scones and Bones on Baker Street: Sherlock's (maybe!) Dog and the Dirt Dilemma*, and *The Rascal in the Castle: Sherlock's (possible!) Dog and the Queen's Revenge*. Brenda states: "It was fun to write from Dr. Watson's point of view and not have to worry about fleas, smelly pits, ralphing, or scratching at inopportune times."

454

Stephen Seitz has reported for newspapers as politically diverse as the *Brattleboro Reformer* and the *New Hampshire Union Leader*. He has covered everything from natural disasters to presidential campaigns, and has interviewed an original cast member from every *Star Trek* television series. Other notables include James Earl Jones, Jodi Picoult, Jerry Lewis, James Whitmore, Senator George McGovern, and many others. He is also the host of cable TV's *Book Talk*. Sherlock Holmes has been a part of Steve's life since the age of twelve, when, while putting homework off, he discovered *The Hound of the Baskervilles* in the stacks at Brooks Memorial Library in Brattleboro, Vt. More than forty years later, he is still an avid Sherlockian and speaks to scion societies on occasion. Naturally, more of his Sherlock Holmes stories are on the way.

Shane Simmons is a multi-award-winning screenwriter and graphic novelist whose work has appeared in international film festivals, museums, and lectures about design and structure. His best-known piece of fiction, *The Long and Unlearned Life of Roland Gethers*, has been discussed in multiple books and academic journals about sequential art, and his short stories have been printed in critically praised anthologies of history, crime, and horror. He lives in Montreal with his wife and too many cats. Follow him at *eyestrainproductions.com* and *@Shane_Eyestrain*

Matthew Simmonds hails from Bedford, in the South East of England, and has been a confirmed devotee of Sir Arthur Conan Doyle's most famous creation since first watching Jeremy Brett's incomparable portrayal of the world's first consulting detective, on a Tuesday evening in April, 1984, while curled up on the sofa with his father. He has written numerous short stories, and his first novel, *Sherlock Holmes: The Adventure of The Pigtail Twist*, was published in 2018. A sequel is nearly complete, which he hopes to publish in the near future. Matthew currently co-owns Harrison & Simmonds, the fifth-generation family business, a renowned County tobacconist, pipe, and gift shop on Bedford High Street.

Robert V. Stapleton was born and brought up in Leeds, Yorkshire, England, and studied at Durham University. After working in various parts of the country as an Anglican parish priest, he is now retired and lives with his wife in North Yorkshire. As a member of his local writing group, he now has time to develop his other life as a writer of adventure stories. He has recently had a number of short stories published, and he is hoping to have a couple of completed novels published at some time in the future.

Tim Symonds was born in London. He grew up in Somerset, Dorset, and Guernsey. After several years in East and Central Africa, he settled in California and graduated Phi Beta Kappa in Political Science from UCLA. He is a Fellow of the *Royal Geographical Society*. He writes his novels in the woods and hidden valleys surrounding his home in the High Weald of East Sussex. Dr. Watson knew the untamed region well. In "The Adventure of Black Peter", Watson wrote, *"the Weald was once part of that great forest which for so long held the Saxon invaders at bay."* Tim's novels are published by MX Publishing. His latest is titled *Sherlock Holmes and the Nine Dragon Sigil*. Previous novels include *Sherlock Holmes and The Sword of Osman*, *Sherlock Holmes and the Mystery of Einstein's Daughter*, *Sherlock Holmes and the Dead Boer at Scotney Castle*, and *Sherlock Holmes and the Case of The Bulgarian Codex*.

Kevin P. Thornton has experienced a Taliban rocket attack in Kabul and a terrorist bombing in Johannesburg. He lives in Fort McMurray, Alberta, the town that burnt down in 2016. He has been shortlisted for the *Crime Writers of Canada* Unhanged writing award six times. He's never won. He was also a finalist for best short story in 2014 – the year Margaret Atwood entered. We're not saying he has luck issues, but don't bet on his stock tips. Born in Kenya, Kevin was a child in New Zealand, a student and soldier in Africa, a military contractor in Afghanistan, a forklift driver in Ontario, and an oilfield worker in North Western Canada. He writes poems that start out just fine, but turn ruder and cruder over time. From limerick to doggerel, they earn less than bugger-all, even though they all manage to rhyme. He also likes writing about Sherlock Holmes and dislikes writing about himself in the third person.

William Todd has been a Holmes fan his entire life, and credits *The Hound of the Baskervilles* as the impetus for his love of both reading and writing. He began to delve into fan fiction a few years ago when he decided to take a break from writing his usual Victorian/Gothic horror stories. He was surprised how well-received they were, and has tried to put out a couple of Holmes stories a year since then. When not writing, Mr. Todd is a pathology supervisor at a local hospital in Northwestern Pennsylvania. He is the husband of a terrific lady and father to two great kids, one with special needs, so the benefactor of these anthologies is close to his heart.

Peter Coe Verbica grew up on a commercial cattle ranch in Northern California, where he learned the value of a strong work ethic. He works for the Wealth Management Group of a global investment bank, and is an Adjunct Professor in the Economics Department at SJSU. He is the author of numerous books, including *Left at the Gate and Other Poems, Hard-Won Cowboy Wisdom (Not Necessarily in Order of Importance), A Key to the Grove and Other Poems,* and *The Missing Tales of Sherlock Holmes (as Compiled by Peter Coe Verbica, JD).* Mr. Verbica obtained a JD from Santa Clara University School of Law, an MS from Massachusetts Institute of Technology, and a BA in English from Santa Clara University. He is the co-inventor on a number of patents, has served as a Managing Member of three venture capital firms, and the CFO of one of the portfolio companies. He is an unabashed advocate of cowboy culture and enjoys creative writing, hiking, and tennis. He is married with four daughters. For more information, or to contact the author, please go to *www.hardwoncowboywisdom.com.*

Mark Wardecker is an instructional technologist at Colby College. He is the editor and annotator of *The Dragnet Solar Pons et al.* (Battered Silicon Dispatch Box, 2011) and has contributed Sherlockian pastiches to *Sherlock Holmes Mystery Magazine,* Solar Pons pastiches to *The New Adventures of Solar Pons,* and an article to *The Baker Street Journal,* as well as having published other fiction and nonfiction.

Darryl Webber is a journalist and author who lives in Essex, England. As well as penning stories under the banner of *The Secret Adventures of Sherlock Holmes* with fellow writer Duncan Wood, he also works for a number of newspapers and runs a film blog called *Chillidog Movies.* Darryl was born in Romford, Essex in 1968 and studied art and design at college before becoming a compositor at his local newspaper. After taking a career break to do a psychology degree at the University of East London, he retrained as a journalist and has held various senior editorial positions in newspapers in the southeast of England, specialising in culture and the arts, as well as working on the sports section of *The Sunday Times.* In 2016, Darryl co-authored a book called *The Man Who Fell To Earth* about the Nicolas Roeg film of the same name starring David Bowie. In this year, he became a part of the team that runs the Chelmsford Film Festival. Darryl's favourite stories from the Conan Doyle Canon are "The Bruce Partington Plans", "Silver Blaze", and "The Blue Carbuncle", and he firmly believes that the game is always afoot.

Sean Wright BSI makes his home in Santa Clarita, a charming city at the entrance of the high desert in Southern California. For sixteen years, features and articles under his byline appeared in *The Tidings* – now *The Angelus News* – publications of the Roman Catholic Archdiocese of Los Angeles. Continuing his education in 2007, Mr. Wright graduated *summa cum laude* from Grand Canyon University, attaining a Bachelor of Arts degree in Christian Studies. He then attained a Master of Arts degree, also in Christian Studies. Once active in the entertainment industry, in an abortive attempt to revive dramatic radio in 1976 with his beloved mentor the late Daws Butler directing, Mr. Wright co-produced and wrote the syndicated *New Radio Adventures of Sherlock Holmes* starring the late Edward Mulhare as the Great Detective. Mr. Wright has written for several television quiz shows and remains proud of his work for *The Quiz Kid's Challenge* and the popular TV quiz show *Jeopardy!* for which The Academy of Television Arts and Sciences honored him in 1985 with an Emmy nomination in the field of writing. Honored with membership in *The Baker Street Irregulars* as "The Manor House Case" after founding *The Non-Canonical Calabashes, The Sherlock Holmes Society of Los Angeles* in 1970, Mr. Wright has written for *The Baker Street Journal* and *Mystery Magazine*. Since 1971, he has conducted lectures on Sherlock Holmes's influence on literature and cinema for libraries, colleges, and private organizations, including MENSA. Mr. Wright's whimsical *Sherlock Holmes Cookbook* (Drake) created with John Farrell BSI, was published in 1976 and a mystery novel, *Enter the Lion: a Posthumous Memoir of Mycroft Holmes* (Hawthorne), "edited" with Michael Hodel BSI, followed in 1979. As director general of The Plot Thickens Mystery Company, Mr. Wright originated hosting "mystery parties" in homes, restaurants, and offices, as well as producing and directing the very first "Mystery Train" tours on Amtrak beginning in 1982.

The MX Book of New Sherlock Holmes Stories

"This is the finest volume of Sherlockian fiction I have ever read, and I have read, literally, thousands." – Philip K. Jones

"Beyond Impressive . . . This is a splendid venture for a great cause! – Roger Johnson, Editor, *The Sherlock Holmes Journal,* The Sherlock Holmes Society of London

In Preparation

. . . and more to come!

Publishers Weekly says:
Part VI: *The traditional pastiche is alive and well . . . .*

Part VII: *Sherlockians eager for faithful-to-the-canon plots and characters will be delighted.*

Part VIII: *The imagination of the contributors in coming up with variations on the volume's theme is matched by their ingenious resolutions.*

Part IX: *The 18 stories . . . will satisfy fans of Conan Doyle's originals. Sherlockians will rejoice that more volumes are on the way.*

Part X: *. . . new Sherlock Holmes adventures of consistently high quality.*

Part XI: *. . . an essential volume for Sherlock Holmes fans.*

Part XII: *. . . continues to amaze with the number of high-quality pastiches . . .*

The MX Book of New Sherlock Holmes Stories
Edited by David Marcum
(MX Publishing, 2015-   )

MX Publishing

MX Publishing is the world's largest specialist Sherlock Holmes publisher, with several hundred titles and over a hundred authors creating the latest in Sherlock Holmes fiction and non-fiction.

From traditional short stories and novels to travel guides and quiz books, MX Publishing caters to all Holmes fans.

The collection includes leading titles such as *Benedict Cumberbatch In Transition* and *The Norwood Author*, which won the 2011 *Tony Howlett Award* (Sherlock Holmes Book of the Year).

MX Publishing also has one of the largest communities of Holmes fans on *Facebook*, with regular contributions from dozens of authors.

www.mxpublishing.co.uk (UK) and *www.mxpublishing.com* (USA)

CPSIA information can be obtained
at www.ICGtesting.com
Printed in the USA
BVHW071927020619

549897BV00001BA/6/P